THE TRIP INTO MILKY WAY

A Novel

GARY PAUL CORCORAN

Also by Gary Paul Corcoran

The Last Love of Eleanor Sands
It's Always Christmastime In Cratchitville
Postmark: Paris ~ Destination: Unknown
The Tribe
The Twelfth Commandment
Afghan's Lipstick Warriors: First Chronicle
Afghan's Lipstick Warriors: Darkness Falls

From the Michael Devlin Series

South On Pacific Coast Highway
Love in a Dying World

Also by Gary Paul Corcoran
Storm Cloud Rising
Purgatory: Origins
The Slow Train to Rishikesh

ACKNOWLEDGMENTS

Marilyn, who read my first, frail efforts and was kind enough to speak of unbridled genius, not the deplorable craftsmanship involved, Chris, who selflessly assisted in dotting the I's and crossing my T's of the original manuscript, the boys at Jacks By The Tracks, for a lovely hole in the wall in which to write this tale, and to everyone else who read this work with sincere interest along the way, especially Jim and Luana, who once entrusted their vacant home to me, my computer and a box full of papers, to Peggy for civilizing me early on, and without whose kindness I might well have been lost, my father, for being Irish and the gift of his Irish tongue, my mother, who spoke so often of following your dreams, though so few of her own were ever realized, to all the boys in Penal del Estado, who together with me endured that strange detour along the road of life, to Win, for being such a noble pal, when probably I didn't deserve as much, and finally, to every friend and stranger who offered kindness to this lost and troubled young man along the way.

Published by Stargazer Press
Charlestown, Rhode Island
http://garypaulcorcoran.com/

Printed in the United States of America
ISBN 978-0997126518

Visit us and blog with the author at
http://garypaulcorcoran.com/

Author Foreword

In 1992, I took a 3rd floor apartment in the Lottie Roth Historical Building, Bellingham, Washington, having abandoned all to write my first novel. Blissfully unaware of the long and winding road ahead, I had convinced myself that said novel would be finished and in the hands of a willing publisher by the end of the year. Fortune must shine on the blind and the ignorant. Had I known what awaited me, I might well have shrunk from the task.

In searching for a suitable place to start that summer, I settled on what was my greatest misadventure from the sixties; incarceration in a Mexican prison for smuggling. Now there was a story to tell! But having an idea is the easy part of writing. Anyone who has attempted to transfer the often fleeting drivel of human thought onto paper soon learns this fact. Only with an untiring willingness to suffer insult and injury, and to endure endless hours of demanding work alone, born of a great love for words, does a fledgling writer begin to master this craft. There is no wishing it so. Decidedly a fledgling writer in the summer of '92, I was at once learning to write seriously, learning to write a novel and grappling with how to structure this particular tale.

Regarding *Milky Way*, Leary's tongue in cheek quip comes to mind. If you remember the sixties, you weren't there. It was at once an absurd and slyly illuminating assertion. Of course I remember the sixties, but to have lived that era to the hilt was to have left behind a lot of brain cells, and I did. That said, I would not trade my surviving memories for all the money in the world.

This is now the third rewrite of *Milky Way*. In the 2010 edition, I added the early scene in the Santa Cruz Mountains, its inclusion driven by the loss of my eldest brother. Our times together in Ben Lomond, however brief, were a beloved part of my journey from nest to manhood to enlightenment and to omit them would have been a sin. If nothing else, it was a way to memorialize a handful of treasured moments, now relegated to a wistful past.

In the 2016 edition, I added the LSD trip, now central to the opening scene. I took more than my share of psychedelics back in the day and how can one possibly tell a tale about the sixties without including at least one journey through the proverbial looking glass? Those trips were equally a part of my odyssey into enlightenment and to omit them would have represented an even greater sin.

This latest revision was driven by three main factors. First, I was made increasingly aware over the years of the many typos littering my several novels. I'm a great content editor, but lousy with copy. It did not help that I was consumed with ghostwriting for much of two decades, leaving little time in a day for my own literary efforts. Publishing in those years was too often a harried and slapdash affair. For any typos still left in my wake, I must beg for the reader's forbearance and forgiveness.

There was also the matter of emotional clarity. Richard Hofstadter once referred to his tome, *The American Political Tradition* as a young man's book. I could ascribe the same appellation to this novel. One of the great challenges in writing *Milky Way* was to look back over the years and feel on a visceral level the way I had felt as a man of twenty. As fortune would have it, the older I get, the more in touch I am with those wild and often bewildering emotions.

Finally, I continue to grow as a writer. Thus, in reading through this novel for typos, it was impossible not to edit equally for content. All of the above factors combined for what was a significant rewrite, not of the storyline itself, but of the forces placed upon the characters herein and how those forces affected their decision making and interactions with each other.

In the end, this is simply a coming of age tale, set in the sixties, with the Vietnam War as the main antagonist. That war exerted a crushing force on everyone who grew up in the era, but especially the young men. It warped many, broke some and made a few stronger. I am both humbled and proud to say I'm still standing and doing what I can to make this a better world, which remains the fundamental lesson I derived from that magical journey.

For Rosie, who always encouraged,

who always believed…

THE TRIP
INTO
MILKY WAY

1

Eric and I stood side by side that frosty, harvest evening, the darkened street of old Craftsman homes towered over by sycamores and those towering trees now barren with the onrush of winter. There were four of us, Chris, Eric, Michael and me and together we had been searching the general neighborhood for fifteen minutes or so, trying to find the house associated with the directions my childhood sweetheart Sarah had given me. The directions went something like this.

"Take the first left off of Glassell, then the second right and look for the house with dormer windows and a covered front porch."

And I had been just stoned enough not to ask, the first left from which direction? Never mind that every house in the neighborhood had a covered front porch and second story dormer windows of some sort, any one of which could have fit Sarah's description.

While paused there in our fruitless search, Chris marched farther up the sidewalk alone, looking in at each house.

"It's Marc Anthony, off to conquer Gaul," I said of him.

Eric lurched forward in laughter, his hands shoved down into his front pockets.

"It's true," I said. "All he needs is a sword and some sandals."

I imitated Chris' stout, stiff-legged gait and Michael laughed too. I looked over at him. His laughter had made puffs in the cold air. Still smiling, he playfully made a few more puffs.

Up the sidewalk, Chris had stopped in front of a house and looked back our way with mock fright before starting across the front lawn. The dead sycamore leaves scattered beneath his weighty footsteps. When he marched up to the front porch and attempted to see in through the front windows, Eric said "Wow" and backed down the sidewalk, not wanting any part of that scene.

Chris ultimately relented and rejoined us.

"Good thing we're not like grunts over in 'Nam."

He marched mechanically around in circles with a pretend rifle over his shoulder, a lost soldier.

"This is such a bummer," I said.

"Wow, mellow out, brother," Eric said. "We'll find the place."

"Yeah, by the time I'm dead."

Chris mimicked my serious demeanor. That got a chuckle out of Michael.

"Real funny," I said. "I guess you guys enjoy being lost."

Chris patted me on the shoulder now, as if to dispense wisdom. I gave him a look. I almost gave him an elbow.

"Let's go find a phone booth and call her again," Michael said.

"No," I said and headed up to knock on the door of the house right in front of us. "This has to be the place. If it isn't, I'll just ask if they know Sarah."

"Wow, far out," Eric said like I had gone off stalking elephants.

"I'd better keep an eye on him," Chris said. "Some redneck with a shotgun might answer the door."

He followed me up to the porch and again tried to see in through the front windows but the curtains were closed and the house looked empty. In fact, the entire block looked to have been abandoned.

I knocked and waited, my heart racing in the silence.

We had been standing there for a number of seconds when the curtains parted on a window next to the front door and Chris did his Charlie Chaplin shtick, like he was trying to escape around a corner on one leg. Michael and Eric laughed out on the sidewalk.

A moment later, Sarah opened the front door.

"Far out, Clay," she whispered and gave me a hug. "You found it."

"Yeah, after wandering around lost forever."

"Sssshhh. There are people tripping inside."

"Well, those were the most screwed up directions I've ever been given."

"I told you the address."

"I know. I forgot to write it down."

2

Sarah smiled knowingly at Chris and waved for Michael and Eric to join us.

"Remember, be quiet. People are tripping."

Sarah held the door open until all four of us were inside. Candles flickered in the darkened living room. People were flopped out here and there on the old sofas and stuffed chairs. Some of them I knew. Some I didn't. Some were our age. Some were a few years older. Shelley, one of our classmates, was sitting at a desk in the corner, wearing a white lace gown and drawing pentagrams. The Grateful Dead was playing softly in the background.

Sarah led us out to the kitchen.

"So, are all of you going to trip?"

"I am," I said.

"And you guys?"

"Sure," Michael said.

"T r i p p i n g," Chris said like he was making fun.

"Wow," Eric said, rubbing his chin. "It's like a heavy decision."

"Well here. Let me show you."

Sarah opened the refrigerator and pulled out two tiny glass vials. The vials were filled with colored liquid.

"The blue is 250 mcg, the purple 500 mcg. If it's your first time, I'd recommend doing the blue vials. The purple can get pretty heavy."

I had tripped before and handed Sarah ten dollars for a purple vial. The blue vials were five dollars. Sarah knew people up in the Bay area who got them straight from Owsley. I unscrewed the top and drank the liquid. There was no turning back now.

Always one to jump off of cliffs like me, Michael bought a purple vial and drank it down. Chris and Eric went round and round and finally settled on the blue ones.

We joined the others in the candlelit living room with Dylan playing now. Someone rolled a joint and passed it around.

Later, as if by magic, the four of us found ourselves in a back bedroom.

"Wow, I think I'm coming on," Eric said.

"Wow, I think I'm falling in," Chris said.

Eric laughed.

"Yeah, far out."

"I think I'm coming apart," Michael said.

3

We were still riffing on that one when Sarah came in to check on us.

"How are you guys doing?"

"We're coming apart at the seams," Chris said.

Sarah put a finger to her lips, reminding us again to be quiet.

"By the way, have you seen Zach?"

The four of us looked at each other and shrugged. Sarah was about to leave when we heard something rustle in the closet. She went over and slid the door open. There was a guy scrunched up in the corner, trying to hide behind the overcoats.

"No! No! No! Keep them away! They're going to eat me!"

Sarah got down in a crouch.

"What's the matter, Zach?"

"I'm just a little dormouse and those big cats want to eat me for dinner."

As if truly believing in this outcome, Zach scurried out the door on his hands and knees. Sarah shrugged at us and went after him.

"You do kind of look like a cat," I said to Chris.

He meowed, licked his chops and pretended to stalk after Zach.

Later, the four of us were lying on our backs together, tripping on the point of infinity in the corner of the ceiling. Time had disappeared. Life was eternal.

"Wow, the colors," Eric said.

"Wow, the patterns," Chris said.

"Our parents have been lying to us," Michael said.

He had a way of distilling things down to their essence.

Sometime later, I remembered the world.

"It's Friday night and Robin Glen's playing Chapman."

My friends laughed.

"No, let's go watch it."

"Wow, brother," Eric said. "That sounds totally crazy."

"No, it'll be cool. Like watching gladiators in the Coliseum."

"Wow, that's like way too much violence for me right now."

"I'll go," Michael said.

"Onward with the expedition," Chris said.

Out in the living room, everyone thought we were crazy for wanting to go outside but the world was calling me. It always was back in those days. I had to be moving forward, going somewhere new.

4

"You're sure you're going to be okay?" one of the older guys asked.

"Yeah," I said and yanked the door open, not noticing the slide bolt had been latched. The door casing came off the wall with the door.

"Oh wow," someone said.

There was laughter and the guy who had been worrying about us came over to help me with the broken pieces.

"You're still sure you want to go out there?"

"Yeah, yeah, I'm cool."

Embarrassed, but undeterred, I stumbled out onto the front porch. Chris, Michael and Eric followed.

"Be careful," Sarah whispered from the door.

"We'll be fine," I said.

The door closed quietly as we headed down the walkway. Turning up the sidewalk, we looked back at the house and broke out laughing. It was anthropomorphic, like Huxley's automobile, the dormer windows upstairs, eyes, the covered porch a nose. The stairs led down into a gullet.

"Looks kind of serious," Chris said. "Like Clay."

I made a face and all of us went down the sidewalk laughing. It felt good to be outside with the towering trees and starry sky. The crisp night air was alive with colors. The entire universe was alive with colors.

Two blocks farther on in the old neighborhood, we came to a small market. No one was hungry but it seemed necessary to go in and explore the place. After wandering around lost amongst all the packaged crap for several minutes, we stumbled back out onto the street, laughing.

"Wow," Eric said. "Like none of that stuff even looked edible."

"We be fryin' us up some Spam for dinner," Chris said like a soul brother.

I gazed up at the stars. The Milky Way spanned the sky. In the quiet that followed, I heard a crowd cheering.

"Wow, the football game," I said and started in that direction.

"Oh wow, I totally can't do this," Eric said.

At the next cross street, I saw it terminated to our right at a chain link fence bordering one end of the football stadium.

"Hey, look. We can see the game from here."

5

The four of us walked down and stared through the fence. The teams were huddled opposite each other in the distance, awash in bright stadium lights. When the next play ran, we cracked up. Each squad appeared to be moving around like a single, many-legged organism. Another play ran, accompanied by more cheering from the crowd. We stood there for a long time, entranced. The game was both miraculous and absurd to us. The idea of winning or losing had lost all meaning.

"Wow, I'm hungry," Eric said out of the blue.

That brought on even more laughter.

"I want food," Chris said like a caveman.

"How do you feed sea grass swaying in the tides?" Michael said.

"You wait for plankton," Chris said.

Having philosophized our way across town, we passed a burger joint and broke out in another round of laughter.

"One slab of cooked crap on a bun," Chris said.

You may as well have offered us tire tread to eat.

We found a little Italian restaurant and ordered pasta.

"Tuscany," I said to the scent of the red sauce on our plates.

"Tuscaloosa," Chris said.

"Tuscaroni," Michael said.

He and Chris broke out in song.

"Tuscaroni...that San Francisco treat."

Late that night, lying alone in bed, the fleeting bliss of my trip slowly dissolved back into my many uncertainties, the draft being foremost among them. If you were a young man, 'Nam was always there waiting for you. It was the first thing you heard on the news every night.

"Good evening, today in Vietnam..."

That was every anchorman's stock in trade, the ensuing images flickering in millions of darkened living rooms across our nation, with a running tally provided in an upper corner of the screen by each network, for how many men had been shot dead and wounded, our side and theirs, for that day and the entire conflict. Progress in Vietnam came to have no other guise. The war had warped into its own sweltering, malarial infested jungle bummer acid trip, the concept of winning or losing it forsaken long ago. You simply counted bodies now to keep score.

6

On occasion, the newscasts led in with another story, like when Apollo 8 had orbited the moon or riots had broken out in one of America's cities or pissed off college students were out protesting around the nation. And there were the assassinations. Something like that always commandeered the headlines for a week or two, but for want of anything more compelling to announce, 'Good evening, today in Vietnam,' was how the news always started, the images of rice paddies and napalm having steadily burrowed their way into America's collective consciousness and words like Khe Sanh and Mekong Delta and the Ho Chi Minh trail having become part of our everyday vernacular, the same as Tang and Skippy peanut butter.

Lying there that night, I felt sick to realize how much of our earlier innocence had been stolen away from us. In a matter of five, six years, we had gone from Johnny Mathis and hula hoops and cocktail parties around the backyard swimming pool to the Beach Boys and early Beatles, to now everything being about gooks and napalm and the war draped around everyone's neck.

But there was no turning back. No matter how much I longed for those simpler times and what had been lost, there was no turning back. Vietnam had made certain of that.

2

The next day, the boys and I drove out to Irvine Park, still doing our best to mellow out from that trip. The lake and picnic areas were overrun with a Saturday crowd so we hiked up to a remote hilltop and spread out our blankets under the shade of an old oak tree. We had a fine view of the lake and whiled away the afternoon drinking wine, smoking joints and watching the swans and row boats glide here and there around the sparkling blue water.

I was scheduled to register for the draft the following Monday and an awareness of that obligation hung over that day and my entire weekend. My birthday was in late October and a notice from the draft board had arrived the very next week.

Monday after school, I followed the address on the registration card over to the local draft board. The office turned out to be in a nondescript glass storefront in the old part of town. I was expecting guys in military uniforms. Instead, I found two secretaries at their desks and a man in civilian clothing. They were all smiles and seemingly surprised to see me. The man came over and shook my hand

Hell, I thought. They never would have missed me. Now my name's in the lottery and chances are, this time next year, they'll be sending me over to have my ass blown off in 'Nam.

The next morning, the boys stopped by to smoke a joint before school. I explained the scene at the draft board.

"Don't even show up," I said while choking on a hit.

Right away, my friends were tripping over that advice, certain that MPs would be kicking down their doors.

"I know," I said. "That's what I thought. Only they acted like they didn't even know I existed. When I walked in the door it was like, 'Oh wow, thanks. Most guys don't even bother to show up'."

My friends cracked up but remained unconvinced. I had another toke off the joint and passed it on.

"I mean it. The minute I walked in there, it hit me. It's a numbers game. Don't show up and you're one of millions. Show up and you're suddenly on a first name basis with those pigs. Better to be one in a million. They don't have time to be chasing you around."

The joint came back to me and I took another hit.

"I'm telling you guys. If I had to do it all over again, I never would have shown up at that bummer place."

Michael swallowed the roach. Chris got out the eye drops. I hit the air spray.

"Okay, off to Bartley's philosophy class," Chris said. "If a man is chained to the inside of a cave and nobody sees him, does he exist?"

"He sure thinks he does," Michael said.

There was laughter.

"I'm so sick of Plato's Republic. It's like it was written by the same petrified bastards who run this country. I'd rather be force fed Leviticus."

There was more laughter and talk of scoring some hashish that evening. We lived adjacent to miles of hills and open country and were always driving up there to get high and talk about the world.

As we headed out the door, the conversation returned to Vietnam. A guy we knew had gone over there to fight for his country the previous summer. They had sent him home in a box two weeks later.

"I'm totally serious," I said, reemphasizing my point. "Don't even show up when you're called to register. Worst case scenario, they'll come looking for you if the Russians invade."

Less than a month later, I got kicked out of school. The people who ran the place had told me not to wear my moccasins on campus and to be sure and wear socks no matter what kind of shoes I had on. So I wore my moccasins again, without socks, and when I got into an argument with Bartley in our philosophy class, he turned me in.

9

My old man came home from work that evening, heard the news and got into my face. Called me a bum. And who did I think I was, wearing moccasins? Sitting Fucking Bull?

That led to us duking it out in the living room. My mother somehow got between us and told me to go wait outside. I went to sit in my car. My nose was bleeding. I had a black eye.

What a prick. The old man had sold our house the previous summer and moved us into an apartment complex. He was always selling stuff and moving us a few miles farther down the road.

My mother came out a short while later, brushing away tears. The old man was kicking me out of the house. At eighteen, I was no longer his legal responsibility and that was that. My mother handed me two hundred dollars.

"Why didn't you stick to your plans of going to college? We were prepared to pay for everything. Now look at you."

She brushed at my tears, kissed me goodbye and disappeared back into the apartment complex. I sat there alone, cast out into the world.

There was a thought to go in and retrieve my Japanese prints and Buddha figure and antique calligraphy pen, the detritus of earlier days, when I was a young boy writing haikus and all was well in the world. What had happened to me? I was once a gentle soul. Now I was at war with everything.

I sat there alone for a spell before heading over to my girlfriend Lisa's place. She answered when I knocked and came outside, quickly closing the door behind herself. Her parents weren't all that fond of me either. In fact, I had nowhere to go. Lisa went in and snuck out with some bedding, then consoled me with kisses before going back inside.

I found a place up in the hills to hide and slept on the backseat. Days turned to weeks with me wandering around lost. I had no idea what to do with myself. Had it been another era, I might have willingly signed up to go kick some ass in Southeast Asia but had yet to find one person who could properly explain to me why we were over there in the first place. No one wanted to be in 'Nam anymore. The only talk now was of how to extract ourselves without too much embarrassment. A great nation and we were getting our asses kicked by an army of little men in black pajamas, taken to the woodshed by a tiny country that struggled to field a modern jet. It didn't seem to matter how much napalm we dropped on those folks or how many B-52 sorties we conducted up north, next thing you knew, they were overrunning Saigon again.

'Peace With Honor' was the slogan our tricky new president had used to get himself elected, but peace with honor was limping home with our tail between our legs, by any other name, and limping home with our tail between our legs was not a thing you could easily sell to the American people.

Dropping the big one was another option, but wiping half a nation off the globe was an even harder sell, even to the most gung-ho, gun loving Americans who thought dropping bombs on other people was a godly good use of our time. So the horror of that war dragged on another week, and those weeks kept turning into months, simply because no one could find a convenient way to save face and back out the door all in one motion; even though the death of one more soldier over there had ceased to make one damned bit of sense.

So you turned on the news and there it was again, that all too familiar mantra.

'Good evening...today in Vietnam...'

The usual film clips followed; a lot of stuff with napalm exploding and archival footage of B-52s cutting loose with thousand pounders. Frequently you saw a handful of our soldiers hunkered down behind a patch of elephant grass, thankful for that much cover as AK-47 and mortar rounds popped off in the rice paddy around them. Or perhaps they had just taken a hill or some other ostensibly meaningful patch of jungle, or it was the next day and the Vietcong had taken it back. Or it was between firefights and you saw our unshaven soldiers standing around with peace symbols painted onto their helmets, looking for all the world as if they had bivouacked through a love-in at Golden Gate Park, except there was no joy left in their eyes as they stared back at you through the camera.

Night after night, you tuned in to watch more Vietnamese villages being strafed with napalm and more frightened villagers running for their lives down some muddy road, their skin and clothes on fire, their neighbors lying there scorched and dead. Straw huts burned in the background. Women in conical hats held their children and wept. These were the images of war and they did not change, only the people who happened to be suffering in them.

The nightly war updates routinely ended in this fashion. An incoming chopper would touch down somewhere alongside a rice paddy and a handful of grunts would drag their maimed and dismembered comrades towards it through the muck. The injured were lifted gingerly into the open bay and the chopper quickly took off again. The last thing you saw were the soldiers holding onto their helmets as the elephant grass was flattened around them.

At times, these battlefront reports were juxtaposed with the war here at home, the one in Newark or Detroit or Jackson, Mississippi. The streets of our cities were in flames and the National Guard had been called out to restore order. The rioters threw rocks and Molotov cocktails. The soldiers shot back with tear gas and such.

Just as frequently you saw students demonstrating at one college campus or another, and usually in response to the government action that had led to the riots. You saw the students march. You saw them chant. You saw them get out of control. You saw the cops arrive and get even more out of control. Sadly, you saw a once simple world being clubbed right out of existence.

3

The calendar turned from that year to the next but the war dragged on and was still there to confront me. Somehow I had to choose; go fight in 'Nam, sign up for college and apply for a deferment or go on the run.

Going to war was already a nonstarter. I had no desire to kill my fellow human beings, any more than I wanted someone taking shots at me. As a young man, all I wanted to do was lie in fields and watch clouds pass overhead.

Lisa had gone off to college that summer and my plan was to join her for the fall semester; find a junior college, take some classes and work on that deferment. At least we'd be together and with any luck, the war would soon blow over.

I had packed my boxes and given notice for the room I was renting when a Dear John letter arrived in the mail. Lisa had found herself a new man. Crushed, and with the war still barreling at me, I quit my job, sold my car and ran off to see the world.

I was in southern France that autumn when my money ran out. I arrived back to New York a few weeks later, that much closer to the draft, but without having devised a realistic plan to avoid it.

While passing through customs at JFK, I decided to go visit an old friend at Cornell. Rick was in his freshman year and living in a campus dorm. After a day on the road and much walking, I tracked him down and we headed off for something to eat at a bar.

The talk was mostly of old friends and times and places. My trip overseas naturally came up. The war did, too.

When it was time for Rick to get back to his studies, he took me across town to a big, clapboard house. Dorm rules what they were, I wasn't allowed to stay with him but he was sure these folks would let me crash at their place for a couple of nights.

A fetching young flower child answered the door, listened with a smile to Rick's explanation and welcomed me inside. I thanked Rick, gave him a hug and wished him well with college.

The young lady and a friend were making bread out in the kitchen. I grabbed a chair and talked with them as other people came and went. The house appeared to be a relatively typical campus scene from the late sixties; a tribe of young people living together, smoking dope, engaging in free sex and generally abusing the university's notion of a higher education.

Seated in their darkened living room later that night, I found myself surrounded by a band of ersatz revolutionaries. There were Army fatigues and field caps and Castro-style beards to go with it. Cigar smoke filled the room. A Che Guevara poster hung from one wall. The discussion was of how to start a revolution down in Chile.

I was amused. How in the world were these Castroistas going to stage a revolution in South America from an old clapboard house in Ithaca, New York? Youthful rebellion, I concluded, and would have left it at that, except they all seemed so damned serious.

Sipping java in a coffee shop the next morning, I noticed an article in the paper about a bomb going off in some government offices outside New York City. The bomb had pretty much destroyed the place and the Feds considered it a small miracle that no one had been injured as the result.

When I arrived back to the clapboard house later that afternoon, several of these Castroistas were gathered together in the living room with curtains closed. There was a glance my way before their whispered conversation continued. The whole scene felt like a bummer.

Heading upstairs, I noticed the door to the basement had been padlocked and it suddenly hit me. These freaks must be the ones behind that bombing. I'd better get my ass out of town.

On the highway that same afternoon, I found the experience back in Ithaca troubling my thoughts. I had always pictured myself as part of the movement, but that basically involved doing my own thing, and in a peaceful manner. It definitely didn't include Marxist revolutionary dogma or blowing up government property. Maybe I was just greatly apathetic, or a coward at heart. I wasn't so sure I could have articulated the difference between those two things at the time, but I knew this much for certain. If you thought wars and violence were a suitable way of resolving conflicts, you could leave me out. Find me a quiet place in the sun and I'd be happy.

Back on the West Coast, I rented a room in an old boardinghouse and got a day job slopping hash at a local diner. I fell in love and took some classes at a nearby junior college but had soon dropped out from a profound sense of boredom. And all the while, that fleeting exposure to the revolution went on haunting my thoughts. It really had me down, to think that some people were willing to die for their beliefs…and I was not.

What peace of mind I had was due mostly to my new girlfriend Laura and the turn-of-the-century neighborhood where I lived. Grand old stone buildings lined the town plaza and retirees gathered on benches in the afternoons, feeding pigeons. And though the plaza and everything remaining from the town's pioneer past had grown a bit dilapidated over the years, they had yet to talk of tearing those things down for a new strip mall or gas station.

It was only when you got out into the suburbs, where I had grown up as a boy, that you found another sort of war being waged; where every time you turned around, another orange grove had been uprooted, another old ranch house turned to sticks and one more piece of the town's pastoral past plowed under for development. Acres upon acres of clay soil cut raw beneath the sun, survey sticks jammed into the ground everywhere, the little orange and pink ribbons flapping in the breeze, like grave markers to a forgotten world.

But at least I never saw a bulldozer or tract house under construction as I came to and from the old boardinghouse where I lived, and aside from my work, and spending every possible moment I could with Laura, I had started to dream of the next wondrous adventure in life and if anything bothered me greatly, it was that Chris and Eric and Michael had all gone off to attend college and my once unshakable feelings of invincibility seemed to have vanished along with them.

4

It had grown late that spring afternoon and as was typical of me in my youth, I started down the wooden stairs in great leaps and bounds, off to retrieve the mail and oblivious to the ruckus my boots were making all around the old boardinghouse where I then lived. As I flew past the second story landing and down the last flight of stairs, the old widow who owned the place came out of her apartment, hair done up in a bun and her left arm akimbo. The look on her face suggested she might give me a notice.

"Clay, you absolutely must stop making such a big ruckus around here."

"Sorry, Mrs. Millstadt. I'll try to do better."

I tiptoed the rest of the way down the first-floor hallway and slipped out the front door with the door to Mrs. Millstadt's apartment closing behind me.

Outside on the front porch, I was treated to a jigsaw puzzle day. It had rained overnight and the snowcapped mountains glistened on the far horizon, the same as they had when we were young boys and girls walking to and from school, our cheeks all rosy and our hearts full of cheer. The last thing on my mind were all the ghastly things that men did to each other in the name of God and country, but with the mail in hand, I spotted the draft notice and you may as well have shoved me off a cliff backwards.

Stunned, I marched dismally back up to my room, ruing my total lack of preparation. Being in this position was as much my fault as anything else. My birth date had come up number eighteen in the lottery and I had basically stuck my head in the sand in response. Of course things were going to turn out this way.

Up in my room, I sat down at my desk and stared briefly at the envelope before tossing it into the trash. There wasn't much point in opening it. I already knew what the damned thing would say.

Time passed. Mrs. Millstadt's laundry flapped lazily in the breeze below my window. A thousand ideas for how to escape flashed through my head, but none of them the least bit realistic.

Later, I heard Mrs. Millstadt retrieving her laundry and came back to the moment. Afternoon was turning to dusk outside. The mail still sat on my desk. A letter from Eric was on top of the pile so I opened it, hoping tales of his adventures at BYU would serve to distract me. Instead, his letter was mostly a rant about the war. Whiner, I thought. His number had been picked 306 in the draft. They were never going to call his ass up for duty.

As I read through the rest of Eric's letter, I found myself glancing repeatedly at the draft notice in the trash. It was a rather innocuous looking thing for all the significance involved; only slightly larger than a legal envelope, with a perforated strip along the top. It could have been a lousy traffic ticket, if not for the draft board's return address printed in the upper left hand corner.

In the end, accepting that ignorance was no form of escape, I retrieved the notice and extracted the letter from inside, seeing straight off that I was in one hell of a fix. The Army had scheduled me for induction in two weeks. I should plan on a long day, starting at a processing center in LA and ending with a bus trip up to Ford Ord. I might want to bring along a toothbrush and sack lunch.

As darkness fell outside my windows, the knowledge of my circumstances burned in my heart. In all likelihood, a tour in Vietnam awaited me; off to fight a war I dreaded and abhorred more than anything in the world.

The ensuing days rushed by with me vacillating over my choice. One voice said acquiesce. Another voice said run. The Bhagavad-Gita came to mind, Krishna reasoning with Arjuna. Why not march down into the field of battle with no fear of my death? After all, this world was all in passing. Yet I found little peace in these thoughts as the time to report drew steadily nearer.

When the day finally arrived, I hitchhiked up to LA, having reluctantly decided to accept my fate. The instructions led me to the back of a long line, where a thousand other young men stood waiting to have their heads shaved and asses checked.

As expected, I quickly passed their physical and psychological tests. Next stop was a haircut and formal induction, but while waiting there in line, a vision of my own death swept over me, sloshing about in a sweltering jungle, fetid water up to my crotch, leeches sucking at my putrid flesh, the scent of wild orchids in the humid air, the call of exotic birds echoing among the trees as the staccato bark of an AK-47 rang out and blew off my head.

Sickened by my decision to report in the first place, I slipped out of the line and entered a building next to the induction area. A maze of long hallways led me back towards the street. Uniformed sentries stood here and there, each one of them with a rifle in hand, each one of them eyeing me as I passed by. I jumped at every voice, expecting someone to bark out a command at any second.

After what had seemed like an eternity, I pushed open the front door and emerged onto the smoggy streets of LA, a free but troubled man. It was time to hide. I heard those words in my head but hardly knew what they meant. All I had was the inertia of an impulsive decision at my back.

My first thought was to call Laura but I knew she had a voice class at that hour on Mondays. Besides, I knew what she would say. You should have gone back to school and applied for a deferment, a course of action I had put off one semester after another, until now, when it appeared to be too late.

My decision-making in this regard bordered on madness. I knew it but seemed incapable of changing my behavior. As a young man, I bristled at being controlled, a resistance to authority so complete, I even revolted at sitting in classrooms. My heart cried out for wide-open spaces, to live and do as I pleased, yet walking alone down the back streets of LA, I knew little of freedom.

Having walked along for the better part of a mile, I thought of my eldest brother Anthony and decided to give him a call. He lived up in the Santa Cruz Mountains and Northern California was definitely a better place to be hiding out than where I was now.

At a small Mexican market, I stopped for some change, located a phone booth and made the call. Anthony listened patiently while I poured my heart out to him. I would have gone on quite a bit longer but he interrupted me and suggested I hitchhike up to his place. He too thought I should go back to school and try for a deferment, but of course I could come up and stay for as long as I needed to sort things out.

I was on the road all that day and arrived about ten in the evening, greeted at the front door of the cabin by Anthony wearing overalls, a flannel shirt and tennis shoes, and with his curly hair down to his shoulders. His wife Mildred scraped together a meal for me out in the kitchen and we talked until late, our conversation returning again and again to the war and my plight.

A bed had been made for me in a small room off the kitchen and I lay there alone that night, haunted by my decision. Federal agents would be knocking down the door first thing in the morning. It now appeared that moving forward was my only hope. All sorts of ideas about where to go came to mind, but, once again, none of them appeared to be the least bit realistic when viewed in the light of day.

I fell asleep to the sound of a creek gurgling beneath the cabin and awakened around eight the next morning to Mildred stirring in the kitchen. The scent of blueberry muffins wafted into my room. I heard Anthony stirring a short time later and the crackle of a fire in the fireplace. Blonde on Blonde came on the stereo, something heartfelt and sincere. I lay there with the memories of my youth digging into my heart—that night we had tripped at Sarah's place and a thousand other dear adventures—all of it so damned close but now completely beyond my reach.

Before getting up, I read a few pages from The Hobbit and the morning was now filled with pleasant dreams of the Shire. Wood elves were making mischief out in the forest. We'd all go off on a grand adventure with Gandalf and live happily ever after.

Anthony and Mildred headed off for their day at the university a short while later. Their two Weimaraner pups flew out the front door with them. Anthony called to me before closing it.

"Keep an eye on them."

I waved and watched the dogs disappear into the forest, tongues hanging out and nipping at each other's heels.

Alone now, I poured a cup of coffee and went out to sit on a deck off the kitchen. The creek exited below me and trickled down a glade. Occasionally, I heard the dogs barking in the distance or a car passing up on the narrow mountain highway, but otherwise it was quiet.

Amidst the silence, a large Tomcat plopped up onto the railing and another one soon followed. They hissed menacingly at each other before settling in to lick their paws from a distance.

Thinking to fashion a bit of peace in the world, I went inside and returned with two bowls of tuna, but in place of peace, I quickly had a full-scale war on my hands, ears pinned back, hissing and snapping. Then the dogs came sprinting home and commenced to have a grand time, barking and leaping up at the cats from the forest floor.

The dogs eventually tired of their sport and disappeared back into the forest. In need of a nap, the cats resigned themselves to a fragile peace. I smoked a joint and dreamed of saving the world. All was quiet there in the forest.

Later on, I ate two of Mildred's blueberry muffins lavished with butter, pulled on my boots and walked down to the San Lorenzo River with a fishing pole. Before I knew it, the autumn sky had grown pale and Mildred and Anthony were arriving home to make dinner.

I spent another day in much the same way, then another, and another one, and soon most of a week had disappeared. The war was still there but receding from my thoughts.

Late that Friday afternoon, Anthony came into my room and sat on the bed while I was reading. He looked serious.

"Mom called me today at work. A couple of guys in suits stopped by the house looking for you."

He studied my reaction.

"I don't know who they were exactly. You know her. She was too flustered to ask. At least she told them she had no idea where to find you."

"But she called you. What if they had tapped her phone?"

Anthony shrugged.

"I doubt it."

"Yeah, but you don't know."

Anthony shrugged again.

"What are you going to do? You've got to hang somewhere. Lay low and I'll help you find a job."

Anthony patted me on the leg.

"Things will work out. Just remember, you're not the only one in this position."

With that, he went out to help Mildred make dinner. I lay alone with my thoughts. What in the world had I done? It must have been something more than dodging the draft. A million other young men had done the same thing. It made no sense for them to come poking around my parent's place like that.

I worried over things all that night and the next day and for several more days to come. Another week flew by and I jumped at every unexpected knock on the door, but nothing much happened, except that I worried a lot.

Anthony did help me find a job with this old hippie, clearing dead trees from the forest. Our days were spent cutting logs into shorter pieces and splitting the pieces into firewood. The job barely paid enough to survive but had one great advantage. I was outdoors and free to dream from dawn to dusk.

Mostly I dreamed about Laura and a world in which wars did not exist. Or, being more practical, of a world where nothing worse than a slap on the wrist and a tour in the National Guard awaited me. At times it seemed that the peace process might actually succeed but my hopes were repeatedly dashed. Laura remained in the south, out of my reach, and the negotiators in Paris went on squabbling like spoiled children. They couldn't decide on the size of the negotiating table, let alone how to end their damned war.

And all the while my life went on in its shadow world, where in the first few moments of consciousness each day, I would pretend my problems did not exist. Then, accepting that they did, I went off to work in the forest and dreamed all day of miraculous solutions. I spent most evenings in general merriment with Mildred and Anthony, only to find the same circle of anxieties and illusions awaiting me when I lay back down to bed.

5

Spring had turned to summer and summer to fall and I had hitchhiked down to visit Laura twice during those months, and was in fact just then returning from a third trip to LA with renewed hopes in my heart. After months of pleading with her, Laura had at last expressed a willingness to transfer colleges and move up north with me.

Having arrived back to Santa Cruz late in the day, I hiked over to where Old Route 9 met Coast Highway and stuck my thumb out. A young man stopped to pick me up a few minutes later and we started up the road beneath a sun speckled canopy of trees. The nearby San Lorenzo River came into view here and there, skipping whitely over pebble and rock, and it was a good river, filled with steelhead in those autumn months of the year.

The highway eventually wound up and over a mountain pass and down into a sunlit valley and soon after entered a stretch of dense, dark forest. Seeing the handmade street sign tacked to a redwood up ahead, I gestured for the young man to pull over. We talked a bit more before he continued on his way. I turned down the gravel lane towards our cabin. The gloom of twilight had gathered among the redwoods and filled the forest floor with the quiet of that hour.

A memory popped into my head as I walked along; of the many times Anthony and I had flown past our street on the way home, the two of us immersed in one discussion or another and not realizing we had missed the obscure street sign until we were a half mile up the narrow highway, forced by our inattentiveness to continue on to the village market in order to turn around and using that as an excuse to stop and buy a bottle of Spanish Port for our troubles.

I felt good having these thoughts and to see the creek gurgling beneath our upraised cabin but the usual trail of smoke was missing from our stone chimney, as was Anthony's car or any other signs of activity, and that was odd. Anthony and Mildred were typically home at that hour.

Going over the little bridge to the front door, I noticed a padlock around the doorknob, of the sort real estate agents use when selling a property, and a jolt of alarm shot through me. Something was terribly wrong.

Unable to see through the front door or the curtained windows, I went around to the creek, climbed up onto the back deck and stared in through the kitchen door. The wood floors had been swept clean and glowed faintly in the dim light. The closet in my room was open and everything gone from it. The cabin was completely empty.

I climbed back down from the deck and impulsively circled the cabin several times, checking every door and window, unwilling to accept my own sensory perceptions. My brother, his wife and their two dogs were gone. I was homeless in the gathering dusk and had just hitchhiked four hundred miles to discover this fact. It seemed impossible to believe. There had to be an explanation, yet nothing I considered made any sense. Before vanishing in this way, why on earth hadn't Anthony bothered to call me?

Sick at heart, I went around front and started up the lane towards our neighbor Nita's place. No doubt she knew what had happened and if nothing else would offer me a place to sleep that night.

Halfway up the road, Nita's boyfriend appeared from around the far side of her cottage and loped up the stairs like a bear coming back to its den. Nita opened the screen door and the two of them kissed before Jack slipped inside.

I paused in the lane, the image of Jack's Levi jacket etched in my mind. A yin yang symbol had been stitched to the back, a reminder of his legendary status among the Merry Pranksters and of my own uncertainties as a young man. There was a thought to go camp in the woods in place of troubling Nita but I went on up to her door and knocked. I needed to know what the hell had happened to my brother, my youthful insecurities aside.

23

The latest Stones' album started to blare out of Nita's house.

'Well, you heard about the midnight rambler...creeping round your bedroom door'.

I knocked on the door with the sound track echoing all around the quiet forest. When Nita failed to answer, I knocked again. Finally, she appeared.

"Clay!" she said at seeing me outside her screen door. "Come in, come in."

The door creaked open. Nita was holding a wooden spoon in one hand and used the back of the other hand to wipe the sweat from her brow. Her cheeks were red from standing over a hot stove. She offered me a radiant smile and a peck on the cheek.

"Come in, come in," she repeated and hurried back to the kitchen, her fluffy, black Afro swaying about as she went.

"You know Jack," she shouted over the music.

Jack sat hunched forward on the sofa, his dark eyes studying me.

I felt another jolt of adrenalin. Did he know about my tryst with Nita? The two of us had slept together back in the spring, when I first moved up to live with Anthony, which probably meant little or nothing to her, given the times. Nita was a free spirit at the vanguard of the Bay Area counter-culture movement and a seamstress to a number of its creative icons, and had no doubt slept with a lot of those men, too, but she was still Jack's lady and for all the free love in the sixties, I doubted his magnanimity under the circumstances. He probably felt about Nita the same way I felt about Laura.

Not knowing what to say, I excused myself and went into the kitchen.

Nita was busy with her pots and pans on the stove. She also had something baking in the oven. She checked that and stirred the contents of a pan, all the while dancing to the Stones. She wiped the sweat from her forehead one more time and smiled somewhat sadly at me over her shoulder.

"Roll a joint!" she said and pointed to her stash on a bookshelf.

I did as requested and held the joint to her lips while she cooked. We both took several hits and I placed the roach in an ashtray.

Seated at Nita's breakfast nook, I felt the drug take effect and the shock of my predicament melt away into spiritual detachment. My former home was merely a painting on life's canvas now, a fleeting moment in the space-time continuum, surrounded by redwoods at dusk and framed by Nita's kitchen window. Only the music seemed a bit incongruous under the circumstances. Recognizing my unease, Nita scurried off to turn down the stereo.

"Sorry," she said upon her return. "Anyway, I suppose you saw the cabin was empty."

I nodded.

"It was crazy, Clay. Absolutely crazy. The whole thing blew up in a matter of days. Mildred caught Anthony and Joni screwing down in the woods. Which I think Mildred would have dismissed but Anthony had already gone off the deep end and by the following week, he and Joni had run off to Europe and Mildred had gone back to live with her parents in Hawaii."

Nita smiled sarcastically over her shoulder at me.

"I guess she had pictured Anthony going over there to work in her old man's shipping business at some point. Imagine that. Anthony taking a corporate job."

"Yeah," I said.

Nita studied me and went back to her cooking.

"Maybe you didn't see this coming, Clay, but things weren't all that great for them after the Peace Corps. Anyway, our friends around the valley helped disperse all their stuff and next thing you know, poof, everything was gone and the place was empty."

Nita waved as if it was some sort of grand magic.

"The cabin's for rent, if you're interested."

"I couldn't afford it alone," I said. "Do you know what happened to my stuff?"

"Oh, it's scattered all over the place. You know how it is with hippies, Clay. You may as well have left your stash lying around. I can give you some clothes if you need them."

"No, I'll be all right. I've got my backpack down at the cabin. I'll sleep by the river tonight and head back south in the morning."

"Don't go south," she said. Nita placed the wooden spoon down and took hold of my face with both hands. "Think of your draft situation, Clay."

"I think about it every day, Nita."

"Then you should know. The last place you want to be right now is down in LA."

Jack appeared in the doorway and leaned there, twirling a feather in one hand. I looked back at Nita.

"Laura was planning to come up and live with me in a few weeks."

"So? Call her and explain. Or better yet, don't say a thing. Just let her show up and take it from there. You know there are places you can stay with friends. Then in a month or so, the two of you can afford to get your own place."

"No, I've got to go down there and explain what's happened. She won't understand."

I did not want to admit to the arrogance I had displayed. 'You need to move your ass up north here where I can take care of you'. And now I had nothing to offer Laura but broken promises.

"Sit still," Jack said. "Let the universe turn. Everything will find its proper place."

He had said this while still twirling the feather in his hand.

Yeah, right, I thought. How easy to dispense wisdom when it wasn't your life and your woman. I doubted he'd be saying the same thing if Nita was involved. I looked back at her, suppressing my anger as best I could. She tussled my hair.

"You can sleep on the couch tonight, okay?"

At this, Jack abruptly returned to the living room. This was followed by the loud thump of a book dropping onto the hardwood floor. The message was clear. Jack didn't approve of the energy. Nita smiled at me again, doing her best to keep two male elk from locking antlers in her kitchen.

"Come," she said and filled a bowl with soup on the dining table. "At least have something to eat."

I sat down and waited for her to bring me a spoon.

With barely a hint of daylight remaining, I walked back down to the cabin and climbed up onto the wooden deck one more time. Leaning over the rail, I stared down towards the river. The creek gurgled beneath me. A woodcock called in the distance. Otherwise the world was quiet. I half expected Anthony's dogs to come running out of the forest from their Bodkins adventures. So many times my brother and I had lingered there with the umbrage of dusk gathering around us; Anthony standing along the rail, his freshwater pole dangling over the creek, laughably expecting an errant steelhead to appear, and me seated at the redwood table, the two of us talking up the world together, a joint passed between us, the dream of the sixties lingering in our trail of smoke and good conversation.

I broke down then, seeing how all of that had been taken from me, never to return.

When my heart was somewhat stilled, I climbed back down from the deck and started towards the river. The forest was nearly black so I had to feel my way cautiously among the undergrowth and fallen branches.

I chose a place to camp under a redwood, some distance back from the river, where I could still hear the whisper of the trees over the rushing water. I had no candle or lantern to read by and was left to my thoughts. The Vietnam War dug into them immediately. It seemed impossible to believe, that at that very moment, on the other side of the world, men stood fearfully amidst the fetid swamps and rotting foliage of a tropical jungle, ready to blow each other to hell.

Not wanting to think of the war, I recalled pleasanter days, when I had bummed my way across Europe, a Moroccan satchel over my shoulder and the world in front of me. Life abroad had been a wondrous adventure, filled with sidewalk cafes on warm summer nights and good conversation and endless discovery, so that returning that winter to face the draft had felt like a death march, and all the more so when learning that my number had been picked at the top of the lottery. It had only been a matter of time before that draft notice arrived in the mail, as it did.

And then I had met Laura, my one impulse since that moment being to steal away with her, to escape the war and all my troubles. With her love, I felt invincible and had no fear of being a man without a country and imagined that I would love her always and these thoughts nearly made me leap to my feet, determined as I was to go south and be at her side, despite what Nita and Jack had told me.

This flow of dreams and desires and regrets went on working in my heart. I wanted to hold the woman I loved in that very instant. I longed to find our place in the sun. And all the while, uncertainty worked within me, as though the gods were pressing a great weight down upon my chest.

6

Sometime late in the night, I was awakened by a clap of thunder and sat up anxiously. It had started to rain. I sat there watching and expecting to be soaked at any minute but the redwood shed the rain off nicely and kept my area dry.

Satisfied, I lay back down with my thoughts. They were the same ones that had been troubling me when I fell asleep earlier — where to go and how to eat and what to do with my life — and it was very late before I found sleep again.

At dawn, I awakened with the wind surging and moaning in the treetops. At least the storm had started to break. Glimpses of blue sky peeked through the gray clouds streaming overhead. I pulled the sleeping bag tighter around my neck, not wanting to face the day.

In time, I grew tired of my thoughts and got up to gather my belongings. To be homeless and nearly broke was to be haunted as a man and going forward was the only form of peace I could find.

Retracing my steps up the glade, I paused for a moment to stare at my former home, then leapt over the creek and went up and around to the gravel lane. It was now puddled with rain so that my boots gathered mud as I walked along. Passing by Nita's place, I paused again, wishing I could have one of her croissants and a cup of coffee, but there were no lights on or signs of anyone stirring so I continued on up to the highway.

Huddled against the bitter cold, I stuck my thumb out at hearing a car approach but the driver flew right by me. Some minutes later, another car came by without stopping, and another one. My hands grew numb and my nose began to run. Visions of gingerbread and fires in a hearth danced in my head.

After waiting a good long spell, a young man stopped and got me down to the coast. I was famished and headed towards downtown Santa Cruz, thinking to warm myself in the Catalyst Café for a few hours over coffee and muffins before heading south.

As I walked along, I recalled my last exchange with Laura and the look on her face. Either you're coming with me or you're not. I had offered a young woman in college little choice, and even less security, which together with my other fears and uncertainties, turned my spirit in a great, anxiety-filled rush to head south and remedy the mess I had wrought.

Have one coffee and a muffin and get back out on the road. I had to make everything all right. To hell with dillydallying around in the Catalyst.

At the top of Chestnut Street, the town was spread out before me on that bleak and stormy day. A single, white church steeple stabbed into the gray sky. My thoughts turned back to another bleak November morning, when a President's casket had rolled through the streets of our nation's capital, a black horse with its tail aloft, the barricades lined with people holding handkerchiefs to their faces, their breath making frosty puffs in the cold morning air.

How in God's name had we remained so hopeful after that tragedy? A few stray bullets and our merry, Sunday evening singing alongs with Mitch Miller national odyssey had been sent careening down its alternative path, the imprint of one man's courage holding the hearts of those who believed in him steady for almost five years, until they shot his brother too, and whatever frail reed of hope and innocence that remained had been trampled in the streets of Chicago that same summer, the obvious all too obvious at that point. If you attempted to get in the way of the machine, it would simply run you over, and that was where I stood that day, the wheels of war and psychedelics still spinning on the wreckage of my abandoned dreams, my logic and bearings shot and left to think, what a sad and lost world it had become, a world that longed to change, but no one seemed capable of changing it.

Tiring again of my thoughts, I turned onto Pacific Avenue and into the downtown district, confronted there by an assortment of hippies huddled against shuttered storefronts, most of them, like me, with nowhere to go on that cold, bitter morning. I passed four of them, three men and their female companion shivering under an old army blanket. One of the men called me "brother" and hit me up for some change, then called me an "asshole" a few paces later for having failed to accommodate him. I flashed a peace sign and kept going, not wanting to argue or to delve any further into the cultural train wreck of my generation. It was like trash along the side of the road, better left ignored if you weren't prepared to clean it up.

Besides, there were more practical matters to address. All my belongings were damp from the rain. I needed to wash up and brush my teeth. Then I'd have a warm, banana-nut muffin, chase it down with a big mug of café au lait and hit the road. My hope was to reach Big Sur by midday. I expected the sun to come out and warm my bones, and if things went well on the road, to be in Laura's arms by nightfall.

With all this worked out in my head, I arrived at the Catalyst Café, pushed open the wooden door and paused inside for a few moments, allowing my eyes to adjust to the cavernous, dimly lit interior, with all its nooks and crannies. The only illumination came from a lofted glass ceiling, making it hard to see past the haze of spectral dust drifting in the center of the room. The fragrances of freshly brewed coffee, baked goods, incense and herbal tea filled the air. A Jefferson Airplane album was playing in the background.

My vision adjusting, I spotted a vacant table and had started in that direction when my friend Eric appeared out of the spectral dust.

"Wow, brother," he said and gave me a hug, then stood back at arm's length with his 'the universe is all in passing' smile.

"Far out, Eric. What are you doing in Santa Cruz?"

"I escaped Provo for the Thanksgiving holiday. My parents think I'm back in my dorm studying for finals."

I kept glancing at his short hair, not having seen him since the previous summer, when he went off to attend BYU. He looked like someone had just freed him from boot camp, but that was the price you paid for accepting a free education from your Mormon parents. It also symbolized the fundamental difference between Eric and me. If my parents had tried to ship me off to BYU, I would have told them to shove it.

30

Eric noticed me staring at his hair and attempted to pull at it.

"Wow. At least I don't have to worry about the cops shaking me down."

I smiled at his wry observation and sat down at the empty table. Eric set his morning paper down and joined me. Serious now, he had started to speak when a young waitress appeared to take our orders. When she left, I began to spread my things out to dry. Looking up, I saw Eric still staring at me.

"What? What's going on? Have you seen Chris and Michael?"

"Oh wow, yeah," Eric said with a chuckle. "Chris left college to attend this acting school in St. Louis but I guess he sort of felt like it was going nowhere so he went to New York. Then Michael and Myron joined him and the last I heard they were starting a band."

"Wow. That's far out."

"Yeah," Eric said. "I was thinking to ditch college and join them."

"That'll really trip your parents out."

"I know, huh?"

Without the war hanging over his head, Eric's life was still a picnic. He could do as he pleased. Run off to New York or St. Louis. Whatever. I did not want to feel bitter about it, but I did.

He had started to lean across the table and speak when the waitress reappeared, this time with two mugs of coffee and my muffin. Eric leaned out of the way and watched while I quickly went about consuming the muffin.

"What?" I said in response to his continued stare.

In place of words, Eric opened the paper and turned it around to face me. It took a moment for me to notice the article about the Weather Underground, and another moment to read how several of its members had been arrested in Ithaca for conspiracy. I turned to the back pages and found the names of those indicted.

I was among them.

"Fuck," I said. "It must have been when I went to visit Rick at Cornell."

I explained about my encounter with those Castroistas.

"I only slept on their couch."

"I guess the Feds aren't making that distinction."

"Fuck," I said again.

My mind raced back over the events of the past year. It would explain why those two Feds had come poking around my parent's place. Evading the draft would rarely get you that kind of attention. They'd have to bust you for something else first and nail you on a background check. But blowing up a federal building? I was now in the crosshairs of every domestic and international law enforcement agency on the face of the Earth. A few more bad breaks and I'd have my picture hanging in the post office.

I quickly weighed how much money I had left. $25. That wouldn't get me far, let alone allow me to take care of Laura.

"What are you going to do?" Eric said.

"I don't know."

For once, I felt utterly bereft of a plan. Always in the past, one scheme or another had come to mind, some way of crossing the Seven Seas, or at least getting to the next place where I might rest my weary head, but now, even my most practical ideas for escape seemed ridiculous.

The front door opened abruptly as another patron came in, reminding me of the bleak weather outside. I had no real desire to brave the highway that day, and was feeling less and less inclined to do so with every minute I delayed inside the warm café. Fanciful solutions to my problems flashed through my brain. I would be Beorn, the changeling, gatherer of honey and tamer of bears. Build a cabin up in the mountains and live in the way that I chose, detached from society and all of its madness.

Nita's words came back to me, too; sit still and wait for Laura to arrive. Perhaps Nita was right. I should go back and find some way to rent our old cabin. At the very least, I should stay here in Santa Cruz, where it was safe. I had put my foot down and it was best to leave things like that. Resolve was precisely what a woman wanted from a man.

Then apprehension jumped to my heart again. I had no money to rent our old cabin, and even if I did, then what? Sooner or later, the Feds would come knocking.

A stream of other notions passed through my head but none of them did a thing to change my situation. I felt driven to move on that day and the impulses of my heart appeared to be my only guide. I wanted to hold Laura in my arms that night. I wanted to love her and know that I was loved in return.

Eric and I talked for most of an hour, and I hated to part with his company, or the warmth of the café, but the time came to say goodbye and I marched back through town on that cold, dreary day, driven on by things that I did not understand.

Out on Highway 1, the wind blew hard and froze me to the core. I huddled with my arms across my chest and cursed the weather. Half an hour went by before someone stopped to pick me up, and for what turned out to be a short ride that only got me down to the artichoke farms around Castroville.

From there, I caught another quick ride to Moss Landing and stood waiting in the cold again. A generating plant towered over the inland side of the highway. Trawlers and various pleasure craft bobbed inside a harbor jetty on the other side. Clouds passed by swiftly overhead and ship masts stabbed into the cold, gray sky, the only point of reference on that dreary day.

Other hitchhikers appeared along the highway and took their places at roughly fifty-yard intervals behind me, honoring the unspoken highway etiquette of the "peace and brotherhood" generation, waiting for your ride in turn. I was first in line but time passed and no one stopped to pick me up. I glanced over my shoulder. Everyone back there looked to be all cheerful about the adventure at hand. I felt more like some wretch in A Thousand and One Nights, torn from my home and condemned to a life of wandering. There were visions of being back inside the warmth of the Catalyst Café. I thought of Laura. An endless stream of hopes and fears and expectations swirled through my head.

A short time later, a car pulled to the side of the highway up ahead of me and dropped off a young couple with backpacks. I watched anxiously, fearing they would jump the queue, but they came along as hoped. When they offered to share a joint with me, I accepted, then regretted my decision when the man asked if we could hitchhike together. I looked up the highway, aware that people behind us were already starting to grouse. You did not let people cut in line that way. Worse for me, a driver might pull over, interested in picking up the chick and only having enough room for two people, in which case, I'd be left behind. I had been down this road before and told them I'd better go it alone. The couple marched off to take their place at the back of the line, trying to act cool but clearly disappointed.

I had another vision after smoking the joint: the power of the world turning in circles, with my generation like asteroids, solitary, irrelevant and drifting off towards the outer reaches of our solar system, cut off from everything central. We were all going off to live in the country. What a joke. We had trouble paying the rent, let alone the determination to maintain an alternative existence.

Around mid-afternoon, I got past Monterey and down into Big Sur. The blue sky broke through the cloud cover and my countenance brightened with it. The surf churned along the rocky coastline. Cypress trees swayed and whispered in the wind. The mountains rose up in a vertical grassy incline on the opposite side of the highway with pines dotting the higher slopes. I felt the peace one finds amidst so much beauty.

An older couple in a sports car was the first to come along. They had the top down and their long, gray hair blew in the wind. They both waved and smiled as they motored by me. I waved back, knowing they would have stopped had there been room. I pictured them as professors from the Esalen Institute or maybe old friends of Henry Miller. I was drawn to their seeming enlightenment and wanted to grow old and happy with Laura in that way, with love and laughter forever in our hearts.

More time passed without a single car coming by. I had only the sea and blue sky and my thoughts to entertain me.

My hopes rose at the sound of another approaching vehicle but it was a big motor home with a square couple and they went around the next bend like I wasn't even there. I was alone again with the sky and the coast and my thoughts. Several cars and motor homes passed by over the next half hour but no one stopped.

I leaned against my pack for a spell then grew restless and paced back and forth, my thoughts fixated on Laura the entire time. The memory came to me of how we had met, while one of my friends was selling mescaline to three students in Laura's dorm room. Laura had pulled me aside while the deal was going down, asking if I wanted to join her for a walk. The moon was full that night with a warm wind blowing out of the desert and Laura's long, flaxen hair had swayed wildly with the trees beneath the starry sky. Laura eventually led me to a nearby school playground and rocked me back and forth on a swing while serenading me with her angelic voice.

With my old boarding house but a few blocks away from the college campus, Laura had visited me regularly, our conversations often conducted with one of us lying on the bed while the other marched back and forth, gesticulating dramatically and generally making a Shakespearean fuss. I could not have adored a woman more, not only for her beauty and mystical nature, but for her intelligence and wit. She was truly everything I desired in a woman and I imagined nothing would make me happier than if we could go away somewhere and live our lives in peace.

I was so thoroughly tripping out over these reveries, I failed to notice that a red Corvette had pulled to the side of the road several hundred feet up ahead. I grabbed my pack and rushed forward, excited at the prospect of moving on, but when I got within thirty feet, the driver honked and sped away in a cloud of dust. I heard laughter as his passenger flipped me off through the open window. I dropped the pack and kicked at the dirt. It took me several minutes, pacing up and down the highway, before I had calmed down again.

Fuckers, I thought and sat back down to wait for a ride.

An hour later, I gave up and hiked several miles down to the lagoon at Little Sur. Twilight was falling as I rounded the last bend in the road and saw the turquoise lagoon and towering white sand dunes out near the sea. The highway looped in around the lagoon and out to the other side before disappearing around the next bend. I watched several groups of people camped alongside the lagoon for a minute before making my way up into the woods alone. Late into the night, I heard the sound of their merriment mixing with the distant sound of crashing surf.

The next morning, I broke camp late and hiked down to the highway. Cars came and went where the highway made its long, sweeping turn around the lagoon. The sea was visible here and there in the other direction, beyond the towering white sand dunes.

Several old school buses and Volkswagen vans were parked along the lagoon's edge with a number of people bathing in the turquoise water, men, women and children among them and everyone naked. I found my own place along the lagoon, stripped down and waded in with a bar of soap. Within seconds, a man had offered me a hit off his joint.

"Where are you headed, brother?" he asked.

"LA."

"Oh fuck."

Everyone within earshot laughed.

"Shit, you'd better give him another hit," someone said. "He's going to need it."

"Hey, brother," one of the kinder souls said, "we're all headed up into the mountains to stake a gold claim. You're welcome to join us."

It occurred to me in light of his offer that a singularity of purpose was my primary problem. I kept thinking of my life as a straight line, when life was anything but straight, and as long as I remained determined to fight this law of physics, I could expect the commensurate frustration and grief.

Indeed, why not go along? Yet, I glanced around at the naked mothers breast-feeding their children, and the kid crapping on the ground behind a school bus and the entire chaos of this entourage and knew I would never be at peace in a crowd. I thanked the man for his offer, hurried to finish my bath and hiked back up to the highway.

On the road south that day, waiting for the next ride, I heard the Irish side of me, the part of me that was like the sea: rootless, restless and detached from the course of history. I imagined walking the coastline of every continent in the world, with nothing more complicated than the song of the sea in my ears. Then another part of me chimed in: the man who wanted stability to go with his independence, fancying an eyrie high up on a cliff above the coast, and with a lady at my side.

Eventually, I just found myself depressed about my impending arrival back to LA, knowing it was madness to be headed that way. I was like a moth to light. After all, if I wanted to be safe, I was certainly moving in the wrong direction. And yet, I felt incapable of suppressing my love for Laura and when I imagined the two of us being together on a shared journey through life, I did not have any reservations at all.

The day passed with my thoughts going around and around and without any abiding logic, other than to think that money was the primary solution to all my problems. There were few options available to me without it, except to go around and around in the same pointless circle. Thus, I focused my mind on getting a job and saving money and being able to take care of Laura in the way that I wished. If I was lucky and caught good rides, I would be in her arms that night and love her greatly and tenderly and we would work together towards our goals. To hell with war and the sixties and everything else.

I pressed south all day, passed San Simeon late in the day and arrived a few miles south of Gaviota at nightfall, bummed to think that Laura's love would have to wait another day but realizing there was little point in forcing the issue at that late hour. I could see a small market not far from the highway off ramp and hiked down there, broke my last twenty-dollar bill on a sandwich and bedded down in a field alongside the sea. For hours I lay there watching anxiously as cattle gathered at a nearby fence. Occasionally, cars passed by in the darkness. I dwelled on Laura and did not sleep until late.

Around noon the next day, I got let off at the Fourth Street onramp in downtown LA, depressed by it all, just as I had expected. The distant mountains were lost in the heat and smog. Even buildings half a mile down the road had disappeared from view. Graffiti covered the concrete wall alongside me. Telephone wires crisscrossed the sky. My only thought was to press on from that hell as fast as I could. Laura was so close now: only thirty miles away.

There were many delays and much walking along sun-blinded avenues but I arrived to Laura's dorm room and knocked. My heart raced with the anticipation of seeing her but another young woman answered the door. Acting as if my presence was a big drag, she told me that Laura had moved off campus the previous day. I followed her directions to an apartment across town and knocked again. After several moments, Laura appeared at the door, fresh from a shower and wearing a silk kimono. She had a towel in her hands and was drying her long, flaxen hair. An older man with a beard was seated on the sofa behind her. He glanced up with a somewhat bemused look and went back to rolling a joint.

"Can we talk?" I asked Laura. She came outside but left the door partially opened.

"There's really nothing to say, Clay."

"But I love you. I came back to take care of you."

"It's a bit late for that now," she said.

37

I started to remind her of all the promises we had made, about loving each other forever and ever, but stopped, seeing it was pointless. The woman was gone. I turned away and heard the door close behind me.

7

Not having any better ideas, I headed for Newport Beach. There was a thought to head down to Mexico instead, but once again it took money and I had little of that. All of my options felt empty and wretched. I called a few old friends along the way but no one was around. I even considered visiting my mother, just to say hello and feel some of her kindness, but I knew I was not welcome there by my father.

Late in the afternoon, I walked over a bridge and found a place to sit along the harbor. Boats came and went and my dreams came and went with them.

I reasoned that if I could get back to Europe, the authorities would never find me. Maybe I could work my way over on a cruise ship. I pictured myself sailing around the Mediterranean. That sounded great, until I realized I would have to cut my hair and wear some sort of snappy uniform.

Other scenarios came to mind, like working my way over to Europe on a merchant ship and bumming around the Greek Isles as a cook. My mind churned with one scheme after another, but in the end, they all felt hopeless. Everything in this world required money and I had $15 left to my name.

At sunset, I got up to walk and saw that day's headline on a newspaper rack. The Vietcong were pressing Saigon again. The war would not end soon, and neither would my odyssey. Maybe going to war was not the worst thing that could happen to me.

As twilight set it in, the question of what to do next with my life came to a sudden head. I had stopped to reflect at a street corner when a cop cruised by in his black and white and did a quick U-turn before the next intersection. I was just what that pig had been looking for all day, a longhair with a rucksack and nowhere to go.

He went by like he was in a parade, his pink skull visible through his butch haircut, his fat neck pressing at his buttoned collar. I pretended not to notice him but all of my foolish decision-making loomed up in front of me: walking out of that induction center, my inadvertent involvement with the Weather Underground, my failure to follow through on a college education and my headlong journey back to this crucible of straight culture.

I continued down the sidewalk, pretending not to see the cop as he came alongside me a third time but knowing full well what he wanted me to do; act like prey and run. And even though that was how I felt on the inside—a guy climbing chain link fences with German shepherds at his heels—I also knew that the cop had no way of knowing my thoughts unless I actually did run.

He finally headed down the peninsula and out of sight for good. What a bummer. I headed for a nearby plaza, purchased two pieces of fried chicken with a bottle of red wine and went in search of a place to crash for the night.

The beach itself was no good. The cops patrolled it from dusk until dawn.

After wandering around a bit, I settled on a bridge crossing over Coast Highway. When no one was watching, I crawled up under the girders, spread out my sleeping bag and opened the wine. When the chicken was gone, I stretched out and continued sipping the wine. The image of Laura making love to another man sat on my chest like a thousand pound rock. What a fool I had been, expecting loyalty when I had little to offer in return.

So I dreamed of a life that did not yet exist, where I had a woman to love me and we were glad for each other's company at the end of the day. I would work hard to provide a home and be worthy of her companionship. I made that solemn pledge to whatever gods might be listening.

For now, though, it was red wine alone under a bridge, and red wine was better than white wine whenever you crashed out in the open. It helped to keep you warm and find sleep. All the better to forget dreams that seemed so far away and impossible to reach.

In the hour just before dawn, a truck rumbled over the bridge, startling me from my sleep. In that grainy first light, the bridge columns and buttresses stood around me like grim sentries. Then I saw Laura in my mind, snuggled up warmly in bed with her new man and closed my eyes to the pain.

To hell with LA, I decided. I'm hitchhiking back up to Big Sur as soon as the day grows warm. Then I remembered my lack of money and practical needs, for which lying in gentle fields was of no use whatsoever.

Amidst this ongoing debate, another car passed over the bridge above me, then another one. They came by more quickly with each passing minute. The day grew brighter and the traffic increased to a constant roar. Civilization had awakened. It was the din of commerce, of dog eat dog; the clamor of people going off in their quest to survive and provide for their children, children who would grow up to have more children of their own, with all of those children wanting to reproduce, again and again, on and on, exponentially, every last soul of them wanting more cars and gadgets, until somewhere in the unspeakable future, there would be nothing but traffic and commotion covering every square inch of the Earth.

What anguish. I could not understand the motivation of my fellow human beings, given the obvious result. Surely there was another path along which our species might evolve. Why not take a few weeks to think things over? At least slow down for a month or two and consider the various options. Yet such reflection seemed utterly hopeless beneath the onrush of morning traffic.

Ultimately, hunger overtook my thoughts and I sat up. I had to eat. I had to play the game or perish. I dressed, rolled up my sleeping bag, crawled down among the oleander bushes bordering the sidewalk and waited until no cars or people were passing by before slipping out into plain sight.

Half a mile down the highway, I found a gas station and used the john to clean up, then went in search of a job at various restaurants around town. I had experience as a cook and it offered a free lunch.

All day long, I filled out applications, but if the boss happened to be around, I got a quick look over the application and a shake of his head. We'll call you if there's an opening. I went back out into the bright sunlight, growing ever more resentful, yet knowing the rejections were my own fault. I had no address, no phone number. I smelled like a bum.

That night after darkness fell, I crawled back up under the bridge and lay on my sleeping bag, my restless mind dreaming up various ways to improve the area around me: boxes for clothes, perhaps a small end table, some books and a flashlight. I nearly brightened at the prospect until the world beyond me came back to my thoughts; lovers sleeping in their homes, with refrigerators and carpet under their feet. All I had was a bottle of bourbon and some lousy feelings. It took most of the pint before I found sleep.

The next morning at dawn I lay there, no more willing to face the world than I had been on the previous day. All I could think of were places to escape, but all the places I wanted to go required the bullion of modern life: money.

Eventually, I got up to face the bright morning, led to action once again by my hunger and anxieties. Applications and more applications, each time having to tell the same lies. That day went by and another one without success. I cursed God and all that was holy.

On the fourth day, I set aside a central canon of my young belief system and stopped by a barbershop. It was a joint catering to old veterans, a buck seventy-five for a haircut, but the only place I could afford. The barber laid into me with a set of electric clippers, finished the job with a splash of cologne and held up the mirror. My face turned red. I looked like a Marine. I paid him and went back out onto the sidewalk, cursing that son of a bitch.

My destination was a bistro where I had submitted an application on the first day. It was right on the harbor waterfront and had a great atmosphere.

The restaurant had yet to open but the manager was out by the cash register when I stepped in, talking with a waitress. He was a short man with a moon-shaped face and a Hawaiian shirt. He glanced at me with a smile, acted as though he had never seen me before and told me to fill out an application. This time I concocted a phony address and phone number.

The manager reappeared from his office a short time later, looked over the form and asked if I could start right away.

"Sure," I told him.

I punched in a time card, put on a white smock and went to work chopping up barrels of romaine and red cabbage. From time to time, my hand involuntarily felt the stubble around my ears. I haven't sold out, I told myself. I'm not a defeated man.

The manager turned out to be a kind soul and a hipster of sorts, despite his age and receding hairline. Mickey was his name and he offered me much needed encouragement. I grew to like him a great deal.

Realizing my plight, Mickey offered me a small advance as I clocked out on the second day. I checked the papers and located a nearby boardinghouse. It turned out to be another grand old Victorian home, run by another old widow, but it was situated on a bluff above the highway and had a view of the harbor and sea.

No drinking or overnight guests in the rooms, I was told in taking the key. I understood: no noise or trouble.

I went upstairs, lay on the bed and experienced the strangeness of my new surroundings. The walls were lined with darkened floral wallpaper. The toilet was down the hall. My fellow boarders were mostly old men and pensioners. I felt lost in time — somewhere back in the '40s — but I was truly grateful. I had a home and could dream of better things.

The following afternoon, while arriving home from work, I passed one of my fellow boarders out in the hallway, this flaccid old geezer who had already scowled at me for beating him into the john that morning. While I fumbled to get my key in the door, he asked me why I wasn't in the war.

"I'm 4-F," I told him. "I've got flat feet."

He looked suspiciously down at my shoes and back at me.

"You're a liar," he said and started off towards his room, muttering to himself about what an unpatriotic bastard I was.

I closed the door in a panic. What if he turns me in? I paced the floor, certain the old man would do it. How far could I get with my upcoming paycheck? Every few seconds, I peeked out through the window curtains, expecting to see the Feds pulling up.

The next morning, I awakened with renewed fears about the war. It was beyond me to explain how I could forget it for one second. Perhaps it would be best if I turned myself in. At worst, they would put me in jail, where I could sit and write a book. Learn to carve. Engage in any number of peaceful activities. Anything would be better than this endless anxiety.

I had hardly considered this option when my mind revolted. I could never willingly choose confinement. If it came to that, I would much rather be a man on the run.

As I lay there, I felt gratitude for my job. However modestly, it would allow me to save. Someday soon, I could go off and find my place in the sun. Excitement stirred in my heart at the thought.

I heard people getting up and moving around in the boardinghouse. Someone went into the bathroom. I heard water running and imagined it was the crabby old man. There were farts and coughing. The toilet flushed. I waited my turn.

Finally, whoever had been in there went down the hall and into his room. I jumped out of bed, eager now about getting to work, eager to be off and see the world again. Maybe I'd bum down to Mexico, as I had planned. Or go back to Europe and see all the lovely places I had yet to see. The world was filled with so many possibilities when you were a young man.

I worked that day, feeling rather spry in this newfound determination and certain nothing could steer me away from my course, until the kitchen door swung open during lunch and my eyes met with those of a petite brunette. She smiled, and in that instant, all the straight lines in my life were swept away, my destiny now curved like a light beam around a brilliant star.

The woman had pale skin and long, perfumed hair and a small birthmark on her heart-shaped lips. With the white blouse and red lipstick, she seemed French. Whatever else she was, the effect on me was completely erotic. I dreamed of her all that day and through the night with every imagined scenario.

Anticipating her return the next day, I kept one eye out front during lunch and was thrilled to see her step out of a green TR4. Her entrance into the restaurant came with delightful laughter and playful bantering with the staff. I gleaned from her conversation that she worked for an insurance company across the harbor. I heard someone call her Caroline. When another gentleman tried to corral her attention, I grew jealous and went out front, wearing my white frock like I was a GI in World War II. When Caroline offered me a playful smile, I winked back casually in return. Whatever my previous plans, they had seemingly gone out the window.

When Caroline returned for lunch the next day, I slipped outside and left a note under her windshield wiper, then watched with heart racing as she made her departure, wondering how she would react to my words of love. She noticed the note but placed it in her purse and climb into her sportscar with barely a glance. I was crushed. She may as well have tossed it away. There wasn't even a look back at the restaurant as she started the engine and drove off.

Now I felt foolish. I had presumed her interest in me and left myself vulnerable.

Having tossed and turned all night, I went in for my usual shift the next day, dreading Caroline's arrival. As soon as I heard her voice out front, I hid at my chopping board and felt greatly relieved when she finished her lunch and left. A few minutes after her departure, a waitress dashed into the kitchen and handed me a note. It was from Caroline. I resumed my work, lacking the courage to open it. I imagined it to be a nicely worded rejection.

At five o'clock, I left for the day and opened the note in the parking lot. My heart jumped. I let out a holler. There was a kiss inside, made with her red lipstick. Her name and phone number were beneath the kiss.

Wow, I thought, what a sexy, classy doll.

I called her from a phone booth on the way back to the boardinghouse and she laughed upon hearing my voice, and laughed again when I asked her to have dinner with me the following evening. Everything about her was accompanied by good cheer.

I spent all night fantasizing, but when Caroline failed to show up for lunch the next day, I began to fear the worst. I pictured her having reservations. Women were prone to whimsical changes of mind. My experiences up to that point had given me every reason to believe as much.

After work, there was just enough time for me to dash across Coast Highway to the boardinghouse, change clothes and dash back across to another restaurant alongside the harbor. I walked up to find Caroline parked out in front. She got out of her TR4 and gave me a hug.

"You didn't come in today," I said.

"I had to work through lunch...Did you miss me?"

I nodded. She looked around.

"Where's your car?"

"I don't have one."

She smiled and gave me another hug.

"Shall we?"

I took her arm, profoundly grateful for this salve to the wounds that Laura had left in my heart.

By way of explaining my lack of a car, I regaled Caroline with tales of my recent travels overseas. I had just returned from bumming around the world and was still getting my feet back on the ground. Caroline had rarely been past the county line, let alone outside of California, so to her I may as well have been a swashbuckling pirate.

I purposefully left out the part about being a draft dodger and wanted for various other crimes, and may have embellished my adventures a bit along the way, but every good story required its dose of literary license.

8

The next day, a Friday, Caroline arrived for lunch and I saw she was wearing a pair of high-heeled sandals, open at the back with a narrow hourglass strap across the toes, her beautifully sculpted feet revealed, the precise digits adorned with red nail polish and aligned like the erotic piano keys to my heart. I had mentioned loving that kind of shoe. I hadn't expected her to come in wearing them the next day. It was everything I could do to keep from seducing her on the spot. "That's my gal," I wanted to shout out but remained in back, having exchanged a smile and wave with Caroline when she first walked in the door.

At one point, a waitress came into the kitchen with another note. It was an invitation from Caroline to share dinner with her again that night. I peeked out through the kitchen door and gave her a wink.

Over dinner, she kept staring at me with bedroom eyes.

"What?" I asked finally.

"Oh, just wondering if I can take you home with me tonight."

I must have blushed because she laughed and tickled me under the table.

"Well, look at Mr. Worldly now."

I did my best to look nonchalant but ate the rest of my dinner filled with butterflies.

Having thought long and hard about my failures with Laura, I pleased Caroline again and again that night, starting down her pale body and rose petal skin with kisses and pausing at her tiny patch of hair before continuing down to her lithe ankles and delicate feet and returning again to her animal scent.

After some time, she pleaded with me to stop.

"Oh my god," she said, kissing my face. "Seven times. I can see your women never stray."

She was soon asleep but I lay there awake until late, haunted by the memory of Laura. As much as I had tried, my love for her would not go away.

The next day at work, a big Saturday brunch crowd had come in, doing their best to forget the weekly grind. There was much laughter and gaiety and champagne flowing.

My personal melancholy remained, my thoughts a redux of the previous night's struggles. Bliss. Regrets. Guilt. Animal hunger.

In the end, I decided that the best tonic would a bit more sex with Caroline but had no expectations of seeing her again that day. She had talked of going up to visit her mother in Burbank.

At a little past one, a waitress raced through the kitchen and dropped a small, gift-wrapped package on my cutting board. One of Caroline's trademark lipstick kisses had been placed on top. I stole a quick look out at the boisterous crowd but she was nowhere in sight.

With the kitchen a frenzy, I had to wait until my next break before opening the box. A key to Caroline's place was inside, along with a new toothbrush. The accompanying note read, 'See you after work.'

How brave. Or maybe she had rushed off, feeling vulnerable, the way I had felt after leaving a note on her windshield. But probably not. A woman knew what she had, and that a man could hardly resist it.

I got off at three and found Caroline waiting for me out in the parking lot. We kissed passionately through her window before I walked around and climbed into the car. It was a long time before we could pry ourselves apart and discuss where all this was headed

"I want you to come live with me," she said.

Her dark eyes searched mine, waiting for an answer.

"Okay," I said.

We kissed again for a long time before she drove off.

At the boardinghouse, Caroline waited outside while I packed my things and returned the key to the landlady. On the way back to Caroline's place, we stopped to buy a bottle of French wine and in the fading light of a winter afternoon, poured two glasses full, put some romantic music on the stereo and danced slowly with our clothes falling piece by piece onto the living room floor.

Over the ensuing days and weeks, I realized that I had never really experienced a mature love affair. I had never lived with a woman before or known the pleasure of dwelling on a woman's kindness all day, knowing she would be waiting for me when I arrived home from work, a gorgeous smile, a dress and high heels, ready to pour a glass of wine when I walked in the door.

In this, I developed my first habits of living together, often the one cooking while Caroline sashayed about the house, lighting candles and changing the album and generally being sexy. We frequently bundled up after our evening meals and took long walks down by the sea. One night, we took a ride on the Ferris wheel at the Fun Zone and laughed like children, our legs dangling high up in the sky and our hearts climbing up to the stars.

The holidays came and we decorated a tree. We found a bluesy Christmas album and danced to it in the living room with brandy eggnogs. One cold, windy wintry afternoon, we packed a picnic lunch, took it down to the beach and huddled snugly together on the leeward side of a lifeguard tower, drinking our wine and eating our lunch with the hum and snap of the wind at our backs.

Caroline and I were dear friends in those hours, on a mystical ride through the universe, all of it preceded or followed with sex. We hungered for that more than anything: at dawn, in the middle of the night, over her coffee table in the fleeting hour of dusk, her work dress thrown hastily onto the living room carpet, the eyes of my pale tigress glowing ardently at me from over her shoulder.

Nothing, it seemed, could go wrong, but for the secrets I kept. Caroline thought my number was 318, not 18, and knew nothing about my real draft status, or that I had been indicted for blowing up a federal building. I wasn't entirely sure why I maintained these deceptions, but one led to another, and another, until the secrets began to eat away at both me and our relationship.

Not that Caroline didn't have her own secrets to maintain. She had been raised by a strict Catholic mother, so that my very existence had to be denied, never mind the fact that we were living together out of wedlock.

Adding to this doomed formula, I willingly became Caroline's mentor, knowing full well that students ultimately had to reject their mentors and mentors came to despise their own creations. Nor was I ready to admit that I felt like a little boy in comparison. Caroline had credit cards and a checkbook and was planning a future, whereas I had never thought much beyond the following day.

And there was Laura's shadow, looming over everything that Caroline did in my mind. When it came to intelligence and erudition, it was no contest. Caroline was bright but had never read a book of any consequence. Yet, I went on with the charade, for fear of the pain that would result were Caroline to depart with her affections.

One night after work, she wore a headband and I had to smirk. Christ. What did she know about the sixties? If she wanted to be hip, try selling all the distressed maple furniture. Her place looked like a Levitz showroom.

"Stop grinding on me!" I yelled when badgered about my education. "I'm not ready to go back to college, all right?!"

Perhaps I had imbibed a bit too much wine, and apologized for my behavior in the morning, but it was yet another deception. How could she know that Yale fight songs and Princeton ivy were no longer in my future?

As the two of us became more and more like strangers, my urge to move on grew proportionately. I had not forgotten my vow, that I would always cherish being loved by someone, and love that woman with devotion in return, but Caroline and I had become like my parents, two people slowly destroying each other from a lack of respect, and I refused to go down that road.

For this, I accepted most of the blame. I had chosen a woman based on beauty, a smile and red toenail polish, ignoring my need for intellectual camaraderie.

One night, when the President came on to explain his reasons for invading Cambodia, I threw my shoe at the TV. We had become a war-mongering empire, invading small, defenseless countries at will. No wonder everyone hated us. Yet in trying to explain the history of the conflict to Caroline, she just sat there with a blank smile. It was hopeless. We were like two figures in a cubist painting, existing on different planes. Save for the glue of our sexuality, there was nothing left holding us together.

50

A few days after the invasion of Cambodia, I had the day off and happened to get word of the shootings up at Kent State. I quickly turned on the TV and sat there watching the Fourth Reich unfold. My impulse was to go out and fight in the streets too but felt eviscerated by my fear of incarceration. Chances were, if I got caught out there, they'd lock me up for treason or send me to 'Nam.

Out of the blue, a knock came at the front door and I freaked, certain that the Feds had found me.

With a cautious peek out the window, I saw it was Eric, standing in the bright afternoon sun wearing muslin clothing and sandals. There were several days' growth on his chin and his chestnut locks were down to his shoulders. Jesus had just materialized out of Galilee.

I quickly opened the door and gave him a hug.

"Fuck, Eric, it's good to see you."

"Wow, you too, brother. Far out."

He was so effusive, he nearly jumped out of his sandals.

"Come in, come in," I said with a quick look around before closing the door. "I'm kind of freaking out here. How did you find me?"

"Your mother gave me the address. Don't worry. She knows enough to keep it from the law...Wow, your father's like on this major bummer. I spoke to him first."

"I know. I grew up with it."

I didn't want to think about my father. I nodded at Eric's long hair.

"How in hell did you accomplish that in the shadow of Brigham Young?"

"I wore a BYU baseball cap whenever I went outside. The beard is just from the past few days...Wow," he added while taking in the cottage. "I feel like I'm back at my parents' place."

"So do I." I explained to him some of my recent conflicts with Caroline and showed him a photograph of her.

"Wow, brother," he said. "I can see why you sold out."

"Yeah, you should talk, oh Gandhi of the Latter-Day Saints."

Eric laughed and settled into a lotus position on the carpet. A well-worn copy of the Bhagavad-Gita appeared from inside his shirt.

I chuckled.

"Reading that war manual of yours again, huh?"

He laughed.

"It's all about acceptance, brother."

"Yeah, right. That's what they tell you at the induction center."

Eric laughed again.

"So tell me. What happened?" I asked him.

"Oh, I just split, brother. Two days ago. Right after the invasion. I couldn't take the deceit any longer."

"Did you hear what happened at Kent State?"

"No, what?"

Eric seemed deeply saddened as I explained the four dead students. I joined him on the floor and watched the events unfold. Over and over, they showed the National Guard units opening fire on the student protesters and then a shot of this young woman crouching beside her fallen girlfriend, arms held out in disbelief and anger.

"And to think we were celebrating Earth Day just two weeks ago."

"Wow, far out, I know."

"Our leaders have gone mad, Eric, and either we shoot back or run for the hills."

"You know, Jesus was mad, too," he said while pulling at the ends of his hair.

"What's that supposed to mean?"

"Wow, brother," he said with a laugh. "I'm not like the enemy."

"All right, all right. Go on."

"I'm only saying, it's possible to be mad and peaceful at the same time. That's why I'm going to join the march at the capital."

"And I'm not."

"Wow, brother, I love it. You always did your own thing."

"My own thing? You of all people should know I'm stuck. I can't afford to go out there and act like Abbie Hoffman."

"Maybe you'd have more peace if you went to face it."

I looked out the living room window at the gathering shadows.

"Don't think I haven't considered it, but I always come back to running. It must be something primeval in me."

"Far-out imagery, brother. I'm like seeing cavemen sprinting across the open savannah."

"I have some hashish," I said. "But I don't know if you really need it."

Eric laughed.

"Oh, man, far out."

His face glowed even more so at the prospect of a good high. We sat on the floor, puffing and coughing and time drifted by.

Then Caroline arrived home early from work, reminding of the talk she wanted to have, a talk I very much dreaded. Fortunately, Eric was there and the two of them started rapping. When the sixties came up, Eric played the role of guide and teacher, a thing at which he was always much better than me. On and on they went, with me listening absently, my mind in faraway places.

In a moment of silence, Eric met my gaze, like he understood my thoughts all too well. Why sit and jive about the sixties? If it was that important to you, get back out on the road and live the experience.

Out of the blue, Eric said, "Wow, I was thinking the other day of going over to live in Hawaii."

"That's a far-out idea," I said. "That sounds really groovy."

Visions of trade winds and palm trees rustled through the afternoon. I saw myself bumming down through the South Pacific, looking for my place in the sun.

"Have you forgotten about going back to college?" Caroline said with a playful tickle of my ribs.

I pushed her hand away without responding. Eric looked down at his feet.

"I hear there's like this whole new sixties scene going on over there."

Eric looked up at Caroline.

"Clay's planning to sign up for summer classes," she said with a look at me. "We're into the sixties but we have to plan our future. We're hoping to buy a home and have a baby someday."

I stared out the window. When I thought of children, I thought of my own chaotic childhood and those hot, restless classroom days filled with static electricity. I had no real desire to perpetuate the species. We were all so fucked-up, why add to the misery?

I looked at Eric. Caroline stood up.

"I'm going to change."

As soon as she was gone, I motioned for Eric to join me on the back porch.

"Wow, brother. She's not into it."

"I know. Let's go."

"Wow, right now?"

He looked saddened more than excited.

"Yeah, let's go. I'll see if she'll give us a ride to the airport."

"I'm going to Hawaii with Eric," I said back inside.

Caroline stared at me, stunned.

"You're welcome to come if you want."

"What about school? Our home? A baby?"

"I changed my mind. I'm not ready for that."

I heard the sound of Eric washing up in the bathroom. Cars passed by out on the street.

"And what if I go?" Caroline asked me. "What about the furniture? My car? Our jobs?"

"I don't know. Leave the furniture. Leave the car at the airport. Who cares?"

Tears came into her eyes.

"Look, I'm sorry. We just don't get along. Can you give us a ride to the airport?"

Crushed, she wandered out to the kitchen. I heard water running and the sound of dishes being washed. I imagined her shock. I went into the bedroom and found my backpack. In five minutes, it was ready to go. I returned to the kitchen.

Caroline turned to face me with tears in her eyes.

"I'm sorry."

"You're sorry."

"Okay, I don't know how to do this. I'll call Mickey and have him send you my last paycheck for the rent but can you give us a ride to the airport?"

Caroline threw the dishtowel down on the counter and went to grab her purse. Eric and I waited while she pulled her TR4 out of the garage. Eric climbed in back and we started through the back streets towards the freeway. We had smoked some hashish on a restless afternoon and were gone. It had never occurred to me at the time to question my decision.

An hour later, we were passing the vast refinery works around Alameda. The sky had turned orange over Signal Hill. Then we were in front of the airport terminal, with the bustle of cars and people rushing by us, and that feeling of excitement one experiences only at airports in the hour of twilight.

I stared at Caroline, not knowing what to say. The driver behind us honked so I got out. Eric climbed out of the back. I went around to kiss Caroline but she drove off before I got to her door.

Inside the terminal, Eric and I secured two standby seats on the next flight out to Hawaii. We were already in line waiting to board when Caroline reappeared. She kissed me sincerely then and I wiped away her tears. She was brave and beautiful and I felt awful about leaving her behind.

"I'll call you, all right?

She nodded and waited for me to say something more.

"I'll send for you as soon as we get settled."

Caroline reached out a hand, as if to hold me back but the line went forward and we were gone down the jetway, swept away by the rush of bodies.

9

I saw Santa Monica and its pier far below my window, with the edge of the continent arcing from there up towards Malibu and Zuma Beach. Parallel rows of surf surged at the coastline, as far as the eye could see. Then the jet made a wide turn above the Pacific and the only thing visible were tiny white boats leaving wakes here and there in the blue sea. Then they too had disappeared.

I turned my attention back to the cabin. With three rows of seats and two aisles, the DC-10's interior seemed as wide as a theater, much bigger than any plane I had flown in before, and filled with the same quiet chatter you might hear before a Saturday matinee. Of those not conversing, most had gotten lost in a book or magazine. Some, like me, were just gazing around the interior.

My ears ached increasingly as the plane gained altitude. Then it leveled off and my ears popped. Flight attendants started down the aisles with beverage carts. One of them pulled down a movie screen up ahead and passed out earphones. The captain's voice came over the intercom. We were at thirty-seven thousand feet. Our expected arrival time in Honolulu was a bit over four hours. It was safe to unbuckle now. There were tidbits about our Hawaiian destination and he clicked off. People got up and began to wander about the aisles. The cabin quickly filled with cigarette smoke.

The hour had been near sunset back at LAX but at this higher altitude, the sun was still well above the horizon. I watched it off to our port side while calculating our speed and the speed of the Earth's rotation and concluded that we would be landing in Honolulu just before or after sunset. My restless mind moved on to imagining Hawaii and how it would feel to be in a tropical setting.

When the stewardesses arrived with the beverage cart, I ordered a cocktail. During my time with Caroline, the idea of a drink had become quite natural to me. It had begun as a vehicle for fun making, but I had learned a few quick pops also masked a lot of boredom and inconvenient emotions.

I looked over at Eric. He was reading from his Bhagavad-Gita.

"I forget. Is there something in there about scotch on the rocks?"

Eric looked up with a laugh.

"Not exactly."

"I know. A lot of stuff about accepting your fate."

He laughed again.

"Sorry, brother."

"Why? You didn't draft me."

We both laughed now. The stewardess stood there waiting.

"About that cocktail," I said.

"Oh yeah, sorry."

Eric ordered something with rum in it and we toasted to our new adventure.

"How are you feeling, brother?"

"Okay. I'm going to feel a lot better after I down a couple of these."

"Far out. Are you going to get drunk and tear up the fuselage a bit?"

I chuckled. It was as if the universe went off in an infinite number of directions in Eric's mind, all of them equally acceptable. There was none of that reflexive, knee jerk reaction you expected in another human being. He seemed to view disaster and being seduced by an exotic courtesan with the same sense of wonder. He was spiritually evolved in a way I admired yet found impossible to understand.

A thought occurred to me.

"What would you have done if your number came up 18?"

"Wow, brother, I don't know. Run probably."

We laughed.

"Oh great and glorious Krishna," I said. "Well, thanks anyway. For a man already on the run, those words were encouraging."

We were quiet then and Eric went back to his book. I stared out the window. My thoughts were of Caroline. The vision of her all alone stabbed into my heart. A part of me longed to be back there, sharing a glass of wine and some laughs. We'd make love in that smoky hour of dusk. And yet, I knew this was for the best. We had become like junkies, addicted more to security than any joyousness. Maybe that wasn't true for her, but it was for me.

As always at this crossroads, I remembered Laura. I had loved her heart and soul, in a way that I had never loved Caroline.

Then what did I know? Maybe you only got to love one person in that way and all the rest of your romances were spent in quiet desperation.

This is for the best, I told myself again. There are too many secrets and lies now and I'm tired of hiding them all away.

I felt free for that moment. Sad but free. Then I was picturing Caroline all alone again and wanting to rush back and rescue her.

During the next four hours, I kept reevaluating my speed calculations and found that they had been more or less correct. The sun was just setting behind the mountains of Oahu as we glided in for a landing, and I could feel the palm trees rustling in the balmy, tropical breeze outside my window, exactly as I had imagined it. What a relief to be away from LA. If something like a refinery existed in Hawaii, it would be a small dot in an ocean of beauty, not a mechanical monster consuming the world.

Once the plane had come to a full stop, everyone stood up and started reaching for their belongings in the overhead storage. I stayed seated with Eric while the other passengers milled about restlessly. I noticed a crew wheeling a set of metal stairs out to the plane. Unlike in LA, or at any other big city airport, there was no enclosed jetway leading into the terminal.

When it was our turn, Eric and I filed out into the twilight. The trade winds rustled in the palm trees and in our ears and was like a woman's kindness after too many years alone.

We were met on the tarmac by Polynesian women in traditional garb, each one with long, black hair and wearing a lei. They placed a lei over Eric's head, then one over mine. I looked back several times as the two of us moved off in the direction of the terminal.

The doors to the terminal were wide open, allowing the outdoor ambience to blow right inside. Bamboo wallpaper and native wood took the place of plastic décor.

We found the baggage claim on the same level. Two young men and their female companion happened by as we stood there waiting for our backpacks to appear. Both men were wearing shorts and Hawaiian shirts. The lady had on a serape-like dress.

"Where are you coming from?" she asked us.

"We just got in from LA," I explained.

"So what are your plans? Where are you headed?"

Eric and I looked at each other and shrugged.

"We don't know. We don't have any."

"Come with us," the taller of the two men said. "We'll give you a ride out to Makaha. It's free to crash there on the beach and no one will hassle you."

"Wow, how far is it from Honolulu?" Eric asked them.

The taller man shrugged.

"Thirty, forty miles."

"Wow, and you'll just take us there?"

"Sure, why not?"

"Oh, wow," Eric said, glowing now. "This is totally like the sixties again."

"The sixties are just getting started here in Hawaii."

"Wow, brother," Eric said, laughing. "This is so totally groovy."

The five of us walked out to the parking lot together, talking away about life on the islands. Among the sea of cars, the taller man guided us to a Volkswagen bus, opened the side doors and waited while Eric and I climbed up onto a raised bed. Closing the doors again, he went around to the front seat and got behind the wheel. Eric and I handed our leis to the lady for their dashboard and our conversation about life in Hawaii continued. I lay back on the bed and watched the shadows and light play upon the ceiling as we motored through the backstreets of Honolulu. No one said a word about the war but it was there in my thoughts, always there in my thoughts.

Soon the city fell away and we came to be driving out a rural highway. Pineapple fields went on for miles and miles, the terrain sometimes flat, sometimes gently rolling. We shared a bowl of hash with our new friends and they shared many important things with us about living on the islands.

In time, we motored over a line of hills and arrived at the coast. A few miles north of Makaha, Eric and I were dropped off on a completely dark and empty road. Hills rose up on the inland side and a forest of bamboo separated us from the adjacent sea.

59

"Good luck, brothers. There's a market just down the highway if you're hungry in the morning."

"How do we get through this jungle to the beach?" I asked.

"Just look for a trail."

With that, the driver turned his Volkswagen bus around, waved a final time and headed back towards Honolulu. Eric and I were completely alone.

"Man, it's dark," I said.

"Yeah, brother, look at all the stars."

The Milky Way girded the evening sky. Both of us gazed upwards for several moments in silence.

"Which way?" I asked Eric.

He pointed north up the highway with a shrug. We went in that direction with the forest of bamboo continuing to separate us from the sea.

Eventually we located a trail that led towards the shore but it quickly became impassable. We retreated and searched for another one. The next path went a bit further but terminated at a bog. Not wanting to test its depth, we again retreated. Several more attempts led to the same failure. At times we caught glimpses of the shoreline but it appeared to be unreachable through the bamboo forest. Going farther up the highway, we tried another path, and another one, but each time the way became impassable. After repeated attempts with the bamboo tearing at my skin, I cursed out loud.

"Fuck!"

Eric bowed his head in silence when I glanced over my shoulder. Mr. Serenity. He never got pissed at anything. I wanted to throw him into the bog.

At last, we found our way out to a crescent cove where palm trees leaned over a steep shoreline and rustled in the trade winds. It was enchanting and peaceful and in stark contrast to my bitter mood.

Eric and I found a level place back among the palm trees and set our packs down. Eric started up the beach alone. The apology I had thought to make caught in my throat. So I had gotten pissed. There was no point in humiliating myself.

While Eric wandered down the shore, I unrolled my sleeping bag and lay on my back. Low clouds raced in from the Pacific and disappeared with a rush over the mountains behind me.

I glanced over and saw Eric coming back down the shore.

"It's like we're on a great sailing ship!" I called out to him.

"Yeah, far out," he said coming back.

"Hey, get your sleeping bag out and we can smoke a bowl of hash. These clouds rushing by are really a trip."

Eric went about arranging his things in silence. I waited until he was comfortable then lit the bowl. We lay together smoking and coughing. The palm trees rustled overhead. The clouds kept rushing in with the balmy breeze. I lay there struggling with my thoughts.

"Hey, I'm sorry about getting pissed back there," I said.

"It's all right, brother," Eric said.

He smiled sadly and looked back up at the sky. I did too, thinking those were the hardest words I had ever spoken. I wasn't even sure they were sincere, but it was the best I could do. For the past two years, I had used the war and everything it had done to my life as an excuse for my anger, when in reality, I was just an angry young man who trampled all over other people's feelings.

In all of this, I remembered Caroline and the many times I had lashed out at her in anger, never offering an apology. Well, there was nothing to do but go forward. It was a bit too late to go back and fix things now.

The next morning, Eric and I bathed in the sea and smoked a bowl of hash. That led to laughter and conversation and just enjoying the balmy, tropical morning.

After a spell, I started to pack my things. Eric started down the cove, looking for shells.

"Hey," I called out after him. "Maybe we'd better get going. I'm hungry and we don't have anything to drink. You know, that guy said there's a market a few miles down the road."

"Sure. I'll be back in a minute," Eric said and continued down the beach.

I stared after him.

He returned fifteen minutes later and went about putting things away in his pack. It was very deliberate, each item carefully folded and arranged. I stared with growing impatience.

When he was done, we retraced our path through the bamboo and what had seemed like the Black Forest in the dark of night was almost comically simple in the light of day. Nearing the highway, we came across a graveyard of appliances, in various stages of rusting away and being overgrown by tropical vines. It appeared that Hawaiians simply tossed their appliances to the side of the road whenever they quit working. There were dozens of washers and dryers and refrigerators, just twenty feet from the asphalt.

"Far out," Eric said. "Even junk looks groovy in paradise."

I smiled.

"I don't ever want to leave this place."

"Yeah. I figure to hang around here for a long, long time."

We sat with our backs against our packs, waiting for someone to come along.

"Let's smoke another bowl of hash," Eric said.

We did and continued waiting. Not one car had come along. Eric stroked his beard, lost in thought.

"You know, Clay, you could probably go live under a waterfall or something. I mean, I doubt they'd ever come looking for you here."

I smirked.

"What?" he said.

"Why don't you go live under a waterfall?"

"I'd like send you letters and stuff."

"Yeah, right. 139 Jungle Way."

He laughed.

"Maybe we should start walking," I said after a few minutes.

"Patience, brother."

He was gazing up at the palm trees over our heads. I stared at him until he looked at me.

"Wow, brother," he said. "It's like you're going to roast me or something."

"You've been reading my mind."

I laughed with him this time. Then we were silent and I sat there trying to understand my emotions. I really had been thinking to roast him.

Sometime later, this stout young Hawaiian pulled over to pick us up and we motored along the winding road, sometimes shrouded by jungle, sometimes with the sky open above us but always with a tropical feeling in the air. Eventually we came to a little village by the sea where the Hawaiian lived. Eric and I found the small market and took our supplies down to another remote stretch of shoreline, where we played in the surf all day and spent another night.

10

The next day, we took the highway around the back side of Pearl Harbor and into Honolulu. We were nearly broke so I asked one of our rides about work and he told us to go down to Waikiki. Dozens of hotels lined the shore and each one had its own restaurant. It was a cook's paradise. Help came and went like drunken sailors.

Having walked the mile or so from downtown Honolulu to Waikiki, I went in to look for work at the first hotel we came across. Eric waited outside with our gear.

The hostess went off to find the manager. I stood there looking out to sea. It was like in the postcards. The surf seemed to be breaking out for miles and Hawaiians in outriggers and on long surfboards were riding it in towards shore.

The manager appeared and invited me into his office. When he handed me an application, I explained that I had just arrived to the island. I didn't have a place yet or an address. He asked me some pointed questions about how restaurant kitchens worked and my experience and promptly hired me on as a cook. I asked if he could take on Eric as a dishwasher too and he agreed.

All that morning from my cook's station, I watched Eric work, wondering how he would take to washing pots and pans, and to his credit, he went about it with great pride, like a man polishing telescope mirrors.

Halfway through the shift, the restaurant manager told me to take a break and join him in his office.

"How would you like to go work on the big island?"

"Why? What do you mean?"

"I've been assigned over there to run a new hotel and I need an assistant manager. It would include a nice salary, a free place to live and a company car."

I immediately thought of Eric. It meant saying goodbye to him but what the hell. Eric wasn't about to join me in the stockade, or under a waterfall. I told the manager "yes" and spent the rest of the day, feeling excited about the opportunity.

That evening, at the end of our shift, Eric and I slipped out the back door into an alley. Day was turning to dusk. The sound of passing cars echoed up from the adjacent boulevard. In that lovely moment, trouble seemed to be a million miles away.

Thinking to camp along the shore for the night, we had turned in that direction when the manager and the chef suddenly appeared. By the look on their faces, I figured I knew what was up. I had slipped several pieces of fried chicken into my pack during the day, so Eric and I would have something to eat that night.

"Where is it?" the chef said. He was a short, stout man with a fiery temperament.

"I don't know what you're talking about."

"Where's the chicken?" the manager said. "Out with it or I'm calling the cops."

Humiliated, I pulled a greasy brown bag out of my pack. The chef took the bag and kicked it down the alley with a curse.

"You can forget about that position on the big island," the manager told me.

"What about our wages?"

He smirked at the chef and looked back at me.

"You really want to go to jail, don't you?"

"Over a couple of pieces of chicken?"

"Get the hell out of here...You're just a fuck up," he added on their way inside.

I made a gesture to let him know what I thought and the chef lurched at me. The manager restrained him at the open door.

"Go on, get the hell out of here, before I really do call the cops."

They went inside and slammed the door.

"Bastards," I said.

"Wow," Eric said. "That was a big deal over four pieces of chicken."

"Fuck," I said, bummed about the lost opportunity.

Eric put his arm around me.

"It's all right, brother. I know you were just looking out for us."

"Yeah. Jean Valjean with his drumstick."

"At least they could have let us keep the chicken."

"Here, have a piece."

I kicked at the broken bag. The chicken was everywhere by this point.

Eric found a reasonably well-preserved breast, brushed it off and offered to share it with me. I declined and we started off down the alley towards the shore. The humiliation and lost opportunity kept working in my head.

At Kalakaua Blvd., we crossed over to the beachfront boardwalk. It was just past sunset and the sky was orange along the horizon. Parents were straggling up from the shore in the fading light, dragging their ice chests and beach chairs and kids with them, off to their cars and the warmth of home. Some had surfboards and rafts and stopped first to return them at a wiki wiki looking rental kiosk.

Eric and I went about selling some of our hash. Half of it was soon gone but we now had enough money to buy food supplies for a week or so. We stopped for sandwiches and a bottle of wine and walked down the shore towards Diamond Head.

Once we were well past all the oceanfront hotels, we made camp under a gathering of palms and ate while sharing the bottle of wine. Our conversation went on late into the night, but behind it all, that lost opportunity continued dogging me. And like any man wounded by his failures, I longed to be comforted and kept thinking of the woman I had left behind.

Well before dawn, it started to rain and we were forced to find refuge under the adjacent bluff. I could not find sleep again. My thoughts went round and round. There had been boyhood dreams of being a foreign correspondent. I had taken French and studied journalism. Now I was hiding under a rock. I drank more wine to drown the feelings.

Daylight blossomed into a beautiful morning in the South Pacific. I decided to quit worrying and just enjoy this place. There will be other opportunities, I reassured myself.

Eric and I swam in the ocean first thing. Afterwards, he wandered down the beach alone. I lay on my towel and listened to

65

the palm trees rustling overhead. Eric was nearly back from his walk when he stopped to speak with an old beachcomber.

"Wow, brother," he said, returning to our camp. "That old man's been here since the end of World War II. He's really cool. Walks the beach every morning. I asked him about camping and he said lots of people do it on the east side of the island. Plus, he heard there's a free concert today at a place called Sandy Beach."

"Where's that?"

"I guess just a few miles on the other side of Diamond Head. What do you think?"

"I was thinking to go look for another job. We'll be out of money before long."

"Hey, it's cool, brother. Let's just go with the flow and worry about money tomorrow."

"Yeah, all right. Across the Seven Seas and all that."

"Yeah, brother! I love it! Off to see the world!"

"On a hundred dollars."

"Hey, we'll be cool."

I took solace in Eric's presence. Besides, the day was so damned lovely, the last thing I wanted was to go on worrying.

We packed up and started on a trek through a suburb of clapboard bungalows, all of them looking as if they were up on stilts with their raised foundations. It was a long walk out to the highway and the sun kept going in and out of the clouds. One moment it was hot on our skin. The next moment it had slipped back behind the clouds and all was shadowy again. Back and forth it went, as if the moods of the gods were changing.

At the highway, a young soldier soon came along and got us as far as the backside of Diamond Head. He worked at a radar facility inside the volcano and told us about being in the military. We told him about our adventure getting to Hawaii.

"Wow, far out," Eric said when he let us off. "He's like this really cool guy and everything we've been fighting against at the same time."

I looked at the military installation off in the distance. It bristled with radar equipment.

"Let's hope they don't miss the Japs this time."

Eric laughed.

"Wow. You know, I was reading where Roosevelt like just let that happen to get us into the war."

"Are you surprised? I mean, the Gulf of Tonkin, right? Isn't that the way they always get us into a war?"

We sat there trashing the government until the next ride came along. The highway now followed the shore with the sun slipping in and out of the clouds and the sea shifting from blue to green along with it. A few miles farther on, the driver pulled into a little market at the mouth of the Niu Valley. That was as far as he was going.

We got out and stood there for some time before a young couple from Pennsylvania stopped to pick us up. Serendipitously, it turned out they were also on their way to the concert at Sandy Beach and before long we were joining a stream of cars pulling into a dirt parking lot beside the highway.

The shoreline was down below a short bluff with the sea off in the distance, and more sage-green in color than blue. Scores of dark-skinned Hawaiians peppered the surf, their dark skin and coarse hair like aboriginal visions. Eric and I made camp and watched them bodysurfing. The Mokes had their own special style to the sport, hurtling at each other from opposite directions of a wave before diving out with a war cry at the very last second.

"I'm going to go out," I said.

"Far out, brother. I'm just going to lie here and dream for a bit."

Out in the surf, I quickly caught a wave and found one of the Hawaiians hurtling at me from the opposite direction. I pulled out just before we collided and he rocketed by below me while letting out a war cry.

After several waves, I swam out past the surf and floated on my back. Hills rose up across the highway, looking luxuriant with their jungle foliage. I noticed Eric talking with some strangers and then heading down the shore with them. When I came out of the water, he was back and had constructed a small lean to with some driftwood. I dried off with my towel and lay down in the shade.

"This so totally groovy," Eric said.

"Yeah."

"Some people I was talking to said that local bands hold concerts down here every week."

"Far out."

"Hey, what do you think about tripping?"

I looked over at him. The setting was beautiful with everyone around us in good spirits. If you were going to trip, this was the kind of atmosphere you wanted.

"Okay," I said.

Eric got out our page of blotter acid and tore off two hits. Time passed and Eric wandered away again.

I had been lying there watching the sun go in and out of the clouds and the colors changing when I suddenly realized I had come on. Polynesian symbolism flitted here and there among the surf and palms and jungle hillside. Someone was playing Santana's *Oye Como Va* and I found my heart soaring with the beauty of its melodies, in what was so different from the raw angst and psychedelic madness of songs like The Doors' *When the Music's Over* or even the playful defiance of Hendrix's *Third Rock from the Sun*. So the Bay Area rebellion was over, I thought, and an entirely new spiritual dynamic was being expressed in song. Love, peace and brotherhood, without divisions of race or class or generations resonated into the tropical paradise around me, until I felt almost terrified by the truth laid bare at my feet; all the fractious struggles created by the Vietnam War would be over one day. Only love lasted forever. All of us had to find our own peace. To go on fighting was to play the part of a fool.

I was tripping on these thoughts and wondering what had happened to Eric when he suddenly reappeared with two ladies. I watched him give them two hits. They shared a joint of their homegrown bush with us and the four of us sat there talking for what seemed like a long time. Then the ladies started to come on and disappeared with a laugh.

Soon after, the band arrived in a van. The double side doors opened to reveal a PA system in back. One man ran a power cord over to the restroom. Another played at the sound controls. The musicians set up a makeshift stage in the shade of some palms trees and the music began.

Their folk-rock sound had touches of Hawaiian music and was a nearly seamless transition from the Santana tape that had been playing earlier. Melodies soared up into the sky and became part of the clouds. The surrounding hills and jungle foliage vibrated with Polynesian symbolism and beauty. A spontaneous love-in emerged with people dancing together along the beach as though there were no strangers.

Then it was dusk and the concert was over. The musicians disbanded as quickly as they had appeared and a steady stream of headlights began pulling out of the parking lot. Many people remained there along the shore, getting high and talking together but Eric and I felt lost. We had no home and no idea where to go. There was no camping allowed on Sandy Beach.

The young couple who had brought us there came along and asked if we needed a ride. Eric and I shared a look.

"I guess we don't know where we're going," Eric said with a laugh.

"You should try the campground at Hanauma Bay."

Eric and I shared another look and shrugged.

"Come on, we'll take you," the wife said. "A bunch of young people camp there and have luaus and stuff. It's really cool. People come from all over the island to party. Come on. It's just up the road."

Eric and I followed them up to their car and were soon headed back in the direction of Waikiki. Five miles farther on, the husband pulled left across the road and into a large parking lot. Eric and I climbed out. Dirt trails ran off into the tall shrubs on our left. We saw tents pitched here and there among the trails but no sign of people.

"Just go down to the beach," the wife said. "You'll find everyone down there."

"Far out," Eric said.

We waved goodbye and watched them pull back onto the highway. Off to the west, the rounded crest of Koko Head rose up against the twilight sky.

"It looks like Jonah's whale," I said.

"Yeah, far out."

"Like the whales drawn on ancient maps."

A short wall constructed of volcanic rock bordered the cliff's edge and partially blocked our view of the bay. We could see the water sparkling off in the distance but not the shore directly below the cliff. We headed across the parking lot in that direction, eager to check out the scene.

69

"Wow, look brother," Eric said when the shoreline came into view.

A village of tents was strewn along the west end of the bay and a large group of people were gathered around a bonfire adjacent to the tents.

"Wow, this place is a trip," he said.

We stood there taking in the moment. The bay was horseshoe shaped with coral reefs that bristled whitely from the incoming surf. Farther out, the reefs were submerged and eventually disappeared into the darker waters of the outer bay.

Drawn to the happening along the shore, Eric and I started down a trail that ran along the steep cliff. At the bottom, we turned right down the beach towards the bonfire. Glancing over my shoulder, I saw more people arriving. Another couple was just leaving and said goodbye on their way past us.

In a fire pit adjacent to the bonfire, we found a four-foot long yellow fin tuna baking in the coals. The upper flank had been well ravaged. Seeing that we had just arrived and were a bit unsure of ourselves, a young man invited us to dig in. There were paper plates and utensils on top of a small table and a tub filled with ice and cold beer next to it. Eric and I were soon enjoying the meal. Someone handed him a joint. He passed it to me. I passed it on to the next person and in this manner, we were quickly absorbed into this village of vagabond souls.

11

I awakened the next morning to the whisper of coconut palms high above my head. White clouds drifted by not far above their towering trunks. Memories of our late-night luau and the mystical moments of the previous day's psychedelic trip flitted in and out of the balmy breeze like sprites.

One thing was clear. My life had been totally simplified. The war and all its anxieties seemed to exist in another galaxy now.

I threw open my sleeping bag and gazed at the nearby village of tents. It began about a hundred feet from where I lay and continued all the way out to where the sandy shoreline terminated at the rock walls of the volcano, and appeared to have evolved as a matter of whimsy, one person wandering in to make camp, then another one a few days later, and so on, until it had grown into a colorful shantytown with meandering pathways. I saw several folks making breakfast and many others just sitting among the tents, talking and laughing and smoking joints.

The campfire rings and picnic tables were a short distance down the shore the other way. There was a bath facility beyond the campfire rings, constructed of brown volcanic rock and keave trees shaded that stretch of shoreline. A ranger station stood at the far easterly end of the bay, constructed of the same volcanic rock. The state and national flags fluttered together from an adjoining flagpole.

Just beyond the bathhouse and up against the cliff, an orange parachute had been wound through the barren branches of one keave tree. A man with long, wispy blonde hair sat alone under the tree in his beach chair. He was wearing a tattered baseball cap and sunglasses and stared out to sea in silence. People came and went from the nearby showers without speaking to him. I wondered who he was. I saw no sign of Eric and wondered what had happened to him too.

Noticing a large bunch of bananas tacked to a nearby palm tree, I went over and broke one off, half expecting someone to bark at me but no one said a word. I returned to my sleeping bag amidst the gathering of palm trees and ate in silence. How to stay in this little paradise? That was the question working in my mind. I had found a sanctuary from the madness of the world and did not want to leave it ever.

The sun cleared the volcano's eastern wall, leaving a line of shadow and light across the bay. I remained in the shade but the white water surging over the inner reefs was already sparkling in bright sunlight.

Two women were snorkeling out among the reefs and one of them had her body fixed at the outermost edge, looking down to where the sandy sea floor sloped steeply away into the navy-blue water. Something out there must have caught her attention because she pulled up her mask and called excitedly to her friend. The friend paddled over and the two of them lay there half submerged in the aquamarine water, the gentle surf surging over their tanned, bikini-clad bodies.

There was a thought to swim out and join them but I checked the impulse. Ever since the humiliation of being fired in Waikiki, my mind had toyed with the idea of calling Caroline. Fantasies of our joyful reunion at the airport played in my head. We were going to live happily ever after, as if our previous troubles had never existed.

But something told me to stop. All my life, I had been running from one woman to the next, wounded in love and longing to be fixed. I had lived in a circle of love, loneliness and longing. It was time to question these impulses. Spend some time alone. Get a job, save my money and see how things looked down the road.

Reasonably content with my decision, I lay down and grew lost in the sound of tiny waves slapping at the pebbly shoreline.

Slap...swiissssh...then slap...swiisssssh again.

The sea also murmured as it passed over the reefs and something ancient came through these voices, and from the dozens of coconut palms rustling overhead. I lay quietly with dreams of old sailor maps and uncharted Polynesian atolls passing through the day. A short while later, the sunlight reached my camp area but the palm trees kept things nicely shadowed directly around me.

In the next half hour, I spoke with several people as they passed by, was offered a glass of guava juice by a couple and shared a bowl of hash with them. Nature called and I went to use the bathroom. After showering, I passed by the man sitting under the parachute and said hi to him but he just stared out to sea without responding.

"Where did you get the parachutes?" I thought to ask.

"Take a wild guess," he said without moving.

I nodded, realizing he had been in 'Nam and I had not and that it was probably best if we left things right there.

I had gotten a few paces in the direction of my belongings when he called out to me.

"Are you Clay?"

I stopped and looked back.

"Yeah."

"Your friend Eric left word for you. He went off to the North Shore early this morning. Said he'd be back in the afternoon…in case you got lonely."

There was a hint of mirth behind his dark sunglasses, and maybe even a bit of kindness.

"Thanks, uh…"

"Stan," he said, filling in the blank.

"Yeah, well, I appreciate the news. I *was* starting to feel rather desperate about the whole thing."

I made a point not to acknowledge my sarcasm, any more than Stan had acknowledged his, and walked away.

On the way back to my sleeping bag, I asked more pointedly about camp etiquette and learned that only the expected hippie credo applied. As long as you didn't bother anyone else, it was do your own thing. I also got wind of someone heading into Honolulu and bummed a ride with him. An idea had occurred to me while lying there in the gathering of palms. The area was up for grabs, if for no other reason, because the trees were too close together for anyone to pitch a tent. However, that was perfectly suited for my intentions.

Arriving back late that afternoon, I immediately went to work installing my new hammock. Folks quickly gathered around the little grove of palms to watch.

"Wow, far out," one of them said. "I wonder why nobody thought of that before."

I too wondered. It seemed like the idea had been implanted into the brain of every American child—a shipwrecked man lying in his hammock while native girls waved palm fronds and fed him tropical fruit.

Once the hammock was properly installed, I climbed in and folks slowly started to wander off. I was alone with the sun setting over Koko Head. The coconut palms rustled high overhead. Clouds drifted along the horizon like barges.

Eric came back after dark and found me. I hadn't moved for several hours.

"Oh wow, brother. Far out. I bought a tent, but..."

"A tent's cool. At least you can store your stuff."

I got out and allowed Eric to try the hammock. He enjoyed it for a moment then sat in the sand nearby and told me about his day's adventures up on the North Shore. It had been a groovy trip so we agreed to do an encore tour the following day.

Things were relatively quiet around the camp that night—no luau, no wild parties, just a bunch of people sitting around getting high and talking away a balmy tropical evening in the South Pacific. Eric and I shared some hash and got to know our new neighbors.

Conspicuously, Stan never moved from under his keave tree or endeavored to participate in any of the festivities.

In the morning, Eric and I took our time getting high and showering and having a bite to eat but eventually heading off for the North Shore along the leeward side of the island. On the way, we stopped at a little palm-covered market in Waimanalo so I could buy some rubber sandals and a pair of shorts. We had lunch with Eric's new friends at their beach bungalow in Haleiwa, returned along the same leeward side of the island and stumbled into another luau in progress as twilight settled in.

We had not asked that first night but now learned the genesis of these events. Big trawlers periodically pulled into port from the Pacific, laden down with yellowfin tuna. The call then went out from a temp agency in Honolulu for work at a local cannery and several folks from the bay were on that list. From there, it was simply a matter of throwing one of the tunas over a back fence during your shift and hauling it down to Hanauma in the trunk of a car. How word of these events spread spontaneously all over the island, I had no idea, but we again had scores of people gathered around our fires that evening.

As the days drifted by, Eric and I made another trip up to the North Shore and also hitchhiked up to Makaha one day, on the windward side of the island, having stumbled in on a surf contest. The break was a half mile out and the swells looked like they were an inch tall, not twenty feet. Mostly, though, the two of us just hung around Hanauma or bodysurfed at Sandy Beach and otherwise avoided the bustle of Honolulu for over a week. It remained a far off and distant place until the last of our funds ran out.

Down to my own last dollar, I hitchhiked into Honolulu and quickly found work as a chef's helper at a little joint called The Bistro. It was on the backside of Waikiki, safely away from the usual tourist traps, and mostly catered to well-heeled businessmen. You could always find elegant looking women seated at the bar, their perfumed hair and laughter mingling with the general chatter around the dining room.

The chef was a grouchy old Russian who yelled and screamed all day long, worse than any chef I had ever known. I could not make a sauce to his liking and nearly quit in anger several times, but every afternoon when it was time to clock out, I would head back to Hanauma Bay with gladness in my heart, knowing my hammock and tribe of friends awaited me in that twilight hour.

Now and then, I would head for Waikiki through the backside of town, where apartment buildings crowded the sidewalks and the native people chattered at me from their balconies as I passed by.

"Hey, Haolie boy, you looking pretty lost."

I always joked back but found this scene a bit sad and depressing, these once daring voyagers now reduced to living in a tenement. Some called it progress, but I had other words for it.

It was usually dusk by the time I arrived to the boardwalk in Waikiki, where young native boys would be stacking surfboards in upright rows against the last blush of orange sky and the usual swarm of folks would be streaming up from the shore in the fading light. And invariably the memory of Caroline would turn in my heart in that moment. We had kissed and danced and made love so many times in that smoky hour, but there my feelings always died, the things we had shared like a star in the twilight sky, beautiful and haunting, but far, far away and impossible to reach.

The weeks of summer passed swiftly by, and during that time I saw less and less of Eric. When I nearly got busted with a friend of mine for selling grass down on the boardwalk in Waikiki, Eric stroked his beard with an all-knowing look.

"I see you headed for a disaster, Clay."

He had learned to divine with the I Ching and I guess he figured he could tell the future now. Stan had taken to calling Eric *His Maharishiness* and I played along. I knew it wasn't kind of me but divination did not seem to have much use for a man on the run.

Whatever else you could say, Eric and I slowly drifted apart. Our history remained, but the warmth between us was mostly gone.

Then one day he decided to go live with some folks on a coffee plantation on the big island. The plantation had a lot more to do with harvesting magic mushrooms than growing coffee beans, but either way, Eric was off. Before he left, he took a moment to explain why he hadn't thought to invite me.

"We seem to be on different spiritual paths, brother."

I assumed that to be true of most everyone in this world but drove him to the airport in Stan's car without saying a word.

From the terminal, I watched as Eric appeared out on the tarmac. The balmy breeze was blowing his long hair all about. He climbed the stairs and waved a final time my way before disappearing inside. The plane soon taxied out onto the runway and lifted into the sky. I drove back to the beach and my hammock, left to reflect on how my past kept disappearing. Caroline. Eric. So many old friends and familiar places were now gone.

I spent several days battling these wild urges to return home and was actually ready to buy a ticket when someone brought back news of the Soledad shooting. A judge was dead. Angela Davis had been charged with murder and she and all the Black Panthers were on the run. Lying there in my hammock at Hanauma, with palm trees rustling overhead, the late sixties angst seemed to exist in another dimension, and gratefully so. I promptly set aside any notions of flying back to the mainland. Who needed riots, shotguns and street paranoia?

A few days later, on what was a typically balmy evening, the trade winds blew these three old hobos onto the beach at Hanauma. A couple of us were seated at a picnic table when they wandered up. Introductions and tall tales ensued. They seemed quite charming until a tray of Sterno appeared and our new guests began inhaling the vapors. Suddenly, we had three trolls on our hands, arguing under a bridge.

"You don't know what the hell you're talking about, Sully, you goddamned fool. It was Dayton not Youngstown where we met that broad."

"Aw, fuck you. It was goddamned Youngstown and I'm the one telling the goddamned story here."

On and on it went. We promptly retreated to a safe distance and discussed a course of action.

"Take their Sterno," someone suggested.

"Shit, let's just run them off," someone else suggested.

"I don't know, man," a third guy said. "That could get violent."

Meanwhile the three hobos were still back there arguing among themselves.

"I say we try the pot patrol," another guy suggested.

This was the primary conflict resolution method used at Hanauma. If folks got into a squabble, you lit up a joint and a few tokes later, the concerned parties usually couldn't remember what the hell they had been fighting about.

After some discussion, everyone agreed on this course of action and a joint was shared with these old coots, but it hardly made a dent in their fried brains. They went on arguing.

We went to bed that night, hoping they would simply drift away with the trade winds, but they were there in the morning and the saga with the Sterno repeated itself the following night. To make matters worse, a voodoo practicing Carob Indian arrived amidst this ongoing spectacle and various belongings around the camp came up missing. When apprehended, our new voodoo chief flashed dolls fashioned from coconuts, driftwood, crustacean shells and seaweed, threatening to transform one or all of us into animal form.

Paralyzed by an aversion to violence, people in camp came up with all manner of wild schemes to end this disruption, but nothing worked and the chaos went on for several more days. Then, one evening, I came home to find the three hobos were gone.

"What happened?" I asked.

"I guess they just got tired of the scenery," someone said.

And as if to complete the circle, the mad Carob pulled up stakes the next morning and a big luau was thrown to celebrate the restoration of our peaceful home. It was a typically balmy evening and people kept pouring in from all over the island. A massive tuna roasted in the fire pit and joints were making the rounds.

In talking with this young lady from Waikiki, I became enchanted. She was possessed of exotic beauty and a hip mind. There was no talk of having kids and buying a house.

Before departing that night, she scribbled her address down on a piece of paper and invited me to stop by and visit her the next day.

"I work during the day. At The Bistro?"

"Oh, I love the place...so come by afterwards."

"Okay."

I lay awake late into the night, dreaming of new love.

After work the next day, I followed her directions through the backstreets of Waikiki and eventually found her place up on the third floor of an apartment building. I knocked on the door and waited. It opened a moment later, but only a crack.

"Oh, hi," she said.

I saw a young surfer looking kid sitting on her couch with his legs stretched out on the coffee table.

"Sorry," she whispered. "Maybe another time."

I shook my head and walked away. The memory of Laura's betrayal burned in my heart. I had felt myself falling in love when the encounter had meant nothing to this woman, beyond a coquettish flirtation.

I started towards home on foot, following Ala Wai Boulevard over to Paki and Paki to Monsarrat Avenue. When I came to the barren landscape at the backside of Diamond Head, I stuck my thumb out. The lyrics to *Help* were playing in my head. When I was younger, so much younger than today, I never needed anybody's help in any way. Looking back, it struck me that Laura's abandonment was just karma for my own cruelty to women, and Caroline was just one more example of how heartless I had been. I had always treated women like trash and felt a sudden urge to call her. I wanted to say I was sorry. Devotion was far more important than I had ever realized. Yet something told me to stop. Calling Caroline at a moment of weakness made her little more than a consolation prize.

A few minutes later, a man I knew from camp stopped to pick me up and we traveled along Kahala Avenue with the sea flashing into view between the houses. At Kalanianaole Highway, he turned left and kept talking but Caroline continued dogging my thoughts. I was sorry for what I had done and wanted to go back and do it all over again.

Back at Hanauma, I felt a chill in the air and went over to grab a jacket from among my belongings. It was one more reminder of how the times were changing. After living under the sun and the stars for six months, with little more than a pair of shorts and sandals to my name, it was getting on towards the end of the year and I now faced the prospect of winter rain blowing all around my hammock and makeshift canopy.

Bundled up, I went over and joined a handful of campers at a fire ring. A joint was being around. The talk was of faraway places.

Looking around the camp, I saw more new faces than old ones. Only a handful of souls were left over from when I had first arrived to Hanauma, and a sense of camaraderie had been lost with these continuing departures. Also, the tuna fleet had been idled with the deteriorating weather, putting an end to our luaus. Save for Stan sitting under his keave tree up by the cliffs, silently staring off to sea, the bay was a far different place now.

As we smoked the joint and listened to FM radio, a disc jockey broke in to announce that Janice Joplin had just been found dead.

"Oh man," somebody said. "What a bummer."

Everyone stood there stunned. Jimi had died just a few weeks earlier. A generation was crashing and burning on its way to hell.

A short while later, Lennon called in to the disc jockey and suggested that maybe the dream was over. It was time to get on with our lives.

"Screw Lennon," someone said to cheerless laughter.

The joint continued around the fire ring with Lennon's words troubling my thoughts. It did seem that history was finally catching up with us, that it was time for my generation to grow up and become like our parents. I had been so busy running from the war, I had never even considered this eventuality.

Two more months quickly passed by and in my hours at the bay, I mostly lay in my hammock with the trade winds swaying me this way and that. Not liking the choices before me, I did my best to pretend they did not exist.

12

One evening, getting on into December, I was standing around the campfire with some friends and smoking a joint when a new man appeared from out of the shadows. His tentative approach reminded of my own arrival on a night long ago. With his golden colored hair tussled about his forehead like straw, it was clear this guy had been swimming in the sea that day. His blue eyes sparkled but betrayed some unspoken sadness. With his small, sensuous mouth and fine bones, I thought of the Little Prince.

"Clay," I said and held out my hand.

"Kip," he said.

"Here, have a hit."

Kip did and passed the joint on to the next person.

"You know, you kind of remind of this chick Sarah I know."

Kip got this bemused look on his face.

"I hope not too much," he said.

"Well, she's definitely better looking."

We both laughed.

"Where are you from?" I asked him.

"Tucson. I just flew in this afternoon."

"Wow, that sounds like a bummer place."

"I don't know. I just grew up there." Kip raised his eyebrows with a smile. "This is definitely a better place to be hanging."

Kip and I ended up talking away the night and when the last of the revelers wandered off from our luau, he spread out his sleeping bag close to my hammock.

In the morning, we had a swim in the bay and after tripping on a number of ideas, decided to head out to the windward side of the island. A short while later, we were on our way up towards the parking lot with some joints and a bag of granola for munchies.

Without warning, Kip abandoned the path and scampered up the steep slope and I scampered up after him. Kip was all smiles when I caught up and we crossed the parking lot towards the highway, talking away. I thought of Eric then and realized that the two of us had never shared that kind of wild spirit. Eric was more cerebral and inclined to scratch his chin in thought.

Across the highway, Kip and I stuck our thumbs out with each passing car. A short while later, a refugee from Czechoslovakia picked us up in an open Jeep and we went along with the wind blowing in our hair.

When this guy Dominik heard of our plan, he threw in his lot with us and we were soon motoring around the backside of Pearl Harbor. Miles and miles of pineapple fields followed. Then we came out to the windward side of the island and turned north up the coast. The road went on past Makaha for fifteen miles and came to an end. A jumble of volcanic rock stretched out as far as we could see.

"Wow," I said. "I always thought you could drive all the way around to the north shore from here."

The three of us climbed out and walked forward among the rocks.

"I can make it," Dominik said.

Kip and I shrugged, doubting it.

"No, I can," Dominik insisted. "Let's just see what happens."

Dominik was soon inching cautiously forward across the maze of volcanic rock. Less than a mile into the adventure, we were met with huge boulders, divided by crevasses big enough to swallow the Jeep.

Wandering farther ahead on foot, Kip and I came across four, heavy wooden planks and called out Dominik.

"Hey! Looks like someone's been through here before!"

Back at the Jeep, we placed two of the planks across the first crevasse, two of them across the next one and Dominik inched slowly forward. Hearing the planks creak and groan, he opened his door to have a look.

"It's okay," he said and closed the door.

After inching forward another ten feet, Kip and I were able to pull the first planks free and move them on to the following crevasse and an hour of the morning passed away in this manner, navigating a few hundred yards. Eventually the terrain leveled out again and we left the planks behind for the next adventurer.

Some miles ahead, we came to a point and an abandoned lighthouse. Wild grasses grew up out of the fine, white sand. The point was otherwise hauntingly barren.

Dominik parked and the three of us climbed up to a catwalk near the top of the lighthouse. All was quiet except for the sea and the wind. This was where the north and west sides of the island met and the sea sloshed milky-green against the rocky shore. We smoked a joint and lay there at that desolate crossroads of the Pacific with the wind whispering quietly in our ears. It was well into the afternoon before we could shake ourselves free from our dreams and move on.

Back in the Jeep, we followed the road north to where it became a narrow trail and snaked high up into the mountains. An hour later, we saw the North Shore far below and the trail eventually led us back down to the sea. Motoring around to the east side, we stopped a final time in the fading twilight and swam where countless reefs bristled whitely out to the horizon.

That evening, Kip reminded that it was nearly Christmas. I had lost track of time and completely forgotten.

Thoughts of Caroline came to mind with the holidays. The two of us had spent the last one happily together.

I lay awake late struggling with whether or not to call her. The impulse always came up hard against the other things. It had been too long. Surely she had found another man. Anyway, why involve her in my desperate situation?

And then there were my feelings for Laura. They had never gone away. Crawling back to Caroline was just a consolation prize.

Two days later, the park ranger stopped by and tacked a notice up by the bathroom entrance. People gathered around to have a look as soon as he had driven off. It was a new set of rules giving everyone until the end of the week to move up to the campground area at the top of the bay. Then we would be given a seven-day pass and when that expired, we had to move on.

Rumors abounded about who was responsible for this change in policy. I remembered seeing a busload of Japanese businessmen in dark suits a few weeks earlier, peering down from the top of the bay and figured that was the reason. If they were investors planning to turn the islands into a tourist destination, the presence of a bunch of hippies camped on Hanauma Bay was definitely problematic.

Whatever the real cause, the dream of Hanauma Bay was over and the remaining tribe slowly picked up stakes and drifted away.

One afternoon, Kip and I went to visit some old friends at a beach campground on the leeward side of the island. The same rules applied there. Seven days and you had to move on.

A family of Hawaiian natives happened to be camped nearby and we sat talking with them at the end of the day. Octopus and mahi mahi swung from a makeshift clothesline in front of their tent, drying in the wind.

"You in trouble now, Haolie boy," the old man said as the sun went down. They didn't have a care in the world. Anyone of Hawaiian descent was free to ignore the seven-day rule.

They all laughed, but it wasn't funny. Unable to thumb our noses at the authorities, we had to accept the inevitable. Many of our friends had already made plans and were returning to the mainland.

At Hanauma, new folks kept arriving to the campsites adjacent to the asphalt parking lot, oblivious to history and how a great and wondrous epoch had come to an end a week or so earlier. Kip and I were still among these people. We now had two days left on our pass.

We had been around the island together that day but Kip had disappeared upon our return. I was on my way back from the shower and looking for him. It was sunset and I came across a group of young folks from Texas. They had moved into the campsite next to ours that same day.

They seemed like a good lot, the men with long hair and the women gypsy-like in their clothing and manner, but they were also of a new generation that drank hard whiskey and played hard Texas rock. The men were busy fashioning a ten-foot long log into a totem pole while passing around a bottle of Jack Daniel's. Each man was offered a jolt from the bottle then encouraged to go after the pole with an axe.

When I asked if they had seen Kip, they shrugged all around and offered me the bottle of Jack Daniel's as consolation. I took a drink, passed the bottle and declined my turn at the axe. I was not in the mood for making totem poles.

Not seeing Kip anywhere, I walked over to the cliff's edge and sat on the rock wall. It was a lovely sunset, awash with pastel colors. Wispy clouds were rushing in from the sea. Stars twinkled high overhead.

Down on the shore, Stan sat alone in his camp. Everyone else had gone away but him. He had respectfully told the ranger where to stick his orders and you wondered where it would end. With the police, I imagined, but as of that moment, nothing had been done. Stan sat in a beach chair next to his tent. The orange parachute flapped lazily above his head. I decided to go down and say hello.

Stan glanced over once at my arrival and resumed his impassive vigil out to sea. Opening a second beach chair, I sat down next to him.

"How're you doing there, Clay?"

"I'm all right, Stan. How are you?"

"Well, hell, if I didn't know better, I'd swear there wasn't a goddamned problem in the world."

"Does seem that way."

Stan didn't answer.

"What are you going to do, Stan?"

He looked at me again for a brief moment.

"Oh, I've thought of swooping in here with a Huey and lighting the place up a bit. That ought to get these sonsabitches to reconsider their goddamned rules. What do you think?"

I let the question hang in the air, amused by the imagery. So many veterans had returned from 'Nam, only to find themselves in another kind of war — with the very people who had sent them off to fight in the first place. Being at odds with the authorities myself, it was comforting to think of Stan bringing a bit of armament to the contest. Then, it seemed rather odd to be considering such things on a balmy evening in the South Pacific.

"Where will you go?" I asked again, wanting to know Stan's true intentions.

"Shit, Clay. You won't let a man have any fun."

"Just worrying about you, that's all."

"Yeah, well, I guess I'll go back to San Diego when it's all over. Start a flight school. Something like that. What about you?"

"I don't know. I had thought to stay here on the islands, but now…"

I noticed Stan staring at me and felt relieved when he looked back out to sea. He cleared his throat.

"Well, speaking of worrying. There were a couple of dicks down here earlier today, asking about you."

I did my best to look unconcerned but Stan was far too observant to miss my reaction.

"Yeah, I figured as much," he said. "I didn't want to say anything but it's just as well you know. They weren't in uniforms, just nice clean-cut pricks, trying to hide it with a couple of Hawaiian shirts."

Stan chuckled to himself.

"Like you wouldn't notice a bear hiding behind a tree. Anyway, I told them you had moved on months ago. Can't say what they learned from anyone else."

I felt sick and got up to leave. My eyes met Stan's.

"Clay, let me give you a bit of advice, for what it's worth. Just keep going. There's no reason to go back and face that bullshit. It's only war and you don't want to be there."

I nodded.

"How long has the trail been cold? Six, seven months?"

I nodded again.

"So you can figure it'll take them that long again. Maybe more. If you're lucky, you'll find someone to love you. Help you to hang on. Then the whole goddamned thing will be over before you know it. We'll all look back someday and have a good laugh."

That seemed impossible, though I took his words in the way they were intended. When you were on the run, it was a comfort to think anyone cared.

"I'd better get going," I said. "Kip and I were thinking to cook up some mahi mahi tonight.

I had started across the sand when Stan called out in a final gesture of kindness.

"Hey, if ever you're in trouble, come see me. Poke around the airport there in San Diego. I won't be far."

I nodded and hurried up the path towards our campsite, dogged both by what Stan had just told me but also by a memory from earlier in the day. Kip had insisted that we stop by Hickam Air Force Base on our way back from the North Shore. When I had asked him why, he had ignored my question and led me out to a grassy field at the end of the runway.

"Just lie here with me."

We got down flat on our backs.

A few minutes later, a B-52 took off overhead, weighted down with so much pay load, it looked like a stuffed goose trying to lift off from a pond, the jets screeching as the plane lumbered into the heavens, the sky torn to shreds by the ungodly strain of those engines at full throttle.

In the silence that followed, Kip had looked over at me with a smile. The world was quiet around us again, enough so that I could hear gulls calling out on the harbor. Then the next B-52 came screeching by overhead.

How Kip found such things entertaining, I could not understand but a day of palm trees and tiki tiki huts had been turned into a vision of death and mayhem, the specter of those planes raining bombs down on Hanoi haunting the rest of my day.

And now this, the Feds still after me, despite all the months gone by, as if they had all the time in the world, and the money to go with it, which they did. Don't you fuckers ever give up, I wanted to scream, but of course they didn't.

In all of that, I was faced again with my complete lack of preparation. I had grown lazy in paradise. I had saved little money over the previous six months and went about beating myself up over my ongoing lack of foresight.

Stan's advice haunted me too, and dropped like the gallows through my heart.

"If you're lucky, you'll find someone to love you and help you to hang on."

I had been provided that gift not too terribly long ago, only to toss it aside like a paper cup. And for all the reasons a man might yearn for comfort on his journey through life, I longed for what had been lost, though doubting Caroline still cared in return. Why would she? Nearly eight months had gone by without me bothering to call her.

Hounded by these thoughts and regrets, my strides grew ever swifter until I was in a flat out run at the top of the bay, both relieved to see Kip and disappointed to find that he had hooked into the scene with the Texans. It was a reminder that another one of my fleeting friendships was about to end. What did Kip need with a man in my position? He was carefree and gregarious to a fault, fitting in everywhere, while I was a wanted man and increasingly distrustful of my fellow human beings.

Determined to extract Kip from those axe-wielding heathens, at least for a moment, I marched resolutely in his direction. One of the Texans welcomed me with a nod as I pulled up. The women were engaged in a Bacchanalian dance around the fire. The totem pole ritual was still in full swing. Kip stood in the glow of their bonfire, not noticing my arrival until the last moment.

In that instant, someone offered me the bottle of bourbon, not seeing the seriousness of my mood, or perhaps because of it. I took a slug, passed the bottle to the nearest reveler and asked Kip to join me out in the darkness beyond the bonfire. He put his hands upon my shoulders once we were alone, still smiling.

"W w w well how are, how are things going there there, pilgrim?"

It was Kip's Jimmy Stewart impersonation and a pretty goddamned good one. Kip had been talking to me in that manner since the day we first drove around the island together and on occasion I had indulged him by playing John Wayne in return. But I was in no mood for bullshit at the moment.

"I need to get off the island, Kip."

"W w well, now now, now wait, now wait a minute there, Pilgrim."

"Look, I'm serious, Kip, so please can the Jimmy Stewart routine. At least for a minute, okay?"

Kip remained smiling but the look in his eyes had saddened considerably.

"All right, Kip. I don't mean to be a dick but please."

Kip nodded at the short wall along the cliff.

"No, let's go up on the point. It's best if I get out of sight."

Kip's countenance brightened at the suggestion of a good climb and we started off through the campground together. Coming to the asphalt parking lot, we crossed it in the silence. Each time a car passed by on the highway, my heart raced at the prospect of the Feds coming back to find me.

At the far end of the parking lot, we struck out through a tangle of trees and heavy brush and circled the upper rim of the bay. After several hundred yards, the brush fell away and the mostly barren flank of Koko Head loomed up ahead of us. Kip and I climbed the craggy promontory and in five minutes were seated with our backs against the warm rock, gazing northeast across the sea towards California. You could see each cloud staggered a bit lower than the last, revealing the curvature of the earth, and somewhere in all of that, the idea came to mind of loading a big V8 up with gas and barreling out towards the four corners and lower Rockies with a thousand miles of flat plains and the whole, vast continent in front of me. Suddenly, all that open country was like a narcotic.

Quiet in our thoughts, nothing disturbed the silence, save for the muffled sound of waves breaking against cliffs far below us. I looked over at Kip and began to explain my predicament, uncertain just how far I intended to go with this thing but eventually revealing all that had happened, from Ithaca to the induction center and concluding my story with what Stan had just told me about the two plainclothesmen. I had never explained any of this to Kip heretofore and he listened with his usual half-sad, half-bemused smile.

"Anyway, I can't get Hickam and those B-52s out of my mind. It was a reminder of how fucking powerful the government is. How foolish of me to think I could defeat them by burning my draft card. It was always going to turn out this way, with me like a duck in a pond and all their guns aimed at my feathery ass."

I glanced over at Kip, who was stroking the peach fuzz on his chin, as though recalling the history of our generation with great fondness.

"I'm glad you find this amusing."

"Hey, brother. I was just thinking of a solution."

"Yeah? And what would that be?"

"Let's fly to Tucson. When I was younger, I used to smuggle bush across the Mexican border. We could do that again. Take our money down to Mexico. Start a little restaurant on the beach somewhere. Get us a couple of Mexican gals and live like kings. We'd have it made."

A great many thoughts rushed through my mind on that balmy evening, but mostly I wondered what self-destructive impulse was encouraging me to give Kip's proposal serious consideration.

No, I decided. This was bad business. My gut told me to ignore him.

"What do you think?" Kip said when I had failed to respond.

"Well, I see two things wrong with your plan at first glance...Tucson and smuggling. Leaving aside any pesky little details I might have ignored."

Kip smiled and continued on as though my concerns were of no consequence.

"I figure we could backpack about five thousand dollars' worth of bush across the border each trip. Say, twice a week. We could have a couple hundred grand in our pockets in less than two months. Think of what all that money could do down in Mexico."

"Yeah," I said noncommittally, though the idea already had its claws in me. Leaving aside the smuggling aspect, every bit of Stan's suggestion was contained in Kip's plan. It was on the wrong side of the law, to be sure, but desperation had no degrees when you were on the run. 'What the hell' became your default response to every new danger.

Probably I should have anguished more over the issue than I did, but I saw myself flipping burgers and tossing hash browns on some remote island in the Pacific for the next however many years, always looking over my shoulder and wondering when the dicks in Hawaiian shirts would pop up, having located me on the basis of my W-2 form, and in light of that fact, the decision became much easier. There was a perilous road ahead for me, either way, but with Kip's plan there was a pleasant mirage at the end — money — and all the freedom it had to offer, including a balmy hideout on the beach in Mexico, which was considerably more alluring than anything I had dreamed up.

"When were you thinking to leave?" I asked him.

"We can take the next plane to San Diego, if you want."

Kip had not turned to look at me in saying this. In fact, staring straight ahead, he appeared to have become a very serious man.

I too looked back out at the lights on the darkening sea and imagined them to be my hopes and dreams, twinkling in the great, yawning abyss. What did I know about destiny and what was waiting for me up ahead? All a man could do was go forward, leaping from one star to the next, and try not to worry too much about the black, unknown spaces in between.

13

Our flight got into Lindberg Field about three that morning. The long, narrow, one-story cement block terminal was painted institutional green and looked more like a bus stop in Wichita than the airport of a fairly major city. A few bums lying around with brown paper bags would have fit right in.

We had sandwiches in a coffee shop before stretching out on some plastic seats near a boarding gate. A few hours later, with dawn blushing on the eastern horizon, Kip and I did a splash bath in the john and caught a shuttle out to the freeway. The sky was gray that morning and our mood was gray along with it. We had gotten very little sleep and several cups of black coffee did little to undo our weariness.

It was a weekday morning and a steady stream of cars raced up the onramp and by us. I stuck my thumb out first, then Kip took his turn. Fifteen minutes went by before someone stopped. It was a short lift and two more rides of a similar length followed. The last ride was with a young guy rushing off to work with a cup of mini mart coffee in his lap. While talking with Kip, a discussion of our days in Hawaii came up.

"Man, I've got to get out on the road," the guy said.

I listened from the back seat, weighing my life against his. A man on the run versus a young guy in a polyester suit, already being worn down by the daily grind. It wasn't much of a choice.

In El Cajon, Kip and I caught a ride over the mountain. The sun came out in El Centro and two farm boys from Iowa picked us up a short time later. They were hauling a '57 Chevy on a flatbed trailer.

The Chevy needed a lot of fixing but those boys were as excited as hell about taking it back to the farm.

At their suggestion, we stopped at a market for a loaf of sliced bread, some cheese and salami, a jar of mayonnaise and a case of beer. Kip and I made sandwiches in the backseat. Everyone told tall tales, and by the time the beer was gone, the farm boys had dropped us off in Tucson.

Kip led me straight over to a district of old houses adjacent to the university. It was dusk and students came and went along the sidewalks and front lawns. The entire neighborhood was something of a college frat party.

I joined Kip on a front porch while he knocked on the door. Kip's dealer friend answered and led us through a front room littered with people. In the relative peace and quiet of the kitchen, Kip and the dealer went about discussing their business. I sat to one side, stunned by Kip's sudden transformation. He and the dealer talked about price, quality and quantities. I took advantage of every joint that found its way into the kitchen, further shocked to realize I had been in Hawaii less than twenty-four hours earlier, still riding the crest of the Bay Area psychedelic movement, but now lost in this dusty, five and dime desert town, without bearings, the cultural revolution reduced to a Cat Steven's album and a bunch of coeds playing massage therapy games out in the parlor. My entire young life seemed to have been a terrible waste.

Kip dragged me home to his parent's place later that night, where the two of us slipped in through a back door unnoticed. In the morning, his mother cheerily made us breakfast and listened to an abridged version of our tales from afar. I definitely lied about who I was and where I had been. Mrs. Prescott was a smart, well-kept woman in her early forties and I didn't trust her as far as I could throw her.

The ranch house itself had money written all over it; money that you knew went back a long, long way. So far back, it felt easy and comfortable. Indian artifacts were sprinkled among the stone and tile décor and the pool and sprawling lawn area outside the open windows transitioned gracefully into the adjacent desert terrain. Far beyond and below the pool, the city of Tucson came into view.

"Have some more to eat," Mrs. Prescott said and ladled another mound of scrambled eggs and potatoes O'Brien onto my plate. "We've got to put some meat on those bones."

I had grown lost momentarily in her silk pants and blouse when Kip suddenly put the morning paper down and excused himself. Mrs. Prescott shooed me away when I took my plate over to the sink.

Kip was already backing his blue, sun-bleached '65 Mustang out of the garage by the time I reached the driveway. I climbed in and we headed down the road, the windows open and the wind blowing through our hair.

Kip had been reticent to discuss anything about our destination, other than to say we were headed for the border. Beyond that bit of information, he had provided me with a pair of old Levi's and some hiking boots. I could not get a word out of him otherwise.

About twenty miles north of Nogales, Kip turned off the highway and started working his way southeast along a crisscross of old ranch roads. Alfalfa fields sprang up, reminding me of the Nebraska plains, only here arid mountains rose up around us in every direction.

Kip eventually turned onto a switchback road that wound up into the hills for several miles. At the crest, he pulled off behind a large outcropping of rock and parked. I climbed out and followed him around to the trunk. He pulled out a camouflage cover.

"Here," he said, handing me one end of it.

With the cover spread over the Mustang, Kip led me around to where the hills dropped steeply off to the south.

"That's Mexico," Kip said with his nose pointed in the distance.

"Okay, so?"

"So, let's go."

Without another word, he leapt over the edge and scrambled down the steep incline in a wild descent. I was hard on his heels. In a few minutes we had reached the valley floor and proceeded to march along a dry, sandy creek bed. Mesquite and saguaro grew thick along the banks of the creek. We passed the bleached bones of a dead steer on the desert floor. The rising sun peeked over the mountain but our way was mostly shrouded in shade.

A mile farther on, we came to a clearing with three clapboard buildings. One of them was tall and narrow and had large pipes running through it. Kip walked over and sat in the shade of that building with his back to the weathered siding. I opened the door and went inside to look around. It was a pump house and the glass meters were covered in a layer of dust. The whole place looked abandoned. I went out and around to another building and opened its door. There were a few hand tools on the wooden shelves, along with some soiled rags.

I went back out and sat on a tree stump across from Kip. A barbed-wire fence ran behind me, east to west. I expected there were cattle around and ranchers, but we saw neither of them. There were only the sounds of the wind in our ears and the rattle of insects out in the brush.

Kip appeared to be listening for something but I had no idea what. We hadn't talked much the whole day so I was in the dark, other than to know we were on a scouting mission of some sort. Kip had picked a stalk of dry grass and was chewing on it. I tried one but soon tossed it away.

"What exactly are we doing?" I asked him.

Kip pointed his chin at the barbed-wire fence that disappeared out of sight in both directions. A number of tumbleweeds were gathered against it where the creek bed ran underneath and headed south.

"That's the border."

"Okay," I said. "So now what?"

"We wait until dark and go across."

"Why wait until dark?"

"Because that's when we're going to bring the grass across. We need to simulate the exact conditions in order to have a proper dry run."

"Oh," I said, surprised again by his sudden transformation. The wistful, carefree vagabond I had met in Hawaii was now a field general. It occurred to me in that moment how serious this entire enterprise actually was. We were consciously preparing to engage in a felony of major proportions. My heart beat wildly in my chest, just thinking about it, and that was without the grass involved.

Kip pulled a topographical map out of his back pocket, carefully unfolded it and pointed to a lookout station in the mountains above us.

"The border patrol people are up there with infrared binoculars. We have to stay down in the creek bed and whatever arroyos we can find and keep out of sight. Sometimes we'll have to crawl on our bellies."

He pointed out various other features in the surrounding terrain and explained our objective was to reach a dirt road leading out of Nogales and return to this place before the night was over, without being noticed. The road on the Mexican side passed five miles directly south of our present location. If things went without a hitch, we would make a real run the following night.

Now and then during the day, the subject of Hawaii came up. I recalled the time Kip had constructed a catamaran out of two surfboards and various pieces of lumber, the whole thing performing modestly well before it broke apart over the reefs. We both had quite a laugh over that because Kip had invested so much time and energy for a five minute ride.

Silence followed.

We had already talked about politics and how the world was filled with senseless wars and hatred, and how, not all that long ago, we had thought we could change these things. Now, we were just trying to find some place to escape.

The day dragged on with the two of us waiting, Kip more patiently than me. If there were any ranchers or border guards or cattle around, we never saw any and the sun was soon setting over the mountains to the west. The day turned to shadows and our trek into Mexico began.

There was something of a rush as Kip jumped over the barbed-wire fence, even though nothing had changed in the gentle night. The border was utterly artificial. It represented fear and distrust of some sort and ran silently off beneath the desert stars.

Now in Mexico, Kip spoke as a Mexican Jimmy Stewart and welcomed me into his country. I laughed at his shtick and jumped over to his side. The laughter quickly faded as we began our journey in earnest.

In time, the sunken creek bed in which we walked rose up to the level of the surrounding terrain and spread out in a formless delta. To go any further in an upright position meant exposure to the lookout tower so we got down on our bellies and crawled along for several hundred yards. Then Kip slipped over into an adjoining arroyo and the two of us were able to stand upright again. That arroyo led us southwest. The lights of Nogales were visible far off in the distance.

Marching along on the desert floor was different from what I had imagined. Whizzing by at sixty miles an hour, it basically looked barren, not this maze of brush and rocks shifting endlessly under our feet. There were no straight paths. Thorns tore at your flesh and clothing. Every time I tripped and cursed, Kip told me to be quiet and I told him what he could do to himself.

About two hours into the march, the road came into view. Kip dropped down into a crouch and signaled for me to do the same. We waited there for ten minutes, watching for any sign of movement, after which Kip unceremoniously signaled for us to turn back the way we had come.

Several miles into our return trek, I had grown dead on my feet when Kip suddenly fell flat on his stomach and motioned for me to do the same. When I failed to do so with the proper degree of urgency, he gestured sharply in my direction. We lay there staring at each other in the darkness.

Moments later, I heard footsteps off in the brush and saw human forms appearing out of the darkness, not more than fifty feet from where we were hiding. Kip opened his eyes wider at me as if to say, see, you dumb shit. I offered him the finger in return.

The lead coyote came by first, followed by a line of wetbacks with their heads down, as if chained to the hopes in their chests. These people did not appear to be any kind of threat but the coyote could have a gun and no telling what he'd do if he stumbled upon us unexpectedly. In any case, I got Kip's message. You did not want your karma getting mixed up with anyone else's karma out here along the border, especially not with the border patrol pointing a set of infrared binoculars in your direction.

Kip waited until they were well out of earshot before we resumed our march. A few hours later, we were in Kip's Mustang and on our way back to Tucson. The eastern sky was turning rosy with dawn.

Kip stopped at a café so we could have some breakfast. I was tired and sore and set on getting some sleep.

Still on the fence about this smuggling business, I knew one thing for certain. I had no intentions of heading back to the Prescott ranch. I smelled danger lurking beneath Mrs. Prescott's good looks and potatoes O'Brien.

After the meal, Kip took me over to the university district to find a motel. I settled on a kitchenette. It had orange Formica countertops, a stainless-steel sink and a stove and small refrigerator with matching yellow colors. A weekly rate was available, in case I decided to stick around.

Kip told me he was off to see his dealer. He'd be back at four o'clock. In the meantime, I should get some rest.

Before he left, we pooled our money together and had enough to buy thirty kilos in Nogales later that evening. If we got back without a hitch, there would be nothing to worry about. If not, we would be in jail with a whole new set of problems. Kip told me not to think like that but I had yet to learn how to compartmentalize my mind in this manner.

I was reminded again to get some sleep and Kip went out the door.

14

Kip whipped his Mustang into the diner parking lot at precisely four o'clock and disappeared around back. He was punctual. I had to give him that much, though I would have been perfectly happy with him being late under the circumstances, or not to show up at all. I had begun to feel a bit like a man with a cop car bearing down in the rearview mirror, all lights flashing, and wondering what to do with the bag of grass in my lap; probably a little worse than that.

The door to the diner opened and Kip came in. A blast of warm air came in with him. He ambled over to the table and sat down. His disheveled straw hair partly covered his blue eyes but I could see the lightheartedness in them was completely gone. This was no longer Jimmy Stewart in *Harvey*. This was *The Naked Spur* edition, the determined frontier gunman in Levi's and cowboy boots. Kip was not about to be dissuaded by any of my arguments. I could see that much.

"How are you feeling?" he asked and reached for a menu.

Sensing that he didn't really give a crap about the answer, I stared off in the distance, uneasy with what I was about to say. It came out like a blast of hot air.

"You know, Kip, I'm not so sure about going forward with this smuggling business."

His eyes flashed over the menu, something like bullets darting out of a pale blue sky. Then he went back to the menu.

"Okay, Kip, I've been giving it a lot of thought and have decided it's one thing to break the law on moral grounds. It's quite another to do so for money."

Kip lowered his menu all the way this time and stared at me.

"Perhaps I'm doing it on moral grounds."

"Oh yeah. Like what?"

He smiled as one all-knowing. It was a nice smile, but I wasn't so sure I trusted the motives behind it.

"Do you enjoy the herb?" he asked.

"Of course."

"It's the organic, spiritual, peace-bearing stuff of gods."

"True, but it's also illegal."

"Then don't smoke it," he countered. The smile disappeared and he went back to his menu.

"Hell, Kip, that's not the point."

Kip snapped his menu closed and stared.

"Then what is?"

"I don't know. It just seems like we're getting a long way from the righteous cause we started with."

"Fair enough," he said. "But just remember, you were the one who was looking for a way out."

"Yeah. Yeah, I guess I was."

"So? Come with me if you want. Or don't. It's your choice. I'm going either way."

With that, Kip leaned back in the booth. I looked out the window, uncertain of my logic now. It had seemed so clear to me earlier on, while lying alone in my motel room. A young man caring about things and having ideals; I had been that way not so terribly long ago and perhaps only wanted to be that way again.

At the very least, it seemed prudent to hesitate at this crossroads and consider our options before going forward, but Kip's sense of conviction just made me feel all the more confused. Was this really about morality, or simply another attempt to mask my cowardice? Not long ago, there had been the occasion to ask the same question as it concerned the war. I had not liked the answers then and didn't like the answer I was finding now.

These reflections were disrupted by a waitress pushing through the doors to the kitchen. Country music came with her. The doors closed and she stood over us, pad in hand. Her strained smile went with her bleached blonde pageboy hairdo. I was reminded of older women, their femininity reduced to a butch. This waitress had already arrived to that place in her twenties. A few extra pounds had been part of the journey. She noticed me staring at the hair and took Kip's order first. He ordered a burger and grabbed the front page of the local paper. I tried a sandwich and added a glass of milk.

Kip's burger arrived and swiftly disappeared. I nibbled at my BLT. We were waiting for Danny, Kip's friend in the Air Force.

A few minutes later, Danny walked in, looking like he had just stepped out of a Norman Rockwell painting. Danny was all Adam's apples and gangly awkwardness. It seemed odd having him mixed up in this business.

According to Danny, half the base was getting high. You wondered how their commander would take the news.

Before I had chance to get any further with that thought, Kip stood up and threw some money on the table. Danny and I followed him out into the desert heat. I climbed into the back seat of Danny's Volkswagen. Kip climbed in front. Kip's Mustang remained in the back of the restaurant. The owner, an old acquaintance, had allowed Kip to leave it there. It saved a lot of explaining to Mrs. Prescott.

Danny zigzagged across town and took an onramp onto the highway headed south. We drove in silence, all of us staring forward without a word.

It grew hot inside without an air-conditioner so Kip rolled down his window for me. In response to the warm wind blowing in my face, I moved over to the other side. Speeding along, a great many doubts and dreams and regrets passed through my head. Where was I going? What was I doing? All that kind of crap. Outside, the desert was carpeted with gold and magenta flowers.

An hour later, we arrived to the outskirts of Nogales. The sun had fled behind the mountains. Only a transparency of pale-yellow remained above the dark peaks. We crossed into Mexico and all that was tremulous about our mission grew that much more tremulous with the onrush of dusk and change of cultures.

On the Mexican side of Nogales, orderliness and prosperity quickly transitioned into poverty and haphazard civic engineering. People were gathered around curbside food carts in the fading light.

We came to a stop sign and Kip pointed left. Danny turned.

"You guys want to stop for anything?" he said.

"Just keep driving," Kip told him. He hadn't bothered to look in Danny's direction.

101

"What, are you mad at me or something?"

Kip looked at him this time.

"You want to stop for something?"

"No." Danny fidgeted with the steering wheel for a moment. "I just thought maybe you might."

He smiled.

"You know, could be the last time for a while." Kip shot him another look and Danny's face turned red. We rode along in silence after that.

The asphalt streets came to an end and we started out a dirt road. Kip pointed to the left again and we ascended into the hillside slums. In the twilight, Danny's car jostled slowly through the ruts. The scent of human waste came on the evening breeze, sweet and putrid. Peasants were gathered around metal drums outside their shacks with fires burning, watching as we came up the hill. Naked children stopped to stare at our passing. Dogs looked warily too.

"They probably think we're lost," I said.

"No one could be this lost," Kip said. Danny chuckled and Kip again shot him one more look. I understood Kip's concern now. We had only one reason to be in this neighborhood and these peasants probably knew it.

Kip pointed at a dirt driveway and had Danny park behind a van. There was a carport over the van, both of these things impressive additions in this neighborhood.

Guillermo, the owner, came out to greet us.

"Come inside, my friends." He motioned for us to hurry. "Come."

Danny was halfway to the door when Kip sent him back into the car.

"Danny's leaving."

I did not wait around to hear the conversation and joined Guillermo inside. The strange sensation of rough ground came through his carpet.

"Please," Guillermo said and waved at the sofa. I found a place that wasn't too worn and had a seat.

Guillermo went in back and whispered sharply at his wife in passing. The faces of their curious children quickly disappeared from a doorway. Guillermo's wife herded them further into the darkened room and closed the door.

102

Thirty kilos were stacked on the coffee table in front of me, each block wrapped with red cellophane over Manila paper. I lifted one and felt its weight.

Guillermo passed by on his way to the kitchen. It was divided from the front room by two sheets of old plywood. He returned with a beer for me. It was cool, not cold. I assumed he had run low on ice.

I heard Danny drive off and Kip came in. Kip also received a beer, took a drink from it and methodically unwrapped one of the kilos. A pungent aroma billowed into the room when the wrapper came off.

"It is good, my friend?" Guillermo said. Kip pried open the flowery stems with his hands. A bud was placed in his mouth and savored. He carefully resealed the packaging.

"It's good," he said. "Not too tight." He checked the taste in his mouth again. "No sugar."

"No. No sugar. Never any sugar, my friend."

It was one of those inexplicable things the Mexicans had tried during the sixties, curing grass with Coca Cola, possibly to hide the scent, or perhaps as the result of some eclectic Mexican taste. In any case, it had bombed with the American market and tended to slash the value of herb in half.

Everything to his liking, Kip handed Guillermo the money. Guillermo counted it while we loaded our packs. The three of us went out to the van. It was almost dark now and most of the neighbors had gone inside. The carport served to keep us out of sight.

Kip and I climbed into the back of Guillermo's van and closed the door. There was a mattress but we remained sitting up, watching in the darkness as Guillermo backed out onto the road. It was the same rough ride going down as when we had come up. Kip and I both grabbed hold of the wall panel to keep from jostling back and forth.

At the bottom of the hill, Guillermo turned right. I could see the western skyline through the back windows. A hint of light was still visible above the now black mountains. I looked the other way to where stars were punching holes in the warm night. Guillermo's silhouette moved at the steering wheel, fighting with the washboard road. I lay down next to Kip. He was staring up at the roof of the van.

"Are you worried?" I asked him quietly.

"No," he whispered back.

"Hell, I am."

"All right, maybe a little." Kip looked at me and back at the roof of the van. We rode in silence again.

Thirty minutes later, Guillermo pulled to a stop. Kip and I got out and hoisted the packs over our shoulders. There were no signs of civilization around us, nothing except for the open desert and the distant lights of Nogales.

"Adios, my friends," Guillermo said. "Buena suerte."

Without another word, Guillermo got in the van, turned it around and started back towards Nogales. I noticed a flash of white in the darkness: a brief smile from the general before he turned to march.

Kip chose our course and I followed on his heels, attempting to be animal like in my awareness, my senses constantly focused and alert, but thoughts inevitably filtered in. When my mind returned from thinking about a past lover or the memory of a fishing village along the Aegean Sea, I was met with the sound of our feet plodding through brush and rock, or another saguaro looming ahead, its arms outstretched like a bandito.

An hour passed with thorns grabbing at my legs and rock turning under my boots. Then we were crawling up the dry wash and the border fence was there, with everything I feared now magnified a thousand-fold.

Kip signaled to stop. The pump house and other structures were fifty yards across the fence from us. All was quiet in the darkness but I had an ominous feeling. The customs people were lurking in the shadows, just waiting for us to cross the fence. Until then, we would not have broken any laws in the United States. If we dropped our packs where we lay and crossed the border fence empty handed, it would mean at worst a slap of the wrist. With the grass, we were looking at twenty-five to life.

Everything inside of me said to turn back and run, but Kip suddenly bolted upright and ran at full speed towards the fence. And not wanting to be left behind, I ran after him.

After a wild, fifty-yard sprint, we reached the border and threw our packs over to the other side. Kip vaulted over the fence first. I followed and nearly landed on top of him. After scrambling to get the packs back over our shoulders, we ran just as wildly along the dry creek bed and then scrambled up the steep slope with the same sense of wild urgency. With every stride, I expected to hear the command. Halt! Or simply the sound of gunfire and a bullet piercing into my back.

15

Shortly after dawn, Kip and I stepped into a café bustling with construction workers and businessmen, truckers and secretaries, men and women of all stripes and colors, some reading the morning paper, some gabbing away, some gulping down pancakes and eggs before the seven o'clock bell; altogether representing the restless pistons of America's sprawling economic engine and everything I had come to dread as a young man. Routine. I dreaded routine more than I dreaded bullets.

Exhausted from our overnight enterprise, Kip and I found an empty booth in the back and settled in. I was relieved just to be someplace warm and out of the cold.

A middle-aged waitress appeared with a big smile and took our orders for bacon and eggs. Kip grabbed a discarded copy of the morning paper. I took in the café. Most everyone had turned a head to check out the two, long haired hippies as we came in but no one was paying attention to us now.

I looked back at Kip, wondering what made him tick. While waiting on that mountain road, I had passed the time restlessly, often pacing back and forth. Kip had sat there as calm as a cat.

I guessed that would always be the problem for me. Waiting. We had waited several hours for Danny's Volkswagen to materialize up on that mountain road. We were waiting now for Kip's connection to get out of bed. Once our load was delivered, we would be waiting to cross the border again. Then, after meeting Guillermo and making the long hike to the border, we would be waiting for Danny to reappear. And if not for me waiting for a war to end, this whole entire enterprise would never have been set in motion.

My entire life seemed to be about waiting.

Later that day, Kip and I took the money from the dealer and rented a one-story ranch house out in the far western suburbs of Tucson, which also happened to be as far as you could get from Mrs. Prescott and still be in town. It was definitely the other side of the tracks. The streets weren't paved. Weeds had overgrown everyone's front yard. The homes were spaced far apart and most of our neighbors appeared to have their own secrets to hide.

Once it was dark, we carried a small safe out into the desert behind the back of our house and buried our cash, using a large saguaro as a signpost.

The next day, I had a thought and asked Kip for a ride over to a head shop by the university. I wanted to see if they had the Wilhelm translation of the I Ching and they did.

"What's this?" Kip asked when we met back up at the cash register.

"It's a Chinese oracle."

Kip looked it over while I paid the hippie chick who ran the shop.

I did not bother telling Kip about Eric and my introduction to the I Ching. I had once dismissed a man for seeking wisdom and guidance from it, the same as I was hoping to do now.

Back at the house, Kip and I figured out how to divine the oracle using pennies. Eric had employed the yarrow stalks but the lady at the head shop was temporarily out of them so we made do with three coins.

Wanting to create the right mood, we lit some candles and played a Ravi Shankar album softly in the background.

The first reading was to determine when we should cross the border again and the hexagram Duration came up. There was a six in the beginning and a nine in the fourth place. The first part of the message seemed clear. Wait. Don't act precipitously. The second part was not so clear but Kip and I decided it must mean that we should find other routes across the border and not use the same one over and over again.

When the signs were again fortuitous three days later, we made a second run. We went twice the following week and a month raced by without the least bit of trouble. All the while, our earnings continued to accumulate out there in the safe.

Kip became convinced that the success of our enterprise was due solely to consulting the oracle but I credited his impeccable planning as much as anything else. Kip had enormous patience and finely honed instincts. He was part army general and part Indian scout.

Inclined to kick back and contemplate the world, Kip read the I Ching from cover to cover, learned how to use the yarrow stalks and was soon using the oracle for everything he did. Forever restless, I went for long walks in the desert and in those hours alone came up hard against the rebellious streak inside of me. Somewhere long ago, I had been a quiet, introspective young boy. Now it seemed as if I had been strapped to a missile and hurtled into this world. I liked to blame the war, but it went back much further, back to some deep-rooted wound that had taken place in my childhood. Whatever it was, I had no peace unless I was moving forward.

Caroline was in my thoughts, too, but each time my hand reached for the phone, thinking to call her, I shook my head and let my hand fall back to my side. What was the point of getting her involved now, with this mischief? When it was over, I kept telling myself. I would call her then, but the longer I waited, the more doubt crept into my heart, doubts about my own intentions and doubts as to whether or not she would still be waiting for me.

Winter was a lovely time to be in the desert, with the lightning storms against the darkened skies and the desert floor carpeted with wild flowers. But Tucson was also a strange place to be living out the last gasp of the sixties, the counter-culture movement caught in a nauseating death spiral between lingering '50s conformity and a still visceral frontier past. The freaks never stood a chance in that hick, backwater town. By the time some local college students finally got a protest march organized, the cops were ready with riot squads and turned the event into target practice. With a bit of tear gas and some rubber bullets, the entire spectacle was over in a matter of minutes, all the hopeful young students summarily thrashed and running for their lives in the fraternity area outside the university. In the end, Lennon appeared to have been right. The dream was dead.

The biggest excitement we had that winter was in the wake of the Sylmar earthquake, when a caravan of cars and Volkswagen buses materialized out of the desert sands along Interstate 10, water beds and bean bag chairs strapped to their roofs, the hippies proclaiming that California was about to fall into the ocean. Of course it didn't and following a two-week party, everyone headed back to California.

In the restless hours between runs, I grew curious about how a man might survive out there in the barren desert all alone and began toting home books on the subject from the local library. Kip was already an expert in this field and took me for an expedition out into the backcountry one day. We came to be lying at the edge of a towering cliff, gazing like a couple of Army scouts at this equally towering crag of rocks far across the valley.

"That's where Cochise made his last stand," Kip told me.

"Far out."

"Yeah...In a way he never surrendered." He stood up and dusted himself off. "Not that it mattered."

His words worked in my head all the way home.

"It must have mattered to him," I said as Kip was pulling into our driveway

"Hmm?" he said.

"I said it must have mattered to him."

"Mattered to whom?"

"Cochise."

"Oh. I didn't know you were still thinking about that."

"It's kind of hard to forget."

I started to say more but wasn't sure I could explain what was in my heart.

As spring turned towards summer, the weather grew increasingly hot and dry, and I grew increasingly restless with it. Then, without warning, the end to our smuggling came. It was a Saturday morning, late in the month of April, and Kip had been to see the dealer following our latest run across the border. He barged into the house looking a mixture of shock and rage.

"What's going on?" I said.

He headed straight for the kitchen and came back with a beer.

"It's over," he said, sitting down opposite me.

"What's over?" I said.

"Smuggling."

He took a long drink and began rubbing his forehead.

"Okay. What happened?"

"Frank had two guys from Detroit at his place this morning. Said he knew them from college or something. They pulled a gun on us. Took everything."

"Shit."

"Yeah. It's a sign. Time to move on."

"Maybe we should consult the oracle."

"You need an oracle to tell you when there's a gun in your face?"

Kip and I sat there staring at each other.

"Wow," I said. "You don't suppose it was karma for selling that shitty dope to those other guys from Detroit?"

Kip met that suggestion with a fierce look. I shrugged back. What did I know, but at one point that winter, Kip had sent Danny down to meet Guillermo alone. Danny's tires were stuffed full of grass and he made it back to the US side of the border just fine, but instead of stopping to have the tires stripped out in Nogales, as planned, Danny panicked and raced straight back to Tucson. When he pulled into our garage that morning, the car smelled of burnt rubber. The grass in the spare was fine, but the rest of it had been reduced to black powder. We weighed out a pound and it was little more than an inch in the bottom of a large baggie.

Unable to move this bush through his usual connections, Kip heard of two guys from Detroit shopping around for some bush and invited them over the next day. "Oh wow!" they kept saying to each other as they smoked a joint of that stuff. "This shit is fantastic."

Once those guys were safely out the door, we had a good laugh. In fairness to us, the shit did get you high, but the energy from the transaction had never felt clean and I always wondered about it.

"Karma..." I suggested again.

"Whatever," Kip said. "I thought for sure they were going to put a bullet in my head."

He pointed at his forehead.

"The fucker had the barrel right there, between my eyes. Finger on the trigger."

"Well, at least you're alive."

"And finished with smuggling," he added.

It struck me there in the silence that a whole new set of decisions confronted me now. I had grown so thoroughly accustomed to our routine — march and bury the money, march and bury the money — that I had failed to consider what I would do with myself next. I shrunk even more so from the idea of calling Caroline, now that the hour was here. Even if she hadn't found herself a new man, I was no longer certain of my own motives. If I had learned one thing in my young life so far, it was that life only went forward. You could never go back.

In the emptiness of the desert morning, a cactus wren called from outside our back door. The clock ticked on the wall. Kip drank from his beer.

"You still planning to come to Mom's party today?" he said.

"I guess so."

"You don't have to."

"Neither do you."

"Anything to keep her off my back."

"You could always move farther away."

"Yeah, well, until then."

Kip stood up.

"I need to get some sleep."

So did I and awakened with the afternoon sun warm and bright in my room. There was a thought to skip this party business over at the Prescott spread but Kip poked his head in through the bedroom door.

"Are you coming?"

"Yeah, sure. I'd better keep an eye on you."

I got up to shower and a short time later the two of us were winding up Old Spanish Trail. Lost in my thoughts, I watched a plane fly overhead and into a cloud. Kip parked and the plane came out the other side. A few moments later, it disappeared over the adjacent mountains. The cloud followed in that direction. I looked back at the parked cars. A Maricopa County sheriff's cruiser was visible among them.

"Great. Your Uncle Charlie's here."

"Just don't make trouble."

"Me make trouble? I know that son of a bitch has it out for my ass."

"I told you. He's under indictment for a shady land deal right now and it's got him a bit back on his heels."

"It's got him pissed off. That's what it's got him."

"Well, don't talk to him."

"I smell a bear in the cave," I said, shutting the door. "So don't go deserting me."

"You fret too much, Clay."

We passed through a wrought-iron gate and started up a long, gardened walkway with me still grousing.

As we approached the carved front door of the adobe house, it opened for us and David stood there, the fiancé to one of Kip's sisters.

"Hey Kip."

He smiled and shook both our hands. David's perfectly coifed, shoulder length hair had me transfixed. It was a reminder of how corporate America was now selling the sixties back to the hippies who had made it happen. The portrait of a general in full regalia hung on the wall behind David and some gently pasteurized folk-rock played in the background.

With my brain on vapor lock, I left Kip talking to David and went looking for the bar. I found it under a rented canopy out in back with a pleasant view of the surrounding pool area and desert beyond.

A black bartender wearing a perfectly pressed white suit mixed my drink and handed it to me from under the shade, complete with napkin and a colorful swizzle stick. I promptly discarded the swizzle stick, tasted the whiskey-soda and looked up to find Mrs. Prescott headed my way.

"Well, hello there, Clay," she said with her delicate hand extended.

I took it without answering, ever wary of the calculating mind beneath all her smiles and perfume and silk blouses.

"Where on earth have you been?" she pressed on. "We haven't seen you in months."

"Just busy with college."

"Oh, good for you! You're going to school! That's wonderful! Tell me all about it. What are you taking? What's your major?"

I had begun to regret opening my mouth when Mr. Prescott called out to her and waved with his hand. She waved back and returned her attention to me. I smiled.

"Duty calls but don't you go running off on me. I'm dying to hear all about your curriculum."

She touched my arm and headed on her way. I enjoyed her fine figure strutting across the lawn while marveling at her lack of sincerity.

Seeing Kip at one of the shaded lawn tables, I went over and collapsed next to him.

"I don't know whom to fear most, your mother or the sheriff."

"They don't trust each other, if that gives you any comfort."

"Not really."

We watched the chattering lawn party in silence.

"David depresses me," I said after a spell.

"Why?"

"I suppose because he's a symbol of our lost struggle."

"Think of David as a brief way station along the path to spiritual enlightenment."

"Yeah. Maharishi with a textured do."

Kip smiled.

"Styled hair is really *in* these days."

"You're a kind soul, Kip."

He blinked his eyes fetchingly.

"But seriously. This whole business with the establishment selling the revolution back to us. It really pisses me off."

I tossed down the last of my drink.

"Define pain," Kip said absently.

"A bummer," I said.

"Then why do you add to it?"

"Did anyone ever tell you that you ask too many questions?"

He smiled and lit up a cigarette.

"Oh shit," I said. "Here comes the sheriff."

16

Charlie was upon us before I could blink, his fork stabbed into an overburdened paper plate, his right paw offered up for a handshake. I shook it reluctantly. He took a deep breath and tugged on his pants, which had nothing to do with his actual waist size. Like most men with a pot gut, the sheriff had his pants buckled about two inches above his scrotum. A recent haircut had left his face as naked as a field after harvest. His pomade glistened in the hot sun.

"Gentlemen," he said while staring in my direction through a pair of aviator sunglasses.

"How're you doing?" I said, staring at my own reflection.

The sheriff looked over at Kip.

"Your Momma tells me you're plannin' to go over to the universty next semester."

"That's the plan, Uncle Charlie."

"Yessir," the sheriff said, getting back to the food on his plate. "Be good to follow in your friend's footsteps here. Isn't that right, Clay?"

"Nothing like a good education, sir."

Sheriff Prescott bent his head down and shook it from side to side, revealing the few remaining wisps of hair left on top of it.

"Damn strange though," the sheriff went on. "Yessir, damn strange."

The sunglasses came up to face me again.

"Cuz I happened to check on that fact. Bein' that other's people's business is my business."

I nodded, beginning to feel cornered.

"Oh sure, with a few heads turned here and there, I can know just about anything around this town." He sampled his potato salad and spoke right through it. "And it seems like they ain't never heard a you over at the universty."

"Must be an oversight," I said.

"Is that so?"

I nodded.

"Well, I considered that possibility too and twisted a few more arms but I'll be damned if I could find any proof of you bein' enrolled over there."

"Well, maybe you're just not on top of your game these days, sheriff. What with that shady land deal and all."

Sheriff Prescott stiffened like a snake had bit him in the ass. He studied me from behind the sunglasses.

"My problems ain't shit compared to what some people's gonna have."

The sheriff looked over at Kip and paused to let that soak in.

"You boys have yourselves a nice day."

With a parting nod, he ambled over in the general direction of the bar and stopped to chat with Mrs. Prescott. Both of them glanced our way while talking.

"Good going, Clay," Kip said. "When are you going to learn to keep your mouth shut?"

"Probably never. And I thought you said they didn't like each other."

"They don't." Kip stood up suddenly. "We'd better get the hell out of here."

"Why? I haven't had nearly enough fun yet today."

We both tossed our paper plates into a garbage can. I headed out the gate. Kip stopped to say goodbye to his Mom before joining me.

"Well, you've definitely stirred up a hornet's nest now," he said as we walked down the path to his Mustang.

"What do I care? I'm getting my ass out of town."

"Okay. What do you want to do for the rest of the day?"

"I don't know. Why don't we stop by the universty?" I said, imitating the sheriff.

Kip smiled.

"Yeah, real funny, Kip, but I'm serious. It's time to move on and that could be tonight if I can find a flight out of here."

Kip backed the Mustang out onto Old Spanish Trail and headed down the hill.

"Where are you thinking to go?" he said.

"I'd like to head to Europe but I'm a bit paranoid about using my passport right now. At least flying out of Tucson."

Kip turned into Sentinel Park and lit up a joint. He took a puff and handed it to me. I leaned my arm out the opened window. The sheriff's words kept turning around in my head.

"My problems ain't shit compared to what some people's gonna have."

I was going over them about the third or fourth time when the sirens went off and my high came crashing down in a nauseous knot of law and order. The world was suddenly moving in slow-motion.

"Bummer," Kip said while glancing in the rear-view mirror. "It's Charlie."

"Fuck."

"Yeah. That bastard must have followed us."

"Brilliant deduction."

Somehow Kip got over to the side of the road. I ate what was left of the joint. The veins in my neck felt like rope. My heart was trying to clear my rib cage.

"Just don't say anything, Clay."

"Well, you know me, Kip. I'm just dying to engage Charlie in some sort of metaphysical discussion."

"Shut up. I've got a baggy under the seat."

"Oh, great."

Kip reached for the baggy and shoved it down his pants.

"And remember, don't say a word."

"You've already said that."

"Shut up, Clay."

A moment later, the sheriff was punching his head through Kip's open window. His deputy had come around to my side of the car.

"Well, fancy meeting you boys again." The sheriff had a look around the interior. "What's the matter? Your friend not feelin' social like anymore?"

"What do you want, Charlie?" Kip said.

The sheriff thumbed his nose at a suitcase on the back seat

"Plannin' on going someplace?"

116

Kip used the suitcase to ferry our dope over to the dealer and had forgotten to take it back inside after that morning's adventures. At least it was empty.

"What do you want?" Kip said again.

"Well son, it seems like you was pushing the speed limit a bit back there."

"Bullshit. I was doing twenty-five."

Ignoring Kip for a moment, the sheriff stood up and checked inside his left ear with a pinky. He checked the pinky to make sure nothing was there and sighed. Sweat had stained the back of his khaki shirt.

"Yessir. Well, maybe you was at that but I reckon it's a damn good thing we pulled you over."

He stuck his head back inside the car.

"Cuz it smells like you was havin' some kind of 'lectrical fire."

The sheriff had a quick look over the roof at his deputy.

"Don't it smell that way to you, Clyde?"

Clyde pretended to smell something.

"Yep. It sure does."

The sheriff smiled and gave Clyde a nod, and he wasted no time in opening my door. I stepped out with that crazy feeling of backing off a ten-story building.

Kip had gotten out with the sheriff and leaned against the hood.

"Go on," he said with a wave of his hand. "Get it over with but you're not going to find a damned thing and my mother's going to be all over your ass when she finds out you've been harassing me again."

"Now hang on there, Kip. Ain't nobody harassing nobody." He went back to prying around in his ear. "But since you offered, why we might just be able to keep you from burnin' yerself up."

"Oh, bullshit."

The sheriff watched me while Clyde assumed the duties of searching the Mustang. Thirty seconds later, Clyde reappeared with a misplaced bud and a roach. Charlie smelled the roach and broke it open. The filling blew away with the breeze, followed by the paper. Then the sheriff held the bud in his paw, as if he were assaying its weight.

"Now what's that you were sayin', son?"

Kip stood there leaning against the hood, staring off into the distance.

"Yeah. I suspected you might quiet you down a bit."

The sheriff found his handkerchief and wiped at the sweat on his face.

"Well, I reckon we're gonna have to book ya."

He motioned to Clyde, who snapped me against the car, spread eagle. After he had emptied my pockets of some change and my wallet, he cuffed me and led me back to the patrol car.

"You may as well lock it up, Kip."

"Bullshit. You're not taking me in and you know it."

"Nope?" He turned to stare out over the desert. The Sierritas were off in the distance with a bit of snow still on their highest peaks.

"That's where you're wrong, son. Your mother put me up to this. She said she wanted you clean or in jail, and didn't care which. She figures if you're gonna go bad, you may as well taste the water now. Might save you some grief down the road."

He took the time to fling a paw in my direction.

"As for him, ain't nobody goin' to worry over that piece of shit." He leaned back on the car next to Kip and sighed like a man who wished he had something better to do.

"I reckon there is one alternative," he said, turning towards Kip. "That's if you're willing."

The sheriff used the handkerchief to wipe the sweat off the back of his neck now.

"What's that?" Kip said.

"Well, there's nothing that'd make your mama happier than if you went back ta school like you said. And no shittin' around."

Charlie glanced up at the phainopepla, singing and fluttering its black wings atop a saguaro across the road. In the otherwise silent afternoon, all of us had stopped to watch it.

"What about Clay?" Kip said, interrupting the sojourn.

"Like I said, son. He's going up. It's some folk's opinion that he's mostly responsible for your turnin' out bad."

"That's a crock of shit, Charlie."

"Well, let's just say that it'd make your mother happy to put it in those terms."

"All right Uncle Charlie, spill it."

118

"Well, I figure ta keep this bit of evidence downtown as a measure of your sincerity."

He assayed the weight of bud one more time and stuck it in his top pocket.

"Now if you was to get yourself back in school. Stickin' to it, mind ya," he added with a smile. "Why I imagine this could have a way of disappearing."

"Yeah," Kip said. "The way a lot of shit disappears down there at the station."

"You best watch your tongue, boy."

The sheriff's hand had come up reflexively but stopped midair when he remembered who he was dealing with.

"Let's just stick to the matters at hand, son."

He wiped at his forehead with the handkerchief and tucked it away in his back pocket.

"Okay, Charlie, I'll talk to my mom about getting back to school. You can stop worrying yourself about that."

He studied the sheriff.

"What about Clay?"

"I told you, son. He's going up."

"Look, Charlie. I'm as much to blame as Clay in all of this. Just let him go and I'll make sure he's out of town by tonight."

The sheriff eyed Kip, then me, and spat on the ground near his shoes.

"I'd be a damn fool, doing that."

"Just do me this one favor, all right? And I'll never ask you again."

The sheriff took a deep breath.

"I'd have a helluva time explaining this to your mother."

"I'll take care of her, Charlie. Hell, you know as well as me. The minute Clay's gone, she'll be off both of our backs."

The sheriff looked at me and back at Kip.

"All right, goddamn it. I'll give that son of a bitch about four hours, and if I see him after that, I'll throw the book at him."

The sheriff pushed away from the car, disgusted with himself.

"Just for good measure, I'm takin' him in to print him."

"I thought we had a deal?"

"I said for good measure. That ways I can always find him if the occasion arises. Follow us down to the station and you can pick him up when I'm done."

The sheriff came back to the patrol car, got in and looked over the seat at me, as best as his broad girth would allow it.

"Amazin' how some people comes to havin' so much trouble all of a sudden." He smiled once and turned back to start the patrol car.

We headed over to the station like it was a funeral procession. Then Clyde marched me upstairs, one hand on my cuffs, the other on my shoulder. While I waited to be fingerprinted, Kip came inside and started to explain the situation.

"I got it. I heard the whole thing from the back seat of the squad car."

Once Clyde was done with me, he marched me over to the sheriff's office. The sheriff waved for Kip to come inside too.

"Kip here can fill you in on all the particulars, but let's just say, I don't wanna have ta see your face around these parts ever again...Ya understand me?"

I nodded.

"All right then. Get out of my sight. Both of ya, before I change my mind."

Kip and I headed for the front door. The sheriff followed us outside and stood there watching while we climbed into the Mustang. Kip was just stomping on the accelerator when the sheriff called out with a final thought.

"And don't you go fucking with me, Kip Prescott!"

Back at the house, Kip and I stopped to face each other.

"What are you planning?" he said.

"Cross the border into Mexico. I don't see where I have much choice. That fucker has my prints and I'll give him about 24 hours before he figures out who I am...If it takes him that long."

"Maybe we should consult the oracle?"

"To turn a phrase, why would I need the oracle to figure out I'm about to be busted?"

I started off towards my bedroom.

"Excuse me while I pack."

Five minutes later, I returned with a suitcase. Kip was sitting at the kitchen table with the I Ching open.

"The oracle says don't go south."

"Yeah? Well screw the oracle. I'm not going down there to smuggle."

He shrugged and placed the Book of Changes down. I grabbed a bottle of mescal out of the cupboard.

"Want a drink?"

"Sure," Kip said.

"Oh shit," I said, seeing smoke.

I had inadvertently left an electric griddle on that morning and Kip had placed the I Ching right on top of it. The coils had burned a round hole through the back cover.

"Bad sign," Kip said.

He thumbed through the back pages to see how much damage had been done. I filled two glasses and cut open a lime. Kip set the book down and watched me. I licked some salt, took a shot and chased it with one of the lime wedges. Kip followed suit.

"You want some company?" he asked me.

"You're not worried about this oracle business?"

He smiled.

"I'd better keep an eye on you."

"What about your bargain with the sheriff?"

"I'll get back to school someday." He tossed back another shot and handed me the saltshaker. "But not right now."

"Now don't you go fuckin' with me, Kip Prescott."

He smiled again. I took another shot and looked out the back door. The late afternoon sun was casting shadows across the desert floor.

"I do owe you a big thanks, Kip. If it wasn't for you, I'd be slinging hash somewhere and looking over my shoulder."

"Hey, maybe it's time to go down there and open that bar on the beach."

"Sounds cool, doesn't it?"

"Yeah…Were you going to call Caroline?"

"I don't know. Let's just head south and see what happens. I'm not going to feel safe until we're on the other side of the border…What's the plan, anyway? I really don't have any idea where to go or how to get there."

"Let's take the train down to Mazatlán and see where the road leads us from there."

"Okay. Sounds good. Be nice to see the ocean again...How do you propose we get to Nogales?"

"Take the Mustang. I'll call Danny and have him pick it up tomorrow."

"And this?" I waved my hand across the room.

"Leave it," he said with a smile. "We'll be lucky to get out of town."

I smiled and turned my attention to the surrounding desert.

"Guess I'd better go grab my share before we leave."

Kip looked out back too. It was late afternoon and we had never uncovered the safe except at night. We both shrugged.

"We'll just pretend we're taking a walk," he said.

We wandered far out into the brush before circling back to the safe and dividing the money up into even thousands. I stuck my half into my satchel. Kip took what he needed and covered the safe back over with sand.

Back at the house, we finished packing and turned everything off.

"Ready to go partner?" he said.

"Sure. One last shot?"

I poured two jiggers full while he cut another lime.

"To the sheriff," I said.

"He's going to be pissed."

We touched glasses and downed the shots. With a final look around the house, I followed Kip out the door.

17

Down at the border, Kip parked the Mustang at a 24-hour supermarket and called Danny from a phone booth. When he was done, I called information and asked for Caroline Leroux. Nothing came up so I tried her mother. They had a number for Mrs. Leroux but when I called it, the phone just rang and rang.

In those fleeting moments of a dying day, I accepted my fate. It wasn't meant to be, and probably just as well. As I had reasoned back in Hawaii, you only got one shot in this life at loving a woman heart and soul, the way I had loved Laura. Who was I, asking Caroline to play second fiddle?

Kip had wandered off a short distance but was waiting when I got off.

"Did you find her?" he said.

I shook my head.

"No answer."

He smiled and put an arm around my shoulder. The frontier lawman was gone. The happy go lucky Jimmy Stewart was back.

"Let's go have some fun, partner."

"Yeah, well, at least get our asses into Mexico before Charlie comes looking."

We started over a bridge and came to the border a few blocks farther on. A Mexican guard welcomed us into his country with a flamboyant wave of his hand. That was something of a triumph. In America, we were hippie scum. In Mexico, we were honored guests.

Strange new sensory information instantly bombarded us. The scent of meat frying on taco carts, car fumes and human waste. Mariachi music played somewhere. Broken old men and half naked kids loitered along the sidewalks. So did feral dogs. If you were poor, you struggled to eke out a living in Mexico, and most everyone in these cheap border towns was poor.

A number of shopkeepers stood in their doorways, watching us pass by. One of them hit us up.

"Hey meester, where you going right now? Maybe you want some girls? I know where you find some girls. Very beautiful girls, Señor. Perfect for you."

Kip shrugged at me with a "why not" smile but I kept walking.

At the first major intersection, he flagged a battered Ford taxi. It had dents everywhere and a fender missing. The driver accelerated away from the curb in a cloud of smoke. The windows were open and my eyes began to burn. Amidst the madness, Kip and I began to laugh. Somehow, our wild, desperate journey had been stripped of its façade. We'd all be dead soon, so why worry.

"I don't think we're going to make it there alive," he said. "And there's something I've been dying to tell you."

"I know. You love me."

"No. I think you're the world's biggest pain in the ass."

We doubled over in laughter.

I was still struggling to catch my breath when that business with the I Ching passed through my thoughts. Don't go south. I looked over at Kip and looked away, unable to escape the image of the I Ching going up in smoke. It was the sort of thing that would piss off the gods.

We had been passing through the grim back streets of Nogales and came to the train station. I paid the driver and he drove off in another cloud of smoke. Kip crossed himself and we started over to the station. It was comprised of a small brick building, surrounded by a sizable stone plaza. A crowd of people stood waiting to board the train, like so many silhouettes in the dusky light. There were a good many Americans among the Mexicans. The train hissed and brooded on the tracks.

Kip and I walked over to the ticket booth. I kept an eye on our suitcases while Kip looked into the tickets. A man inside the brick building spoke with Kip through a small window. Kip came back and shrugged.

"The train leaves in fifteen minutes but it's booked up."

"Bribery?"

"That's been known to work from time to time in Mexico."

"Shit, when hasn't it?"

"Good to see you're getting back into form, Clay."

"It's a lot of work being the world's biggest pain in the ass."

We headed off in the direction of the train with Kip laughing.

As we waded through the crowd, we were greeted warmly by most Americans and exchanged a few "What's happening?" and "Peace, brothers," along the way.

Kip found the conductor and spoke to him in Spanish. After a brief discussion, Kip pulled out a twenty dollar bill and placed it in his hand. It quickly disappeared.

"Aver," he said.

For twenty dollars, he would see.

Kip smiled at me and gave the man another twenty. We were shown to the baggage car.

Inside, we were greeted by a large dog in a cage. He let us know how he felt about our arrival. I turned to argue with the conductor but he was already gone. Kip and I threw our suitcases in with the other luggage and headed back outside.

"It's going to be a long night," I said.

"Between you and the Mexicans, I think I'm going to cry."

Kip pulled a flask out of his back pocket, took a drink and handed it to me. The Mescal warmed my insides.

"Thanks," I said. "Now what?"

"Let's go talk with the other Americans."

"You go. I'll stay behind and work on being miserable."

Kip smiled and went off alone. I leaned against the train and stared at two Mexican kids clinging to their mother's dress. They stared back at me with big eyes. When I made a face, they clung even tighter to their mother. I looked up and saw Kip rapping with two hippie chicks.

Feeling restless, I started along the train in the growing darkness. One of the cars was a saloon. That buoyed my spirits. Kip found me a few minutes later.

"What's happening?"

"I got word on some groovy places to stay in Mazatlán. We can even just crash on the beach if we want to."

125

"I think I'll rent a nice villa somewhere. I mean, what else am I going to do with all this money?" Kip smiled at me in return. "By the way, I'm getting awfully hungry."

"You should have eaten more at my Mom's place."

"You're right. I don't know what came over me."

Kip laughed and placed his arm around my shoulder again.

"I'm glad we're here together, brother. You're the best friend I've ever had."

"I'll second that, Kip."

A call went out from the conductor and people began to converge on the train.

"By the way," I said. "I saw there's a bar on the train."

I pointed up the tracks and we started moving in that direction, with much of the crowd moving against us. The people came in groups and you had to decipher their bonds, then cut through them where you could.

I reached the car with 'Cantina' painted on the side and turned to find Kip fifty feet back, talking with a Mexican family.

"By all means, take your time," I said when he pulled up.

"What's the hurry?"

"All right, you dawdle. I'll go grab some seats."

I turned and nearly ran over a young woman and had begun to excuse myself when everything strange and wondrous about the universe flashed through me. I was standing face to face with Caroline. She stared back. Neither one of us knew what to say.

"God, this is so strange," I said, reaching down to hug her.

I felt ambivalence in her embrace. There were two male companions over Caroline's shoulder. I pulled back to look in her eyes.

"I'm sorry. I tried to call."

"Not very hard, I think."

"No, well. I am really sorry…I can explain…This is Kip, by the way. We met in Hawaii."

Caroline introduced us to her companions, Tom and Bill. Everyone stood there sharing looks. I was wondering what those two men meant to her. A lot had been said behind my back. That much seemed certain.

"Sort of mystical, running into each other this way," Kip said.

"It is trippy," Caroline said.

Those two clicked immediately and started talking. While they did, I stole another look at Tom and Bill. Tom had long, dark wavy hair that half hid his face. With his hands in his pockets, he seemed like an overgrown kid. Bill had wire-rim spectacles and reminded me of my 5th grade teacher. Strict. Taciturn. From Kansas. Forty years of age and a ponytail seemed to be the primary differences.

"Are you really going to Mazatlán too?" Caroline said to me.

"Yeah."

"Onward to Mazatlán!" Kip proclaimed.

I met Caroline's eyes. I had forgotten how damned beautiful she was. My failure to call and all my mixed-up unresolved unspoken emotions stood between us. So did these two men and all the things I didn't want know.

"¡Vaminos!" the conductor called out.

"Guess we'd better get on board," Kip said.

I helped Caroline up the steps. Tom and Bill followed us, then Kip. The conductor closed the door and the train slowly picked up speed.

"Do you have a berth?" Caroline asked me.

"Yeah. The baggage car." She laughed. "It's a long story."

Caroline went down the aisle a few doors and opened one.

"This is yours?"

She nodded.

"Nice."

The sleeper car was small and dark and their suitcases were piled onto one of the beds.

"It beats the hell out of the baggage car."

"Sorry," she said. "If it was bigger, we'd make room for you."

"It's all right. We've got room to lie down. It's the rabid dog that has me worried."

Caroline laughed again.

"Maybe we could talk for a few minutes alone?" I said.

Caroline glanced over my shoulder at Tom and Bill. Tom brushed the hair away from his face. Bill stared. Kip was smiling behind them. There were other bodies trying move past us down the aisle

"I'm headed to the cantina," Kip said, getting the drift.

When Bill and Tom failed to follow, Kip encouraged them along.

"Come on. Let's go join the party."

The two reluctantly followed him down the passageway. Tom looked over his shoulder several times before disappearing into the next car.

With them gone, Caroline and I went into the small cabin and closed the door. Her dark gypsy eyes flashed in the shadows and her tongue licked absently at the birthmark on upper lip, the way she had always done.

"It's like I just went out to grab the morning paper."

"And never came back," she said.

I looked out the window at the passing town. The memory of what I had said at LAX dogged my mind. I'll call you as soon as we get settled. I looked back to find Caroline still staring at me.

"There were things I never told you about my life and I honestly thought it was best to spare you the trouble."

"You might have gotten my opinion."

I nodded, still staring into her dark eyes.

"It's Tom, isn't it?"

She barely nodded. When I looked away, she pulled my face back.

"What did you expect?"

"Hell, I don't know. Anything but this."

I pulled my chin free and looked back out the window. The train was picking up speed.

"I'm sorry," Caroline said. "Tom and I are just friends now but he was good to me when I needed it. I realized at some point that he was simply my attempt to forget about you."

I stood there, feeling worse for what she had just said, not better. Caroline reached out and shook me.

"What did you want me to do? I had no idea if you still cared about me."

"I know. You couldn't have. And once weeks had turned into months, that became another reason why I didn't call. I dreaded this very thing. I nearly picked up the phone a thousand times. First in Hawaii, then in Tucson." I shook my head. "I guess I was always waiting for the right moment and it never was. Then all of a sudden Kip and I were crossing the border and I had to try. I called your mother's place about half an hour ago."

Caroline stared.

"What happened in Tucson? Is that your secret?"

"No. Well, maybe that too. I just have a lot to explain and don't feel like I can do it in a matter of a few minutes."

"You know, this is really what I came to hate about our relationship, Clay. After you left, I realized I knew so little about you. Your life was just this great big mystery to me."

"I know. I'm sorry. I just wish it was like I had expected. To feel this great joy at seeing you again. Not this fucked up mess."

Caroline was staring out the window thoughtfully.

"Well, it is such a trip, running into each other this way so maybe we ought to just drop all the questions for now and try to enjoy it."

"Yeah, sure," I said.

"Oh, come on." She shook me playfully. "Let's see that smile."

My feeble attempt made her laugh. I leaned down to kiss her lips, wanting to feel her love and warmth, but when I went to pull her tighter into my embrace, she pulled away.

"I'll always love you, Clay, but I don't think we can ever go back to the way it was." She touched my face and searched my eyes. "That's the way I feel right now."

We stood staring at each other in the growing darkness.

"Come on," she said, trying to tickle me again. "Let's go join the party.

"All right."

Out in the passageway, Caroline locked the door and we started down the passageway.

"I really like Kip," she said.

"Yeah. He's been the best of friends."

She stopped at the door to the next car and reached up to kiss me.

"I do love you, Clay. Those feelings for you have never died, okay?"

"That's nice to hear. I never stopped loving you either."

We continued forward two more cars and reached the cantina. It was standing room only. I pushed through the crowd while pulling Caroline along behind me. We found Kip seated at the bar. He let Caroline have his seat.

"Drinks?" he said.

"Two margaritas?" I said with a look at Caroline.

She nodded and Kip called to the bartender. He turned back, looking a bit drunk already.

"Did you know this moment has been happening forever?" he said to Caroline.

His eyelids were slowly blinking.

"I guess I didn't," she said with a grand smile my way.

I hugged her discreetly with one arm and looked around the crowded cantina. When my eyes met Tom's, he looked away. The train clicked and clacked down the tracks. The horn called. There were scattered lights among the distant black hills.

Our drinks came and we toasted.

"Welcome to the journey across the Milky Way," Kip said.

"Oh, let's drink to that!" Caroline said.

I hung back and let Caroline rap with Kip. My mind was elsewhere, struggling with this confluence of destiny and mixed-up feelings. No doubt there was magic in this moment. Life had brought us back together. But there remained my love for Laura and my inability to feel the same way towards Caroline, like it was forever and ever.

Troubled by these thoughts, I hadn't noticed her standing in front of me. She held out a closed fist and stared up into my eyes.

"I have a surprise for you."

She flashed her hand open briefly, revealing two tiny squares of paper in her palm. The figure of a man with long hair and a frock was printed on both. Caroline came near and whispered in my ear.

"If you want."

"Tripping here?" I said.

She pulled back to look at me.

"Is that so strange?"

"Yeah, maybe."

"Do you think it will hurt, Clay?"

"I don't know about that. I just wonder if you know what you're getting into."

"It's only your fears."

"Oh, yeah. My little guru."

She grabbed my ribs and tickled me. I saw Kip over her shoulder, smiling, and Tom and Bill seemingly brave enough to take the plunge. Not wanting to be the one hanging things up, I held out my hand. When Caroline put the piece of paper into her mouth, I swallowed mine. A tincture of adrenalin and regret rushed through me the minute it went down. As always, there was no turning back now. I called to the bartender for two more margaritas and tried to give in to the gaiety of the moment, but I felt a bit like someone had just kicked me off the back of the train.

18

Nothing existed before this moment...and nothing after it. The only dimension was now.

I was suddenly aware of the Hindu monkey gods, chattering away in every corner of the smoky room. The king of all monkey gods stood behind a wooden alter, wearing black and white. He turned and placed a vessel of frothy green liquid on the altar.

"Cinco pesos," the voice said.

A finger pointed at the wrinkled paper. I shook my head. Take whatever you need. The paper was worthless to me. The hand took several pieces and disappeared. I drank to complete the sacrament and turned back to face the chattering monkeys. A galaxy of smoke swirled above their heads, the destiny of the universe written in its vaporous strands.

A straw-haired man appeared out of nowhere. I stared into his sparkling blue eyes.

"I know why Mona Lisa smiled," he said.

"Are you Tarzan of the cornfields?"

Erotic ivory fingers wrapped around the golden-haired arm. A warm breeze tickled my ear. A voice came with it.

"I think we're coming on."

The ivory fingers pulled and I followed out through a door. Standing still, the warm black night rushed by us. Soft-footed creatures scurried warmly about my legs. A horn beckoned from up ahead.

Out of nowhere, a thief with greasy hair appeared. His shifting eyes and cunning smile announced that he was no good.

"Clay, he's coming for us."

"Just close your eyes and he'll miss us."

Then the man was upon us, Shiva, the destroyer, smiling at our impending doom. Light flooded the darkened space. The monkey gods laughed uproariously and chattered. Then darkness swallowed them and the light again.

Clay, he missed us."

"Yes, it's magic."

"But where can we go?

"I thought you knew."

"No," she said. "You have to lead the way."

When I did not answer, Caroline squeezed me more tightly.

"Don't you know?"

Then I remembered the berth. It was through the door up ahead. A door that led to another door, and another one, and another one, until the end of time.

"Come, this way," I said.

I did not understand my own words. I only knew to keep moving forward. I would be Caroline's noble knight and take her there.

We entered a place drenched with stale sweat and urine. Many dark eyes stared at us. The sad, dark eyes of men chained to the oars of their ships. Only their eyes moved as we passed by them. We moved quietly so as not to reawaken Shiva. Then darkness came again, then another place of sad men, then darkness again. Then we were standing in the infinite hallway. It had no beginning. It had no end. Caroline collapsed against the wall and held out a key to me. I stared.

"In the hole," I heard her saying. Her hand reached out and pointed.

The key went into a hole and the door magically opened. Then we were alone in moonlit darkness, aware of having clothes on our skin.

Caroline sat down on the bed and unzipped my pants.

"It is beautiful," she said and pressed her lips. I gasped.

"I didn't love anyone."

The failure of this now haunted me. I had been more hapless than faithful and stood cuckolded.

Magically, Caroline had removed her clothes.

"How did you love him?" I asked.

"Clay, please."

"Show me."

"Please," she said again and began to cry.

"Did you love him like me?" I said.

When she did not answer, I pressed her onto the bed and thrust my manhood into her womb. She gasped and stared at me through the tears.

"I have to know."

"I wanted it to be like you," she said.

"Was it?"

"No. It was never the same."

I pounded her womb hard while she wept. Then the sky was falling around me and I lay there for a long time, crucified between heaven and hell.

Later, I grew aware of the train shifting beneath us.

"Where are we now?" Caroline said.

"Lost, I think."

The sex had been like flowers tossed upon a sea of great sorrow, and now that the flowers had floated away, only the sorrow remained. Caroline's body was no longer mine. Things would never be the same. Caroline kissed my face tenderly but I was Prometheus, locked in stone and unable to return her affection.

"Clay," she said. "Do you remember when we met? How we were going to be together forever."

I nodded.

"Well, it took me a long time to accept that you had walked away from that."

I looked over at her, still locked in my pain.

"I don't know how to forgive," I said.

Then suddenly my mind was on another train, this one leaving Paris, having said goodbye moments earlier to my dear Guinevere. I had waved back before entering the train station, expecting we would meet again one day, but then the gendarme's impassive gaze had met mine through the window, at the very moment the train was pulling away from the station, and I knew. Each moment in eternity was forever there, and forever gone, like the face on a passing train, and the only freedom was in letting go. All things passed away and only fools tried to hold on.

I stared into Caroline's eyes, aware this second chance was some kind of magic, but unable to mend the wound in my heart. I only knew I had to be like the train, to be straight and true and go forward. Either ride it or get off. Forgive and forget, or never see this woman again.

I buried my face in Caroline's womb and tried to tear out the awful pain, the click clack, down the track dying sorrow, the passing of all things eternally into life and death, into torment or enlightenment.

Aware that Caroline had been pleased, I crawled back up beside her, feeling somewhat redeemed.

"Do you forgive me?" she said.

I paused, thinking.

"No. It's my fault. I should have called. I only wish Bill and Tom weren't around to remind me."

"But they're my friends."

"I know. I just wish they weren't around."

"Clay, you have to accept this. Tom and Bill are very special to me."

I looked away.

"Clay," she said and shook me gently. "Please. I've never loved a man the way I love you."

I understood the intent of her words but they still wounded me. And not knowing what else to do, I pulled her close and tried to drive out the sorrow. Just the two of us rolling down the tracks of life, searching for some way to hold this all together.

"How long do we have?" I asked in the darkness.

She was silent for a moment before pulling away.

"My summer classes begin in a month."

"Is that important to you?"

"It's my career," she said. "I guess that's important."

"Doing what?"

"You never listened, did you? I told you I wanted to work in film."

"Doing what?"

"I'm doing make-up and wardrobe right now but someday I'd like to direct."

Direct. Somehow that wounded me too.

"I have money. And plans."

I searched her eyes and waited.

"And those plans can include you."

"Clay. I can take care of myself."

I looked away again. This goddamned world. I had been reunited with Caroline, only to discover that she was not where I had left her.

"Can we at least spend some time alone?" I asked.

"I get this feeling that you're trying to steal me away."

"Well?"

"Well, I don't want to abandon my friends."

"But you don't mind abandoning me."

Caroline shook her head. I hung mine, realizing what I had said.

"I'm willing to be open," she said.

"All right. I'm sorry. I suppose that's all I can ask."

She reassured me with the stroke of her hand and a kiss.

"You are my special potentate and will always be impotentate to me."

I couldn't help but smile.

"Aw, there you go," she said.

"Yeah. I guess it's nice being impotentate again."

Caroline snuggled up close to me and together we listened to the train going down the tracks. Sometime later, Caroline got up to dress and I watched each new article of clothing go back in place with regret. When she was done, I got up to dress too and we stood there facing each other in the cabin. I kissed her hands.

"I want it to be like it was again," I said.

"I don't know, Clay. I think you're trying to bring back something that never existed."

She was right but still I wanted it to be like it had been. She tried to reassure me with kisses again.

"Come on," she said, shaking me. "Let's go join the fun."

"Okay."

Caroline mimicked me and tickled my ribs.

"Seriously, Clay. Isn't this amazing? Meeting like this again?"

And as if her words had picked the lock to my heart, I broke down. And seeing my tears, Caroline cried too.

"Oh, this is so much fun," she said after a minute.

She went into the tiny bathroom and blew her nose.

"Can we go have some fun now?" she said, coming back out.

"Yeah, sure," I said.

Caroline laughed on her way out into the passageway.

With the door locked, we started back towards the cantina, passing through the many cars we had navigated two hours earlier, but with none of it seeming quite so strange now. From a journey through the stars, we had landed back on planet Earth, the oarsmen of the slave ship but peasants now, trying to get some sleep.

Stepping into the cantina, we found it even more crowded than before, and with four mariachis now playing in one corner.

"We have found the cha cha corner of the cosmos," Kip announced at our arrival. Caroline looked at me with a smile.

"I need a drink," I said. "And you?"

She shook her head and went off to see Tom and Bill. I ordered another margarita.

Kip was talking to me amidst the general revelry but I hardly heard a word. All my focus was on what to do about Caroline. She reappeared a few minutes later with the somewhat drunken mariachis in tow.

"Come on, Clay! We're doing the Conga!"

I had wanted her all to myself. Instead, I watched as a strange man placed his hands on her hips, this growing train of people heading out the cantina door with the mariachis leading the way.

"Dahdah dahdah dah dah Dahdah dahdah dah dah."

"Come on, Clay!" Caroline called again as she disappeared.

What the hell. I flipped the bartender a ten. He gave me a bottle of tequila and I grabbed the next waist going by.

About two in the morning, the conductor begged us to stop. A number of us returned to the cantina but most people had gone off to sleep.

The train pulled into Los Mochis at three and those of us still manning the cantina went outside to stretch our legs on the empty platform. A scent of the sea was now in the air, along with a sense of things beginning to rot under your feet. The dry desert air had turned tropical and muggy.

An old woman appeared out of the nearby village streets and ambled along the tracks with a colorfully painted metal tray hanging from her neck. The tray was piled high with steaming shrimp.

"¡Camarones! ¡Camarones, si hay!"

"She's got the camarones, Kip."

"She certainly does."

"Go grab some beer. I'll get the shrimp."

He went inside. I paid for the entire tray and the old woman transferred them onto a sheet of wax paper.

"Go home where it's safe," I told her. She waddled off, understanding the money but not my words.

I welcomed everyone outside to join in the feast. Kip returned with the beers and the cold, bubbly carbonation went down nicely with the shrimp. Caroline sat there with her head against my shoulder, nibbling absentmindedly on one of them. Many people milled along the tracks, feasting and talking together. The beer began to take effect and mellow the descent of my fading psychedelic journey.

The engineer blew the whistle and people hurried to get back onboard. I left the remainder of the shrimp for the dogs and helped Caroline onto the landing. The train slowly gathered steam, letting out a long, mournful cry.

A shadow crossed my mind, the memory of a sheriff in Tucson. Something told me the hunt was on. He must have run the prints and learned the truth by now, and was no doubt kicking himself for letting a big fish get away. I turned towards the bar, my gut full of adrenalin.

Caroline pulled me to a stop.

"I need to get some sleep."

Tom and Bill were lined up behind her. My impulse was to run them off. It would have been all too easy to make an ass out of myself, but I kissed Caroline and told her I would see her in the morning. The three of them headed off towards their sleeper car. I turned back towards the cantina, modestly content with my position in this rut.

19

Kip and I held up our beers to an American couple on their way out the door. We were now the only ones left in the cantina. I glanced over at Kip. He looked half drunk, half mad. I glanced at myself in the mirror. I looked half drunk, half mad.

A lot had happened in the past twelve hours, from that scene with the sheriff to being magically reunited with Caroline to the psychedelic trip we had taken, a trip that had been reduced to the likeness of radio wave static between my ears. I wasn't sure where I was. I wasn't sure where I had been. I wasn't particularly sure where I was going.

The bartender stood there drying glasses as if it were an art. I grew lost in the squeaking sound of his towel against the glass, that and the click clack sound of the train going down the tracks. It seemed to be getting on towards dawn though no light had yet appeared along the horizon.

Kip slapped a twenty on the bar and asked for two margaritas. I thought that was a terrific idea. Clearly, the bartender did not. He stopped with his artistry and stared.

"Señores, please. You come back this morning and we start all over again."

"It is morning," I said, figuring I had outflanked him but he just shook his head and went back to drying glasses.

Not having the stomach to argue, Kip and I stood up and stumbled out of the cantina. Our objective was the rear of the train, but for two drunken sailors, it was an expedition worthy of maps and Mausers and much planning.

Along the way, we passed in front of Caroline's cabin. I pointed at the door and whispered.

"My little señorita's in there."

Kip cautioned me with a finger to his lips and I saluted him.

"Si, generalissimo."

Just then, the train jostled around a bend and the two of us fell against the cabin wall, laughing. That led to an older man opening his door and glaring at us. We stood at attention and saluted him too. The man cursed in Spanish and closed the door.

Kip and I resumed our quest for the baggage car, stumbling from side to side down the narrow corridor and then through several passenger cars, doing our best to keep quiet but pissing off more than a handful of people along the way. When we reached our destination, we saluted each other as if it had been some great conquest.

Opening the door to the baggage car, we found the dog had yet to change countenance. I followed Kip's lead and threw some luggage on the floor as a makeshift bed. I passed out with the dog showing me his impression of a smile.

A few hours later, I awakened in the sultry weather of Sinaloa. The fickle sprites of last night's ecstasy beckoned to me briefly, but were followed quickly by a wave of nausea. My brain synapses had been fried. My clothes were pasted to my skin. From the lofty ascent of our psychedelic journey, I had crash-landed into the squalidness of Mexican culture. All my thoughts became focused on one thing, stilling the pain in my head.

When I rolled over, the dog growled at me. I bared my teeth in return, which only made things worse. The scent of its warm breath spurred me to sit up. The memory of Caroline sleeping with Tom got me to my feet.

I'm going to put an end to this Tom business, I thought. Until then, it's get drunk or get out of Mexico. That didn't make a great deal of sense, but I thought freshening up and having a drink were both splendid ideas. I placed this Tom business on the back burner until I could marshal my forces.

After locating the men's room and gaining my turn, I threw some toilet-paper on the filthy floor, stripped down to my underwear, splashed water all over my face and upper body, dried off with the previous day's shirt, brushed my teeth, got into a fresh pair of shorts and shirt, slipped back into my sandals, urinated and almost felt like a new man.

Kip was in the passageway when I came out.

"You know where to find me," I said and headed down the passageway.

"Save me a spot," he said before closing the door to the bathroom.

I left my suitcase in the baggage car and gave the dog something else to get excited about before heading off for the cantina. I felt raw and ethereal all at once. Flashes of the previous night's trip were still sparking in my brain. Dawn was blossoming on the horizon. Passing from one car to the next, I could feel the day already growing hot.

We had entered a dry country of gently rolling hills dotted with papaya groves and the occasional palm. It was the sort of land where a man might settle down, build a home and allow things to grow around him.

That sent my mind off on a fantasy. I'd disembark right here and now, build myself a big hacienda and dig in some roots, fan myself on hot summer days with a dog beside me on the front porch; images that quickly came up hard against the wild, restless part of me and dissipated into the sultry morning.

Let's just get that drink, I thought. In a few hours we'll be arriving at the ocean and I can go to work on this Tom business. There had to be some way to extract Caroline from his grasp.

I went into the bar with that plan parked in my head. The first patron there, I slapped a twenty-dollar bill on the counter. The bartender stopped polishing glasses and came over.

"Buenos dias, Señor. ¿You see? Now we starting all over again."

"That's right, my friend, and I mean business, so let's see a beer."

The bartender pulled out an ice cold Tecate and plunged the can opener through the metal top, leaving two triangular shaped holes.

"That's pretty good for you, Señor. You working hard last night."

"Yeah. I was working hard last night."

I liked the sound of that, much better than the way I had framed things. As he placed my change down, I took the first drink, staggered from the punch and took another one. There were more fleeting images of last night's adventure, and a material pain now beginning to float in a sea of carbonation. Detail returned to the

141

chaos in my mind. I tossed down the rest of the Tecate and squeezed the can. The bartender replaced it without asking. Kip came in and sat beside me.

"Get my partner here a beer."

I pushed money across the bar.

"Jyesss. Him working pretty hard last night, too."

"You hear that, Kip?"

"Si."

We toasted.

"It has a certain ring to it."

"I'm finding everything has a certain ring to it this morning."

I toasted to Kip's sage observation and drank. When it appeared he had caught up with me, I ordered two margaritas. We belched alternately and ordered another round. Caroline came in a short while later.

"Hi," she said and gave me a kiss. "Oh, your lips are cold."

"How are you feeling?" I said.

"A bit fuzzy. How do you think?"

I pushed my drink her way. She laughed and took a sip.

"Have as much as you like."

"That's enough," she said, "I need something to eat."

Kip groaned.

"What's the matter, Kip?" she asked facetiously.

I gave Caroline my seat and she whispered something in my ear. I whispered something back. She gave me a commiserating look.

"Can that wait?"

"I had prepared myself for that answer."

She handed me the key with a kiss.

"Later," she said with another kiss.

I took Kip and marched down to her cabin, passing Tom and Bill along the way. They said hello and kept walking, plainly not any happier to me than I was to see them.

I unlocked Caroline's cabin and found the roach where she had instructed. Kip and I took a few tokes and quietly waited for the drug to take effect. I opened the window to clear out the smoke. My headache grew far away. The entire universe mellowed.

"Who needs aspirin," Kip said on our way back to the cantina.

I stopped him before going in and explained what I had planned.

"Don't worry about me, Clay. Maybe I'll find a little señorita of my own down here."

He opened the door to the cantina and waited for me.

"You understand, don't you Kip?"

He put his arm around my shoulder.

"Of course I understand. Love is love. I would do the same thing in your shoes."

"But let's stick together, all right brother? I don't want you to disappear."

Kip slapped me on the shoulder with a smile and we headed into the bar.

"Two margaritas," I said to the bartender.

When the drinks came, I saluted Kip

"To the goddamned best friend I've ever had."

"To the goddamned best friend I've ever had."

We touched glasses and drank.

Caroline eventually returned from having breakfast with Tom and Bill and the party resumed, though with considerably less anarchy than the previous evening. All the while, the tropics increasingly engulfed the tracks, our journey south as though entering the world of Kipling's tales; the verdant greens all sunny and sparkling and a scent of the Pacific in the sultry air as we dropped back down to the coast near Mazatlán.

I listened absently to the conversation around me, content to make my plans in secret. I reasoned that getting Caroline away from Tom and Bill was like splitting a log. A man only required the smallest of cracks to start his wedge in. With that in mind, I spoke quietly into Caroline's ear.

"Will you trust me to make some decisions?"

She turned her head to meet my eyes.

"Such as?"

"We'll set a time and location to meet the others for dinner. Then find a quiet place to be alone."

She waited for more.

"That's it," I said.

Our eyes remained locked for a moment.

"I don't see why it's necessary," she said. "I mean the secrecy of it."

"Just so we can talk."

"All right," she said and turned away. We touched hands for the rest of the journey but did not say much. There had already been enough chatter along the way to Mazatlán.

When the train pulled into the station, Kip and I went out ahead of the others. There was a slight breeze coming in off the ocean. The morning sun was already hot on our heads. Kip chased the scents on the breeze with his nose.

"A little bit of Hawaii, isn't it?" I said.

"Yeah. Can't wait to jump in the ocean."

"Yeah, wow. I don't know why but I just pictured Charlie in a pair of swim trunks."

"Barrel style," Kip said.

"I don't know. I kind of pictured him going for the bikini look."

I pretended to be Charlie tugging at his low riding belt buckle and we both laughed.

"Yeah, I could see that," Kip said.

A moment later, the others disembarked from the train and came towards us.

"Are you going to hang with Tom and Bill?" I asked Kip quietly.

"I might ride along with them for a while. Purely for entertainment's sake."

I kissed Caroline on her forehead to make my role plain with her.

"Any suggestions where we can meet tonight?" I said.

"Where are you going?" Bill said.

"I'm running off with Caroline," I said. "So? Any ideas?"

"Do you mind us asking where?"

"It doesn't matter. We want to be alone."

Tom stood there looking hurt.

"It's okay, you two," Caroline said and gave both her friends a hug.

"You got any ideas?" I said to Kip.

"Yeah, somebody told me Señor Frogs is a happening place."

"Okay. Señor Frogs it is. About sunset? That way we don't have to check our watches?"

Tom, who had been staring at Caroline, looked away when I pulled Caroline under my arm.

"Well, if there's nothing more, we'll be on our way."

I grabbed the two suitcases and started out towards the street with Caroline.

"See you guys tonight," she said over her shoulder.

When I glanced back, Tom averted his eyes. As much as I hated knowing that he had been intimate with Caroline, he obviously felt even worse about me taking over for him.

Out on the street, we quickly found a taxi. The driver jumped out and helped us to place our suitcases into the trunk.

"Something to eat?" I asked Caroline inside.

"I wouldn't mind a bite. You're probably famished."

"The Mercado," I told the driver over the seat and we were on our way.

"I wish you'd try to be nice to Tom," Caroline said when I had leaned back next to her.

"I thought I was."

"Not really."

"I'll try harder," I said.

"You turkey," she said and tried to tickle me.

I got hold of her hands and kissed her lips. Then everything stopped as we stared into each other's eyes.

"I'm glad you're here," I said.

"Are you?" she said as if I had touched the old wounds.

"Of course. It's everything I've been dreaming about for the past year."

Caroline stared into my eyes. I stared back for a long moment and kissed her again.

"What's inside?" she said and tried to peek into the satchel.

"A passport," I said, battling with her hands.

"Hmm hmm. And what else?"

"And some other things."

"Oh. Some other things."

I smiled and glanced out the window, not wanting to discuss its contents yet. Everything would be revealed in good time. Caroline let it drop and we rode along in silence.

Downtown, the driver pulled to a stop in front of the yawning, dark entrance of the Mercado. The building itself was brilliantly white in the morning sun. The scent of butchered meat and fish and a thousand other things spilled out from the cool air inside.

While the driver retrieved our luggage, I dug out a twenty dollar bill. He thanked me profusely and drove off. Caroline and I were left standing by the building. Hundreds of people came and went from the Mercado entrance.

"What'll it be?" I asked her.

"What do you want?"

"Hmm, seems a bit late for eggs and coffee."

"You just want an excuse for a beer."

"Probably," I said.

She tried to tickle me again. I laughed and pointed at a cocinero along the sidewalk. Several people were already seated beneath the yellow and white umbrella.

"All right," Caroline said.

We ended up ordering fish tacos and beers. The bustle of the city went on all around us.

"It reminds me of European cities," I said between bites.

"Why?" she said.

"I suppose because it was built up before the car. It makes a big difference when you don't have all the parking lots."

She smiled.

"Of course, there weren't nearly as many Mexicans in Europe."

"You," she said.

"You," I said in return.

"They are a strange people, aren't they?"

"They are many people," I said. "Which leads to their identity crisis."

Caroline swiped at the flies.

"Why do you say they have an identity crisis?"

"You try founding a nation on defeat."

When it was clear she did not understand, I wiped my mouth and explained about Cortez and Montezuma.

"Ready to go?" I said when she had finished her tacos.

"What do you have planned?"

"Like I said. Find a nice quiet place where we can talk."

"Where?"

"I don't know. I'm winging it."

She shrugged as if to say she wasn't overly concerned yet. I kissed her on the forehead and flagged a taxi. The driver and I spoke over the seat in Spanish. I added hand gestures to compensate for my lack of subtlety. The driver finally understood and drove northwest towards Olas Atlas. I settled back in next to Caroline.

"What were you two talking about?"

"About finding a place in the old part of town," I said. "I hope." She laughed.

"Why the old part of town?"

"I don't know. It just sounds more charming, doesn't it?"

"I guess so."

"Like I said, I'm winging it a bit."

"This doesn't look like the old part of town," Caroline said when the driver pulled to a stop in front of the Banco Nationale.

"I need some travelers cheques," I said. "Can you wait here?"

"Sure."

"I'll be right back," I said and closed the door.

Inside, I asked the clerk for a safe deposit box. She gave me forms to fill out. I put two names on the account. Also, I opened a checking account and placed enough money in there to fly two people around the world in style. As an afterthought, I had the clerk put two names on that account, as well.

She escorted me into a clean, well-lit corridor and left me alone. I placed the contents of my satchel inside a metal box, holding back enough to live on for a few months. A few minutes later I was back in the cab.

"Well, Mr. Bond, are we done now?"

"Soon," I said and waved to the driver.

Caroline pinned her hair up as we drove. I kissed her exposed neck. It was warm and sweaty from the tropical heat.

"Oh, this is really groovy looking," Caroline said when the driver reached the Olas Atlas district. We were surrounded by colonial era buildings.

The driver negotiated a hillside of narrow streets and parked in front of a white, two story building. An ornate wrought iron railing bordered the balcony upstairs and wooden doors led out onto this balcony. Lounge chairs were visible behind the railing. It seemed to have a sweeping view of the shoreline. I caught a scent of the ocean breeze.

"Is this where we're staying?" Caroline said.

"I think so. Hang on while he talks with the owner."

The driver climbed out and went to knock on a large, hand-carved door on the first floor. A moment later, an old lady answered. The two of them talked and the driver returned to explain what he knew. I motioned to Caroline.

"Come on, kid. Let's go have a look."

Caroline took my hand and scooted across the seat. The driver led us up a flight of stairs, opened the door and allowed us to enter before him, Caroline first.

It might have been mistaken for a beach house in California. The furniture was a bit worn, a decade out of style, pictures that said there was something on the wall, nothing more. It was thoroughly unpretentious, a place to relax, everything there to accommodate that purpose, and to cause you to go out on the balcony. Then none of the other issues mattered.

The blue ocean sparkled in the distance, with glimpses of bristling white surf here and there among the jumble of red-tile roofs.

Caroline went through the front room and onto the balcony. I nodded at the driver and the two of us started downstairs.

"I'll be right back, sweetheart."

Caroline took in the view without looking back.

The landlady and I spoke for a few minutes. When I felt my interests were clear, I paid her for a month's rent. She thanked me and closed the door; no need to be seen again.

I turned to the driver.

"Nadien, Señor," I said.

"Nunca, mi amigo."

I looked at him for a long moment before handing him a hundred dollar bill. Then I was his amigo, for sure. He gave me his card. We shook hands and he left. I went upstairs and found Caroline in the shower. I invited myself in.

When we were done, I dried off with a towel and went out on the balcony to wait. The many things I wanted to say were working in my mind.

I felt safe for the moment. The only link was the cab driver. If someone started to ask questions, he would give me a chance to bid for his loyalty. You had to guess the American authorities would make a showing. Not so much here in the old part of town. They'd sip their drinks around the Zona Dorado and wait, where they wouldn't have to get their hands dirty doing it. They would count on a man like me getting lonely and slumming around the tourist bars for a bit of action.

Either way, they would be looking here in Mazatlán, assuming the sheriff ran my prints. It figured he would, especially when his nephew came up missing. Logic would dictate that, in our haste, the two of us had fled across the border. It wasn't hard to follow the trail from there. Nogales wasn't renowned for its airport and the train pointed right at Mazatlán. That said, the only likely way for me to get busted was if I attempted to leave the country by plane, or if I broke another law, or my luck just ran out.

Short of foolishness, I was free from the war and all its madness and had enough money to hide for many years now: possibly even for the rest of my life with a cautious investment or two. I savored the power that money could bring. The entire world lay before me. Only one question remained. Would Caroline join the expedition? My plans now seemed rather hollow without her.

As she went from the bathroom to the bedroom, I caught a brief glimpse of her through the balcony door. Then she came out of the bedroom and towards me across the tile floor, naked save for a robe.

So much beauty. So many secrets I had withheld. I wasn't sure I could manage it all. And despite all my confusion, I wanted this woman madly, the one thing I could not control.

20

Caroline and I lay on the chaise lounge with our feet playing little games together. The world was quiet save for the rustling of a nearby palm tree and the distant sounds of the city. When I looked into her eyes, I saw a reflection of the white plaster buildings around us. Gazing down at her lithe ankles and delicate feet, I felt an urge to make love again and much preferred that idea to the task at hand. Each time I thought to explain what I had failed to explain heretofore, my mind stalled. There were the things I was willing to tell Caroline, and things I would never confess. How could I tell her about Laura? To do so would be cruel, and spell an end our renewed love affair.

I looked back into Caroline's eyes. God help me. How to keep this all sorted out. I already felt corrupt, just thinking about it.

"So?" she said.

I sighed deeply.

"So, for starters, I was drafted. I reported to the induction center in LA one day then decided to walk out at the last minute."

"I don't understand. How could you just walk back out?"

I explained.

"I never signed any papers while I was there but I don't know. I could be a deserter. Or just another draft dodger."

I saw Caroline's mind working.

"I know. I should have told you." I held her close and kissed her forehead. "Anyway, I guess I'm a wanted man."

"You seem to be guessing a lot."

"It's a manner of speaking. Of course I'm wanted. I just don't know exactly for what. They came looking for me at my parent's place. And then in Hawaii."

I left out the part about smuggling and being indicted with the Weather Underground and added those to my list of half-truths.

Caroline reached out to touch my face with a look of compassion.

"I'm sorry, Clay. I know it must be awful, being on the run like that but I was taught to face my problems."

"Oh, that's great, Caroline. I appreciate the advice."

"I'm sorry, Clay, I..."

"No, I'm not going back to face that war. Do you want to go over there and have your head blown off?"

"Well, I'm not saying that you..."

"No, Caroline. That's what it means. Either I go to prison or go over there and fight and die in a war I don't even believe in."

"All right. I understand." She shook me gently. "I know it's a difficult choice."

Incensed, I stared at some boats out on the sea.

"Okay, let's drop it for now," she said. "Is that all you were going to tell me?"

I continued staring out to sea, unable to let it go.

"Please?" she said.

I turned back and stared.

"Look, the point is, I didn't tell you these things at the start and then there were all these secrets between us and they kept leading to more secrets and seemed to take on a life of their own. Maybe that's why I left. I couldn't stand the lies between us anymore...Anyway, I'm sorry. I can see now that my deceptions had a lot to do with the way I treated you."

"But I don't understand the Hawaii part. Every day I waited for the mail. I jumped each time the phone rang."

She shook me with her feet to get my attention.

"You say you still loved me. Why you didn't you even bother to reach out?"

I met her eyes.

"I thought about it many times. But leaving you alone seemed to be the kindest thing I could do. I had no right to drag you into my problems."

She shook her head.

"Oh. So you think I'm lying about that too?"

Caroline recoiled from the tone of my voice. I went back to watching the boats, even more incensed now. Of everything I had just told her, that was probably the most truthful part.

After some moments, I turned back to face Caroline.

"Look, I am sorry. I really mean that. Now can we go find a bar somewhere and have some drinks and skip the lecture?"

Caroline continued staring.

"What?" I said.

"Well, you have to go back sooner or later, don't you? I mean, you can't go on running for the rest of your life."

"No? Let's say I go back and they put me behind bars. What's the good of that? I may as well enjoy my freedom as long as I can. Anyway, I have enough money to hide in comfort now. For a long, long time. It's only a matter of where, and whether or not you'll come with me."

"Listen to you, Clay. Hide. It's become a way of life with you."

"Goddamn it, Caroline. A simple yes or no will do."

"I'm sorry. I just don't believe in running."

"Oh fuck. I should have expected this."

"Okay, Clay. I'm just getting the same old feelings now."

"The same here. I forgot how fucking straight you can be."

"Thanks," she said, looking away.

"Well, why do you suppose we ran into each other on that train platform?"

She played with her lip.

"So I could slug you for being such a mean bastard."

"Yeah? Well go ahead and get it out of your system. Then maybe we can move on to the real choice in front of us."

She stared at me, thinking.

"We're together," she admitted. "I guess I'm trying to make sense of that."

"And how shall I act in the meantime?"

"You just want to make love, don't you?"

"And is there something terribly wrong with that?"

After a few moments, searching my eyes, she arose and pulled somewhat defiantly on my hand and we were soon all hair and flesh and honey in the back room.

Sometime later in the day, I awakened to a car honking in the distance. The threads of a dream still enveloped me. Everything in the world seemed far away and indiscernible. It was that old feeling of having landed in the wrong galaxy, with no way to get back home.

Caroline awakened soon after me, saw that it was late, kissed me on the lips and hurried off to shower. I lay alone in the fading light of a late afternoon with the distant sounds of the city layered over my still troubled conscience.

When Caroline returned, I watched her dry off. And seeing her flesh dimple from the breeze, I sat up to kiss her shoulders and tawny back and eventually pulled her gently on to the bed, wanting only to remain in our dream and to make love again and again.

Having made ourselves late by our passions, we went running down the steep, narrow streets to our meeting. At one point, I stopped to let Caroline catch her breath and we tried walking.

"Oh, it makes my ankles sore," she said. "It's better running."

Down on the main boulevard, we stood waiting for a taxi to appear. The shore was just to the other side of the opposite buildings and a fine breeze blew in from that direction. When a pulmonia appeared in place of a taxi, I flagged the young Mexican driver. Caroline and I squeezed into the back. I told the driver, Zona Dorado and off he went.

Clearing the point, we saw the sun setting. The sea looked metallic blue with the sky orange along the horizon. People were gathered below the seawall to our left in the growing dusk, some on their towels in the sand, some in the surf. Farther up, lights had begun to sparkle along the crescent shoreline.

"Caroline?" I said.

"Yes?"

"Remember never to talk about what I told you."

"I guess I already understood that, Clay."

"Okay."

"I do have one more question."

"Okay."

"You told me you had a lot of money. Where did it come from?"

"Kip and I did some smuggling in Tucson."

I felt her staring and turned to meet her eyes.

"Is there anything else you're not telling me, Clay?"

153

"No," I said.

After a moment, she leaned her head against my shoulder and we were silent with our thoughts.

At Señor Frogs, we found the place packed with people spilling out into the aisles. I heard a shout and saw Kip waving from the back of the restaurant. A waiter greeted us halfway and carved a path through the intervening hubbub. Two chairs appeared from in back. Our friends pushed their chairs aside and made room for us to sit down.

There were three new faces at the table; a couple, by the way they touched, and another man. Caroline said hello and went over to talk with the woman. I winked at Kip.

"How do you like it?" Tom asked me.

"Groovy," I said, acknowledging his olive branch. What the hell. I didn't like him but there was no point in making things worse.

"This is Steve and Robby," Tom said again. "They're staying next to us at the campground."

I reached out to shake their hands from across the table.

"This is my wife Kristine," Steve said.

Kristine acknowledged me with a smile and went back to chatting with Caroline. I liked her, and her boyfriend Steve. They were like a troubadour couple; both pale, she with a long mane of red hair, he tall and thin with cinnamon ringlets. They both had good, kind, intelligent faces, but I immediately disliked their friend. He was short and had restless hands. They stopped the moment I looked at them, then started again. Instinct told me to avoid this man. Life was a contest to him, a contest in which he had to compensate for being too short. His coarse hair seemed to be an apt metaphor for his personality. It spread out as if carrying electrical current.

A waiter came to take our orders and returned soon after with two double shots of mescal. It was a ritual with every meal at Señor Frogs, we were told. I knocked down my shot. Caroline came around the table and tried hers. We both laughed when she gasped.

"Here, chase it with a bite of lime."

She did and pushed the remainder of her shot towards me.

"You can have the rest."

I downed it and found another lime.

"You really like that?"

"It wards off disease," I said with a kiss of her still wet lips.

The food came and we ate amidst much revelry. I kept watching Robby. His personality was obnoxious. He had to be the center of everything.

"So, where are you staying?" Bill asked me over the crowd.

I shrugged and kept eating.

"Caroline?"

"I guess we'd like to keep that private."

Unhappy with the answer, but unwilling to fight, he went back to his discussion with Kip.

"What brings you to Mazatlán?" Steve asked me.

"The waters."

Steve smiled.

"And you?"

"School break," he said.

"What's your major?"

"Pre-med."

"Kind parents."

"My parents couldn't send me to shoe shine school."

I shrugged and went back to my meal.

"Kristine's putting me through college," he went on.

"Even more noble."

"There's a reward at the end."

Kristine elbowed him playfully in the ribs and offered me a smile.

"Anyway, it's nice to get away for a while," he said. "Work on my suntan."

We both looked at his pale arms.

"Yeah, you're off to a great start there, Steve."

I pushed back from my plate. Some of the others had finished eating, some not.

"I'll tell you what I'd like to do while we're down here," Robby said. "Score some grass."

He ran his hands through his wiry hair in saying this. His eyes came to rest on me.

"You know what I mean? Take it back and make a few bucks when we get home?"

I made a cursory look around the restaurant, to make sure no one had been listening, and leaned over the table.

"Well, whatever you do, it's probably best to keep that shit quiet."

"Hey, what's the big deal, man? We're in Mexico."

Robby leaned back in his chair and slapped his hands behind his head.

"Robby," Kristine said. "Be cool."

She was sweet, but emphatic about it.

"Like, whatever man. I don't see what you guys are so worried about. Like someone's going to bust us for saying *grass* down here?"

"How about just shut up about it," Steve said.

"Hey, up yours," Robby said. "No one fucking tells me to shut up."

He brought his chair down and called for the waiter, a little Napoleon.

"Anyone else want another margarita?" he asked.

There were looks and shakes of the head around the table.

"I know, let's go dancing," Kristine said.

She stood up and went around the table pulling at everyone's sleeve.

"Come on," she said. "It'll be fun."

She ruffled my hair going by.

"Want to?" Caroline said.

"Sure, let's get out of here."

The two of us stood up. Everyone else did too, except for Robby. He sat there sullenly, waiting for his drink.

"We'll be in the same place," Kristine said to him. "Okay?"

A little of his armor came down with her kindness, but not much.

Kristine led us to a bar along the beachfront. The interior was lit up from both strobe and black lights. The band members were dressed in white suits and glowed phosphorescently. The strobe lights made them appear and disappear. The whole scene was like a tacky version of a club on Sunset Strip. When the din and bizarre lighting became too much for us, Caroline and I went for a long walk down the shore. Upon our return, we found the others out on the street, wondering what had happened to us.

"And what are you two espionage agents planning for tomorrow?" Bill wanted to know.

"Don't have any plans as of yet," I said.

"We're talking about hiring someone to take us upstream into the jungle."

"Sounds like fun." I looked at Caroline.

"Sure. I'd like to go see the jungle."

"Where and when?"

"Why don't you pick a time and place?" Bill said.

"How about the Mercado. Say nine o'clock? We can have a bite to eat before we head out."

I flagged a pulmonia while the suggestion was tossed about.

"Good night then," I said when everyone agreed. "See you at nine."

Caroline waved as the driver circled in the parking lot. Back in Olas Atlas, we started up the long hill in silence.

"Tired?" I asked Caroline along the way.

"Very," she said.

At the villa, I opened the carved front door for her. She went up the stairs with me following. We were quickly in bed. Caroline had turned her back to my chest. I pulled her long hair aside and kissed her neck, and then her shoulders.

"I love you," I said.

"I love you, too," she said with a look back to kiss my lips. The tension caused by that movement made a seductive crease along her waist and I kissed that area too.

"I hope you'll come with me."

"I do wonder about it," she said with her face turned away.

"There's hope?"

"Seeing the world would be fun, Clay. I just don't see how we could enjoy it being on the run."

"We'd be very comfortable. There are a lot of people who dream about the way we would live."

"People don't dream about being on the run."

"Everyone's worried about something. What's the difference?"

"You have an answer for everything."

"Everything but you."

I squeezed her ribs and she squealed playfully.

"Tell me more about how we would do it."

"I'm not certain," I said.

"We can't just get on a plane?"

"I don't think so. Not now. Not with the sheriff."

"There's a sheriff?"

I explained.

"I'm sure he said something to the Feds so I'm also pretty sure they'll be keeping an eye out for me down here in Mexico."

I kissed her neck and shoulders again.

"You still haven't answered my question."

"About where we would go."

"And how."

"Obtain some forged passports on the black market, I suppose. Maybe take a boat down to Costa Rica. Fly to Brazil and then Africa. We could slip into the Adriatic quite unnoticed from someplace like Tangier."

"That sounds awfully complicated."

"It might be. All you're trying to do is to avoid the obvious. Everyone's lazy, even cops. I would want to get to someplace neutral, such as Costa Rica. There is nothing unusual about flying from there to Brazil, or from Brazil to Africa. But from here to Europe? If I were an agent, that's a route I'd be keeping an eye on."

"Are you guessing again?"

"A bit. I hope I'm being logical too."

"But you could be wrong."

"Yes, I could be wrong."

Caroline looked back and searched my eyes.

"Are you satisfied for the moment?"

She looked away and snuggled up tighter to my body.

"You were planning to leave the country without me, weren't you?"

"Well, Jesus, Caroline. How could I have known? Like you said, let's try to live in the moment."

She turned over and put her head back on my chest.

"You're lucky," she said. "You know that?"

"I don't see how."

"No, you are."

"Then luck has not made me happy."

"What would make you happy?"

"Knowing you'll be with me."

She crawled on top of me.

"That will make you happy for a little while."

"Don't say that. Not for just for a little while."

"But not for all your life."

I stared back, silenced by my ongoing deception. Yes, I had known that feeling once. For all my life. For all eternity. For all the marbles, but I did not feel that way now. I felt passion, but not eternity.

"You're such a complicated man," Caroline said and lay back down beside me.

I remained silent, feeling like I might explode from the pressure building inside, and the secret I dared not express.

21

I went to sleep troubled and awakened the next morning to my ongoing inner battles. The war. The Feds on my trail. The secrets eating away at my soul.

I was about to take one more trip on that merry-go-round when I heard Caroline in the shower and felt again the magic of us being reunited. The palm trees rustled outside. A cock crowed. Mariachi music played somewhere in the distance. Two women were conversing in Spanish down on the street. The Seven Seas seemed to be calling from just beyond our balcony. Why not stop worrying for one goddamned day, Clay, and just enjoy yourself?

Caroline came out of the bathroom with a towel wrapped around her torso and curled up beside me. Her body was still warm from the shower. I pulled the towel away and kissed her belly in place of a confession. When I reached her patch of hair, she let out a cry and we were soon lost again in the sweetness of love making.

Afterwards, Caroline saw the time and jumped out of bed.

"We're late again, Clay! Please hurry!"

I headed in to take my shower.

"Maybe you'll have to be more efficient with your orgasms."

"You turkey!" I heard her say from the other room.

Our laugh filled chase continued out the front door and over the hill, away from the beachfront. The narrow, winding streets descended steadily down towards the commercial district and the busy sounds echoed up from it more and more as we drew near, until we turned a corner into the bustling city.

Merchants had washed down the sidewalks and draped their storefronts in red and green bunting. We passed several restaurants with chickens roasting on spits in open windows and I had developed quite an appetite by the time we reached the Mercado. Tom and Bill stood alongside the main gate in the morning sun, looking unusually somber, even for them. Kip and the others were nowhere in sight.

"Hi," Tom said as we approached.

Caroline gave him a hug, and then Bill.

"Where's Kip and the others," I inquired.

"They're somewhere inside," Bill told me.

I peered into the vast, shaded interior. It was a virtual square block teeming with merchants and customers.

Deciding it was best to wait, I walked over to a nearby stand and ordered six raw oysters and a cold beer. The old woman quickly handed me the beer with a napkin and went to work shelling the oysters. When she delivered the first oyster, I dipped it into cocktail sauce and devoured it. Caroline had come over to watch.

"They look horrible."

"But a familiar labor of love."

She slapped my shoulder.

Kip appeared just then out of the darkened interior of the Mercado with an old Indian at his side. His dark, watery eyes exuded mirth at seeing Caroline slap me and he encouraged her to do it again with a grunt.

"The old man says he can guide us upriver," Kip announced to everyone in general. "A place where most tourists never go."

Steve and Kristine appeared from out of the Mercado, along with Robby. Kip came over with a smile and had a look at the oysters.

"Help yourself," I said and shoved the plate his way.

He dressed one up with cocktail sauce and slurped it down.

I glanced in Steve and Kristine's direction. They were talking with Bill and Tom, seemingly about the excursion. Caroline was talking to the old man about his turquoise jewelry. Robby was pacing around restlessly with his hands in his pockets. The man made me nervous, just watching him.

Suddenly the entire entourage was headed towards Steve's panel wagon.

"Whenever you two are ready," Steve called out to Kip and me.

"We'll be right there," I called back.

Kip and I split the final two oysters and hurried to catch up.

161

We were soon motoring north along an open stretch of coastline. At the old man's instructions, Steve turned up a dirt road into the jungle. Speckled sunlight filtered down through the trees. Strange calls echoed from near and far. Kristine lit a joint and the drive turned into a laugh filled journey.

After several miles, we came upon a home made of wood and bamboo along the river. The old man pointed for Steve to park beside it. The home had dried palm leaves for a roof and palm leaves as window coverings. Two of those windows overlooked the front porch and the coverings were tilted open. The porch served as a dock and had a boat tied to it.

The jungle had been cleared around in back and planted with banana and papaya trees. I went around that way to use the outhouse and returned.

Kip was speaking with the owner of the hut in Spanish. He was a tall, dark man with graying hair combed straight back, and rather distinguished looking for someone subsisting in the jungle. His face showed no expression. Kip came over to the rest of us.

"He'll take us upstream for ten dollars," he said.

"That's what all the discussion was about?" I said.

"Negotiations," Kip said with a smile. "It always sounds more complicated in Spanish."

"Who's going to pay him?" Robby asked.

He was shifting around with his hands in his pockets, as usual. I shook my head and pulled out a twenty-dollar.

"Tell him to keep the change, Kip."

Robby went off to look at the boat like he knew something.

"Think we'd have any luck trolling for crocodiles?" I said quietly.

"I don't know. He's mostly gristle," Kip said.

"You guys are so mean," Caroline said and slapped my shoulder.

The Indian was amused and encouraged Caroline to hit me again.

Everyone climbed on board and our distinguished looking guide headed upstream with his motor on low. All of us grew quiet in the speckled sunlight. The water was dark and broken only by our wake. A band of monkeys chattered and scampered higher up into the canopy as we passed by. We continued hearing them from far off.

162

When we motored past a water snake, I glanced at Robby and smiled. He stared at me as if he knew my thoughts.

An hour later, we arrived at a shallow waterfall, barely a man's height and spanning the river in a straight line. Below the falls was a large pool dappled in sunlight. Long forgotten Aztec kings came to mind. The royal procession would have come here to bathe. A rock ledge bordered one bank and offered a smooth platform from which to enter the dark water. The water was tepid but felt cool in the fierce jungle heat. A clearing in the trees left a line of sunlight in the river thirty feet below the pool.

Our guide pulled up to the rock ledge and tied the boat to some vines. Everyone disembarked except for the two old men. They relaxed in the boat and talked. I followed the smooth rocks to the falls.

"Clay, where are you going?" Caroline called after me.

I pointed and climbed towards the top. She followed.

"Watch out for crocodiles," Kip called out.

"You turkey," she said. "Why did you have to say that?"

I pulled her up over the top and we went along the river laughing. When we came to a clearing, I sat on a fallen log in the sun. The rumbling bass drums and melody of Poinciana played in my head. I remembered hearing that song on a jazz station when I was a boy and how it had brought to mind jungle imagery just like this.

Our friend's voices could be heard faintly in the background, mixing with the jungle sounds. When I looked over, Caroline was undressing.

"Aren't you worried about the others coming?" I said.

"I don't care," she said. She was naked now with her painted toe nails in the leaves and bark. She sat on me, wet, so that I knew what had been in her thoughts. My head fell back and the light played upon our bodies. I heard the distant calls. Then blood filled my ears and I felt myself falling wildly through time. Then I was back in the moment again.

"I wanted to please you," I said.

"You always do."

"I feel empty somehow when I haven't."

"This is all I wanted right now."

She was lovely with her breasts up high and her soft slender waist beneath her ribs.

"I love you," I said.

"I love you, too."

I had thought to say 'always' but had never felt that way about Caroline and did not understand why. She was so very lovely, and so many other good things that a man would want in a woman. She stared at me with her dark eyes, her whole being exotic and beautiful and speckled with sunlight in the jungle.

"Do you think everyone falls in love this way?" she said.

"How do you mean?"

"Screwed up and then getting better."

"I don't know. Let's hope not."

She laughed and tried to tickle me.

"Well we did, so there."

I nodded, studying her.

"I'm scared," she said.

"Yeah?"

She nodded.

"Well, join the club. I've been running scared for a couple of years now."

"I don't know how you can do it."

"What else am I going to do? I've accepted that I'll never have peace until this war is finally over."

She kept staring in the speckled sunlight.

"I love you too much for my own good," she said. "That's what I meant when I said I'm scared."

"Oh," I said.

I caressed her back and reached up to touch her breasts with my lips and soon our lovemaking had started all over again.

When we were done, I watched her put on her swimsuit, standing gracefully on one leg, and then the other, her red toenails still erotic looking in the leaves and bark. I stood up and pulled on my trunks. We walked upriver to explore a bit further and started back.

"I'm going over the falls," I said.

"Don't," she said.

"Come on. It'll be fun."

"No it won't. We'll probably get killed."

"No we won't. Come on. The pool is deep below the falls."

I held out my hand.

"Clay, please don't. You're going to get hurt."

"Okay. I'm going to be dead here soon. Will you want to live without me?"

"Oh stop it," she said.

"You'd better come along."

I started out into the water and she reluctantly followed me. The bottom was soft.

"Ooooooooh. It's awful, Clay."

"Float," I said and paddled out towards the center of the river. The current slowly took me downstream. I looked back and saw Caroline paddling behind me, looking like a wet cat.

"Come on! Get your speed up!" I shouted at her before going over the falls. Caroline tumbled over as I came up. I helped her to the pool's edge. She looked a bit stunned.

"Are you okay?" She pushed the hair out of her face and laughed. "You're fine," I said.

She smiled and kissed me with her wet lips.

"Where were you two?" Kristine asked.

We crawled up on the ledge and let our feet dangle in the water. Kip had left some papayas there along with a knife. I sliced one open.

"We went exploring and swam back," Caroline said.

"They went exploring," Kip said.

I met Tom's eyes and smiled. He looked down at the water and paddled his legs from the ledge.

"Exploring, my yes," Kip said.

"Well, we did," Caroline said.

I offered her a slice of papaya. She ate it with glances at Kip.

"It sounds fun," Kristine said. "I want to go." She climbed out of the water and waited for Steve to join her. He did so without much enthusiasm.

"Now kids, don't go off exploring for too long," Kip called out after them. "We'll be wanting to head home soon."

Caroline kicked water in Kip's face. He splashed back and it became a playful fight. I reclined on the smooth stone and enjoyed the sun and their laughter. Shade moved slowly across the bright spot down the river.

Later, everyone became uncomfortable with being wet. My hands were white and wrinkled in the dark water. Steve and Kristine finally returned.

"Let's go dry off," I said.

"Steve wouldn't jump with me," Kristine said while we got onboard. Steve shrugged and scratched his head in response. Enthusiasm moved slow in Steve, or not all. He definitely wasn't one to jump off of cliffs.

We headed downstream and arrived back at the hut around four. It seemed much later under the jungle canopy. Kip took what was left of the fruit and we drove back to Mazatlán.

The town had gone on busily in our absence. I felt exhausted and wanted to spend a quiet evening with Caroline. She agreed.

"Let's eat now," I said to the others.

"I'd like to get out of these wet clothes first," Bill said.

Everyone quickly agreed with his idea.

"You can go home and get cleaned up after we eat."

No one moved.

"Come on," I said and grabbed Caroline by the hand.

Everyone followed us reluctantly to a restaurant around the corner. The kitchen was open to the street with dozens of chickens turning on a rotisserie in the window. We sat at a picnic table around to the side and had a feast delivered to us with cold beer. We ate with our hands and squirmed in our wet clothes but felt better to have been fed.

We agreed to meet again in the morning at the Mercado, ostensibly for an outing at the beach and said goodnight. Dusk was settling over the streets now. Caroline and I strolled along hand in hand. When our eyes met in the glass of a storefront, Caroline stopped and tugged on my hand.

"Why do you love me now?" she asked.

"What do you mean, now? I loved you back then too."

"But it's different now, Clay. What has changed? I need to know."

"I've changed. You've changed. I don't know. It's hard for me to explain."

"Why?"

When I started to walk, she pulled on my hand again.

"Please. I need to know."

"I don't know. It's like trying to explain life. People grow and change and I've realized how much I admire you now."

"Really?"

I nodded.

"I have my insecurities too, Caroline. I was living under a bridge before I met you."

"Really?"

"Well, for a few nights, anyway. I had never planned much and then everything fell apart on me up north and next thing you know, I'm calling a bridge my home."

"That sounds really awful."

"It wasn't pleasant but it led to us meeting. And to being here now."

I kissed her sweetly and we continued up the street, both of us silent, both of us lost in our secret thoughts.

Having walked down to the seafront, we turned south towards Olas Atlas and eventually arrived to the narrow, winding street leading up our villa. Thoughts kept passing through my mind and I kept stopping them before they came out of my mouth, and with each one I had harbored a new secret. It was a great deal of work keeping things hidden inside.

That night, while Caroline slept, I sat on the balcony wrapped in a blanket, enjoying the wind off the ocean and considering where things stood. My thoughts careened this way and that, only to congeal again around the apprehension of being a fugitive. When you included another person, things became even more complicated.

Perhaps Caroline was right. Running from things had become a way of life for me, staining my every thought and deed. Being truly selfless, and thinking only of her, I would have slipped off into the night, never to be seen again. If not for the loneliness, that decision would have been easy.

Sleep came hard that night and I awakened in the morning wanting to know Caroline's decision. After we had showered, I led her by hand out to the balcony and made her sit down.

"This looks serious," she said.

"It is. I'm going for the passports."

"Clay, did you think I was ready to join you?"

"No, but I have to move on. I'll get everything ready. It will be nothing to throw away one extra passport."

She squeezed my arm.

"I'm honestly considering it. That's all I can say."

"I'll understand either way. I know you love me."

She shook her head sadly.

"No, I won't go back," I said.

I got up to call her a taxi. Once I had provided the driver with instructions, and he had driven away, I made myself a drink and went to think things over on the balcony. In the end I decided to try the old Indian at the Mercado and called another cab.

I found him inside the main gate, seated on a backless wooden chair, erect and patient, like a wizened Aztec shaman. He grunted and waved for me to sit across from him. There were flies on the freshly butchered meat nearby. The scents of a thousand raw things filled the air.

Observing some unspoken etiquette, I waited a few minutes before I told him what I wanted in my lousy Spanish. He understood and pointed out towards the entrance to the Mercado.

Together we stood up and headed out to the streets. Some blocks down and around a corner, we came to a door recessed between two storefronts. Above the door was a sign with a man's name printed on it. The name was followed by the word, licenciado. It was a title I had seen in other places but did not know its precise meaning. I knew this much. The title hadn't afforded its owner much in the way of wealth or panache. The sign was faded. The paint was peeling away from the door. The door led up a long flight of worn stairs.

Going down a narrow hallway on the second floor, the old man knocked on one of the doors. A man in his thirties answered. He wore a ribbed, white tank top and black pants. His soft, brown skin was moist with sweat. The room contained a workbench and single bed. The old man and I were invited in. The owner made a final check of the hallway and closed the door behind us.

We sat down and I explained my needs to the forger. He nodded that he understood. I asked to see his work and he showed me an American passport. It was very good. I asked him what he needed. Just bring him the photos, he said, that was all.

He wanted two hundred apiece, American, which was cheap. I had heard of people paying five hundred in Barcelona, and the peseta was worth less than the peso. I didn't know if the exchange rate mattered, since they always wanted to be paid in American dollars. I informed him that I would be back with the photos the next day. We shook hands and he showed us to the door.

I asked the old man to take care of everything. I would give him half the money in the morning with the photos, the balance when I picked up the passports, plus a hundred for his trouble. He nodded. I left him at the Mercado and walked back to the villa. Feeling tired from my restless night, I crawled into bed and slept.

When Caroline came home late that afternoon, she undressed and crawled into bed with me. Later, we shared our experiences from the day. Caroline and the others had taken a boat out to an island and a remote beach. It sounded lovely and we agreed to go there the next day.

"Everyone's driving down to San Blas with Steve and Kristine tomorrow morning," she said.

"And Robby."

"Yes."

I offered her a lugubrious smile.

"I can see why you wouldn't like him," she said.

"Who could?" She tried to tickle me.

"Let's go with them," she said.

"No. I wouldn't ride with them because of Robby. But we can meet them down there if you'd like."

"Can we?"

"I suppose," I said. "But it would only be a stop on our way out of the country."

"I would feel better somehow."

"Sure, I understand. Let's plan to meet them down there in a few days. That way we'll have time to talk."

"Okay."

"Are you sure about this, Caroline?"

She studied me.

"How do I know? Nothing has been certain with you, Clay."

I looked away.

"I'm sorry," she said and pulled face around. "I'm sorry."

I nodded and looked away again, gathering ever more secrets in my heart. I had lived my life in broad brush strokes up to that point. Now I found myself faced with vexing little pinpricks and at a loss as to how to deal with them. I knew there was truth in what Caroline had said, but I still hated hearing it.

When we met with the gang for dinner that night, Steve roughed me in on their plans. They expected to stop here and there along the way, but would definitely be down to San Blas in three days, no matter the diversions. We all agreed to meet in the main plaza then, at sunset.

Everyone drank quite a bit over dinner. Caroline and I took a stroll along the shore on our way home. My head was busy gathering more secrets. By dragging Caroline along, I made her an accessory to my crimes. I wondered if she realized this. I started to say something but stopped, fearing it would only add to her reservations.

When we got back to the house, I made another drink. The sting of Caroline's earlier words was digging at me again. Nothing has been certain with you, Clay. As if I had chosen this path.

"Clay? What's bothering you?" she said.

"Nothing. I'm okay."

"Please don't lie to me."

She came to put her arms around me but I held them away.

"Don't say I'm lying to you."

"I'm sorry but I can tell something's troubling you."

She reached out again and again I held her away.

"You don't have to call me a liar."

I went out onto the balcony. She followed me.

"Clay, please?"

"There's nothing wrong, damn it!" I stared down at her. "Now leave it alone."

She rubbed her forehead and sat down. I went into the kitchen and poured a large glass of mescal. I saw her legs on the chaise lounge through the doorway. To hell with her. I drank the glass and looked again through the doorway. She hadn't moved. I went back and sat down.

"I'm sorry," I said.

She put a hand to my face.

"How can I help but worry about you?"

"I'll be fine. Please. I'm just concerned about getting out of the country."

She kissed me and stood up.

"I'm sorry, Clay, but this makes me question again whether it's best to go with you."

With that, she went off to bed. Once I knew she was asleep, I brought the bottle out to the patio. I awakened much later to find a blanket over me. Feeling remorseful, I crawled back into bed with Caroline. She stirred briefly and reached for my hand.

In the morning, I arose before her and took a shower. We met in the kitchen.

"I'm sorry."

"Try to be good to yourself, Clay."

She grabbed my hand and looked at my fingernails. They had been chewed to a nub.

"I'll be better once we're safe," I said.

She bit her lip and slowly shook her head.

22

While Caroline went about dressing, I rummaged around in the drawers of the kitchen for a phone book. Amidst the candles, scissors, pens and old coasters, I discovered a dated copy. That led to several out of service phone numbers. On the fifth try, I located a photography studio still in business and within walking distance of the Mercado.

I went to tell Caroline and found her brushing her hair at the bathroom mirror. Her shoulders were bare and I kissed them. The brush stopped and our eyes met in the mirror.

"Will it ever be easy for us, Clay?"

I sagged in response.

"That sounds so heavy."

"Well, it is sort of heavy, being on the run."

"Going to see the photographer ought to be un-heavy enough."

"You turkey."

She turned to wrestle with me and our playful struggle had soon led us back to the bed.

On our way down to the beachfront, I felt a new peace come over me. Maybe this was the way of life. You took the good with the bad and didn't make too much of either. It felt miraculous that Caroline and I were together and I was grateful for her companionship and maybe nothing else mattered. You accepted things as they were at any given moment because that was the only reality you would ever know.

At the photography studio, a man with curly black hair and a red scarf welcomed us inside. His shabbily decorated storefront and studio betrayed his artistic aspirations. We shook hands and moved on to the passport photos. He seemed capable enough for that.

When the photographer suggested we come back later to pick up the photos, I told him we were in a hurry and that got me a look. While he was in the dark room, I sat there worrying over that and every other potential problem. Nothing was certain. We might not even make it to the border.

Back at Mercado with the photos, I left Caroline outside while I went in to find the old man. He was seated alone on his wooden stool. I handed him the package of photos and two hundred dollars. He placed both of those inside his peasant shirt and started out to the street in his stiff but upright gait.

I returned to Caroline in the bright sunshine.

"Shall we take something to eat?"

"Yes," she said. "There's a bar but they don't serve any food."

We walked into the darkness of the Mercado and left with a grilled chicken, cold beer, and a few pieces of fruit. Caroline bought a straw hat and looked fetching with it on her head.

As we walked to the harbor, I stole repeated glances, disarmed by her beauty. What if Caroline decided not to come with me? I felt desperate to think of the journey ahead all alone. My great feeling of peace had evaporated into the tropical morning, but later, once we were on the small boat and it had cleared the breakwater, I felt some measure of it return. There was only the sea and the sun and Caroline and it seemed as if nothing could take her love away from me now.

Leaning over the starboard side, I broke the fresh water with my hand. Caroline leaned her head against my shoulder.

"What are you thinking, Clay?"

"About another boat ride I took once."

"Where?"

I did not want to answer. I was in love with another woman then, with another set of problems, and assumed telling Caroline about this would only create yet more problems. A moment passed before she troubled me further.

"Were you sad that day?"

"Yes. I was sad that day."

"But you're not sad today, are you?"

"No, I don't know what I am. Not sad."

"Not sad?"

I met her eyes.

"No, not with you here."

The captain pulled into a small lagoon and up close to the shore. We climbed out into the clear, shallow water. He would be back with the boat at sunset, he told us. We thanked him and walked up onto the sand.

To our right, the shore was dotted with palm covered cabañas, most of them occupied. The cabaña closest to us served as a bar and a handful of gringos were gathered around it, drinking. The bartender had several bottles of booze and mixer and a cooler filled with ice. Mexican families stood in the surf nearby with their clothes on. A handful of Americans were lying on their towels in the sun, glistening with tanning oil.

I looked across the bay at the busyness of Mazatlán.

"Let's go over to the windward side," I said.

"Do you think we can?"

"I think so. I saw an isthmus on our way over."

"An isthmus," Caroline said.

"Yes, the island's very isthmussy."

We started down the shore and away from the others, having more fun with the word isthmus.

Eventually the sandy shore turned into a rocky trail along the coast and our fun day became a saga, the struggle symbolic of my compulsive need to escape the world and everything in it.

"Come on," I said, looking back at Caroline.

She kept falling behind. I marched forward alone, growing perturbed with my own nature.

In time, I saw a small patch of sandy shoreline up ahead and waited for Caroline to join me.

"Isthmus be the place!" I said when she caught up.

She laughed but wiped her forehead, looking weary.

"Let's stop here."

"No. I don't want to be looking at Mazatlán. Come on."

I helped Caroline up and over a carapace of rock and down onto the windward side of the island. It was completely abandoned for miles. We spread our towels out in the sand with the shade of the cliffs directly behind us. Caroline promptly took off her dress and waded out into the surf. I joined her.

Refreshed, we had started back in towards shore when I noticed several squirrels trying to make off with our lunch.

"Damn it," I said and chased after them. Caroline laughed. When I returned, we lay on our towels and listened to the murmuring of the surf.

"This is nice," she said.

"Our lives could be simple like this."

She looked at me. I ran my hands along her waist and hip.

"Plus we'll probably get to speak Italian."

"I speak French."

"We could go there too. They usually understand each other."

I rolled over and stared at the squirrels. They sat on their haunches, watching us from a safe distance.

"Are there always squirrels?" Caroline asked.

"I don't know." I looked back at her. "Everywhere I have been."

"I think you should go back and face this thing, Clay."

"You have made that abundantly clear."

"So, will you?"

"Maybe someday, but not now. Not the way things are in the States. They'll hang me."

"It would be over with and we could get on with our lives."

"I'm not going in for weekends, Caroline. You might not see me for many years, except through a plate glass window."

"But this other way," she said. "It seems so uncertain."

"Everybody has their uncertainties."

"Clay, some people lead very happy lives. Homes, families, jobs. That seems very secure in comparison."

"And boring."

"You always have an answer."

She placed her head on my chest as if listening to my heart. We were quiet for a spell, during which time she looked into my eyes several times and away again without speaking.

"Maybe I'll go with you, Clay."

When I failed to respond, she shook me gently.

"Aren't you going to answer?"

"Are you wondering if I'll be happy to have you there with me?"

She nodded.

"Yes, very happy."

"You don't seem like it."

"I know there will be moments. There will be times when you'll want to run back home."

"Is everything about running now?"

She stared for a moment before burying her head back in my chest.

"I don't know. I didn't make this world the way it is. But somewhere deep down inside of me, I am very happy to think you will be there."

"None of this feels very happy somehow."

"I'm worried about you, that's all."

"I thought it was my decision to make." I reached down and felt the warm skin on her back.

"You're right. If I worry it becomes meaningless."

"I guess I have to be there for you, Clay."

I pulled her close into my arms.

"Thank you. It brings me such peace to know you will be."

She shook me half playfully.

"Oh, Clay. I love you too much for my own good."

I pulled the towel over our bodies and we lay with our faces close in the shadowed silence. I knew the world was out there, beyond Caroline's dark eyes, beyond the sound of the sea, waiting for us with all of its uncertainties, but here, there were only our dreams.

"Can we still go to San Blas?" she asked me.

I kissed her.

"Yes. We'll take the train as far as Tepic."

"Then what?"

I kissed her again.

"Then a taxi, I guess."

"Who are we going to be?"

"For now, a French couple. On our way to Rio."

"Do you think our French is good enough?"

"We won't need much. If they don't believe us at first, we won't need any."

"Can I write my mother?"

"All right."

"What should I say?"

"That you're fine, with some friends, but don't know where you're going."

I became aware again of Caroline's troubled childhood and how it had defined her perception of men. Her father had left her mother when she was young, so she seemed drawn to healthy father figures and repulsed by them all at once. Either way, I was forever picking women who had similar issues. I could have started a club. Then, at least Caroline's father had not beaten or abused her. That sort of thing was almost impossible to overcome.

I heard the squirrels chattering amongst themselves and lifted the towel to look. The dry hills rose up behind them. I pulled the towel back, not wanting to let our dream escape.

"She'll ask a lot of questions," Caroline went on.

"Hmm?"

"I was saying my mother will worry."

"Tell her you're happy."

"She'll still worry."

"They always do."

She laughed and tried to tickle me.

"Like you don't."

"I worry."

"When should I do it?"

"Before we leave Mazatlán. The farther from our destination the better."

"Clay?"

"Yes."

"I feel it. I feel what it's like now that I've decided."

"We'll be all right."

"You've grown addicted to it, haven't you?"

"To what?"

"To the excitement."

"Maybe. It's the loneliness I have trouble overcoming."

Towards the end of day, we went for a last swim, jumping over the waves together, with the sea an emerald green and the wind spraying surf in our faces against the late afternoon sky. Caroline looked at the shore and laughed.

"Where did you put the food?" she asked.

"I wrapped it in the towels."

"Look," she said. I turned towards shore and saw the squirrels beyond the surf. When one of them tried to drag the towel away, I yelled. It scampered off a bit and stood on its haunches.

"To hell with it," I said.

"They're hungry," she said.

"Yes. Let them have what they need."

In the coolness of the dying day, we returned to our towels and drank our last beer. The beer was warm but at least the carbonation tasted dry after the salt water. I ate what was left of a chicken breast and threw the rest to the squirrels. Caroline and I pulled the towel back over our heads. Beyond her, I saw the choppy sea was turning a deep blue with the fading sky. My mind grew lost in more dreams. Caroline's eyes were there studying me.

"Do you really want to be with me?" she said.

"Yes, I want to be with you."

"Always?" she said.

"I hope it will be always."

She was back to studying me.

"We'd better get back," I said. "The sun's going down."

We gathered our things and returned to the leeward side of the island. The world was over there, a half mile across the bay.

On our way back along the rocks, we heard laughter and found a few people still seated at the bar upon our return. The sky was orange to the west but midnight-blue overhead. We decided to have one drink and sat chewing on the cool ice in our margaritas, immersed in enjoyable conversation until the boat captain pulled into the lagoon.

"What shall we do tonight?" I asked on our way back across the bay.

"I don't care. We can stay home if you like."

"I thought it would be nice to have a few margaritas on the veranda."

"All right. If we don't get drunk."

"We won't get drunk."

"Okay," she said.

We bought a fresh bottle of mescal, some mix and a bag of ice on the way home. There was no blender so Caroline took a towel and beat the ice over the counter. I watched her with amusement. We made a pitcher and went out on the balcony. The chipped ice worked out very well.

In that quiet moment, with the palm leaves rustling overhead, I shared some of what had happened in Tucson. Caroline laughed over my portrayal of the sheriff. Then both of us grew silent.

"It feels so strange," she said.

"What do you mean?"

"Your life. My life. They've been so different."

"Be thankful you weren't born with a pecker."

When she slapped at me, I grabbed her hand and kissed her fingers. I stared into her eyes.

"You are such a beautiful woman."

"And you're such an unfathomable man."

"Yes, well, I want you and that's all that matters."

We left the empty pitcher in the kitchen and went off to bed.

I ran my hand along the length of Caroline's body, especially lingering along the slender hollow of her waist and somehow comforted by this aspect of her form. When I went to kiss her neck and shoulders, she rolled over, on fire.

Later, when it appeared that Caroline was asleep, I got up and headed for the kitchen with a drink on my mind. I felt restless and wanted to move on. I wanted to be away from Mexico. Something about Mexican culture had never felt familiar to me. Their music, that one song with variations, their failure to make a decent loaf of bread, the list went on and on. Caroline spoke before I reached the door.

"Where are you going, honey?"

I stopped and stared in the direction of her voice, seeing only darkness.

"Clay, please don't drink anymore."

I shrugged and went into the kitchen, not wanting to answer to her or anyone. There was a brief attempt to crush the ice but that turned into a chore so I poured the mescal and mix over plain ice cubes.

Caroline appeared in her chamois.

"This is what I fear," she said.

"What? A margarita?"

"Drinking ourselves to death."

"You're making too much out of it."

"Clay, how much can you take?"

"I'm not questioning your behavior, Caroline."

"I'm not getting drunk every night."

"Thanks, Caroline. Now if you're done lecturing me, I'll get on with my cocktail."

A veil descended over her face and she left the room. I regretted those words but downed my drink and made another. To hell with her. I wasn't about to apologize. I grabbed a blanket and went to lie out on the balcony.

It was early the next morning when I awakened. Caroline was out in the kitchen cleaning up. The previous evening came back to me with a stab of remorse. I was feeling badly on several accounts. I went in and sat at the kitchen table Caroline watched me look at the bottle of mescal and back at her.

"Go ahead, Clay. I won't stop you."

"What are you thinking, Caroline?"

"I'm thinking I can't go with you."

"Please. Don't you remember how close we were yesterday?"

"Sure, and I remember how far apart we were last night."

I hung my head.

"Well, wouldn't you worry if you were in my shoes?"

I looked back up at her, not really knowing how I would feel.

"Look at you, Clay. I think you can escape everything but yourself."

"And you really think going back would be easier?"

"If running destroys you, then what do you have?"

I got up, went into the bedroom and returned with five thousand dollars.

"There," I said, dropping it on the kitchen table. "It's yours. You can put it in an account somewhere and leave any time."

She said nothing.

"I want you to come with me, but I'm not going back to face those fuckers. Not now. You may as well ask me to face a firing squad."

I took a shower, dressed and stopped in the kitchen for a shot of mescal. Caroline pretended not to watch.

"I'm going for the passports," I said. "I hope you're here when I return. If not, I'll understand."

I stopped at the door.

"The money is yours, either way." I closed the door and hustled down the stairs.

When I reached the Mercado, the old man was nowhere in sight. I bought a beer and made myself comfortable in the shade. Meanwhile, the adrenaline was wearing off and remorse had started to kick in. I had not even bothered to kiss Caroline goodbye and felt like hell over that. Then I felt angry again. I faced twenty years in prison but Caroline kept acting like it was a picnic.

In the end, I just felt empty. The two of us had become like strangers again in three days' time. I wanted love to be simple. Instead it was this big complicated mess.

Amidst the bustle of a Mexican city, with the sounds of the Mercado echoing around me, I searched for some explanation for the emptiness I felt, something other than the truth I knew. I loved Caroline, but was not 'in' love with her, not in the way I had been in love with Laura. I did not understand why. I just knew this to be the truth.

Anyway, Caroline was probably right. It was best if she left. I had nothing to offer her. Who knew how this thing would turn out? My young life was about survival and little else.

I would take the passports, return to the villa and leave things up to fate again. The decision was hers to make.

I was well into my second beer by the time the old man walked in from the street. I joined him in back of a large price board and quickly examined the passports. They were fine so I gave him the additional three hundred dollars. The passports went down my pants.

I was ready to leave when I noticed the two dark forms against the bright sunlight of the main gate. The pork pie hats and Hawaiian shirts said everything I needed to know. It looked like some dicks had followed the trail of the passports. If correct in that assumption, these boys were hard workers.

Assuming they could see my face, I smiled and engaged in small talk with the old man as if I didn't have a care in the world, all the while sizing up the Mercado. A dash for the back door was out. They had too clean a shot down the main aisle. My only hope was a side door to the left of an adjacent meat counter. If it was locked, I was fucked.

With one more casual look in the direction of my adversaries, I pulled the partition around to cover my path and bolted for the door. Everything was moving in slow motion now. Shouts and footsteps echoed in the background. This door knob had better open. It did and I bounded out into the bright day, flinging the door closed behind me. I was a good fifty yards down the street when I heard it open again.

The street was bustling with enough people that I had little fear of being shot in the back. I also had little hope of getting away in a straight run and cut across to a side street, then right at the next corner. My objective was the maze of streets going up the hill but I had to lose my pursuers before that point.

On the next block, I came astride a long length of apartment buildings, all of them joined together and distinguished only by their color and facades. Halfway down the block I heard the sound of their shoes behind me.

"Freeze or I'll shoot!" one of them shouted.

Go ahead, you bastard. I dashed up some stairs and into one of the residential buildings. At the end of a long hallway, I rushed out the back door and came face to face with a fire escape. The pavement was fifteen feet below but I made the leap with hardly a moment's hesitation.

Hitting badly, I scrambled to my feet and started down the block, limping now and looking over my shoulder. I saw the two dicks come out the door and start down the fire escape. Out of sheer panic, I had added another hundred yards to my lead.

I had reached the maze of streets winding up the hill but did not stop until I had come to the top. By the looks of those two agents, I had the luxury of a few moments to catch my breath and get my bearings straight. They were plenty out of shape and would have a hard time keeping up with me.

Then the urgency of my situation jumped in me again and I started down the other side of the hill, became lost, cursed several wrong turns and found myself on the right street as a matter of sheer luck. A few minutes later, I was closing the front door behind me and dashing upstairs. My options were nothing to envy. My escape was temporary, at best.

Up in the living room, I saw the money still sitting on the table

"Caroline," I called out quietly.

I checked the bedroom and peeked out at balcony before closing the curtains. It was a damned lousy time to be going for a walk. My impulse was to go look for her but I knew that was an even lousier idea.

Needing something to calm my nerves, I headed out to the kitchen and immediately saw the piece of stationery folded up on the counter. Before summoning the courage to open it, I downed a shot of mezcal. With one glance at the message, I felt a kick in my gut.

Dear Clay,

I'm sorry but I've decided to go back to California. I'm not leaving because of your problems, but because of what they are doing to you. You're not the same man I met in the bistro last spring.

I wish you luck, as I know what your freedom means to you. I still love you and if you decide to come back and face this thing, I will stand by you. But I can't watch you destroy yourself.

If I never see you again, I hope you will forgive me.

Caroline

I wadded up the paper and threw it across the room. There was another impulse to chase after her, but where? The train station? The airport? Two places I did not want to be seen. I took the bottle and sat on the living room sofa. I drank and tried to forget. Seeing there was nothing to do but get out of town, I called my friend, the taxi driver.

While waiting for him, I burned the note and went about wiping doorknobs. It seemed silly but I did it anyway. Then I packed my suitcase, placed the money from the table into my satchel and stood there watching through the curtains with the bottle of mescal in my hand.

When the cab arrived, I went down and told the driver what I wanted. He declined initially but I showed him a hundred dollar bill and that got him interested. I was careful not to show him too much cash, or seem too desperate. I told him the lady had run away and it was too long to wait for the train. I had to catch her. He understood that. I added another hundred dollar bill.

"Dos mas hay ya, mi amigo." He seemed to sense the danger but bit his lip and took the money.

I climbed into the back seat, cracked the window for some fresh air and slouched down out of sight as much as possible. The driver headed for the main highway. Along the way, I worked on the bottle and propped myself up from time to time to check on the passing road signs.

Once we had turned from Tepic down towards San Blas, I felt safe enough and sat upright. Being a bit drunk, I initiated a conversation with the driver about las mujeres and how they always did us wrong. It was a lousy conversation but conveniently masked the bitterness I felt inside.

So, the end of another romance, and with it, another layer of scar tissue. I looked forward to seeing Kip, and even the others. Hopefully I could find a quiet cantina and set up residence until things cooled down a bit.

Someday, I would head back to Mazatlán, retrieve my money from the bank and move on to more pleasant surroundings. To hell with women. To hell with love affairs.

It was midafternoon when we pulled up to the main plaza in San Blas. There was no one in sight. I climbed out and paid the driver. He nodded sympathetically. I must have looked the part.

The driver turned around and headed back up the dusty road. The cloud of dust lingered well after he was gone. So did the image of his taxi. The dents, the cracked yellow paint, the missing hubcaps, none of it had seemed quite so cheerless back in the bustle of Mazatlán.

I stood there with Caroline's departure haunting my thoughts. It appeared that there were some things you could easily forget in life, and some you could not, and I was on my way to understanding the difference.

23

Dust from the dirt streets of San Blas had left a grim patina on all its white plaster buildings. Here and there around the large plaza, a car had been parked, looking equally dusty, but I did not see a single human being. Discount a few stray dogs sleeping in the shade and the town appeared to have been abandoned.

There being no cantina in sight, I hoisted my suitcase and started towards the far side of the plaza. It too was empty and exuded all the charm of a shuttered amusement park. With the tropics, I had expected colorful tiles, parrots, the festive air of one of those early Disney cartoons. Instead, I came to the central fountain and found its cistern filled with dust in place of water.

I moved on, searching for any signs of life among the surrounding plaster buildings but nothing moved, not in front of the sad looking businesses along the block nor within their darkened interiors. Something was terribly wrong in the town of San Blas.

Then I heard children's voices and turned to find two young girls peeking out from a darkened doorway. Our eyes met and they retreated back inside with squeals of laughter.

That was comforting. These people were known for disappearing.

My spirits were further buoyed at seeing a sign for Jorgé's Cantina on the street farthest from me. These people were also known for making a good margarita.

I headed in that direction and came to another dirt street. A set of concrete steps on the opposite side led up to an elevated walkway. The cantina was a few doors down on my left. I slipped inside with the sounds of the surrounding jungle in my wake. A man with dark hair and mustache stood behind the bar.

"Hola Señor. Please, sit down."

He waved his hand at the bar top as though offering it me.

"I am Jorgé. Anything you want."

"Are you granting wishes or mixing drinks, Jorgé?"

"We try to make you happy anyway we can, Señor."

I swatted at the flies.

"Let's say we start with a margarita and see how that goes."

Jorgé smiled broadly.

"That's good, Señor. You need a drink."

"Yeah, I worked hard last night."

"Yes, you working too hard, maybe."

Since this conversation wasn't going anywhere close to where I wanted it to go, I decided in my best interest to leave it alone. I took another swipe at the flies and turned to review the cantina. There were two old men in a corner. They both eyed me momentarily and went back the business at hand: a siesta. Their beers were half empty and making dark rings on a wooden table.

I returned my attention to Jorgé and found him devising the margarita in a martini shaker, not a blender. He poured the margarita through a sieve and into a glass, leaving behind the ice. There was no salt around the rim of the glass. The mixture was lime green, mildly frothy and very cold. I saluted him, took a drink and quickly downed the remainder. It looked like Jorgé and I were going to be in business for a good long while.

"Where do visitors stay in town?" I asked while he concocted the second margarita. Jorgé poured my glass full and eyed me thoughtfully.

"You like the camp?"

I shook my head.

"The hotel is very clean. And cheap."

Again, I shook my head.

"Ah. If you are willing?" He rubbed his thumb and fingers together. "A little money and sometimes you find the nice house."

I nodded.

"Si. The best for you. A little while, you talk to the lady, Faith. She knows."

"Faith?"

186

"Si. She is long time here in San Blas. She tells you everything you need to know."

"And you expect her in?"

"Oh, si. Everybody in here pretty soon, Señor. Cinco de Mayo."

"Today?"

"Si. You don't know?"

I looked around at the dearth of activity.

"No. I had no idea."

Time passed and Jorgé continued doing what he did best. I lost track of the drinks.

By the time the crowd started to drift in, I had had enough time to grab the world by the throat and slap it around a bit. Not that it had done me or anyone else any good, but there was a temporary sense of satisfaction, a feeling that I knew what was wrong with everybody and everything and how to fix it, when in fact, I was a man with a jaded heart and a bad reputation, working on a hangover, in the cantina of a dusty, nowhere town, lost and hung up in a country where I did not want to be. Hard to see where I had any particular wisdom to offer the guy on the next barstool. I could buy you a drink and tell you a story or two. That was about it.

For what it was worth, I wished Caroline well. I had no expectations of changing the world, or the way my own life had played out, but under different circumstances, I could imagine things arriving at a more favorably ending. Something I wasn't likely to find out. I had failed a woman in various ways, faced the future without her and felt as empty as a man could feel. It was my burden to wonder if Caroline felt the same.

As the shadows of dusk settled over the town, I continued to pour booze over these thoughts and feelings. Meanwhile, more and more celebrants had appeared in the plaza outside, draping the town in red and green bunting and displaying the nationalist sentiments that were to be expected of the Mexican people, given the occasion.

Thoroughly tired of mankind and all its frivolities, I made no effort to go out and join them. Anyway, I had developed a deep sense of affection for the cantina. The cantina was my country and I its loyal citizen.

Long live the cantina.

More time passed and the drunken revelry increasingly invaded Jorgé's Cantina, particularly in the form of boisterous, testosterone laden men, marking the territory around their space with garritas, the Mexican equivalent of some redneck yelling 'yahoo'. As always, the place went to hell with a crowd.

Jorgé graciously offered to stow my suitcase behind the bar and I went out for a walk. People danced to a mariachi band and children laughed and played in the warm evening air. There was gaiety everywhere I turned.

I made my way to the far side of the plaza and sat on a short stone wall. The mariachi band had segued into a melancholy love song and the haunting melody drifted on the wind, wanting to pluck the hopes right out of my heart.

Well, Clay. Here's your glorious place in the sun. The freedom you have longed to find for the past two years. Ever since my flight from that induction center, I had dreamed of this moment, the money and freedom to go anywhere in the world, yet that freedom seemed useless to me now. I was ostracized from family and friends and the woman I loved had just left me. I was homeless at the edge of the world. Dying for one's country began to sound attractive.

A group of Mexican children approached me as I sat there and one of the younger boys held out a box of candy. I paid for the entire thing and they collectively ran back from whence they had come. I tossed the candy here and there at a gathering of the town chickens.

A thought entered my heart then, a thought so narcotic in its allure, I could hardly resist it. The solution was so simple, the pain over in seconds, and I very much wanted the pain to be over.

Battling these thoughts, a fetching American woman happened by and smiled in passing. I offered an obligatory wave and looked down again. She continued on for a few more paces before stopping abruptly and turning back.

"Is everything all right?" she asked.

When I failed to answer, she sat on the wall beside to me and leaned over to look in my eyes.

"Yeah, sure," I said with a glance her way. "Everything's fine."

She sat upright again and looked out over the festivities.

"Well, whatever else you are, you're not a very good liar."

I brushed away sudden tears.

"Oh dear," she said with another effort to look in my eyes. "You're not thinking to…"

I continued staring down at the ground. She began rubbing my back.

"Look. You can talk to me, okay? Whatever's going on with you, I'm here to help…In any way that I can."

I had started to look back when she suddenly burst out laughing. I turned away, ready to take the knife from my heart and stick it into hers.

Then, amidst my grief and anger, the nature of her double entendre struck me. I looked up and shrugged.

"Sure. I suppose you could hold the gun and I'll somehow manage to get in the way."

She sat upright and placed a finger to her lips amusingly.

"I don't know. I suspect the authorities are going to frown on my part in this enterprise."

"I won't tell a soul…Promise."

She laughed and we were back to staring at each other. Her gray eyes sparkled with warmth and mirth. Her beauty aside, her fluffy, angora-like hair was the color of pearls, making it hard to guess her exact age. She could have been anywhere from thirty to fifty, though I was inclined towards the lower end of the scale, simply because she had nice skin and the figure to go with it.

When she held out her petite hand to me, I found it to be much warmer than the night.

"I'm Faith."

"Oh, hello Faith. I'm Clay and I guess I was looking for you."

"Oh?"

"Yes. I had thought to find a home for rent here in town, but, you know…"

"Well, it is getting rather late in the day. Perhaps you'd like to get yourself better organized and shoot for tomorrow."

She laughed again at her latest double entendre.

"Come, come," she said, pulling on my hand. "I'm headed over to Jorgé's for a drink. We'll toast to your success."

I met her eyes and looked off.

"Oh, come on," Faith said and pulled me to my feet.

We started back towards the bar with Faith's arm locked in mine. Children emerged from the darkness around us waving sparklers and Faith chased them and it ended only when several mothers came to gather their children away. Faith returned to take my arm and we strolled with fireworks going off all around the plaza.

"So tell me, Clay. What brought you here to San Blas?"

"I'm a fugitive from riots and mayhem, mostly. With the obligatory doomed love affair thrown in."

"Well, whatever turns you on, as they say."

"Actually, I have absolutely no interest in riots and mayhem...And I don't appear to be any good at romances."

Faith laughed again.

"Clay, you're just having a hell of a time, aren't you?"

"You know, things seemed to be going just great a few days ago. Then suddenly, here I am, abandoned at the end of the world."

"Well, we'll just have to have that little drink and see if we can sort things out."

We had arrived at Jorgé's and found the cantina standing room only, and little of that. The packed interior was sour with the scent of stale beer. I pushed ahead and held Faith's hand to keep her from being swallowed by the sea of bodies behind me.

When Jorgé saw us, he waved towards the end of the bar.

"Hola, Señora."

"Hola, Jorgé," Faith said.

"See. I told you she is coming, Señor."

I nodded in honor of his wisdom. Jorgé produced a bar stool for Faith from behind the bar and looked expectantly at both of us.

"Any last requests?" Faith said.

"Two margaritas and a cigarette, Jorgé."

Not understanding my humor, he went about his business. I gave the crowd a once over and met Faith's eyes.

"So, abandoned," she said.

"That's my side of the story."

The drinks came and I threw some pesos on the counter.

"To life," she said. I held up my glass.

"And all its endless misery."

Our glasses met and we drank.

"Well, that was a lousy toast," she said.

I shrugged.

"What do you want me to say? It's been a lousy movie so far, with a lousy ending."

"For which we are wont to shoot ourselves."

I quickly downed my drink.

"Sorry, Faith, but I'm just not in tune with your humor right now."

"Oh well, Clay. Over the course of a lifetime, I've learned to develop a measure of detachment when it comes to l' aahhhmour."

"And I've come to find that bitterness is more fitting."

"Understood," she said, looking forward. "It's usually what happens when we attempt to get other people to do what we want them to do. Heartache and misfortune."

"I'll grant you that much."

Faith acknowledged my comment with a shrug and a drink.

"Would you care to elaborate?"

"I don't know. Definitely not here."

"That's right. A man with a past."

I stared.

"Well, it just so happens, I have a bottle at my place, if you'd like to get a few of those skeletons out of your closet."

"I'll accept the drink. I don't know about the rest."

"Okay, one for the road it is."

She downed her drink and stood up. Jorgé passed me the suitcase and I saluted him as we departed.

It occurred to me on our way out that I was reasonably sober, and also that drunkenness was not a very good spectator sport.

Faith led me along the elevated sidewalk in the direction of the sea, and then right and away from the store fronts at the first dusty street. The homes bordering it were mostly hidden away behind vine covered walls. The music and hubbub slowly died away behind us.

Faith turned down a shorter lane and opened a gate for me. I went ahead of her down a vine covered path. The scent of orchids filled the warm evening.

At the end of the path we came to a small yard and a one story plaster house. Faith opened the arched front door and encouraged me to go in ahead of her. I entered a tiled living room lit by moonlight. Faith hit the light switch and continued into the kitchen. More lights came on. The décor was warm and cheery with yellow and green murals painted on the white plaster walls of the kitchen.

"Please," Faith said. "Put your suitcase down and have a seat while I concoct the potion. I won't ask you what's in the satchel."

Growing conditioned to her laughter, I pulled a chair away from her pine table and sat down to watch the enterprise.

"Describe your feelings," she said and sliced through the lime in her hand.

"Like I've been brought to a sacrifice."

"Well, we can certainly accommodate, if you'd like."

She made a few playful thrusts with the knife before returning to her chore.

"Tell me, Clay, what has gone so wrong in your life?"

"It's that bad…"

"Few people arrive in San Blas all alone and with no place to stay. Never mind the face."

I proffered a saturnine grin.

"Oh heavens, yes. That's a decided improvement."

"What makes you so happy?"

"Who says I'm happy?"

"Then why are you always laughing?"

"I find life amusing."

"And I find it's mostly tragic."

"And I've learned the two go hand in hand." She studied me briefly before returning to her concoction. "After all, if we couldn't laugh at our grief, we'd all go mad."

Faith came with her chilled pitcher and corralled me out onto a brick patio. There were wood and leather chairs around a wooden table. I sat opposite Faith. She poured two glasses full and pushed one of them across to me. We both settled in to a warm night in the tropics.

"To a long life," she said as a toast.

I drank and put the glass down.

"You didn't like my toast?"

"What the hell."

I held my glass up to her this time.

"To a long and inscrutable life on a planet going mad."

"I liked my toast better," she said.

"It always sounds better without the nagging little details."

Faith guffawed. I drank and gazed up at the stars.

"Well, I have to admit, Clay. You have my curiosity up. How in the world have you become so cynical at such a young age?"

"A war? The aforementioned world going mad? Did you need me to provide more evidence?"

Faith nodded her head slowly, commiserating now.

"I know. The war has been really hard on men of your generation."

"More like hell. You come forth, all filled with hopes and dreams and expectations, only to find yourself in that vice?" I shook my head. "I struggle every day, trying to understand my fellow human beings. What the hell motivates people? "

"You mean, nobody's told you yet."

She laughed. I stared.

"Oh well, sorry," she said while drawing a finger around the edge of her glass. "It is difficult. We each have our own destiny to fulfill but they eventually get all tangled up together and it becomes rather hard to sort out which is which."

"I suppose there's living in a cave."

"We come here alone. We leave the same. I'm not so sure how you explain what happens in between."

"Hell."

Faith laughed.

"I suppose my point is, when we interact with other people, it can bring bliss but it can also bring sorrow so you'd better be ready for both. And it's sure to be both."

I reached out and touched her hand.

"Now who's being cynical?"

"Well, only an itsy bitsy teeny-weeny little bit," she said playfully.

I waited, but nothing more came. Faith refilled our glasses. Time passed and we came to be staring into each other's eyes.

"What?" she said.

"What? Did you want me to draw you a picture? Guy meets girl in a dusty little town at the end of the world?"

"And so, blinded by their bliss, they leap headlong back into the fire."

"Hey. You're talking to a guy who's written the book on jumping into fires."

193

Faith laughed and stared up at the distant stars. A warm breeze stirred the vines above us. Drawn by her beauty, I pulled Faith's head around and kissed her lips. We remained with our faces close, lost in each other's eyes.

"I don't think I could have gone through with it," I said.

"Most of us have come face to face with that moment, Clay. Sadly, those who succeed have forgotten that life is good. Essentially good..."

She sipped at her drink.

"Then what the hell are you going to do if it isn't?"

"Execution at dawn, as planned."

I took a long drink and looked back up at the stars. We held hands and enjoyed the evening in silence for a good long spell.

"Well, back to the issue at hand," I said. "Do you have any idea where I can spend the night?"

"I had assumed you were staying here."

"You know I want you."

"There, there," she said and met my stare. "No, I'm not prepared to sleep with you tonight. And don't give me those puppy dog eyes."

She stood up and went off with the empty pitcher and glasses. I heard the sound of glass meeting tile on the kitchen counter, then rustling in a closet somewhere down the hall. I looked over my shoulder and found Faith turning the sofa into a sleeper. I stood up and went to join her.

"Just like home," she said, fluffing the pillows.

"Thanks. I really appreciate the hospitality."

"That's quite all right."

I joined Faith on the sofa and put my arm around her shoulder. She leaned her head on mine. After a few minutes she pulled away far enough to look into my eyes.

"We'll talk in the morning. Though I won't have much time. I'm due in Tepic about ten. Maybe you'd like to go with me."

"I probably shouldn't."

"Well, fine," she said, feigning offence.

I tickled her and she laughed.

"Can we meet when you get back?"

"Sure. We'll talk about it over breakfast."

"All right."

"Good night, Clay."

"Good night, Faith."

I lay awake late into the night, still doing battle over my relationship with Caroline. I could see that it was mostly sophomoric when compared to Faith's maturity and intelligent conversation, and yet my heart ached for what had been lost. Whatever else I was feeling, I kept thinking Faith would come back down the hallway but she never did.

I awakened in the morning to the sound of her rattling around in the kitchen and the scent of bacon frying. It was something you rarely smelled in Mexico. With a peek, I saw Faith bustling over the stove. I closed my eyes again, feeling as if I could sleep for a hundred years. The battle over two women was ongoing in my heart.

A minute later, I sat up and swung my feet onto the floor. The movement caught Faith's attention.

"Good morning there, sleeping beauty."

"Hi."

"Did you sleep well?"

"Yes. What there was of it."

"And how do you feel?

"Virtuous," I said.

"And isn't virtue a pain in the ass."

I smiled, having grown accustomed to her laughter.

When she turned around again, I slipped into my pants and shirt and folded up the bedding as best I could. I noticed a clock on the kitchen wall. It was a little past eight.

"Mind if I use the bathroom?" I said.

"I'll mind if you don't."

I went off, laughing with Faith this time.

A few minutes later, I was taking a seat at the pine dining table. Faith had arranged colorful place mats and cloth napkins on the table. The napkins were bound in wooden rings. The yellows and greens in her murals seemed even more festive in the morning light.

"How you survive down here."

"Imports." She brought over the bacon and eggs and went to retrieve the toast.

"Such as?"

"Indian craft. I have several outlets in California."

195

She put the toast down and took a seat.

"Thank you," I said.

"Oh, well..."

She made a gesture that said she was happy to do it.

"And that's where you're going this morning?"

"Yes. The local tribesmen come down from the mountains once a month and I try to get in and out of there without being shot in the ass with poisoned darts." We both laughed. "What are your plans?" she asked.

"I need to lay low for a few days. Maybe longer."

"Well, I'm sure you could be made to feel welcome around here. Assuming Interpol doesn't come knocking down my door."

Seeing the look on my face, she bit her nails in mock fright.

"Oh dear, I really have struck a nerve, haven't I?"

"Is there a camp down by the beach? A place where the young Americans like to hang out?"

"Yes. You follow the road out of town and turn left at the coast. There's a place called Mother's. It's a bit of a walk."

"Okay. I guess I'll check around town first."

"You're expecting someone?"

"Yes, some friends. We're supposed to meet in the main plaza later today. I can always hang out at Jorgé's in the meantime. And try not to drink too many of his margaritas."

"Well don't come back here if you do."

She dug into her eggs with a smile. I did, as well, wondering just how serious she was. The eggs were delicious. I chased them down with black coffee.

"So, about seeing you tonight, dearest Faith. I'd really like that, if you can avail yourself."

"Well...since you put it that way..."

Later, she took the empty plates into the kitchen. I followed and tried to lend a hand but she shooed me away. Outside, I closed my eyes and enjoyed the speckled sunlight. My heart was restless as always but I thought this wouldn't be such a bad life, living here with Faith. She came outside and locked the door.

"Are we ready?"

"Yeah. You know, I may as well just walk over to Jorgé's."

"Getting a head start, I see."

"There's always more coffee."

She laughed but her eyes were studying me. I smiled back and joined her on the way out to the street.

24

With the tropical sun burning down on my head, I hurried over to the shade across the dirt street. I had changed into my sandals and the dust felt like warm flour between my toes. Mysterious calls echoed out from the jungle around me, the same jungle that had swallowed an entire civilization not all that long ago. When it came to being swallowed, the little town of San Blas did not look like it would put up much of a fight. It was comprised of a few dozen streets and the jungle rose up boundlessly in every direction around it.

I came to the street bordering the plaza and stopped with a look down towards the sea. The road beyond the plaza was shrouded by more jungle and disappeared out of sight in that direction.

I turned left towards Jorgé's Cantina and slipped unnoticed into the crowded bar. There were young Americans, mostly, peppered here and there with a few Mexicans. I found a stool in front of Jorgé and ordered a Corona. That seemed like a reasonable compromise between coffee and another margarita.

"Tell me, Señor Clay? Everything okay for you?"

He looked over his shoulder while cracking open the beer.

"As well as can be expected, Jorgé. And you?"

"Oh, every day is fine for me. Si, never any problemas."

He set the beer down and wiped the bar top in front of me. I saluted to him.

"Then here's to never having any problemas."

I drank and set the beer down.

"By the way, I'm looking for some Americans. Six of them, actually. One of them is a lady with long red hair."

"Who knows, Señor? Many, many Americans in here last night."

"Pela roja." I gestured to show how long.

"Oh, si, si. Late last night. Yesss, I remember the lady. Muy bonita."

"Do you know where they're staying?"

"At the playa?" He shrugged in saying this. "You wait. They are here for breakfast maybe."

I considered walking down to the beach but decided to try patience. It appeared that I could use some practice at particular enterprise.

Time passed and I ordered a margarita. It was a little past noon and I was onto my third margarita when Kristine walked in through the door.

"Look, it's Clay."

She joined me at the bar, followed by Steve, Robby and the rest of the gang.

I sensed Bill and Tom standing behind me and turned to face them.

"Where's Caroline?" Bill asked.

"We had a fight."

"So, where is she?" Tom said.

"I guess California."

"What do you mean, you guess?" Bill said.

I looked from Bill to Tom and back again.

"Why don't you guys can the big brother routine."

Bill stared at me with his usual pail of water expression. Tom came forward and brushed the hair from his face.

"Hey, we like came down here with her, man, so we kind of feel responsible for her safety."

"Yeah? Well, you can have the job, Tom. All of it. But don't think it includes keeping track of me."

"Well at least tell us where you think she is," Bill said.

"I already told you. California. We had a fight. I went for a walk on my own and when I came back there was a note saying she was headed home."

"Well, what else did it say?" Tom asked me.

I started to get up but Kristine put her hand on my shoulder.

"That's personal," she told him.

I stared at Tom and Bill until they left for the other end of the bar. They glanced my way several times while talking quietly among themselves.

"Do you think she's okay?" Kristine said.

"She had plenty of money."

Kristine consoled me with a hug.

"Sorry," Steve said. "Well, guess we'll have lunch."

"You want to join us?" Kristine said.

"Thanks, but I've already eaten."

She rubbed my back went over to sit with Steve and Robby at a table. Tom and Bill joined them. Kip sat down with me at the bar.

"Welcome to the lost city of San Blas," I said.

"Yeah…Bummer about Caroline."

"Yeah. What was it you once told me? I don't pretend to control women."

"Did I say that?"

"Well, somebody did…Sage advice, by the way."

He smiled, patted me on the shoulder and ordered a margarita from Jorgé. I looked to make sure no one was listening and told him about my escape.

"Wow," he said.

"Yeah."

I turned away from the bright sunlight in the doorway.

"You know, I met this lady named Faith last night. She lives here in town and I'm thinking she can help me get out of this country."

"Why don't you sit still for a spell? Let things cool off."

"I've thought about it, but come on. They're on to me again. I'd probably be safer in the States right now. Where were you, by the way?"

"We went off the main road at Tuxpan and down to what they call the marismas. Or as we call them in the States, swamps. The flies and mosquitoes were eating us alive. We'd hardly settled in when everyone said fuck it and we got out of there."

A robust lady with a big smile and red lipstick came to take Kip's breakfast order. Jorgé produced Kip's margarita and Kip saluted me.

What about the others?" I nodded towards the table.

"They're heading down to Oaxaca."

"Screw Oaxaca. I've seen enough jungle to last me a lifetime. Tell me more about your trip."

I did my best to listen but found my mind lost in various faraway destinations. I was drinking a beer and having Paella in a waterfront dive on Mallorca when Kip's food came. We headed over to join the others. Kip pulled up a chair next to Tom and Bill. I sat as far away from them as possible. I considered them a plague and assumed they felt the same. God knows, they probably thought I had killed Caroline and buried her body somewhere.

During the meal, a drive down the coast was planned. When I kicked in on the adventure, Tom and Bill begged out. Steve offered to take them back to camp but they declined.

With all the plates cleared and the bill paid, everyone but Bill and Tom piled into Steve's panel wagon and we motored down the long, straight road towards the Pacific. The town of San Blas abruptly came to an end beyond the plaza and a jungle canopy engulfed us. The inside of the van quickly filled with marijuana smoke and conversation. A mile or so later, we exited back into bright sunlight.

Steve turned left at the coast and continued on past their campground. A few miles farther south, the white sand beach and barren coastline shoreline dead ended at an estuary. The estuary narrowed beyond a sandy point and wound up into the jungle.

Kristine immediately shed her clothes and ran down to the surf. Steve shrugged and did the same. The rest of us followed. We swam in the sea and eventually made ourselves comfortable in the warm sand. I tried to ignore Kristine's nakedness but it was not easy. She was a statue coated in white sand with a tuft of orange hair protruding.

Everyone grew restless over time and agreed to drive up into the jungle along the estuary. The sound of the surf grew faint as we moved away from the sea, then faded altogether.

"Wow, look at that," Kristine said.

A decaying trawler sat aground the middle of a mud flat, fifty yards from the road. Steve parked. Kristine looked at us over the front seat.

"Come on. Let's go see what's in it."

She climbed out, pulled up her pant legs and was quickly up to her knees in the mud.

"Come on, guys," she said, laughing. "Where's your adventurous spirit?"

"Maybe someone should stay behind," I suggested. "In case you get into stuck."

"Nonsense. You're nothing but a bunch of old women."

"Looks like she intends to make a day of it," I said.

"I'm waiting on the road," Robby said.

"Hell, what's the big deal," Steve said. He rolled up his pant legs and gave chase. "Maybe there's some brass left on board."

I doubted that but had no intention of waiting on the side of the road all afternoon. I followed Steve. Kip came along and then Robby.

Walking in the mud was like walking in chocolate pudding and required that you pull your leg straight up with each step in order to maintain your balance. I heard a sound behind me and turned to find Robby had not absorbed this lesson quite soon enough. He had pretty much taken a dunk. It was difficult to lend him a hand under the circumstances.

"Goddamn mother fucking son of a bitch! Mother fucker! Mother fucker!"

He moved frenetically in several directions before deciding to head for the dark waters of the estuary. I figured it was his best shot, too. He fell again several times in his haste, cursing the whole way.

"Son of a bitch! Goddamn fucking mud!"

The string of expletives trailed off in the distance.

"Fuck! Fuck! Fuck!"

Having reached the trawler, the rest of us did our best to contain our laughter. I hurried around to the bow, reminded of cut timber as Robby fell into the estuary. He emerged from the turbulence underwater with a film of mud flowing down from his wiry hair. Everything about him was brown except for his eye sockets and flesh-colored lips.

"Are you okay, Robby?" I called out.

"Oh yeah, Clay. Just fucking great. How are you doing?"

I watched his mouth move, thinking he needn't be so sarcastic.

"Just wanted to make sure you were all right." It was difficult to pick the right words under the circumstances. When he failed to respond, I finished my thought. "We'll be waiting for you onboard."

He stared at me, blinking through the muddy film on his face.

In the end he chose to head downstream towards more solid footing. I turned back along the top deck. The wooden planks had been polished into a dull gloss by the salt air and smelled of the sea. I quickly inspected the gutted fo'castle for anything of value and joined the others in the stern.

"Think he's okay?" Kristine asked.

"He's fine. He went downstream to go ashore."

"He has the worst luck," she said.

"He has the worst karma," Steve said.

"He certainly has the worst language," Kip said.

There was laughter and a few words spoken, then everyone grew quiet. It seemed as if I could hear echoes from the past, the distant cries of men who once stood on this deck and brought fish up from the sea.

I had entirely forgotten myself when I noticed Robby staring at us from the road. There were looks and a general stirring for the journey back to shore when we heard a faint drone echoing up from the direction of the sea. A panga had cleared the waves and was coming our way. All of us went over to that side of the ship and watched the boat grow larger. In time, we were able to make out the features of an older man at the rudder. A young boy stood in front of him. The man cut the motor and came astride of us. The boy waved at three bulging gunnysacks bleeding brine into the hull of the boat.

"Looks like oysters?" Kip said.

"That is what I suspect, Señor."

"Ask him what else he has," Kristine said.

"¿Que tienes?" Kip shouted. The young boy pulled open a sack and displayed one of the mottled-gray shells.

"¿Y pescado, tienes?" The boy held up a large, silvery fish.

"¿Quieres?"

"¡Si quieres!"

The old man motioned to some mangroves just above the mudflat and restarted his panga. As we made our way to shore, he guided his boat in that direction. Once onshore, we hurried up the road with our muddy feet gathering dust as we went.

The boy was steadying the boat against the mangroves when we arrived. The old man pulled opened one of the sacks and several oysters spilled out into the bottom of the boat.

"¿Cuantos quieres?" he said.

We indicated the entire sack.

"Diez pesos."

I laughed and pointed at the yellowtail.

"¿Y con pescado?"

"Veinte," he said.

Kip gave him fifty pesos and waved off the change. The boy took the money without hesitation and helped us unload the sack of oysters. Kip held the large yellowtail by its tail.

"Wow," Steve said. "Twenty pesos for all this? Even fifty pesos."

"That's the same as fifty bucks in Mexico," Kip said.

Steve joined me in grabbing the sack of oysters. The old man started the motor and headed upstream. The boy waved one last time as the panga disappeared around a bend. Somewhere in the jungle, a young wife waited for the old man and her boy at the end of a day. Caroline came to mind then. Women always did in that fleeting hour of dusk. My heart wanted everything to be simple like that, a woman waiting for me somewhere in this world, her kindness washing the loneliness from the hours of my life.

"Let's go barbecue in the plaza," Kristine said on our way back to the truck.

"I'm taking a fucking shower," Robby said.

"Sure. We'll stop and grab the hibachi from camp."

Steve stopped at Mother's, where we all showered before driving back to San Blas.

The plaza was crowded with Mexican families at dusk, the adjacent streets lined with cars and young Americans. Smoke from barbecues spilled up into the onrushing night, along with laughter and music.

I left the others and went to look for Faith at Jorgé's. She was having a drink at the bar.

"Well hello!" she said. "I see you've survived another day!"

I sat down and nodded at Jorgé.

"How was your trip?" I asked.

"Good. No poison darts."

She pulled up her dress playfully. Jorgé set my drink down and took his fee.

"How are you feeling," she asked.

"Better. I didn't think too much."

"Oh. That's usually a good sign."

I sipped the margarita and explained what we had done. Faith laughed quite a bit about Robby's misadventures.

"I need to talk with you alone," I said.

"Don't tell me you've rescheduled the execution." She put a finger to her mouth. "Let's see. What all will I need? Some popcorn, a cold beer, hmm hmm hmm hmm hmm, what else?"

I found her ribs with my hands and made her suffer.

"Okay okay," she said at last.

"Are you hungry?" I asked.

"A bit, yes."

"We have some fresh yellowtail outside."

"By all means," she said.

Faith and I took a moment to finish our drinks and wandered out to stroll the plaza in the dusky light, met with companionship and good cheer at every stop, each little gathering with its unique tribal signature, our journey leading us around the entire town square and back to our companions, where we feasted on the yellowtail and drank cold beer with stars beginning to poke holes in the warm evening sky.

Later, a group of musicians from Mazatlán arrived and we danced to their Latin music in the street, the cool, metallic tones of the vibes player spilling up into the night sky, those haunting melodies gone in search of their ancient birth in some distant galaxy. Then they played Poinciana, the same song I had heard in my head while making love to Caroline in the jungle but a few days earlier, the same song I had heard over the radio in my youth, when all was well in the world, and here it was again, having materialized in this far flung place, just as Caroline had materialized on that train platform in Nogales, and it was as if the universe was trying to inform me, that everything would be all right, that goodness would always be at my side, that each journey through this world inevitably led towards greater truth and enlightenment. And with these thoughts my gaze turned northward, wishing I could fly home on wings that very second. I was ready to face my destiny without fears. I would be a freedom fighter against the war and lay down my life so that others would not have to suffer the same fate. There was nothing I could not endure or overcome with a loving woman at my side.

Lost in my reveries, I had wandered off alone in the crowd and was there for several minutes when this dream world vanished and I was back on Earth, a mortal thing, and with the brilliant clarity of but a few moments earlier dissolving into renewed doubts.

Feeling like a stranger in a strange land, I went to find Faith.

"Can we go to your place?" I asked her over the music.

Quickly discerning the seriousness of my mood, she nodded and took my arm.

"Let me say goodnight to the others."

In doing so, I learned that Steve planned to head south the next day. Kip was thinking to go with him. I was undecided and left after agreeing to meet them for breakfast in the morning.

Turning down Faith's street, the music followed us for a few hundred yards before the jungle's brooding silence completely swallowed it. Faith turned the key in her door and entered the living room before me. I slumped down onto the cane divan. Faith turned on a lamp and joined me.

"What's going on?" she said.

"I think I just had a spiritual experience...Something happened. I had this sudden revelation where I felt like I could see everything with utter clarity and it came with this feeling that I should go back and face my problems. You know, that it was going to be all right."

"I have no idea what your problems are, Clay."

"I know," I said and explained everything to her.

She listened intently and touched my face when I was done.

"You dear sweet boy. You do have a past."

I sighed.

"I don't know. At times it all seems so insignificant and on the other side of the universe, but then I realize they won't give up and I feel so goddamned hopeless. I don't want to go to jail or die in Vietnam but I hate this feeling of being cut off from everything dear to me more than anything. And there, back in the plaza, it just suddenly felt like going back to face things was the right thing to do."

I broke down then and she took my head in her lap, giving comfort, and then made gentle fun of my grief and got me to laugh. It was awhile longer before I spoke up.

"I trusted you."

"That was foolish."

"Okay. Maybe I'll shoot you instead."

"Yes. Blaming someone else is that age old answer to all our personal problems."

"So? What would you do, if you were in my shoes?"

"Well, first of all, Clay. I'd be very wary of acting impulsively upon this revelation you've just had. It is not unusual for people under great duress to have such experiences. You think by surrendering that you'll bring a climax to your hardships, when in fact, you'll just end up in jail and probably have done nothing to change the course of the war."

I stared at her.

"You've completely taken the air out of my heroic vision."

"Oh...sorry."

I buried my head in her bosom again.

"It's the loneliness, Faith. Sometimes I feel so empty and apart from everything. Then I despise myself for being weak and needy."

"I should think that that's what any person in your shoes would have to decide. You're on a path that has cast you apart from your own society."

Faith got up and opened the French doors. There was a late breeze blowing in from the sea and it disturbed various papers around the room. When she sat beside me again, I took her hand and kissed it in gratitude. When I looked up again, she was staring at me.

"I want you," I said.

"I'm so much older, Clay."

I kissed her nose and her lips gently.

"I don't care. You're as lovely as spring to me."

"You say awfully nice things when you want something."

"Oh stop. I mean it. With all my heart."

"You know, Clay. All women are like little school girls. They want a man to be gallant. They also don't want to be hurt."

After a moment, she nestled in my arms, I assumed deciding to trust me. I sat stroking her hair, wondering how to make sense of my own feelings. I loved Caroline and was compelled by this profound desire to go back and make things right with her, but I also felt a profound desire to love Faith. In no small measure, she had saved my life. I had seriously thought of ending it twenty-four hours earlier. Now I felt determined again, even angry and ready to fight.

I stood up and gently pulled Faith towards her bedroom. Our clothes came off slowly while we kissed beside her bed. I tasted Faith's naked flesh, wanting to thank every little part of her, my kisses slowly descending along her supple body until my mouth was locked upon her sweetest of places. And I stayed there until she was satisfied, and then she came after me, a black silhouette with white teeth flashing.

"Oh Faith," I groaned. "You know me so well."

"You see," she said and kissed me there tenderly again. "You only need imagine what would delight yourself."

Unable to restrain myself any longer, I pulled Faith on top of me and watched her move ardently against the pale light of the window.

Afterwards, she lay beside me as quiet as a kitten

In the morning, I awakened to the scent of coffee brewing and my thoughts careening all over the place. As Faith had said, this newfound impulse to face my legal problems would probably accomplish little, other than to see me locked up in prison for many years. Plus, by making love to Faith, I had created a whole new set of lies and deceptions between Caroline and me. And yet I felt driven by some unspoken need to return and make amends with her. Why, I did not understand. I could not tell if the impulse was a sick or noble one. I just felt driven forward now, as if by galloping steeds.

I saw a shadow coming towards the door and braced for the encounter. Faith came into the room wearing a long gown and crawled on top of me.

"Good morning," she said.

"Hi," I said. "Have you taken a shower?"

"Yes."

I started to get up but Faith held me down playfully.

"Don't think you can fool me, Clay. I know you're planning to run back to your little princess."

I smiled uncomfortably.

"I'm sorry," I said. "I can't lie to you."

"It's all right. There's a closeness of spirit that comes when a man and a woman talk honestly with each other and what follows is hard to resist."

She kissed me.

"I wouldn't have believed your bullshit anyway."

She went to stand up but now it was my turn to restrain her.

"Please, just stay here and hold me for a while."

We lay there for a long time without speaking.

"I don't know how to thank you," I said.

She pulled her head back to look at me.

"I hope you are always so kind to the women you meet."

"I will try," I said.

"I suspect you will."

She stood up and held out her hand.

"Now come have a cup of coffee."

"I'll be right there."

I showered and dressed, all the while grappling with my impulses. I wasn't so sure about turning myself in to the law, but I knew I had failed to come completely clean with Caroline and properly respect her and her independence and the need to make things right had completely possessed me.

I met Faith in the kitchen.

"What are you doing today?"

"Attempting to get rid of all this crap I bought yesterday. And you?"

"Looking for a way back to the States."

She raised her eyebrows.

"Sitting tight for a spell and giving your impulses some thought, that went out the window?"

"I guess it's not in my nature," I said.

Faith poured me a cup of coffee without answering.

"I'm being honest," I said.

"Yes," she said. "I suppose you are."

After studying me for a moment, she smiled.

"You know, Clay. You're probably the only person I've ever known who could manifest more trouble by telling the truth than not."

"Thanks...So what do you think?"

"I suppose you could go up with my driver."

"When?"

"Sometime in the next few days. I'll know later today."

"All right. How about if I buy you some breakfast?"

"Very well. You go on ahead. I have to check on some things but I'll be up in a bit."

When I hesitated, she shooed me out the door.

I found Kip and Robby already seated at Jorgé's when I arrived. The cantina was host to the usual mix of Mexicans and Americans. Most of them were having breakfast. The other members of our group were nowhere in sight.

"Where's the gang?"

"Bill and Tom took the bus down to Puerto Vallarta," Kip said. "Steve and Kristine are having a moment alone...Robby's taking it pretty hard."

"Up yours," Robby said.

Kip smiled at me.

"Are you ready to order?"

"No, I'll wait for Faith."

The waitress brought three more beers. Kip decided to wait with me. Robby ordered his meal, refining the codes of imperialism along the way. I felt badly for the waitress. When he was through with her, he leaned back and stared at the ceiling. I had this vision of him as Shiva, dormant between kalpas. It was frightening to think he would awaken.

He did.

"You know? I'm sick of this place. I can't wait to get back home."

"I suspect the Mexicans feel the same way about you," I said.

"Yeah? Well, screw them."

He mulled over my comment for a moment.

"And screw you, too."

"You're probably right about me. But the Mexicans have good cause to be a lot less gracious than they are, considering all the crap they've taken."

"To hell with them. They live like dogs anyway."

"Poverty will do that to you," Kip said.

"Is that my fault?"

He pounded his chest with a fist to emphasize the point. I looked at Kip and we both nodded.

"Yeah, yeah we think it is," Kip said.

"To hell with you fuckers."

He went back to staring at the ceiling.

Not long after, Steve and Kristine appeared. They said hello and hurriedly dragged Robby out the front door. I looked at Kip. He shrugged and returned to nursing his beer. I did likewise. Presently, Steve returned and asked us to come outside. We followed him over to the panel wagon. Robby was pacing back and forth with both hands running through his wiry hair.

"What's happening?"

"You're not going to believe this," Steve said.

"Try me."

"This sand cleaning machine came down the beach half an hour ago and dug up a hundred kilos. Right in front of our campsite."

"It was amazing," Kristine said.

"Tuition fees," I said.

"Yeah, we took our share and packed it into the panels," Steve said.

"There were others?"

"Most of the camp. Every bit of it was history in less than two minutes."

Robby took a break from his nervous pacing.

"Can you fucking believe it? Huh?"

"Somebody's going to be pissed," I said.

"It's their tough luck," Robby said and climbed behind the wheel.

"We're breaking camp," Steve said. "Thought we'd see if you wanted a ride."

"I could be interested, Steve. Will you stop by on your way out of town?"

"Sure. We'll have one for the road, either way."

"Sounds good."

I gave Kristine a hug and watched as they joined Robby in the front seat. Kip and I returned to our beers.

"I don't like it," he said.

I looked him over.

"Karma?"

"Nothing's free, partner. You know that."

"Can you imagine the guy who buried that stuff?" I said.

"He'll be looking at his maps, all right," Kip said.

"He'll be looking for his gun."

We laughed, but it wasn't a very good laugh.

"What about you, Kip?"

"I'd better keep an eye on you," he said in his dreamy manner. "Anyway, I like your idea of heading over to see Europe. What do you think?"

"That would be cool, Kip. The two of us and a couple of gals. We'll just bum around with no idea where we're going to end up at the end of each day."

"Yeah, sounds groovy," he said.

We returned to our beers and our private thoughts. Mine were of Caroline. To hell with turning myself into the law but I still felt a powerful urge to set things right with her. I heard Faith's voice, telling me to sit still, but the prospect of hitting the border in forty-eight hours and holding Caroline in my arms was impossible to resist it.

Faith showed up and I filled her in while we waited for our breakfast.

"My truck's going north in two days," she said. "Why not wait?"

"I'm in no hurry," Kip said.

Faith stared at me.

"Don't worry. I'll be okay."

"It's just a feeling, Clay. Just a feeling."

"I've got one, too," I said. "And it just can't wait."

A short while later, Steve, Kristine and Robby returned from the beach and we all joined together at the bar for a margarita. Faith had coffee, stealing quiet glances at me as she sipped. When our drinks were done, everyone walked out to the street.

"Thanks again," I told her.

"For what?"

"For saving me from the firing squad."

She smiled and gave me a big hug.

"Be careful."

"I'll try."

"You're sure you don't want to wait?"

"I told you. I can't."

"You won't."

212

"All right. But I can't help what I feel."

"I know," she said, "I guess I figure I could run your life better than you can."

"I wish it worked that way." She beat on my chest playfully. I kissed her forehead and waved to her through the rear windows as we pulled out of town.

I had noticed her wrinkles in the morning light but loved her just the same. I loved her in many ways, but more than anything, I would always remember her wisdom and laughter. Then she was lost in the trail of dust. Steve honked once as we went around the turn and I lost sight of Faith for good.

25

The land rose up in lofty peaks to the east, mottled in lime and emerald and every imaginable tint of green. In the sultry heat, ominous looking clouds cloaked the highest peaks. Aztec mythology came to mind, like one of those Mexican paintings on black velvet, where a warrior stands high up on a mountain ledge, holding the willing maiden in his arms. I wanted to hold Caroline in that way; without the neurotic self-doubt and soul searching of modern times, just a man and the woman he loved, while the native drums kept time along the tedious road to Tepic.

I came back to the moment and found Steve working away at the steering wheel. Kristine sat next to him. Robby sat by the door. Kip and I were lying in back. The drone of the truck reminded me of riding in Guillermo's van, though those moments seemed to have been in another lifetime now.

I wiped the perspiration from my face one more time. The day grew steadily darker with clouds. A short time later, the rain started. I heard it pounding on the roof of the panel wagon in large drops.

Kip sat up and looked over the front seat.

"Can you see anything?" I asked him.

He lay back down.

"No. It's coming down in sheets."

I sat up and looked out the small, rear windows. There was the dark sky and the jungle getting wet and the water spraying up from the wheels onto the highway. I lay back down and dreamed of Caroline. I wanted to hold her right then and an automobile was never fast enough. Nothing was fast enough when you were trying to get back to a woman.

Through the drone of the engine, I heard snippets of the conversation up in front. They were worried. I was too, but only a little. I planned to hike across the border. I had done that enough times already. I would not be facing the border patrol in a big, green panel wagon with forty pounds of marijuana hidden inside the walls.

Kip told me a story about when we were in Hawaii and it brought back a flood of fond memories.

"Sometimes I wish we had never left," I said.

"It's a beautiful place," Kip agreed.

"I wonder what happened to old Stan. He used to call us hippies 'white flour children'. The war did something to him."

"It's done something to all of us," Kip said.

I looked over, thinking I might better see what was going on in his head.

"Well, screw the war," I said. "I grew up thinking we were really going to change the world. Then 'Nam came along and now everything's just a giant mess."

"We changed the world a little," Kip said.

"Yeah, maybe a little."

"Maybe with a new president."

"Yeah, maybe with a new president."

We both were quiet then. As with all political diatribes, our conversation met with an uneasy demise.

When Steve stopped for gas in Acaponeta, Robby took over driving. Out of boredom, I tried again to watch out the back windows but it rained and there was little to see so I lay back down and talked with Kip.

When we grew silent, my thoughts turned again to Caroline. Surely we had met on that train to Mazatlán for some reason. With her by my side, I'd be willing to face anything. I'd be a warrior for peace. My name would be in the papers.

I was fine with that vision for several miles until my aversion to confinement leapt forward and I was ready to jump out and catch the next bus back to San Blas. Drinking margaritas at Jorgé's and loving Faith beat the hell out of incarceration any day.

There were so many hopes and dreams and fears churning around inside of me, it was impossible to keep them straight. And all the while, the rain sprayed up from the back wheels of the panel wagon.

The storm broke just below Mazatlán and we stopped there for lunch. The sun felt hot on the back of my shirt when we got out in front of a restaurant. I ate in silence while Robby argued with Steve and Kristine. All of a sudden Robby wanted to go sightseeing. They wanted to drive straight through.

"I think you should get to the border as quickly as possible."

"Who asked you?" Robby said.

"You could get into an accident. Any number of things."

"What? Are you trying to make us paranoid?"

"He's right," Steve said. "The longer we're here, the more chances there are for something to go wrong."

"He's the one in a hurry."

Robby thumbed his nose at me. But no one else wanted to stay and he gave in before the waitress took our plates. His eyes told me how he felt. He'd like to leave me on the side of the road somewhere.

The rain started to come down again twenty miles north of Mazatlán, the big drops pounding away on the metal roof. Kristine rolled a joint and passed it back, but not before she had patched a run with her spit. I took the moist finger of paper and herb and finished it with Kip. We laughed quite a bit after that, about the many panics we had experienced crossing the border, about Stan and trying again to imagine Sheriff Prescott in swim trunks. I was still adamant that he would go with the bikini look. Kip was sure he would wear them barrel style. Either way, he painted a hilarious picture.

Then there was silence and I thought again of the journey my generation had been on and how it seemed that there was no place left for us to go, no place left for us to call home. Then I came back to the rain, pure and simple and without motive. It poured in sheets over the little square windows and onto the highway. I fell asleep to the wipers slapping at the rain, back and forth, slapping at the rain.

I awakened in the last light of day. The rain had stopped and the jungle had given way to dry, grassy hills, and the hills were dark from the rain and laced with gold at dusk and the folds of the canyons had filled with darkness. We were back in Sinaloa, the rolling landscape disturbed here or there by a shack, a few palms and groves of papaya. The shacks were makeshift hovels mostly and surrounded by fences that would need repair with every strong wind. Kip and I watched from behind the front seat.

"God, you wish you could help these poor people," Kristine said.

"Poverty's a necessity," I said.

"That's an awful thing to say."

"If financial success is the objective, somebody has to lose."

"Plow them all under and start over," Robby said.

Kristine sighed and stared out the window.

"If the rich weren't so greedy," Steve said.

"Yeah," Kristine said, sounding hopeful.

"They'd probably be happy if everyone would just leave them alone," Kip said.

Nothing more was spoken until we reached the outskirts of Culiacan. It was night and humid and the streets were crowded. Gone were the peasant clothes and sandals of Nayarit. The Mexican dandies now wore cowboy boots and jeans and big, ostentatious looking belt buckles and had their hair greased back. Six hundred miles away but you could already smell the border.

Robby found a liquor store and parked. Kip went in to buy some beer and all of us walked up the street to eat at a cocinero.

After several tacos, I drank down the last of my beer and placed the empty bottle back in the case. Kristine wrapped up the extra food and opened the last beer. All of us were taking in the setting in silence.

"Should we stay?" Steve asked.

Everyone looked ready to move on except Robby. He still looked defiant.

"Let's go camp at the beach," he said.

"The gulf is forty miles away," I said.

"Like I already told you, Clay, nobody's asking for your opinion."

Rather than deck him, I turned to watch traffic.

"He's right," Steve said. "The beach is way out of our way."

"So what?" Robby said.

"How far would we go?" Kristine said.

Everyone followed Steve back to the truck. He grabbed a map from the cab and spread it out on the hood.

"Los Mochis. Or maybe Guaymas," Steve said.

"Guaymas is on the coast," I said.

"Hey. We're planning this, okay?" Robby said.

I stared at him.

"It's less humid in Guaymas."

"We can drive to Los Mochis and see how we feel," Kristine said.

"Yeah," Steve said. "Let's just gas up and go."

He folded the map.

I went in to buy another six-pack of beer and a bottle of mescal. Steve was at a gas station across the street, filling up the panel wagon. I walked over and handed him some money for gas going by.

Back inside the truck, I cracked the seal on the mescal, had a drink and shared it with Kip. He had a drink and handed the bottle to Robby. Steve climbed in and started the wagon forward. The city soon fell away and darkness surrounded us. I felt the warmth of the mescal mixing with the hopes and dreams in my gut.

Later, I heard Kip snoring and poked my head over the seat to talk with the others. When I tired of the conversation, I took the bottle and tried to get some sleep of my own. My mind went around and around in circles. I held onto the bottle as an anchor.

We pulled into Los Mochis about eleven. It was a town that made you want to keep moving. Even Robby could see that. Steve found an open service station and topped off. I went around back to find the outhouse. It was foul. I felt sorry for Kristine when she came around back. I saw her open the door, close it with disgust and squat under the folds of her dress. Back around front, I leaned against the truck and waited. Kristine returned with a weary smile.

"Would you like to get some sleep?" I asked her.

"I'd love to."

She looked at Steve.

"Sure. You guys ride up front for a spell," he said.

"Are we going through?" Robby said.

"It's only three hours to Guaymas," I said. "It's less you'll have to drive in the morning.

He shrugged. He had lost some of his fight since Culiacan. I grabbed the mescal, had Kip sit in the middle and the three of us tried to get along for a few hours. The booze helped to loosen Robby up. I pretended to be him when he had fallen into the mud. He laughed and told us about growing up in Chicago. He was a pretty decent guy when he wasn't fighting the world.

The hours and miles passed by and the terrain transitioned into the Sonoran Desert. Saguaros clipped by like telephone poles. Clusters of stars glowed in the clear, arid sky. The hills were matte black along the horizon. We smoked another joint and passed the bottle and pushed on through the night.

About two in the morning we saw a sign that read Playas. Robby turned onto a washboard road in that direction. The road ran straight across the desert terrain and on a gentle slope down towards the gulf. I lowered the window to let some fresh air in. It was good to smell the dry desert breeze off the gulf. It was a clean smell after the rotting scent of the jungle.

Near the gulf's edge, we found vehicles parked randomly here and there but no restroom or organized campsite of any kind. Robby cut the engine, turned out the lights and glided in from a hundred yards out. As we came to a halt with a crunch of gravel, a few heads popped out but they quickly retreated, satisfied we weren't federales or banditos. Our gang got out and discussed what to do in hushed voices.

There wasn't much choice when it came to the sleeping arrangements. Steve and Kristine took the back. Robby slept across the front seat. Kip and I took the ground. We were donated two sleeping bags, which was some consolation against the rocky terrain.

The dry desert breeze was fighting with the moist gulf air as I drifted off to sleep. I heard the sound of the sea lapping against the rocks and thought of Caroline's gentle touch. I thought of making love to her in clean, fresh sheets. I was tired of sleeping bags. I was desperately tired of the road.

Early that morning, I awakened while the others still slept. Kip looked once and went back to sleep. I went down to the sea alone. There was a dab of pink to the east, but to the west and out over the water, the sky was still dark.

I climbed down to a smooth ledge of rock bordering the gulf, took off my sandals and sat with my feet in the water. The sea slapped lazily a foot below the ledge. There were tide-pools along the ledge that would be underwater at high tide.

The sky grew lighter, revealing the sea bottom below my feet. Looking out across the gulf, the water was darker where the bottom dropped off about fifty yards from shore. A fog bank shrouded the shoreline on either side of me, leaving a mosaic of cliffs drifting in and out of the mist.

I became aware of how fleeting and precious each moment was, especially with people you loved, and how the moments you shared together so often slipped by without notice. Then, being alone, you were ready to sell your soul to have one of them back. I wanted Caroline in that way. I wanted to tell her I loved her and make everything all right again.

I heard movement behind me and turned to find a young man picking his way down the shallow cliff. He came and sat next to me with a beer in his hand.

"Frank," he said, holding out his free hand.

"Clay."

We shook.

"You one of the folks that came in late last night?"

"Yeah. Sorry to wake you."

"No sweat, brother."

We sat together watching the sky bloom from pink to pale yellow and finally to blue. The waters changed with it. The sun rose over the mountains behind us. I saw the mist lifting off the cliffs farther up the gulf.

"Ain't freedom lovely?" he said.

I looked at him.

"Sure. What makes you say that?"

"Oh. Some folks came down yesterday. Said they had passed a van full of Americans being arrested at the checkpoint."

He looked at me and shook his head.

"That'd be a bummer, wouldn't it?"

"Where's this checkpoint?"

"About ten miles north of Hermosillo."

"Smuggling?"

"Oh, probably. Not much else can go wrong down here, other than getting into a car wreck."

I heard sounds and turned to find Kip, followed by several men with scuba gear. The divers walked down to our left and put on their equipment. Kip stripped off his clothes and dove in. He came up smiling and leaned on the ledge beside us, his straw-colored hair waxed against his face.

"This is Frank. Kip."

Kip smiled and stuck out his hand.

"Frank here was telling me that they busted some folks above Hermosillo yesterday for smuggling."

Kip looked at Frank and back at me. The smile was gone.

"You guys aren't smuggling, are you?"

Kip shook his head. Frank looked back at me.

"Well, just the same. I wouldn't drive five miles around here with a joint on me, let alone try to make the border."

He got up and crushed his can.

"Time for seconds," he said and headed up the cliff.

"What do you think?" I asked Kip once we were alone.

"What all did he say?"

I explained about the checkpoint. He nodded and rubbed his chin.

"Think we'd better catch the train?"

"Suppose so," he said.

"What's their plan?"

"They want to hit the border at rush hour. Figure they'll get lost in the traffic."

"When are they leaving?"

"Around noon."

"So, four or five hours to kill."

"Yeah. One of the campers told me the movie set for Catch-22 is about a mile south of here. Runway and all."

"The movie stunk," I said.

"We're not going to watch the movie."

"Yeah."

"Let's tell them about our plans later," he said.

"Yeah. They might leave us."

"Think we ought to tell them about the checkpoint?"

"I think we should."

I took off my clothes and dove in the clear water. It was surprisingly warm but refreshing. Two ladies came down as I got out. They said hello and took off their clothes. We talked, then Kip and I got dressed and returned to the truck. We explained what we had heard.

"What do you think?" Kristine asked Steve.

"No one's ever going to look behind those carpet squares," Robby said.

"I noticed one square is coming loose," Steve said. "We need to take care of that before we head any farther north."

"We can stop for some glue in Hermosillo," Robby said.

Kristine looked at me.

"You'll be all right if you stay calm," I said.

She wished I hadn't told them. You could see it in her eyes. I found a taco left over from the previous night, ate it and chased it with warm beer. It felt good. It felt good to be alive and free. To hell with turning myself in. All I wanted now was to be in Caroline's arms. If things went well on the road, I could be in LA in twenty-four hours.

Everyone agreed to kill some time at the old movie set. We came across a market along the way. It was a little shack with mostly empty shelves. We bought a six-pack and headed south. The gravel road crossed the asphalt runway at the end farthest from the gulf. Steve cut the engine and coasted down past some wooden shacks near the middle of the strip. The gulf was blue in the distance. Once he had stopped, all of us climbed out to explore the abandoned set. Kip and I walked over to one of the shacks. It had a door knocking quietly in the wind. The wind whistled in the weathered siding. We picked a spot in the shade and sat by ourselves. The hot sun had already turned the runway into a boiling mirage, all the way down to the gulf. We drank our beers in silence.

"You know I'll have to hike across the border," I said after a spell.

Kip smiled his dreamy smile.

"Want me to pick you up?"

"Yeah, tomorrow morning. I hope."

"Then what?"

"I don't know. Try to make things right with Caroline. If I can find her."

I shook my head.

"What?" Kip said.

"Oh, I had this grand revelation back in San Blas. About turning myself in. It was the night before you guys showed up."

I explained about the music and stars and the sense of inspiration I had felt.

"I was going to go back and join David Harris in prison. Be a big hero to the cause. With Caroline at my side, I could do anything...But fuck that."

Kip chuckled.

"Yeah, I'd rather be bumming around Europe again. You still up for that?"

"Sure," he said.

"Yeah. I'll try to get her to come along with us, but if not..."

"Maybe it will work out."

"Yeah, I'm kind of doubting it, but whatever happens, brother, I ain't going to prison."

Kip smiled his dreamy smile again.

Steve came to find us later. Kip and I followed him over to the panel wagon. I looked in the back. They had made everything neat.

"We've decided to take the train from Guaymas," I said.

Steve shrugged. Robby was staring at us as if we had ripped him off for taking a ride this far. Kristine spoke up.

"Sure, you guys, we understand. No sense in you taking a risk."

"You'll be all right."

"Well, let's go," Steve said.

I climbed in back with Kip and Steve shut the door.

26

Steve muscled the wagon up a dusty road to the highway and turned north towards Guaymas. The sparkling blue waters of the gulf were visible off to our left for several miles. Then the town of Guaymas grew up around us and the gulf was lost from view.

After a several wrong turns, Steve found the train station. I got out with Kip to check the schedule. We had missed the morning train and there would not be another one until later that evening. There was however another train that pulled into Hermosillo from the east in two hours.

"We've got time to catch that one," I said.

"What's the hurry?"

"I don't want to sit around here for ten hours."

Kip shrugged and looked off into the distance.

"What?" I said.

"I think we should wait?"

"Look, like that guy Frank said, the checkpoint is north of town. So what the hell could happen between here and Hermosillo?"

"A lot. You never know."

"Well, stay if you like. I'm taking the ride to Hermosillo."

I walked back over to the panel wagon.

"What's up?" Steve said.

I explained about the other train out of Hermosillo. Kip came up and leaned with his back against the truck.

"You don't mind, do you?" I asked Steve.

"No. Happy to give you a lift."

I got ready to climb in back. Kip stood there looking off in the distance.

"Are you coming?"

"Look, we could have some lunch and a few beers and walk around town."

"I'm leaving, Kip. Make up your mind."

Kip kicked at the ground and climbed in with me.

"We'll be in Nogales before sundown," I said.

Kip lay on his back and stared at the roof of the truck without another word. I patted him on the shoulder.

There were some attempts at conversation up front along the way but it soon died in the desert heat. The mountains were dry and the wind blew through the truck like a hair dryer.

"We need to find that glue," Kristine said as we neared the outskirts of Hermosillo.

"We'll find a store," Steve said.

"Fuck, man," Robby said. "Let's just go."

He looked back at me. His face was flush with paranoia. I leaned back against the wall of the panel wagon, eager to get away from him and his bummer energy.

Kip got up to see where we were going and pointed at two old men sitting out in front of a café.

"Pull over here, Steve, and I'll ask these two old relics where the train station is."

Steve pulled the wagon to the side of the road.

"Ask him where we can find that glue."

Kip jumped out and struck up a conversation with the two old men. The rest of us sat inside the truck watching.

"I'm taking the wheel," Robby said. He got out to switch places with Steve.

"You're sure?" Steve said.

"Yeah, man. I'll feel better if I'm driving."

Steve climbed over Christine. Robby got into the driver's seat. Kip was still talking with the two old men. The one with a battered straw hat gestured and followed Kip over to the truck.

"He says it would be easier to show us."

"What, the glue or the train station?" I said.

"The glue. He said it's nearby and the train station's on the other side of town."

I wondered what this man wanted and looked at the others.

"Oh, man," Robby said, running a hand through his hair.

"All right, tell him to get in," Steve said.

The old man climbed in back with Kip and me and went up to lean over the front seat. Robby drove away. While I stared, the old man turned to smile at me. He had a mouth full of bad teeth. His eyes were brown and jaundiced looking. There were thick protuberances beneath each one. He smelled of old sweat and stale alcohol.

Impatient, I got up to look over the seat with him. We had started up into the hills behind town on a dirt road. There was nothing up here that we wanted and I was about say as much when the old man motioned for Robby to pull over in front of a shack.

"Vaminos," he said.

Kip followed him inside. A moment later Kip reappeared. The old man followed him out but stopped on the front porch. Kip came back to the truck.

"What the fuck is going on?" Robby said.

"He's trying to sell us some pot."

"What the fuck! Let's get out of here before we get our asses busted!"

Kip climbed in. Robby jammed the transmission into reverse. The old man turned his head from the dust as we pulled away. Robby was pushing hard down the hill along a maze of rutted dirt roads.

"How did we happen to get onto that subject?" I asked Kip.

"Best I can figure, he heard glue and thought we wanted to get high."

I shook my head at him.

"Think maybe you'd better brush up on your Spanish?"

"Might have to do that," he said with a smile.

I looked back at Robby, thinking to tell him, you can drop us anywhere near the station, when I noticed his eyes darting looks in the rear-view mirror. I looked that way and saw a red Baja bug racing around us. The driver quickly straddled the road out ahead and pulled to a stop, forcing Robby to stop too. The driver jumped out with a gun. He was alone and in street clothes and we were a good half-mile from the respectable part of town.

"Pull around him!" Steve shouted. "He's probably a fucking bandito!"

Robby tried but then a big sedan also pulled across the road up ahead. Three men got out and also trained their guns on us. The first man had pulled something out of his top pocket and waved it at us.

"It's a fucking badge!" Robby said.

I leaned forward.

"Look, Robby, remember this. They don't know a thing, so act like it."

"Aw fuck, man. We're going to get busted. We're going to get fucking busted, man. I know it."

"Cool it!" Steve said fiercely but under his breath. He glanced once at Robby and looked ahead.

The first man was approaching us cautiously, his revolver in both hands. His three partners were leaning over the hood of the sedan, still giving him cover.

Robby sat there with his hands gripping the wheel.

"Just relax, Robby," I told him. "They don't know a thing."

"You already fucking said that."

The man came around and motioned for all of us to get out of the wagon. After a cursory look inside, he called for his partners. They rushed over and quickly had us leaning against the side of the truck with our legs spread. Reflexively, I recoiled from the hot metal but the man frisking me kicked at my ankles, causing me to fall forward again. I leaned there with all my weight held up by my fingertips.

Once these men were certain we had no weapons, they relaxed and allowed us to stand. The cop who had shown us his badge carefully looked us over and stopped when his attention came to Robby. He smiled and pointed at his eye and back at Robby. This motion was repeated several times, as if to say, I can see you're guilty. And Robby fell completely apart in response.

"You," he said and gestured for all of us to get back in the wagon.

He climbed back into his Baja bug and waved for us to follow. The sedan pulled around behind us. Robby dropped the wagon into gear and moved forward. I spoke up.

"They may or may not find the stuff, but if they do, you should take the fall, Robby."

"Forget it, man!" he shouted back at me.

"Why not? They already think you're guilty."

227

"I'm not taking it alone!"

"If you won't spare your friends, you could at least spare me and Kip. This isn't our scene."

"Go fuck yourself! All right!?"

"He's probably right, Robby," Steve said.

"You can all go to hell!"

He looked around quickly.

"Who's going to help you if we're all inside?" I said.

"Oh, what? Like you've got money?"

"I do. More than you can imagine, Robby, and I'll play fair with you if you play fair with us."

"Right. You don't even have a car."

I sat back and stared into space. Kristine looked at Kip and me hopefully.

"Is it true? About the money?"

Kip nodded. Robby saw him in the rear-view mirror.

"Bullshit!"

"You had best see if you can talk some sense into your friend," I said.

"Why should I take the rap for everyone? Huh? Tell me that."

"Because you're driving. We could be hitch-hikers for all they know. Anyway, it's not going to make you feel any better to have us in jail too."

Disgusted with him, I leaned back against the wall. There was nothing more to say. I heard Kristine working on him.

"Please, Robby, maybe nothing will happen. But if it does? Don't you see? You could save everyone."

"No!"

"Please. We'll do everything we can to get you out."

"Forget it!"

"Oh come on, Robby. Just think it over, okay?"

"Forget it. All right?"

That was it. Kristine gave up. He would or he wouldn't. I met his eyes in the rear-view mirror. I didn't think he would.

We followed the lead car onto a long gravel driveway and parked in front of a stone courthouse. Once out of the wagon, we were escorted up wide concrete steps and in through an arched opening. Someone guarded us in the foyer while our fate was discussed in the next room. We heard voices and laughter. A woman stuck her head around the corner and smiled before disappearing again. Presently, a uniformed guard came out and led us up a long flight of stairs. At the top of them, we were led into a room. There was a square table with chairs. The guard closed the door and we were alone.

Four sash windows filled one length of the room and were open. The adjacent wall was lined with suitcases.

"Fuck, look at that," Steve said.

"What?" I said.

"Those two suitcases over there on top. They're some of the ones that the beach cleaner dug up."

"God, do you think they got busted too?" Christine said.

"Fuck, it sure looks like it," Steve said.

I went over and forced one of the lower suitcases open. It was filled with marijuana. They all were. I tore off a chunk of herb and put it in my mouth. Kip came over to inspect the herb with me.

"Man, will you guys get away from there," Robby said.

He was pacing the room and running his hands through his wiry hair. Our eyes met.

"I'm telling you, man. It's a set up. They've probably got a two-way mirror in here."

"Robby, they don't even know what a two-way mirror is."

I went back to the windows. There was a dirt courtyard twenty feet below us with a stone wall connecting the outer wall of the courtyard to the building. This connecting wall began directly under the windows and was as wide as a man's body. A well-placed jump would place you neatly outside the jail in a matter of seconds, but then what? I looked at Kip. He shook his head. I examined a few more of the suitcases and went back to sit down.

I didn't think they would find the marijuana. It was well hidden. Besides, Kristine and Steve would back us up. We were only hitch-hikers.

Robby paced around the room. Kip remained at the window.

"Are you going to sink your friends?" I asked him.

"Shove it, Clay."

"We've already been through that, Robby. As I said, I promise to help you if you cooperate. Otherwise?"

"Oh yeah. Big shot."

He turned to the Steve and Kristine.

"Did you hear that? He's a big shot."

I stood up and went back to the windows. The town was quiet in the heat of the day. No one was in the courtyard. There was a clear path to the outside, unless someone happened to be waiting on the roof.

"I'm really scared," Kristine said, grabbing hold of Steve's arm.

"Just relax. Everything's going to work out."

I watched him hug her. I could see he didn't believe it. Neither did she.

Like a bird in an open cage, I wanted to flee, but it wasn't that easy. If I ran, it would not be good for the others. Then they would definitely tear the truck apart, if they had not done so already.

Therein lay the dilemma. If they found it, these windows and this opportunity would slam shut for good. My heart raced while weighing the matter.

Just then, the door opened and a kindly old man in civilian clothing came in.

"You are comfortable?"

He looked and waited for our response. Kristine spoke.

"Yes, we're fine. Can we go soon?"

"Yes." He made a gesture with his hand. "Only one minute. We are sorry to have trouble. We find nothing."

He smiled more broadly at Kristine.

The cop who had pulled us over came in and spoke urgently with the old man. The old man waved him off at first. Then he read Robby's eyes. Robby had seen the screwdriver. All of us had seen the screwdriver. The one who had pulled us over had found the panels. The two men left abruptly, closing the door behind themselves.

"Goddamn it, they're going to find it!" Robby said.

He began to pace the room more intensely now.

"Fuck, man. They're going to find it for sure."

"Shut up," Steve said.

But it was true. I went to the window. The words came through very loud and urgently, but as if locked in amber.

NOW! GO NOW!

But there was that other thing. Death. What if someone was waiting on the roof to shoot me and my young life ended here, my blood soaking into the dirt of a dusty Mexican town on a dying afternoon.

But the words kept screaming at me.

GO! GO NOW!

I hesitated. It might all work out and I would have lost my life for nothing.

But the words kept screaming at me.

GO! GO, YOU LOUSY COWARD!

Wanting my freedom more than anything else in this world, I had one foot out the window and was ready to jump when the door swung open and two guards with M-1's rushed in. One of them quickly yanked me back into the room and closed the windows. The other one motioned for us to sit down.

Our chance to escape was over. The trap had shut.

The kindly old man came in right after the guards, but he wasn't so kindly now. We had watched while he made a fool of himself and he was angry. A woman followed him in and interpreted.

We would be questioned one by one. Then we would be transferred to the state prison here in Hermosillo. Within 48 hours we would be allowed to see an attorney and given an audience with a member of the local consulate. Everything else would be explained at the prison. He left with the interpreter. The guards remained.

I started to say something to Kip but was cut short with the wave of a rifle barrel. And so it began. They broke Robby, just as I figured they would, and he had implicated Kip, of all things. Impulsively, when asked how he could have bought the marijuana without speaking Spanish, he had told them Kip was the interpreter. He had never thought to tell the truth, or say nothing at all.

After bringing him back, they took Kip, then me next. I told them I was a hitchhiker and didn't know a thing. I still had hopes they would let me go.

Once they had taken all our statements, the guards left. I went back to the windows. There were guards on both sides of the courtyard now. As I stood there, the others discussed their fears but they weren't mine. They feared what would happen to them on this side of the border. I feared what would happen once they discovered who I was. It wouldn't take the Americans long to figure it out, a few weeks at most.

Well, there was nothing to do but keep my mouth shut. Anything could happen in the meantime.

A guard came in and spoke to us in Spanish. Kip nodded and turned to the rest of us.

"He wants to know if we're hungry. It will be too late to feed us by the time we get to the prison."

Everyone agreed. The guard asked me another question. Kip smiled.

"What," Steve said.

"Would we like some beer?"

"If he's offering, sure, I'll take a beer," Steve said.

Kip nodded. The guard left, closing the door.

"Hey, we forgot to tell him which kind," I said.

Kristine, who had been crying, looked up at me and hung her head again.

The guard returned later holding five plates stacked on top of each other, each of them covered with foil. Having passed them around, he opened each beer with a can opener before leaving.

We ate in silence, mostly. The food was good, very simple and good. When it came to the last beer, I encouraged Robby to take it. He was in bad shape.

Having finished my meal, I belched and pushed the plate away.

"Well, I suppose I should roll a joint."

"God, Clay. You have such a macabre sense of humor."

I looked at Kristine.

"What difference does it make now?"

She shook her head and looked away. I shrugged at the others. What did it matter? We were going to prison and nothing we thought or said or felt would change that fact now.

Within the hour, they started to book us. I was taken first and placed in a holding cell downstairs. While I sat there waiting for the others to arrive, my mind busied itself with rearranging the events of that day. Things seemed fairly straightforward in hindsight. All I had to do was wait for the next train. A few hours enjoying the sights and I would be a free man. The thought of it dug at my heart.

A guard came down a bit later with Steve. Kip arrived next, then Kristine and last of all Robby. With all of us together again, we were led outside and placed in the back of a van with bench seats along the walls. A guard sat by the back door with an M-1 in his lap. The driver worked his way through a succession of dark, empty streets. The inside of the van was dark too except when we passed by a street-lamp and the others faces would be lit up briefly in the light and shadows.

At the outskirts of town, the driver started circling up a steep hill, the road winding around and ever higher, until we came to the top and the prison. A parapet stood at each corner and a stone foundation wall buttressed the prison where the hill fell away. All in all, it looked hard and unkind and impenetrable.

We were led up to a black iron gate. The guard inside opened it. He had a holstered revolver with the holster catch conspicuously unfastened. Now transferred to his care, the other guards returned to the van and drove away.

We stood in a long, arched tunnel. The white plaster walls around us were worn and soiled from many years of grief.

The guard led us down the tunnel and into a freshly painted office. A large desk was situated in a prominent position with bookshelves lining the wall behind it and a family portrait pointing our way. The young man in the photo had pale skin, soft, handsome features and sad eyes. He also had a lovely wife and two contented young boys who did not appear to know yet that such places existed.

A window with bars looked out over the city. The city lights dispersed little by little until there was nothing but the blackness of the desert beyond them.

The guard placed our files on top of the desk, instructed us to sit and left, locking the door behind himself. I noticed a box of cigars next to our files.

"Maybe they offer you a cigar to go with the beer," I said.

Kristine shook her head. Kip smiled. Steve and Robby just stared at me.

After some minutes, the door opened and an urbane looking man in his late thirties came in. He was older and sadder than the man in the picture, but still handsome. He nodded at us, sat down at the desk and picked up our files, perusing them one by one. With each new file, he spoke the name listed on it and looked up to see which face went with the name. When it came to Kristine's file, he merely looked up with a nod.

Once he had satisfied himself, he placed the reports down and rubbed his eyes, as though it had been painful.

"Do you understand the charges against you?" he asked.

His English was clear and carried only a trace of his nationality.

"I'm innocent," I said. "And so is my friend Kip here."

"Fucker," Robby said under his breath.

The warden snapped a look at Robby and looked back at me.

"It's true," I said. "We were just hitchhiking and I want to know when we can expect to be released."

The warden studied me and the faces of the others before looking back at me again.

"That is for the courts to decide."

He gave me time to absorb that much before continuing.

"You are in Mexico now and in our country, unlike your own, a man is guilty until proven innocent."

Kristine gasped as if she had taken a sap to the head. I felt badly for her. It was bad news for all of us. Our fantasies of an early release had just fluttered away like papers off a cliff.

"When can we make a phone call?" I asked further.

"Tomorrow. If not then, the next day. Also, I will arrange a meeting with your consulate as soon as possible."

He got up, walked over to the window then turned to face us.

"The consulate will assist you with an attorney and any personal matters, but I must warn you not to have false hopes. Our legal system is very long and bureaucratic in nature. There are some Americans who have been here for over seven years now."

He returned to his chair. His face was pale and solemn beneath his thick, black hair, but all in all he seemed kind, if kindness mattered under such circumstances.

He went on to explain in more detail the nature of our few rights and privileges and responsibilities. I hardly listened, lost in thoughts of what was to come next for me, once the American authorities got wind of my fate.

The director pushed a button, jarring me from my thoughts. The same guard appeared and escorted us further down the long, arched tunnel and deeper into the bowels of the prison, a journey that was becoming all the more dark and surreal to me, given the marijuana I had eaten.

We came to a stairwell and were led upstairs. At the top landing, we were ushered down a short hallway and into another room. As was true of everywhere in the prison except the director's office, the white plaster walls were soiled as if from countless years and countless hands. The guard told us to wait and departed. The door was left open.

From beyond the walls, I heard a muffled din. It was the sound of many voices, of all humanity, of all hopes and dreams and despair.

A short time later, I heard footsteps slowly climbing the stairs. And behind it, the din, the low, muffled din of a thousand voices, a poison to my spirit.

Why had I been in such a hurry? I looked at the others and saw the same misgivings in their eyes. If only we could have back that day.

The footsteps were coming down the hallway now. I turned towards the door, waiting to see who came with them.

27

The first light of dawn had blushed in the eastern sky, revealing in murky detail the layout of the long, narrow prison cell where I lay. Bunk beds lined both walls and other men slept in them, some snoring. The prison was otherwise still and quiet.

I had been given an upper bunk in the night, had slept little and was awake now, my mind pacing back and forth with the restlessness of a tiger. Over and over, I kept replaying the events from the previous day, unable to change them, but unwilling to accept the result. This was the end of the line for me. If there was a way out, I could not see it. Throughout the night, I had tried to conjure some way to escape these foot thick plaster walls, only to find despair and frustration. I longed to be back out on the open highway and move freely, but was trapped.

After our brief indoctrination, a guard had led me straight through to this cell, leaving me with but a scant mental picture of the prison layout. Anyway, that gutful of grass had made the short walk seem like a carnival ride through a house of mirrors.

Now, in the dim morning light, the grim feel of the place was more clearly revealed to me. The soiled plaster walls and bare concrete floors reeked of impoverished Mexican outposts run by dissolute officials.

There were two windows opposite me, both imbedded with round, black iron bars in place of glass, and a total of ten bunk beds, six along the inner wall and four on the wall with the windows. In the center of the cell, between the windows, an enclosure made of wood and woven blankets stood against the wall. That was the bathroom. Inside, there was an old toilet, a sink and a bucket. A water pipe came from high along the wall and fed down behind the curtain. To flush the toilet, you filled the bucket. Why the Mexicans had connected the water pipe to the sink and not the toilet, I presumed only they could explain.

There was a second-story balcony outside the windows, encircling a rectangular courtyard below it. The balcony had no awning along its two sides but was recessed under a tile roof on both ends. The courtyard below was the size of a basketball court and had many cell doors around it, as did the second story balcony. On both levels and at both ends of the prison, short hallways extended out from the shaded verandas towards the exterior walls, with more iron gates and presumably more prisoner cells. One of the gates had an Indian blanket hanging over it, suggesting that one could have privileges and upgrades.

My prison cell was near one end of the balcony, allowing me a view of that shaded veranda and adjoining short hallway. A large, arched opening stood at the end of the hallway with the same black iron bars running through it. I had no view of what was below the opening but it appeared to look out into an open yard of some kind. I could see a stone wall beyond that area, along with a parapet anchoring a corner of the prison. The peak of the hill rose up beyond the parapet.

My attention turned to the single bed at the end of the room farthest from the gate. It was positioned perpendicular to the others and had a curtain surrounding it for privacy. The word CABO was painted on the wall next to the curtain. The lettering was done up nicely in black script. I had been told that you answered to this man when it came to issues within the cell.

I watched a fellow prisoner stir and go inside the enclosure, disgusted with everything I heard. The man pulled back the curtain, poured the bucket of water down the toilet, refilled the bucket from the adjacent spigot and went back to his bunk. The whole cell now stunk. That was Mexico: never enough money to do something right unless you were wealthy.

Another man went to the toilet and back to his bunk. Other men began to stir and use it in succession. I tried to ignore it all.

A loud clang echoed up from the lower level of the prison, followed by rapid footsteps and voices, all of it distant and muffled.

"¡Vaminos, hombres...La cuenta!"

I heard numbers being called out in response, briskly, and in succession.

Another clang followed, then more footsteps, the clang of another gate and the brisk, orderly count being conducted again.

"¡Vaminos, hombres!...¡La cuenta!"

This procedure continued around the entire lower level.

Everyone in our cell was awake now with some of the men standing in the narrow passageway between the bunkbeds, talking quietly. A minute passed and the main gate to the second floor flew open and footsteps came down the balcony. The counting of prisoners continued cell by cell in our direction.

Then I saw a guard in a gray uniform and cap march by the windows, followed by a Mexican prisoner with a clipboard. The two of them turned down the short hallway leading to our cell. The guard unlocked the door with a large key and flung it open. The prisoner with the clipboard called out.

"¡VAMINOS, HOMBRES...LA CUENTA!"

Anyone still in bed at this point hit the floor. I jumped to the floor in my underwear. The young Mexican inmate came briskly down the aisle with his clipboard, placing a check by each number as he heard them called out.

"¡UNO, DOS, TRES, CUATRO, CINCO!"

The guard followed along behind him, looking impassively at each face.

When they got to me, everything came to a halt. The kid slapped the clipboard against my chest. I looked from him to the guard. His gray officer's cap was askew and soiled from hair oil and the years in general. He stared at me, waiting. Every Mexican in the cell was staring and waiting. I shrugged. The punk slapped me again with his clipboard, but harder than before.

"What number, Señor?"

"How the hell do I know?" I said.

My impulse was to take the punk's head off.

"Numero seis," someone whispered.

"Pinche cabron," the guard muttered. He ordered everything to begin again. The Mexican with the clipboard went to the front of the cell and started over.

"¡UNO, DOS, TRES, CUATRO, CINCO!"

"Seis," I said.

The fat guard jerked the clipboard from the punk's hands and jammed it into my throat. His face was six inches from mine. The scent of stale booze mixed with his hair oil.

"Pinche gringo. ¿Que numero?"

"SEIS," I said, as loud as I could through the clipboard. He nodded at me slowly for a moment before handing the clipboard back to the punk. They continued on their way.

"¡SIETE, OCHO, NUEVE, DIEZ, ONCE, DOCE!"

"You greasy son of a bitch," I said while rubbing my throat.

"Ssshhh," this kind young Mexican prisoner said to me.

He smiled sympathetically but I was ready to take his head off too. I wasn't accustomed to taking orders, even if they did come with my best interest in mind.

The guard and his punk with the clipboard had reached the end of the aisle and came back the other way.

"¡DIECIOCHO, DIECINUEVE, VEINTE!"

Their count completed, the two men went out the door. The young prisoner closed the door. The guard with the keys locked it. The door to the cell across the hall was opened and the count began anew.

The young Mexican who had tried to help me shrugged as if to say, only God could understand and went about making his bed. All the Mexicans were making their beds.

I looked out the window, aware of the countless voices again, the whispering and chattering of a thousand lost souls. The reality of my situation burned in my heart. Ten hours did not seem very long to wait for one's freedom, now that it was lost.

Of course, there were countless other ways that my life might have turned out differently. If not for Kip, I would not have found myself in Tucson, and hence in Mexico. If not for Eric showing up, I would never have run off to Hawaii. If not for running off to Hawaii, I would never have met Kip. If not for the war, I would never have met Caroline, leading to that day when Eric showed up at our doorstep. On and on it went, until I was back in the womb. Finally, I was standing there in a Mexican prison, and nothing I said or thought was going to change things.

Robby came to mind. That fool. He had never won a poker game. I would have bet my life on that one. That cop hadn't suspected anything until Robby freaked out. I wondered where they had put him.

Then I remembered the slow, measured footsteps ascending the stairs and the emotionless looking man in his thirties who had come with them. Maximillian was his name; pale skin, black hair combed straight back. He was also a prisoner and fluent in both English and Spanish. His job was to explain the rules and answer any questions we might have before they led us off to our cells. One thing had become abundantly clear in conversing with Maximillian. He didn't give a crap about us and our personal fates. He was looking out for number one and nobody else.

We had been invited to call him Max. I figured to be calling him Maximillian, if it were all the same. Somehow, he did not look like any Max I had ever known.

From that room, a guard had taken us one by one to our cells, my personal journey down those darkened hallways like some strange carnival ride, high as I was at the time. The cabo of my cell had been awakened to receive me and he issued a set of rules I was to obey before assigning me to the last available bunk and going back to bed. Most of the prisoners in the cell had awakened and their whispers went on for some time before everyone was back to sleep.

I felt my bruised ribs and wondered what the guards had done with Kip. When they started to separate us in the night, I had protested and was silenced with a club.

I was still grousing over that memory when the cabo parted the curtain to his sleeping area and stepped out. He wore a white tank top and black pants and stood there combing his thinning hair straight back. He put the comb away and checked his nails. Over his bed, a framed print of the Virgin of Guadalupe hung on the wall. This was the patron saint of Mexico. She had a large, red heart that was suffused with a radiant glow.

Needing to urinate badly, I stepped behind the curtained enclosure provided for that purpose. When I was done, I poured the bucket of water down the hole and started to leave, then thought better of it and filled the bucket as I had found it.

All the other prisoners were milling about at this point, waiting for the count to be completed in the other cells. I had learned that once this was done, our cell door would be unlocked and we would be free to roam about the prison as we saw fit. Beyond the gate to our cell and through the two windows, I could see other men milling about in other prison cells, anticipating this impending moment of freedom.

The cabo came down the aisle and ordered me to make my bed, then stood there giving instructions. When my handiwork had left a little fold of the sheet beneath my blanket, he told me to straighten it out. Satisfied at last, he walked back to his bed, combing his hair again. I considered ways to straighten him out.

I had been given two sheets and an old army blanket, and no pillow. Some men had nice blankets and real pillows. As before, I sensed a degree of commerce and capitalism at work here. I would have been happy just to have a pillow. My jacket wadded up under my head had left me with a sore neck.

Tired of the long wait, I started to climb back up on my bunk but the young Mexican kid cautioned me with a wave of his hand. Apparently getting back on your bunk before breakfast was one more cause for getting clubbed.

When the cell door opened, everyone rushed out with a cup and bowl in hand. I drifted out with them. They had turned right towards the chow line. I turned left down the short hallway outside our cell, drawn by the arched opening and view of the Sonoran Desert. The opening was taller than a man and reached almost to the concrete floor. I stepped up onto the bottom ledge and stared out at the wide vista. Freedom was that close, less than a hundred feet away.

Hunger eventually overtook me and I went to see what they served for breakfast. A table with a large pot had been arranged at the end of the long balcony to my left. The serving line formed on the opposite side and went all the way around the balcony. Each man received a ladle of whatever was inside, along with a cup of coffee. A young Mexican hurried by and I caught a glimpse of the offering. It looked like watery Crème of Wheat. I decided my hunger could wait.

In the courtyard below, a similar ritual was playing out. I leaned over the plaster railing, looking for Kip. I wanted to know if he was all right. I wanted let him know I was sorry. He had been right. We should have waited in Guaymas.

Failing to see Kip, I returned to the window and climbed back up onto the lower ledge. The scent of damp sagebrush wafted in the air. A cool breeze tickled my skin. Several buzzards soared up and disappeared out of sight with the morning thermals. The glow of dawn had brightened to a clear blue sky. The Sonoran Desert looked so damned peaceful.

While attempting to block out the din of a thousand restless voices, a dream from the previous night returned to my thoughts. Caroline and I had been driving around Hawaii together, white clouds drifting across a clear blue sky, happily in love. Then, without warning, our car began to fall apart and Caroline was sucked beneath the wheels. The dark dream lingered within me, infused with a thousand regrets.

As more men returned to the surrounding cells with their bowl of gruel, I caught the scent of sausage being cooked and considered going to investigate but decided against it. It would be pleasant to have a warm, hearty breakfast, but not so pleasant watching someone else eating theirs. Besides, I gathered that sticking your nose where it did not belong was one more cause for getting a club to the head.

Two Mexicans gave me the eye going back into our cell. I assumed this was for having commandeered the window. Then I realized that they had little reason to be happy in this place, with or without another stinking gringo.

I looked out over the desert again. The sun had risen and the breeze had warmed with it.

How ironic, I thought. After the many narrow escapes, to fall for the oldest trick in the book. Love.

Someone somewhere was going to have a good laugh. It wouldn't take them long. The Mexicans had finger-printed us. No doubt they planned to turn the prints over to the consulate, which in turn would forward them along to the State Department in DC, which would no doubt forward them along to the FBI. I tried to picture some prick with a crew-cut kicking his feet up on his desk and slapping his hands behind his head with a smile.

Given the bureaucracy within the State Department, I had two, maybe three weeks at the most to get out of this hole. But how? I touched the soiled plaster walls with my hand. They were a foot thick, plus the bars in the windows were barely far enough apart to poke my head through. Even if I could somehow collapse my rib cage, there was a thirty-foot drop into a dirt courtyard. Assuming I survived the fall, there was little chance I would walk away without a broken leg. And even if I did, there remained a twenty-foot wall around the courtyard, with a parapet and armed guard at either end. If by some miracle the guards ignored me and I got over the twenty-foot wall, I would be faced with almost two hundred miles of desert to cross; like walking through a hot oven.

I stared out at the desert floor. It was already a mirage along the horizon at this early hour. The saguaros and desert brush appeared to be floating on a lake of molten fire. It was pleasant enough in the alcove of the window, but when I reached my forearm out into the light, it burned from the desert sun.

Freedom was right there, as far as I could throw a rock, but a man unprepared would die out there from exposure; maybe four hours before he was delirious, eight if he was lucky and it would be over, the body shriveled to a husk, the spittle caked like salt around the lips from heat prostration. And all those considerations were only academic unless you could get through the bars and overcome the other hurdles.

To that end, I needed money. You could buy anything in Mexico, even your freedom, but I needed someone who could get into my bank accounts in Mazatlán. With money, perhaps I could bribe the guard when they took us to court. I assumed they had to take us to court at some point.

If it ever came to me crossing the desert on foot, I had learned enough during those idle hours in Tucson to believe I could make it. A few essential things and I could survive.

While I wrestled with these questions, someone came by and slapped me on the leg. I turned around to find two Mexicans looking for trouble.

"Vaminos, hombre," one of them said.

He tried to push his way into the window, thinking I would leave, but I shoved him back. At this, he spit on the concrete floor and challenged me to a fight. I smirked. He could have his horseshit machismo. I had the window. Let him climb up here and take it from me.

I was about to turn away when I noticed two men hurrying down the hallway. The man who had spit did not see them coming and received a good crack upside the head with a club. I winced at the sound of his skull meeting wood.

With that man now dazed and bleeding on the concrete floor, the one with the club yelled something and two other men appeared from around the corner. They lifted the wounded man to his feet and dragged him off. His friend was ordered to clean up the spit and blood.

The Mexican with the club looked hard at me and left with his fellow enforcer. I had no idea how these men came to have the power to mete out punishment, but clearly spitting on the floor was taboo and standing in the window was okay. In no mood to press my luck, I abandoned the window and resumed my search for Kip.

Circumventing the man with the mop, I stepped from the shady hallway into the brilliant sunlight of the balcony. Somewhere in the prison, a radio was playing mariachi music, reviving memories of my brief sojourn in Mazatlán with Caroline. I followed the balcony east until I was out of the sun and leaned over the plaster railing. The western end of the balcony was lit up like a projector screen, the white walls almost impossible to behold. The red tile roof above them wavered in the heat.

Below me, the line of sunlight had progressed halfway across the concrete courtyard. The serving tables had been cleared away and a group of men were engaged in a game of basketball. A crowd stood around the perimeter, watching. Backboards on either end of the courtyard were mounted to metal poles. The poles had been welded to car wheels, tires and all. The tires appeared to have been filled with concrete for ballast.

I counted sixteen Americans downstairs, but there was no sign of Kip or Steve, or even Robby. Unable to see the area directly below the balcony where I stood, I started around towards the opposite side.

On my way, I noticed two black men staring at me from across the balcony, and looking none too friendly about it. Assuming they were Americans, I headed that way. I really didn't care what they thought of me. I just wanted to know what the hell was going on around here.

Passing along the eastern veranda, I found a man shining shoes in the north facing hallway. Two other men were waiting their turn in the shade. Another tall, arched window looked out at the desert in that direction.

At the opposite end of the veranda, there was the window that looked out at the hill rising up behind the prison wall. The wall was very high and had parapets on either end with a guard in each one.

Reaching that window and looking down, I saw into a small courtyard that contained two, elevated concrete water basins. Each basin had a shallow curb around it and a finely polished working surface of approximately three feet by ten feet. Men stood there with water sluicing through the basin, washing clothes in the morning sun.

My curiosity satisfied, I turned back towards the shaded veranda and passed the corner cell with an Indian blanket hanging over the entrance. The scent of fried food wafted out. My impulse was to peek in but I already knew that such intrusions could warrant a crack in the head. I turned left down the long balcony opposite my cell and had gotten a few paces when I spotted Kip. He was looking up at me from the shade of the opposite balcony. An almost imperceptible smile crossed his face. I found a vacant place along the railing and leaned over to wait. Kip walked around beneath the eastern veranda in order to avoid the basketball game.

"Are you okay?" I asked when he reappeared below me.

He nodded.

"And you?"

I shrugged.

"Did you get your call?"

"No," he said. "Did you?"

I shook my head.

"I'm hungry," I said.

"Didn't you eat that swill this morning?"

"No."

"I tasted it. The coffee has saltpeter in it."

"Great."

"We can buy food if they give us our money," he said.

"Let's ask them for a ride to the border instead."

"Yeah."

"I'll drop you down a note as soon as I find some paper," I said.

"Okay."

"Have you seen Robby?"

"He's in his cell. He won't come out." Kip pointed in the direction of the northeast corner. "Have you seen Steve?" he asked.

245

"No. I haven't seen any Americans up here." Kip pointed in the direction of the black guys. "I know. I was going to ask them what's happening."

He nodded and asked me about Kristine.

"They took her right after they took you," I said. "The women are below us, on the north side. That's what I was told."

"She took it okay."

We stared in silence for a moment. The basketball went flying by Kip's head and he ducked. Someone out of my vision threw it back into the court and the game resumed. Kip looked back up at me.

"I'm going to see if they'll give us a chance to meet out front," I said. He nodded again. "You ask first if you get a chance."

"Okay," he said.

We stared at each other again.

"I guess I'll keep looking around."

"Yeah. I'll send you a note, too," he said.

"Don't call home until we talk."

He gave me a thumbs-up and started to walk away.

"Kip?"

"Yeah?" he said, turning back.

"I'm sorry."

"Don't go south," he said with a resigned shrug.

"Yeah. I should have listened."

He smiled.

"Me too."

He let that thought linger before walking away.

I pushed away from the rail and started towards the two black men. They were both leaning over the rail in the sun. One of them turned his head to size me up briefly before turning back to watch the basketball game.

"Don't be sendin' no note down there, you honky motherfucker."

"Why's that?"

He pushed away from the rail and got in my face as if I had challenged him. He had coarse black skin, a flat nose and a very large afro. The afro was big enough to have offered shade, if I had been on the right side of him. I stood my ground and stared. He glanced back at his friend.

"Did you hear that, Muddy, this motherfucker wants to know why?"

246

In keeping with the color of his skin, Muddy was more mulatto in appearance. He also appeared to be more impartial.

"Yeah, I heard it, Leon. So go ahead and set this honky straight before he gets his dumb ass in trouble."

Leon turned back and reviewed me in the hot sun.

"I'm gonna tell you, just to save your dumb white ass from the hole. Because that's where they're gonna throw you if you start passing notes between floors."

I rubbed the sweat from the back of my neck and parked all the things I had been thinking to ask Leon. Setting aside his bad attitude, he was actually doing me a favor.

"Thanks for the tip," I said and continued down the balcony.

"I should have let your ass rot," Leon said.

I ignored him and kept walking.

"That's what I should have done. Hey! Hey, I'm talking to you, honky!"

I suspected their lousy attitude was the result of too much prison time and made a mental note to avoid them. Leon and Muddy could make this dismal place even more dismal.

Having reached the far end of the balcony, I turned left down another wide, shaded hallway and found a man with a large griddle cooking tortillas. The griddle resembled a three-foot wide conga drum. There were stacks and stacks of tortillas on top of it and a line of men waiting to purchase them. Penniless, I stared, hoping that lunch would be better than breakfast.

I turned back the other way and came alongside an iron gate beneath the shaded veranda. Beyond the gate, an arched foyer led to a set of tall, wooden doors. This was the main entrance to the upper floor. There were two small cells on my side of the main gate with Indian blankets over both the windows and doorways. The aroma of fried food again emanated from within.

A long sink hung from one wall of the shaded veranda itself and men were lined up there washing dishes. I headed back towards my cell, increasingly famished and depressed.

On the way, I saw Robby had made an appearance at the far end of the courtyard. He didn't notice me, but I saw him, standing with his hands in his pockets and staring wretchedly as men came and went from a small cell that functioned as the mercado. Each man entered empty-handed and left with a brown paper bag. Through the doorway, I saw open boxes of onions and tomatoes and peppers. A man served meat from behind a counter.

Tired of everything, I decided to try and sleep. The heat had become oppressive. I wanted to get out of the sun if nothing else.

Back in my cell, I found it empty. I climbed up onto my bunk. Paint was peeling off the ceiling above me. More mariachi music played in the distance. My mind decided an indictment of my life was in order. In little more than twelve hours, I had been clubbed for protesting prison rules, had fought with a couple of Mexicans over a window and had found myself in a civil war with two black men. And the very sight of Robby made me want to get a gun. I did not play well with others, it seemed. Conflict followed me everywhere I went. Why not go to war? Evidently I was very good at it. Only the freedom to head down the road a few more miles had allowed me to ignore the truth of my nature up to this point. My heart burned with the despair of men who are unable to escape their own failings.

As I lay there with these thoughts, another black man appeared at the door of the prison cell and sauntered down the aisle, jouncing a cane as he did. His muslin shorts and mesh swamp shoes invited comedy. His physique commanded respect. I prepared myself for more trouble but the man smiled at me, displaying a gold tooth.

"Good day, sir," he said in a deep voice that betrayed southern roots. "Colonel Green. Gentleman farmer and philosopher."

He offered his large, brown paw. I shook it, thinking he would squeeze me much harder than he did.

"Clay Matthews, deceased."

He laughed soundly.

"We heard you were here and assumed you to be hungry."

"Who are we?"

"Well, if you'll come along, we'll attend to your questions and hunger all at once."

28

Green made his way among the many restless, unhappy Mexicans crowding the balcony, tapping his cane jauntily along as he did. I followed behind him, effectively blinded by the morning sun and not seeing the passing faces until they were right on top of me. Two things were abundantly clear. None of these men held any affection for Green and none of them were prepared to tell him as much. Everyone we encountered stepped grudgingly out of his path, and by way of extension, mine.

I was preparing to ask Green my next question when I found he had stopped in front of me.

"Sorry about that, Green," I said, standing back from our collision.

"Most folks call me Colonel Green."

"Okay, Colonel. Shall I salute when I say that?"

He laughed soundly again.

"You know, Green, there's a lady in San Blas you just have to meet."

"Is she good looking?"

"More than that, she laughs on the same order of frequency as you do."

"I look forward to the occasion."

"Under any other circumstance, I would say let's go immediately."

Green smiled sadly and continued on his way up the balcony. I followed him forward and to the right under the eastern veranda.

"Your other questions?" Green said over his shoulder.

"Well, first of all, I was wondering what happened to my friend Steve."

"You will find him residing comfortably inside."

We had arrived to the alcove at the southeast corner and the door to the cell where I had smelled someone cooking earlier that morning. Green pulled back the Indian blanket and waved me into a twenty by twenty foot room populated with young Americans, eleven of them, including Steve, Green and me. There were the same window openings with black iron bars — one of them overlooking the wash area in back and one looking out over the balcony and courtyard — and the standard bathroom enclosure. What remained of wall space was lined with bunk beds and storage shelves and otherwise pasted over with magazine pictures. A large, circular fan was chewing up all the hot, humid air with the roar of a prop plane and Strange Days by the *Doors* was playing quietly in the background.

"Gentlemen," Green said. "I would like you to meet Clay Matthews. By his own account, deceased."

Everyone acknowledged me with a nod or a wave. Two were playing a game of chess. One was busy cooking. Another one lay on a top bunk reading and two others stood by a window, looking out towards the wash area. One of the parapets and its guard was visible off in the distance.

Steve got up and shook my hand.

"Sorry for the bummer," he said.

I shrugged.

"I might want to kill Robby but I don't see you at fault. Anyway, I'm just glad to see another gringo at this point. I was thinking I was up here all alone."

"Hardly. There are at least twenty-five of us up on this level."

"Where? I haven't seen another American all morning. That is, besides Leon and Muddy."

"Most of them have private cells like this and those who don't hide out with the ones who do until lunch. There's not much use eating the breakfast they serve us."

I acknowledged this truth and made a further scan of the room. Aside from a significant library of books, records and magazines, the makeshift kitchen, the stock of canned and fresh food and the magazine pictures plastered all over the walls, there were boxes of clothes shoved under the lower bunks and laundry drying on ropes hung between the upper bunks.

I looked again at Steve. His gaunt frame was always slightly hunched over, as if weary, but even more so now.

"By the way," I said to everyone in general. "What the hell happened to Muddy and his sidekick Leon?"

"Someone attempted to sell them into slavery," one man said.

"Casualties of an uncivil war," said another.

Green laughed.

"I take it you've met them, Mr. Matthews."

"No, I was engaged in a pissing contest with them. That's different."

Green laughed again and went back to writing in a notebook. Steve saw me staring at the food preparations.

"Have you eaten?" he asked me.

"No. Did you try that swill this morning?"

"Yeah. You weren't missing anything."

"Yeah. I couldn't seem to get past the resemblance to craft paste." He smiled. "Have you been in here all morning?"

"No. I only met Green at the gate ten, fifteen minutes ago. I told him about you."

"Where were you?"

"Down talking to Kristine."

"How is she?"

"All things considered, pretty good. We'd both like to kill Robby."

"He'll probably suffer more alive."

"Yeah, come to think of it."

I went back to staring at the food preparations. It was hard to ignore.

"Ah, Mr. Matthews, you look as if you can't believe your eyes," Green said.

"I feel like I'm dreaming."

He laughed soundly.

"Mr. Matthews, we're all dreaming in here."

He liked the sound of it so much he laughed again. The two men at the window came over and introduced themselves.

"General John Haynes, retired."

I shook his hand and the other.

251

"Sergeant McTavish, 101st Airborne."

"Clay Matthews, deceased."

McTavish had a craggy face softened by round spectacles. He studied me without malice or mirth. Haynes was a man more or less my own height, six-two, six-three, with a long, narrow face further lengthened by a Van-dyke. His deep-blue eyes balanced a ruddy complexion and straight, well-proportioned nose. He looked at Green with a smile.

"Perhaps we should offer Mr. Matthews the extra bunk."

"He would be a splendid complement to our campaign," Green said.

I looked at Steve and then from face to face, not at all comfortable with being singled out under the circumstances. It smacked of privilege.

"You'd charge someone to move in?" I said.

"No no, Mr. Matthews," Green said. "You pay El Presidenté for the privilege."

"Who the hell is that?"

Green smiled.

"No one has clued you in yet?" Haynes asked me.

"Apparently not."

"This entire prison is run by the Mexican inmates, at least on the inside. The director picks the baddest mother fucker around, usually someone who has robbed some banks and killed a few people. The threat of violence tends to keep the other inmates in check. The president is then free to pick his own regime, vice president, captains, right on down the line. There's one on each level. Basically, the only thing the director and guards do is to make sure we stay locked up."

My mind quickly considered the ramifications.

"And who keeps an eye on El Presidenté in this scenario?

"You're starting to grasp the problem," Haynes said.

"So, Mr. Matthews," Green went on. "About taking the bunk."

I had already considered the advantages and disadvantages of his offer and realized, given the reality of my plight, it was best to leave well enough alone.

"I don't have the money, Green. At least not for the moment."

"Payment arrangements can be made," Green said.

"With all due respect, I'd be satisfied with a fork and a plate right now."

"Ah yes, Mr. Matthews, please forgive me. I'd nearly forgotten your hunger. As you can see, the kitchen help is whipping up a late breakfast just for you two."

Green slapped me on the back with a smile in saying this. I went over to shake the hand of the young man cooking. He had long, silky blonde hair and the face of a pubescent boy.

"Clay."

"Don," he said and returned to preparing the chorizo and eggs without another word. There were roasted green chilies, salsa, avocados and tortillas to go with the eggs.

Green spoke to me on his way out the door.

"McTavish and I are going on reconnaissance. Haynes here will fill you in while you're eating. I'll take you down to see the president when we get back."

He had dropped his affected speech in saying this. I revived it with my response.

"I will look forward to our continued discussion, Colonel."

Green smiled, revealing his gold tooth, and then broke out in laughter.

"Yes indeed. Mr. Matthews will be a fine complement. Wouldn't you agree, McTavish?"

"Subject to the proper review, as always, Colonel."

I watched them go out the door. McTavish was dead serious about something. It bled right through his craggy face and floppy blonde hair. Maybe he'd just been locked up in this Mexican prison for too many years, like Leon and Muddy.

Don handed Steve and me plates and we wasted no time in satisfying our hunger. I glanced up to see Haynes studying me from against the end rail of a bunk.

"What's with all this 'gentleman, farmer' crap?" I asked through the food.

"Just something to kill the time."

I nodded, understanding that and sorting through all the questions in my head.

"By the way, if you've got room, take Steve. I'm planning to break out tomorrow."

He laughed.

"We'll take that into consideration. Anything else you'd like to know?"

"How many Americans are here?"

"Roughly sixty. Actually, I think sixty-five with you and your friends, but it tends to change from day to day."

"What about those other people?" I said to Steve. "You know, those suitcases we saw at the police station?"

"Yeah, I heard from Kristine that it was two couples. The women are with her and the men downstairs."

"Bummer. I told Kip when it happened, it felt like bad karma."

"Why didn't you tell us that?"

"Would it have stopped you?"

"Probably not."

"Yeah."

The chess game broke up in a draw. The board was put away and the two men headed out the door, introducing themselves as they went by.

"Joe Delaney."

"Glenn Palmer."

"Clay Matthews."

Glenn's oval face was reminiscent of a medieval troubadour. Even his straight, dark hair was cut in a bowl. Joe was heartland America, a bland face and bland smile with coke bottle glasses and the remnants of acne.

"Under any other circumstances," Joe said going out the door.

"Under any other circumstances," I repeated and went back to the food. The fan droned loudly behind me, the hot air it produced mixing with and muffling the sounds of the basketball game going on downstairs. I looked back at Haynes.

"You were saying? About the rest of the Americans?"

"Oh yeah. There's another cell like ours across the way, ten in there. And another five guys scattered around in the big cells like you and Steve. The others are downstairs. Roughly forty of them down there. It can change from day to day, depending on who gets freed and who gets busted."

"How did you rate this spot?"

Haynes rubbed his thumb and fingers together.

"It's that or you know somebody."

The man reading a book snapped it shut and jumped down, offering his free hand on the way by.

"Francis."

"What are you reading?"

"Spengler's *Decline of the West*. You know it?"

"Know it? I'm living it."

Francis smiled and headed out the door.

Steve and I had soon finished our meals and Don went about cleaning up after us. There was something sad about him that I couldn't quite place; like his father had beaten him. Then, maybe he just didn't like prisons.

I joined Steve at the back window. Several Mexicans were bantering away while doing their wash in the yard below. Water splashed all about their bare feet and clothing. Life went on. Nothing was new under the sun. I turned back to face Haynes.

"I wonder about my money. Our money."

"Whatever you used to have, you can forget it," he said.

"I rather expected that."

"You're lucky to be alive. They shot one guy out on the highway. He must have had more than his life was worth."

"How would you know?"

"You don't, for sure, but his wife says he left Los Mochis with ten grand and three hundred kilos. They brought his body in the next day with enough grass to explain the shooting. The bulk of his load and the money had disappeared."

I pictured the scene. How completely helpless you would feel; a brief struggle, the disbelief and terror, then boom, garbled neuron brain wash fading to nothing. What a world. I got back to my own problems.

"I have money but I need to make a phone call." I turned to Steve. "How about you?"

"Kristine called home. Her father will be down in two days."

Green and McTavish came back in.

"Are you ready to meet El Presidenté?" Green asked me.

"Hell, how do I know? From what you've said, the man's a bastard."

Green put a hand on my shoulder.

"Come," he said. "I believe the two of you will get along just fine."

I followed him out the door and down the length of the balcony with the hot sun on our backs. Along the way, we passed Leon and Muddy.

"Gentlemen," Green said going by. "Good to see you engaged in peaceful activities."

You could see they had something planned for Green and it wasn't pleasant.

Once we had reached the western veranda, Green turned to face me.

"I'll do the talking."

"If I put up the money, is it possible to pass this thing on to Steve?"

"It's non-transferable," he said. I shook my head. "Mr. Matthews, you seem very reluctant to accept this opportunity."

"It's nothing personal. But I like it where I am, the food aside."

"Trust me, Mr. Matthews. One day soon you'll be thankful that I persuaded you."

Hardly convinced of that, I followed him down the short hallway, past the tortilla maker, and to the door of a cell. There was only one other cell in that hallway so this was as private as you were going to get and still be in the prison.

A blanket veiled the door and two men guarded it. Green addressed them in Spanish and one of the men poked his head into the room. A moment later, he held the blanket aside.

I followed Green into a den of thieves. Beer and mescal bottles littered a row of tables to one side of the room, along with several plates of half-eaten food. A pall of smoke hung in the air. I counted seven men sprawled out in chairs behind the tables, all unshaven and looking half drunk.

There was one who didn't look drunk and had the eyes of a tiger. I assumed him to be El Presidenté. He waved at two chairs opposite him. We sat and Green nodded respectfully. With a glance at me, El Presidenté returned the gesture.

"¿Que quieres, Señor Verde?"

Green started in with some idle talk and built up to his request. El Presidenté listened with the whites of his eyes shifting in the darkened room. Having heard all that Green had to say, he took a moment to reflect before answering.

"Dos mil pesos."

"Dos mil es bien," Green said.

When I started to say something, Green cut me off. I knew what he was thinking. Better to pay El Presidenté's price than try to negotiate. There would be less cause to argue when we told him he had to wait for the money.

El Presidenté had noted this exchange while eyeing me warily.

"Aver," he said and held out his hand.

Green shrugged and explained it might take a week, maybe more. El Presidenté told us to have the money wired. Green asked him for the phone call. Things went back and forth from there. We left without any promises. He would see about the phone call and think about the rest.

Green turned on me when we got outside.

"You do not follow instructions very well, Mr. Matthews."

"It's my money we're spending," I said.

"That is beside the point. You gave him reason to doubt or you may well have been moving your gear in at this very moment."

I shrugged.

"That's true, Mr. Matthews, it's your life and you're free to do with it as you please."

He placed his hand on my back.

"But next time, please, desist from interrupting my negotiations, or you may truly find yourself deceased."

Green offered a smile in saying this, but it was a smile I no longer enjoyed seeing. He could have his damned country club. I spotted Steve on the opposite balcony and excused myself.

Volleyball had replaced basketball in the courtyard and Robby had joined in. He played the game the same way he lived his life, like he had something to prove.

I joined Steve along the rail. Robby looked up, saw us and quickly looked away. I turned to Steve. The sun was directly over our heads.

"Let's get out of this heat," I said.

"Sure. Your cell or mine?"

I smiled and followed him over to his. It was the same thing as mine, only fifty feet away and on the next hallway perpendicular to the balcony.

"How's Kristine?"

"She's fine. There are fewer women so it's less crowded. Sounds like they have it better down there in most ways."

"Did you get a call through?"

"No, she did. Her father said he'd call my folks. I hate to think how they're going to take it."

"They'll freak out, of course. Did you talk with Robby?"

"Yeah."

"What happened?"

"The jerk's going to sink us all. He says he heard that if you get more than five years, you can't obtain a fianza. It's some kind of bond deal. The Americans have been paying it and skipping town."

We waited quietly while two of El Presidenté's men came by on patrol. They eyed us and moved on with their clubs.

"Who are these guys?" I asked.

"Green said they're called cabos, same as the guy in the cell. Only these guys can crack your head open."

"So I've noticed…Back to this fianza business."

"Robby says if he takes the whole rap, he's sure to get more than five years."

"How does he know?"

"He doesn't. He's just paranoid."

"That's understandable."

"I wouldn't mind so much, except for Kristine."

I nodded. It was definitely bad having her in here, and yet I envied him a bit. She was so close, and Steve knew she loved him.

A breeze stirred through the open window and my thoughts jumped to the months ahead. Those same windows, which now let the hot desert winds blow through would be equally permissive when winter arrived and the cold Pacific storms blew out of the north. It explained the value of blankets.

Just then, someone announced the arrival of lunch in the courtyard below and the two of us went outside to lean against the railing. The volleyball game had been disbanded and the net removed. The basketball backboards had already been dragged to one side and out of the way.

The main gate opened and two men came in bearing a twenty-gallon pot. The sheer weight of it required that they hurry in syncopated steps. A trail of steam trailed in their wake. Two more

258

men rushed in with a matching pot and the gate was shut with a clang behind them.

A long table had been arranged to accommodate the serving operation and men were soon stepping up to have their bowls filled. Each man received one ladle and was expected to move on. Two men with clubs kept order.

Robby took exception to the ration he had received and was rewarded with sharp words and the wave of a club. He moved away, glaring at that man, for which he received more sharp words. Robby hurried to his cell with a final look of resentment over his shoulder.

"I don't think he'll survive this place," I said.

"He won't survive me if anything happens to Kristine."

Our eyes met.

"I've got an urge to take a nap," I said and pushed away from the railing.

"Yeah, I'm pretty beat, too. Think I'll have one last walk around the joint."

"Talk to you later."

"Sure. I'll pick you up for dinner."

I watched Steve walk down the balcony and disappear into the crowd.

The lunch ritual had also begun upstairs, with men queuing up along the south side of the balcony. I turned down the hallway and into my cell. Several Mexicans were already in there eating. I climbed up on my bunk and looked down on the fare. It was soup and one of the Mexicans was just then removing a chicken's foot from his broth.

Maybe Green wasn't such a bad guy after all.

I lay on my back and stared again at the peeling paint on the ceiling. Layers and layers had been applied over the years, like the years of a man's life, the years and years of passing time while you waited to be free again.

This being imprisoned wasn't as bad as I had imagined it to be. If I pictured myself stuck in this place for the rest of my life, it would be crushing, but I had hopes of escaping and those hopes required only one thing; getting in touch with Eric.

Accordingly, I needed to make a phone call and my impulse was to press the issue but I decided to sit tight. Best to wait and accept their terms. No matter the impulse, those were the things that would work for you in here: patience and gratitude. They owed you nothing.

I thought of Caroline as I lay on my bunk and how I had embarked from San Blas with such noble intentions, only to have it come to this. Seemingly, I knew very little about life.

Without answers, weariness soon overtook me and I fell asleep.

29

Late in the afternoon, I was jarred awake by a great roar outside the windows of my cell. I sat up, for that brief second unsure of who I was, or where. Then I remembered and settled back in quiet despair.

A crowd was gathered all along the balcony outside and roared again. I lingered there on the bed, damp with sweat from the afternoon heat and still captive of my dark dream. The dream had been about the bullfights in Madrid; the peasants cheering in the late afternoon and the noblewomen waving their handkerchiefs, the sun cutting a line of light and darkness across the stadium as the bull faced death, its flank painted red with blood.

When the Mexicans cheered again, I gave in and jumped down from the bunk, curious to see what was going on down in the courtyard. Forcing my way through the men along the rail, I discovered the reason for all the commotion. In the gathering dusk, two men were boxing, one American, the other Mexican and the American was taking it badly. With a straight right, the American's head wrenched backwards and the Mexicans cheered again. The sheer violence of the blow had made me wince.

I was not a fight fan but my father had shown me films of Sugar Ray Robinson when I was a boy and this Mexican reminded me of that boxer. He moved with the suppleness of a cat.

The American swung wildly and the Mexican countered with two swift punches. One led to a slump of the body, the second to another violent jar of the head, and another round of cheers from the Mexicans.

Someone should have stopped it. Several Americans tried to intervene but the cabos wouldn't allow it. They had their reasons for seeing this thing through to the end.

A few punches later, the American fell hard to the concrete and two of his buddies were allowed to carry him off. Meanwhile, the Mexican's mouthpiece was removed and his gloves raised in victory. An old man had started to rub down his body with towels.

In pushing away from the rail, several of the Mexican prisoners gave me a good shove with their shoulders. I let them have their moment, knowing this anger was not directed at me personally. It was simply pent up frustration directed towards the gringo in general. We had beaten them in war, for which they still harbored a great resentment. In fact, their whole history was rooted in failure. Machismo was the Mexican art of conjuring pride from defeat.

Below, the courtyard had been cleared and men were soon queuing up at the serving tables again. It was suppertime in Penal del Estado and I had been told what to expect—beans—the same thing every night. The response by Mexican inmates was unwarranted in the mind of an American. A bowl of pinto beans hardly seemed to justify the mad rush.

With men on the second floor rushing to queue up on the opposite balcony, I went the other way, my sights set on Green's cell. I was rank. I hadn't taken a shower or changed my clothes in three days.

The late afternoon sun had reached into the recesses of the eastern veranda, leaving it awash in golden light. I went along half blind while skirting the first Mexicans to have received their bowl of beans. When I pulled back the curtain to Cell 47, everyone looked up at me.

"You see, gentlemen?" Green said. "Mr. Matthews knows how to find his way back home."

"When I start calling this place home, you can truly consider me deceased."

"Home is where you find it," one said.

"Home is where you make it," another.

"Home, home on the range," another one sang.

There were smiles and laughter. Green continued.

"You may be entirely correct to say that, Mr. Matthews, but trust me. You have yet to appreciate the true splendor of your surroundings."

"And when do you suspect that will occur?"

"When the stars come out, Mr. Matthews, when the stars come out."

I looked around at all the bemused smiles in the room, dumb to the reason behind their humor but having learned not to rule out anything.

"To the matter at hand, Colonel. I would like to take a shower."

"Hmm. That is a stickier situation than meets the eye. So close to the evening repast, that is."

"It couldn't be any stickier than the way I feel."

"Yes, and it has become quite evident to the rest of us, as well."

There were more smiles and chuckles but I wasn't amused.

Seeing the seriousness of my mood, Green guided me out the door and back through the golden light of the eastern veranda. When he found two cabos, he slipped them four Marlboro cigarettes and made his request. They looked me over before nodding in the direction of the showers. Green thanked them and pointed at a hallway perpendicular to the veranda. I nodded my appreciation to the cabos and they nodded back without emotion. Their attention returned to policing the dinner line. I caught up with Green.

"Why the formality?"

"It would be most difficult if everyone decided to take a shower while dinner was being served."

"When have you ever known everyone to do the same thing at the same time?"

"In war, Mr. Matthews." He laughed at his own comment. "In war, of course."

The iron gate to the shower room creaked when he opened it. Ten galvanized pipes protruded from the wall at eye level. That was it. There were no showerheads and only one handle for each pipe.

"Cold water?" I said.

Green nodded gravely.

"And what do I do? Run around the prison a few times to dry off?"

"How about this, Mr. Matthews? You brave the waters and I'll retrieve a towel."

"Thanks."

I salvaged an abandoned piece of soap from a corner of the shower and turned on the valve, yelping a bit at the first blast of cold water. By the time I was rinsing off the last of the soap, Green returned with the towel. He also had a fresh T-shirt and pair of shorts in hand.

"These will have to be fumigated," he said of my dirty clothes. He placed the clean clothes down on a crude, wooden bench and threw me the towel. I dried off and got dressed while we talked of various things.

"Green, you're sure you don't mind feeding me?" I asked when I was done.

"Mr. Matthews, when we eat, you will eat. And your friend Steve, as well."

"The hospitality will be reciprocated."

"That is a funny thing about this place, Mr. Matthews. You can never get very far from the effects of your behavior."

I studied his eyes, having already considered this fact earlier in the day. If you had ever fancied that you weren't your brother's keeper, you definitely were now.

I grabbed my dirty clothes and headed for the balcony.

"There is one thing you can do," Green said as I caught up with him.

"What's that?"

"Go retrieve your share of beans."

"Why?" I said.

"Just do it, Mr. Matthews, and Don will make you most happy that you did."

I placed the dirty clothes in my cell and returned to Cell 47. Don handed me a bowl and I went to stand in the long food line. Don took the beans when I returned, drained off the excess water and dumped them into a bowl with all the other beans. In short order, the entire lot of them had been dumped into a pan of hot lard. The beans snapped in the grease. Chopped onions and tomatoes were folded in. Don had large green chilies roasting on the other grill. When those were done, he separated the charred skin from the soft, inner flesh. I stood back, watching this enterprise.

When the food was ready, everyone grabbed a plate from a table in the center of the room and took their share of tortillas, beans, chicken and chilies. Chopped cilantro and grated queso were there for garnish.

"So, tell me, do they eat this well on the outside?" Haynes asked me as he settled onto his bunk.

"Who cares?" I said through a mouthful of food.

"Why obviously I do, or I wouldn't have asked."

"People could be starving out there and you'd envy them."

"Ingrate," someone said.

"Let him eat cake," another.

"He eats well for the envious," McTavish said.

There was much nodding with full mouths.

"What is the mood of the country these days?" Haynes said.

"This is a pretty safe place by comparison."

"That bad?"

"It's war out in the streets. At least it felt that way to me."

He shook head. "And here I sit, a general without a battle." He received a pat on the back for his feigned grief.

"One of the networks is coming down to do a story," Francis told me.

McTavish took notice when my mood darkened at the suggestion. I met his eyes and returned to eating. McTavish stared long before going back to his meal.

"A bit of battle-front journalism," Delaney said about the network people coming down.

"Yes, I can see it all now," Haynes said. "Battle fatigues and helmets."

"The place was overrunning with those bastards in 'Nam," Delaney said. "I might even be on a first name basis with a few of them."

"Perhaps we can get someone cracked over their head for amusement," McTavish added dourly.

"The word out of the consulate is they're quite sympathetic," Francis added.

"I suggest you hold out for copyright," I said.

"A businessman," someone said.

"Worse, a barrister."

There was laughter.

With time, darkness filled the room. Each of us in turn piled our empty plates on Don's cutting table. Someone reached back and pulled the Indian blanket to one side from the balcony window, allowing a dim light to filter in with the evening breeze. The sounds of the prison drifted in with it.

"It will almost be sad to leave this chapter of history behind us, don't you think, Mr. Matthews?" Green said.

His gold tooth gleamed in the umbrage. I looked around at the other faces in the shadows. It appeared that everyone was waiting for me to give an answer. Uncomfortable with their stares, I got up to lend Don a hand with clearing the table. I was eyed further for my efforts but no one made an effort to stop me.

"You could wash the plates if you'd like," Don said.

Remembering the long sinks at the west end of the prison, I gathered up the plates and slipped out through the gate. The many Mexicans crowded along the balcony railing regarded my passage with disdain.

I reached the sinks and got in line to wait my turn. The last light of day had lent a golden glow to the soiled plaster walls.

In due course, it was my turn and I began rinsing off plates under one of the faucets. Hearing someone curse behind me, I turned to find the man who had battled with me over the window that morning. He wore a bandage on his head.

Not wanting more trouble, I ignored him and went back to washing the plates. He pushed his way up to the faucet next to me and stared. When I looked his way, he tossed a bowl of water in my face. I quickly returned the favor and he took a swing at me. By the time two cabos ran up, I had him by the throat and pinned against a wall. A crowd of Mexican prisoners had quickly gathered in the hall around us, eager to see a gringo get his ass kicked.

With the cabos separating us, a voice barked out and the crowd quickly parted. The cabos spun me around to face El Presidenté. He had two of his capitans at his side.

The cabos explained what they knew. El Presidenté listened while reviewing both my adversary and me coldly. When the Mexican tried to defend his reasons for starting the fight, he was cut short with one look. No one bothered to ask my side of the story.

Having heard enough, El Presidenté nodded towards his cell. The cabos led us to the door. The blanket was pulled back and someone shoved us inside. It was the same room where Green had come to lobby on my behalf earlier in the day and the same dissolute looking men were sitting around the tables. The room was darker but little else had changed.

One of the capitans ordered the cabos to clear everything from the center of the room. El Presidenté took his place behind a table. My adversary and I were made to stand in front while he and his men sized us up. There were references to our height and build and money was tossed on the table.

A minute went by with this cabal of thieves engaging in their fun and laughter. Then the curtains parted and a cabo rushed in with two pairs of boxing gloves. One was quickly laced onto my hands, the other onto my opponent and we were shoved at each other. I looked in the direction of El Presidenté. He was tossing down another glass of mescal in the darkened room.

"¡Vaminos, muchachos, vaminos!" he said with a flourish of his hand.

Eager for this fight, the Mexican was quick to throw a roundhouse punch at me. I brushed aside his gloves, which brought jeers from El Presidenté and his men. Distracted by a look their way, the Mexican caught me square on the temple with a right and with an uppercut to my chin. Staggering on rubber legs now, I swung back wildly and went for a clinch. This elicited more jeers and cursing and the pounding of shot glasses on the wooden table.

Seeing there was nothing to do but win this fight, I held up my guard and took a pounding to my body and gloves until my head had cleared. Then I went after my adversary. He was helpless against my longer arms and I used this advantage to jab him repeatedly. Growing frustrated, he took a wild swing, allowing me to catch him with a straight right and a left hook. I kept out of his range and slowly beat him down.

Sensing defeat, the Mexican charged me, causing us to crash over a table. Food and bottles went flying. Laughing, El Presidenté motioned for his honchos to shove us back into the center of the room.

The Mexican was half blind now from a cut over his left eye. His nose appeared to be broken. He staggered at me throwing wild punches and I shoved him back. I kept expecting El Presidenté and his men to put a stop it, but they were not thinking of his health, only of the money his failure had cost them.

When the Mexican tried to charge me again, I caught him square in the jaw with a right and he fell backwards onto the table. El Presidenté's men promptly tossed him back at me with disgust.

"Perro," one of them said.

He toppled to the floor in front of me and was still. El Presidenté appeared to be satisfied with this outcome. It would seem he had bet on me.

Two of his cabos lifted the vanquished man up violently by his arms. His eyes came open as they unlaced his gloves but there was no longer any awareness in them. Another man parted the curtain and the two cabos dragged my foe out to the main gate. One of them called for a guard.

Another cabo came over and unlaced my gloves.

"Vaminos," he said with a slap on my back and a wave at the door.

The cabo guarding the door lifted the curtain for me and I emerged into a darkened hallway crowded with Mexicans. They were silent, realizing the victory was mine, not theirs. I went to the sink where the fight had begun and washed the blood from my face and body.

"¿Donde va?" I asked someone about the man I had beaten.

"El hoyo."

I looked about, expecting to find compassion, but the Mexicans had none. You lost, and for that, they threw you in the hole. Better him than me. Still, I felt badly for the man. He had failed twice in one day.

The crowd parted again and El Presidenté strutted by, giving me a pat on the back as he did. It was only a hint of the abrazo, the Mexican embrace, but to touch a man in public, especially a man below you, that was very rare in their country. I had been given an honor and the men stood out of my way as I started back towards Cell 47. No one would dare to mess with Clay Matthews now. At least not until some future action by El Presidenté rescinded his previous gesture.

His entourage turned the corner onto the balcony and came face to face with Green. El Presidenté smiled at Green and nodded at me. He said something to his cabos and moved on. They came by and instructed me to follow them back to my cell. Green came alongside me.

"What's going on?" I said.

"You have been granted passage to Cell 47."

Once we had arrived to my cell, the two cabos watched while I gathered my few possessions.

"Vaminos," the head cabo said, growing impatient.

When I was ready, he and the other cabo escorted me over to Cell 47. As a precaution, the lead cabo poked his head in through the curtain and had a cursory look around the room before allowing me to enter. Satisfied, he waved me in and went on his way.

"Welcome," Haynes said to me and went about clearing the empty bunk.

"Nobody will fool with Mr. Matthews now," Green said. "Not if they know what's good for them."

I deflected a barrage of questions and jokes about the fight while placing my few belongings away. When I was done, I turned to face the room, feeling none of their mirth.

"You don't seem very content with your victory, Mr. Matthews," Green said.

"My victory just meant someone else's defeat."

"Would you have preferred being the one thrown in the hole?"

"No, I'd prefer there wasn't a hole. Or the pretense to humanity by a bunch of animals. That's what I'd prefer."

"I'm sorry you feel that way."

"I'm not blaming you, Green."

He nodded and went about his business. I looked around the room, uncomfortable with my place in it. Glenn had started out the door with his guitar so I followed him. It was now the twilight hour. A handful of bare light bulbs illuminated the balcony and courtyard below, but they were spread far enough apart to leave much of the prison in shadows.

Glenn made himself comfortable in a window alcove and began strumming a Latin ballad. Mexicans quickly filled the balcony around him. I listened to a few bars before pushing away from the railing and moving on, not wanting to be reminded of women and what they did to men's hearts.

In the darkened recesses of the eastern veranda, I came across a game of five-card poker, Mexican style. El Presidenté was at the table, along with six other men. In Mexican poker, each man received one card up and one card down. You bet and received another card down, and another, until you had five or had folded. It was all bluff and El Presidenté's face was perfectly suited for the game. He looked up at me briefly and back at his cards without showing the least bit of emotion. I thought being in a poker game with him left something to be desired. Who would dare to take El Presidenté's money?

Aware that a crowd of men had gathered under the balcony where I stood, I continued around to the far side, wanting to see what had attracted them. Haynes had come out and was leaning over the balcony. He greeted me with a smile. I took up a spot alongside him.

In the courtyard below, several women were milling about in spaghetti strap gowns and high-heels, each of them with their hair piled up on their heads. A few dozen Mexicans were loitering around them, lighting their cigarettes and generally fawning.

"Breaks your heart, doesn't it?" Haynes said.

"They allow women in here?"

"They're inmates like us."

"And prostitutes," Green said, coming up.

"You mean these are the women inmates from below?"

"No, no," Haynes said.

I reviewed his sly smile and looked below again.

"All right, out with it," I said.

"Those are the ladies from Cell 13," Haynes said.

"They're ladies but not women."

"In this case, there is a difference," Green said.

With greater scrutiny, the subtleties slowly became apparent to me, the shoulders a bit too angular and bony, the feet too large, the hips narrow and lacking the usual flair.

"They're transvestites?"

"You've hit the nail on the head, Mr. Matthews," Green said.

"And men screw them?"

"Indeed they do. For a fee."

As we stood there, a Mexican emerged from the wide hallway leading to Cell 13 and started across the courtyard with a contented tug at his belt buckle. A moment later, one of the courtesans reappeared, hair and makeup flawlessly arranged.

"That's it? And no one gives a shit?"

"Do you use that word with irony, Mr. Matthews?"

I lowered my head. They laughed.

"I believe he's faint of heart," Haynes said.

"He has no taste for the exotic," Green said.

"It doesn't seem very macho," I said. "Going about poking each other in the ass."

"And indeed it's not, Mr. Matthews."

"And so?"

"It depends entirely on which side of the equation you find yourself," Haynes said.

I pondered this for a moment.

"You mean it's okay to poke someone?"

"You catch on quickly, Mr. Matthews."

"And if you found yourself on the wrong side of the equation?"

"A one way ticket to Cell 13," Haynes said.

"Well, it would be a damned shame if you got carried away one night, now wouldn't it?"

"I suppose it depends on how much you enjoyed the experience."

He and Green laughed. I thumbed my nose in that direction.

"And anybody can go in there?"

"If they have money, Mr. Matthews."

"Americans?"

"Some of them," Haynes said.

"Nothing's sacred," I said.

"We're talking about biology," Haynes said, "not religion."

"Yes. You must consider, Mr. Matthews, no one forces anyone to participate." As he spoke another lady escorted a man down the darkly lit hallway.

"Do we have a Cell 13 up here?"

"No," Haynes said. "But a few of the ladies are allowed up here each visiting day."

"What, so we can light their cigarettes?"

"No, so a man can rent a cell and have his way with them."

I shook my head.

"Wouldn't you rather have a woman?"

"Most certainly, and we do. But not everyone can afford to pay a woman prostitute. The ladies from Cell 13 price themselves competitively."

"And they allow prostitutes in here on visiting days?"

"They allow everything in here on visiting days."

271

"Drugs?"

"Drugs. Lots of drugs. El Presidenté controls the traffic, of course, and takes his cut."

A cool breeze gusted down from the mountains just then and the ladies below pulled their shawls up over their shoulders. The chatty little games of love went on with their admirers. Glenn's song of romance echoed all around the prison. I looked over at El Presidenté. He was checking his cards and keeping a wary eye on his domain. A beer and a growing pile of chips sat in front of him. I caught the scent of marijuana wafting from some unseen source. The utter futility of being in this prison suddenly struck me.

"Why lock us up? We're doing in here exactly what we would be doing outside."

"Yes, we've pondered that same thing many a night."

"And?"

"We have yet to come up with a rational answer."

"And therein lies the dilemma, Mr. Matthews. How do you find a rational solution to an irrational set of circumstances?"

I looked at Green.

"There's everything in here but death," I said.

"I wouldn't rule that out," Haynes said.

With that, I pushed away from the balcony and continued on my stroll.

Halfway to the main gate, I heard a loud crash coming from the direction of the eastern veranda and turned to find the poker table had been upturned. El Presidenté and his cabal stood facing a man. He was holding his stomach with one hand and reaching clumsily at the air with the other, as if in search of the cards and chips now scattered all over the floor. It was clear from the bulge in the man's bloody shirt that he had been gutted. Unable to stand any longer, he fell across the upturned table and did not move again.

El Presidenté barked a command and several of his cabos began herding all the prisoners towards their cells. A long knife was taken from El Presidenté's hand and carried off to the showers. The now lifeless Mexican was searched. A small knife was found and handed to El Presidenté. The dead body was carted off to the main gate. The card table and all other evidence of this incident were swiftly removed.

The courtyard below had been emptied, as well. There were shouts, the rattle of iron doors and a murmur of many voices. On my way to Cell 47, El Presidenté went past me. His eyes met mine. His little pat on the back meant nothing now. If necessary, he would kill me just as readily.

"What was that you were saying about death?" Haynes asked as I entered the door.

I rolled out my blanket and crawled into bed, not much in the mood for his or anyone else's conversation. It had been a long, long day, the events of it seeming to drift back over months and lose all perspective, to be out of time and place and without beginning or end. And to think, only five days earlier I had been lying on a white sand beach with Caroline, so much hope in my heart.

Green came over to my bunk a short while later. There was kindness in his voice.

"Don't despair, Mr. Matthews. Someday we shall all look back at this adventure and laugh."

"Yeah, no doubt."

"Don't despair," he repeated. "Your patience will be rewarded."

"Well, speaking of patience, I'm still dying to make that call."

"I'll make sure that it's arranged in the morning."

"And to talk with my friend, Kip."

"I'm certain we can arrange that, as well. The director is really most accommodating, if your requests are presented in a reasonable fashion."

"Then tell him I'll take my continental breakfast in the lobby. Say, at eight."

"He's not that reasonable."

Haynes came over and handed us both a large, plastic tumbler.

"What's this, the arsenic?"

I smelled the cup and bolted up at the waist, smelling it again.

"Sake, Mr. Matthews. Or as best as we could approximate."

I took a drink and choked. I took another drink, but more carefully this time. It seemed to be a cross between wine and hard liquor.

"Why sake?"

"It was rice or potatoes," Haynes said. "Those are the only two grains readily available."

I toasted to them and took another drink. Haynes and Green returned to their clandestine meeting. All of the men save for Don had joined together in a far corner of the room. Don lay alone on his bunk, thumbing through a magazine.

I heard voices outside and presumed it was some sort of investigation into the murder. It not yet being my turn to die, I returned to matters of living. If only I could get to that safe deposit box in Mazatlán. Then I'd be in business.

Braced by the sake, dreams of escape again took shape in my head. Then, I had always seen my life as a straight line between two points and when you looked at it that way, anything seemed possible. But straight lines only existed in Euclidean geometry, while I lived in a world of relativity and quantum mechanics, where nothing was predictable, except for unpredictability. And how did one plan for the future, given that set of facts? I was grappling with that paradox as I drifted off to sleep.

30

It was morning again in Penal del Estado and the first brilliant shaft of sunlight had just then peeked over the hill, like Jesus in the morning, looking down upon all the lost souls. A dog began to bark, somewhere beyond the kitchen. A loud clang echoed up from below. I looked to see if anyone had stirred. They had not so maybe it wasn't la cuenta. I really wasn't in the mood for la cuenta yet that morning.

I turned my attention to the collage of magazine pictures pasted on the wall above my head. There were young people placing daisies in the rifles of soldiers, Marilyn Monroe, Castro, men taking fire in 'Nam, President Kennedy at his inauguration, Hitler, a college football game in the fall, Martin Luther King, Che Guevara, black protesters being blasted with fire hoses in the deep South, Iggy, The Beatles, circa Abbey Road, a hydrogen bomb being detonated over the Pacific, The Beatles, circa Rubber Soul, President Kennedy's casket being led through the streets by a black horse, kids splashing about in a backyard swimming pool, a woman with a beehive hairdo doing the hula hoop, Thanksgiving dinner in the Midwest, a woman wearing a mini skirt in Piccadilly Square; on and on it went. Behind the pictures was a foot thick wall. Somewhere in the distance, the melodies of mariachi music had begun to play on a transistor radio and I was there, the unwitting prisoner of this bizarre Mexican dream, longing to be free, or anywhere else in the world.

The main gate opened and I again expected to hear la cuenta begin, but the footsteps came down the balcony and hurried past our cell without further event. I jumped down, emptied my bladder and splashed some water on my face. Don was making his bed. He smiled sadly at me. Everyone else was still snuggled up in their blankets.

I recalled Eric telling me once that all life was an illusion. I stared at the walls, trying to make them disappear.

When the effort failed, I crawled back into bed. The sunrise was now so brilliant above the adjacent hill, I could not bear to look out the window. Instead, I went back to perusing the pictures on the wall. Hopefully this day would be modestly better than the last one.

Some minutes later, the gate downstairs clanged open and the unmistakable sound of la cuenta commenced. The kid with the clipboard called out and numbers were shouted back, the ritual accompanied by swift footsteps and more cell doors clanging.

In the desert outside, nothing remotely resembling this sort of harsh discipline was ongoing. If the orderliness of ants had such severe regulations attached to it, it was well disguised. The world of nature appeared to be as carefree as a sunny spring day.

I heard la cuenta being repeated over and over again on the lower level of the prison. Then all was quiet.

A few minutes later, the main gate opened upstairs and the count moved swiftly down the balcony towards our cell. Then they were at our door.

"¡LA CUENTA, HOMBRES!"

The door was unlocked and bodies hit the floor. The same punk I had encountered the day before marched in, followed by the same guard. The punk half smiled at me, like he couldn't care less that El Presidenté had patted me on the back. Then who knew? Maybe that man wasn't El Presidenté any longer.

Either way, there were no hitches this morning and the two men were quickly out the gate.

McTavish pulled out a bucket and began to fill it from a spigot fastened to the wall. While the bucket filled, he retrieved some soap and mixed it with the water.

"What's the occasion?"

He waited until the bucket was full and he had shoved a mop into the soapy water before speaking.

"Visiting day."

"In here?"

"We figure to spread them around the jail a bit."

"So we have to mop the floors?"

"You catch on fast, Matthews."

"Why on Sunday?"

"You'd have to ask the Mexicans."

Haynes chuckled and came over.

"They open the gates every Wednesday and Sunday from ten to four and half the town shows up. And the Mexicans like to put on a good show so we clean things up a bit."

Green came over and joined us.

"Actually, it's not the worst idea, Mr. Matthews. A bit of soap and water cuts down considerably on the roaches."

McTavish remained leaning on his mop, waiting. The other men in the cell were at work, getting all the boxes up off the floor.

"What do you want me to do?"

"Stay out of the way," McTavish said.

"How?"

"Dance."

Now Green laughed.

"This is the one time you're allowed to stay on your bunk between the count and breakfast. You'll find most of the prisoners choose this method."

"Guess I'll dance around a bit."

"As you wish, sir."

I heard the main gate open and close. A few minutes later, a cabo arrived to reopen our cell. I went outside to watch the proceedings. Men were busily connecting hoses to the spigots along the balcony. Another crew stood at the ready with floor squeegees. All of them were barefoot and had their pants rolled up.

When someone shouted from the courtyard downstairs, the spigots upstairs were turned on. McTavish began mopping furiously inside our cell. When he was done, a man with a hose rushed in and rinsed all the excess soapy water out the door. Two men with squeegees followed him, funneling all of the excess water out into the hallway and from there to the balcony. Holes along the base of the railing had been unplugged, allowing the soapy water to cascade down to the courtyard below. This process was being duplicated all around the second floor, accompanied by shouts and

277

laughter and a wonderful esprit de corps. Mariachi music added an additional flair. I moved this way and that, staying one step ahead of the furious activity.

Once all the excess water had been funneled downstairs, the holes were plugged, the mops and squeegees stored away and the entire process repeated on the lower level, with men using the soap and water delivered from above to scrub the courtyard. More soap and water poured out from the rooms and hallways downstairs, this entire deluge guided into a central drain in the courtyard. Within half an hour, it was over, the entire jail now clean and the wet concrete drying in the morning sun.

I stood at the railing and watched as men dragged benches and tables into the courtyard below. Others draped green and red bunting on the walls. All the while, men came and went from the showers. A number of Mexicans were already dressed and milling about the courtyard in black pants and white shirts. Mariachi music played in the background. The place sounded like a carnival but looked as grim as Sunday mass.

I waited for Kip to appear and waved him over. He had a towel over one shoulder and a bar of soap in his hand

"Did you get your call yet?" I asked him.

"Nope. You?"

"No."

We stared with a thousand things unsaid between us.

"Everything okay with you down there?"

Kip shrugged.

"I haven't gotten into any fights."

"Yeah. I'll tell you about it later. Hopefully we'll have our visit today." He nodded. "Remember, whatever you do, don't call home yet."

He nodded again and went off to shower. As always, he seemed calm. He couldn't possibly be having as bad a time down there as I was having up here.

Remembering my dirty clothes, I went to grab them from the cell. The guard at the main gate had me write my name on the bag. The clothes would be washed and returned the next day.

I went back to our cell, looking for Green but he was not there. Steve and Haynes were talking alone. Don was busy cooking. Francis lay on his bunk reading. Everyone else had gone outside.

"What's up?" I said.

"They're letting Kristine up today," Steve said.

I looked at Haynes.

"Are we going to clear out for them?"

"We were just discussing that."

I nodded.

"By the way, what happened to El Presidenté?"

"Looks like a wash," Haynes said. "They're calling it self-defense."

"You wouldn't expect anyone to argue with him."

"His word is scripture to me."

I sat on a bed. Morning sunlight from the window was still infusing the room with a blinding light. I watched Don cooking but all I could see was a golden glow where his body should have been. His hands kept appearing and disappearing as if from another dimension.

A Mexican called out from the door and came in with a paper bag. Don opened it, inspected the chickens and paid the man.

"Gracias," Don said.

"De nada," the man said and left.

"By the way, where's Green?" I asked.

Haynes had gone to look out the balcony window and looked over his shoulder.

"Taking a shower."

I stood up.

"Better do that myself."

I headed out the door, crossed the shaded veranda and got in line. *Labyrinths of Solitude* by Octavio Paz came to mind as I stood there. What were the Mexicans if not a violent clash of cultures? Aztec versus Spanish. Black versus primary color. Human sacrifice versus Sunday morning confessional.

Briefly lost in my inquest, I promptly reeled myself back in. What the hell did I care? My only concern should be how to get out of this place.

I passed Green on my way into the shower room.

"Think I can get that call today?"

"After the gates clear, Mr. Matthews. Perhaps by noon."

"And Kip?"

279

"Come back to the cell when you're done and we'll write El Presidenté a note. He'll send it down with the guards."

"Thanks. See you in a few."

I went in, turned on the spigot and prepared myself for a blast of cold water.

Upon my return to the cell, Green assisted me in writing down a request to visit with Kip, which we handed to the cabo guarding El Presidenté's door. It appeared that El Presidenté wasn't taking any visitors that day. As to the call, we received a shrug. They would see what they could do. I found a comfortable spot along the railing on the eastern veranda and did my best to wait patiently. It was the one thing at which I had most failed in life and there weren't any signs of improvement that morning.

Preparations for visiting day were now complete and the entire balcony upstairs was lined with men, waiting for the doors to open. The Mexicans were dressed for Mass, the Americans for a beach party.

While standing there, I noticed an American come out of his private cell downstairs and stand in front. He was wearing a nicely pressed Hawaiian shirt and dark shades. His coarse, closely cropped hair was combed straight back. He would have made a fine pimp. I also noticed a wire leading from the TV antenna on the roof down into his room. The man had himself a virtual penthouse in a ghetto.

Then, who was I to judge? I had been eating like a farmhand while others went hungry.

Promptly at ten, a bell rang and the process of admitting people from the waiting area behind the gate into the prison began. Men stood in one line, ladies in another and were directed one by one into separate enclosures, where a guard of their own sex joined them, wearing a rubber glove. It left little to the imagination.

Having been inspected, people were then allowed through the gate. An old lady came in first, carrying two large mesh bags. A young Mexican greeted her, took the bags and led her off to his cell. Variations on this theme were repeated as each person arrived. Many people quickly sought shade on the benches under the balconies and in the covered verandas. When the encounter involved a man and a woman, they usually disappeared. There were children and old ladies and everything in between. Every old woman I saw was wearing a black shawl and fondling rosary beads. Men who had no visitors milled about in groups, watching the others. As in all of life, some interactions appeared to be grave in nature, some involved laughter.

Vendors had set up their wares on long tables in the hallways at either end of the prison and people strolled by, inspecting jewelry and tacky native trinkets, and sometimes buying things. A mariachi band arrived downstairs and moved from the sunny courtyard to the shady hallways and back again, serenading lovers and everyone else in between. It could have been the streets of any Mexican town.

Shortly before eleven, Kristine arrived. Her eyes looked particularly blue against her pale skin and long, red hair. She had the bearing of royalty, or so it seemed to me in that moment: wise and always kind. I went over to say hello.

"Clay, I'm so sorry this happened to you."

"Likewise. We all look a bit foolish."

"God, I know. I wish we'd never seen that stuff."

"Yeah, I've tried to undo the past until I'm back in the womb."

"Yeah."

When a couple of El Presidenté's henchmen walked by, clearing traffic, they took the opportunity to have a good look at Kristine. Steve responded by putting his arm around her.

"Let's get out of sight," he said.

Back in our cell, Kristine was introduced all around. A bit of small talk ensued. Then everyone slowly filed out until only Steve, Kristine and I remained.

"How are they treating you?" I asked.

"All right. It sounds like our food is better. And it's mostly quiet. Except when they let the crazy men out."

"What crazy men?"

I looked at Steve.

"I guess they're down in a yard where we can't see."

"I think they're just mentally ill or retarded or something," Kristine said. "But the guards treat them like animals. They're free to wander around the yard outside our windows from two to four each day and when they stare in at us, the guards beat them back with clubs. It makes me sick."

"How did they end up in here?" I said.

"That is their crime," Steve said. "Being nuts."

"God, these people are fucking medieval."

There was silence between us.

"Have you talked any more to Robby?" I said.

Kristine looked at Steve.

"It's hopeless," he said. "He's totally convinced that if he takes the rap alone, he won't get a fianza."

"We're really bummed about it," Kristine said. "Especially for you and Kip."

"Don't put it on yourselves."

"I know Robby's a good man at heart," she said, looking at Steve. "I still think he'll come around."

"I'm not getting my hopes up," Steve said.

"Yeah, I'd say that angle's hopeless."

I stood up to leave.

"I'll see you two later."

They smiled uneasily and squeezed each other's hand. I walked out, pulled the curtain closed and shut the iron gate behind me. Making love in there, with all the pious Catholic symbolism draped around you and mariachi music playing in the background. Very strange. Though I presumed you'd forget all that soon enough.

I had been seated alone for a spell, off on another riff about Mexican culture, when something struck me. No older Mexican men had come to visit. The Mexican prisoners were surrounded by everything from sons and daughters to wives and lovers and grandmothers, and even a handful of brothers, but not one male patriarch. No big surprise there. Getting thrown into prison wasn't very machismo.

I was on my third or fourth lap, trying to understand the Mexican mind, when Green appeared and told me my wishes had been granted. I went to the main gate and a guard led me downstairs. Like so many Mexicans, the guard appeared to have ingested too much booze and bad food over a lifetime, but he seemed kind. It was visiting day, so a brief truce had been called. The guard informed me that I would be allowed to make a phone call after my visit and opened the door to a small room. Kip was waiting inside. I sat down next to him.

"Well, my friend. This isn't exactly the way we had pictured things turning out."

"So, we've got time now to figure things out."

I raised my eyebrows.

"Sorry, Kip, but I'm not on the same wavelength. I know an American jail awaits me on the other side of the border and probably have one chance to get free before that happens. I just need your help."

"To do what?"

"Don't call your parents. Or anyone in your family. At least not until they take me to the first hearing."

"Sure. If that's all you need."

"What I need is a helicopter but they'll probably be landing one in the parking lot for me at any moment."

"I'm done with fighting," he said. "Acceptance is the only answer I can see."

I stared but held my tongue.

"I hear it's about two weeks before they take you to your first court appearance. What have you heard?"

"The same. They have you make a second statement and then you can wait a long time before anything else happens. One guy down here has been waiting a year. Another guy got sentenced in three weeks."

"It's impossible to understand the Mexican mind."

"It's the same as anything. You have to accept things for what they are."

We were back to staring. I tried to distill my thoughts down to a few words. There weren't many to suit the job.

"I should have listened to you in Guaymas, Kip."

"It goes back much further than that."

"I know, but goddamn it. I remember standing at that train station. We were free. We had all the time in the world."

"We're free now, Clay. It's all a matter of perception."

"Give me a break, Kip. We're in a fucking Mexican prison. Now tell me you don't want to get your ass out of here?"

"Sure, but I'm here until I'm not, so I'm not going to go crazy fighting my karma."

I shook my head and looked away.

"And there I was, off to make things right with Caroline. Fuck. I wish I was back in Jorgé's having a beer."

The guard reappeared and waved for Kip to join him. Kip reached over and patted me on the knee.

"Just be patient," he said. "Before you get yourself into any more trouble."

"I could figure you'd say some shit like that."

He gave me another pat and stood up to follow the guard. A few moments later, the guard returned and led me down to a room with a phone. He stood by the door and pretended not to listen. I was trying to reach Sarah, with hopes that she could find Eric. They had grown up on the same back country road, but who knew where that Bhagavad-Gita toting space cadet was now. While the phone rang, I thought of those days gone by, when the world was young and so were we and filled with blind hope.

Then, crackling through the phone, I heard Sarah's voice.

"It's Clay," I said in return.

"Clay! You sound far away!"

"I am."

I quickly explained what had happened.

"Clay, you have such strange karma."

"Yeah, yeah. Don't get me started."

"So what's going on? How can I help?"

"Find Eric. Do you know where he is?"

"I heard he's living down in Encinitas. But why Eric?"

"I really can't explain that right now. Suffice it to say, without him, all my plans are screwed."

"What should I tell him?"

"To come visit me and be sure to have at least a hundred dollars extra. And the sooner the better. I'll explain the rest when he gets here."

"I'll drive down there today," she said.

"I wish I could."

"I'll bet."

We exchanged a few more thoughts and memories.

"Please tell him to hurry," I said before hanging up.

I quickly cursed myself. I had meant to have Sarah call Caroline. Then it was probably best if she didn't. The only thing I had to offer Caroline was more trouble.

I nodded at the guard and we started back upstairs.

"Someday, you go home, Señor," he told me.

It was a kind thought but ran against the grain of my own. His gun hung loosely from his holster, reminding me of the vow I had made the day we were arrested; never hesitate again. My heart pounded at the thought of overwhelming him. He did not look to expect it, but I remembered the long march through the desert and knew it had to wait. However impulsive I felt, it had to wait.

When the guard opened and closed the main gate behind me, it struck me more vividly than before that I had lost my freedom. Even that short walk downstairs had come with a feeling of liberation. I longed to move about in wide-open spaces as I saw fit. Why was that so important to me? Was it something good? Or something primitive and dangerous and better discarded? Kip had seemed so serene.

I spent the remaining visitor hours trying to find such peace but failed. It just wasn't in me. I squirmed and changed positions all day, my mind still pacing like a caged tiger.

31

At four o'clock, a bell rang and the prisoners started en masse back towards their cells. I ran into Green on the balcony outside Cell 47.

"What's going on?"

"They find it prudent to sequester us while the visitors are leaving."

"What would stop you from just walking out?"

"They give you a pass when you come in and if you don't have it at the end of the day, you don't leave."

"Why not forge one?"

"Why don't you, Mr. Matthews?"

"I think I will."

Moments after I had followed Green into our cell, a cabo came around to lock the door. A fresh shipment of food supplies had arrived during the visiting hours and Don was busy at his table, preparing dinner. There was also a cake to one side, filled with holes where it had been probed for weapons and contraband, I assumed. It was a nice cake but no one had bothered to try it yet.

I went to the window and watched the visitors move in a slow procession towards the main gate. The sun had disappeared below the roof of the prison, leaving the courtyard and procession bathed in a dusky light. People chatted among themselves. There was laughter. The older women had placed their black lace shawls over their heads and were working away at their rosary beads.

Ultimately, a single line formed as people neared the main gate and every person was stopped briefly by a guard before being allowed to pass. My heart went out the gate with each one of them.

Once the last visitor had disappeared, a guard locked the gate. A bell sounded and la cuenta began. I climbed up on my bunk. The body count moved from the far end of the prison towards our cell.

While I lay there with my thoughts, everyone other than Don gathered to one side of the room. There was an occasional glance my way as they whispered among themselves.

Later, with the count concluded, our cell door was reopened and I went in search of Steve. He was leaning over the opposite balcony, the portrait of a farmer looking out over his fields.

"How's it going Clay?" he said as I walked up.

"About the same. And you?"

"I could use a decent meal."

"We're never satisfied."

"Not for long."

I leaned over the rail with him.

"It's nice they let Kristine up here to see you."

"I'd just as soon she was on the outside."

"Well, as long as we're making wishes," I said.

"Yeah, that's true."

We were silent for a spell. I glanced up at the cirrus clouds passing by high overhead and pulled off my shirt. Many men had done so in the sultry heat. You hated to think what summer would bring.

The fortunate American with the private cell was leaning against the wall by his door. Several of the ladies from Cell 13 were leaning against the same wall nearby. The entrance to Cell 13 was three doors down and around a corner, where a short hallway led back towards the kitchen courtyard.

"You know the guy down there? The one by the doorway with the short, coarse hair?"

"Yeah. I heard his name's Rene."

I smiled.

"Of course."

"What?"

"I think he's pimping for Cell 13."

Steve looked back at Rene.

"Yeah. I could see that."

A thought had been kicking around in my head over the past twenty-four hours and I paused there now, considering whether or not to share it. In the end, I decided to go ahead.

"Something funny's going on in Cell 47."

Steve looked over at me.

"Yeah? Like what?"

"This is strictly between you and me."

"Sure."

"I'd swear they're planning a break-out."

"Seriously?"

"I don't know but it sure feels that way."

"Fuck. They'd just shoot you."

"I know. But even if I don't join them, it puts me in a tough situation."

"Yeah. They'll think you're guilty, no matter what you do."

"Would you go out?"

"Hell, no. I have Kristine to think about."

"Yeah. You can't very well leave her behind."

I stood up from the rail.

"I could be imagining things."

"Well, whatever. I won't say anything."

"Thanks. I'd appreciate it."

A moment passed with us staring down at the workings of mankind.

"I hope I'm wrong," I said.

Steve joined us in Cell 47 for dinner and we spent the evening over a game of chess. It was a decent match, but my heart wasn't into it. My thoughts were with Caroline, wondering what she was doing on a Sunday evening and wondering if she had paused to think of me.

I conceded the match in the end and took a final stroll with Steve before lock up. A late wind had pushed down from the mountains, bringing a bit of relief from the sultry weather. The prison was quiet. The ladies had given up for the night. Only Rosa remained out front, engaged in a bit of non-vocational flirting. At the northeast corner of the balcony, Steve and I stopped before going our separate ways. I looked up at the stars.

"I can't help but wonder if somebody's up there in a similar situation, looking back at us."

Steve shrugged.

"Probably. Given the odds. I imagine things are pretty much the same, no matter where you go in this universe."

"Yeah, shitty."

He chuckled

"Yeah, but things have a way of turning out for the best in the end, given enough time."

I stole a glance at Steve, suspecting he had been secretly exchanging notes with Kip.

The final bell rang and Steve went down the balcony towards his cell. I turned towards mine. Once the door had been locked, Haynes pulled the curtain back and watched until the guards were gone.

"The coast is clear," he said and let the curtain drop.

The second he did, Green, Haynes and McTavish got in my face. Their smiles were gone.

"We're going out tonight," McTavish said.

I looked from face to face.

"What do you want from me?"

"Silence, to begin with," McTavish said. He went over and dragged one of the bunk beds away from the far wall.

"I have no reason to stop you," I said, looking at Green. "Though you might have forewarned me before inviting me into your plans."

"Aren't you going with us?" Delaney said.

I shook my head. Green shot a look at Delaney and he went back to the business of tying sheets together.

"Well, it looks as if fate has involved you, regardless, Mr. Matthews."

I stood eye to eye with Green.

"Okay. How do you intend to get out?"

Green nodded at Francis, who was just then cutting the cake in half. Three flexible diamond blades had been baked inside of it. Francis removed them and rinsed them off in a bucket. Haynes tried the frosting.

"Mmmm. A terrible waste of culinary skill."

I turned my attention back to the blades. I had seen them used in the construction trades and figured a man could work his way through one bar every half hour or so. You would have to cut two different bars and each of them twice, so roughly two hours to get down into the wash yard. I looked back at Green.

"Okay. You're in the wash yard. Then what?"

Green gestured to where twenty feet of water pipe ran along the base of the wall behind the bunks. This included an assortment of pieces on the opposing wall and around the toilet, enough there to make a long hook and get you over the outside wall. McTavish worked at the pipe, turning the long run away from a coupling in the corner with two small pipe wrenches.

"What are you going to do about the water?"

Green showed me a short nipple with a plug on the end. Someone had damned in front of the door with bedding. Francis was preoccupied with cutting the first bar. Haynes had gone to watch the guard in his parapet through the other window. The others were tying sheets together along with Delaney. The sheets would be used to rappel down from the window and into the yard below us. Green searched my face. The esprit de corps went on around us.

"You've obviously been planning. But I don't rate your chances for success very high."

"You have a better plan for escape?"

"I might."

"Then you've been holding out on us."

"You've been holding out on me."

"We thought you worthy, Mr. Matthews. But telling a complete stranger about our plans couldn't be risked."

I tried to put myself in their shoes. It was understandable, but didn't change my position.

"Look, I don't know what you have planned, if and when you get over that wall. But I've got my own reasons for doing what I'm doing and I don't think they're any of your business, any more than you thought this was mine." I waved my hand over the enterprise. "So do what you've got to do."

Green reviewed me seriously. "Just stay out of the way then."

"Hell Green, I'll help if you want but I'm not going out. Anyway, you're better off if I don't. Who's going to pull the sheets back inside the cell?"

"The sheets were for getting down from the outside wall."

"Okay. So we'll use them here instead. It'll save a lot of racket."

He nodded and took watch at the window facing the balcony. The bunks had been pushed back in place, the hook made from the water pipes hidden behind them. Glenn and Joe mopped up all the water from the floor and stashed the wet bedding under a lower bunk.

I took a seat on one of the lower bunks and watched Francis work at the saw. When he tired, I relieved him. Very quickly, the grip and constant motion numbed my fingers. The muscle and tendons in my forearms began to burn. A depression from the blade grew raw in the flesh of my palms.

I focused on the guard in his parapet, seventy-five yards distant from me. It was a moonless night and pitch black but I felt certain his eyes were focused in my general direction. All the while, my arms moved to and fro with the quiet grinding of the saw.

Suddenly the blade pulled through the first bar and everyone froze at the sound; one end of one bar down, three cuts to go. I motioned for someone to relieve me and Delaney took over.

A few moments later, the guard stood up to pace the wall and Delaney moved back from the window. When the guard sounded off that all was well and returned to his parapet, Delaney went back to work.

Growing restless, I got up from my spot on a lower bunk and stared outside. Something wasn't right. McTavish waved me back but my concern remained. I whispered to Delaney.

"Do you remember the guard wearing a red hat?"

Delaney peered through the darkness and looked back at me.

"I don't know. Why?"

"Because I'm pretty sure he wasn't wearing one before."

McTavish motioned for us to be quiet. I waved for Green and Haynes to join us. When the rest of the men gravitated towards the window out of curiosity, McTavish shooed them away.

"What is it, Mr. Matthews?" Green whispered.

I explained about the hat. Green, Haynes and McTavish joined heads and discussed the matter at some length, all the while darting glances at the guard.

"I think we're just getting paranoid," Haynes said.

"No one remembers seeing it before," I said.

McTavish scratched the bowl of hair on his head.

"Hell, it doesn't matter. We're going out."

"If they're on to you, you're sitting ducks," I said.

"Well, if they're on to us, why the hell don't they just march in here and bust us?"

"I don't know. Maybe they just want an excuse to shoot you in the back."

I looked outside one more time before climbing back up onto my bunk. It was a red officer's hat and I knew it had not been there before. Still, McTavish was right. It didn't make any sense for them to sit back and wait, unless they really did consider shooting you a sport.

A few minutes later, the main gate clanged open and every man dove for cover in his bunk. Footsteps proceeded haltingly down the balcony, as if someone was checking each and every cell.

With everything in our cell pushed back into place, it looked completely normal. We were fully clothed, but you would have had to come inside and pull back our covers to discover this fact. With a cursory glance, all would look to be in order.

I heard rustling and saw the curtain on the door parted with a club. A head looked around briefly and the curtain fell closed. The footsteps continued on around the balcony. Later, whoever had come to investigate opened the main gate. It clanged shut again and every man jumped to his feet.

"They know something," I said.

McTavish eyed me suspiciously.

"You're fucking paranoid. Let's get back to work."

He returned to cutting bars. I returned to my bunk and cursed my fortunes. I should have refused Green's offer, certain that their mission was doomed to failure and that I would be thrown into the hole with them, helpless if Eric did come. The window of opportunity would have passed and the next time I saw daylight, it would be under FBI escort.

Time passed to the constant grinding of the blade on iron bars, the stillness otherwise broken only by the occasional muffled voice and shuffling of feet. The first cut on the second bar went through. The guards called out again.

Sometime later, the second bar give way. It was time to go.

I jumped down and helped Francis pull the pipe out from behind the bunks. McTavish made the final twist of the hook and we aligned it on the floor with the window. Delaney tied off the sheets and gave the knot a good yank.

Now, everything had to go click, click. The next time the guard walked the wall, every man had to be in the courtyard from the moment he stood up to the moment he sat down again, maybe three, four minutes; and then only when his back was turned.

We waited. Fifteen minutes passed before the guard started his next watch. At the right moment, I threw the sheets out the window. McTavish scrambled down, followed by Francis, Don and three others. I pulled the sheets back up before the guard turned back. Only Haynes, Green and Delaney remained.

We waited again as the guard came towards us, our faces well back of the window.

"Sure you're not coming out?" Delaney whispered.

I shook my head.

"Give me liberty or give me death," he said with a chuckle.

It wasn't anything I would have said under the circumstances. Green shot him a look and put an end to the foolery.

When the guard turned his back to us again, I tossed the sheets out and waited while the others grappled down, one on top of the other. I shoved the pipe out when they were done, untied the sheets and dropped them into the wash yard before the guard returned to his parapet. Then I hunkered down out of sight and watched from the window's edge. My heart was pounding in my chest. I could only imagine how they were feeling.

When the guard started his walk half an hour later, McTavish moved the pipe into position. The guard made his far turn and McTavish hoisted the hook end of the pipe over the wall. It hit with a bang and everyone froze. Then McTavish was shoving Don upwards. Delaney started up the pipe right after Don. The two of them were nearing the top when the gate to the wash area crashed open.

Things happened rapidly then. I heard rifles being cocked and various orders shouted out in Spanish. Don and Delaney slid down the pipe almost on top of each other. Everyone in the courtyard was herded against a wall and searched. Simultaneously, the main gate opened upstairs and footsteps approached down the balcony, but rapidly this time and certain of their destination. I barely had time to get my clothes off and return to bed before the cell door flew open. There were two guards with M-1's and a handful of El Presidenté's men.

They ordered me out into the hallway and inspected the cell. More orders were being barked out downstairs. I heard the main gate open and presumed this meant the others were being herded down to the hole.

A guard brought my clothes out of the cell and told me to get dressed. As I did, I noticed something out of the corner of my eye. It was McTavish, using the exposed electrical wires on the west wall of the central courtyard to reach the roof. He had a knife clenched between his teeth. The two guards facing me did not see him. I quickly looked away so as not to invite their attention.

McTavish had nearly reached the roof when I heard someone bark out "¡Alto!" from down below. The two guards watching me promptly turned and aimed their rifles. McTavish had his right leg lifted over the roof when a second command came.

"¡Alto!"

When McTavish disregarded the order and started over the top, a loud report rang out. It was followed by a dull smack that died before it could echo up into the night sky. McTavish's body had stiffened but his hands were still desperately trying to keep hold of the conduit. Then his body went limp and fell backwards with the back of his knees caught on the wires. There was a pop and the lights went out. Electricity arced in the darkness, as lightning does against a night sky. McTavish's hair and arms hung freely but his body was jumping from a load of 220.

"¡Vaminos!" one of the guards said to me.

As I was being marched out to the gate, I looked up one last time. The knife was still clenched reflexively between McTavish's teeth.

32

From the main gate, I was marched down to the first floor. One of the guards went off to retrieve a flashlight. The second one kept his rifle at my back. When the other guard returned, he opened a heavy wooden door and started down a stairway hewn from sandstone. The other guard encouraged me from behind with the rifle. The precise beam of the flashlight bounced down the stairs ahead of us. There was nothing to see as we descended deeper into the bowels of the prison, not even a handrail.

The stairs terminated at a corridor that had been hewn from the same sandstone. I was guided to the right by the rifle at my back. We marched past several more heavy wooden doors on the left. Each door had a small opening near the top. A foul stench emanated from each opening.

The guard with the flashlight opened the last door. The other guard nudged me inside with his rifle and the door was closed. The guards turned back down the corridor, the darkness around me growing complete as the glow from their flashlight disappeared.

I found the wall and cursed. Something had crawled over my hand.

"Matthews?" a deep-voice said.

"Green."

"And thus we are mutually assured of each other's presence."

"Anyone else?"

"Don."

"Delaney."

"That's it?"

"They must have put the rest of us in another cell," Delaney said.

"That is a brilliant bit of deduction, is it not, Mr. Matthews?"

"Do you know what happened?" I said.

"Don't keep us in the dark," Green said.

I heard Delaney chuckle.

"They shot McTavish. He's dead."

There was silence.

In my mind's eye, I saw the swashbuckling image of McTavish still alive, with the knife clenched between his teeth, when he was neither alive nor swashbuckling anymore. He was dead and irrelevant to our survival.

"Is everyone all right?" I asked.

There was silence.

"Yeah. Yeah."

That was Delaney and Don. Green had not answered.

"Green?"

"The nobility of your concern is touching, Mr. Matthews."

"I didn't ask you if you were enjoying your birthday party, Green. Are you all right?"

"I am saddened to know that people have died, Mr. Matthews."

"What the fuck did you expect?"

"Yes, yes," Green said. "But please allow me my moment of grief."

Deciding that the truth was in order, I explained my past and reasons for wanting to steer clear of their enterprise. I left out the money but confessed to most everything else. I also made clear that secrecy remained critical to my future plans.

"We should never regret wanting to be free," Green said.

"Yeah, well, I'm guessing our only goal now is to stay alive…By the way, what is that god awful stench."

"The hole where you perform your bodily functions Mr. Matthews. Hence the name."

Curious, I inched down to the far corner of the cell and counted my steps coming back.

"What are you doing, Mr. Matthews?"

"Measuring."

"And what do you surmise?"

"It's twenty feet one way, more or less."

Needing to urinate, I move cautiously in the direction of the stench, leading with one foot and then the other, like a blind man with a cane.

At a spot roughly midway between the walls, I was startled by something solid on the floor. I reached down and felt for the object with my hand.

"What is it?" Green said.

"I just kicked the bucket."

Delaney chuckled.

"Curses," I said.

"What is it, Mr. Matthews?"

"Roaches! They're fucking everywhere."

"We've all got to make a living, sir."

I swiped at whatever was crawling on my legs, urinated and headed back towards the cell door in the darkness. I had reached the wall when I heard the sound of someone else urinating.

"That you, Green?"

"That's me."

I inched over until I touched a body. In the darkness, I could barely make out that it was Don and slid down next to him. I heard Green heading back and taking a seat. Delaney was between him and Don.

"Hell of a way to treat a war hero," Delaney said.

"Were you?" I said.

"Purple heart…Twice."

"What about you, Green?"

"No, I was never decorated."

"But you were in 'Nam."

"Yes. I lacked either your brains or your audacity."

"I don't know. Sometimes I wish I had been there. I look at my life and realize I've never sacrificed shit for anything. It kind of leaves you feeling hollow."

"I had men die in my arms," Green said. "That will definitely leave you feeling kind of hollow."

"Yeah, I suppose."

"Don't worry yourself," Delaney said. "You weren't missing a damned thing."

It struck me there in the ensuing silence how some of us had gone off to war and some of us had refused but we had all ended up side by side in the same damned hole, all of us with our share of misgivings.

A short while later, I sensed Don crying and reached out to squeeze his shoulder. He squeezed my hand back.

"It's going to be okay, Don."

I didn't know what else to say to him.

Time passed. I felt the occasional roach probing at my skin and swiped it away with disgust. Finally, I fell into a fitful sleep.

Much later, power was restored and a dim light filtered through the opening in the door, enough to make out the corners of the cell, the bucket and the dark hole in the floor next to it. I got up to urinate again.

The others curled up on the floor and went back to sleep. I overcame my own revulsion and curled up with them.

Awakened by the door opening, I watched as a guard shoved two buckets of fresh water inside, along with eight slices of white bread. Being the closest, I was told to retrieve the other bucket.

I reasoned it must be dawn and this was breakfast. The bread wasn't much of a meal. Having chewed both slices to a pulp, it felt as if I had eaten a pea.

"I've been on better slave ships," I said when I was done.

There was more chuckling.

"You don't know anything about being a slave, Mr. Matthews."

"Like you do, Green," I said.

"Far more than you."

"Well, thanks to you, my knowledge is growing."

Green was silent in return.

"Hell, I wouldn't mind hitting the oars today," Delaney said.

"The gentle rolling of a swell," I said.

"The scent of sea spray in the air."

"Please, gentlemen, you're making me queasy."

"What's the matter, Green? You can't swim?"

All of us laughed, except for Don. Green broke the silence.

"What happened to McTavish?"

"They said stop and he didn't."

"Where was he?" Delaney asked.

"Climbing that exposed conduit up the western wall."

"Was it fair, Mr. Matthews?"

"Fair as it gets around here."

"Oh God, we're all going to die before it's through."

Don fell against my shoulder, sobbing now. I tried to think of something comforting to say. Had his anguish not been so visceral, I would have told him to suck it up and be a man.

"Hey, we'll all be home for Christmas someday soon," Delaney said. "A long way from this pit."

For most of that day, Delaney's hopeful prophecy went on fluttering about in my brain, along with visions of rosy cheeks and gingerbread and Christmas cheer.

Some hours later, they brought us bread again and changed the water. I assumed it was dinner time in Penal del Estado. Heartened by our pitiful meal, we told stories about the sixties. It seemed truly wonderful, looking back, but there was nothing more to say and a long night of silence followed. We did our best to sleep, as much as the roaches would allow it.

Assuming we had been fed morning and night, it was three days when they came and took Don away; the morning of the third day. After the evening bread they brought Francis in.

"What happened to Don?" I said.

"They let him out. They should be letting you out soon. We told them you had nothing to do with it."

"Why haven't they questioned us?"

"They're taking their time. They only questioned us last night."

"Why did they let Don out?"

"We told them he was forced. They know he's weak. They couldn't picture him planning a break-out."

"Have you heard about McTavish?" I said.

"Yeah. The guard told us last night."

"Too bad about McTavish," Green said. "Too bad."

"I guess he wanted it more than anybody," Francis said.

"Yeah. He had the most to lose," Delaney said.

"How long had he been in here?" I said.

"Five years on a twelve year sentence, and no one to help him on the outside."

"You expect the consulate would do something about it."

"Mr. Matthews, you cannot possibly be so naïve. Why should the government wish to get us out when they are the ones responsible for us being here in the first place?"

299

"Why would they care about us being locked up in a Mexican prison?"

"As you once said, Mr. Matthews, there's a war going on in the streets of America."

"Sure. But what's that got to do with us? We never made it to the border."

"It's gringo politics," Delaney said. "The Mexicans don't care but they've been trained to pull over anybody with long hair and a beat up van."

"What the fuck for?" I said.

"For them, it's the money. The Mexicans get to confiscate our dope and sell it back to us. Meanwhile, the Americans don't have to dirty their hands locking us up, or pay for our incarceration."

"We're a sick nation," I said.

"We're a frightened nation, Mr. Matthews."

"Well, as you know, I'm a real threat to society."

"You are in here for what you represent, not what you did."

"The mayor of Hermosillo is one of the biggest dealers," Delaney said. "Portillo, what's his name?"

"Juarez," Green said.

"To hell with the Mexicans," Francis said. "They're all corrupt."

"We will be thankful for that corruption when we pay our fianzas and go home," Green said.

"We wouldn't be in here if it wasn't for their corruption," Delaney said.

"We wouldn't be in here if we hadn't broken the law," Green said.

No one spoke for a spell.

"How did they miss McTavish in the first place?" I said.

Francis answered.

"When they came through the gates, he hid behind one of the wash basins. He must have circled around behind it because I know a guard went back there to look."

"Did you see him?"

"No. We were already down here but kind of figured. There were only two guys in here longer. Muddy and Leon, and you see what it's done to them."

"Yeah."

The next morning, they took Green. He was gone about an hour. Then they took Delaney. Delaney never came back.

"What do you think happened to him?" I said.

"Who knows? Maybe they put him in the other cell," Francis said. They never came for me.

By the fifth day I had open sores and the roaches came to feed on me. I had no energy left, not even enough to swipe them away. Fifty push-ups and fifty jumping jacks each morning had settled into staggering over to the hole twice a day, and I was barely able to do that.

There were only shadowy dreams left, much of it about Caroline, but sometimes about Kip and Hawaii too. Lovely memories that were swallowed by vague anguish and the rope twisting in my gut. I was asleep. I was awake, no longer certain of the difference. My perceptions had become like more delirium.

By the next day, I was too weak to stand up and crawled over to the hole in order to urinate. The urine burned my legs but I lacked the energy to do anything about it.

No one spoke for hours. Then I heard movement and saw Green sitting up.

"Tell me a story, Matthews...."

"Mr. Matthews to you...."

"Mr. Matthews...."

"I don't remember any...."

"Please. I need a good laugh...."

"Is there any laughter left in the world...? Green....?"

"I am no longer certain."

It was quiet.

"Did you happen to pass through Haight?" I asked him. "In '69?"

"A sad time," he said.

"Yes. The magic had blown away. All that we had tried to create, all that we had dreamed was possible in this world, it was all diminished to a sad carnival of freaks, folding up its tents at the outskirts of town."

"Many things have been blown away," he said.

I saw his eyes in the darkness.

"But we did do something to change the world, didn't we, Green?"

"Yes...No. It is a difficult question."

"But it was magic once."

"It was magic once."

"And now this."

"And now this."

It was silent again for a while.

"Well, forgive me, Green. It wasn't much of a story. And I failed to make you laugh."

"Ah, but you did help me to forget.

On the sixth day, two guards opened the door and called my name. I had to be helped down the tunnel and up the stairs. The brightness at the main gate was blinding. When my vision returned, I saw for the first time the deep sores clawed into my skin and my heart jumped.

There were no interviews with the director, no lectures on behavior. Nothing was said or done about my health. The guards simply led me downstairs and deposited me in a cell. My new cabo assigned me a top bunk. Fortunately, Don was there to help me climb up.

I was nearly asleep when Kip came in with a bowl of water and a towel. As he washed me, I tried my best not to cry out in pain. At times I watched Kip's blue eyes and how they sparkled like the color of the Caribbean Sea.

"I see Hanauma Bay in your eyes," I said.

He smiled. I liked remembering the sea. Maybe things would be better now. I felt sure they would get better now.

I awakened late that same day, still lost in a world of delirium and dreams. My only wish was for the chatter of a thousand voices to go away. I turned towards the wall and went back to sleep.

Later, I felt a hand on my shoulder and turned to find Kip with a bowl of soup in his hands. The soup had potatoes and zucchini in it. He placed a pillow under my head and fed me, spoon by spoon. It hurt terribly at first, to feel the sharp, hot finger penetrating into the hollow space of my gut. Each spoonful brought tremors. The nausea made me stop several times.

Unable to take anymore, I waved Kip off. He adjusted my pillow and blankets before going away.

When I awakened, the cell was locked. Everyone was asleep. I considered urinating in bed but forced myself to climb down and use the toilet. It was the part about getting back up that troubled me.

Back at my bed, I clenched my teeth and made the leap, the sores on my belly ripping and stretching. I stifled my yelp and lay down, thankful for the comfort of a bed and the stillness of the night. It was bound to get better. Something always came along to make life worth living, something to save us from the senseless drift of time without measure or meaning.

I tried to think of all the good things I once knew and hoped I might have them back again. I would cherish them more than ever now. Of that much I was certain. I said a prayer—that no one else would ever have to endure the things I had endured—and at last found sleep

The next morning, I climbed down to urinate and became aware of my own stench. I made it through la cuenta only by holding onto the bed frame.

When the cell was reopened, I staggered out in search of Kip. I wanted to take a shower but needed a towel and some fresh clothing. All my clothes were as soiled as the ones I was wearing.

Along the way, I saw men scrubbing the upper balcony and felt sick. It was visiting day, meaning I would be required to sit around alert and upright for six hours, and quite possibly out in the hot sun. I wasn't sure I could stay awake for that long and they put you in the hole if you fell asleep on visiting day.

My search for Kip assumed a level of desperation. Water was now flooding down from the upper balcony. I needed someplace to hide.

At last, I saw Kip, heading to take his own shower and caught up with him.

"How are you feeling?" he said.

"I can't stay awake for six hours, Kip."

"Hang on, we'll figure something out."

At the showers, Kip bullied his way through the crowd inside and carved out a spot for me on the wooden bench. The Mexicans stared when I sat down. You could see that my reputation had preceded me and they were hungry to finish me off. I slumped over with Kip standing protectively at my side.

When it was my turn, I took the first blast of cold water with another yelp. Water to my sores was like salt on a skinned man. The soap made it worse but I forged ahead until I was clean and felt greatly renewed. All I needed now was someplace to sleep away the day.

When I was dressed again, Kip took me to his cell and had me lie down on his lower bunk. He went over to speak with the cabo. They conversed in Spanish at some length, after which the cabo came over to look at me. A kind man, he smiled, felt my forehead and nodded at Kip.

"Esta bien," he said and left.

"Stay here," Kip told me. "I'll be back soon."

I watched with failing strength as men prepared for the visit. It was something like matadors getting ready for a bullfight. I enjoyed it, as much as was possible. Then I found myself asleep again.

I was reawakened by Kip tucking a blanket into the bunk over my head. I attempted to sit up but he held me back.

"Stay put," he said.

"All right, generalissimo."

I lay back down in the now darkened space. When Kip was done, he pulled back the corner of the blanket near my head. Light came in.

"It's my shroud of innocence."

"Yes, today you are the saint of all lost souls and whores."

"I would like to be that saint," I said. "I would make him a very good one."

Kip smiled and sat on the edge of the bed.

"Have you talked to Danny?" I asked him.

"He was here Wednesday. He said he can't come much right now because of his base duties."

"Did you tell him about the safe?"

"No. I'll wait to hear what my parents have to say. In any case, I don't want to leave him with the temptation for too long."

"Am I messing things up for you, Kip?"

"No. It doesn't matter that much right now."

Someone had turned up the mariachi music and it wafted in with a warm breeze through the windows. The scent of fresh tortillas came with the music. The festive air of visiting day was upon us.

"I suppose I slept through breakfast."

"Would you like something to eat?"

"Yes. Something."

Kip dug into a box under the bed and produced an apple. It was small and green and very tart.

"Is that okay."

"It's okay." I chewed on one bite and let it settle into my shrunken stomach before I spoke again. "Explain to me what's happening."

"Nothing so far."

"No news of our trial?"

"I already told you. It's not a trial. They take you in for that second statement and that's it. It's supposed to be your chance to clarify your first statement but Max said they almost always go by the first statement."

I stared at him.

"Why do we never see Maximillian?"

"He lives out by the shop. Next to the kitchen."

"That would be nice." He nodded. "But you don't know when?"

"Like I said, it usually happens in the first three weeks. They take you to the courthouse and put you under oath, and you make a statement to a secretary. Then you sign it, and they bring you back. Then you wait."

"I have to practice waiting," I said.

"It helps if you meditate."

I nodded, not wanting to think about mediation. I would need to practice that too.

"Are you going to hire a lawyer?"

"Probably. Robby has one. His father came down and took care of everything for him. His lawyer said there's nothing you can do until after the second statement. Then the district attorney recommends a sentence, and the dance begins."

"Has Robby changed his tune?" Kip shook his head. "The bastard."

He shrugged. I looked up and saw Don coming in from his shower.

"Hi Don. How are you?"

He seemed embarrassed by his prior moment of weakness.

"Okay. How are you?"

"Still weak, but better."

"What about the others?"

"It's not good. Someone should tell the director. They may start dying if no one does anything."

"Do you really think the director cares?"

"He might. If he knew how bad it was. Do you know what happened to Delaney?"

"He's out too," Don said.

"Here?"

Don nodded.

"He paid his way out. They took him to the hospital yesterday. He's okay, I think."

I nodded. I was running out of strength and things to say when Robby came in.

"Hey, thought I'd come by to see how you were doing."

"Not bad, considering."

He shifted his feet.

"Well, I'm as sorry as anybody, if it makes any difference."

"Thanks."

"I did the best I could."

"I know you did."

"Shit, I'm in this thing, too."

"Get Kristine out of this. That's all we're asking, Robby."

"I'm doing whatever my lawyer tells me to do."

"Is that in lieu of your conscience?"

"Hey, screw you. I came over as a friend."

I started to sit up but Kip held me back. Robby flipped me off while backing his way out of the cell.

"You're still just an asshole, Clay."

"Go on," Kip told him.

"Pretend it's *your* own girlfriend!" I called after Robby.

The cabo came down the aisle and made a gesture with his hand.

"Calma Señor, calma."

I apologized and he left us.

"Like I figured, it's no use trying to reason with the prick."

Kip stared.

"Guess I'd better get dressed before the gate opens," Don said.

"Thanks for stopping by."

"Are you coming back to our cell after the visit?"

"Yeah. Are you going to cook?"

"Yeah. They brought me down the hot plate and stuff."

"That'll be good." He started to leave. "Can you ask about my clothes?"

"Sure…See you Kip."

"Game of chess?" Kip said.

"Okay," Don said. "I'll meet you over by the kitchen."

During their brief conversation, I had closed my eyes and a picture feeling had passed over me, like a cloud bringing shade on a summer day. I could not see the cloud in my mind. I only knew the great peace it had brought for one moment. Then the cloud was gone, along with my fleeting moment of peace. Was this the transcending Kip had encouraged me to seek?

I opened my eyes and found him staring at me.

"When's the next train to Nogales, Kip?"

"About half an hour."

"Good. I'll wait this time." He smiled sadly.

"Get some sleep."

"Wake me when it's over."

"I'll check on you later."

"Thanks."

He started to leave.

"Kip?"

"Yeah."

"Just until we go to court. That's all I'm asking."

He nodded and dropped the curtain on me. I drifted off to sleep with visions of Hawaii and Kip's straw-colored hair tangled over his face and the clear seawater dripping down his tan skin. I saw white clouds passing overhead and heard the palms whispering and the slap of gentle waves along the pebbly shoreline and was far, far away in my lovely dreams.

33

There was a flash of light and then darkness again, followed by a lady's playful laughter. Still entangled in my dreams, I pulled the blanket aside and found a young woman of sixteen or so standing in the aisle between the beds. She had a doll's face, skin to match and short black hair. She was a bit plump, but with a face like that, the weight hardly mattered. A young Mexican inmate and his girlfriend stood nearby, distracted by their petting.

"¿Qué quieres, Señorita?" I asked of the young woman.

She smiled.

"¿Está enfermo?"

"¿Por qué quieres?"

"Quiero saber. Nada más."

"Yo también."

Not understanding my humor, or the intent of my lousy Spanish, she came over anyway, tucked the curtain back and sat on the bed next to me. Her girlfriend said something in Spanish and went out the door with her inmate boyfriend. I looked back at the young lady. She wore a short dress, which seemed to be growing shorter, despite her repeated efforts to keep it down by her knees.

When I placed a hand on her soft, plump thigh, she pushed it away. I tried her back and she jumped up. She wasn't very playful now.

"You American all the same."

"Todos los hombres quierent egual."

She shook her finger at me and stormed off. About fifteen pounds less and she would have been breathtaking. I lay there, savoring the mental image of her high heels and bare legs. She certainly did justice to a pair of black pumps.

Aroused by my curiosity, I climbed out of the bed and got to my feet. I was still a bit shaky, but if sexual appetite represented any kind of barometer, I was on the mend. I shuffled over to the bathroom, splashed some water on my face and wiped it away with my shirt. I started to comb my hair but promptly gave up. Nothing but a shower and more rest could possibly improve my appearance.

I walked out into the bright sunlight and made my way across the courtyard. My shirt felt like it was being torched to my back. The tropical season had begun to move up from the gulf in earnest.

I found Kip sitting against a wall with several other Americans.

"You look much better," he said.

I sat next to him in the shade.

"I feel better."

He introduced me to the other Americans, names I did not recall a second after Kip had spoken them, but they were attached to good faces.

"Like to have a look around?" Kip asked me after a spell.

"Sure. I could use some fresh scenery."

We started in the direction of the southwest corner.

"For one thing, Señor, as you well know, we have los fuegos down here."

"Si, Señor. Upstairs we could only watch los fuegos with much envy…Have you heard more about the guys in the hole?" I asked as we walked along.

"They got thirty days."

"They're not going to last thirty days."

He glanced at me with his sad smile.

"Look at me after six days."

"I know, but I don't think the consulate cares. They come by and pretend to be concerned, but nothing ever happens."

"I think they at least have to keep us alive," I said.

"I think we have to consider ourselves alone."

Kip stopped to look at me.

"It's what we wanted, isn't it? To be free of our parents and society? And now we're going to go back and beg for their help?"

"I hate it when you ask those kinds of questions."

"I know you do."

309

We started walking again.

"We're still the sons and daughters of American citizens, and if we start dying, the press will turn it into a major bummer for Nixon."

"I think they know where that line is," Kip said.

"Well, let's hope it doesn't take one of us dying to find out."

We came to the alcove in the southwest corner and turned down that way. A man sat there with his family in the shade. Two lovers stood at the far wall. By their overt displays of passion, I assumed they were unable to afford a room, or were finding it hard to wait their turn. The family looked up at us and went back their business, which was trying to corral several young children.

Of all the corner alcoves, this was the only one that had no window opening at the end. I looked at Kip.

"The kitchen's back there."

"Of course. They wouldn't want you to see them making chicken foot soup."

Kip laughed.

"Did you get one too?"

"No, but I saw it."

We turned back and passed the main gate. The upper main gate and covered western veranda were directly above our heads.

"This is our presidential suite," Kip said. He pointed to a large cell that bordered the main gate. There were blankets on the windows, the same as upstairs.

We saluted and continued into the opposite alcove, which had a window facing north towards the nearby mountains. A twenty foot high perimeter wall blocked out everything but the very tips of the arid, brown peaks.

"The view's better upstairs," I said.

"Think you could see the Patagonias on a clear day?"

"No, but you could damn sure dream about it."

"Dreaming's good," Kip said. "Dreaming and meditation are our most important salvations in here."

"Oh to meditate for a thousand years."

Kip smiled as we turned back towards the courtyard. The greatest place of shade at this time of day was created by the northern length of the balcony upstairs and that six foot wide area was packed with bodies from end to end. Kip and I hurried out into the brilliant sunlight and made our way over to the alcove in the northeast corner. The window there was crowded with people but I saw briefly down into the dirt courtyard. A few of the so-called crazy men were wandering about in the sun. A guard came along and prodded one of them with a stick. He squealed and ran off.

Disgusted, I turned away with Kip and we walked under the eastern veranda. In the southeast alcove, we looked out through a locked gate at the wash yard. The bottoms of the long, smooth wash basins were dry now but still glistening in the hot sun. I looked over at the wall where McTavish had hung his hook and pipe. The wall was pockmarked with small holes.

"The firing squad," I said.

"Sort of," Kip said. "The Mexicans tell me this was Pancho Villa's headquarters at one time and he gave every prisoner a chance to escape. Then he shot them as they tried to climb the walls."

"Things haven't changed much."

"Not much."

I heard a voice calling out to us from around the corner.

"Oyer! Oyer hombres!"

I looked at Kip.

"That's the padilla," he said.

"Padilla?"

"Purgatory. One step up from the hole."

"The Mexican imagination is to be admired."

"Yes," he said.

I looked around to make sure no one in the hallway was listening to us, then looked back through the bars into the courtyard.

"I have two questions for you," I said.

"I don't have many answers."

"It's about escaping."

He nodded.

"I'm waiting for a friend to show up. With money, I hope. To bribe the guard when we go to court."

"Do you think you can make the border?" he said.

"I doubt by car. I'll probably head south, or cross the desert on foot."

"I think I'd head south."

"There are some other choices to be considered, but it's academic until my friend Eric shows up."

311

I looked at Kip.

"The question is, do you want to come, and if not, will you loan me the money if Eric doesn't materialize?"

"I don't know."

"About which?"

"Either of them."

"The money?" I said.

"I think you're crazy, but I guess that's your business."

"I hope we haven't come to moralizing with each other." He shrugged. "Well, as to the other."

"You mean escaping?"

"Yes."

He looked down and shook his head.

"I'm not sure."

"Do you want my opinion?"

"Okay."

"I wouldn't. The chances are this guard will take the money and shoot me in the back. In your case, you've only made things worse on yourself. Me? I've got nothing to lose."

"Your life..."

"If the Americans get a hold of me, I'm looking at twenty years."

"But maybe it wouldn't be so much. Maybe you're only looking at five or ten years. That wouldn't be so bad."

"Tell that to McTavish."

"He was desperate."

"So am I."

A man came out of a cell behind us, followed by a woman in a red dress. She was growing older, probably in her mid-forties, and showing her age. The corset and tight dress and abundant make-up helped, but not much. She would have made a decent wife but was struggling as a whore. I imagined her to be a bargain. As the woman worked on her looks, the owner of the cell brought another man down the hallway. The two entered the cell and the owner closed the door behind them.

I thought of all the things that made this place what it was; from a corrupt regime to the whores and fags, the life and death, the stores and craftsmen, the desire and pain of it all. It was not very unlike the rest of the world, if you could get past the spatial limitations.

312

"Maybe choice is an illusion," I said.

"We made quite a few of them to end up in here."

"Maybe we should stop making choices?"

He smiled.

"I think you always have to make choices," he said.

"I'd definitely like a few of them back."

"Maybe what's important is to accept the ones we've already made."

"I hate it when you say shit like that."

Kip smiled.

The man in the padilla called out again. I looked at Kip. Now the man shouted. He wasn't happy, that much was certain.

"There's somebody who's not happy with the choices he's made," Kip said.

"Yeah. Let's get out of here."

"Sure. What landmark would you like to visit next?"

"Oh, the bordello, of course. I've been dying to see it."

"By all means. Follow me."

We turned from the alcove and started along the southern wall in the bright sunlight. Single cells lined that length of the courtyard, along with the doors to them. The Mercado was among those cells. Back among the shadows, a man stood behind a counter that displayed raw meat, chickens and cheese. One wall was lined with fresh fruits and vegetables, everything from tomatoes to onions to limes and papayas. The other wall was lined with canned goods and sundries.

Two more doors further on, we came to a short hallway on our left. Cell 13 was down at the end of this hallway. A window looked into a small courtyard, which included the back door of the kitchen. A row of garbage cans lined the kitchen wall. The whole place smelled like a dump in the hot sun.

As Kip and I turned into the hallway towards Cell 13, two transvestites loitering in the shade of the entrance tried to hit us up. We ignored their overtures and received some bitchy chatter.

Down at the end of the hallway, it took some time before the curtain over Cell 13 opened and we were able to catch a glimpse inside. Blankets had been hung from floor to ceiling, creating private quarters. There were plants and candles. All in all, it was very flowery and feminine.

313

Rosa, the madam, stood behind her podium inside, like a dinner hostess. Rosa was the least attractive of all the transvestites and also the toughest. She eyed us and thumbed her nose.

"¿Que quieres?"

"Nada, Señora," I said and made eyes at her.

"Entonces, vaminos."

Behind Rosa, I heard someone crying out, "oi, oi, oi...oi mi amor."

It sounded like torture, but when you got right down to it, sex would always sound that way, if a person didn't know any better.

With a final wink for Rosa, Kip and I walked back into the bright sunlight and turned west to where we had begun. The other Americans were still sitting against the wall. I heard *Procol Harum*, originating from Rene's cell. When I stopped to peek inside, Rene got up from his bed and came outside.

"Hey, what's happening, brother?" he said to me.

"Same old shit, how about you?"

"Everything's groovy here."

"Try the hole," I told him. "It's a real change of pace."

Rene's nose twisted up. He looked around, like he half expected to be mugged, and retreated back into his cell with the iron door closed behind him.

"King Rat," I said.

Kip nodded.

"I watch him at night. I think he's very lonely."

"He'll be bummed to find out you can feel that way for free."

"I see you're getting right back into form, Clay."

"Yes, and hardly off my deathbed."

Kip and I returned to the group of Americans we had left sitting along the southern wall. Some had gone. Others had taken their places.

Don sat apart from the others, his head hung down between his knees. I went over and crouched beside him.

"What's wrong, Don?"

He looked up and wiped at his face. He had been crying again.

"Oh, nothing," he said and put his head back down. I placed my hand on his shoulder.

"Maybe you should talk about it?"

He shook his head without looking up.

314

"This place is getting to me, that's all."

"It's getting to all of us."

He didn't say anything.

"It's okay, Don. You're not the only one who feels like crying."

He looked up at me now.

"Yeah, but I'm the only one who does."

He half laughed at himself.

"Maybe you're just more honest than the rest of us."

"I definitely cry more."

His next attempt at a laugh died into a miserable look and his head went back between his knees. I squeezed his shoulder gently, hoping to have some positive effect on him, but he did not look back up.

The bell rang to end the visit. I squeezed Don's shoulder one more time and stood up. Kip was waiting.

"There'll be a lot of crying now," I whispered as we started across the courtyard together.

We were about to part ways for our respective cells when I caught a glimpse of Robby sneaking around in the other direction.

"Looks like he got stoned and lost his way," I said. While we watched, Robby slipped into the door of Rene's penthouse. "Well I'll be damned. The fucker bought his way up."

Kip shrugged and turned towards his cell.

Back at my bunk, I found myself chewing on that image of Robby, unsure why I found him so detestable. It wasn't the private cell alone. Maybe once a person did something bad and never made up for it, then everything they did afterwards seemed rotten to you, whether it was or not. I guessed that was the way I felt about Robby.

That night Kip came by to help Don prepare dinner. After the dishes had been cleaned up, Don indulged us with some of the bush he had purchased from El Presidenté. It came in a tin foil package, half an inch wide by two inches long, and the joint he rolled was mostly paper, but it got us high and lent a new dimension to our nightly stroll around the cheap Latin bordello that had become our home.

We were about to call it an evening when a group of young machismos came around and made several lurid gestures in Don's direction—grabbing their crotches and blowing kisses his way—

315

that sort of thing. I looked at Don but he appeared to be no more troubled by it than he was by any of his other ongoing burdens. I looked once more at these men. Their gestures had seemed innocent enough on the face of it, but Don was defenseless, and that was not a good thing to be in a prison.

34

Dawn arrived again at the prison and everything was the same as it was, and the truth began to sink in, how my emotions would drift this way and that with the passing days. How hope would come to me, followed by despair, then laughter at times, followed again by despair, but always there would be these hours upon hours of waiting and longing, and for what, except to be somewhere else, always expecting that in this other place, I would be happier than where I was now. And no matter what I thought or felt or hoped or dreamed, I would come back from my distractions to realize I was staring at the walls of confinement.

Again that morning, the guard and his sycophant came to conduct their grim ritual and I stood in line to shout out a number for men who really didn't give a damn if I existed, just as long as I didn't make trouble or try to run off somewhere.

Once la cuenta was over and they had reopened our cell, I went for a stroll, eager to have my shower, like everyone else, but knowing it was best to let them fight it out for an hour or so. By nine, you could walk in and shower at your leisure.

Back at my cell, I found Don pasting magazine pictures on the wall above his bunk with that white swill they called breakfast. It worked for that as well as anything else.

His mother had sent him a Look magazine pictorial of the sixties and I wandered back through the all too familiar memories: Haight, Woodstock, the magic bus, the many faces full of hope and wonder. What had happened? How had things gone so terribly wrong? I was immersed in these thoughts when Delaney came in with my clothes.

"Clay, you're a survivor," he said and handed them to me. They were clean and neatly folded.

"And you're a bastard." I climbed down gingerly and gave him a hug. "How the hell are you?"

"Oh, I'm a survivor, too."

I nodded at the clothes.

"You trying to buy my friendship?"

"It was worth a shot."

"Not after what you pulled."

"Hey, sorry, man. I didn't mean to leave you behind."

"I know...So where did you happen to find these?"

"El Presidenté had them stored away."

He put his arm around Don and smiled.

Watching Delaney, I wondered why I had forgiven him his deed and not Robby. My imprisonment wasn't Robby's fault, any more than Delaney was responsible for my trip to the hole. They were both just trying to save their own asses, but at least Delaney hadn't lied. Maybe it was as simple as that and I just couldn't pity Robby as the result.

Anyway, Delaney's nondescript face and thick glasses made it rather impossible to sustain visceral emotions towards the man. It was a face so bland and utterly unmemorable in its features, it stirred no emotional response in you at all. You were always left with a vague feeling that you had known him somewhere else before, a feeling that countless souls from countless past lives were locked within that Wonder bread mug.

Delaney was déjà vu in the flesh.

"By the way, you can call me Joe," he said.

"When I get ready to forgive you, I'll call you Joe. In the meantime, it's Delaney."

"You're not really mad at me, are you?"

"Don't get yourself a penthouse and it might pass."

"It's survival, Clay, and you know it."

"Don't expect me to like it."

"I'd get them all out if I could."

"I know. I know you would."

He pretended to give Don a punch and Don winced.

"We ought to do something about getting them out," I said. "I'd feel a lot better if we tried."

"Yeah. I still think our best shot is the consulate," he said.

I shook my head.

"What?"

"I think Green was right. They don't give a crap. And I don't think the director understands how bad it is."

A troop of Mexicans left the cell, making a great deal of noise on their way out.

"We'll talk about it later," I said. "I'm off to take my shower here in a minute."

He gave me a thumbs-up and marched out.

This consulate business had me worried. They had seen Kip already; the same with Steve and Robby. I personally had no interest in meeting with the consulate but you had to wonder why hadn't they called me. If they knew who I was, they wouldn't be ignoring me, and if they hadn't connected the dots yet, they would have paid me a visit, just like the others. It didn't seem to make sense, either way.

Getting nowhere with it, I gathered my things and headed for the showers, with one look back at Don as I went out the door. He was the only one remaining in the cell. All the Mexicans had gone off.

I took quite a while cleaning up my old sores. They had scabbed over and itched intolerably. I crossed paths with Kip on the way back.

"Robby had a visit from his lawyer this morning. We're scheduled to go to court next Tuesday."

I thanked him for the news and continued back towards the cell. Next Tuesday; that seemed impossible. I had yet to hear anything from Eric, and once he arrived it would take at least two days for him to retrieve the money. And that still left the issue of bribing the guard and planning an escape. I had to pressure Kip about the money again. Danny could probably have the money down here the following day.

Absorbed in my thoughts, I hadn't noticed the two Mexicans standing near the entrance to my cell. When I went to enter, they tried to stop me, then parted when four other Mexicans inside came down the aisle. None of them belonged in our cell.

"¿Que paso?" I asked them.

One of them showed me a knife going by.

"Cuidado, hombre. Cuidado."

He punctuated his threat with a smile.

I was thinking to show him the proper use of a knife but had already heard the animal-like sounds coming from the far end of the cell and ran that way, realizing that these were the same bastards who had taunted Don the previous night.

Sure enough, I found him lying on the floor behind the last bunk, his pants down at his ankles and his arms clasped around his knees, naked to the cold, concrete floor and moaning rhythmically. They had made a real mess of him. I grabbed a wad of toilet paper and cleaned him up as best I could. When I tried to wipe his face, he struggled with my hands.

"It's all right, Don. It's me, Clay."

My words of reassurance did little to quell his anguish. I did my best to get his pants pulled up and more or less dragged him down the cell. My attempt to hoist him onto his bunk failed for a lack of strength.

"Don. Please help me."

He grabbed hold rather helplessly. I banged his head several times but somehow got his body over the edge. He went on moaning and convulsing as I arranged some blankets over him. My thought was to go for help but I remained there rubbing his back and thinking it through, more afraid to leave him than anything else.

Kip came in after a few minutes.

"Delaney is looking for you. Said he wants to..."

I cut him off with a gesture and herded him back to the entrance. Kip's eyes turned gray when I explained what had happened. When he bolted for the door, I grabbed his arm to restrain him.

"Kip. It won't do any good to start a fight. You'll end up in the hole."

"I accept being here, Clay, but I don't accept them treating us like animals."

The sound of men shooting hoops echoed around the courtyard. The orange ball flew past the window against a blue sky. I saw a group of inmates gathering in the hallway outside. Kip tried to pull away.

"Let go of me."

I pinned him to the wall, knowing he could beat me if he wanted.

"Kip. I learned upstairs. There's a certain way of going about things. Let's ask Delaney before we do anything stupid."

Kip looked back at Don.

"It's survival, Kip. It's whatever we have to do to get out of here alive."

"There's no point in surviving if we have no dignity left."

He pulled himself free and started down the hall. I grabbed at his arm, but he pulled away. Just then Joe turned the corner and saw us struggling.

"Come on guys. There's enough trouble in here already."

"It's not us, Joe. It's Don."

I nodded at the door. Joe poked his head into the cell briefly and came back.

"What's wrong with him?"

"The Mexicans violated him."

"All right, that's it. We're going to see El Presidenté."

He started down the hall but I grabbed his arm too.

"Why the hell would he care what happens to us?"

"He knows he can't mess with us unless we're causing trouble."

"I don't trust him. I say we go to the director."

"That'll take a week, minimum," he said. "And you still have to go through El Presidenté."

"There has to be a way to get to him sooner," I said.

Delaney shook his head.

"What do you think, Kip?" Joe asked.

"It can't wait. I won't watch those fuckers strutting around for another minute, let alone weeks."

Joe looked at me.

"You want results today, you go see El Presidenté."

I studied him, his eyes looking back as though a fish-bowl. I didn't like having to trust El Presidenté. I didn't like it at all but Joe had been in here longer and knew the ropes better than me.

"Okay, Joe," I said, looking over at Kip and back. "We'll wait here."

Kip and I went back into the cell and stood near Don. At one point, I told him we were going to get justice. I thought it might make him feel better but he probably didn't care. He probably didn't care about anything right then.

Kip and I said little to each other while we waited. The sound of the basketball game ebbed and flowed outside the windows.

Once, Don opened his eyes as though he had felt the nightmare resuming and his anguished moaning commenced all over again.

A minute later, we heard approaching footsteps and four cabos marched into the cell. There was the feeling of cold, impartial justice to their enterprise. These men weren't here on any mercy mission.

"Vaminos, puta," one of them said.

Don cowered against the wall.

"¡Vaminos, puta!"

When Don failed to respond, the cabo reached up and pulled him off the bed by his hair. I mostly caught Don, but his left knee cracked hard against the concrete. One of the men kicked him in the stomach.

"Arriba, puta. Pinche chingada. ¡Vaminos!"

I tried to intercede and caught a club across the temple for my efforts. That cabo stood guard over me while two others backed Kip against the opposite bunk. The remaining cabo lifted Don to his feet by the hair. Don yelped and they all laughed.

They showed by way of charades that Don was to roll up his bedding and follow. Don cried as he gathered his stuff and was marched out of the cell.

I pushed my way through the throng outside and hurried across the courtyard. Kip was at my side.

"Where do you think they're taking him?"

"Cell 13," I said. "I knew I shouldn't have trusted that bastard."

"I'm going to find Delaney," Kip said and raced off towards the main gate.

I cleared the crowd in time to see Don herded down the hallway and into the door. Their assignment complete, the cabos marched back towards El Presidenté's cell.

The spectacle had momentarily silenced the prison, but once the outcome was clear, the Mexicans broke out into a chorus of derisive cheers. They had stuck it to the gringos big time. They had made an American the chingada. They suggested to me by way of words and gestures as I entered the hallway. Go on. Give it to him good.

I shoved Rosa aside and forced my way into the cell. She and all her gay friends were chattering at me like a pack of monkeys. One of them caught me with his nails and I slapped him a good one in return. He gasped and held his face.

I found Don on a bunk in the corner.

"Don, I'll get you out of here." I shook him when he failed to respond. "Just don't let them hurt you anymore."

He looked up through his red, swollen eyes. Then he collapsed back on the bed.

"Go away. Please. Just go away."

He was lost and there were no words to console him. I got up and left with one last squeeze of his arm.

The cabos wasted no time in escorting me to El Presidenté's cell. One man went ahead of me. One man held my right arm behind my back. They brought me before the man everyone feared; the man who had purportedly killed more than thirty other men, two of them cops, but I didn't think he looked so fierce. He looked more like a plumber to me.

He said something I was unable to understand but it was translated.

"He wants to know why you go there and make trouble, Señor."

I stared at El Presidenté, daring him to beat me down, daring him to come across that table and face me with his fists.

"That's my friend you threw in there. He was raped by your people."

El Presidenté listened to the translation, appearing to be perplexed. He said something rather quickly.

"He enticed those men."

"Did you ask him his side of the story?"

They talked among themselves. Then El Presidenté concluded something, which was translated.

"It no matter, Señor," the man said with a smile. "Once you get it." He made a gesture. "That's it. You go to Cell 13."

"Fuck all of you."

El Presidenté waited for a translation. Everyone waited. The cabo grimaced as he spoke the words, as if they were his own.

In the silence that followed, El Presidenté reviewed his men, measuring the damage to his authority, then returned his attention to me and spoke with the sharpness of glass. His words were translated.

"For going where you did not belong and saying this thing, you clean up for thirty days."

"Fuck you."

This did not require an explanation. El Presidenté kicked over the table and his men surrounded me. The first blow came from behind. I lurched forward from it and went down from a punch to the side of my head. As soon as I had struggled to my feet, another blow came. I tried one more time but felt a boot on the back of my neck. Nauseous light patterns spun around me with lead weights attached.

Two men yanked me up. I prepared for the next blow but instead, one of them placed a cigarette in my mouth. I assumed that was for taking a beating without complaint.

"Hombre," he said, lighting the cigarette.

El Presidenté patted me on the back. I inhaled and blew the smoke to one side, not at all satisfied. They must have sensed my determination because they began talking among themselves. One of them translated.

"Okay, Señor. We send them to the hole for a while. These men no good. It's okay. But your friend, he stays."

I started to say something but he stopped me.

"This is Mexico, Señor. ¿Comprendez?"

Yeah, I understood. It was the unwritten law, like a woman giving up her virginity before marriage. She was automatically a whore. There was no gray area, no middle ground. It was part of their society and no cultural platform existed from which to question these values.

I wanted to fight but saw it was no use. We would have to protect Don where he was. Nothing further would happen to him except perhaps a bit of humiliation. I figured we could carry him through that all right. It wasn't that much worse than what he had already experienced.

I nodded and El Presidenté patted me on the back again. I had to fight back an impulse to deck him. What the hell. We were in their world and they would never know what we thought of it, or of them. I finished the cigarette and put it out on the floor.

"Hombre," one of the cabos said and patted me on the back. I pretended to punch him and his friends laughed.

"Que verga."

I received one more pat on the back on my way out the door.

I stopped at the sink and washed the blood from my skull. My face was in one piece. They had been careful to avoid hitting me where it would show. They knew enough to keep up appearances.

I wandered back to my cell and climbed up onto my bed. A crowd of Americans followed me in. Joe came over to my bunk.

"What happened?" he said.

"I was going to ask you the same thing."

"Hell, I never expected that to happen."

The crowd of Americans was growing restless behind him. It had the scent of a street fight. The Mexicans had crossed a line. We were hippies and thus outcasts, but we were Americans. El Presidenté would not understand the politics involved, but the director would. If a riot broke out, it would be very bloody before justice was found.

"Hey man, what happened to you?" someone spoke out from the back.

I winced and shifted my weight.

"I told them something they didn't want to hear."

"I'm going to the consulate," someone said.

"To hell with the consulate, let's go kick some ass," another one said.

"They're going in the hole!" I shouted in an effort to restrain them but they started en masse out the door. I closed my eyes.

"Delaney, stop them."

"Are they going to let Don out?" Joe said.

"No."

"Then I don't think I can."

I turned to look at Joe.

"This is something we can't change. You may as well try to bring Montezuma back."

We both watched as the angry mob swarmed the courtyard. A riot felt imminent. Joe turned back to me.

"What am I supposed to do?" he said.

"Take care of Don where he is. And make sure he knows those guys are going down."

"I don't see how that's going to change anything."

I closed my eyes again.

"Neither will more blood."

"I'd better go see what's going on," Joe said and left.

There were further sounds of rebellion out in the courtyard. When I opened my eyes, Kip was standing there.

"What was that you said about restraining myself?"

"Getting the crap beat out of me was easier than watching it happen to you."

"It looks like they worked you over pretty good."

"Yeah. I wasn't conscious for most of it."

He looked away and out the window.

"I was right. It's pointless."

"What's pointless?"

He looked back at me.

"Fighting. All you can do is turn inward."

"Yeah. Let me know when you have that thousand year meditation handy."

"It's turn inward or get ready for a very long bummer."

In that moment, I finally got Kip, or at least saw more clearly the difference between the two of us. He had tried battling the world once and found it wanting. I had tried surrendering once and found that wanting. Acceptance was as contrary to me as fighting was to Kip. In any case, we had settled back into our more natural quantum states and things appeared to be more or less normal again.

Out in the courtyard, I heard what sounded like the law being enforced and jumped down from my bunk. Kip joined me at the window. Four of El Presidenté's capitans had those responsible by the arms and were herding them towards the main gate. It appeared as if a struggle had taken place.

Expecting the Mexicans to be pissed, I found them jeering and taunting the condemned. They savored power being wielded, no matter the nationality.

I got back up on my bunk. Kip went off to investigate. He returned with Joe a short time later.

"They're looking after Don all right," Kip said. "He won't say much but he understood what had happened."

"He seemed to be relieved," Joe said with a shrug.

The three of us stared at each other.

"I suppose we can invite him over for dinner," I said. "Some way to make him still feel a part of us."

"We'll check on him later," Joe said. "Get some sleep."

He patted me on the shoulder and left.

"What about the others?" I asked Kip.

"It's calmed down quite a bit. They're still talking about going to the consulate, though. To get him out."

We stared at each other.

"I need your help, Kip."

"Something tells me you're headed for another catastrophe."

"I'm trying to get out of one," I said.

His mouth twisted up.

"What?"

"Why don't you stop struggling for once?" he said.

"Maybe it isn't in me, Kip. But I'm asking for your help, not your advice. I want out of here."

"I'll see what I can do."

After a moment, he walked out. Alone, I closed my eyes and drifted off to sleep. If only a man could sleep for twenty years. That would be the way to do time. Wake up and find it was all over. Maybe the world would be a better place by then.

Despite our best efforts, Don refused to come out that night, or the next day. The hours passed by even more slowly as I waited and fretted over Eric's expected arrival. As a backup plan, I had hopes that Danny would show on the next visiting day, but that was all I had; hopes. Kip and I had used up our phone call privileges for the week and the mail was too slow now for my purposes.

I slept for long periods and rarely got out of bed except to eat and shower. Visiting day was upon me again and I would need all my strength to get through it. Kip and Joe made regular visits to Don but had little to report in the way of progress.

"He told us he feels safe," Kip said.

"It's like they brought a lost little kitten home," Joe said.

"You don't suspect they're abusing him, do you?"

They looked at each other and shrugged.

When visiting day arrived, Don joined the entourage of ladies from Cell 13 to take a shower. It was customary to clear the area for them and the usual adolescent chirping from the Mexican inmates took place as the procession passed by. If any of it was directed specifically at Don, he was well shielded. The ladies had him surrounded like a newborn calf.

I tried to make eye contact but Don never looked up. Something had caught my eye, though, and I looked for it again upon his return. It was difficult to see through the others. There was only the quick flash of something in the sunlight and Don was gone back to his cell.

I had staked out one of the window coves early and was killing the day with a game of chess when the young Mexican lady from the previous visiting day appeared in front of me. She had a cake in her hands and was obviously quite proud of her efforts. When I laughed, she took it the wrong way.

Realizing we had to put the damned thing down somewhere, I had Joe assume my place in the chess game and led this young lady off towards my cell. Halfway there, it hit me. I may have been a wayward young man, stuck in a Mexican prison, but I was a wayward young gringo, and this little doll was obviously seeing her ticket out of Hermosillo.

Well. She wasn't wanting for ambition. That was for sure.

"¡Mira los hoyos!" she said in anger about the holes the guards had poked into her beautiful cake. I gestured to let her know it was okay and that appeared to have the proper effect. She sat down on a bed and patted the place next to her. I asked her name and she gave me about four of them. I plucked Rebecca out of the lot and said it out loud, gathering it was the most important one.

"Si," she said and patted the bed again.

I spent the day attempting to derive something meaningful from Rebecca's conversation, without much luck. Mostly we were left to a game of charades. Rebecca spent most of her day attempting to keep her skirt down. In between all that, I experimented with what I could touch and learned it was her hand.

When the bell rang at the end of the day, Rebecca made it clear that she would return on Sunday. I started back to my cell and crossed paths with Joe along the way.

"Hey Matthews, starting a family in your spare time?"

"Don't get me started, Joe."

"She's a beautiful gal."

"Yeah, but she's got marriage on her mind. I'd better wait for another one to come along."

"You think like that and you'll grow old all alone."

"You grow old either way," I said.

"Well, fine. Don't marry her."

"Why don't you?"

"If she's not good enough for you, what makes you think I'd have her?"

"And if you won't marry her, why should I?"

Delaney stood there scratching his head like he was trying to get the cobwebs out.

"It's gotten too complicated for me, Matthews."

"And that's the problem with marriage, Delaney."

He laughed.

"Okay, okay. You win. I'd better get back to my bachelor's pad."

"Yeah, maybe I'll see you later."

"By all means, stop by for dinner."

"About eight?"

He winked through his glasses and plodded off to his cell.

Back in my cell, I stood at our window, watching Rebecca as she waited in line to leave. A thought had occurred to me earlier in the day. Marriage or not, surely there was some way I could use this situation to my advantage. If nothing else, there was no reason not to encourage this charade.

When Rebecca looked my way and waved, I waved back. Then she was lost in the crowd and gone out the gate.

I gaze up at the sky before climbing back up onto my bunk. Ominous thunderheads were gathering over the prison. A storm had eased up from the gulf and stalled against the mountains and the sultry air that came with it was stifling.

Right in the middle of la cuenta, the rain broke and came down hard, splattering up onto the plaster window ledges and into our cell. I saw the guard and the kid with the clipboard running across the courtyard.

Dinner was served up in the hallway by Cell 13. I took my beans and hurried back to Joe's cell. Kip was there. I shook the rain off my clothes and hair before sitting down.

"Did you notice anything strange about Don today?"

"Nope," Joe said. "Haven't seen him."

"And you, Kip?"

"He looked embarrassed, I guess. Other than that, no."

I watched Joe cooking the meal in half an inch of lard. He cooked everything in half an inch of lard. He was a mess cook at heart. I missed Don.

The cell was empty except for us. The Mexicans always cooked outdoors, even in the rain. There was something tribal still in them; ten guys half soaked and crouched around a hot-plate under the balcony, like it was a campfire.

"Did you notice anything?" Kip said.

"I thought I saw him wearing an earring."

"You're nuts," said Delaney.

"I'm not sure, mind you."

"About which?" he said.

"About the earring."

"Yeah, 'cuz we all know you're nuts." He enjoyed his joke as he went about his cooking. "He's out of his mind, Kip."

Kip smiled but otherwise kept his thoughts to himself.

When the meal was finished, we put the plates in a pile and went out to stand under the balcony. The rain let up a short while later. When the clouds parted, the last ray of sunlight glowed on the tile roof. We stood against the wall directly across from Cell 13 and waited.

About an hour passed with the usual clientele coming and going. The ladies milled around toying with the potential customers, the way prostitutes will.

Then Don appeared. He was taking it slowly, but he had definitely gone over the line. His hair was curled and he had a knit top pulled down over one shoulder. No lipstick yet but he was wearing an earring. With his silky blonde hair and angel face, the Mexican males were in heat. They had all dreamed of having an American bitch and Don was probably as close as they were ever going to get to one.

He was definitely the prize of the stable and you could see Rosa keeping a tight handle on things. When one of the customers came too close, she slapped him away. Perhaps she was jealous. Perhaps she was just giving Don time to work into things.

"I don't believe I'm seeing this," Delaney said. "He's a fucking fag."

"Why don't we talk to him?" Kip said. "Find out what he's thinking."

"Find out what? The guy's a fucking fag."

"Kip's right. We need to talk to him."

"Shit. You talk to him."

"Okay, I will."

I got up and crossed the courtyard. Don saw me and looked the other way. The other ladies closed ranks around him.

"¿Qué quieres, hombre?" Rosa said.

"Nada de ti."

"Que verga," she said, straightening her gown.

I ignored her and attempted to make eye contact with Don.

"Don, are you all right?"

There was no answer. I had to look through several faces to see him.

"Don! I just want to know you're all right."

"What do you care?"

"Come on, Don. Of course I care. We all care."

"I know you're all making fun of me so just fuck off."

"Don, I don't know what anybody else is saying. I just came over here to make sure that no one is abusing you."

"I'm fine, okay?"

"Are you sure?"

"I said I'm fine."

"Okay, as long as this is what you want."

"God, you fuckers will never understand me."

With that, Don ran off to his cell. Rosa lit into me with a string of curses. I went back to sit with Joe and Kip.

"I guess it's what he wants."

"I told you. He's a fucking fag."

"Look. He's an American, so let's just try to give him the understanding he needs, all right?"

"I'll give him some fucking understanding," Delaney said and grabbed his crotch.

I couldn't help but chuckle.

"All right. Come on. This is a matter of dignity, Joe."

"Aw fuck him. If that's what he wants, fine."

I stared long at Delaney before turning away. I knew I didn't understand freedom all that well and had little room to speak for others. Perhaps Don was finally out of his own prison. Perhaps he was freer than the rest of us now.

Whatever the case, we did not see him again that night.

35

The following morning, Joe handed me a twenty-peso note and sent me over to the mercado for eggs and chorizo. A lot of sad faces were there to greet me as I approached from across the courtyard, all of them Mexicans. They looked sad when I walked in. They looked even sadder when I walked back out. Men with a hole in their guts watched as I marched off to eat like a lumberjack.

It was that bowl of swill they served up for breakfast every morning. You couldn't doctor it into something toothsome no matter how much you tried.

Back at Joe's cell, he grunted when I handed him the chorizo and eggs and his change. He hadn't bothered to look up. His pan was already sizzling with the usual pool of lard.

Kip was telling Joe how his great-uncle had chased a particular Mexican villain down into Mexico. I had already heard the story back in Tucson and went over to sit at the window with my thoughts.

With it being a Saturday morning, laundry hung from clotheslines all over the courtyard. A carefree feeling came with it; something like when you were a kid and your mother was pinning up sheets on a blustery spring day.

The main gate opened upstairs, breaking me from my reveries. Two cabos came down the balcony marching an old man along between them.

"They're dragging in a new prisoner," I said.

Joe and Kip came over to look. The old man appeared to be a peasant, lean and wizened with age. His gaze was downward. The cabos took him into a cell and came out alone. An American stopped to explain.

"The old man had put all his money into a load of kilos and was walking to the border when they nabbed him. Up in the mountains somewhere, just him and his donkey. At least that's what I heard."

The American shrugged and left.

"Aw man," Delaney said. "Goddamn. Can't they leave nothin' alone?"

I turned from the window and looked at Joe.

"What the hell are you going to do?"

"I can't believe it," he said.

"Wonder what they did with the donkey?" Kip said.

"Hell, the usual interrogation, then the firing squad," Joe said. He looked at me. "Burros are tough."

Joe went back to his cooking.

"Aw man, I can't believe it. I can't believe anyone would do that to the poor old guy...Jesus."

A short while later, as Joe was ladling the last of the omelet onto my plate, something hit the courtyard concrete with a dull thud. This was followed by a buzz of voices. I went to the window and saw that the old man had thrown himself off the balcony. The top of his head had cracked open like a walnut. Kip ran out the door and kneeled over him. A trail of blood was inching its way towards the drain in the center of the courtyard.

The old man's face was turned in my direction and I thought I could see crosses over his eyes. I told Joe about it.

"Do you see it?"

"Yeah," he said. "I see it."

Then the crosses disappeared.

"He's gone now, Joe."

"Yeah. He's in a better place."

"It wouldn't take much."

"Anything would be better than this rotten, fucking hole."

"Let's hope he's with his donkey," I said.

"Yeah, let's hope he's with his donkey."

Kip returned to the room and stared off absently. There was blood on his shirt. All the Americans had drifted back to their cells, or at least off to a safe distance. The Mexicans were crouched in a rough semi-circle around the body, uphill from the trail of blood.

They murmured quietly among themselves from time to time but mostly just squatted there reverentially.

The omelet had sat there growing cold this whole time. None of us had bothered to touch it.

"You still hungry, Clay?"

"Not much, Joe."

"Yeah. Me neither."

"How about you, Kip?"

Kip shook his head. He was staring out to where the body had been. Joe offered the omelet to the Mexicans in the cell. They divided up the remains and quickly devoured it.

Half an hour later, a handful of authorities from outside the prison arrived and milled about the corpse, pointing at it, rolling it over on its side once or twice, as though it were wild game that needed to be measured and weighed. An hour passed before they took the body away. By that time, the trail of blood had grown dark in the sun. It had stopped just short of the drain. Two men dragged out a hose and washed and scrubbed the concrete until only an inconspicuous outline of the blood remained. You had to look hard, but it was there.

In reverence for the dead, the director came over the intercom and said a few words. It was unfortunate, but life went on.

"I know what we need," Joe said. "Just wait here. I'll be right back."

He started out of the cell as if on a mission. I looked back at Kip.

"We need to start talking about buying our way out of here."

"With what?"

"Well, plainly, you'd have to trust Danny."

"Not that I don't. Or trust you, for that matter, but what's keeping you from getting into your own funds?"

"A slight snag."

"Which is?"

"Eric's name is on my bank accounts in Mazatlán."

"And you can't find him."

"Hell, I can't look for him."

"That's a fine mess," Kip said.

"It seemed like a brilliant idea at the time."

"It's better than nothing."

"Not much, but yeah."

335

I stared at Win until he looked back at me.

"So, what do you want me to do?"

"Get Danny to bring ten grand down here on Monday and we'll bribe the guards on the spot."

"And like I already said, Clay, it sounds like you're headed for another disaster,"

"Goddamn it, Kip."

"Look, I just don't want to see you dead."

He thumbed his nose in the general direction of where the corpse had been.

"I figure that's a choice I can make for myself."

"And the same holds for me."

"Twenty years in prison, Kip. That's what I'm facing."

"You don't know that. Even if you served ten years, you'd get out with a long life ahead of you."

"Ten years…"

"Granted, it wouldn't be pleasant. But you'd survive. I question whether you'll survive this prison escape."

"Damn it. Don't put up the money, but don't pretend to live my life for me."

He stared.

"I haven't said no yet, Clay."

"Well you haven't said yes."

"I'm thinking about it."

"Well, think quickly."

Kip looked out the window. I stared down at the floor, fuming. Before I got too far with my emotions, Joe returned and unwrapped a gallon jug from some newspapers.

"Presidential stock," he said and patted the jug affectionately.

I watched him unscrew the cap, guzzle down a good swig and gasp. I took a drink that nearly came up through my nose.

"Tastes a bit like Southern Comfort," I said.

"A bit chalky, but yeah, pretty close."

I tried it again for good measure and passed it to Kip.

"No thanks," he said and got up to leave.

"What's wrong?" Joe asked him.

"It's pointless," Kip said, looking at me.

"This whole situation is pointless," I reminded him.

"Well it's for sure we're not going to solve our problems with a bottle."

He turned down the narrow aisle between the bunks and headed out the door.

"Come on, Kip," Delaney called out after him. "We're just trying to pass the time, bro."

"Let him go."

Joe stared after Kip. I took another drink and passed the bottle. Joe took another belt and put the cap on. The warmth was growing inside of me.

"What did you pay for this crap?"

"A hundred pesos."

"Hell of a deal, Joe."

"Yeah. Say, what do you suppose is wrong with Kip?"

"Don't ask me. I don't understand him. Don't know if I ever did."

"Hell, he's just feeling down."

"We're all feeling down. Now give me that bottle."

Before long, the two of us were skunked. Delaney started in on politics.

"Screw politics, Delaney. It's the blind leading the deaf and dumb."

"Yeah," he said. "When I get out of here, I'm going up into the mountains or something. Get as far away from civilization as I can."

"Everybody says that."

"No, it's true. We've got to start a new life. Something we can call our own."

"People have tried that, Joe. It always looks great on paper. Then comes the hard work. Hippies never much liked that part of the equation."

"You know, you called me Joe. Does that mean I'm forgiven?"

"No. It just slipped out."

We passed the bottle back and forth for a while in silence.

"How about a joint, Delaney?"

"If you're nice and call me Joe."

"All right, Joe. Start rolling."

He reached under his bunk, dug around in his network of boxes and produced one of those foil packages you bought from El Presidenté. He rummaged further and produced a package of rolling paper. With several Mexicans loitering around in the cell,

Delaney hung a blanket over his bunk and twisted up the joint in privacy.

"I admire your preparedness, Joe."

"Shit, I figured right from the start. The only way to get through this mess was to stay fucked up."

"Makes sense to me."

"Hey, if nothing else, it kills the time. You sit around here staring at your shoes for too long and you'll go bonkers."

"How long were you back from 'Nam before this happened?"

"Shit, about two months. They hadn't hardly patched me up and sent me home when I got this wild notion to go see Mexico."

He lit the joint, took a deep hit and passed it to me. I took a hit and passed it back to him, gasping.

Like the joint Don had rolled, this one was mostly paper, but within minutes my synapses were arcing. Cosmic symbolism scurried around my mind with delightful randomness. We sat on Joe's lower bunk, our backs against the wall, pillows under our heads and reasonably comfortable in the sultry heat.

Life had resumed in the prison, almost carefree in its quality, as if no one had died in the courtyard two hours earlier. I heard the ladies from Cell 13 laughing in the wash yard. They would be standing side by side in the sun, their hair pinned up, their legs bare, soap and water getting their blouses wet, bantering playfully to the men watching them from beyond the gate.

I smelled tortillas cooking in the muggy gulf air, and hair oil. Someone was getting his hair cut. Someone was having his shoes shined. Someone was on his way to court, where he would be told that he could not leave the prison for a very long time. And it didn't matter if you felt happy or sad about these things, life went on.

Joe and I sat there for what seemed like an eternity, listening and surrendering to the listless Latin dream.

"You know," I said, breaking the silence. "Most people would give their left arm to be in our position."

"Yeah. We've got it made, don't we?"

"Free room and board. Nothing to do but contemplate the universe all day."

"Danger and adventure at every turn."

I thought of that poor old man. What sorrow had driven him to abandon all hope? Why didn't we all give up?

338

"What do you suppose freedom is?" I asked Joe.

"It's strange, isn't it? If I was on the outside, I'd be working my ass off somewhere, wishing I could sit around all day and do nothing."

I nodded.

"I'm really beginning to think that choice is an illusion?"

"Yeah," he said. "But I still reserve the right to choose my own illusions."

"I love that feeling of getting out on the highway, don't you? No idea where you're going? The wind in your hair?"

"Yeah. I think the automobile is the modern equivalent of a nomad sprinting across the vast primordial plains."

"I've had that very same notion, Joe."

"Yeah?" he said.

"Yeah. I wonder if it isn't just motion and change. That's all we really crave. Motion and change."

"Yeah. Like man equals mc2."

"You're on a roll, Delaney."

"I wish I was."

"Well, hell, let's have a toast."

We worked on the booze again in silence.

"Why don't we take a stroll, Delaney? What d'ya say?"

"Yeah, sure. I can work on my suntan."

"I'm dying to see the ladies."

"Frolicking in the soapy water," Joe said.

"Yeah, those little tarts."

We crossed through the hot sun, stopping for a moment where the old man had died. A faint outline of blood remained. An American sat in the shade nearby, doing a watercolor.

"You forgot the corpse, Dean."

"Real funny, Joe."

Joe shrugged at me and we moved on.

"Must be from the neo-obscurest movement," Joe said.

"It lacks humor."

"It certainly lacks a dead body."

We laughed at our joke and went off to look through the opening to the wash yard. It was exactly as I had envisioned it from Joe's cell. Rosa was there holding court with the other ladies. There was a little feminine lift of their shoulders when they looked up and noticed us staring. I looked at Joe.

"Would you?"

"Oh, I suppose. On a deserted island."

"Hell. You'd do it right here if I told you it was okay."

"So would you," he said.

"Have you ever wondered why people are so touchy about it?"

"I know the Mexicans have answered one part of the problem."

I looked at him.

"You scandalous dog, you."

"I know," he said.

We watched for a while.

"But really, Joe. It must be something primitive, like an unspoken medical taboo."

He looked at me skeptically.

"Christ, Clay. You're getting complicated on me again."

"Naw. Look at it this way. Anal sex is a dirty business. I could see a few guys having their dicks fall off and boom, it's gotten a bad reputation in the cave-dweller circuit."

Joe laughed.

"Hey, look at Don," he said.

I caught a glimpse of him as he went to hang some laundry on the line. He was wearing a babushka and lipstick. His nails were painted red.

"He's got a lovely face, Joe, you've got to admit."

"You getting hot there, Clay?"

"Hell, maybe. It's been a long time."

"You're sick."

"And what does it matter if I am? Our little life of illusions is over pretty fast. So what if a guy's happy having someone poke a pecker up his ass. Who are we to say?"

"Yeah. I guess there are more miserable things in life."

"Miserable people, Joe. And miserable people have forfeited their right to judge."

"Yeah," Joe said. He blew a little kiss towards Don and we headed down the hallway towards the courtyard. It was lunchtime and the usual table was being set up.

The Mexicans loved beans, but lunch was actually your best shot at a decent meal. It depended on how greedy the cook was that day.

We stood by the gate and caught a glimpse as the Mexicans scurried by with the pots.

"Shit, Joe. Looks like kidneys again."

"Don't kid yourself. Kidneys and cream? That's the high life."

"If you're a cat."

"Come on. I'll make you a peanut butter and jelly sandwich."

"Makes me think of school days, Joe."

"Sure. Falling leaves and young sweethearts."

"You really know how to romance a guy."

"Yeah, Clay, we'll have to get together when we get out of here."

"Are you kidding? I hope I never see you again."

"You'll feel different tomorrow."

"Differently, Joe. Get your goddamned grammar straight."

"What, are you joining the miserable now?" he said. I thought about his question before I answered.

"No, Joe. I'm sorry. I didn't mean to be hard on you. I'm just restless. Hell, maybe I am miserable. Probably just a bastard at heart, but I didn't mean to be hard on you."

"Naw, Clay, you're just upfront. It's cool." He gave me an armful of encouragement and we went into the cell.

Joe got out the Skippy and jelly and lashed them onto a couple of slabs of white bread. We took turns chasing down the lunch with that rot gut brandy and killed the afternoon with a few games of cribbage. I was too far gone for chess. I was nearly too far gone for cribbage.

I tried not to think of things I could not have but my mind was on Eric and my hopes for escape. I played the game and tried to be at peace with exactly where I was right then, but failed.

Late that afternoon, Joe and I washed away the rest of our drunk with a long shower. On the way back to his cell, I stopped. Something was calling to me.

"What?" Joe wanted to know. He had stopped to turn around.

"I'm going down the hall to watch the desert."

"It's the same damn thing."

"I know. But I have to look."

"Suit yourself."

"I'll stop by this evening."

"Call first," he said.

I left him and walked into the shady alcove at the northeast corner. It was nothing, just as Delaney had said, but I wanted to be alone, alone as a man could get with a thousand restless souls around him.

The window was empty and I stood there in thought. A glimpse of the mountain peaks was visible to me above the stone wall. There was the harshness of mankind's world and then everything out there quiet at the close of day. All I wanted was one more shot. Just one more shot. I felt certain I could make it turn out differently this time. I said a little prayer to that effect and remained quietly by myself for another half hour before returning to my cell.

That evening, when the Mexicans had gone outside to cook their meal, Joe offered to take me one step further down the road to iniquity.

"Let's shoot some smack."

"You're a walking drugstore, Joe."

"You don't want to?"

"How would I know? I've never tried it."

"You've never tried slammin' some drag?"

"The thought has never occurred to me."

"It's cool, man. You just sit and stare at your tennis shoes for eight hours."

"Sounds like a real thrill."

"It's eight hours you won't have to worry about any more."

"Hell, I don't care. What do I do?"

"Just hang loose."

He reached under his bunk and pulled out a bag of sugar. Hidden inside of it was a small, wooden box. Inside the wooden box was a kit. I watched as Joe laid everything out.

"You're going to do this right here?"

"Hang on," he said.

With everything ready, he lit a candle and waxed it into a bowl. Then he pulled the blanket down over his bunk. A flat metal tray sat on his lap as a workstation. The heroin was in waxed paper. He carefully sprinkled a small amount onto the spoon and added a measure of water with the syringe. This was cooked over the candle until it boiled. A small piece of cotton was placed in the spoon as a strainer. The boiled fluid was retrieved back into the syringe through the cotton. Joe handed me a belt.

342

"Tie this around your left arm."

I did as told.

"Tighter."

I gave it another cinch and Joe snapped the crook of my arm with his middle finger, searching for a good artery. Satisfied, he slid the needle into my flesh. A teardrop of blood gathered where the needle had gone in. Delaney pulled on the syringe and my blood flowed into the glass tube, thick and dark. When Delaney knew he had the needle in clean, he told me to let go of the belt. I did and he simultaneously compressed the plunger. There was a split second delay, then a fifty-pound weight landed in my gut. My urge was to sit up but a white-hot cannonball slammed into my head. The metal gate to an elevator closed. The elevator climbed twenty stories and before I could catch my breath, the elevator doors blew open and someone kicked me out. That fifty-pound weight had me falling fast.

"Oh man, I'm falling. I'm flying. I'm flapping."

"You're slammin', brother."

I could not speak. There were no words to speak anyway, only a nauseous odium of wild beasts stampeding out of my brain. My heart was a pit of depravity. I was cilia flagellating mindlessly in a sea of cosmic excrement. I wanted to escape but could not move. I never saw Joe slammin'. It could have been minutes or hours, I wasn't sure. I was a slab of grey light on a hard bed. There was another dim light next to me. We were staring at our shoes.

"I need some fresh air," I said.

"What do you think this is, a camping trip?"

"I just need some air."

"Well breathe, you dumb shit."

"There's nothing to breathe."

Joe made the miraculous journey forward and opened the curtain. The heavy blanket of air dispersed with a feeling of cool lips blowing ice down my pants. It was a nice thought.

"I would like to have a lady right now," I said.

"What the hell would you do with her?"

"Look at her naked. Look at her and touch her ivory flesh."

"I've never heard that one before," he said.

"The smooth, elegant beauty of a statue."

"What?"

"With pubic hair."

He laughed.

"Do you believe in God?" I asked Joe a bit later.

We had gone back to staring at our shoes.

"Maybe one of us is God," he said.

"God's a prisoner."

"And loneliness is his sin."

I looked over at Joe.

"Wouldn't that be just like this world, Delaney. God's doing twenty to life for having a heart."

36

I lay on my bunk the next morning, thinking hope was the ultimate form of denial. I was broke and in bondage. A woman had left me of late over my sundry problems, problems that, in all likelihood, would soon lead me from this hellhole into a far more efficient and antiseptic version of it. A place where I could expect to be for a very long time and my only chance to remedy this predicament depended on a guru-slumming space cadet who was nowhere to be found. It was truly remarkable that I expected everything to work out all right. Perhaps I had gone mad and didn't know it yet, but so much the better to pass the long, long years ahead.

That day went by and nothing changed. That evening, Joe and I started back in on his jug of presidential stock. We were sprawled across his bunk with our legs in the aisle. I had not entirely recovered from the previous evening.

"So what do you think of smack?" Joe asked me.

"Delaney, if someone's stupid enough to try that shit twice, they deserve exactly what they get." He looked at me with surprise. "Of course, that's just one man's opinion."

"I take it you didn't like it."

"I already know I have feet. And I'm sufficiently aware of the fact that there are shoes on them. The only confusion may lie in how far they are from my head at any given time."

"Well, I won't take it personally," Joe said.

"You can take it any way you like."

I unscrewed the bottle and took a slug.

"What do you say we go carousing?"

"Sure, let's go have some fun," he said.

I had a final drink, belched and stood up.

"Let's not be overly selective, my friend. Carnage and mayhem will do just as well in my book."

Joe finished off the bottle and stood up with me.

"Shall we?"

"By all means, sir."

We wandered out into a courtyard teeming with men, the urgency of their affairs no different than if we stood along the streets of the next dusty little Mexican town.

I noticed Rene and Robby checking in for a bit of poker action at El Presidenté's pad and dragged Joe in that direction. Any American was welcome to play at El Presidenté's table, as long as that person had money, and Robby and Rene had plenty of that. They stood at the gate, waiting their turn to go in. Rene had the air of landed gentry about him. Robby had hands in his pockets, as usual. I made a gesture like I was polishing my nails on my shirt.

"El Jefe," I said and nodded at them.

The guard at the door smiled.

"Looks like they left the limo at home tonight," Joe said.

"Yeah, boys. Kind of dangerous slumming around this low rent district all alone."

"You're just pissed because you're broke," Rene said.

"You're right, Rene. And I especially envy the shit out of the little general here."

I tried to straighten Robby's collar.

"Fuck you, Matthews," Robby said, pushing me away.

He ran his hands through his wiry hair once and placed them back in his pockets. The feet kept shifting nervously.

"You know, they cut your balls off if you win," Joe said.

"Well hell, then Robby's got nothing to worry about. Cuz he ain't got any."

"Screw both of you," Robby said.

Joe and I hung around having fun until someone drew the curtain back and welcomed Rene and Robby into the smoke-filled cell.

I drifted down towards the nearest alcove alone. Several Mexicans were singing a love song nearby and the melody knifed into my heart. What had happened to me? I once had hopes and dreams but somehow those things had been stolen away long ago.

It seemed then that there was nowhere to turn. I had tried and tried to make things come out all right but had failed. Had I been on the second floor, I might have thrown myself off the balcony like the old man.

Joe caught up with me. I was wiping at tears

"What's the matter there, Clay?"

"Oh, nothing, Joe. Just feeling a bit lost all of a sudden."

"You need another drink?"

"Sure, Joe, take me."

"Let me get a pack of cigarettes first."

I sat down against the wall opposite Cell 13, my heart filled with despair. I wanted to fly away, far, far away from this place. Joe came out of the Mercado and sat down beside me. He lit two cigarettes and handed me one.

"Would you look at that," he said.

Don had come out with the other ladies wearing a spaghetti strap gown and high-heel shoes.

"He's gorgeous, Delaney."

"Look at the Mexicans. They'd sell their kids to fuck him."

"I'd sell my kids to fuck him."

"You're sick," he said.

"I'm human."

"You want me to loan you some money, Matthews?"

"Yes, please."

"You are sick."

"I know. I'm going to go see if I can get it for free."

I wasn't too popular in that neck of the woods so the ladies kind of hissed with my arrival. I ignored them and made my way towards Don.

"Hi Don. You look real nice." He turned away. The other ladies tried to herd me off, and none too gently.

"I mean it," I said. "I'm still your friend." While waiting for his response, I was escorted further out of harm's way.

"I like the gown, by the way."

I went back and sat down.

"He looks real nice, doesn't he, Joe?"

"Fucking gorgeous."

347

"Hey, man, he's doing his thing."

"He's doing somebody's thing."

"All right," I said and got up. "It's your thing, do what you wanna do."

"Gringo loco," some Mexicans said going by.

I gave them a gesture to let them know what I thought and continued with my choreography.

"I'm having a tough time with my moves tonight, Joe."

"You're crazy, Matthews."

"I know. Now how about that drink?"

I pulled Joe up by his hand.

"I'll meet you back at my cell," he said.

Joe returned a few minutes later with a fresh jug. We drank for a while more but the fun had gone out of it.

I stood up.

"I need a break, Joe."

"What the hell're you gonna do?"

"I don't know. I've just been drunk too long."

"You'll feel different in the morning."

"Differently," I reminded him. "Anyway, good night. I'll see you tomorrow."

I felt like hell the next morning. After la cuenta and breakfast, I slept again. I wanted Joe to rescue me but figured it was time to clean up. There was always a possibility that Eric would show up and I would need my wits about me. A little before noon, about the time I was preparing to take a shower, Maximillian came in. I doubted he had good news and I was right.

"The consulate is sending someone over to talk with you today."

"So?"

"From what I gather, they have some questions about your identity."

"Isn't that strange? I'm having problems with it myself."

He stared at me, as cold as raw liver.

"It sounds pretty serious."

"Considering the present circumstances, that's a real revelation."

He adjusted his horn-rim glasses.

"Just be ready at one."

"I'll check my schedule."

I watched him walk out, wondering where the hell Eric could be. Probably on a mountaintop somewhere, consuming psychedelics. I felt hope slipping away. So much for thinking that everything would work out in the end. Actually, I was surprised it had taken them this long.

Well, whatever it was, they didn't know the whole story yet or they wouldn't be sending the consulate over.

The guards called my name immediately after lunch. I went to the main gate. The director personally ushered me into his office. He left, closing the door behind him.

A man in his forties got up from behind the desk and extended his hand. He was classic Establishment; tall, ivy-league, the hair combed back and thinning, his hands soft and well-manicured. He wasn't fat but there was a distinct lack of attention to his carriage, as if he considered it merely an appendage to support his head.

"Peter O'Donnell."

"Clay Matthews."

"Yes, I know. Please, have a seat."

He gestured, allowing me to sit before he joined me. He took very easily to his position behind the director's desk. It wasn't new to him. I stared and waited. He was thumbing through a file.

"Tell me, Mr. Matthews, how are they treating you?" he asked without looking up from his paperwork.

"Random torture and starvation aside, things couldn't be better."

He looked up from his file.

"I want you to know that we take the matter of your care very seriously."

"The evidence is ubiquitous."

He considered this for a moment.

"We are in a very delicate situation down here, Mr. Matthews."

"Just call me Clay."

"You are obviously an intelligent young man. I should think you would appreciate the complex nature of our relationship with Mexico."

"You'd invade the goddamned country if it served your interests."

"Your thinking is from another era, Mr. Matthews."

"Clay."

He looked me over carefully, contemplating his course.

"In keeping with our concerns, we have attempted to contact your family and have encountered a certain difficulty in that regard."

We stared at each other, waiting to see who would break first, and since I didn't give a crap what he thought, I was in a fundamentally sounder position. Besides, I knew what he wanted to know and wasn't about to tell him. As suspected, he broke first.

"It seems no one knows who you are. We have yet to receive the trace of your fingerprints from the FBI but it appears obvious that you're not Clay Matthews. That person does not exist. In the meantime, we thought you could help us clear up this mystery."

"It's got me baffled."

"Mr. Matthews. You don't seem to appreciate the seriousness of your situation."

"Let me get this straight. I've been in here two weeks, during which time I was thrown in the hole, nearly starved to death, beat up, and, for all intents and purposes, left to rot. Yet you hadn't the least bit of interest in coming to see me. Now, suddenly, you've developed an insatiable concern for my well-being, and all because you don't know who I am. Does that pretty much sum it up?"

"You tried to escape, Mr. Matthews. You can hardly blame the Mexicans for that."

"I didn't try to escape. I was transferred into a cell with some men who attempted to do so. But that begs the question. If you were incarcerated in this hole, wouldn't you try to escape?"

"I do not go about breaking the laws of other nations, so I'd have no reason to be in this situation."

"Not without the cover of law you don't."

"Mr. Matthews, I'm running out of patience. Are you going to assist us or not?"

"No. The question is, are you going to assist us?"

"Yes or no, Mr. Matthews."

"You figure it out."

He got up in disgust, pressing the call button under the desk. The door opened and the guard motioned for me to follow. As I got out of my chair, O'Donnell offered me one last clarification.

"I am instructing the authorities that you are to be held in the highest security until we have resolved the matter of your identity. In case you had any further notions of escape."

"You're suddenly very influential, aren't you, O'Donnell?"

"Good day, Mr. Matthews."

"Up yours, O'Donnell."

The guard led me out. O'Donnell's knuckles had turned white on his stack of papers. I had the smug satisfaction of kicking the hangman as he placed the noose around my neck.

It would seem the trap had closed. Even if Eric arrived, there would be no window of opportunity unless they took me to court, and O'Donnell had just taken care of that.

I went back to my cell and lay on my bunk. It was strange how the imagination deluded a man until the very end. In a matter of days now, I would be whisked away in a plane and marched down antiseptic corridors to my fate. And through all the years of confinement I could think, if only I hadn't cared.

Kip came in to see what was up. He stood at the foot of my bunk.

"They're on to me."

"Clay, it was inevitable."

"Kip, I need money." He shook his head. "Yeah, some friend."

I stared up at the ceiling.

"Why do you always fight things, Clay?"

"Since when is freedom a crime?"

"Freedom is something inside."

"Go to hell, Kip."

"I'm sorry. I'm not going to watch you get shot full of holes."

He turned to leave.

"Hey, Kip?"

"Yes."

"Just out of curiosity, if you were in my shoes, would you want me to give you the money?"

"Clay, acting impulsively is the only thing you know how to do. And the one time I went along with this propensity of yours, this is what I got."

"Aaahhhhh. So it is my fault we're in here."

"No, I don't blame you for the decision I made. But you asked me a question. What would I do if I were in your shoes? Well, instead of waiting ten hours for a train, I went along with one of your wild impulses and here I am. Here we are."

He let that sink in a moment before turning away. I stared after him, sorry we had ever met. Why did people always figure they had the right to tell you how to live and die? People who had no idea how to run their own lives, but were sure they could run yours.

Well, screw him. All I wanted was to escape this hole and thought it entirely natural for a man to feel that way under the circumstances.

37

One more sultry day was fading to late afternoon when they brought the new American into our cell. He was a short man with stout legs and a slight torso. The two parts of his body did not seem to match. Above it all, he had an intelligent looking head with gray eyes and a strong brow.

At a little past middle age, he did not look to be the sort of American you would find in a Mexican prison. They had assigned him Don's upper bunk.

"How are you doing?" he said with his bedding in hand.

"Not bad," I said from my bunk. "Given the circumstances."

He nodded and went about making his bed.

While he did, I noticed the plastic hands. They were pink and had the hideous quality of prank barf about them. Tufts of dark hair had been attached to the back, but that only made their appearance all the more hideous. I looked off at the pictures Don had left on the wall, not wanting to stare. When the blanket dropped to the floor, I swung my legs over, thinking to lend him a hand.

"I can do it," he said without looking back.

I returned to my prone position but my mind would not leave it alone. What was beneath the plastic hands? His actual hands must have been even more hideous, or why bother wearing the fake ones?

While he struggled with making his bed, I squirmed with another thought. Sooner or later, he would have to climb up onto his bunk and, I assumed, need my help. And that assumed he ever got the bed made, about which I had my doubts.

"The name's Clay," I said, deciding that conversation was better than silence.

Miraculously, the man had gotten his bed made and turned to face me. A jolt of anxiety came with his stare. Would he reach out to shake my hand? I braced myself for the moment.

"Glad to meet you, Clay. I'm Harry."

I waited but the offer of a handshake never came. Harry had no doubt been through this before and knew my thoughts well.

"Where did they pick you up, Harry?"

"Guaymas."

"Ah yes, Guaymas."

"You know it?"

"I know if I had been willing to wait there for a train, I would be a free man today."

"A man is only free if he believes it."

I gave him another look.

"Let's just say a bit freer than I am right now."

"Freedom isn't relative. Otherwise, it would have no meaning."

I shrugged and looked away, hating it when people were so sure of themselves. I figured if I was in the dark, everyone else ought to be, too. Joe walked in about this time and came over to introduce himself.

"Howdy, I'm Joe," he said.

I watched the expression on Joe's face as his hand started up and promptly went back down. He had done quite well, I thought.

"Harry," Harry said.

"Well, good to meet, Harry, and if there's anything we can do, don't be afraid to ask."

Joe thumbed his nose in my direction.

"You're in good hands here with Clay."

I grimaced over his choice of words. Harry looked from Joe to me and back at Joe again.

"When do they feed you?"

Joe laughed.

"The question is, what do they feed you?"

"I'll take whatever they slop out right now."

"When was the last time you ate?"

"A late dinner yesterday."

354

"Yeah, you're good and hungry. I'll tell you what. Why don't you and Clay come over in half an hour? I'll throw something together."

He looked at me.

"Sure, Joe. Thanks. I'll fill him in and we'll be down in a while."

He nodded.

"Hey, Harry, don't let it get you down. We stick together around here."

He patted him on the shoulder with a smile and left. Harry looked at me.

"Guess I'll lie down for a spell."

Staring up at the ceiling, I could see Harry's struggles from the corner of my eye. He had one foot on the lower bunk, his forearms wrapped around the bedpost and was attempting to stretch his right leg up and over the top bunk. He nearly fell several times and it was all I could do to restrain myself.

When he finally succeeded, I breathed a sigh of relief.

The stifling heat wore on in the listless afternoon. I heard the guards call someone to the gate. There was a clang of iron. Mariachi music played somewhere in the prison. I smelled cheap cologne and the usual scent of fresh tortillas. Several flies were playing keep away over my head.

Imprisoned by a thousand restless desires, all I wanted that day was to walk out into the fresh air, a free man, to drive off towards the horizon without a damned thing restraining me. Instead, I was lying next to a man who desperately needed help but would not accept it, a man who had given his hands somewhere back down the road but nevertheless proclaimed a great knowledge of what freedom meant in this life. A great deal more about freedom than I did, in any case.

I wanted to know. I had to know.

"What happened, Harry?"

There was a moment of silence.

"I was shot down behind enemy lines in Korea."

I heard voices whispering at the window and looked out to see a group of Mexicans peering in for a better look.

"¡Vaminos, hombres!" I barked and offered them a gesture to go with it.

The men left, but not without a curse for me and a final effort to see Harry's deformity.

"So you were a prisoner of war?"

"For two and a half years." He looked over at me, knowing what I wanted to know. "I was hung by my thumbs for eighteen months."

The thought left my mind blank. I tried to conceive of the pain and torment but had no parallel experience to inform me.

In an otherwise a beautiful world, what horrible things men did to each other. I considered my simple dreams: to live in peace and love someone dearly, to wander the Earth and know its beauty. It was more than a lifetime. Why hang someone by their thumbs?

Our little squadron of hippies being incarcerated in a Mexican prison did not seem like such a big deal all of a sudden. In little more than two weeks, I was desperate from a mere loss of freedom to move about as I pleased. Compared to what Harry had been through, this was a picnic.

"How did you survive?" I asked him.

"By wanting to."

"Did you ever think of giving up?"

"At times, but I always came back to the things I loved, to all the things that I thought were worth living for and I wanted to see them again."

"I've had those same thoughts. Then there are times when I think it would be easier to give up."

"But you haven't."

"No. I suppose there's always a thread of hope left."

"Time passes. You can't control that but you can leave here a wiser man or a bigger fool."

"I guess I'm stubborn, Harry. All I can see is me being locked up and wanting to get back out on the highway."

"Be nice, wouldn't it? A full tank of gas and the wind in your hair."

"You're breaking my heart."

"Sorry, my friend."

I met his eyes and looked back at the ceiling.

"I don't know. I guess I'd be out there thinking of something else I couldn't have."

"It's not easy, keeping your mind and body in the same place...At the same time," he added with a look in my direction.

I nodded and stared out the window. A Mexican was getting his hair cut in the courtyard. It was going to be a hot one. You could feel it. Time went by.

"Harry," I said. "What did they bust you for?"

"Cocaine."

"That doesn't sound like you."

"I have a prescription for liquid cocaine. For my hands."

"And they busted you for it?"

"I don't think they understand."

"You don't belong in here, Harry."

"Well, I'm hoping the consulate will straighten things out in good time. Of course, you never know."

"I'm sure everyone in here will go to bat for you."

"I'm not really worried about it. I intend to kick back and read some books. Let time take care of things."

"What do you say we look into that meal?"

"Sounds like a plan."

I jumped down and waited. It was becoming an ordeal.

"Please, Harry. Let me help you."

"Grab my legs."

He came down backwards. I waited in front while he urinated and we walked down to Joe's place beneath the shade of the balcony. Every man stared, but Harry held his head high and pretended not to notice.

Joe welcomed us with some chopped steak and chilies, eggs and a basket of hot tortillas. We spent the day together and all the Americans came around to offer their support. I don't think the message was lost on anyone. Compared to the Korean War, our plight was almost laughable.

Later that afternoon, Joe went to petition El Presidenté for a lower bunk and permission was granted. A Mexican kid was told to swap with Harry. We also sent a note to the consulate, hoping to have Harry's prescription returned.

That night, before we slept, I saw Harry's hands and understood why he wore the plastic hands. His real ones were essentially claws—a thumb and one finger — neither of which looked much like a thumb and a finger. He could grasp and manipulate things with them in a primitive way.

357

We awakened the next morning with preparations for visiting day in full swing. Men scrubbed the cells and yard down with soapy water. Mariachi music played in the background.

After the bell, Rebecca arrived with a nice meal and another cake.

"Que horrible, que horrible," she said at seeing Harry's hands.

She spread the food out on a bench and encouraged us to eat.

"I think she's worried about it getting cold," I said.

Harry looked up at the sun.

"I don't think blood could get cold in this weather," he said.

I nodded my head.

"Yeah, I think it could, Harry. I think it could."

Rather than explain the old man's death, I offered Harry one of the rolled up flour tortillas. They were filled with meat and beans and potatoes. Harry took a bite.

"Delicious," he said.

Rebecca stared on while I took a bite of my own.

"Muy sabroso, Rebecca," I said with the first bite. "Muy sabroso."

That appeared to satisfy her. She handed me a napkin. Harry had been watching all this intently.

"When a woman cares for you like this, you should marry her."

I looked at Rebecca. She seemed to understand his words were about her, but not their meaning.

"I don't know, Harry. I've found love to be more trouble and heartache than it's worth."

He shook his head.

"You think like that and you'll die a lonely man."

"So, what's worse?"

"Your loneliness can't cook."

I laughed.

"¿Qué dija? ¿Qué dija?" Rebecca said, shaking me.

Still chuckling to myself, I looked into her dark, determined eyes. Perhaps Harry was right. I should marry this woman and be satisfied. Life was simple. I alone was making it complicated.

After the meal, I was about to set my plate down when a pair of jeans and moccasins appeared in my vision. It had been a long time, yet, by the very way this man stood there, I knew who it was and looked up to meet Eric's sad but smiling eyes. His chestnut colored hair had grown back down to his shoulders. His beard was short and showed a hint of red. As if to suggest irony, he was stroking it. I set the plate down and stood up to give him a hug, then stood back to look into his eyes.

"I had given up hope," I said.

"You're eating pretty well for the hopeless."

I did a quick review of the surroundings while looking at him.

"I've been meaning to have a talk with the screenwriter."

He laughed and winked at Harry.

"He always complains about the movie, even though he wrote the script."

"This is Harry."

Eric saw the hands and gave Harry a pat on the shoulder. His attention turned to Rebecca. He smiled at her but did not receive a smile in return.

"And this is Rebecca."

"Eric," he said and held out his hand.

"Ewrreek," she said.

She shook his hand, still without smiling. Eric laughed and she did not appear to like his laughter, either. When I excused myself and started off alone with Eric to talk, she liked him even less.

"Be nice to get out of this heat?" he said.

"That's pretty impossible."

"Maybe just get out of the sun?" he said with a laugh.

"That we can do."

We crossed the courtyard and headed towards the shady alcove in the southwest corner. I looked back once before we disappeared and found Rebecca staring. Her legs swung back and forth from the bench. Her black eyes looked like bullets.

"Does she come with the room and board?" Eric asked me.

I laughed now and looked back one more time, expecting she would still be there and staring in the exact same way when we came back into view.

"Her only fault is she cares too much," I said.

We sat down against the wall.

"I suppose Sarah filled you in."

"Yes," he said. "And you are?"

"Still Clay Matthews."

"It seems to fit."

"Yes, I suppose the old Clay is dead and gone."

"So what's in a name," he said.

359

"The consulate has been wondering that very thing."

He nodded knowingly.

"Then the chase goes on, I take it."

"The last time I checked, they were still baffled," I said.

"They're in character."

I smiled and studied his face while he took in the surroundings. There were two Mexican families in the hallway with us and a pair of lovers, doing what lovers and families do. Eric appeared fascinated by it all.

"It has Fellini written all over it."

"I really don't have time for the film potential, Eric."

"You're always missing the artistic resonance, my friend."

"It's hard when you're in a hurry."

He looked me over.

"Since when this newfound self-awareness?"

"Since I met this immovable object."

I patted the hard, plaster walls behind my head. We sat in silence for a moment.

"What got you busted?" he asked.

I explained. Eric smiled frequently, laughed a few times and pulled on his beard all the while.

"What do you think?"

"You know, Clay. Maybe you are better suited for war, after all."

"And don't think I haven't considered it."

I smirked to myself, remembering something.

"What?" Eric said.

"Oh, that last day in Tucson. Kip had consulted the I Ching just before we left town and it said, 'don't go south'. I figured the oracle was telling us to stop smuggling, but so much for over interpreting."

Eric shrugged.

"The meaning's not always that clear, and usually not all that literal."

"And sometimes it is," I said with another pat of the wall behind my head.

Eric laughed.

"Yes, well, I suppose the question now is, how do we get you out of here?"

"Money," I said.

Eric nodded and gazed off dreamily at our surroundings. Then he was back in the moment.

"Well, if it's money you need, I'm afraid I can't be of much help."

"In fact, you can."

"How so?"

"When I deposited the money in Mazatlán, I put your name on the account."

"Splendid. It shouldn't take me long to figure out which one and leave you here to rot."

"I did it because I trust you."

"You're a fool on top of everything else."

"Probably...It's the Banco Nationale, downtown. There's a safe-deposit box. You'll find a savings account book in there but you won't need it. Bring ten thousand dollars and whatever you want for your efforts."

"And then what?"

"I don't know," I said.

"The plot thickens," he said with a laugh.

"You get back here with the money and I'll thicken up a plot for you."

He got up and pulled me up by my hand.

"What about your signature?" he asked.

"I don't think you'll need it, but just in case."

He produced a small pad from his back pocket and a pen from his shirt and worked on his beard while I scribbled a note and signed it.

"This should take care of it."

"I'm on my way," he said.

"Eric, you know this is going to get dangerous so I'll understand..."

"Yes, I've considered that but my life is so boring otherwise."

"We can trade places if you'd like?"

He laughed again.

"I think I'm content with a bit part here and there."

I gave him a hug.

"Got enough to drive down?"

"I don't know. Probably"

"We're scheduled for court on Tuesday."

"I'll do what I can."

"Please, Eric. Hurry. This is my only chance."

"So much for turning over a new leaf."

"As soon as I'm done with this immovable object, I promise to wash my hands of haste forever."

"Hmm? Why do I doubt you?"

"Probably for good reason. But there's no other way."

Eric shook his head with a smile. I stopped him before we headed back towards the gate.

"I just need to say this. For me. I'm truly sorry for the way I acted back in Hawaii. You know, I…"

"It's all right, brother. I forgave you long ago. We're all just fumbling around in the dark, trying to find our way."

"Well, it's never been all right with me. There I was making fun of you for consulting the I Ching. And now look at me for having ignored it…"

I shrugged and looked around.

"I suppose you'd find this hard to believe, Clay, but the grass sometimes looks greener to me as well."

"What? You mean you envy my impetuous, headlong behavior?"

He laughed.

"Well, not entirely. I doubt I'll ever be able to jump off cliffs the way you do, but there's something to be admired about it. A man like me could think himself right out of existence."

"Yeah? Well I'd trade a bit of your thoughtfulness for the jam I'm in right now."

Eric shrugged in his sage manner. I gave him another hug and watched as he went out the gate. I walked back and squeezed in next to Rebecca. It took a moment for my vision to adjust from the sun to the shade.

"Nice guy," Harry said.

"Hmm? Oh yeah, Harry. A nice guy."

I felt Rebecca reaching for my hand and gave it to her without looking. Not satisfied with that, she began to play with my shirt buttons. I ignored that too, lost in thought.

The guard was the key. Everything depended on the guard. Money could corrupt anyone in Mexico, at least anyone I needed to corrupt. But who was he, and how could I get to him?

While I went around and around with that question, the image of Eric handing his pass to the guard worked in my mind. I had been looking at that issue from every angle over the past two weeks, unable to get past a vague sense that I was missing something. Something was there but I just couldn't see it.

Frustrated, I worked again at the question of the guard. The shadow of O'Donnell's words hung over my restless thoughts.

38

While Rebecca and I sat holding hands on the bench, Delaney came by and dragged Harry off for a cold drink. It had gotten to be that kind of day; oppressive, even in the shade. The heat made you want to tear your shirt off. It conjured dreams of bristling white surf and alpine meadows. You understood the Mexican mind. When it was hot, take a siesta. Everything can wait until tomorrow.

Rebecca pulled on my arm again, wanting more attention, but I remained lost in thought. It all came down to the guard.

Just then, an old Mexican woman waddled over and took Harry's space on the bench. Her middle-aged son squeezed in next to her. I glanced at them. The old woman was wearing a black dress and black shawl. Her hands were working on a set of rosary beads.

Always with the blackness, these Catholics, and it troubled me. Forget the mariachi music. Let's play dirges instead. Make a day of it and crucify someone in the courtyard.

Growing more uncomfortable with the old woman's presence, I pulled on Rebecca's hand and took her for a stroll around the prison. Meanwhile, my mind kept working on this guard business. Probably the best man to ask was twenty feet down in a hole, dying of starvation. Green would know. So would Maximillian, but he couldn't be trusted. He had too much to lose. Getting other people to do your bidding was always the most difficult piece of the puzzle.

Perhaps the best course of action would be to bribe the guards on the way to the courthouse. It might come down to that. Have Eric follow the van on Tuesday and flash some money on the spot. There would be less opportunity for double-crossing, but it had a wild, desperate quality to it that even I didn't like. Of course, all this presumed I could get someone to take me to court in the first place, which left all of my other hopes as grim as the gallows.

Yet I felt my heart beating wildly in my chest and knew I had a shot. I had a shot now, however crazy the whole thing might turn out to be.

When the bell rang and the visiting hours came to a close, I returned to my cell and again watched through the window bars as Rebecca made the slow procession towards the front gate. She looked back several times and waved to me.

When it was her turn to leave, she paused in the foyer and spoke with one of the guards. He held his rifle aside and gave her a hug. Good god. I pressed my face to the bars and called out Rebecca's name. She looked my way. The guard did too, glaring.

"Escribes mañana, con su apartamento. ¿Bien?"

Rebecca nodded. I waved a final time as she disappeared.

One of El Presidenté's cabos came by and told me to shut up through the window. None of the Mexicans inside the cell looked happy with me, either. Goddamned gringos. It was bad enough we had screwed them over for half their empire. Now we were trying to run off with their pretty young women too.

After la cuenta, Harry got comfortable with a book. I flopped out on my bunk and stared at the ceiling.

"You going to marry that girl?" Harry said.

"Huh? Oh yeah, sure, Harry. I think I will. Think I'll do that."

He must have seen I was distracted because he went back to his book without another word. I returned to my thoughts. They were filled with all kinds of wild plans and uncertainties.

For one thing, if Eric and I did manage to bribe a guard, there was no telling how much time I'd have before the authorities got wind of my escape. Ten, fifteen minutes? Who knew? It wouldn't be much.

If and when we cleared the outskirts of town, Eric would have to drop me south of the check-point and rendezvous with me farther north the following night. Once at the border, I would have to march across alone. Of course, that assumed they wouldn't be checking the entire highway, and that was a big if.

The other option was to go south, something they probably would not expect. There were numerous diversions in that direction that might work to my advantage, including a boat ride across the gulf, but it was a matter of going farther from safety and in its own way becoming a more perilous journey. In either case, it required that Eric's car had not been identified during the escape.

If we went south, some alteration of our appearances would probably be necessary. To the north, I would need to spend at least one night and perhaps two in the desert alone, waiting for things to cool down.

If everything went awry, it meant a long march to the border. It wouldn't be a camping trip, but if it came to that, I knew I could make it.

I visited briefly with Harry and Delaney that evening but avoided Joe's cornucopia of mind-altering substances and returned to my cell early. As soon as the lights went out after lock-up and everyone was asleep, I began to construct a list for Eric. Several times, I hid my enterprise while someone got up to use of the toilet, but mostly the prison slumbered while I worked in the dim light filtering in from the courtyard.

Late the following afternoon, Rebecca's letter arrived. I quickly scanned the amorous dedications, wrote the address down on a separate piece of paper and disposed of the note. It seemed there was nothing to do but wait now.

I went to stare out at the desert, hungering for the moment. I imagined myself on my way to the border with a great vista of hills and mountains before me, thoughts of escape that came with both excitement and dread. There might well be guns and bullets and dying alone beneath the sun. I lived more in days to come and days gone by than in the moment.

Hearing footsteps, I turned to find Kip approaching down the short, dimly lit hallway. I stared down at him from the window ledge.

"I talked with Robby last night. He said they're taking the two of us to court in the morning. Then Steve and Kristine in the afternoon."

"So?"

"The lawyer said you hadn't been scheduled to go."

"What do you want me to say?"

He nodded.

"Just thought I'd let you know."

"Thanks for the news."

He left without another word. Joe came and invited me over for a meal and some drinks. I joined him for the food.

"What the hell, Matthews? You going good on me."

"No, Joe. Just not feeling right the past few days."

"You're going good on me."

"I wouldn't do that. Let's get Harry. He'll drink with you."

Needing every good meal I could get my hands on, I thought it would be best to keep Joe entertained.

The next day arrived without any sign of Eric. I jumped at every strange sound, fearing they would call my name, when I wasn't ready for them to call my name now.

Before lunch, they called Kip and Robby and led them out through the main gate. When they returned, I questioned Kip about the trip.

"They put us in a room full of desks and secretaries."

"And?"

"Asked us the same questions."

"How about the guards?"

"There was only one. And the driver."

"Have you seen the guard before?"

"Yeah. The same one that watches the main gate during visiting days."

So it was the man Rebecca had embraced. I wasn't sure if that was good or bad news. It could be worse. It definitely could be worse.

"What about Robby?"

"Same story."

"It figures."

I went back to waiting.

After lunch they took Steve. It was late when he returned. I watched and waited for some sign of Eric but he failed to appear.

The night passed without any news and I began to fear the worst. I pictured Eric peering into the safety deposit box and deciding, screw Clay. After all, how long could it take a man to drive down to Mazatlán and back?

By nine the next morning, the prison was ready for another visiting day. The place sparkled. The Mexicans all looked dandy. The gates opened, and not long after, Rebecca came in.

She wanted to know why I hadn't written her.

I took her to a quiet place out of the sun and professed my undying love in broken Spanish. Then I explained what I wanted her to do. She stared at me with her black eyes and shook her head. I pretended to be angry and demanded to know. Who was the guard? She confessed it was her uncle. I became angrier and more determined. I told her if she loved me and wanted me to marry her, she would do this one thing. Otherwise, I never wanted to see her again. Her lips trembled. Tears trickled down her cheeks. I stood over her and pressed my case until she surrendered.

She was very beautiful to me then and I thought I might even marry her someday, but now was not the time to think of such things. Once Rebecca had dried her eyes, I explained in more detail what I wanted her to do. She stared up at me and nodded without a word.

Visiting time was nearly over when Eric made his appearance. He strolled in with the usual calm.

"You took your sweet time," I said.

"After seeing all that money, it took me the better part of a day to decide whether or not to rip you off."

He smiled at Rebecca but again did not receive a smile in return. She was obviously having trust problems with him.

"Where do we stand," he said to me.

"We seem to have hit a snag."

"Ah, for want of a nail..."

"Yes. Come on, I'll explain."

I told him everything I knew and all my plans. We knocked it around for a while, refining a point here and there as we thought it through. Then I explained the plan to Rebecca in Spanish. She was to meet with Eric in an hour at some pre-arranged location, a place of her choosing.

"Hotel San Anselmo," she said. "En la cantina."

I looked to Eric. He smiled.

"Keep your hands off my woman."

"You're not being very generous, given the circumstances."

"Maybe but I can't seem to stop myself from being territorial." He smiled. "So, how's your Spanish?"

"Lousy. It works with charades."

I looked at Rebecca.

"¿Entiendes?"

"Si." She nodded obediently. I gave her a kiss of reassurance and waited with Eric as she passed through the gate. She spoke again with the guard.

"What happens if he sells us out?" Eric asked me.

"They shoot you in the back."

"Hmm," he said while pulling at his beard.

I handed him my shopping list. He reviewed it briefly and stuffed it into his moccasin.

"I presume you know what you're doing," he said.

"I think so, but I've been wrong before."

"Hmm," Eric said again. "You know, this shooting in the back business has me a bit worried."

"It's very quick," I said, "I've seen it done."

"Yes, well, as long as it's quick."

I assured him it was and the two of us went for a stroll around the prison. We circled several times from veranda to veranda, reviewed the whorehouse and kitchen and the empty wash yard and the mountains to the north. We talked of life and of longing and skirted the question of death. We returned to the main gate when the bell rang.

"Now, if only they'll take me to court."

"I'll see if I can arrange something for tomorrow," he said.

"Thanks. At least it has the air of hope about it."

Eric gave me a hug and got into line. I went back to my cell. I had done everything in my power to beat this train to the crossing, but it was always that way with me. Watching Harry read a book in our cell, I could not understand his calm. Then, for me, this was hanging by my thumbs, until something worse came along.

I went to see Kip after la cuenta and all the visitors had gone.

"If things work out, I'll be gone tomorrow."

"I wish you luck."

"I doubt I'll be seeing you again."

"You never know," he said.

"No, but I wanted to ask you to give me a few more days before you call home."

"I can wait that long."

"Good. If I don't see you again, good luck."

"I hope you make it," he said.

369

We shook hands.

"It's mostly been a pleasure," I said.

I went to find Joe. He and Harry were sprawled out on Joe's bunk, swapping war stories over a bottle of rot gut. Joe had bought himself a sombrero and serape.

"How's everything going, Pancho?" I asked him.

"Hey look, Harry, eet's Señor Clay, mucho big hombre."

He made a gesture to emphasize his point, took another slug of the booze, wiped his lips with the back of his hand and offered me the bottle. I waved him off.

"Hey Harry, mira. Heeem mucho too good for us, eh?"

"Oh hell, if it'll make you happy, give me the goddamned thing."

He handed it to me defiantly. I took a short drink and handed the bottle to Harry.

"How's the life of a bandito, Harry?"

"Fine. His proclivity for mind altering drugs aside, Joe's a pretty square guy."

"Cuidado, hombre, or I feexs you, too."

Harry seemed unfazed by the threat.

"So listen, Pancho," I said. "I came by to let you know. Eric will be wiring you some money this week. I don't want you wasting it all on booze and drugs."

"Dat's okay, Señor. We take your money either way."

I took the bottle from Harry, drank again and returned it to Joe. Joe tried to say something but belched and had forgotten what it was by the time he had reorganized his thoughts. I left him with a drunken grin on his face. Harry winked as I went out. It was life in the foxhole.

The night was clear and warm with a dry breeze blowing down from the mountains. Stars sparkled high above in the black sky. I had a sudden thought and crossed over to see Don. He was lingering among the coterie of ladies gathered near Cell 13. Most of the ladies had their backs pressed to the wall. It was a line of hookers in tight dresses, waiting for a john.

There was the usual display of hissing that accompanied my arrival. Rosa had a word for me under her breath. Ignoring her, I stared at Don.

"¿Que quieres?" Rosa asked me.

I continued ignoring her, waiting for Don to look my way. With his gown and the blonde hair piled up on his head and the lipstick and earrings and soft skin, it would have been easy to get aroused, not knowing any better.

"Can we talk?" I said when he looked at me.

He looked away.

"Please," I said.

Don pushed away from the wall and came towards me as if it implied punishment. Rosa hurled a fresh barrage of vulgarity in my direction. No telling who did what to whom when the doors closed on Cell 13 at night, but it appeared to involve Don and Rosa. Being the bull dyke among them, Rosa could probably have her way with anyone in the harem.

I led Don far enough away so that we could speak privately, but not far enough to exacerbate Rosa's hissing.

"Are you all right?"

"Of course."

It was said with resentful sibilance. I had known gay men before and none of them had ever offered a satisfactory explanation for why they developed that characteristic. Don definitely hadn't exhibited it before. Not that I cared.

"Are you really happy? I mean, are you doing this because you want to or because you're ashamed?"

"God, I can't believe you're asking me this."

Rosa let off with a fresh string of curses at seeing Don's agitation.

"Don, I never saw it before. And after what happened...I thought maybe the shock and the shame at being thrown in Cell 13."

"You can't imagine it, can you?"

"I wanted to hear it from you. That's all."

"Well, it's what I've always wanted, so now you know."

He looked insolently at me and away.

"Hey, the revolution was all about doing your own thing so who are we to argue?"

"Well, thanks, I guess."

"Come on," I said and reached out to give him a hug.

This prompted more threats and curses from Rosa. I couldn't suppress a smile. Somehow it got Don to smile, too.

"You're a real doll, Don."

"It's Donna now."

"Okay, Donna."

He blushed and pulled his shawl over his shoulders.

"Look, I might be gone soon so I just wanted you to know, if you need help, don't be afraid to ask. Joe. Harry. Kip. They'll all understand."

He nodded and headed back to his place. I drifted back that way and gave Rosa a good pinch in the ass when she wasn't looking.

"¡Higo de la chingada! ¡Cabron! ¡La Malinche verga!"

The curses followed me across the courtyard. I went back to my bunk and tried to sleep. I figured I would need it, but sleeping did not come easily. Harry returned about eleven o'clock.

"How are you doing, Harry?"

"Beats the hell out of being hung by your thumbs."

He pulled back the blanket and climbed in with his clothes on.

"You know, someday someone's going to ask me that same question, Harry, and I'm going to say..."

Before finishing the sentence, I looked over and found Harry fast asleep.

The cell was locked at twelve. I listened to the Mexicans whispering in the darkness. Much later, I fell asleep.

The morning began with the same determined footsteps, the clang of iron doors, and the call to attention. I watched the men around me as they sang off their number. It had become routine, the senses dulled by habit in a fortnight. But I was aware of it being a brand new morning, one that had never been before and I took it as such. I had a shower and put on my jeans with a T-shirt. I had thought to pull on my boots but left them in the cell. I would have looked odd wearing boots in the prison. They were at the ready just in case I was called.

The sun had yet to clear the roof so the morning air still felt cool. The scent of the desert was fresh and clean. A wind from the north had been beating back the gulf weather for several days, making life almost bearable.

I walked down to Joe's place under the shade of the balcony. Harry was there and looking the worse for wear. He smelled of booze and was trying to rub the cobwebs out of his brain with his plastic hands.

"How are things going this morning, Harry?"

"That Joe's got me on the skids. I'm not sure I can keep up with him any longer."

When Joe threw some chorizo on the grill, Harry groaned.

"It's fun trying," I said.

Harry groaned again. I slapped him on the back and went over to have a closer look at the food. Joe was as chipper as a jay in springtime.

"Good morning, Clay. Where's my money?"

"You don't forget a thing, do you?"

"Not money I don't."

He looked at me with a big grin. I could picture him knee deep in a swamp in Southeast Asia with that same look. He would cook breakfast in a firefight.

"Hey, just kidding. You don't worry about the money, Clay. I know you'll pay me."

"Maybe."

"Naw, you will."

"How are you feeling?"

"Great. You ready for some breakfast?"

"Sure. I was wondering, Joe?"

"You still trying to get an invitation to Cell 13."

"Look, I'm just asking you to be nice to Don."

"How nice?"

"I'm serious."

"I'll work on it."

Joe spread the food out and the two of us dug in. Harry came over and tried to get some eggs down but was quickly on his way to the head. I did my best to ignore the sounds. We were nearly finished by the time Harry came out.

"Hey Harry, I don't mind feeding you but if you're going to throw it all down the drain like that..."

Joe laughed. Harry hung his head.

"Where you going, Harry?"

"Back to my bunk."

He staggered out at about three-quarter mast. Joe and I split up what was left on his plate, cleaned the dishes and dove into a game of chess. Joe beat me badly. We started another. Lunch came but no call. I lost again. Joe and I got up and wandered out to the courtyard.

"Hey Clay, where's your mind today?"

"I don't know."

He looked me over.

"Must be wedding bells."

"Must be."

"Let's get this game of hoops going. That'll be good for you."

"Sure."

They chose up sides while I went to put on my tennis shoes. Being the tallest, they made me center. I took a beating on the inside from the Mexicans. They loved to take out their every frustration on a gringo. While I ran over to retrieve a loose ball, one of the cabos came up and poked me with his stick.

"Vaminos afuera."

I hadn't heard the usual bell ring and stared at him, perplexed.

"¡Vaminos, hombre!"

"They must be taking you to court, Clay."

I dropped the ball and ran to my cell.

"¡Oyer, afuera, cabron!" the cabo called after me.

"Momentito."

"¡Cabron, vaminos ahora!"

He followed me back to my cell, still cursing as I pulled on my boots and grabbed my coat.

"No es necesario, loco."

I followed him out and waited for the guard to open the gate. There were two men arguing over the orders in the foyer, one of them Rebecca's uncle. He was showing a piece of paper to the guard who arranged transport for all the court visits.

"Aquí es el documento."

That man pointed to the list of names on his clipboard, unpersuaded.

"Sí, pero no está aquí."

"Claro, pero es aquí."

The other guard remained resolute and Rebecca's uncle became exasperated.

"Aquí está !"

"Claro que si, pero lo no tengo aquí."

The guard at the gate shrugged. He had no record of my release. The director wasn't there and the guard wasn't about to do anything without his say so. I stood by, trying to look impartial.

While the two men continued arguing, I grew lost in some framed photographs on the wall. There was one of an American couple in a Cessna. Their heads hung lifelessly inside the shattered windows of the cockpit. There were many holes in the plane and a great deal of blood. It was a reminder to those who would break Mexican laws and attempt to escape while doing so.

Then another photo caught my eye. There were several Mexican and American authorities standing together in an open field, all of them exhibiting the stiff bearing that accompanies such events, like they had gathered around for a family photo. A stack of kilos stood beside them, as big as a house. Two of the men held torches, preparing to start the bonfire.

With the two guards still discussing my fate, I leaned in for a closer look. Taken from a distance, the men in the photo were necessarily very small but one of them in the front row seemed awfully familiar. I had to squint but sure enough, it was Sheriff Prescott, wearing a cowboy hat and a big grin on his face. You could hardly mistake him.

Very strange, I thought. What would have dragged him that far south of the border?

"¡Vaminos!" Rebecca's uncle said to me suddenly.

Somehow, he had prevailed.

I tore myself away from the photo and followed him out the gate, feeling a great rush just to be outside the prison again. The driver opened the back doors of the van and the guard instructed me to sit on a wooden bench. He sat opposite me. The butt of his M-1 rested on the floorboard. The driver closed the door and had soon turned the van around in the gravel parking lot. We started down the hill. I watched the guard. Several times our eyes met but he said nothing.

How would it happen? When would we stop? The city rolled by with those questions working in my head and a tremulous feeling in my gut.

Then I saw the driver pulling into the gravel parking lot of the courthouse where we had been arrested. He stopped in front and came around to open the door. Rebecca's uncle motioned for me to get out. The driver closed the doors and went back around to the cab. While he drove off, Rebecca's uncle marched me up the concrete steps and into the courthouse. He handed his papers to a clerk at the front desk. The clerk searched her records and shook her head. The two of them went back and forth about the whole thing, just like back at the prison, but clearly this clerk did not have my name on her court dockets, either.

Rebecca's uncle eventually apologized for the confusion and escorted me back outside. We stood at the bottom of the steps. He had his eyes focused on a cross street at the end of the courthouse to our right. There were trees between us and that corner of the building.

A minute went by with him staring in that direction. Then a man appeared on foot from around the corner, waved at us and disappeared again. Rebecca's uncle prodded me with the butt of his rifle.

"Vaminos."

I stood there, uncertain what to make of it. He nudged me again.

"¡Vaminos, vaminos!" he said and gestured towards the end of the building.

But this wasn't how I had pictured it happening. If my assumptions were correct, the money had just exchanged hands and I was supposed to make a run for it. But it was a long way from the courthouse steps to the end of the building. I was looking at a few hundred feet of open space with a loaded rifle at my back.

I inched away slowly at first, then gave in to the adrenalin and turned in full flight. Halfway to the corner of the building, I looked over my shoulder and saw the van pulling back into the parking lot.

I heard a shot and saw a spray of gravel kick up, ten feet to my left.

"¡Alto!" a voice shouted.

I heard a second shot go off and wondered if that bastard was just putting on a good show or actually trying to shoot me.

"¡Alto!" I heard him shout again.

Nearing the corner of the building, several more shots went off in succession and a chunk of sandstone chipped off from the courthouse wall, three feet from my head. Whatever the guard had been doing up to that point, he definitely wasn't fooling around now.

I dashed around the corner and found Eric waiting in his old Ford van. I pulled the door open and jumped in. The motor was running.

"Get this roller-skate moving."

He smiled and pulled onto the road. When he had cleared the short side street, he gave it some gas. We hadn't gotten far when I heard sirens.

"What's the matter, didn't you pay this guy enough?"

"I paid him. I presume that's the problem."

"Shit. I had hoped for a little more time than this."

"I can always take you back."

"You son of a bitch."

"How does it feel to be free?"

"Damned exciting."

Eric reached under the seat and produced a bottle of cheap Mexican brandy.

"You want a shot?" he asked.

"Are you attempting irony here?" I said, taking the bottle.

He laughed. I had two long slugs from the bottle.

"Take it with you if you'd like."

"No, I've got enough problems already." I took one more shot for good measure and put the bottle back under the seat.

Eric cut off a handful of people as we raced north towards the outskirts of the city. The afternoon was filled with sirens. I glanced back several times at the road behind us. The various options were turning over in my head.

"I don't think we have much choice now, Eric. What do you think?"

"No. It doesn't seem that way. We aren't heading south. I can tell you that much."

"Did you find a map?"

"Yes, but not the one you wanted."

I grabbed the pack off the back seat and pulled out the map. He was right. I had wanted a topographical map, but this one was good enough. It showed some elevations and many small villages. I located a spot roughly twenty miles north of the checkpoint.

"Here. One mile north of Carbo on the main highway. Look for me there in two days. Park out of sight on the east side of the highway. If I don't show, you'd better head back to the States. I'll call when I get back to LA."

"You're sure you don't want me to give you an extra day?"

"No. No point in it. If I can't make Carbo in two nights, I've been driven off the trail."

We were moving alongside a reservoir now. There were three rivers from the nearby mountains that fed that body of water and I knew I would have to cross at least one of those rivers before this adventure was through. The checkpoint was another ten kilometers to the north.

Once we had cleared the reservoir by a few miles, Eric pulled down a dirt road heading east. It was all open desert around us.

"You'd best get out of here," I said.

"See you in few days."

"If not, thanks ever so much."

"You'll make it, boy. I have faith in you."

"Just be careful," I said and grabbed Eric on his shoulder. Then I closed the door and turned to run.

39

I ran recklessly away from the highway, dashing this way and that through the desert terrain, forced to make wild loops and zigzags around all the mesquite and cardon and brush that stood in my path. At one point, I caught a thorn in my hand and stopped to dig it out. Then I ran wildly ahead again. I exerted as much energy going sideways as I did going forward but that only added to my sense of urgency.

Off in the distance, I saw the foothills and mountains looming up into the sky, the two of them together looking enormous and impenetrable and not at all as they appeared on a map. The very idea of traversing them on foot seemed impossible, as did marching all the way to the border, but one thought rang out above all the others in my mind. I was free. A great joy rose up in my chest to realize this fact. I was free again; to live and die as I pleased.

Once a significant distance had been covered, I stopped for a spell to catch my breath. Then fear jumped in me and I ran crazily ahead again. I wanted to run through the night but knew I had to pace myself. I had to think of the journey ahead. It could possibly be a long one, I thought, not entirely certain what that meant.

I ran for another mile or so and concluded that I had placed a sufficiently large distance between my pursuers and me. No matter what forces were aligned against me, I had achieved a damned good lead.

At the nearest mesquite, I sat down in the shade to rest. Even with the afternoon growing late, the wind was warm and dry. The scent of sage came sharply on the wind. I heard many bird songs, and all around those melodies, a great, abiding silence. And in that silence, another smile crossed my face. I may be hunted as prey now, but at least I was no longer caged in a cell.

In my mind, I tried to imagine the wheels of justice turning. The police would quickly turn this matter over to the Federales. The Mexican army would get involved and the Americans would be notified. I could expect planes as well as dogs. If they knew where to look, they would find my tracks soon enough. I remembered seeing that plume of dust as Eric pulled away in his van. Hopefully no one else had seen it or my wait wouldn't be long.

I hoped for the rendezvous with Eric above Carbo and not the long, difficult march to the border. Carbo was an easy journey. Two days, and from Carbo it would be less than three hours to the border in a car. Of course, I was no more popular in the United States than I was in Mexico, but I could return home without anyone ever knowing it.

Home, I thought. After all I had been through, thinking of America as home seemed rather out of place. Indeed, where was I going? I had been so thoroughly consumed with escaping over the past few weeks, I hadn't thought much beyond those immediate concerns. I was on a headlong journey, hardly knowing what drove me forward any longer, other than to stay alive that day and not have someone count me in a cell when darkness fell.

I looked east towards the mountains and hoped more than anything that I would not have to climb those towering peaks. The other way sounded so easy. I knew it was best not to have such hopes, but I did. I stood back up, gave the pack a tug and started off in a steady march towards the river.

Soon, the sun had touched the peaks of the mountains behind me. Shadows stretched long across the desert floor. Flocks of lark sparrows flushed against the pale sky and quickly settled back into the trees. A change in the wind brought the scent of river brush and a feeling of coolness to the warm afternoon. I marched in that direction with a steady gait.

Before dark, I spotted cottonwoods and came to a maze of brush alongside the river. Pulling the pack off my back, I got out the map. This was a river named Zanjon. It followed a course due north then turned to the west below Benjamin Hill. If I stayed on this side, it would press me against the highway as I marched towards Carbo.

There was too much danger in that choice so I decided to cross to the eastern bank.

Taking off my boots, I rolled up my pants, put the map and boots in the pack, cinched the tie string tightly and fought my way through the seep willows bordering the river. The limbs had a chartreuse coating that rubbed off onto my skin and clothing.

I came to the river and saw that it was slow and dark. Not knowing how deep, I waded in cautiously. Then halfway across, the bottom gave out. I struggled to stay afloat and cursed my luck, knowing everything in the pack was now wet. It wouldn't have mattered so much in the morning, but with the many hours of darkness ahead of me, everything would start to spoil.

Pulled downriver by the current, I struggled towards the other bank, still chastising myself the whole way. I should have explored this crossing more carefully. Then I heard the dogs and realized none of that mattered now. It was the trail of dust from Eric's van. That one little thing had undone my fate.

Fixating on all the things I might have been done differently, I reached the far side of the river and pulled myself under the branches of a seep willow. The water was waist high with a bed of rotting vegetation oozing up between my toes. Expecting I might soon have to run for my life, I hung the pack from a branch, retrieved my socks and boots and pulled them on, then located the Bowie knife and cut a length of plastic tubing. This had been intended for water distillation. I had not envisioned this use. I took my length of rope and tied the pack underwater to some exposed tree roots. Then I waited.

The hounds came closer and grew louder. At times they seemed to be moving away, but always they came back to the scent.

The sun was behind the mountains by the time the men appeared through the trees upstream and stood at the edge of the river. Darkness continued to settle around them as they talked. After several minutes of conversing, two of them left. The other four let the hounds go and waited.

The hounds followed their instincts into the river and came drifting down towards me. The men followed along the far bank. I saw that two of them were gringos.

I went under water well before the dogs came near, using one hand to hold myself underwater and the other to hold the plastic tube in the air. My boots were dug into the brackish mud.

By the sound of their barking, I knew the dogs were drawing near. Then I heard them splash out of the river and climb the bank behind me. The men kept the hounds close with calls and whistles from the other side.

My jaw had begun to ache around the tubing. The muscles in my arms and legs burned. I battled my desire to come up and cursed the men and hounds for their persistence.

Then, through the dark waters, I heard a distant drone. It grew louder and became a vibration. It was a boat. The other men were coming up from the lake. I bit harder into the tubing, more determined than ever to survive.

How badly did you want to be free, Clay boy? Had you thought this was going to be easy? You're lucky to have a chance, I reminded myself, even as the ache in my lips and jaw became a torment. I felt like I had blown up a thousand balloons. My hands ached too. I let go and squeezed hard with them repeatedly in an effort to ease the pain. With my lips growing weak, water began seeping into my mouth. I nearly coughed from it trickling down my throat

Going by the sounds above water, the men in the boat had stopped to pick up the others. Then the boat crossed the river and came toward the trees. I saw the men above me, murky dark forms, ten feet from where I was submerged. One man probed the river bottom with a stick. Another man bent over and searched beneath the limbs of the trees. I pulled the tube underwater and waited. Then the dogs bayed and the boat moved in that direction.

The boat had gone away to the north perhaps fifty feet when the dogs resisted and turned back. The men came with them.

Then, at last, the dogs headed back upriver and the men followed them. I let go of the roots underwater and floated to the surface. My hands were knotted into a closed position. My jaw and cheeks ached, but at least the men and the dogs were gone. I waited until I was certain of this before untying the pack and pulling it out of the water.

My intent now was to make the San Miguel River and follow it north. I probably had but one hope: to lose them on the way to the border. There was time to get a fresh lead before dawn, but they would return in the morning and they would be better prepared. I held onto the idea of meeting Eric at Carbo, but that seemed like an increasingly unlikely prospect.

Once out of the river, I ran for a long spell before stopping to empty my boots and find a drier pair of socks. With my boots back on, I slung the pack on my back and moved out in a steady trot.

Stars filled the evening sky. Distant lights flickered against the black hills. I imagined them to be the lights of peasant families, there at the end of the day, probably with kerosene lamps, preparing a simple meal. I felt drawn to that image. I felt drawn to every simple comfort in life; a cozy bed, a hot bath and a warm meal. Thoughts of Caroline also swirled about in my head; sweet, tender thoughts that had nothing to do with my survival. I concentrated back on my immediate reality; the sound of my boots crunching into broken rocks, my breath, the sound of my jeans whispering as my legs moved, the wheezing, wet sound of my leather jacket. I ran steadily onward marking time with these rhythms.

To the north, a long procession of hills came to its terminus before me and I sensed an approaching decision, and one that I did not like. When I came around the hills and saw down into the valley, my fears were confirmed. The river valley was below me in the distance and mountains rose up around it and marched off into the distance, as far as I could see. If I headed that way, the valley became deeper and there would be no turning back. The only easy way was to turn around and follow the Zanjon. It was that or forget about Carbo.

I decided to go through the pack and assess the damage. I found the compass. It seemed fine. The food, however, was soaked. Eric had tried to protect it with plastic bags, but it had been submerged for far too long.

There were raisins and dates and almonds. If I dried them in the sun tomorrow, they might be salvageable. Much longer in their current condition and they would rot. I ate some, did what I could to get rid of the excess moisture, and placed them aside.

There was a tarp on which Eric had created a camouflage effect with different colors of spray paint. I smiled at the thought of him working away in a hotel room. It was sand colored, with a mottled design of black, brown and green. There were several stakes and some rope with which to secure the tarp. There was also a small spade to hollow out a depression in the soil. Dug at night and in a shady spot, the soil in such a depression would remain cool for many hours during the day, protecting a man from the surrounding heat.

I quickly went through everything else. There was a knife, a bota bag, a thousand dollars, two hundred of it in pesos, a snake-bite kit and some vitamins. And there were the two pieces of plastic sheeting that I could use along with the plastic tubing to distill water.

I decided to take a vitamin pack and eat a few more dates. Then I put everything away and tied the pack shut. I secured the knife to my belt and sat in thought.

The decision was simple, really, but my mind did not want to accept that fact. My mind wanted what was easy, so it told me there was no danger. The authorities would forget about me and give up. If I accepted that idea, there was no need to go down into the valley. I could simply turn back and make my way towards Carbo.

But I knew the territory around the highway would be swarming with men and dogs and planes. The farther away from the highway I got, the bigger the vector and greater my chances.

There was no choice, really. I was compelled to take the hard way. Chances were they would double back on my trail and find my tracks again. It would be foolish to assume otherwise. A long hike through the waters of the San Miguel would make it very difficult for them to find me again.

I stood up and looked back towards Hermosillo. The prison sat high up on its hill, bathed in a yellow light. At this very moment, men would be talking about me. They would wonder if I was free, or if I had been shot. Their hearts would be with me no matter what they thought. I prayed never to know such a place again and headed down to the river.

As I neared the valley floor, paloverde and ironwood rose up around me. I had no vision beyond the next few trees. I had only the compass and the mountains to guide me towards the northeast.

Eventually, I came to a steep bluff and walked along it until finding a path down to the sand below me. I walked along that bed of sand and then the river appeared through the cottonwood and brush.

The San Miguel was wider and shallower than the Zanjon, with far less overgrowth along its banks. The water danced over rocks.

I sat down to rest for a few minutes. My feet were wet and cold. I wanted very much to take off my boots and dry them but knew if I placed a few more miles between my pursuers and myself, it would take them that much longer to find my tracks again. It was an advantage I very much needed and waded in after a few minutes, heading north.

The moon rose over the eastern hills and the river wove gently through the terrain with the moonlight reflected in its glass-like surface. Here and there, the river rippled over rocks but mostly the surface was as smooth as glass.

My boots kicked up the shallow water with each step until my pants and the front of my shirt were soaked again. I struggled at times with my footing in the rocky riverbed, but I leaned hard into it and did not complain.

I thought of Harry and what he had said about freedom. Freedom wasn't relative; otherwise we would never have it. So I imagined myself and the path ahead in that way. The path would become hard, harder every day, but it did not matter. It did not matter that my cold, aching muscles were already crying out for me to stop. It did not matter that I was wet to the bone and miserable. I would not waver. I would be this Clay thing marching resolutely forward, indifferent to every obstacle and discomfort.

Then I thought of Caroline and longed to be a simple man and have a simple life with her. I would forgive all of her propriety and the demands she had placed on me. Maybe it would never be perfect between us but I did not care anymore. I just wanted to start over with one simple truth. I wanted to begin at some point of honesty and be a good man. Whether or not I died before having this opportunity, just thinking it and believing in it was my freedom.

Behind all these thoughts was the passion, and passion was the trick. Character was destiny but character required passion. Nothing happened in life without passion and the thought of Caroline's sweet kisses led me onward. I had no idea where was I going but the desire to hold her again and be a good man became my inspiration.

Hours passed with the river steadily narrowing before me. The moon rose higher overhead and filled the smooth water with white light and the light danced in sensuous undulations between my legs. I lost track of time. It must have been two or three in the morning but I had no watch. It was foolish of me not to have asked Eric for one but I would see dawn in the eastern sky and know when to stop. I decided to go on for at least another hour. Every bit would help. I measured my pace by the splash of my boots through the water, one after the other, breaking holes in the white moonlight.

Then I saw lights far to the east and stopped. I knew from the map that a road ran between Rayon and Carbo, so it had to be Rayon. It was best to find a spot now and stay away from the road and the town.

Hills rose up on either side of the river. I looked to the east for a clearing. I would be out of the early sun that way and better able to flee towards the Sonora River if danger came my way. When I saw the mouth of a small canyon, I followed that arroyo of sand up from the river, then had second thoughts and returned to the river, backing my way up the arroyo while removing my tracks with a branch. It would never fool a dog, but a man could see what he could not smell.

When the arroyo became overgrown with brush, I started up the adjacent slope towards a thicket of paloverde. A few hundred feet above the river, I reached the trees and had started to pull back a low branch when dark forms came crashing out of the undergrowth. Startled, I leapt to one side but felt a sharp pain below my knee. Peccaries, and one of them had clipped me good. Goddamn it. I heard the sound of pack charging up the hill and reorganizing. I checked my leg and felt warm blood oozing from a long, deep gash right beside the flex point.

I rushed to remove my boots and pants and clean the wound. If I kept it clean and dressed each day, I could hope for it to heal. I touched the lip of the wound with my finger and felt nauseous. Better not to think about it. It would have to be all right. I bandaged the wound with a torn piece of cloth from my shirt, then pulled my

386

pants back on and did my best to ignore the pain as I got on with my chores.

Beneath the densest cover, I staked the lower end of the tarp towards the southwest and tied the opposing edge to the branches above me. Then I dug a one foot deep trench for my body, directly beneath the tarp. When I was done with that, I placed my boots in the tree out of sight.

I had filled the bota bag before leaving the river and dug another hole for that. The food drying business would have to wait until sunrise. My jacket would have to wait, as well. A chill wind blew down steadily from the mountain now, and though the jacket was wet and cold, it was my only insulation.

I crawled into the trench, pulled the pack under my head and glanced once at the sky behind me. I wasn't sure but it appeared to be near dawn. I squirmed to get comfortable on the broken ground and ran my finger over the wound one more time. I was free, I reassured myself and closed my eyes to sleep.

40

Startled awake by the roar of a passing plane, I sat up and peered through the branches. An old P-38 raced north up the valley and disappeared from view. I lay back down, concerned, but not too terribly much. It was to be expected. The authorities weren't about to give up but this pilot was merely hoping to find me marching along out in the open like a fool.

Lying back down, I remembered my wound and probed along the lip of it, feeling nauseous again. That was cause for concern. There were a great many things that were a real cause for concern.

I sat up again and peered cautiously through the brush. The rising sun had painted the highest peaks across the valley vermillion in color. A halo of insects swirled above the river. A killdeer skimmed low along the water, looking for a morning meal. I heard a dove call and the click of quail in the brush below. The peace of the countryside surrounded me.

There being no other signs of men, I forged ahead with my duties. First thing, I put on some sweat clothes, knowing this would help me to retain vital moisture. Next, I set everything out to dry under the cover of the paloverde. I drank sparingly so as not to dilute my blood salts and ate some of the nuts and dried fruit as I worked. When I had done all that was possible, I made myself comfortable and watched the river to the south.

From a distance, I heard the plane returning down the valley and ducked back beneath my lair. The pilot banked to get a better view going by. He and the plane then disappeared to the south between the fold of two hills. When it was gone, I poked my head back out to have a look. There was silence in the morning sun. Satisfied, I lay down again and eventually found sleep.

Around mid-morning, I was awakened by a rustling sound in the brush. Thinking it was footsteps; I held my breath and waited. The rustling came again. I lay completely still. My heart beat wildly. Then I understood the cause of the sound and scampered up to find a troupe of antelope squirrels stealing away with half of my dates and nuts. Ants were ravaging what remained. I brushed away the ants as best I could and sealed everything up. The ants would go down when I was hungry enough.

I went back to the tarp and hung the plastic bags in the paloverde, determined to forget this significant loss of resources but my mind would not let it go. I heard the distant hum of the plane and worried over that too. It sounded as if they were over the ridge, scanning the plain between the San Miguel and the Zanjon. I stood up to look but saw nothing.

As the day wore on, the heat became oppressive. My impulse was to tear off the sweat suit. I imagined myself up in the Alps with a cool wind blowing down from the alpine snow. I dreamed of summer surf, the cool, refreshing water enveloping my body. Eventually, I found sleep again.

When I reawakened in the late afternoon, the worst of the heat had passed. I took off the sweats and probed the lip around my wound, uncertain whether or not it was healing. It was sore so I decided to look for some sort of plant to dress it. Having found a clump of aloe vera farther up the slope, I used this to pack the wound and attempted to put the issue out of my mind.

I turned my attention north but was unable to see through the maze of hills and mountains in that direction. Regardless, the river ran north, so as long as I followed it, I could not possibly get lost. The road to Carbo was there and if all went well, I might still make my rendezvous with Eric the following morning. There were no signs of men or dogs so perhaps they had missed my trail. Perhaps they were backtracking. They had little reason to suspect I was prepared for a prolonged desert assault.

In either case, there was nothing to do but go forward. I folded the sweats and placed them in the pack. I took the tarp down and folded it away too. I checked my jacket. It was stiff but dry. So were my pants. I put these things on and tied off the pack. I was ready and turned one last time towards the sunset. The hills had grown dark beneath a fading sky. Cardon dotted the highest ridges like telephone poles. Distant clouds were blushing blood red over the gulf. The smell of the river came up the canyon. I watched the sparrows flock from branch to branch in the trees along the water. The river flowed calmly down the valley towards Hermosillo, reflecting the last light of day.

Then, in this quiet of dusk, I heard the hounds baying. They had found my trail.

I consoled myself with knowing that the dogs would lose the scent again once they got to the river and that it would probably take them all day tomorrow to find it again; if they found it. But I knew it was inevitable now. I must abandon my hopes of meeting Eric. The long march to the border lay ahead. I quickly hid all signs of the camp and started down the canyon.

At least I had a day's head start on my pursuers. If I stayed in the river and got past the road to Carbo without being seen, my chances were good. Somehow, though, I had to lose their hounds. As long as they kept picking up my trail, there would be no relief.

I backed my way down the arroyo, covering my tracks as before and slid down the bank into the shallow river. I could feel the hills still radiating the heat from that day. The river gave off a soft light as I marched. Then the sky faded from midnight-blue and all was black beneath the stars. I sloshed through the cool, shallow waters of the river keeping time.

In half an hour, I had reached the road to Carbo. It ran east and west along a lateral valley like a black line. The lights of Rayon were up ahead on a hill. The lights of Carbo glimmered enticingly far down the lateral valley to my left.

Behind me, the terrain fell away, revealing a distant campfire. That was good. My pursuers had camped for the night. Perhaps news of my trail had yet to be relayed ahead. They had only found it this afternoon.

I turned my attention back to the road, watching from behind some brush. When it seemed clear that no one was waiting for me, I crossed under a bridge and continued north. With each step I felt more confident. It was clear, open country and the river bottom was layered with silt now and easy to walk in.

An hour later I had crossed the lateral valley. Up ahead, the mountains came down on either side of the river, creating a narrow canyon with a tangle of brush and rocks blocking its entrance. It would be harder soon, but it had been a good hike and I had made good time.

I was staring one more time towards the lights of Carbo, wishing I could take the easy way, when a pair of headlights flicked on in that direction and a motor came to life. I ran with a spotlight sweeping the terrain and the vehicle closing fast.

When rifle shots rang out, I started zigzagging wildly back and forth. The arms of the mountain were near but somehow seemed to be moving away, not growing closer.

Then at last I had crashed into the brush surrounding the mouth of the canyon and stopped there to have a final look back. The jeep was a few hundred yards off and jouncing across the flat terrain. I saw two silhouettes against the windshield and assumed them to be Mexican soldiers. Whatever they were, they couldn't follow me in the Jeep and would probably not follow on foot, at least not for long. They had no way of knowing whether or not I was armed and they weren't about to keep up with my wild pace. Still, they had my trail again and all my previous efforts had been wasted.

In desperation, I scrambled up the river, running when I could and clawing my way over falls and other obstacles when it became necessary. Several times, I slipped on the wet rocks and landed wildly in the darkness and the sweet taste of blood began to mingle with the sweat in my mouth.

I ran for what seemed like twenty minutes and stopped to listen. There was only the gurgling of what had become a creek, rising ever steeper ahead of me. It would meet the plain above Escondida and pour me like a funnel into their waiting hands. There was no choice. I had to turn east and away from the San Miguel, but how? The mountains in that direction rose up in a broken carapace of ridges and spires three thousand feet above me. It seemed like an impossible route but I had to try. I had to find a way out.

Foolishly, my mind wasted time retracing my steps and considering what I might have done differently, when there was no changing it now. I could have gone more directly east into the mountains and reached the Sonora, or headed southwest towards the gulf. Had I found a fisherman to transport me across the gulf, I could have followed the coast of Baja back up to California. But wishing for what might have been was fruitless. I could easily be somewhere else, wishing I had taken this route. It was still the straightest shot to the border.

A coyote howled up in the barren mountains as I moved on. Distant stars sparkled in the black sky above me. I stared up, wondering if there was someone up there like me, being chased like game on a warm, desert night.

Through the night, I scrambled forward with scant concern for my flesh. There were thorns in my hands and bruises everywhere. My mind grew numb from the fatigue. Then, late in the night, the moon rose over the mountain and revealed a flat trail ascending among its many peaks. With no other way forward that I could see, I started up that slope, praying it wasn't a dead-end.

The going was easy at first and I was drawn forward by what seemed to be a shallow bluff at the top of the slope, with several canyons above it. However, what had appeared so small from a distance turned out to be a hundred foot sheer cliff. I put my hand on the rock and felt its lingering warmth from the day's heat.

Most of an hour passed with me traversing one way and the other, searching for a way to the top of the cliff. When I reached it, I found three separate canyons rising above me. Forced to choose between them, I took the one on my left and climbed high up into the folds of the mountains, only to be confronted with a mogul of rock formations and the need to retrace my steps.

I tried the middle canyon but was once again forced to retreat. By the time I started up the last canyon, I was delirious. Blood and sweat stung my eyes. My hands were covered with thorns and glistened like a field of tiny grave markers in the moonlight. I pulled out those that I could and broke off the rest against my pants. At least they would not dig any deeper. I took a drink of water and pressed forward.

Eventually, the canyon floor became a bed of sand that had washed down from the surrounding peaks. Encouraged by this, I ran forward with the wash winding blindly among vertical cliffs and steadily narrowing to a trail.

A few minutes later, I had my answer. This canyon also led to a dead end, a spine of rock and brush rising three hundred feet above me. I could attempt to climb it or go back down to the river and try somewhere else.

I sat down, overwhelmed. I was just tired, I decided. There was nothing else wrong with me so I lay down to rest for a spell, drifting in and out of sleep.

Then an invisible urge jumped in me. My body didn't know. It didn't care but something in my spirit told me that I had no choice. I had to go on. Going back was easy. Going back was to surrender. Something in my life had led up here into the mountain.

I looked up again at the sheer climb. Going on might well mean death. It was a very real possibility. Sensing this danger, I considered whether or not to dispense with the pack but decided that whatever danger it posed in a climb, death was a certainty without it. I drank some water and had two dates. There weren't many left. With a deep sigh, I stood up and began the ascent.

The climb became more terrifying with every inch upwards. Each slip of a foot sent shockwaves through my body. Each time this happened, I clung tightly and closed my eyes, hearing rubble bound off rocks and land with a thud far below. Looking down once, I decided not to do it again.

It occurred to me in one of those fearful moments that no one would dare follow me up here. A man would have to be crazy. Even if they found my trail down below, if I somehow made it over the top, it would take them days to pick up my scent again, if they did at all. And the vector would have opened into hundreds of miles of territory. It felt good to think that I might win this battle simply by taking the most difficult route.

My spirits rose further as I came to a shallow ledge and scrambled over the top, sensing the pass through the mountain was not far ahead. Then all my hopes vanished. I had come face to face with a huge dome of rock, like a plug in the end of the canyon. Grass and brush hung enticingly over the top, but sheer mountain walls rose precipitously on either side. I was a hundred feet from my goal with no other way up but across that near vertical dome of rock.

I worked my way up and over to one side of it. A narrow ledge traversed laterally to my right and continued around the rock, out of sight. I checked to make sure I had a solid grip with both hands and extended my right leg, then brought my left leg to it and searched for a new hand grip. As I inched my way forward, I felt the pack wanting to pull me over.

In time I came out over the drop from which I had just climbed and my heart quickened. The further I went, the more the dome pressed me backwards and toward the darkness below.

A few pebbles broke loose while reaching for the next handhold. Then my left foot gave out. I grasped desperately in the darkness and found a crevasse with my right hand, left crucified, for all intents and purposes, with both my feet now dangling in midair. I pressed my face to the rock, too sick to look down.

Knowing there was no other choice, I brought my left hand next to my right one, took a deep breath and reached out for the next handhold. When my hands and arms began to ache, I took a deep breath, and reached out again. My only hope was to keep moving. When I hung on too long, my body began to atrophy.

I thought only of where to reach with my right hand and followed it with my left. I brought them together again and again and time disappeared. The pain subsided with the motion and my panic became concentration.

As the dome turned back, I found myself confronted with another intersecting face of rock. There was a place below to plant my feet but it appeared to be just out of reach. As I hung there, considering my dilemma, the ache in my hands returned. Again, there was nothing to do but go forward.

I reached wildly with my right foot but missed the ledge and the weight of my body tore my hands loose from their grip. I cursed and tumbled wildly backwards into the black abyss, desperately trying to remove the pack and hoping somehow it would break my fall.

My body was contorted into this position when I hit. The inertia caused my knees and face to converge into the same space. I felt the pain of my nose slamming into something solid and heard the sound of it breaking.

I crumpled backwards, somehow awake but unable to breathe. The black sky and all the stars seemed to have frozen in my mouth. Then with a groan, my breath flooded back. I rolled over with blood trickling down my throat and coughed and was there like death for a long time.

Some minutes later, I wrestled free from the pack, looked inside for my sweatshirt out and held it to my nose. I lay down prone again, waiting for the bleeding to stop. Once it had, I felt the flesh of my nose. It had been twisted to the left. Gritting my teeth, I pulled hard to the right. The crunch of cartilage brought nausea. The shock from the pain knocked me out.

When I reawakened, my tongue instinctively ran over my broken lips. I got up on one elbow. The rush of blood stung in my nose.

What had happened? Surely I hadn't fallen three hundred feet. Yet here was the same sand I had left below. I crawled over to where the sand fell away and peered down cautiously. No, the wash ended right here.

I looked up to the rock above me. I had fallen thirty feet into this narrow trail of sand, something I had not seen from above. Ten feet the other way and I would have fallen to my death.

Going up the trail the other way, I came to a shallow ridge and climbed over to have a look. A meadow spread out before me. Elated, I scampered back to retrieve the pack. Once I had lifted myself back onto the meadow, I took time to eat some of the raisins. The sweet fruit came with a spicy hot flavor of ant flesh. I washed all of it down with a good drink of water and put everything away.

It was another hour before I reached the crest and saw the Rio Sonora valley dropping away gently to the east. I could expect to make the river before sunrise.

Looking the other way, I saw the San Miguel flowing far off in the distance to the south, and a dot of light above the city of Hermosillo. There, prisoners were slumbering in their cells.

I beat you bastards, I said out loud. I beat you. I wanted to shout it at the top of my lungs but cautioned myself. There was yet a long, long way to go.

41

In the bitter cold before dawn, the mist covered farmland spread out far below me with the Sonora River winding lazily through it like a ribbon of glass. The lights of towns sparkled along the river here and there and a pair of headlights moved almost imperceptibly in my direction from the south. The headlights paralleled the river for some distance before crossing it and continuing on along the other side.

I retreated to the mesquite where I had camped, pulled out the map and tried to get my bearings with the first light. There were five towns along the river and I appeared to be somewhere in the middle of them. The most northerly, Sinoquipe, was at the top of the valley. I would have an easy walk that night and then be back in the mountains. From there it was a hundred miles to the border: three or four nights if things went well, five if they did not. I folded up the map and lay down.

With time, the sun cleared the ridge to my east, the mist slowly lifted and a patchwork of green crop squares appeared across the valley. The scent of irrigation came on the morning breeze. Chorizo and eggs and a cold beer at Jorge's crossed my mind. I closed my eyes and enjoyed the thought. There would be plenty to eat in a few days.

The morning was quiet but quickly grew hot. I spent most of the day struggling to find sleep. I had bandaged the wound on my leg with the meat of a prickly pear, hoping to hold back the infection. I ate most of what was left of my food supplies. I was nearly out of water.

In the late afternoon, a caravan of army trucks made its way up the valley, the men dispersing here and there to search along the river before moving on. What appeared to be the same plane came up the valley and disappeared but none of this worried me. The authorities had no idea where I was. They were simply covering all bases.

When things quieted down, I tried to sleep again. A thought occurred to me as I lay there. No one in the world knew where I was. There was not a soul who knew whether or not I was still alive. Not even Eric was certain of my plight. The thought made me feel very hollow and apart from the rest of the universe.

I made a second notch in my boots with the knife, two nights so far. I drank again and drifted off to sleep.

With dusk, I broke camp and headed north. The mountains were tall and dark to my left. I descended steadily down towards the valley. The smell of alfalfa mixed more and more with the sharp scent of mesquite and sage as I did. The alfalfa was sweet and finally dominated the other scents.

The river ran darkly through the valley and in the hollows, mist had started to gather. All down and along the river, the sparkling lights of civilization came to life. Headlights converged on the towns, men arriving for an evening meal and a beer in a cantina.

I stayed well back from the farmland until I had passed Huepac then worked my way farther down towards the river. The trail came alongside a field of green peppers. I passed broccoli and early corn and stuffed my pack with everything I could manage. I ate as I marched on towards Banamichi.

In passing one farm, I heard dogs barking and moved higher up towards the hills. It was quiet then and I saw nothing except bats as they whirled overhead. Sometimes they came too close and I swung at them.

It was a long hike to Banamichi and I made sure to get well past it before going down to the river. The river was slow and dark but tasted clean. I filled the bota bag, drank all that I could and moved back away from the dense brush before heading north. It was a good march, but after the previous night, anything would be a good march.

Near dawn, I found the road converging with the river and climbed back up into the hills to avoid it. Later, I came over the lights of Sinoquipe. As usual, the poor had parceled off the hillsides in a mish mash of ramshackle huts and crude, block buildings clinging to the steep slopes.

I hiked up to a lone paloverde and made camp well hidden among the rocks. I cut the third mark in my boots and lay down to sleep. There was a throbbing in my nose, a deep ache in my leg and my hands were red from cactus thorn, but I slept well enough in spite of these things.

A jay came down from the mountain late in the afternoon and awakened me. I poked my head over the rocks and watched people stirring in the town below. I lay back down, hungry for many things in my heart — a good meal, a woman's love, a quick ride to the border — but was glad for one thing. There were no soldiers in sight. It seemed clear that I had lost my pursuers.

Darkness came quickly below the mountain and with it came those same feelings of loneliness. I wanted someone to know me and where I was. I broke camp and headed north, trying to feel grateful, not dismal, but the loneliness kept dogging me. It did not seem in that moment that I would ever rejoin my place among my fellow human beings.

Traversing the hills, I had only a goat trail to keep me from cascading two hundred feet down into a line of brush and cacti. The first row of pueblos was roughly a hundred feet below that. I heard strains of Bavarian-like music coming up from the town, the sounds of it breaking apart in the gloom. The Germans had really screwed the Mexicans, I thought, bringing with them their accordions and polka. I had a brief smile while marching forward.

It was another hour before I had worked my way around the last lights of town and began my descent. I could see the canyon below was narrow and steep and cluttered with brush and trees where the river had claimed the bottom. There would be no place for me to hike but in the rushing water.

I stared at an unpaved road winding along the canyon opposite me but knew I could not take the chance. Any stray patrol would leave me cornered. I consoled myself with the thought of cold water numbing my leg again. My wound had begun to ache over the course of the day and any relief from that was welcome. The thought of having to trudge against the current all night and to fight rocks with every step was not.

A bridge crossed the river up ahead and from there the road began its climb to the north. I decided to get ahead of the bridge before I went down into the river. I now had less than a goat trail under my boots and was unable to stop various loose pebbles from tumbling down the hillside as I inched forward.

With a fresh cascade of debris from my footsteps, I heard voices and froze. The voices seemed to be arguing. Then a spot light came on and swung up my way. I scampered over behind some rocks and watched as the light crossed below me, then higher up.

A volley of gunfire rang out and several bullets struck nearby. I listened and waited. They were searching below me now where the rocks had fallen. Then the arguing began again. It was apparent from the sound of their voices and laughter that they were drunk.

Following another wild volley of gunfire and laughter, the lights went off. They had probably thought it was a wild animal of some sort. Still, it had scared them at first or they would not have been squeezing off rounds. After that, they were just having fun. It grew quiet again as they went back to whatever it was they had been drinking.

I peeked around the carapace of rocks and considered a plan. The brush from the river came up and gave cover to the hillside about a hundred feet from where I was perched. It was bare rock until I got there. I risked being in the open and having more pebbles fall and potentially being caught in the spotlight with nowhere to run.

I waited for some time with the voices and laughter going on as before. They might fall asleep, or I might be waiting all night. I decided to risk it. I couldn't be sitting here in the morning light, not with a narrow canyon as my only means of escape.

I inched cautiously forward with my chest to the rock face and in five minutes had made it back to the cover of brush. When I felt safe, I stopped and took off the pack. I was now a hundred yards upriver from the patrol.

Feeling weak, I decided to finish the raisins and eat the last of the almonds. Then I leaned back with pleasant dreams flooding my mind. I would soon be free and in some lovely place like Europe, without a care in the world.

Smiling at the thought, I spread my arms out and accidentally struck the pack. It was but a glancing blow but enough to dislodge it. I watched in horror as the pack cart wheeled down through the brush, the entire contents spilling out across the hillside along the way.

Shots rang out again, only aggressively this time. Two of the soldiers quickly crossed the road in my direction. The other searched the hill with the spotlight.

There was nothing to do but slide and tumble down after the pack, all the way to the river. Shots zinged through the brush above my head.

Then I was in the river and running madly upstream. The river was shallow and swift and the mountains rose up steeply around me. I glanced back frequently but saw no one and kept running. I no longer had any thought of conserving energy. My only thought was to run onward, as far as I could from that disaster. I was now without anything between me and the unforgiving desert but a knife. The money, the food, everything was lost.

I knew it was imperative for me to make Arizpe before dawn. If they found the pack in the morning, I wanted to be clear of the town. I had to get past the bottleneck.

I stopped for a moment to catch my breath and pick the thorns from my hands but it was useless. There were too many and my efforts only brought more pain. I quickly splashed water on my face and moved on with a steady gait. I ran when it was easy and walked when the river bottom required it, but I pushed hard and did my best not to dwell on what had happened.

I thought instead of what I knew about the desert. There were only two things to worry about: water and heat. The heat I could avoid. As for water, it would be hard to survive if I left the river.

I tried to recreate the map in my mind. I had to get away from the road and the Rio Sonora. They hugged each other for twenty-five miles, halfway to Boachici. There was another tributary coming straight down from the north, but there was the risk of finding a dry creek bed above and being without water. That was a real danger. I looked down at the river. There was plenty of water now. More than I could ever need.

I came upon the lights of Arizpe with the first light of dawn. The road crossed the river about a half mile ahead. I drank well and fought my way up towards the hills to the west through heavy undergrowth. I came across some mesquite a few hundred yards up from the river, stuffed my pockets full of the beans, broke open a pod and sucked the peas into my mouth. They were like pebbles but perhaps they would grow softer with time. At least it was something for my digestive juices to gnaw on.

As the morning grew bright, I ran again. I had to find the tributary and get well out of the range of dogs. I assumed they would find my pack; then maybe not. Maybe they would forget. Those soldiers would likely be nursing hangovers this morning and unwilling to chase after some noise they had heard in the night.

Still, I decided to travel for part of the day. I knew it was foolish, but I was reasonably safe as long as I had water. I tried to calculate how many miles I was from the border now. I thought perhaps seventy. It had looked so damned close on the map.

Arizpe was now well below me and on the far side of the canyon. There were few signs of civilization up here at the base of the hills. I saw no patrols and only a lone pueblo with some chickens in the yard. The scent of cooking came with the wind, something like sausage, though I might have been imagining things. It might have been nothing but the sagebrush around me.

I stood staring at the pueblo for some time before moving on. I could have used a warm breakfast right then but could not afford to risk being seen. I turned away and tried again to chew on the beans.

Soon, I came across the tributary and it was a good, clear stream, shallow, but enough to sustain trout, and there had to be a way to catch trout. The bed of the stream was firm so I began to run. The clear, blue sky grew bright above the dark walls of the narrow canyon.

There were two buzzards soaring in the sky, high above the cliffs. The air was dry and a chorus of desert birds greeted the new day. It was a fine place, cool and green along the stream, a pleasant place to have a picnic.

I laughed suddenly. A picnic, wouldn't that be great? I'm sorry everybody, but time out. I'm having a picnic today. We'll resume the chase at five.

I stopped and caught my breath. I looked up at the hills around me, but no one was there, no one but me.

A fear jumped in me. Was I losing my mind?

Dreading the answer, I moved on. The hunger kept tightening in my gut. Somehow I had chewed the beans and heard my digestive juices working. It was good to have something in my stomach. I pulled out a few more pods and broke them into my mouth.

In time I began to walk punch drunk, my head hung low like a starving animal. I knew it. I knew it was best to stop but I marched on. I thought of the pack and felt vulnerable without it. I tried to remember what I had been thinking when I knocked it down the hill. I was smiling then, but I wasn't smiling now.

Feeling the ache in my leg, I probed around the pain with my hand. It was very sore. My neck and entire body were sore.

I marched on. The sun cleared the mountain and began to bake my head. The brush and rocks radiated heat until everything seemed to be wavering in the dry air but I kept going. Only a little further, I thought. If only the voices would stop arguing. I was tired of the voices. I shook my head, trying to make them stop.

"Go to hell," I shouted. "I don't want to stop."

You're going to die if you keep it up.

"To hell with you. I'm on my way home."

You don't have a home, you dumb son of a bitch.

"To hell with you. I got a home. I got bacon and eggs and all you can eat. Right up ahead."

The dumb fools. What did they know? I began to laugh wildly and fell face first into the stream, then struggled to my feet and stood there hunched over, coughing the water out of my lungs. Fearing my own delirium, I dug my nails into my palm and yelped from the shock.

What the hell? Have I been talking to myself?

I vaguely remembered that there had been voices. I tried to think of how long I had been walking and what I had eaten last. And why I was there in the hot sun. I felt it burning into my skull. I stared up through my hand into the blazing white light. It was a terrible sun. I had to get out of it now.

You're going to see Caroline, remember? It's only sixty more miles, only three more nights. I drank my fill of water, crawled up under a cottonwood, pulled my boots off and remembered to make the fourth mark. I looked at my hands and they were strange things; not like mine. Something was wrong but I was too afraid to ask. Instead, I closed my eyes and fell asleep.

402

42

I awakened late in the afternoon with the grim countenance of a man who has had nothing to eat that day. I cleansed my wounds at the river, drank deeply, pulled on my boots and started upstream. I would not make a sixty mile hike without sustenance. I wasn't so sure I would make the hike in front of me that night but dusk was now descending and with it any hopes of finding food until tomorrow's light.

An hour into my trek, the canyon narrowed to a steep arroyo leading up into the mountains. I soaked my hands in cold water to relieve the pain, drank deeply again and started to up through the brush and rock.

As the night wore on, I grew weaker and fell often and each time it took me longer to get back up. I grew mad with anger and resentments. Where are you, Kip and Caroline? Let's see you endure the same journey as me. I thought not and felt a perverse sense of superiority to them and the rest of the world.

Up and up I climbed, scrambling ever higher, at times moving forward blindly, but always with a thought now of that safe in Arizona. I would show them for abandoning me. Revenge festered in me until it was the only thing driving me onward.

Dawn arrived and in that pale morning light, my spirits sank to see the creek rise up in a series of waterfalls, ever higher into the mountain. I wasn't sure if I could make another climb, the way I had above the San Miguel, but I would try. I had to try. What else could I do? If I fell and died then there would be nothing to worry about anymore. I would no longer be weary and hungry and burdened with the anger in my heart.

The canyon walls rose up increasingly around me as I climbed until there was nothing but a narrow slit of blue sky directly above my head. Scrub pines had taken root here and there, sprinkled in among the mesquite and paloverde. A stellar jay alighted on a nearby prickly pear and chattered at me before fluttering off up the narrow canyon. The sharp screech of two red-tail hawks broke the silence and explained the jay's sudden rush for safety. I saw the hawks crossing the sky above me before they quickly disappeared.

Unexpectedly, I came to the crest and scrambled over to find a level canyon before me. It was a cool and beautiful morning and I hiked on for a spell longer before lying down beneath one of the scrub pines. The sun had come out, warming the day.

I soon found sleep and awakened in the early afternoon. There were four marks on my boots. I stared at them for a long moment before making another one. Five nights. Or was it five days? It hardly mattered. It was five something.

I took off my boots and hung the rest of my clothes out to dry. My lower legs were pallid, my feet white and wrinkled. I checked my hands. They were infected and swollen and my other wound was even worse. I did not want to think about what came next. Best to let it dry for the day, I decided. Only two more days and everything would be all right.

The canyon spread out on either side of the creek for a hundred feet in slabs of smooth shale, piled about like broken plates. Here and there another scrub pine had made a stand or some manzanita.

In my bare feet, I walked gingerly over the shale and found some prickly pear growing along the walls of the canyon, but none of them bearing fruit. It would have done little to fill my stomach anyway. I needed protein. I cut off a piece of its flesh for my wounds and moved on.

Farther up the canyon, I came across some brittlebush in bright yellow bloom but it was useless to me. The only useful stockpile I found was a misplaced salicornia, which I licked for its salt. I thought it best to pick some. I would need salt, especially without food. It would be good for my wound, as well.

On my way back to the creek I stumbled across a small pool of rainwater filled with fairy shrimp. I remembered reading about these pools back in Tucson. The Mexicans called them tinajas.

I fell to my knees and attempted to scoop the shrimp out but they mostly slipped through my fingers. With an idea, I hurried back to the camp and returned with my shirt. With it carefully slipped under the shrimp, I raised up more than a handful.

Back in the shade of the pine, I carefully chewed each fragile shell to a pulp. They tasted like sea brine and conjured a distant memory. Camarones, si hay. I saw the image of the old lady and smiled.

Feeling better for having eaten, I spread my shirt out in the sun and lay down with the jacket under my head. If it rained tonight, there would be more tinajas. The thought of it brought me comfort.

Later in the day, I awakened to the moan of the wind in the pine. The sky was cerulean above me. The air was dry and warm and rising now from the bottom of the canyon. Sitting up, I made a sudden decision to climb the last leg of the mountain in daylight. There would be a plateau above and easier going if I could get out of the canyon before nightfall. I bandaged my wound, got dressed and made my way across the rocks in search of more tinajas. I found none and sucked on the mesquite beans as consolation. I would have better luck above.

I came to a place where the canyon walls once again converged on the creek. There was no way up except among the piles of boulders and various waterfalls. I looked back down at the canyon. It had grown dark in the late afternoon. So had the blue sky above it. The beauty made me think of Caroline, and with her memory came guilt. I did not want to think of her any longer, but she came to me in waves of tenderness, anger and remorse.

I climbed slowly, fighting through the brush, fighting with the pain, slipping and cursing, my hands a constant torment, always a sign I was nearing the top, only to discover another set of falls and another struggle up ahead. The sky darkened to midnight blue and the first stars appeared in the eastern sky.

At last, I came over a ledge and saw the plateau before me. There were arid peaks on my left and far to the east, the Sierras, with their meager snowcap looking lovely and cool in the twilight. But straight ahead the mountains marched in lateral folds across the horizon, as far as I could see. They were dry and forbidding and I dreaded having to cross them, and yet, I was glad in my heart. I could make it now. I felt sure of it. I was looking at the Patagonias,

405

perhaps thirty-five or forty miles away. I was looking at America. It seemed as if I could almost reach out and touch it with my hand.

I stood and gazed across the rugged country for a brief moment longer before striking out again. Not long afterwards, the creek turned west and away from my goal, forcing me to leave the security of this water source. I took a moment to drink well before continuing on. There would be water elsewhere, I reasoned. And food, there had to be food somewhere up ahead.

What trail I found staggered this way and that across the rocks. My feet caught frequently. I lurched forward often and fell at times and found it hard to get back up.

I tried to remember my reasons for going on. Mostly there were vague and distant feelings involving Caroline. I grew possessed with this need to prove my strength to her. I stumbled forward, half mad but determined to show her how tough a man I could be.

Sometime later, I collapsed and slept. When I awakened again, I was better. I walked over the crest of a nearby hill and saw a valley far below, with a highway winding from east to west. I assumed this to be Highway 2, which meant I was still in Mexico.

I looked long at the mountains beyond, trying to imagine how I would negotiate that impossible maze of peaks. There were countless passes, but none of them aligned with the next one. If I took one route it would mean doubling back to make the next crossing, adding miles and miles to my march. I looked longingly at the highway but knew I risked running into Federales or the border patrol.

I skipped and slid and fell carelessly down a thousand foot slope, my body growing further bruised as I went. It would soon be over, I thought, and none of the pain would matter.

Reaching the valley floor, I started out without resting, expecting I could march straight through now. Walking seemed easy. I felt nothing but the numb motion of my body. I would be home before tomorrow night.

I came to the highway and again wanted very much to march along it. It was so nice and straight and flat compared to the mountains ahead. In a car, it was less than an hour to the border.

Then a set of headlights appeared in the distance and I hurried across into the adjacent folds of the hills. From that safe perch, I watched as an army truck rolled by, confirming my suspicions. I had to take the hard way.

I turned and climbed through dense brush, the hunger twisting and tormenting my guts. The hours passed and I gave in to the madness. I knew no beginnings or endings. I fell. I got up. I climbed higher. I put one foot in front of the other. I told myself that freedom was higher, much higher, way up high in the clouds. I concentrated on my knees lifting and falling, mechanically, one after the other.

How much longer? Days? Hours? Until the bells stopped ringing in my ears? Think how close we are. When we cross that ridge, only one more remained.

Then, near dawn, I fell, knowing I should get up and find some protection. I knew it was wrong to be exposed in the fierce sun, but I slept.

When I awakened, there was a raging, hot light above me. I wanted to move but could not. Instead, I dreamed there was water everywhere, crystal clear water. And Caroline would be here soon. Kip too and we would all be friends again.

But there were black wings in the sky. From the turquoise sky came the black wings, circling and circling through the sun.

I had to get to the water. It was there, so close: alpine lakes full of cold, clear water on the horizon. I had to go where the snow turned to icy cold rivers and churning white water rapids, where I could draw tall, cold, glistening pitchers full of water.

But no one came and the water was not there.

I got up and staggered on towards the wavering horizon. Surely there's a lake up in the mountains. And lots of water to get. And lots of sun. The sun is good, too. Everything is good with water. But the water never gets closer and everyone has betrayed me.

I fell as one already dead in the sun. Perhaps whoever made me can make me whole again. I will bake here in the sun and nothing will spoil until they return.

Then I saw the teeth and fur and somehow knew it was over. Low and slinking and with teeth bared, it came. I pulled out the knife and stabbed once but was blinded by the sun. A carnival merry-go-round spun in my mind and Caroline waved to me as she rode by. And in the shadows and darkness of the great wheel, I heard the sound of the devil, and a bright flash from the sky, and suddenly, felt something cool strike my skin.

43

A world existed somewhere far above me, and in that world a boy lay in bed with the pale light of afternoon fading around him. Other children were playing outside his windows on that autumn day and the boy longed to go out and play with them but he was ill and could not. The boy's mother had come home from work and parted the curtains and was now holding his hand and telling him she loved him and that everything would be all right.

I was that boy and my heart jumped at the feel of the leathery, coarse hand holding mine. It was not my mother. Something was terribly wrong.

Needing to understand, I swan up frantically through the dark sea and came to the door of the world and pushed against it with all my might and was met there with a brown, shriveled face and two black eyes. The eyes stared at me without emotion. I attempted to speak but my lips were bound together.

When I attempted to move my extremities, I found my right leg was stiff and ached with a deep, hollow pain. Fear jumped in me and I attempted to sit up, but a hand gently pressed on my chest.

With a look down, I saw my leg was bound in cloth. So were my hands.

Then words came, an airy, raspy voice, speaking in a language I did not understand. I heard another voice answer him, a softer voice, and moved my head to see an old woman sitting on my other side. She was also brown but not so old and shriveled and wore a scarf over her head. There was another woman behind her, both young and fair. Her eyes were black and kind but unmoving, like the other two.

I lay on a bed, covered with brightly colored blankets. There were other blankets on the walls, and herbs and garlic and gourds hanging from the ceiling. There were things from the earth all around the circular hut and the scents of these things filled the room.

The hut was made of adobe with a roof constructed of thatched wood, pitched to a small vent at the center. Through the vent, the sun shone fiercely in the blue sky, but it felt cool and pleasant inside the hut.

I searched my mind for any kind of memory but found only a shroud beyond which I could not see. Exhausted from even that small effort, I closed my eyes again, knowing something terrible had happened but I could not remember what.

Then my escape from the prison jumped in me, and my long, hard perilous trek through the desert, and the whole strange odyssey of my life returned. So who were these people and how had I gotten here? More importantly, had they told anyone of my presence here? Wondering if I was still in Mexico, I tried to sit up again and again the hand held me down.

My stomach growled and the old man nodded to the young woman. She filled a wooden bowl with something from a pot on the stove and brought it to the side of the bed. When I was unable to open my lips, she wiped gently at them with a wet cloth until they parted and then spooned a bit of warm broth into my mouth. The sensation of it going down my throat brought nausea and it was a long time before I could take another spoonful. I watched the black eyes of the young woman as she fed me, one slow spoonful at a time.

When the soup was gone, I used my tongue to probe my cracked lips and found they were hard like leather. With a jolt, the memory of my fall came back to me and my heart pounded. I closed my eyes to the terror of that moment and the other hardships I had endured.

Tired and wanting to sleep, but realizing I had forgotten something, I made the great effort of opening my eyes again. The old man was staring back at me.

"T h a n k y o u," I said.

He nodded and I closed my eyes again.

Time ran swiftly through fleeting hours. A world of darkness became light, then darkness once more. I heard strange chanting and the rattle of something dry, but I mostly slept and lived in a world of dreams. When I awakened again there was daylight. The women were gone. The old man sat next to me. I lay there looking into his eyes, feeling as if I could hear his thoughts in the silence of the day.

I saw all the good things I had known, the stars, the wind, the sun, the green fields and all that was wild and I thought I would like to go outside and see these things again.

When I nodded at the door, the old man grunted and helped me up. He was old and frail looking but had arms like iron. There were two thatched chairs in the shade of the hut and he sat in one.

"I need to use the bathroom."

He grunted and nodded towards the back of the hut. I went around and found an outhouse.

When I returned, the old man was still sitting there. The women worked in a field some distance from the house. It was dry and hot under the afternoon sun and dust lifted up as they worked. They both looked once in our direction and went back to work.

"You speak English," I said.

"Little."

We both looked forward at the dusty fields and beyond to a line of mountains ringing the valley.

"Spanish?"

"English is better."

"My name is Clay."

"Clay."

"Yes, like this."

I grabbed a nearby pot and pretended to turn it. He seemed to understand.

"It is a good name for you." His hand reached out and delicately touched my nose. "But you look more like a raccoon."

I smiled at his laughter.

"What about you?" I pointed to him.

"Jijiwa."

"Jijiwa," I repeated.

I lifted my hands to show him my concern. He grunted and took off the bandages. It was terrible to see. The hands were swollen and covered with a black puss, although the thorns appeared to be working their way out. I pointed again, this time to my leg. It had

411

been hard to walk. When he showed me the wound, I felt sick. It seemed as if I might lose the leg.

He saw my fear and shook his head. He brought water and washed my hands and my leg. He then pulled out what thorns he could with his long fingernails. I grit my teeth at the pain and my eyes watered.

When he had done everything possible, he poured a bit of dry, black powder from a leather pouch and rubbed it gently into my wounds.

"What is that?"

He said something in his native tongue and pointed at a nearby succulent.

"Aloe Vera?" I said.

He grunted.

I wasn't sure if he knew the word but assumed he had dried the plant down to a powder. When he was satisfied, he wrapped my leg and hands with a fresh cloth. He nodded confidently and sat down.

"Thank you, again."

"You are a strange one, coming from nowhere."

"But how did you find me?" I said.

"I was out hunting and saw the great birds."

He spread his arms wide. I nodded. I felt a great weariness at having to speak, but there were so many questions. It was too much for me to order them so I asked them as they came to mind.

"What was the furry thing?"

"Coyote."

I looked at him. He looked back once and looked away. I tried to imagine this old man carrying me on his back.

"You saved my life," I said.

He nodded but said nothing.

"Does anyone else know I'm here?"

He turned, looked into my eyes and went back to watching the women work.

"Your journey may be short, but it not over yet."

That was all he said. The questions continued to pass through my mind, but I let them go and watched and listened. A hawk flew over the mountain. Clouds came and went. The sun grew fierce in the sky. I could take no more and Jijiwa helped me back to the bed. I slept until the women came home from the fields.

That evening the young woman fed me again, this time with tortillas and beans, and a soup that had squash in it. When my stomach was full, I thanked her and closed my eyes, aware of their hands working and their voices speaking as I drifted in and out of sleep. Then it was dark and still in the hut and I slept until morning.

The hut was empty when I reawakened. I got up on feeble legs and walked to the door. The door faced into the morning sun and it felt warm on my skin. A dry wind blew dust across their fields but no one was there. I used the outhouse again and returned to look for food in the hut. The stove was in the center of the room and made of adobe, with the hole in the roof above it for ventilation. I found the soup still warm and ate some of it with a wooden spoon. My body quickly grew weak standing there so I lay down again with my thoughts.

As the memories moved within me, I realized the flashes of light and the sound of the devil on that last day had been lightning and thunder. I felt a sense of wonder to be alive. I would be dead had Jijiwa not stumbled upon me.

In the afternoon, I saw him returning from across the fields. He walked in the manner of someone who was old, but upright and steady, and carried over his shoulder a string of quail. There had been no gunshots, nor did he have a rifle, so I assumed he had trapped them. He hung the quail from the roof poles outside and grunted his approval at seeing I had eaten some soup.

He came over to remove the bandages and examine my wounds. I saw the swelling was gone. The cut on my leg was still open so he cleaned it and wrapped it again. The sores on my hands had shrunk to small dots where the thorns had been. It was as if the Aloe Vera had drawn the skin together. I tried flexing my fingers. They were stiff but the skin had nearly healed. The old man shook his pouch at seeing my disbelief.

"Strong medicine."

"Strong medicine," I said.

We went outside and sat in the chairs. The late afternoon sun had fled from the valley and the mountains rose up all around us. We sat in the fading light with the day yet warm. My mind had thought of two things during the day, pressing questions that I wanted answered.

"How many days have I been here?" I asked.

413

Jijiwa thought for a moment and held up four fingers. That meant he had found me one day, I awakened the following night and there had been the two days since.

"How far am I from America?"

He gestured as if to say I wasn't ready to know this. When I tried to press him, he gestured again.

Still restless, another question came to mind.

"Who are you? I mean, where do you come from?" He laughed and pointed to the sky. "You're Indian?"

"We are Papago." He made a circle with his hand.

"Your wife and daughter too?"

He grunted.

"And there is no one else?"

He sat silently. Realizing he did not speak English well, I thought it was possible he had not understood the exact meaning of my words. Then it occurred to me that the question might well have been taken in several ways. I waited to see what he would say.

"No, they are all gone. Down the mountain."

"And this is where you have always lived? Your people?"

"No. We once lived there, below the mountain."

Seeing that I wasn't satisfied, he went on.

"The Spanish drove my people up here. But no one can live up here."

"But you are living?" I waved my arm across the valley.

"It is hard. I went down the mountain, too." He looked again. "It is harder down there."

As I listened, something more occurred to me.

"I am like you."

I pointed to myself, feeling it was somehow important to do so. He took the time to study me before answering.

"Money-men don't like you?"

"I don't like them," I said.

He laughed and waved his hand away.

"To hell with money-men," he said.

While I laughed, he reviewed me passively. I told him about Faith and the reasons for my journey.

"Honesty is a word we do not have. If a man does not lie to himself, he will always speak the truth to others."

"Then what do you call it?"

He said something in his native tongue without looking at me.

"It is all truth," he said. He looked once and turned back towards the fading western sky. "Each man must learn for himself."

Before dark the women came home with a basket full of saguaro fruits. I saw now that the wife was twenty years younger than Jijiwa but older than fifty. She was short and round and strong. The daughter was soft and fair. I doubted she was twenty yet. She carried the long stick they had used to pick the saguaro fruits. They did not smile at me though their faces were kind. They went about dressing the birds, speaking among themselves in soft voices. Sometimes the old woman laughed. The young woman did not and kept darting looks in my direction. With twilight the two women started inside.

"Do you speak English?" I asked them.

The young one stared at me with her steady, black eyes. The older woman spoke.

"Very little. It is better to forget." She pointed at the old man and went back to her chores.

"What are their names, Jijiwa?"

"Toki and Nai. My daughter is Nai."

I watched her.

"Come, let us eat," Jijiwa said and helped me inside.

I ate well and returned to rest on the bed. It was warm and cheery inside and I nestled between the blankets, enjoying the sound of their voices. I recalled being in the prison and felt thankful to be here, a free man. Before I slept, Nai washed me. I watched her and thought of Kip and the many things we had endured together. I thought of him and wondered how many years he would be locked away over my impulsive decision. Nai finished and I was soon asleep.

The next morning, I awakened early. Toki had made a pot of tea and fed me hard bread that was laden with the jelly from the saguaro fruits. I went outside to eat in the chill morning air. Jijiwa was nowhere in sight.

When I went back inside, I saw that Nai had washed and neatly folded my clothes. While she and Toki worked over the stove, I changed from the loose muslin clothes they had given me. When I was done, Nai took my hand and gently pulled me outside, then

415

motioned for me to follow her towards the rising sun. I watched her walk off for some distance before running to catch up.

Heading east across the valley, the peaks directly ahead of us were dark against the approaching sunrise. I looked back once to where the mountains behind us were lost in a gray mist.

When the sun rose, all the lingering mist quickly dispersed with it. Cool air mixed with my sweat and my body grew warm with the morning sun.

At the base of the mountain, Nai turned south and then east again up a gorge between sheer rock cliffs. The trail ascended ever higher. The sun was hidden and the air was cool. We walked for an hour and I saw only a glimpse of the blue sky directly above the sheer rock walls.

As we marched ahead, the canyon narrowed further and became as dark as dusk. Scrub pines grew out of the canyon walls and were twisted and gnarled by the wind. There was some manzanita, too, but not much else.

We walked on until this chasm opened up to a view of the desert spreading to the east far below us. The distant hills were pink in the mid-day heat, and even farther beyond them were the Sierras and they were bigger than everything and their peaks touched the sky with a narrow band of snow.

Above us, the elements had fashioned a rock shelf out of the mountain, accessed by a steep, narrow path. The shelf was shady and secluded and Nai pulled on my hand, motioning for me to join her but I was reluctant. I had fallen from such places and shook my head. Nai kept pulling on my hand until I gave in.

Climbing up to the ledge brought back all the primordial fears I had experienced from my fall but when we reached the ledge, a strange peace descended over me. A warm breeze rose up from the desert floor, but it was cool in the shade and I felt safe with the rocks close around us. Nai and I gazed out at the vast panorama together and sometimes looked into each other's eyes. The wind whispered softly as it rose through the rocks and cactus. At times I thought I heard voices in the wind, but it was only a way of dreaming, as a child will conjure dreams from the hours of a day.

An eagle flew high up in the blue sky and over the mountain. It circled once and disappeared out of sight and I imagined I was like that, high up where I might see the course of my life, like a river flowing through a valley, to see where it had begun and where it was now and where it might be going. I imagined myself now like one of the ancient sages and realized I had never stopped to examine my life in that way. Even before the war, it seemed as if I had always been rushing from one place to another, that some primal fear had always been driving me forward.

The hours passed in a stream of thoughts and feelings and urges, often restless thoughts and feelings, but I found when I wanted nothing, the world was a simple place. Time passed and other, deeper, unspoken mysteries passed through my heart, mysteries I was unable to understand or articulate, but something told me that this was not the river of my life, that even though a part of me wanted to stay here with these people beneath the sky and never leave, my life flowed through the people I had come to know and love, and that I was needed in that other world somehow.

In the last light of day, when the magic of that hour runs like a child into darkness, I left with Nai and walked down the mountain.

From far across the valley, I saw the wisp of smoke rising in the fading light. It was a lovely sight and a feeling of gratitude for these people welled up inside me. It was enough to be alive and to know that someone cared.

Once we had returned, Nai went inside to help Toki with the evening meal. I sat outside with Jijiwa in the chairs by the hut. Nightfall was rushing upon us again. I looked over into Jijiwa's watery eyes.

"Thank you again," I said.

"Why do you thank me?"

There was kindness in his eyes.

"For saving my life."

"The gods must want you to live another year."

"I don't know, but I feel this great longing to go help my friend."

I looked over at Jijiwa and his eyes met mine.

"There are ways and there are ways. Listen to your heart."

I thought about his words but they were opaque and without clarity to me.

We were quiet, each of us with our own thoughts in that hour. A jay alighted nearby. Then another one came and they squabbled among themselves.

"No one will win that argument," Jijiwa said.

"Perhaps they enjoy arguing."

"For their sake, let's hope so."

I laughed and studied his profile.

"What will you do?" I asked him.

I nodded at the door and he understood.

"We will pass away like the wind."

"How sad, Jijiwa."

"Perhaps, but the young men will not come up the mountain. They are free to drink and gamble and make trouble down there, so why come back?"

"There must be someone?"

"Eh. Who would want their blood? Nai is happy. Perhaps we were meant to die beneath the mountain." Then later, he asked me. "What will you do?"

"Go back to my world, I guess."

"Better to pass away, I think."

I laughed. Jijiwa studied my face.

Night came quickly and we sat down together on the floor of the hut to have our meal. A lamp lit the hut and mesquite in the stove burned and crackled.

At times in the scant light of the lamp, Nai's gaze met mine and in these moments she never flinched or looked away, and it felt as if I was peering into the blackness of night, peering into life itself without all its complications, without all the complications I had known with Caroline and the other women in my life. And in those moments, I thought that Nai would make a good wife and that this would be a good life for me and I longed to be that simple.

Later, when I lay down to sleep, Nai rubbed my neck and back and I surrendered to her kindness and did not want to leave this place, and yet I was not content. A sense that I was needed in that other world continued to haunt me. I remembered that raw, cold day in Santa Cruz and the dangerous impulse I had felt at the time to go see Laura and how it had only led to disaster, and worried now that only disaster awaited me again, and wondered why a man always had these impulses to return to the fire and anvil where his life had been forged.

Seeing my restlessness the next morning, Jijiwa grunted and encouraged me to join him for a walk. We headed west and eventually arrived to a wooded area. We walked on until we came to a glade with a stream running through it. Jijiwa pointed at some trees at the edge of the glade and gestured for me to get out of sight.

I did and watched him approach a nearby thicket. He had a pouch of seeds tied to his waist and backed away from the thicket, spreading a trail of seed on the ground as he went. He then knelt down and waited.

Some minutes later, a quail appeared and pecked at the seeds, stopping to eye Jijiwa frequently, but slowly following the trail towards him. Jijiwa remained utterly motionless throughout it all and the bird came to accept him, until at the last second, he reached out and broke its neck.

He hunted through the morning in this way, and I longed in watching him to possess the same patience, the patience a man would need to stay in this world and love Nai, but I was restless and longed even more so for the world of my birth. It was a place I dreaded more than I loved, but I was drawn back there as a moth was to light.

When Jijiwa and I returned to the hut in the late afternoon, I stopped to help the women tend the fields. Nai stared briefly and went back to work. Toki seemed to acknowledge this exchange with a private smile. I hoed and weeded alongside them until fatigue forced me back to the comfort of the hut. I lay down and slept until dark, awakened by the smell of the birds roasting.

I knew it was time.

Jijiwa sensed my decision and spoke with the women in their language. After the meal, they wrapped food in a pouch and Nai tied it around my waist. She also strung a bota bag over my shoulder.

Jijiwa stood waiting for me at the door. I embraced both women and turned to leave, doubting I would ever see them again.

"If the wind blows this way, you will be back," Toki said.

"I wish it were true," I said and went out the door, haunted by the look on Nai's face and what I was leaving behind.

Jijiwa headed north across the valley and eventually led me into what seemed like a dead-end canyon. The mountains rose high and steep all around us. The canyon veered west at times but always turned back towards the north. We had walked for most of an hour before coming to the summit of a high pass. Then the truth of our location was revealed to me.

Looking northwest across the high plateau, the lights of Nogales were visible, the Patagonias too, and the lookout tower at Washington Camp, then Naco and Douglas as we rounded the mountain. I had been so very close.

Jijiwa stopped and pointed to a trail that descended from the mountain down into the plain below us. With no moon in the sky, I could barely see Jijiwa's eyes in the darkness, mostly the whites of them set against his leathery skin. He put his hand on my shoulder and squeezed.

"If you get lost, go up on the mountain," he said. He pointed up to the peaks. I nodded, not at all certain what he meant.

"Thank you again."

With a final squeeze of my shoulder, he turned and walked away. I watched him disappear, then started down the trail alone.

The way was steep and I fought with my footing, and most of an hour was lost just getting down to the desert floor, but from there I made good time. I had twenty miles to cross before reaching the border, even more so if I steered towards Nogales. Realizing this, and that I might not make it that far before sunrise, I headed due north towards the Patagonias. I would find the best place to cross the border and reconsider things with daylight.

In the wee hours, I crossed a dirt road that led to San Lazaro, then the railroad tracks and saw Los Mattates off in the distance. I stopped in the darkness of a field and ate. There was a quail and four flour tortillas filled with beans. I ate the quail and one of the tortillas and continued on.

By the time I passed the outskirts of Los Mattates, dawn had begun to spread in the eastern sky. I saw it above the lights of Lochiel. The mountains also loomed in that direction, dark and impenetrable.

My only thought was to slip unseen across the border and to that end, I found a sufficiently deep arroyo and made my way along its sandy wash, crawling as necessary, until at last I was staring across an open expanse at the border fence. I lay there watching for a minute with the usual caution before making a final dash across to the American side. Then I hiked a mile or so up into a steep canyon and lay down in the lee of a large mesquite and rock formation. There were decisions to be made and I had a long way to go yet, but for the moment, I was exhausted and needed sleep.

As I lay there beneath the stars, it came to me slowly. It came with a brief smile and sense of triumph. I had made it. I was home. However ambivalent I felt about the whole damned thing, America was still the place of my birth.

In the morning, I would find my way to Nogales, and then to Tucson. Plenty of money awaited me there, money that would allow me to go about things as I pleased, and the primary thing on my agenda was to pay Sheriff Prescott a visit. But before I walked in through his door, I had to make sure my assumptions about him were correct, that he was indeed an influential man with certain Mexican authorities across the border. And even if those assumptions were correct, I still had to render him in a cooperative mood, far more than he was at present.

That last day in Tucson flashed through my mind, and though I wasn't a particularly vindictive man, the son of a bitch had left a bad taste in my mouth and I thought it might be fun to watch him squirm a bit in place of me.

It all hinged on what Sheriff Prescott did late at night. I assumed it was something he did not want the rest of the world to know and in the best interests of my friend Kip, I planned to take whatever time was necessary to find that out.

44

In the bitter cold before dawn, I lay there curled up in the embryonic position, frozen to the core. The ground around me was covered in frost. I glanced over my shoulder at the eastern sky and curled up again. I was waiting for the sun to rise and warm my bones. Until then, I was as miserable as a man could be.

All through the night, I had been thinking about my plan to rescue Kip, the hope being that the sheriff could pull a few strings down in Hermosillo and get him sprung. But if that didn't work, then what? Did I just punt and leave him in there? Various other schemes had come to mind, but they all risked being imprisoned again.

I had lain there for some time, battling with the question of courage and cowardice again, when a shadow appeared on the ground beside me and something poked me in the back. I bolted to my feet and found an old man pointing a .45 at my guts. His other hand held a long stick.

His steel-blue eyes were furrowed nearly out of sight from too much sun and his ruddy face was a graveyard of white whiskers. With his sunken jowls, he was the picture of a man who wore dentures but had rushed out the door with them still on the nightstand. I took him to be an old prospector by the worn boots and plaid shirt and loose jeans tied in front with a rope. With the scruffy cowboy hat, one size too big, and the way his withered neck had shrunken down into his jacket, a turtle came to mind, cautiously poking its head out at the world.

"What the hell are you doing?" I asked him.

"What the hell am I doing? Now ain't ya one ta be askin' questions. Ain't too many folks that goes around taking naps in the Sonoran Desert. Not without a tent and camping gear, leastwise. Or ever that I can recall."

He dropped the stick but kept the gun trained on me with a less than steady hand. I imagined he would be easy enough to overwhelm. He stank of stale whiskey and his reflexes looked to be shot.

"Well, are ya gonna answer me or what?" he said with a twitch.

"What's it to you?" I said, trying to back him up a pace.

"I'll do the askin' for now, sonny."

"I was out for a hike and got lost."

"Now ain't that a sad excuse for a story. Hell, ya look like yer dressed fer a day at the park."

"Whatever I'm doing, I don't see how it warrants that gun in my face."

"I ain't takin' no chances. There's a heap a bad seeds runnin' around these parts and who's ta say ya ain't one of 'em."

"All right. I'm in trouble."

"Well, I figured ya was. Ya look the type, all right."

"It's not what you think. A buddy and I got tossed in the can down in Mexico and I escaped."

"Whereabouts they take ya in?"

"Hermosillo."

"Well then how in tarnation did ya come ta be restin' underneath that mesquite bush? Answer me that."

"I walked."

"Boy oh boy. Ain't that a tale. He just walked up from Hermosillo, dressed for a picnic. Now I know ya's lyin'."

He had started to have a good laugh but caught himself and trained the gun back at my guts.

"Look, old timer, you know a lot more about the desert than I do and only a fool would believe what I just told you. And trust me. I'm not that bad of a liar. The truth is, I need help, and I'm willing to pay you handsomely for it."

"What kinda help ya looking fer?"

"I need a ride to Tucson."

"And that's it?"

"That's it," I said.

423

"What's in it fer me?"

"How about two hundred dollars and a steak dinner."

He squinted from under his hat with the gun still pointed at me.

"Look, old timer, it's damned uncomfortable standing out here in the cold, so if you're not interested, I'll be moving on."

With a final once over, he shoved the pistol down the front of his pants.

"Well, I reckon we can discuss this plan of yers and in a more civilized manner back at my spread. But don't think I won't shoot ya the minute ya start to get outta line."

He amplified this thought with a little tug at his belt buckle.

"Okay, okay," I said, suppressing a smile. "You show the way and I'll try to stay out of trouble."

"Yep, from the sounds of it, ya could use some practice at that particular enterprise."

"What's your name, old timer?"

"Gold Pan Jake. But ya can call me just Jake."

"Clay."

I shook his hand.

"And you're probably right about that."

"About what?"

"About the trouble."

"Hmm," he said, scratching his chin. "Well, let's say ya go on out ahead and I'll follow."

Suppressing another smile, I started up a trail at his direction.

After hiking up and up for most of an hour, we came through a high pass and looked down into a narrow canyon far below. The canyon was mostly dust except for around a shallow creek that ran through it. The creek was lined with shrubs and trees from one end to the other. A small shack was tucked against one wall of the canyon, well back from the creek. An outhouse stood a safe distance from the shack and a battered Chevy pick-up was parked nearby.

A narrow, switchback trail led us down into the canyon. From there, we followed the winding creek over to Jake's shack. The entrance to a mining tunnel was off behind the shack. A weather-beaten sign hung askew by one nail. The first three letters on the sign read DOU. The sun and rain had bleached out the rest. I leaned my head over, but the words remained illegible.

"Well partner, what d'ya think of her?"

I gazed out over the trees and shrubs lining the creek.

"Sure is peaceful. And I imagine hard to find."

"You'd best believe it. Ain't seen another human being around here in over twelve years."

"I suppose there's the upside and the downside to that."

He eyed me suspiciously but went on.

"Ain't no road. Not to speak of. Jest a trail out the far end of the canyon there. Probably bury a station wagon. Last half mile slithers down a narrows that'd like to take yer side mirrors off. It'd wash ya ta kingdom come in a flash-flood."

I looked up at the sky.

"Doesn't seem like there's much chance of that around here."

"Ya never know in these parts." He looked up at the sky as well. "But I reckon not today, anyway."

"Well, Jake, I guess the next order of business is getting me back to Tucson."

"Well, I'm fixin' to have a look at yer money first," he said. He gave another tug at the pistol as a reminder.

"It'll have to wait until we get to town."

"Now I knew I shouldn't a trusted ya from the very start. Ya think I'm dumb enough to fall fer that trick?"

"Make it three hundred, Jake. I just can't do anything until we get to town."

"All right, what's yer bluff, tenderfoot?"

"The money's buried in the desert."

"Hmm. Buried, ya say?"

I nodded. He eyed me suspiciously again but seemed to understand about burying things in the desert.

"Well, I reckon we ought to have us a snort and look things over a spell."

I followed Jake into his shack. It was done up with a twin bed, a plywood counter and kerosene stove for a kitchen and some empty orange crates tacked to the walls. A small table sat under the lone window. One of the orange crates held cups and plates. Two of them held supplies, heavy on soup cans. Another one of the orange crates was covered with chintz cloth. I had a pretty good idea what was hidden inside it and sure enough, Jake pulled the cloth back and produced a fifth of Old Grand Dad. With a couple of glasses in hand, we went out to sit on the porch and worked on the bourbon for a spell. I listened with growing impatience as Jake grew looser by the shot. Finally, I had to stop him from filling my glass.

"Before we get ourselves too drunk here, Jake, how about that ride?"

"Now?"

"Jake, I haven't had a bath or a decent meal in nearly two weeks. Yeah, now, if you don't mind. I've got work to do."

"I'm not one ta trust strangers, but I'm guessin' I'll do it jes this once."

Jake put what was left of the fifth away in the shack, closed the door on his way out and invited me into his truck.

He hadn't been lying about that narrow, rutted trail leading out of his canyon. We went along with Jake alternately slamming on his brakes and flooring the accelerator until my guts felt like they had been run through a washing machine.

Once we had cleared the pass, Jake got onto a wash-board road and followed it straight for twenty miles. Well above the check-point, he turned left and found the main highway.

Jake sprung for a couple of beers in Tucson and we parked on Wagon Wheel Drive, waiting for day to fade to black over the Santa Rita Mountains. Once it had, I marched out to the safe alone. Finding it all right, I could not remember the combination and crouched down beside the nearby saguaro, watching the stillness of the mountains against the sky. I listened to the howling of a coyote. I looked up at the stars. Several minutes went by before the numbers tumbled back into my mind.

As I turned the knob, I felt a pang of anxiety. What if Danny had been here before me? With the safe opened, I grasped desperately at the empty space inside, only to have my heart flood with relief. Kip's money was still there at the bottom.

Damn, I thought. I don't need this kind of excitement in my life.

I made a mental note to call Danny first thing in the morning. I needed to know if Kip had told him about the safe. Either way, it was probably best if I moved it. I didn't need Danny messing up my plans. I took what cash I needed right then, covered things up and walked back to the truck.

"Well, how'd it go, partner?"

"Let's go get a steak."

"Damned if that don't sound good."

426

After the meal, I had him take me to a Travelodge on the edge of town. It wasn't much, but it was safe and clean. I was inclined to catch up on my sleep, but Jake talked me into hitting a strip joint and I felt I owed it to him. Besides, there was something sacred about an old man still having a hard-on.

We went down to the south side and watched a parade of women divulge everything but their innermost secrets. By midnight, I'd had enough.

"Come on old timer, I can't take any more."

I got a hand on his shirt-sleeve and dragged him out the door.

"That's the spirit, partner. Now that ya got yerself an appetite, we can get ya properly fed."

"I just need some sleep," I said out in the truck.

Jake headed down 22nd Avenue with prostitutes working both sides of the street, one of them so young and fair and lovely, I felt all the sorrows of the world in her eyes as we passed by. What in god's name had brought that poor young thing to this destiny?

"I see ya staring there, partner," Jake said. "Now what d'ya say we sidle up to a couple of these prissies? Put a smile on that long face a yers."

"Just keep moving, old timer. Just keep moving."

"Ya don't know what yer missin'."

I waved Jake forward without another word.

No, I knew what I was missing, all right, but I also knew a wild impulse lived within me, an impulse that Jake would never understand, an unspoken urge to rescue that poor young woman, and every poor young woman in the world like her, to wipe away all the pain and sorrow and loneliness on the face of this earth, to right all the wrongs and leave behind a decent and noble and happy place, but I did not have that power. I could only fix my little part of it and was relieved when Jake dropped me off at the motel.

"Thanks again, old timer. Maybe we'll meet again."

"Ya know where to find me, youngster. Bring a steak and yer welcome anytime."

"Thanks again."

I watched him drive off, went into my room, took a long shower and crawled into bed, knowing enough about what I was preparing to do that I didn't care to think about it any longer, at least not for one night. Wanting to put the other things out of my mind too, I

427

turned on the late show, the strangeness of the modern world descending over me in the flickering light. It sure seemed like a piece of crap world we had created, but it was a miraculous place no less. Nothing could totally fuck up our dear Mother Earth, not even mankind. As long as we admitted it was a piece of crap thing we had made for ourselves, and tried to do better, that was all that mattered.

I enjoyed the feeling behind my thoughts. It felt strong and unwavering and I wished that I could explain it to someone else, but I knew I couldn't do that either. The truth was certain, but it was also ephemeral, and if you tried to turn it into a dissertation, it simply disappeared. Only if you and another person had been through similar things could you look at each other in the eye and understand.

Somewhere in the night I got up, took a leak and turned off the television. It was mid-morning before I arose. I got on my knees first thing and said a little prayer. I wasn't sure why. It just seemed like an act of humility was in order. Afterwards, I took a shower and went out for some bacon and eggs.

I learned from looking at the morning paper that it was Monday. I had been on a journey for twelve days. The many episodes of it turned over in my mind as I ate alone.

With all the barbershops closed on Monday, I put getting myself a haircut on the back burner and called a taxi. After a quick trip across town to a western-wear shop, I caught another taxi and had him drop me at the hall of records. After a bit of research, I took the copy of a birth certificate and went down to get a new license.

Next, I hit a used car lot and quickly settled on a white '65 Nova. It was a V-8 two-door with red interior and air conditioning. I drove it away, tags and all, for $800 cash.

Back on Speedway, I headed for the south side of town, looking for a pawnshop. When I saw the word CAMERAS painted in bold letters on a front window, I parked and went in to have a look. After a number of pointed questions, I walked away with a Nikon F-2 and a Fixed 135 telephoto lens. I didn't know cameras and had to take the owner's word for it. You could make out the smile on a man's face from a few hundred yards, and a dollar bill in his hand, to boot.

I knew someone who wouldn't be smiling much when I got through with him. But he'd be ever so helpful just the same.

Lastly, I called Danny and learned that he already knew of my escape. I explained my intentions without getting into a lot of detail.

"You need to keep your mouth shut," I told him before hanging up. He said he would and I figured I could trust him. By way of subtle questioning, I became convinced that Danny was not yet aware of the safe.

I killed a few hours at the movies watching Easy Rider. Goddamned hippies. They couldn't do anything right. I ate well, played some pool down at Danny's Hideaway and gathered my strength.

The following morning, I went to the barbershop first thing and had them clip my long hair nice and short. With the cowboy hat and dark shades on, I doubted my own mother would have recognized me. But it was a haircut any law enforcement official would appreciate and Sheriff Prescott was going to have a chance to do that soon enough.

45

I parked half a block down from the police station and waited for the sheriff to poke his head out the front door. It was about lunchtime when he did and I got right on his tail.

I followed him for two days, from the station to the courthouse to a number of questionable destinations, a cathouse and a few redneck bars among them. I slept in the front seat and burned a lot of film, but had yet to see what I needed. Enough to make him uncomfortable, but my plans required a great deal more than that.

In the restless hours of waiting, I played out the impending encounter with Caroline in my head: everything from blissful reunion to a door being slammed in my face. More than once I thought to find a phonebooth and drop a dime, but it had to wait. I wanted to arrive in LA without a single distraction. Anyway, I had to wait until Sheriff Prescott provided me with the evidence I needed, something that would make him more than willing to lend me a hand, no matter the request.

It came on the third day and drew me into a danger I had not expected. About four in the afternoon, he left the station, but instead of going home, or to one of his many disreputable destinations, he pulled onto Highway 19, headed south. I followed him into Nogales and cursed as he crossed the border. Not the least bit happy with where this was headed, but seeing no way around it, I kept on his tail.

The sheriff parked at a police station on the other side of the border and disappeared inside. Five minutes later, he reappeared, accompanied by his Mexican counterpart. They both squeezed into the back seat of a black Ford Galaxy with Sonora plates. The driver headed west with little regard for the speed limits. Our journey led us through the harsh, industrial side of town. The Galaxy came to the outskirts of the city and kept on going.

As we wound out through desolate desert country, I held back far enough to be inconspicuous. They eventually pulled off the highway, slipped under a ranch sign and headed down a long, private dirt road, leaving a cloud of dust in their wake. I caught a glimpse of a sprawling, one-story house going by.

A short distance past the ranch sign, I parked with the front end of the Nova pointed out towards the road, grabbed the camera and telescopic lens and scrambled up to the top of an adjacent knoll. It was a bit out of range, maybe a hundred yards more than I wanted, but close enough to give me a decent portrait.

I got down low to the ground and peered through the lens. The two sheriffs were standing at the edge of an airstrip. A briefcase had been placed on the hood of the Galaxy. There were several men with automatic weapons milling around nearby.

Close to sunset, I heard the sound of an approaching plane and ducked out of sight as a twin Cessna swooped into view from the hills directly behind me. A few minutes later, the plane had taxied to a stop. One of the gunmen opened the cargo door. The two sheriffs went over to inspect the contents. A kilo was pulled out and placed on the hood next to the briefcase. I started burning film.

Satisfied with the quality of the goods, Charlie opened his briefcase. The Mexican sheriff came around in front of him. I kept the shutter moving with that greasy-haired son of a bitch moving in and out of my subject. The deal done, one of the gunmen gathered up the briefcase and took it into the house, but it had been open long enough for me to get off a dozen clicks with Sheriff Prescott standing there, a toothpick in his fat jowls. I could only hope that I had the money, the kilo and the sheriff in the same frame.

I watched the two sheriffs shake hands while a gunman closed the cargo door. The pilot taxied up the runway, for what I assumed would be a quick jaunt into the States.

I had the camera in hand, watching the takeoff when one of the gunmen began shouting to the men around him and pointing up at the knoll. With everyone staring my way now, what had been a lone gunman easing towards me turned into a full on stampede with live rounds going off.

I scrambled wildly back down to the Nova, the truth having hit me. The man must have seen the setting sun reflected in the lens of my camera.

I had the pedal to the metal by the time the gunmen made the crest of the knoll. A burst of automatic fire rang out and shredded the saguaros to my right. More shots clipped off the back of the Nova as I made a curve in the highway and got out of sight.

I had a head start but that was all. If they caught up with me before I made the border, they would put a bullet in my head and nonchalantly expose the film. If I expected to live much longer, I needed to get back to the States and have it developed. With that done, I could expect to have a very cooperative sheriff. Until then, my life wasn't worth a plug nickel.

Barreling through the backside of town, I found myself entangled in a maze of loops and one-way streets that only a Mexican engineer could love. I knew I was only a few blocks from the border but had somehow gotten turned around in the wrong direction. At the next intersection, I prepared to hang a U-turn with a cop holding up traffic for a mother and her string of five children. They were crossing at a tortoise pace with the children going every which way. I had one eye on the rearview mirror while cursing my luck and every damned Mexican street planner while I was at it.

When the family was safely out of harm's way, I whipped the U-turn. The cop was cursing me and every damned gringo who had ever broken a Mexican law. I kept going and hoped we could leave it at that.

A few minutes later, I was in line at the border and inching my way up to the customs booth. Dusk was a lousy time to be crossing. I worked on the length of my fingernails while watching the traffic behind me.

I was going over a list of things I would never do again when I saw the black Galaxy barreling up on the inside lane. Someone was gesturing out the passenger side window and the driver was honking at everything in his path.

As I neared the customs officer, I put on a face; the one that said I lived at home with Mom, the one that said I was the model of sacrifice and good living.

The van in front of me received a small, yellow piece of paper on the windshield and a wave to the inspection zone. I was thinking this man might not be in the best of moods as I pulled up to his booth.

"Good evening. What's your nationality?"

"American."

"And are you bringing anything back from Mexico today?"

"No sir." He eyed the camera equipment sitting innocently next to me on the front seat.

"How long have you been in Mexico?"

"For the afternoon, sir."

"And what was the nature of your business?"

"Have a few beers. Practice my photography mostly."

I glanced in the mirror and saw the Galaxy going the wrong way in a southbound lane. The Mexican agents had waved them through. I turned my attention back to the customs agent and smiled.

"That's interesting," he said. "I happen to enjoy the hobby myself. Are you getting any good at it?"

"I'd like to think I am. Wouldn't mind making a living at it someday."

"Wouldn't that be nice. I suppose we all have a bit of the artist locked up inside of us," he added with a chuckle.

"I'm guessing so," I said with a chuckle back.

I kept smiling, having no grounds to quarrel with the man or his conversation, not when you looked at the big picture, but with that Galaxy bearing down on me, he was picking a hell of a time to have this chat. When he saw that I was out of fresh insights, he had a cursory look at the back seat and waved me on.

"Good luck to you."

"Same to you," I said and pulled away.

By that time, the Galaxy had come to a stop a hundred feet behind me. The gunmen got out and dashed into the border office with the Mexican sheriff. Charlie joined them, but not before taking a moment to spit in my direction.

I kept to the speed limit, figuring I had nothing to worry about for another half an hour or so. I knew the sheriff didn't stand a chance of getting help from the American border patrol. He'd be too busy putting his foot in his mouth. His best shot was to get a few of his own men to head me off at the pass. He could do that without much trouble.

Anticipating his move, I took Highway 82 east at the outskirts of Nogales, turned north onto the first ranch road, hit the lights and leaned forward into the darkness. Fifteen minutes later, figuring I was mostly out of danger, I turned on the radio. There were only two FM stations in Tucson and I wasn't getting either of them so I flipped over to AM. When I got a country station tuned in, I cranked up the volume and tapped my boots to a good old boy redneck, crooning about starting a fight in a bar.

It took three hours but I made it back to town without a hitch, parked the Nova in an all-night supermarket, walked six blocks to a gas station and called a cab. They could have the car if it came to that, as long as I had the film. I had the taxi drop me at a safe distance from the motel, walked back in the dark and got myself a good night's sleep.

In the morning, I took a cab to the nearest one-hour photo and ordered double prints. I had some breakfast while waiting. I sure hoped Sheriff Prescott was as influential as I imagined him to be. I wanted to get this part of my duties over with and be on my way to California. Still, I couldn't help but relish the next scene, assuming the photos turned out as planned.

With breakfast under my belt, I headed out the door and down the sidewalk in the listless desert heat. The photos were just coming out as I walked in. I paid for them, parked myself under an awning a few doors down and opened the packet. Going through them slowly, the smile on my face only grew larger with each one. There was the sheriff, right down to his toothpick.

I called another taxi, went to the bus depot and placed the negatives along with the extra prints in a locker. Then I mailed the key to the motel and had the cab driver take me over to the police station.

When I asked for the sheriff, the desk sergeant informed me that he was expected back at eleven. I looked at the clock. It was a quarter past ten. I made myself at home on a bench against the wall and watched what policemen did for a living. Mostly they walked from room to room and shuffled papers. That and they made a lot of other people unhappy.

The sheriff traipsed in a few minutes after eleven and checked his messages. The desk sergeant thumbed his nose in my direction.

The sheriff turned my way with a quizzical look on his face. The desk sergeant shrugged when the sheriff looked back.

"What can I do for you, son?" the sheriff called out.

I went over to give him a better look. It took him a minute, but the truth finally got through all that pomade around his brain.

"Well, I'll be damned. Hey Clyde! Look what we got here."

Clyde came out of an adjoining office. It didn't take him nearly as long as the sheriff. Two seconds and he had my arm pinned behind my back, ready to slap the cuffs on me. The sheriff interrupted him.

"Hang on there, Clyde. He ain't going nowhere."

Clyde moved away, though I could still feel him breathing down my neck.

"Seeing as he was generous enough to save me the trouble of finding his ass," the sheriff continued, "I guess we can treat him as a guest. So long as he behaves hisself, of course."

The sheriff looked back at me with a big grin.

"Son, you got to be one dumb son of a bitch comin' around here like this. That or you got a hard-on for four walls. 'Cuz you're going to be seein' a lot of 'em from here on out."

"Maybe. But I was hoping we could have a little chat first."

"About what?"

"I've got a message for you from Portillo Juarez."

The sheriff tried to disguise his reaction, but it wasn't any use, not after what I had seen on the walls of the foyer in Penal del Estado, Hermosillo, and especially not after what I had witnessed the previous evening.

"What the hell are you talkin' about?"

When I reached for my back pocket to retrieve the photos, Clyde's hand quickly intercepted me. I kept smiling. The sheriff chewed on things for a moment before nodding at Clyde. He let go of my wrist and I handed the packet of photos to the sheriff. He inspected the first one and looked back at me. We stood there staring at each other.

"Suppose we ought to talk this over in private, Sheriff?"

He waved Clyde away, motioned me into his office and closed the door behind us. Once at his desk, the sheriff sorted through each photo, slowly at first but picking up speed as he went. He dropped the final photo on his desk with disgust. I was smiling when he looked up at me.

"All right, what do you want?"

"You'll forgive me if I savor this for a moment, sheriff, but it does seem like the tables have been turned."

I imagined him ransacking his brain, trying to find some kind of loophole; enough so that it had his face twisted into a knot. When the heat and the effort had him good and hard-boiled, I tapped once on his shell.

"Amazin' how some folks comes ta havin' so much trouble all of a sudden."

It wasn't nice of me, but seeing as I meant the man no harm, I considered it a minor transgression.

"All right, spill it."

When it came to the moment, and I saw the sheriff actually break, I almost felt sorry for him. Besides, I once owed the man for my freedom.

"You know I could be going up for a long time," I said.

"I've been informed as much."

"Well, if I do, you're going with me."

There was a pause, during which time I imagined him regretting his previous decision to let me go.

"I got no reason to mess with you."

"As long as we understand each other."

He fiddled involuntarily with the photos for a moment and pushed them across the desk at me.

"You didn't come all this way to tell me that."

I looked at the photos and back at him.

"Have you heard from Kip lately?"

"No. And his mother's been all over my ass since he disappeared."

"Well, don't expect a turn for the better."

"You know where he is?" I nodded. "Well?"

"He's in a Mexican prison."

"God Almighty."

He shook his head in disbelief.

"It may or may not be that bad."

"Well, where is he?"

"Hermosillo."

He chewed on this for a moment while staring at me.

"And you want me to try and get him out."

"It would seem you have connections in that neck of the woods."

"Hell, I don't understand those people any better than you do."

"I'm not asking you to understand them, Sheriff. I'm asking you to bribe them."

"With what?"

"You get them to name a price and I'll get you the cash."

He drummed his fingers.

"I'll see what I can do."

I stared at him with a measure of calm. It was the contrast of two intersecting destinies. Mine seemed to be heading in the right direction. The sheriff appeared to be on his way to some kind of hell.

"Is that all?" he said.

"For now. I'm going to California on some personal business. I'll call you tomorrow. I want this over with quickly. Then I'm going to disappear."

I stood up to leave.

"If you want, you can keep those for your personal photo album."

"Go ta hell."

"I expected you'd feel that way, but just so we understand each other, I have the negatives. Or, shall I say, they're in safe hands. If anything untoward should happen to me, they'll find their way to the proper authorities."

"You ain't got nothin' to worry about with me."

I went over to the door and held onto the knob.

"By the way, sheriff. Would you mind taking the tail off my Nova? I'd like to drive it out of town."

 He got up and followed me out the door.

"Take it easy, Clyde," I said, tipping my hat. "Be seeing you around."

Clyde stared at me like a hungry dog with an empty bowl. His eyes pleaded with the sheriff but Charlie made a wave with his hand.

"Let him go."

"But sheriff..."

"I said let him go!"

46

Pushing open the precinct door, I was slapped in the face by a blast of hot desert air. The sheriff's office door slammed shut behind me. I lowered my shades and headed down the precinct steps. I felt a number of things right then, but responsibility for Charlie's karma wasn't one of them. I had my own cosmic justice to face and didn't anticipate the sheriff rushing forward to rescue me.

I caught a taxi to the Nova, drove from the market to the motel, grabbed my few belongings, told the manager to hold my mail and headed west with a tank full of 103 octane.

There wasn't much but sand and cactus to entertain me for five hundred miles, but I didn't much care or notice. The brief, reckless journey I knew as my life, the need to make sense of all the cheap thrills, heartaches and fading ideals, all of it was distilled down to this one passionate moment. I polished over and over what I intended to say and hardly noticed the small towns and telephone poles clicking by me. I kept my eyes on the rearview mirror, made Blythe in less than three hours, refilled the tank, relieved myself and got right back to hugging the center-divider.

The sun was setting in a blaze of orange smog over the Hollywood hills when I came to a stop at the end of the freeway off ramp. I had arrived in Burbank, but it could have been most any other American town. There were the same gas stations, the same power lines, the same heartless clutter.

I found a phone booth and made the call.

"Hello," a voice said, a warm but circumspect voice that I assumed belonged to Caroline's mother.

"May I speak to Caroline, please?"

"She's not here right now. May I ask who's calling?"

"This is Clay Matthews."

There was silence.

"I'm sorry but I don't know when to expect her."

"Mrs. Leroux, I came to clear the air with Caroline but I'd like a chance to talk with you too. May I come over?"

"Well, I'm not sure..."

"Mrs. Leroux, please. I just drove five hundred miles."

There was another long pause.

"Well, I suppose. Do you have the address?"

"Yes, it's right here in the phone book."

She asked where I was, gave me directions and I drove straight over. The home was in an old neighborhood lined with maple trees. It was the sort of place that defied time and a changing world.

I left my Stetson on the seat and went up to knock on the door. I had noticed a rustle of curtains as I climbed onto the porch. The door opened a few moments later.

It was Caroline in thirty years. The eyes were a trifle more enigmatic, the nose a bit more pronounced. I would have smiled, except Mrs. Leroux didn't appear to welcome it. I offered her my hand instead.

"Hi. Clay Matthews. It's nice to meet you."

"Well, yes, please, come in."

She had taken my hand and courteously circumvented the rest.

I went in and closed the door behind myself. I was invited into the living room and did everything possible to minimize the clomping of my boots along the way.

At Mrs. Leroux's direction, I sat down on an old Provincial sofa. She sat opposite me in a wing-back chair. A grandfather clock kept time behind her. Her slacks were straightened while she studied my face. I stared back.

"You act as if you've seen me somewhere before," I said.

"Oh, forgive me, but you don't look anything like what Caroline had described."

"Changing identities has been one of my predicaments, Mrs. Leroux."

"Well, I must admit, an aura of mystery surrounds you. And I can see how that would be alluring to a young woman like my daughter. But I remain concerned for her safety first and foremost. You see, she's all I have."

"I understand. I have felt the same way."

She nodded with her brown eyes studying me. There were noises from around the neighborhood and the grandfather clock keeping time. The moments passed in the gathering twilight. Seeing that Mrs. Leroux had no intention either to encourage or stop me, I went on.

"As a wanted man, I have had to do a lot of things that I would not have done otherwise. Changing identities is one of them. I was just trying to protect myself. I never gave much thought to how that might have affected Caroline. Then I realized it had driven a wedge between us and…well…here I am. Hoping to get everything out in the open, once and for all."

Mrs. Leroux nodded ever so slightly at hearing my admission.

"There is nothing quite so edifying as the truth. Is there, Clay?"

I nodded, not liking the way she had said it, and even less the prospect of laying out my life in front of someone who was so damned proper, but in the end I went forward and told everything as straight as I could, prudently sidestepping the part about being in a Mexican prison, fully aware that I had created another deception in the process.

When I was through, I shrugged and waited. The slow, methodical rhythm of the clock kept marking time in the growing shadows.

"Is that it?" Mrs. Leroux said.

"Pretty much."

In the spontaneity of the moment, both of us laughed but Mrs. Leroux's eyes quickly resumed their steely gaze.

"I don't mean to judge you unfairly, Clay, but you represent a real threat to my daughter's safety, and for that reason alone, I'm not very fond of seeing you here."

Having been scorned for my honesty, anger burned in my heart. I had been rejected in this manner all of my life. Mrs. Leroux played with the loose hairs in her bun.

"You realize," she went on. "If all you wanted was to tell the truth, you could have called."

"Okay, I admit it. I want Caroline back."

"As a fugitive," she said.

"I tend to forget that's how the world sees me, because that's not the way I see myself."

"We are a country of laws, Clay and you have broken them. There is nothing very confusing about that."

She put her hands together and placed them against her lips. Her eyebrows went up. I took a deep breath and tried to reason with her.

"Look around you, Mrs. Leroux. Two generations are at war, and mostly over a war that never needed to be fought. It has complicated the lives of a good many people, not just mine."

"Is that your defense?"

"I'm merely putting things into some kind of historical perspective. If I had been born in the fifties, for instance, I might well have gone to college and worked for an insurance company. Gotten married, bought a house and had a couple of kids."

I waved my hands at the world around me.

"But that's not how it worked out for me."

"So you refuse to turn yourself in and face this thing?"

"As I told your daughter, I don't think so, not willingly, not now, especially not in this political environment. The happiness I've had with your daughter? The world will have to take it from me."

Her eyebrows went up again on that note.

"You certainly seem determined," she said. "Though living on the run does not seem like a very good life. And certainly not one that I would want for my daughter."

"I understand. I have come to accept the hopelessness of my situation, and perhaps it is impossible for us to be together now. I do put her safety above my own. But nothing will change the fact that I love her."

Seeing a glimmer of kindness in Mrs. Leroux's eyes, I was encouraged to go on.

"Consider. Because of a bombing, in which no one was hurt and in which I was not even involved, I have been ostracized from everything I love, Caroline included. Yet, had I been willing to go out and kill and create mayhem in the name of my country, that would have been all right."

She considered this.

"I don't know," she said. "Is that true? No one was hurt?"

"Not to my knowledge."

441

"Well, assuming all that, there still remains the question of your military status."

"True, but any idiot can start a war and that one will go on quite nicely without me."

Her hands entwined, Mrs. Leroux tapped ever so slightly at her lips with her two index fingers.

"I can see you are a very idealistic young man," she said.

"Is that a crime too?"

That won me a cautious smile. The dust drifted between us in the last golden light of day. The moments passed. The maple leaves rustled outside. In the silence, a question I had wanted to ask came back to me.

"Do you think Caroline still loves me?"

"I know she does. Despite my protestations."

I smiled. Mrs. Leroux didn't.

"I love her a lot, Mrs. Leroux."

"I believe you do."

"Then where do we go from here?"

Her eyes were averted for a moment before she spoke.

"You know how I feel. But, ultimately, that is for the two of you to decide. I won't try to interfere."

"I wouldn't blame you if you did," I said.

"There's no point. I learned long ago, there's no controlling her. In many ways, she's much more like her father. Still, she was taught to face her problems and never to run."

I recalled Caroline's words in Mazatlán and her abandonment of me and the same anger flooded into my heart.

"Perhaps we should stop," I said. "While we're ahead."

"Yes, I'm almost starting to like you."

I smiled, despite myself, and stood up.

"I'm sorry. I've taken enough of your time."

Mrs. Leroux stood up with me.

"Yes, no doubt you've tired of talking to this old lady by now."

She self-consciously played with her bun.

"Age has only refined your beauty," I said.

"Hmm. Well, I'm beginning to see why Caroline fell for you."

We stared through the differences that come with age and gender.

"I promise I'll put your daughter's safety first."

"Under the circumstances, I don't see how. But I believe you'll try."

"Okay, well, thanks for hearing me out."

"I hope it was good for your soul."

"It was all right."

She smiled somewhat.

"Know where I can find a hotel?"

Mrs. Leroux guided me out to the front porch by my arm and pointed.

"Go down two blocks, turn right and then left at the first signal. There are a number of places along that boulevard."

"Thanks. I'm sure I can find my way."

"I'll tell Caroline you're here. Just call when you're settled and let us know where you are."

"Thanks. I'll call right away." I started to leave and turned back. "By the way, when do you expect her?"

"Not much before eight," she said.

I nodded and walked towards the car. When I got behind the wheel and looked back, Mrs. Leroux was nowhere in sight.

I followed her directions out to the main boulevard and drove along it until I found something that seemed fitting for the occasion. It wasn't five-star, but close. They had a room on the twelfth floor. I gave my clothes to the bellboy and asked if he could have them ready in one hour. He could. He took my leather jacket and said he'd see what he could do with that, as well.

I called Mrs. Leroux, gave her the room number then crawled into bed, exhausted. There were a million thoughts racing through my mind but I fell asleep a short time later.

The room was dark when the phone awakened me. I was filled with the usual uncertainties. Who was I? Where and why?

Remembering Caroline, I reached for the phone.

"Hello," I said.

"Clay?"

"Yes, sweetheart."

"Hi."

"I have missed you so."

There was a pause.

"I've missed you too. You turkey."

I laughed.

"I suppose your mother has explained?"

"Yes. You're terribly stubborn."

"I am truly sorry about it all."

"I was making love to a stranger," she said.

"No, that's not true."

"Well, it seems that way."

"I just want you to believe in me again."

There was another pause.

"I don't know if that's possible. Not in the way it was before."

I took the blow and let it go. The words hurt, but I did not believe they were necessarily true.

"Will you come to me?" I asked her.

"I still feel you should face this thing."

"I promise to keep an open mind."

There was silence from her end.

"Won't you please come to me now?"

"Okay. Give me a few minutes to change."

"I'm waiting."

"I'll be there soon."

I took a quick shower and waited impatiently for the bellhop to knock. When he did, I took my clothes and handed him twenty dollars for his troubles. I got dressed and spent the next half hour pacing the room.

Finally, I heard a knock and opened the door. It was Caroline, wearing a red halter top, tight white jeans that left her belly-button exposed and high-heel sandals. Her dark hair tumbled down over her exposed shoulders. The woman clearly knew how to disarm me.

I gathered her up in my arms and kissed her passionately, all around her face and lips and then down her tan shoulders and back up her neck again and to her lips. I had begun to retrace my path down her shoulders when she laughed and held me back.

"Maybe we should go inside?"

"I won't let you leave for a long, long time."

She grew serious.

"You scare me, Clay."

"Why?"

"Because you've changed again. I don't think I'll ever catch up."

I saw that she was far away and shook her gently.

"What?" I said.

"I don't know. What have you been doing?" she said.

"I'll have to explain."

"You haven't been in trouble again, have you?" I nodded. "Oh, Clay. What am I going to do with you?"

I put my hands around her face and kissed her once.

"Love me, I hope." I placed my hands on the warm skin along the small of her back and tried to kiss her passionately a second time, but she pulled away.

"Let's go eat," she said.

Disheartened by the seeming distance between us, I went to grab my coat. In the elevator, we held hands and looked at each other in silence, neither one of us knowing quite what to say.

I drove with Caroline directing me this way and that. On a hot summer night, the boulevards were filled with high school kids out for a cruise.

We landed at a darkened bistro and ordered steak and lobster. Over a bottle of Merlot and our meal, I explained what had happened since we last saw each other. I told her about my serendipitous involvement with the Weather Underground and the ensuing indictment. Of my life story, I left out only the part about Faith. There was no need to trouble Caroline with that, any more than I wanted to hear all the intimate details of her involvement with Tom. Caroline shook her head many times, especially when I explained my escape and final journey. Once the plates had been cleared, I poured our glasses full.

"So? Do you believe me?"

"I guess. I don't know who could make up a story like that…But who are you really, if you're not Clay Matthews?"

"I was born Clay Gulland. Clay Matthews died in a car accident at five years old. I found his birth certificate while on a trip up to San Francisco. It wasn't easy. Someone of the same age and same first name? Who had died before receiving a social security card and driver's license? But that way, there's no record of him and everyone new and old would still be calling me by the same first name."

She stared.

"Do I get any points for ingenuity?"

She smiled.

"A few."

I reached out for her hands.

"Look, I just wanted to get that part out of the way because there's a lot more important stuff to deal with here."

"Oh no."

"No no. This is personal. About everything that went down between in the past. You know, like looking down at you?"

"Yeah. I was always trying to be what you wanted me to be...And I didn't understand how lousy that felt until you left."

"I know. And when we met on the train, I knew everything was different but I just couldn't figure out how to deal with the change."

"But a man should know if he really loves a woman, Clay."

I stared.

"See, you don't."

I sighed.

"That's not true. It's just, there's all this stuff inside of me that I don't understand. I've always been restless, wanting to be somewhere other than where I am. I'd be restless with or without you."

Caroline did not seem at all satisfied with my answer and we were back to staring at each other.

"Look," I said. "When I was alone in San Blas, I saw that it wasn't enough to think something. You had to say it out loud, so all this time, from there to the prison to crawling through the desert and mountains, I just wanted to get back here and clear the air. To get to someplace fresh and new and start again as equals. I really did love and respect you."

Caroline squeezed my hands.

"I still want you to go face this thing."

I started to pull away but she held onto me.

"It's the only way I can be with you, Clay."

"I don't know. Anyway, there's something else I must do first."

"Not more trouble."

"I don't know. I don't know think so. Not for me."

Now Caroline tried to pull her hands away.

"Stop. I'm just trying to get Kip's uncle to help me with getting Kip out of prison."

I explained about Charlie and what I was hoping he could do.

"And you really think bribery will work?"

"With enough money in the right hands, yes."

"And then?"

I emptied the bottle into our glasses.

"Once Kip is free, it will be time for me to disappear. I'd really really love for you to come along, but it's okay if you don't. I think I can be at peace now, knowing we've had these moments together. I know you love me, and you know I love you."

I shrugged.

"I can't change the rest of it, Caroline."

As we stared, tears came into her eyes. I held onto her hands and watched them fall down her cheeks, one by one. When the waiter came to clear the plates, Caroline pulled away and wiped her face. There was laughter around us and other background noises. An elderly couple got up from the next table and left arm in arm. I looked back at Caroline. The candlelight flickered upon her beauty.

"Do you remember when you wanted to go with me? 'Anywhere', you said."

She nodded.

"So why can't it be that way again?"

She shook her head slowly.

"I don't know, Clay. I don't know."

"We believed in a dream once. We can believe in it again."

"Maybe, but I've realized some things since we've been apart. I've gotten honest with myself and accepted that running from things is not my nature."

"I know, I know. You've already said as much."

"No. I'm talking about me now, not what someone else has taught me. Maybe it's just part of being a woman, but I'm not comfortable with insecurity."

When I looked away, she pulled on my hands.

"Clay, we're here in this moment. Let's quit trying to be somewhere else."

"Fine."

I stood up and threw some cash on the table. Caroline grabbed her wrap and followed me out to the sidewalk. The evening was still warm and bustling with traffic. Caroline put her arm through mine. I stared in the opposite direction

"You know, Clay, I've decided that people have to start out as equals. Otherwise they never will be."

"Yeah? Well maybe they go backwards that way."

We both stared defiantly and then started to laugh.

"Okay," she said and put her head on my shoulder. "I know one place where we never fight."

"That's true enough."

Caroline held onto my arm as we walked back to the car.

At the hotel, we made love that was both raw and sincere. Afterwards, we lay there with only the sheet over our bodies. I looked at her lumps and mine all entangled. Everything was entangled and not any clearer to me than when I had started. At least I felt cleaner inside. I was thankful for that.

We fell asleep and awakened about three in the morning. I called for room service and the bellhop brought up two beers and a couple of sandwiches. We watched a bad horror movie and had fun with our observations. In the silences, I sensed that Caroline understood my newfound respect for her and felt grateful for that too.

Dawn brightened the room about five-thirty. I had forgotten to close the curtains and got up to do so. Caroline was awake when I came back.

"Clay, let's go to Mass."

"You're kidding, right?"

"No, I feel the need."

"My god. It sounds so heavy."

"Please?"

"All right."

I recalled the many lessons I had learned and decided it was best to acquiesce.

We slept for two more hours and got up to shower. Dressed, we drove to a cathedral across town, leaving behind a bright, sunny morning for the dimly lit sanctum. Caroline knew the ritual. I perused the stained-glass windows and allowed my mind to drift. The many voices mixed together and rose triumphantly up to the vaulted ceiling. I presumed from there it went to heaven, where your soul was saved, and afterwards you went to have breakfast. If it worked, it could save a guy like me a whole lot of trouble.

"Well, I'm all ready for some more sinnin'," I said as we walked to the car.

"You turkey," Caroline said and slapped me on the shoulder.

Back at the hotel, we did as I had suggested. Later in the day, we drove down to Malibu for some Italian food. We walked the beach at sunset and drove back to the hotel in the dark. A freshly made bed awaited us.

"I should probably go home tonight," Caroline said.

"Why?"

"Because, I have to be at school in the morning."

"Please don't leave me. Call your mother and I'll have room service ring us in the morning."

"All right."

I got up to relieve myself while she called her mother.

"Everything fine?"

"Yes."

I called the desk and crawled in bed with her. I felt desperate suddenly. There was always the world trying to come between two people's lives. I kissed her, wishing the world would go away.

"What are you going to do now, Clay?"

"That depends a great deal on what happens with Kip's uncle."

"I have the feeling you're not telling me something," she said.

"I love you."

"That's not what I meant."

She eyed me over her shoulder again.

"Clay? Why don't you at least have a lawyer look into it?"

"That's an idea."

"You have the money," she reminded me.

"Yes, I suppose I do."

"Clay, it could be over before you know it. Then we really could go away to someplace like Europe for a long time." She sounded hopeful. "Wouldn't that be better?"

"No."

"Oh, you turkey." She rolled over and took the covers with her. I pulled both her and the covers back in one motion.

"Look, young lady, I was in jail not all that long ago and there wasn't anything fun about it. I have no guarantees you'd be waiting for me when I got out. So keep that in mind while you get all spry about turning me in."

She stared at me for a moment.

"Yes sir," she said.

"If my situation was hopeless, I guess there wouldn't be much choice. But it would be pretty hard to face four walls thinking you and I could be bumming around the Mediterranean together."

449

I looked into her eyes and knew I had touched something.

"I promise you this. I'll hire a lawyer and have him look into things. When I'm through with this other business. Okay?"

She nodded and accepted my kiss. I pulled her back under my arm and we stared at the ceiling.

"What are you going to do tomorrow?" she said.

"I don't know. Maybe I'll drive down to San Diego and see if I can find Stan."

"Who's that?"

"A guy I met in Hawaii. He was in the war."

"Why would you go to see him?"

"Just To say hello. And for something to do." She turned around and made me look into her eyes. She stared for a moment and looked away.

When she fell asleep, I arose and sat at the picture window. An endless stream of car lights passed along the freeway. It was Sunday night and people were coming back from their weekend excursions, back to their homes, to their lives and a job in the morning. I felt a powerful longing for such routine, and revulsion for it all at once. I hated this life of the maverick but I wasn't sure I could ever change myself.

I turned and watched Caroline sleeping, wishing there weren't things like duty and honor. The idea of being in a village far away with her made me feel content, away from all the madness of this world, but there were some things a man needed to do.

In the morning, the desk called. I answered the phone and placed it back in the cradle. Caroline crawled up on top of me and kissed me. I tried to resist but she kissed me again and again.

"I want to please you," I said.

"We don't have time."

"But I want to."

"I just want to do this now." I let go and smelled her and watched her dark hair toss about her soft shoulders. When we were through, she lay at my side. I did not want her to leave.

"I feel powerful when I please you," she said.

"I know. I feel the same way."

She kissed me and sprung to her feet.

"I have to go."

I watched her get dressed, feeling more lost with every article of clothing that was put back in its place. When she was done, she was enchanting, and I felt helpless.

"Maybe you are too powerful."

She came over and kissed me from my belly up to my lips.

"I'm all yours, big boy."

"Aw, you make me feel so impotentate."

She stared at me with a sad but tender look in her eyes, the memory of her little joke on the train ride to Mazatlán lingering between us, those memories and all the others we had shared like the unseen forces within atoms that kept life from spinning apart.

"Will I be seeing you again, Clay?

"Oh stop."

"Seriously. Are your really going down to San Diego?"

She stood darkly against the bright light from the window so that I could not see her eyes or discern her mood, except by her voice emanating from the light. She sounded sad.

"Yes," I said. "I think so."

"And are you coming back tonight?"

"I don't know."

"Please let me know."

"All right. I'll try to be back tonight."

I sat up and kissed her.

"I worry about you," she said.

"I'll call tonight if I plan to stay."

"Okay. I'll be home studying."

"I'll call."

"By the way, cowboy."

"Yeah?"

"You might want to skip the next haircut."

She kissed me and retreated quickly with a smile.

It was hard watching her leave in those high-heel shoes and tight pants. The image of her haunted me all the way out to the streets. That was the way of love. It began with a photograph in the mind. Then it became a long, slow ache in your heart.

47

The waitress came by to top off my cup of coffee. While she did, I troubled her for a dollar's worth of dimes. She rummaged around inside her big apron pocket for the change and ran off with my breakfast plate. I went to call the sheriff from a phone booth back by the restroom. It was a bit past eight in the morning. I took the liberty of calling him collect.

"What's the good news, sheriff?"

"They gave him ten years."

"What!?" I looked around and cupped the phone. "What the hell are you talking about, ten years? The trial hasn't even started."

"The trial's over with."

"Bullshit! Did you try flashing around some serious money down there, like I told you?"

"I drove down there yesterday, wantin' to do it first hand, but all I got was a lot of no's and people shakin' their heads."

"Sheriff, you know anybody can be bought down in Mexico."

"I'd have thought so but there ain't nobody takin' and I can't tell you why."

"The goddamned American government, that's why."

"Yeah. I reckon you're right on that one."

"I know I am."

There was a silence.

"There's got to be something, sheriff. Try upping the ante."

"Just how much are we talking about?"

"More than anybody down there could think to ask."

"I'll try again. But I wouldn't get your hopes up."

I stood there, fuming.

"Goddamn it. They can't just slap ten years on him like that. There's a process, even in that shit forsaken country."

"Well, it's still *their* shit forsaken country, so I'm guessin' they can do whatever the hell they want."

"All right. And I suppose because of this fianza business, we can't do a damned thing now for the next five years."

"That's what my contacts down there are tellin' me."

"Son of a bitch…And what about the others?"

"That one kid Robby got ten years, too, the other kid and his gal, seven each. Guess they figured when you ran, they all must be guilty."

"All right. You hang on. I'll be back in a few days. And please don't call his parents."

"I'll keep my mouth shut that long. But sooner or later, they've got to be told."

"Just hang on. I'll check in with you again tomorrow."

I got off the phone, depressed by the news and not knowing which way to turn. After some thought, I decided to fill the gas tank and take that drive down to San Diego. A few hours on the road had to be better than listening to my head until Caroline got home from school.

I pulled onto Interstate 5 a few minutes later and right into rush hour traffic. Everyone around me looked pissed; pissed at themselves, pissed at each other, pissed to be crawling along a ten miles an hour, pissed at a society that had conned them into thinking a two car garage, a summer vacation and a three handicap golf game was worth the screwing it took to get there. What a life, every sucker in a hurry, and going nowhere fast.

Forty miles down the freeway, I left behind the miles and miles of industrial wasteland and came into an open country of rolling hills. I saw orange and persimmon groves along the road and tawny hillsides disturbed only by cattle grazing up among the wild oaks.

A short while later, I made the long, sweeping turn at Doheny with more rolling hills on my left and the sea on my right. This went on for another forty miles, down through Encinitas and Leucadia and Cardiff by the Sea and all the little beach towns you thought you might want to visit someday because they had such lovely names, and where you saw rows and rows of rickety old greenhouses along the highway, not a clutter of strip malls.

It was a little before noon when I passed Mission Beach and pulled off at the airport exit. I found a phone booth near one of the maintenance hangers and searched through the yellow pages. There were several aviation schools and I called three of them before I found Stan. He had left for the day, a woman informed me, but I might find him in a little dive down at the far end of the runway.

I found the place without much trouble. A 727 was screaming into the morning sky as I opened the door. Everyone looked up at me and went back to their business. I let the door close and started along the gray Formica counter. A cook was visible through a pass-through window, a cigarette in his mouth. I smelled hash browns and sausage cooking on the griddle.

I spotted Stan at a booth in back and went to stand over him. A dark-haired man with a square jaw sat across the table, nursing a cup of coffee. Stan looked up from the morning paper without a sign of recognition.

"Long time no see, Stan."

A look of both warmth and sadness passed over his eyes.

"Goddamn Bart, I told you the revolution was over."

Stan made room for me and shook my hand. He couldn't seem to keep his eyes off the haircut.

"What d'ya do, Matthews? Get drunk and wake up in an induction center?"

"I had a dream about that once."

"Well shit. Looks like you had more than a dream. Bart, meet Clay Matthews."

Bart shook my hand and returned to his coffee. He had the shoulders to go with his square jaw and an impassive gaze. His face looked unshaven, even though it wasn't. Beneath all of that, he seemed decent.

The waitress brought their food. I ordered a BLT and a glass of milk. Stan had gone back to his paper.

"Have you seen this, Clay?"

He was reading an article on the Pentagon papers. The report had just been released. Excerpts from it were in the dailies. I had read it over breakfast.

"They lied to us. I fought a goddamned war for nothing."

He closed the paper and threw it down in disgust.

"You're not really surprised, are you Stan?"

454

"Hell no, Clay. But allow me my moment."

"If it gives you any peace of mind, I've often felt the same way."

"I suppose you would. All that running around for nothing."

"It's gotten worse."

"Well hell, we've got all afternoon. Lay it on me."

I recounted my brief association with the revolution, being as I had never told Stan about that when we lived in Hawaii.

"No wonder those dicks were hanging around Hanauma," Stan said, interrupting me. "A regular revolutionary."

"I had nothing to do with it. Guilty by association only."

"Sure, sure, so go on."

I told him about Tucson, the money and Mexico. When I got to the part about the prison and my escape, Stan interrupted me again.

"You hear this, Bart? The man feels so bad about not going to 'Nam, he's making up his own goddamned war."

"You're nuts," I said.

"Whatever you say there, partner. Continue."

I explained about Sheriff Prescott and laid it on him.

"They sentenced Kip to ten years."

"Ten years," Stan said.

"Yeah, and nobody seems to be taking any money," I said.

He looked over at Bart and back at me.

"The Americans."

I nodded.

"Yeah, you could see it. There'd be enough money on the so called clean side to keep some greasy Mexican son of a bitch halfway respectable."

"Yeah. So anyway, I just heard the news and I'm feeling pretty down about it."

"Hell," Stan said. "Why don't we just go down and blow him out of that shit hole?"

"Sure, Stan," I said.

I looked back and forth at the two of them. A slow smile came over Bart's face.

"With what?" I said.

"A chopper. You know what a chopper is, don't you, you goddamned hippie son of a bitch?"

"Oh sure, Stan. Saw a picture once."

"Cost you some of that big time money you got stashed away, but it could be done."

"Not that I'm really interested, but are you really serious?"

Stan winked at Bart and looked back at me.

"You're talking junk to a junkie, Clay."

I tried to imagine the whole thing and shook my head.

"It's crazy. I don't even want to talk about it."

"The truth is," Bart said, "we're just a couple of mercenaries looking for a gig."

"We'd best discuss this over a beer," Stan said.

"There's nothing to discuss, but I'll be happy to buy you a pitcher or two before I head back."

"You don't know what you're getting into, Clay. You don't know what you're getting into."

"I think I do, Stan."

I threw some bills on the table and followed their directions to a seedy, waterfront tavern. It consisted of one pool table parallel to the bar and a handful of men with nothing better to do than hang around a cloud of stale smoke all day. There was a view of the harbor out a window behind the bar as consolation.

"Bart here was my main man in 'Nam," Stan told me after we had ordered the beer. "Crew chief, then gunner when the Cobra arrived."

I nodded and looked out at the harbor.

"I'm telling you, Clay, this is a piece of cake."

"You think so."

"You bet your ass."

Bart confirmed this with a nod.

"A little chicken-shit operation like that, we could have breakfast in the States and be back home having a cold one before the evening news."

"You give me a nice quiet job and the evening paper any day, Stan."

"Bullshit. I'll tell you what. Let's run through it. Then you've got a second option."

"Why don't you re-enlist, Stan."

"That's what I'm doing. Now listen up."

I shook my head and went to work on my beer.

They beat the thing around between themselves as though they were planning another sortie into Cambodia. I stared out the window, paying just enough attention to notice they had indeed drifted back to their days in 'Nam. It was quiet for a few moments. Then Stan was back in the present.

"Hell, you could take half the Americans home with you in a stripped down Huss."

I shrugged.

"A Sikorski. 58? Troop transport?"

I shrugged again.

"Never mind. Hell, it doesn't matter. I wouldn't want to be taking automatic fire in a fully loaded Huss. We'd be sitting ducks."

"Remember, I'm only trying to get Kip out," I said.

"Hell, I figured as long as we're there."

"How far did you say it was from the border?" Bart asked me.

"About 175 miles."

"One way?"

I nodded.

They looked at each other again.

"Have to be a Huey, Stan."

"Yeah. A little out of range for a Huss."

"Huey? As in 'Nam?" I said.

"Well shit, he's not totally ignorant."

"Ignorant enough to wonder who's going to borrow it. And return it to the local military reservation."

"We're talking the commercial version, there Clay. A Bell 204."

"Would that one take half the jail as well?"

He shook his head.

"Six, seven maybe, besides us."

"I take it they rent them."

"If you know how to fly it."

We canned the conversation and leaned back to allow one of the hustlers his pool shot. The waitress filled our glasses and ran off to retrieve another pitcher. Stan reviewed me.

"You wouldn't be getting interested there, Clay?"

"I may as well get an education."

"You know, they may not like the way it looks when we get back."

"We haven't taken it yet, Stan."

457

"Anyway, it's like a car, you get a few dents, you take it to the body shop."

"Or a few bullet holes," I said.

"Yeah, well, you'll probably need someone to take care of that on the American end."

"Assuming we go," I said.

He looked at Bart and winked again.

"Don't you worry, partner, I'll get some of that big time money out of him yet."

They smiled, Stan more than Bart.

Outside, the harbor water was turning deep blue in the afternoon wind. My mind was out there and on other things. Stan had been watching me and I turned to meet his gaze.

"How is this Caroline?"

"She's a doll. More than that, really."

"Yeah? Well, I suggest you go off some place quiet, marry her and forget about all this shit."

"Precisely my thoughts."

"Well you ought to take your own counsel then."

"You can be sure I'm not going to take yours."

"Did you hear that, Bart? Just for that, the price has doubled."

We were quiet and drank. I thought of Stan back in Hawaii and the comment he had made about swooping into Hanauma with a chopper, just to stir up a little trouble. I imagined arriving at the prison in that fashion. A sense of power came with it.

"You know, they wouldn't know what hit them," I said.

"You mean down in Hermosillo?" Stan said.

I nodded.

"You'd have some beaners flying, all right," Bart said.

Stan and I chuckled.

"Let's hope it never comes to that," I said.

"You see, Bart? I've got him on the hook."

Bart smiled at me.

"I had never considered how outmatched they would be."

"Well, just remember," Bart said, "if you ever decide to go ahead with this, it ain't the movies."

"Yeah. You can never be sure how these things will turn out," Stan said. "You might never make it back."

"Well, on that note, gentlemen, I'd best be heading north."

"Hell, the day's still young," Stan said. "Let's hit our favorite topless joint and have a little fun...Come on," he said when I failed to respond.

Stan got up and paid for the beer. Bart got up with him.

"All right, but only for a little while," I said.

"We'll have to drag you out of there," Stan said on our way out the door.

They took me over to a joint by the state college, where coeds from the nearby university made top dollar for twirling around a pole. The G-strings came off in the process. Between performances, they mingled with the clientele. Stan had it in his mind that any woman with her clothes half off wanted to get laid. He got slapped in the end and a bouncer asked us to leave.

"Did you see that little bitch slap me," Stan said on our way out to the parking lot. He touched the spot affectionately. "Boy, she was something."

It was a little past seven when we got back to the diner. It was early enough to drive back to LA. We talked for a while against the Nova before Stan climbed into his rig. I followed him over and he rolled down the window.

"Thanks for the thrills, Stan."

"No problem there, Clay. Good to see you again."

I pushed away from the window.

"And don't be kidding yourself," he added. "We've got PhDs in this warfare shit."

"Yeah, I suppose you do. Good luck, Stan. Same to you, Bart."

"The best to you, Clay."

"Yeah, it's time we faced it. That peace and brotherhood crap is all over."

"Maybe, Stan, but we planted a seed."

"Let's hope that's true."

I had turned to walk away when Stan called out again.

"Hey Clay."

I looked back.

"How many 'Nammers did you say were in that jail?"

"Fifteen, twenty of them."

"You hear that, Bart? Sonsabitches risk their life for their country and that's the thanks they get. Hell, maybe I'll go down there and blow 'em out myself."

He circled around the parking lot, still ranting to Bart about it. I watched until the two of them had disappeared down the block.

A thought occurred to me as I stood there, something that had been troubling me since the moment I first reawakened in Jijiwa's hut. There was something I needed to know so I called Caroline to tell her I wouldn't be back that night. It turned out she wasn't home but Mrs. Leroux took the message.

Half an hour later, I was pulling off the freeway in Encinitas. A gas station attendant showed me to a map taped on their wall. I found the street address and followed the directions down to a narrow, winding lane along the ocean bluffs. Having parked, I turned off the motor and listened to the sound of breakers echoing up from the shore far below. The night air was thick with sea mist.

The street was a mix of nice homes and rickety old bungalows. There were empty lots overgrown with palms and mulberry. I made my way down the darkened block on foot, keeping a wary eye on all the parked cars as I did.

Once I found the address, I stood for some time watching the house. The front porch was darkened. A few dim lights were on inside.

Convinced that no one was watching, I climbed up through heavy brush on the adjacent lot and went around to the back of the house. At the top of some stairs, I checked the back door and found it unlocked. I turned the door-knob quietly and let myself in. It was silent: no TV, no radio, no voices. I followed the dim lights down the hallway to the living room. When I came around the corner, I found Eric seated on some straw mats in a lotus position. His copy of the I Ching was opened on the table in front of him. Eric didn't move for several minutes then opened his eyes.

"I was wondering when you'd show up, brother."

"What makes you so sure I would?"

"A number of things. Have a seat."

I made myself comfortable on a futon and leaned against the wall. It was typical Eric. Nothing above knee level and scant little below it; a small table, a lamp, candles, incense and tapestries. It lent itself well to contemplation.

"For that matter, how would you know I had survived?"

"As I said, I have great confidence in you, my boy."

460

"Well, the fact is, I nearly didn't. And of course, worried about you."

"Yes, that did turn into a bit more of an adventure than I had anticipated."

He stroked his beard thoughtfully.

"You must have crossed the Gulf," I said.

"I did. Wow. You know, I thought it might be a good idea to get off the main highway and I was on a back road to Guaymas when I ran into this Yaqui Indian. He eventually guided me down to the coast, but not before an enlightening introduction to the peyote rituals."

Eric laughed with a distant gaze.

"Then what?"

"Then there was a ferry from Guaymas across to Baja, which in itself became another adventure. The people of Baja have yet to become familiarized with the word highway." He laughed again with his distant gaze. "But I got back here with money to spare. And you?"

I told him my tale.

"Wow, brother, you live an exciting life."

"It's not over yet."

"Oh wow, now what?" he said with another laugh.

"I'm hoping I can bribe Kip out of that prison. Then I plan to disappear somewhere, hopefully with Caroline."

"And if bribery fails?"

"Stan was saying we could blast him out with a Huey helicopter."

Eric laughed again.

"I know, but it's not as farfetched as it sounds."

I told him about my meeting with Stan and Bart down in San Diego.

"I have to admit, they've got me going."

Eric continued to stare at me with a sardonic grin.

"What?" I said.

"Once again, I realize that our lives are predisposed to two distinctly different spiritual paths."

"Everybody's on a different spiritual path, Eric."

"Yeah, brother, but some are more different than others."

We laughed at his joke.

461

"Well, Eric, I'm relieved to know you got home safely. I've been haunted by the idea that you went down over my troubles. You know, I keep trying to make things turn out all right, but one disaster seems to follow another.

"Maybe you should stop trying to make things turn out all right for a spell."

"How do you do that?"

"You just sit still."

"Yeah, well, so much for that idea. I'm like a moving train that keeps blowing by the station."

Eric laughed.

'What?"

"Oh, nothing, brother. I figured out long ago. There's no point in interfering with another man's destiny."

"Yeah, I'd screw things up, no matter what you told me."

Eric laughed again. Then we were quiet and listened to the breakers for a spell.

"So, what's going on with Chris and Michael and the band?"

"Oh wow, that was really a trip."

"What do you mean?"

"Oh, Michael freaked out. Thought everyone was using him, so he pawned all the equipment and ran off to Europe."

"Fuck, what a bummer," I said.

"Yeah. The sixties, brother."

"Fuck that. I don't know what that is but it's not the sixties."

"Yeah," Eric said, stroking his beard thoughtfully. "Hey, you're welcome to spend the night."

"No, I'd better keep moving. I've taken enough of a chance as it is."

Eric stood up and gave me a bear hug.

"I'm going to send you some money, my friend."

"Wow. Far out. What am I supposed to do with it?"

"Well, if for some reason I don't come out of this alive, I trust you to take care of Caroline." I wrote down her number. "There may be others. Do what's right and give her the rest."

"Hopefully I'll see you again, brother."

"Yeah, happy trails in the meantime."

I slipped out the back and retraced my steps to the Nova.

When I was comfortable in a motel room, I called Caroline. I told her about my day, omitting the part about helicopters and topless dancers. The news concerning Kip had her worried enough.

"What are you going to do now, Clay?"

"Wait, I suppose. Perhaps go back to Tucson and work on Charlie."

"I'm worried about you."

"Just hang on to your horses, okay? I'll be back tomorrow."

There was a pause.

"Please don't do anything foolish, Clay."

"I won't."

"Yeah, right, you turkey."

"I won't."

There was a long silence.

"I love you," she said.

"I love you, too."

I crawled into bed after we got off the phone and lay there wishing my life were as simple as it had been in those brief moments with Jijiwa. I could not think of any good reason why it shouldn't be, but it wasn't and I wondered how my path and the path of the entire modern world had gotten so screwed up. I lay staring at the ceiling for a long time over that one.

At dawn, I showered and called the sheriff.

"Son, you can just forget it. I got the word. This whole fianza deal is so they can keep the ones they want. Ain't nobody can touch him for five years now."

"Sheriff, there has to be some way."

"You got a hundred grand?"

I hesitated.

"Yes. It can be had."

"Well, that's what I offered them and the answer was still no. Period. Not even some attempt to negotiate for more. Just no."

"What about springing him the way I got out?"

"Uh uh. I fished that around too. They've beefed up security, right down the line."

"I'm driving back tomorrow. Hold off calling his parents until then."

"Shit"

"Just give me a few more days, sheriff. I'm on my way back."

"There ain't no hurry. Except for his folks. That's got to be done, and soon."

I hung up, checked out of the motel and climbed into the front seat with my thoughts. Sometime later, I started the car and headed up the coast. Of the thousand things going around in my head, one of them would not leave me alone.

I crossed over to Interstate 5 at Oceanside and took it slowly up through the Marine base, with nothing but blue skies and the ocean and a big, wide highway in front of me for fifteen miles. There was plenty of time to think about what was important in life, but I always came back to the same thought. I had to rescue Kip. I couldn't leave him behind. I'd never be able to live with myself. Hopefully some other way to solve things would turn up. And once that was done, I promised to go someplace quiet and never make trouble again.

It was a little past one in the afternoon when I arrived back to Burbank. I checked into the hotel, not in the best of moods. I had just witnessed a fifty mile long stretch of commercial and industrial trash, where greed and haste had taken precedence over everything else.

I sent my clothes down to be washed again and called Mrs. Leroux. There was no answer, which was just as well. I was in no mood to hide anything from her or Caroline.

I tried Stan.

"Change your mind there, Clay?"

"I don't know. This bribe business seems to have hit a snag."

"And what? You want to know if we were serious?"

"I suppose."

"You bet," he said. "But you'd better be damn sure you are too."

"It's an option."

"It's an option," he repeated.

"I'm heading back to Tucson in the morning."

"We'll be here."

"What kind of helicopter did you say?"

"Bell 204. It would be nice to have the 1B series."

"What's that?"

"Ask around and see if anyone has the twin turbine. They'll know what you mean."

"But I won't."

"Just have a damn good reason for wanting it. These boys are awfully suspicious about their helicopters, especially around the border."

"Remember, I have the local sheriff on my side."

"It couldn't hurt."

"I'll call you on Thursday."

"I'm looking at my schedule. I'll be here in the office after two."

"I'll call you either way."

"Roger, Clay."

I knew Caroline would not be home until later so I ordered a sandwich and milk and killed the day watching the crap that passed for entertainment on the TV every afternoon. I would have given my right arm for half an hour of Soupy Sales right then.

I called Mrs. Leroux at six and told her I was in the same hotel.

"Clay, you know there are some less expensive motels in the area."

"I only want the best for your daughter, Mrs. Leroux."

Silence followed.

"Well I've been thinking to talk to you about that," she said. "Would you mind stopping by? We can chat while you're waiting for Caroline to come home."

"Oh, I'm beat, Mrs. Leroux. I was about to take a nap. I could stop by tomorrow sometime if that's okay with you."

"Very well. Let's say morning and I'll make you breakfast."

"Thanks. That'll be nice."

There was a moment of silence.

"Then I'll look forward to seeing you tomorrow, Clay."

"Yes. I'll see you then."

I hung up and called room service about my clothes, then dialed the front desk and told them to give Caroline the key when she arrived. The bellhop knocked as I was hanging up. I tipped him, threw the clothes on a chair and took a shower. Then I crawled back into bed and tried to get some sleep.

Before closing my eyes, I looked out the window one last time. The sky was blood red over the Hollywood hills. A stream of cars lit up the freeway. The hills were dotted with the familiar lights of home.

48

I awakened to Caroline's silhouette moving beside me in the darkened room—her arms going up over her head and the whisper of cotton against skin, her thick hair falling back onto her shoulders and the sound of elastic snapping. Then she was naked on top of me and whispering strange things in my ears and it was like the mystery of a summer forest at twilight.

Caroline's kisses started down my belly but I had my own ideas and rolled her over, searching down her belly for the source of her sweet perfumed animal scent and then I was making love to her with my lips and when she could take no more, she pulled hard on me and I crawled up inside of her.

"You are good to me," she said sometime later, when we were still.

"It makes me happy to know you're pleased."

She touched my face and searched my eyes.

"What is inside of you, Clay?"

"I don't know. Sometimes it feels like all the sorrows of the world."

"But why?" she said. "Is there something wrong?"

I kissed her lips again, and for that one moment, there was nothing wrong anywhere.

"Tell me," she said.

"I honestly don't know."

"What are you going to do about Kip?"

"I don't know."

"I know you feel badly for him."

"Yeah.

"Did you call the sheriff again?"

"Yeah."

"And?"

"It looks hopeless," I said.

"Why don't we go away somewhere and give it a little time."

She saw me snap to attention.

"I mean a vacation," she said. "Not for the rest of our lives."

I sighed and lay back down. I wanted so much for her to abandon all with me, for us to find that little village by the sea, where life was simple and the modern world was a million miles away. I had no use for a two week vacation.

In response to my silence, she shook me gently.

"What?" she said.

"It's hard to enjoy yourself when you already know you're coming back."

She shook me again.

"You can let go of it for a little while, Clay."

"I thought you wanted me to turn myself in."

"Clay, I think it's inevitable. But I can understand your reluctance." She got up on one elbow. "Maybe you'll feel differently after you've had some time to reflect."

"Maybe."

"Maybe I'll feel differently," she said.

I stared at the ceiling.

"What are you planning, Clay?"

"I don't know."

"Have you forgotten your promise?"

"No."

"Well?"

She turned my face gently back towards hers.

"I think I'd better head back to Tucson in the morning."

"Clay, what are you going to do?"

"I'm not sure."

"What?"

"Stan was talking about taking a helicopter down there to bust him out."

She shook her head slowly and collapsed back onto the bed.

"It's just a thought."

"You'll do it."

467

"It's only talk," I said. "Anyway, Stan did this sort of thing every day in Vietnam. He says it would be easy."

"Easy to get killed."

"We're only talking, Caroline."

"You'll do it. I can see it in your eyes."

"I can't leave him in there. I would regret it for the rest of my life."

"The way you're going, that won't be long."

"Can you please try to understand how I feel for one minute?"

"I do, Clay, but that? It seems like you're just heading for disaster."

She held her stare to emphasize the point and turned away in frustration.

"I wouldn't leave you in there," I said after a long silence.

"It only implies that you had gotten me into trouble in the first place."

"Fuck it, Caroline. You win."

I got up and grabbed my briefs.

"Where are you going?"

"What the hell do you care?"

"Well then I don't."

I found my pants.

"I'm going to get something to eat. You're welcome to come, if you want."

"Maybe I'd better go home."

"Maybe you'd better."

I was getting into my shirt when she popped out of bed and stormed into the bathroom. I braced myself for the door slamming. I sat down to pull on my socks and boots. When Caroline came out and grabbed her purse to leave, I leapt up to intercept her.

"Let go of me, Clay."

I pressed her hard against the door.

"You don't get it, do you?"

"I said let go of me."

She tried to raise her knee but I pressed my body against hers. She turned her head away in response. I was looking at her fine, long neck.

"I'll let you go, Caroline, but not until you've had a good long look at my side of things."

"Yeah, it's always about your side of things."

I waited until her face turned back towards mine.

"Let's say I do go. I might leave here and never come back."

"Are you looking for sympathy?"

"Some tenderness would do."

When there was no response, I went on.

"It would be easy enough to disappear somewhere with you. A quiet little port on a Greek island comes to mind. I think of it every minute of every day. But I'd have to live with my choice for the rest of my life."

"Why is this one thing so important to you, Clay? You've run away from everything else in your life."

"Go ahead, Caroline. Dig the knife in."

I felt the force in her arms relent.

"I'm sorry. That wasn't fair."

"It's okay. I ask myself the same questions every day."

"So, go ahead. Soften me up for the blow."

"I can't leave him. That's all. You've already seen what happens when a man doesn't have a clear conscience."

She searched my face. I realized I had a crushing grip on her wrists and let go. She shook them without taking her eyes off me. Sensing some spark, I ran my hands through her hair and kissed her lips softly. Her eyes closed for that moment, then reopened. I kissed her again, producing the same result.

Then a tear welled up in one eye and spilled out. I watched as it cascaded down her cheek. I kissed it away from her face, and another. She collapsed against my chest, her arms desperately around me.

"Sweetheart. Everything's going to be all right."

"I hate what you do to me," she said through the tears.

"Here, look at me."

I held her face in my hands. Her lips trembled. I wanted to tell her I would be back, but I didn't know if I would.

"Honey, if I never live another day, I'll always treasure your love and how good you've been to me."

"I love you too, Clay, but I don't know if I can take anymore. I feel like there's always going to be some saga or disaster looming over our lives."

"I'm sorry, Caroline, but I can't promise you anything."

469

"I'm starting to hate you. I'm starting to hate how this feels."

I held her without a word as she cried. After a time, she pushed away and wiped at her tears.

"All this fighting has made me hungry."

I laughed and she shoved me.

"Come on," I said. "I'll buy you a nice burger."

Reluctantly, she accepted my kiss and we headed out the door.

Again, following Caroline's directions, we drove to a diner and ordered a couple of burgers, French fries and two strawberry shakes. I had her feet in my lap. With the burgers done, Caroline had a last slurp from her shake and put it down.

"Clay, I feel myself falling away from you."

"Please. Let me do this one thing, whatever it takes, and when I'm done, I'll find a lawyer. And if everything works out okay, we'll go somewhere far away and I'll never make trouble again."

She stared at me.

"I promise," I said.

She shook her head and looked away.

"Okay, what? You're done? You want to go home?"

"No, I want to make love to you before you leave."

"One last time, is that it?"

She stared with that look of black coal in her eyes. I paid for the meal and we headed back to the hotel without saying another word.

In the morning, after Caroline left, I called Mrs. Leroux and begged out of our arrangements. A friend needed my help in Tucson. It was the lesser of two evils, trading one lie for many. I definitely wasn't going to tell her the truth about Stan and helicopters.

I slipped over to Pasadena, hit a diner for breakfast and from there skirted southeast along the base of the San Gabriel Mountains. By the time I had negotiated my way back to Interstate 10, it was a little past ten o'clock. I had the air-conditioner on and five hundred miles of desert to consider the question. Why should I rescue Kip? I had given him a chance. He could have escaped with me. In fact, he had said it himself. It was only five years. He would survive. If I put his money away in safekeeping, he would have a nice little nest egg when he got out. When the discussion ended there, I was ready to head back to Burbank.

But always a shadow came over these thoughts, and I knew it was my conscience. I saw the image of Kip standing at the train station in Guaymas, kicking at the dirt. I recalled the words I had spoken. "Are you coming or not? We'll be in Nogales by sundown." I saw again that look in Kip's eyes as he crawled into the back of the truck and stared up at the roof.

Who knew what might have been, had we waited ten hours for the next train? Perhaps Kip and I would have ended up in prison somewhere else, but all that was academic. I knew what did happen and it haunted me. And my conscience would not let it go.

I stopped for gas in Blythe, grabbed an ice-cold beer and got back on the road, doing eighty miles an hour. Fifteen miles west of Tucson, I backed off the throttle. The western sky was fading to darkness over Mt. Lemmon. Cirrus clouds wound like ribbons through the sunset.

It was almost eight. I checked into a motel on the outskirts of town and called the station. Sheriff Prescott was gone for the day. I tried Danny. He was on duty. There was nothing to do but wait patiently until morning, the one thing I hadn't prepared myself to do.

After a shower I drove down to the south side and had some Mexican food. The waitress lavished a great deal of attention on me while I ate. I must have looked lonely. Then again, so did she, a woman who had been attractive enough in her time, and still had the figure to prove it, but the voice had grown coarse from all the cigarettes and heartaches and her hair had been one too many colors over the years, trying to match the feelings inside. It was black now and I assumed that was the way she was feeling these days.

After the meal, I went for a walk. The mountains were black along the horizon. Back at the motel, I crawled into bed, turned off the lights and did my best to leave the emotions alone for one night.

In the morning I walked across the street for some breakfast and called the sheriff the minute my eggs had been mopped up. He had just walked in the door so I waited.

"What the hell are you plannin'?" he asked me after we had dispensed with the formalities.

"It's only a possibility, but maybe going down there to break him out."

471

"You're going to get yerself killed. And a lot of other folks along with you."

"I don't need to tell you, sheriff, but there's close to four hundred grand between Kip and me. Now will that get him out?"

"I told you, the Americans have this thing clamped down tighter than the lid on a coffin."

"You see any other hope?"

"Nope. But I still say you're gonna get yerself killed."

"I'm asking for help, not your advice."

"Hell, I'm just getting dragged deeper and deeper into shit."

"All I need is a good excuse for leasing a helicopter."

There was a silence.

"You gotta be nuts."

"Maybe I am, sheriff, but the question stands."

"You tell 'em you're taking a chopper over the border and you'll have fifty Feds up your ass before you hit Nogales."

"They don't need to know we're crossing the border."

"And you're expectin' I'll cover for you."

"That's the general idea."

"Hell, I'd be better off bitin' the bullet right now."

"Maybe so, sheriff. But that still leaves Kip in there to rot."

There was more silence.

"What in hell would I want to lease a chopper for?"

"I don't know. But people do. There must be something you could tell them."

"Maybe," he said. "When you figurin' on doing this?"

"If I do it."

"All right, if you do it."

"Within a week."

"How long you need?"

"We'd better plan on two or three days. You never know what might happen."

"That's just what I was thinkin'."

"I'm not asking you to come along, Charlie."

"And just what the hell would I do if something went wrong?"

"We'd have to figure out some way for you to cover your ass. It might tie in to your story."

"I'll see what I can do."

"I'll call you in a few days."

I rang off and called Danny. He agreed to go down and see Kip on Sunday. Also, I asked if he knew a good body and paint man, someone we could trust. He said he did. We set a time to meet on Saturday. I reminded him to keep his mouth shut and got off.

I spent the remainder of the morning tracking down the helicopter Stan had suggested. Only one outfit in town had it; at $500 a day and $200 per flight hour. When the owner asked my intentions, I gave him a line about doing some research for a university program and that seemed to go over well enough. At least the questions stopped. I killed another hour rummaging through an Army surplus store. When it was two, I called Stan. After a quick hello, he yelled in the background.

"Hey Bart, he's hooked."

"Be serious, Stan. I feel crazy even thinking about this."

"It's not that big a deal, my friend. But you've got to be sure it's what you want to do."

"No, it's not what I want to do," I said. "I just don't see any other way."

"Before you go to war, Clay, you'd better make damn sure there isn't any other way. Because if things go wrong, you'll be thinking about the choice you made for the rest of your life."

I listened to the hum in the receiver.

"You really think we can pull this off?" I asked him.

"I don't see why not. It wouldn't be a fair fight."

"I'm kind of worried about this side," I said.

"It'll take some planning, no doubt about it. We'll need a place to hide, if nothing else. You got something in mind?"

"Possibly."

There was another long silence.

"Well, call me when you think you're ready, Clay."

"Would you mind coming down here for a few days? Just to look things over? I'll pay you for your time and all your expenses."

"Sure, no problem. I've got one flight in the morning. Bart and I could head out by noon."

"And if I decide to back out at the last minute?"

"Hell, pay us for our time and we'll leave it at that."

"You're sure?"

"We'll be there about sunset."

I gave him the name of the motel and told him two rooms would be waiting. He took my room number and signed off.

I started to pick up the receiver again but stopped with my hand in midair. What's the use? Caroline wouldn't approve of what I'm doing. I hardly approved of it myself. I only knew that my conscience was always waiting for me there, right around the next bend.

49

Late that afternoon, I awakened in the listless heat and stared at the ceiling, feeling again like this plan of mine was utter madness. There was a thought to call Stan and tell him I was backing out. Then I pictured Kip in that hour, preoccupied with a game of basketball or making dinner or staring at the ceiling of his cell, his heart filled with God only knew what sort of despair, and I could see no other way forward. I knew how I would feel to be looking at ten years and maybe this was all about me in the end.

Jijiwa's words came back to me too. Go up the mountain. I wasn't sure I had done that, or if I even knew what the old shaman had meant. I was just a man down in a hole, unable to see out of it.

Another thought occurred to me. Why not consult the I Ching? All I had to do was drive across town, buy another copy and sit down with a half open mind, but I quickly dispensed with the notion, fearing the oracle might actually dissuade me from my path. Despite my abundant reservations, I had become a prisoner of my own momentum and did not want anything getting in the way.

Seeing there was still a bit of light left in the day and not wanting to spend the next few hours listening to my head, I decided to get something done. I paid for the extra rooms, stopped by a surplus store to buy some camping gear and pulled onto the highway headed south.

As the miles flew by, I worked on a schedule for this potential mission in my mind and concluded that visiting day was the best time to show up in a chopper. It meant more security, but it also meant a great deal more distraction. It was now Wednesday and

Sunday was far too soon to get things off the ground so I'd shoot for next Wednesday and see how things went.

Seeing a liquor store, I pulled over and bought a case of Wild Turkey, hoping it would do wonders for frontier relations. An hour later, having jostled along washboard roads for thirty miles, I came to a narrow gorge and wound my way slowly between two walls of sheer rock, passing into Jake's canyon with the last glow of day fading above the mountain peaks. Jake was sitting in front of the shack as I pulled to a stop in front. I nodded. He didn't. There was a shotgun in his lap.

"It's a dern good thing it's you, that's all I can say."

"Yeah, I'm not so sure of that."

"What the hell d'ya mean by that?"

"Oh nothing."

I got out to stretch, pulled on my jacket and went around to grab a bottle of bourbon out of the trunk. Jake came over and took the bottle of bourbon like he was holding a baby. I hadn't meant for him to see the whole case, but he did.

"Now would ya look at that. Ain't that a sight for sore eyes."

I closed the trunk.

"Best if we stick to one bottle for now."

"Bet yer life, partner. I'll grab a couple of glasses."

He tottered off in a modest rush. I sat down on the porch. Jake returned with two tumblers and without the shotgun. I poured the glasses half full and we drank in silence. Stars were steadily poking holes in the evening sky. Cottonwoods stirred down by the stream. The scent of water came on the wind. There was the yelp of a coyote far off. The cottonwoods spoke again. Jake finished his bourbon and I poured his glass a bit fuller this time.

"Well, I reckon ya got something on yer mind, tenderfoot, so spill it."

"Oh, I thought I might need some help. Maybe later in the week, if things play out the way I expect."

"What kinda help?"

His head peered out from underneath his frayed hat, white whiskers everywhere. I studied his blue eyes in the growing darkness.

"I may be going down to rescue my friend, and if I do, I'll need a place to plan things. And a place to hide for a few days when we get back."

"So yer figurin' on this place."

"It's as good as any. And I figured you could use the money."

He took a sip of his whiskey and thought this over.

"Well, I'll tell ya one thing's fer sure. I ain't aimin' ta get overrun by a pack of tenderfoots in the bargain."

"No need to worry about that. There'll be three of us at first, maybe seven or eight when we get back."

"And jes' fer a few days, ya say?"

"Just for a few days, Jake."

"Well, now, jes how much would it be worth to ya, havin' yerself a fine stagin' area and all?"

He waved his hand over his spread.

"Oh, I don't know."

I took a moment to replenish the glasses and savor the evening breeze. I looked back at Jake and braced myself for the reaction.

"Can't afford much. Say $500."

"$500?! Why that ain't even enough to buy ya a guided tour!"

"Hang on to your hat, Jake. Maybe we could double that, though it would represent a real hardship."

"Well, it's got a mite nicer ring to it, I'll tell ya that."

He drank his glass dry and I refilled it. After he'd taken a long belt, he continued.

"But it still ain't enough."

We sat in silence for a spell. It was growing dark and I was tired. I finished my whiskey and got up to stretch.

"I suppose you're right. It's not much money. Guess I'll have to look around for another spot."

I took the unfinished bottle of bourbon back to the trunk and caught a glimpse of Jake's forlorn look while closing the lid. I was climbing back behind the wheel when he spoke up.

"Now don't go getting yerself all carried away. I ain't said no yet. It's jes, a man's gotta think things through proper. Give it a fair lookin' over, so ta speak."

I closed the door and leaned against the car.

"By all means, Jake, take whatever time you need."

I already knew he would cave, just by the way his voice had cracked. And not that I meant to be tight with the money, but it had to be this way. If Jake knew how much was involved up front, there was no telling how much he might demand. I figured to give him a generous bonus when it was all through, no matter which way things turned out.

While Jake got right with his decision, I gazed down towards the south end of the canyon. Columbine trees were waving their creamy blossoms in the breeze, reminding me of a woman's softness.

I waited.

"Well, here's the long and short of it," Jake said after a spell. "I'll accept yer terms, but only 'cuz it's a good deed yer doin'. Otherwise, I'd run ya right outta here with a load of buckshot."

In honor of frontier relations, I retrieved the open bottle bourbon from the trunk and handed it to Jake on the front porch. He filled his glass, then mine. I offered a toast.

"Here's to our success, Jake. It's real generous of you to help out us out. It would have been tough to find another spot as nice as this one."

"That's fer sure. Now ya jes' slap that cash here in my palm and we'll shake on it."

"I can't."

"What d'ya mean ya can't!?"

"I don't have the money with me."

"Well then what the heller we jawin' away the night fer?"

I thought this might be a good time for the second bottle of bourbon and went over to dig it out of the trunk. Sitting back down next to Jake, I cracked the seal. The sound appeared to soften his attitude a bit. I refilled his glass and continued.

"I'll bring the money with me when I come back. You can run me off if I don't."

"And don't think I won't."

"You've got nothing to worry about, Jake."

"Ya betcha I don't."

Like most arguments, someone had to get in the last word so I left things like that. We shook hands on reasonably peaceful terms and went back to enjoying the scenery.

After a bit more conversation and whiskey, I retrieved my tent from the trunk and staked it out. Jake watched and offered advice. Watching me appeared to make him thirsty, and every drink of bourbon appeared to make him better at putting up tents. When the moon rose over the mountain, I gave up trying to keep pace with Jake and crawled into my tent. Every so often, I could hear the sound of the metal cap twisting open and being closed again. The sound of bourbon splashing into a glass had disappeared early on.

Much later, Jake's front door opened and slammed shut. I finally slept; knowing neither one of us would be feeling like a jay in the morning.

I awakened about midmorning to the sound of the shack door flinging open. Jake's footsteps headed off in the direction of the outhouse. A few minutes later, the outhouse door flung open and shut again. The footsteps returned to the shack and that door closed, too.

I crawled out of my sleeping bag and marched down to the stream in my shorts, feeling thick in the head. Stripping off the shorts, I dove into the cold water and came up with a holler. The sound of it echoed nicely around the canyon. Jake came in quick pursuit.

"What the heller ya tryin' ta do, raise the devil?"

I got up on dry ground and shook the water out of my hair. In the shade of the cottonwoods, there was still a bite to the morning air. I worked the goose-bumps out of my white flesh and started back towards the car with a determined gate. Jake was on my tail.

"Ya gonna answer me, tenderfoot? Yer likely to bring on the 7th Cavalry."

"You try jumping in there and see what happens."

"I ain't jumpin' in no creek at this hour of the mornin'."

"Well, you ought to."

I cracked open a fresh bottle of Bourbon. Jake stared as I took two good slugs and set the bottle down.

"Well? Are ya gonna answer me? Ya make a lotta noise like that and next thing ya know, I'll have some fool prospector down here looking fer gold in the mine. Well? Whaddya think of that?"

I looked up at Jake, thinking to throw him in the creek. I offered him the bottle instead.

"I ain't havin' me no drink before breakfast."

"Suit yourself."

I went about breaking camp. Out of the corner of my eye, I saw Jake actually sit down with a bowl of cereal. I pulled the Nova around when I was done packing and stopped in front of the shack with the engine running. Jake had finished his cereal.

"See you in a few days," I said.

He grunted. I left him on the front porch with bloodshot eyes and that case of Wild Turkey at his side.

In Sonoita, I stopped and forced down some breakfast of my own. The urge was to sleep off my hangover back at the motel but I compromised with a cold beer on the way back into town. As soon as I was there, I called the sheriff. It was a little before noon. He answered the call.

"I thought you was goin' to give this thing a few days."

"I had a feeling you already knew."

"Who's goin' to fly this chopper?"

"Just remember, sheriff, I'm only feeling this thing out."

"Well, likewise. Now who is this fella?"

"A friend. Ex 'Nam pilot. Why?"

"Cuz, it ain't gonna to look too fancy, me pullin' up with some goddamned long-haired hippie."

"I'm sure we can arrange a haircut, sheriff…So?"

"If I told them we was goin' up to San Carlos to hunt, up on the Indian reservation, they wouldn't think twice about it, that's if the appearances were right."

"Rifles, gear, that sort of thing?"

"That's right."

"I can have anything you want onboard."

"Now I've got a question for you."

"Go ahead, shoot."

"Where the hell do I get off?"

"Anywhere you'd like."

There was a pause.

"All right, I'll arrange somethin'."

"Good. You can say Stan's an acquaintance and I'm an acquaintance of his. You don't know me. You're just taking us up there to hunt. You make the arrangements with the helicopter and I'll give you the money before we go in. We'll drop you wherever you like and say you got sick and got a ride home from the reservation when we bring the chopper back."

"If you get back."

"Okay, if we get back. If we don't, you stick to the story about coming down with something and going home early."

There was a pause.

"I'm warnin' you. If one goddamned thing goes wrong, I'll sell you blind."

"If anything goes wrong, Charlie, you won't need to."

Again, I waited.

"I still think you're crazy."

"You've got a lot of company."

"Let's say we leave this thing in the plannin' stage and I'll keep fishin' around with the money."

"Fine, but go ahead and reserve the chopper and we'll see how things look in a couple of days."

I gave him the name of the outfit.

"When do you want this thing?"

"Have it ready for Tuesday morning and three days."

"I'll go as far as that right now."

"Any other questions?"

"Naw. Hell, you already heard 'em."

"I'll call you tomorrow. Remember, we're doing this for Kip."

"Jesus, god almighty, if his mother knew what we're plannin', she'd have me skinned."

"I've heard that may happen anyway, sheriff."

I pictured the sour look on his face as I hung up.

There was one more thing to do; consult a lawyer about my problems. Ever since Caroline had suggested the idea, it had been working in my head and I was ready to learn the truth. If it was twenty-five to life, I might as well know.

Thumbing through the yellow pages, I picked an attorney solely on the basis of his long hair in the ad. Half an hour later, I was walking out of his office, attorney-client relationship in effect, and with a promise that he would have an answer for me in the next few days.

There was nothing to do now but wait. I still felt like hell from the Wild Turkey so I downed another beer and took a copy of the morning paper back with me to the motel. The proprietor said she would have the maid wash my spare clothes. A Mexican girl came by to pick them up.

I crawled in bed and opened the paper. The president was still talking about peace with honor, whatever the hell that meant. There was an account of a B-52 bombing raid up north. On page 2 there was a story about Vietnam vets protesting the war. Buried further back in the paper, there was an article about the government constructing a bomb shelter in Hawaii, exclusively for VIP'S, just in case of a nuclear attack. The rest of us were expendable. I noticed the department store ads were now promoting a bush-jacket look. 'Harris & Frank does Haight-Ashbury' was already dead. I threw the paper on the floor and closed my eyes. Maybe things were always this way at the end of an era. It would be best to have it over, best to leave the illusions behind. We could try to change the world again in fifty years. I figured it would take everyone that long to get over the disappointment.

I awakened late in the afternoon, took a shower and found I could no longer suppress my impulse to call Caroline. I went outside to the phone booth. My heart beat wildly while the phone rang.

"What are you doing?" she asked right off.

"Waiting for Stan," I said.

"Oh Clay."

"We're only talking about it, honey."

"It sounds like you're doing more than talking about it."

"Okay, we're looking it over."

There was the hum of electricity coming through the line.

"Look, Caroline. This thing will be over with soon enough and if I end up dead, this conversation won't mean a damned thing, one way or the other."

There was more silence.

"Why do you have to be so hard on me?"

"I need to plan my life, and I can't with you."

"I can't help what's in my heart. And I'm only asking you to be patient for a little while longer."

"I feel very far away from you, Clay."

"For god's sake, Caroline. I'm not your father leaving you."

"Thanks."

"Well? Why do we have to do this every time?"

"I don't know. I just feel very empty. And I'm afraid I'll always end up feeling this way with you."

"This one thing, Caroline."

"It's always one more thing with you, Clay."

I tried for several minutes to feel a pulse but she was a million miles away. When I couldn't stand the distance between us any longer, I said goodnight. I had to hope it would be okay when I got back. It wasn't now. I felt emptier than when the conversation had started.

When the maid came by the motel room a short while later, I took the clean clothes from her through a half opened door and got dressed. Out in front, I sat on the bench beside my door. Stars were peeking out overhead. The mountains looked like black teeth against the pale evening sky.

Time passed. The night turned completely black. Then Stan was pulling up front in his truck. He and Bart got out. We shook hands. Stan had a wink and a smile for my western wear.

"Where can a man get some grub and a beer around these parts, partner," he said with a cowboy accent.

"I know a few dives around town."

I helped them get all their stuff inside. They had two duffel bags and a long, wooden box in the back of the truck. Bart and I grabbed the box and muscled it into their room. Bart nodded at the near wall and we set it there.

"Should I be asking you what's in there?"

"It's your life saver," Bart said. "That's what it is."

I put aside any further questioning for the moment and drove them down to the south side for some Mexican food. After ordering, I explained what I knew about the lay of the land and how I pictured the operation.

"That's about it, Stan. You'll have to figure what a helicopter can and can't do from there."

Stan put his arm around me with a smile.

"A regular general, what do you say Bart?"

Bart nodded.

"Could have used you in 'Nam, you son of a bitch."

"It might have been less trouble."

Stan and Bart glanced at each other.

"Yeah, well, maybe not," I added.

The food came and we ate without much conversation. There were a number of biker babes you couldn't help staring at, and an equal number of bikers who didn't want you staring at them. Danny's Hideaway was a good place to mind your own business but I felt reasonably safe with Bart on our side.

When the waitress took our plates, Bart spoke to Stan.

"You know, there's only one thing I'd change."

"What's that?"

"Blow the main gate after we put out the guards. It'll create confusion and give everybody some place to go. Otherwise, we'll have every sorry Mexican son of a bitch trying to climb that ladder."

"Sounds good to me. What do you think, Clay?"

"I don't know."

"Well you'd better know something."

"All right. There's a second, inner gate, but like the front gate, it's just iron bars. I'm thinking a grenade will roll right through one gate and out the other."

"You leave that to me," Bart said.

"Okay, enough of this war crap," Stan said. "Let's have some fun."

"Well, before we do that, I have one thing to say."

"So? Out with it, soldier."

"I'm going through the motions here. We'll set everything up, but I still may decide to back out any minute."

"So get the goddamned frown off your face."

"This is it, Stan."

"Aw, ain't he a sight?"

Bart smiled.

"I suppose you'd like to see some dancing girls now."

"He knows me, Bart, he knows me."

Stan wasn't hard to figure. We headed down the street to a topless joint. It was going on two in the morning before I had corralled Stan and Bart back to the motel. I waited long enough to make sure they were asleep before I drove out to Wagon Wheel Drive. It was very late when I returned.

Stan's persistent knock came way too early the next morning.

"Come on, cowboy, time for some grub."

"All right, all right. Let me shower."

"Well, hurry it up."

We drove downtown and stopped at a diner across the street from the surplus store. I watched them eat and crack jokes in equal proportions. You'd have thought we were going fishing.

The clowning around kept up all the way through breakfast. I ate with growing concern.

Over at the surplus store, they started in on the young sales clerk. He quickly looked disconcerted, both by the jokes and my supply list.

"Prospecting," I told him.

"Looks like you're planning an invasion."

"We are," Stan said.

The clerk half blushed and started down the aisle. I cornered Stan and Bart.

"Will you guys cut the crap? This is serious."

Stan grabbed Bart and pretended to be frightened.

"All right, fuck you two."

I went over to help the clerk. Bart and Stan came over to lend a hand, doing their best to look repentant.

Once the bill was paid and everything had been loaded into the truck, we went across town to buy a generator, a compressor and some assorted air tools. With those items carefully packed into the bed, the load came flush with the top.

"I don't know where you're going to stick that box back at the motel," I said.

"Throw it on top," Stan said. "It's not going anywhere."

"Then we still need some lumber."

"Throw it on the Nova."

I stared at him.

"Uh oh, Bart. Looks like things are getting serious again."

I pretended to club Stan over the head with a convenient tent pole.

"Look. I drove out there once already. The Nova will never make it with a load of lumber on top."

"All right, all right," Stan said. "We can strap it over the cab."

"That sounds better. Let's clean out of the motel first."

"Yes sir, Lieutenant." Stan saluted me and we all got into the truck. Star and Bart commenced to sing.

After we had checked out of the motel, Stan followed my directions to a lumberyard. We bought a bundle of 20-foot 2x4's, some nails and a couple of hammers. I threw in a tool bag for good measure and we hit the road. The truck was on the stops.

The trip down was a merry one from their point of view. When we ran out of FM they switched to country-western, but either way, the singing never stopped. It was getting on towards the end of the day when we pulled into the canyon. We had the windows down and the radio blaring. I knew enough to expect Jake with a shotgun in his hands. He didn't let me down. We found him on wobbly legs out in front of his shack and trying to get a shot off.

Stan looked over at Bart, shrugged and stepped on the gas. Jake let off a round and the windshield blistered. Stan bore down with one hand on the horn. The second blast was a moon-shot as Jake dove to avoid the truck. He was already reloading by the time Stan got the truck turned around. I jumped out and waved my arms at Jake.

"Jake, goddamn it, it's me, Clay."

He clipped the barrel back and fired two more shots that hit nothing. Stan blew by in the other direction. There was laughter coming out of the cab. I jumped to my feet and tackled Jake before he could reload. He was kicking and hollering as I wrestled the gun out of his hands. I found two unused shells on the ground, loaded them and pointed the gun. Jake got to his feet, rummy eyed and smelling of whiskey.

"Open your eyes, you ornery son of a bitch." He peered at me from underneath his hat. "Jake, it's me, Clay. Remember?"

He took another step closer and craned his neck.

"Ya look familiar enough," he said, squinting at me through the dust, "but that don't say yer welcome."

Jake jumped when he saw Stan and Bart coming around from the other side.

"There's three of ya, eh? Well ya best hope I don't get my hands on that shotgun or yer gonna find yerselves full of buckshot, ya sack of worthless tinhorns."

"Friendly sort, isn't he?" Stan said.

"Why you two-bit tenderfoots, I'll show you who's friendly...."

He took a roundhouse swipe at Stan and nearly fell on his ass in the process. I cocked the gun and he jumped to attention with his eyes twitching. He swiped as if something was buzzing around his head.

"I think we're going to have to tie him up," I said, "at least until he comes around.

"Tie me up, eh? Why I'll show ya bun..."

"Shut up or I'll blow your ass up into those mountains over there!"

I felt like hell for talking to the old man that way, especially on his own property, but it sure put the brakes on Jake.

"How the hell do you talk to this character?" Stan said.

"I made the mistake of leaving a case of Wild Turkey with him on Wednesday and I don't think he's stopped drinking ever since."

"Eh, what's that? Did I hear ya say somethin' about Wild Turkey?"

Jake leaned in towards me, licked at his dry lips and did his best to focus through the twitch in his eyes.

"Well, he understands Wild Turkey," Bart said.

"Shit, so do I," Stan said.

"Say, you gents like a good whiskey?"

"Sure do, old timer."

"Well, why didn't ya say so?"

Jake got up real close to Stan and whispered.

"Say, ya get yer friend there to put that musket away and I'll treat ya to the best. Got most of a case left up there in the shack."

"No problem, my friend. You take care of the whiskey and I'll take care of the gun."

Stan put his arm around Jake and they headed off towards the shack. Bart and I brought up the rear.

"How long have you been out here?" Stan asked Jake.

"Since forty-three. Not in these particular parts, mind ya. Just prospectin' in general. And hidin' out from the war."

"Nineteen forty-three," Stan repeated with reverence. "Well, it's a helleva nice place you got out here."

"Hell, this ain't nothin'. Ya shoulda seen my spread up in the Superstitions."

Stan looked back at us with a wink. Jake looked back too, as though something nettlesome had crossed his mind, but he went right back to jawing with Stan.

"That was before ya bunch of tenderfoots was even born, I'm suspectin'."

"I suspect so," Stan agreed

487

Bart followed them to the whiskey. I stopped at the truck, broke the gun and removed the shells.

Their conversation trailed off. The sun had gone down behind the mountains. I thought of Caroline, wishing whiskey was an answer to the god-awful feeling of emptiness in my gut, when I knew it wasn't. Anyway, I might want to turn back, and if I did so, I wanted to be damned sure it was done with a clear conscience, not with a hangover and a handful of cheap feelings.

I heated up some stew on the Coleman stove, knowing the troops would be thankful they had eaten by the time they awakened the next morning. Then I turned in early, hoping to set a good example, but it accomplished little. The tall tales went on until late and grew in proportion to their consumption of whiskey.

I was awakened later by a string of profanity echoing off into the night and looked out through the tent opening. It was Stan and Bart, attempting to raise their tent. I had tried to enlist their support for that endeavor earlier in the evening, to no avail. Now they were trying to do it in the dark, and drunk. After arguing like a couple of hobos for several minutes, they gave up and crawled into their sleeping bags.

I curled back up into mine, wondering what I could expect from these two hardened veterans when the chips were down. So far, it had been a lot of fun and games and little else.

50

The sky had turned a rosy color over the eastern mountains. The fire crackled in the morning cold. The metal coffee pot percolated one last time and grew still. I gave it an extra moment to settle down before pouring myself a cup.

Time passed and a groan emanated from inside of one of the sleeping bags. A head popped up. It was Stan. He had a mad look about him. I nodded at the coffee pot and that elicited another groan.

Bart came up soon after, not looking like he had fared much better. I pointed my nose in the direction of the stream. It took a moment for the message to get through the cobwebs in their brains but first one then the other of them crawled out of their sleeping bags and trekked cheerlessly down towards the water. There was a lull, perhaps a minute, before the hollering commenced. That canyon had a majestic way of magnifying a man's voice.

As expected, Jake came flying out of the shack, trying to pull on his boots and cover ground all at once. He put the brakes on in front of me.

"What the blazes are ya confounded tenderfoots up ta now?"

"You ought to know, Jake. You were the one up drinking with them all night."

He tried glaring at me but his eyelids wouldn't cooperate. Shy a shotgun, and some ammunition, he belched, farted and headed in the direction of the outhouse.

I started breakfast and kept an eye out for Stan and Bart. They reappeared with the color of their skin changed, but not the look on their faces. I worked on the bacon and eggs while they dressed.

Jake came out of the outhouse and went into the shack. I knew what he was having for breakfast. He returned shortly and cracked the seal on a fresh bottle of bourbon. That elicited a chorus of groans. It was a good sign.

"Don't you ever stop, old timer?" Bart said.

"Ya jes never mind. I'd like ta know what kind of shenanigans yer plannin' ta cook up with all this battle gear ya got here?"

He waved at the truck. Stan eyed him once and grabbed a plate.

"You should have shot him."

"Why, ya lousy bunch of tinhorns...Ya jes let me get my hands onta that shotgun and I'll show ya some shootin'."

"All right," I said. "Let's not get started again. There's work to do."

"Well, maybe there is, and maybe there ain't."

Jake came closer and stared defiantly at me from the other side of the fire.

"But I'd like ta see some of this fancy cash a yers before I consent to any changes in the real estate, as it were."

"Okay. If I give you the money, will you promise to keep quiet and stay out of the way?"

"Stay out of the way...why I...Well I'll be a sight more pleasant ta be around, that's fer sure."

"Give him the cash," Stan said between mouthfuls.

I helped Bart with a plate, poured two cups of coffee, then pulled out my roll and counted a thousand dollars. I held it out of reach.

"I promise we'll clean up after ourselves when we're done. In the meantime, let's not have any more squabbling, all right?"

Jake acknowledged my admonition by grabbing the cash.

"And I'd like ta see that shotgun of mine."

"I'm not giving it to you until you're sober."

Again, he tried to look menacing, and again his eyelids failed him. Halfway to the shack, Stan called out.

"Hey, old timer, how about a little snort?"

"Stan, please," I said with a shake of my head.

"A little hair of the dog," he said sheepishly.

"All right. But one and that's it."

Jake came back with the bottle. Stan topped off his coffee and did the same for Bart. Jake took the bottle and retreated to his porch.

It wasn't long before Stan and Bart were chirping away about war and romance. Then, as soon as they had wiped their plates clean and gulped down the last of their coffee, they jumped to their feet.

"Well, what the hell are you waiting for, Matthews? There's work to do."

I poured another cup of coffee and followed them over to the truck. First, we got everything onto the ground. If things went as planned, we would be trying to hide a helicopter in a few days and went about constructing the framework for an enclosure to that end.

"You were damn close," Stan said when we ran short on lumber. I got down from the ladder and faced him.

"I guess we can stitch the canvas together."

"You don't guess in war, Matthews."

"All right, bring the goddamned rope and let's get to work."

"That's better," he said as he went to retrieve the rope. Bart helped me unroll the canvas and we resumed our industry. The sun cleared the higher peaks around mid-morning. Our shirts came off in the heat.

"What was it like, Stan? You know, Vietnam."

"Oh, it wasn't nearly as nice as this, was it Bart?"

Bart shook his head without looking up.

"No," Stan said, "I'd have sold my chopper for a day like this." He looked up once to make sure I was listening.

"You think man can't live without trouble?" I said.

"Seems like it sometimes. You wondering if you're doing the right thing?"

"I'm always wondering that."

"Don't be so rough on yourself. Men choose war rather than deal with questions like that one."

"I imagine there's plenty of questions afterwards," I said.

"Sure. One side's always pissed over how things turned out and start another war, just trying to get back what they lost in the last one."

He slapped Bart on the back.

"You think I wouldn't rescue my buddy, here?"

I let the question hang and looked over at the shack. Jake had disappeared. It was too damn hot to be out in the sun without good

491

reason. There wasn't a breeze in sight. I wiped at the sweat and got back to work.

"You know, when I'm lying there alone at night, it always seems like it would be easy to make this a better world."

"The world is what it is," Stan said. "It's never going to catch up with our dreams."

Stan looked up.

"You worried about the blood?"

"Not mine so much, but yeah."

"We're all going to die, Clay. You may as well do it for something worthwhile."

I looked around at our enterprise, feeling half mad about the whole thing.

"I just hope things go as planned."

"I wouldn't worry yourself too much. We'll be in and out before those Mexicans have time to fart."

Once we had finished with stitching the canvas together, Stan and Bart went up and got comfortable in the mouth of the mineshaft, just to be out of the sun. I put things away and went over to face them.

"I'd best get back to town. Either one of you want to come with me?"

"Neah," Stan said. "We'll stick around and keep an eye on the old timer."

"Where'd he go to?" Bart said, peering out the mine shaft. His head was very bright for that moment. Then he leaned back into the shade.

"Back in his shack. Probably worn out from all the worrying."

"I'd be blaming the whiskey," Stan said.

"Well don't you guys go giving him a hand."

"How do you like it, Bart? A goddamned chaperon."

"Just the same, we're going to need our wits about us."

"Don't you worry," Stan said, waxing serious. "When the time comes, I'll have plenty of wits for both of us."

He jumped out and handed me the keys to the truck. Bart went over and peeked into the shack.

"Snoring away in there," he said, coming back.

The last I saw in the rearview mirror, Stan and Bart had the shovels out and were digging a hole for the generator.

I stopped at the motel for a quick shower, checked the clock and decided to call the attorney. There was a feeling of dread as I dialed the number. The secretary put me on hold. The attorney came on the line a moment later and explained what he had learned. When he was done, I asked how much I owed him. He told me the deposit was enough. I thanked him and hung up the phone. It was sometime before I could think to move. I felt emptier than I had ever imagined. None of my actions seemed to make sense now, in light of the truth.

I called Danny next and made arrangements to meet him at a cafe on Speedway, finished my errands and gassed up. By the time Danny and his friend joined me at the café, I was half finished with my lunch. They sat down opposite me.

"Clay, this is Tony. He's the body and paint man I told you about."

I reached over and shook his hand. Tony was a dark-haired kid with an honest face, and a man that could be trusted when the chips were down.

"Things are a real mess, huh?" Danny said.

"Yeah, but we're going to get him out of that hole."

I looked them over, took into consideration the need for caution and decided there was nothing to do but explain the situation, revealing only what they really needed to know. I got back to my meal while they digested the news. Tony had taken it matter-of-factly, the way I had hoped.

"Boy, you're going to be in a lot of trouble when you get back," Danny said. "Don't you think?"

"If I decide to go," I said. "I haven't entirely committed to going through with it yet."

"Danny's right, though. You're bound to take some flak, if and when you get back."

"There's no doubt we'll have to lay low for a while."

I pushed my plate away and leaned back.

"In any case, I'll give you a thousand dollars and pay your legal fees if something should go wrong."

Tony looked at Danny and back at me.

"What if I end up doing time?"

"I don't see why you would. The only trouble we're likely to have is getting blown out of the sky, or when we take the chopper back, neither of which need involve you. But I'll be square with you, no matter what."

"How do I know that?"

I looked at Danny.

"It's okay, Tony. He has the money."

"What if you get busted? Or even dusted? Then what?"

"I'll give you a note and the name of a friend. He knows where the money is. He'll take care of you. As to prisons and doing time, you'll have to make up your own mind on that one."

I waited.

"Make it two grand and you've got a deal."

"All right." We shook hands. "I have the compressor, air hose and generator down there already."

I dug out two hundred dollars and handed it to him.

"I'd like you to call around and find the right paint. I'll phone you Sunday night with my decision. Stick around the house, okay?" He nodded.

Then I went over everything Danny should tell Kip on Sunday and had him repeat it for good measure. When I felt confident we were all on the same page, I paid the bill and followed Tony and Danny outside. The last light of day was fading in the western sky. They went one way. I went the other.

On the way back to Jake's, I bought an ice chest and a few cases of beer, figuring it was the best way to keep the troops off the hard whiskey.

Stan had a nice campfire going when I pulled up. A half empty bottle of bourbon sat next to Stan, but it appeared he and Bart were under control. Jake had passed out in a sitting position, his chin on his chest.

"He'll never rot," I said.

"Actually, I'm surprised he doesn't catch fire," Stan said.

I laughed.

"How are you doing, Bart?"

"Good, Clay. What did you bring us?"

"A couple of cases of cold beer."

"Aw, you see, Stan. You had no cause to be disparaging his name the way you did."

"All right, I take it all back. Now let's see the beer."

Bart took care of the cooler while I unloaded the rest of the supplies. I stacked the 2x4's, grabbed my own beer and sat against the pile.

"Well, gentlemen, everything else is set. We'll finish up the cover tomorrow and drive back to town."

"What the hell day is it, anyway?" Stan said.

"Saturday," I said and drank.

"Saturday night," Bart said. "We could be having a lot more fun than this."

Stan eyed him once and went back to watching the fire.

"All things considered," Stan said. "This is a helluva nice place."

We watched the sparks jump off the dry mesquite and into the surrounding night. It was dark away from the fire; quiet with a lot of stars.

"Yeah, we could turn something like this into a little paradise. Christ, I was reading in the Whole Earth catalogue the other day. You can turn your own crap into energy, enough to run a little village. Cars, TV's, the whole works."

He looked at us, shaking his head.

"Can you imagine it? The world's poisoning itself to death because of a goddamned doo-doo complex."

Bart and I simultaneously tossed our empty beer cans at him.

"All right, you sonsabitches. You're just lazy like the rest of them."

It was quiet for a spell.

"I'd be happy to have one love affair work out all right."

"Talk about dreaming," Stan said.

"It's a nice thought," Bart said.

"We're inclined to screw things up," Stan said. "It's in our nature."

"Well I've got a perfect track record so far," I said.

Stan shrugged and it was quiet again.

"I guess having a chance to get things right is all a guy can ask," Bart said.

Jake came to with a jolt, counted heads suspiciously, had a snort and quickly passed out again. I got up and replenished our beers.

"What'll it be like?" I asked Stan as I sat down. He glanced up at me once and went back to warming his hands over the fire.

"You mean the break-out?"

He looked up again and I nodded.

"Oh, nothing. Just a long ride down and about five minute's worth of fireworks."

"You think it will be that easy."

"Should be. What do you think, Bart?"

"We went up against five-shack gook villages that were packing more fire power than these boys. What do you figure, Stan, M-1's?"

I nodded, and so did Stan.

"Quit worrying about it, Clay. The moment will come soon enough. Just pretend this is your last night on Earth."

We were mostly quiet after that.

Later, we helped Jake over to his shack. I crawled into my tent and tried to get some sleep. Stan's words kept going around in my head.

The canyon was miserably cold in the morning. A mist lay over the stream. We had breakfast by the fire and went right back to work. The sun eventually cleared the mountain and the day grew hot. All three of us took off our shirts again.

With the frame completed, we spread the canvas on the ground along its backside, leaned some of the extra 2X4s against the framework for a ramp and used the attached ropes to slide the canvas up and over the top. Several times we shifted positions in order to pull at some place that was lagging behind. When it was done, we stood back to admire our handiwork.

"We'll have to do it faster than that, Stan," I said.

"Yeah but I don't want any ropes closer to the center. Not with those blades whipping around."

"We can wax the top rails," Bart said. "That should help. And the extra bodies."

"Yeah," Stan said. "That and the adrenalin should do the trick."

I looked back at the cover. It was over sixty feet long and forty feet wide. The canvas must have weighed half a ton.

Jake had wandered over cautiously as we spoke, like he was coming up on an elephant.

"What in the blazes is that fer?" he asked me. "Ya expectin' an army."

"No, no," I said.

He scrutinized me, no doubt wishing he had his shotgun back. Given what I was about to tell him, that was the last thing I wanted. Either way, it was time to get things out in the open.

"It's for a helicopter," I said.

"A helicopter?! Why ya no good lyin' tinhorn! Ya never said nothin' about no helicopter!"

He stomped the ground and waited for a response. When I didn't answer, he turned and marched back off towards his shack.

"Ya can have yer money back. Every damned last cent of it."

After getting things stored safely away under the cover and making a final inventory, we went to check on Jake. He had a fresh bottle of Wild Turkey beside him on the front porch. All of us joined him out of the hot sun.

A dust devil spun to life down by the stream. There was the usual dry chatter of insects out in the brush. Otherwise, the canyon was quiet.

Sitting next to Jake, I put my arm around his shoulder. He looked up from under his hat like I had sold him a bum horse.

"I'm a damn fool, that's what I am. I should a known better than to trust a bunch of hippies."

"Take it easy, old timer. You'll be glad you met us before it's all through."

"I'll be glad when the whole lot a ya's gone. That's when I'll be glad."

I looked at Stan. He shrugged. Maybe I had sold Jake a bum horse. The poor old guy just wanted the world to leave him alone, but I had tried that, and it wouldn't. I resolved to do something extra special for Jake and got back to the business at hand. When the truck was ready, I leaned against it and looked at Stan and Bart.

"Do we dare leave him the shotgun?"

"Sure, what the hell? It's his spread."

"Bart? You're the one he's going to see first."

Bart retrieved the gun from the mineshaft and gave it to Jake. Jake cradled it across his lap without saying a word. Bart leaned over and patted him on the back.

"I'll be back tomorrow afternoon, old timer. Keep an eye on things in the meantime."

Jake nodded. We climbed into the cab and headed for town.

51

Back at the motel, I went over the list of supplies with Stan and Bart one last time. They went off to get some sleep. I returned to my own room. The day was miserably hot but I had no desire to hear the drone of an air-conditioner right then and filled the bathtub with cold water.

Having cooled myself down, I lay naked on the bed. The afternoon seemed as empty as my thoughts. Maybe it was the other way around. Either way, I was unable to turn off my head. The mission had taken on a life of its own; bigger than me now, bigger than Kip, bigger than helicopters. Turning back no longer seemed to be an option. Considering what the attorney had told me, that would have been best for all concerned; make sure Kip was as comfortable as possible and go someplace far away until the war was over. Forget all these desperate deeds.

Wisdom evaded me like a breeze. I searched and searched for Jijiwa's mountain but could not find it.

Unable to find one moment of peace, I dressed and went out to call Caroline from the phone booth. I longed to hear her voice. I longed to tear away all the emptiness between us. I had no reason to think she would be home at that hour but had to try.

Mrs. Leroux answered the phone.

"I take it you're still in Tucson helping your friend, Clay?"

"Yes," I said.

"I see…Well, I suppose you were calling to talk with Caroline."

"Yes, is she there?"

"No, actually. Something completely unexpected happened."

"Yeah? What's that?"

"A man she had met through one of her classes invited her to work on a movie set. Oh, what do they call it?"

"On location."

"Yes, that's it. Caroline was beside herself when she left. I can't begin to tell you how excited she was."

"Yeah, that's great news. So where did she go?"

"Someplace in Colorado. Let's see, I have the information here somewhere...I assumed you'd want to know."

"Sure."

I opened the phone booth to let out some of the heat. A cowboy was staring at me from a billboard across the street, a sneer on his face, a cigarette in his mouth. The image had faded in the desert sun. The paper had begun to peel away.

I waited.

"Yes, here it is. The post office box is in Durango but I understand the actual shooting location is about ten miles north of there, up in the mountains."

"How long will she be gone?"

"She said about six weeks, but they told her to expect anything."

"When did she leave?"

"Just today. It all happened so fast. I can't tell you how excited she was."

I sneered back at the billboard. I had never been all that fond of cowboys.

"Clay, are you there?"

"Yes, yes, I'm still here."

"You sound troubled."

"Your daughter seems so far away now."

"Well, I suspected something had gone on between the two of you. She had that determined look, like she was forging off on her own again."

"Yeah, and maybe it's best to leave things that way."

"Well, you've got your own problems, Clay, but it's a long road and only time will tell if you two were meant to be together."

"Yeah."

"Are ready for the information then?"

"Oh yeah. Go ahead."

I jotted down the location, exchanged a few more pleasantries with Mrs. Leroux and rang off, wishing she hadn't been so damned gleeful about the whole thing.

Back in my room, I lay on the bed with the images flitting through my head. Caroline rubbing shoulders with the movie crowd, a career, going places in the world. My life was like a bad road movie in comparison. I ate out of cans and slept in the backseat of my car. All I needed was a mangy looking dog.

I decided a bar would be a good place to nurse my feelings and went next door to inform Stan and Bart.

"What's the matter, Clay?" Stan asked me. "Looks like you swallowed the canary."

"Did you want to join me for a beer or not, Stan?"

"It's women trouble, Bart. What do you think?"

"Only one thing makes a man look like that."

"Drop it, gentlemen."

I walked out and climbed into the Nova. Stan and Bart came outside the door to their motel room.

"Big women trouble," Stan said.

"Yes or no?" I said out the window.

"We'd better keep an eye on him, Stan."

"Yeah. Better keep an eye on him."

We had polished off the first pitcher before they bothered to try me again.

"Looks like you're feeling a little better there, Clay," Bart said.

"Yeah, fucking terrific."

"Maybe you ought to get it off your chest," Stan said.

I filled my glass and ordered another pitcher.

"She didn't run off with some other guy, did she?"

"Who knows?"

They looked at each other and shrugged.

"Well, either she did or she didn't," Stan said.

"She went off to work on a movie set up in Durango."

They looked at each other again.

"Hell, that's it?"

"Yeah, that's it, Stan."

I glared when he began to chuckle.

"Take it easy, Clay."

"I'm minding my own business."

"You said she's a good woman, didn't you, Clay?"

"Sure, but put yourself in that situation."

"Men and women are no different," Bart said. "You trust someone or you don't."

"Then I guess I don't trust her."

The beer came and I poured the glasses full.

"Gentlemen, the mission is on."

I held up my mug, but they didn't.

"This is beginning to have a tragic air about it, Clay."

"You just worry about flying the helicopter, Stan."

"Sure. Just wondering why you're so eager all of a sudden."

"I've got one thing worth doing in this life. Now let's get it done."

He and Bart watched me pour the glasses full. When I ordered another pitcher, they were still quietly nursing their last beer.

Back at the motel, I called to give Tony the word and tried to get some sleep. There wasn't much of it and I felt like hell the next morning.

I rang the sheriff first thing from the phone booth.

"It's on," I told him.

"And what if I say no?"

"Hell, we can all go to prison."

"And I believe you're just about that crazy."

"I know I am. But this is one thing that's going to get done and the ball's rolling."

There was a long silence.

"Did you get your friend a haircut?"

"Don't worry yourself, sheriff. I'll take care of my end."

"I'm plenty worried. I don't want these sonsabitches seein' me elbow to elbow with no goddamned hippies. I've made a career of puttin' 'em behind bars."

"I'm well aware of your history, sheriff."

"All right, what time?"

"Eight a.m.," I said.

"I'll be in the parking lot at the airport waiting."

"I suppose we'd better keep this out of the family circles for a while yet."

"You bet your ass we will."

I rang off and called Danny. He had been down to see Kip on Sunday. Kip was onboard. Apparently ten years wasn't going to fly by so quickly after all. Kip knew that if he didn't hear gunfire by the end of the visit on Wednesday, we had called it off. Either way, he was to be prepared.

I showered and drove over to Tony's place. Stan and Bart followed me in the truck. Everyone shook hands and started piling Tony's tools in the bed.

"Did you find the paint?" I asked him.

"It's right here."

Tony pointed at two cardboard flats. We hoisted them into the truck.

"It wasn't easy. I had to make several calls before I got a factory rep. There are a number of different color combinations but it's all standardized."

"Anybody ask any questions?"

"The rep had a few, but nothing to worry about. The other colors I mixed myself. I figured nobody would be matching tints and shades with a lot of guns going off."

Bart was behind the wheel, drumming his fingers. I had one last look at everything. Besides the paint, there were five full jerry cans, some extra sleeping bags, three more ice chests and enough food, beer and ice to last a week. Tony climbed in the cab. I went over to the driver's window.

"You remember how to get there?"

"Sure," Bart said.

"See you tomorrow, then."

He gave us a thumbs-up and drove off. I climbed in the Nova with Stan and headed back to town.

"Let's get some breakfast," I said.

Stan looked me over.

"Sure you can eat with that broken heart of yours?"

"Up yours, Stan."

"That's all right, Clay, old buddy. You'll be glad to see me yet."

He leaned back in the seat and slapped his hands behind his head.

"It's not life until you've lived it."

I thought, great, that's all I need, Stan waxing philosophical on me.

We had breakfast and I took him over to the university. Later, we went to see an early matinee. Stan picked a low-budget motorcycle film. Jack Nicholson had a minor role. I thought he was the only good thing about it. Stan liked all the motorcycles and orgies. It was very hot and bright outside when we left the theater.

"Up for a beer?" Stan asked me.

"Sure."

I drove back to Danny's Hideaway and we made ourselves comfortable in a far corner of the tavern. A couple of bikers got out of control, but some chick got between them and things calmed down, at least for the moment. I refilled the mugs.

"Just like the movies," I said.

"Yeah," Stan said. "Damn this beer tastes good on a hot day."

We drank and kept a cautious eye on the bikers.

"What do you think our chances are, Stan?"

"You already asked me that."

"No, really. What do you think?"

He pushed his mug aside.

"Let me tell you a little story, and this is after I'd been in 'Nam a few years. I dropped into a green LZ one day, six fresh grunts in tow and a week's R&R waiting for me in Thailand. Something told me to pull out, but I went in anyway."

He drank from his beer and looked around before continuing.

"It was an ambush. I spent two hours in a firefight, trapped inside the chopper, a bullet in my leg and a broken arm. By the time reinforcements came, I was the only one left alive. My buddies died trying to save me."

"And your point it?"

Stan drank again.

"The point is, you just never know what's going to happen in the business of war."

"What do you think our chances are?"

"Oh hell, pretty damn good. Bart'll clean the place out before they know what hit 'em. I'd be more concerned about things on this side of the border."

"I expect the place will be swarming."

"Yeah, it might get a bit dicey but, shit, it's a lot of territory to cover and they've only got so many pricks to chase after us."

I finished my beer.

"You think I'm nuts for doing this, Stan?"

He poured our glasses full and took a sip.

503

"Probably, but it makes more sense than that goddamned war I was in. I can tell you that much."

"Think so?" I said.

"I know so."

I took the suds off the top of my beer, thinking I liked Stan, but still not understanding how he was so certain about things. I knew I wasn't. Our eyes met.

"It's all the same, isn't it, Stan? People don't agree, so they fight?"

"Maybe, but it don't matter. You do it because you believe it's a good thing and if you have to fight, you fight."

"I hope I feel that way afterwards."

Stan resumed his reconnaissance of the bar without answering me. Everything was viewed through a thick pall of smoke. A couple of rough looking Mexicans came in off the street. There was a brilliant flash of light and a blast of heat before the door closed behind them.

"You ever wonder why this life had to come with so much pain?"

"Why don't you ask those two bikers over there?"

"They'd probably kick the shit out of me for asking."

Stan smiled.

"Death is probably painless enough."

I nodded and went back to drinking my beer.

"I was thinking of Hawaii," I said.

"That was a helluva time, wasn't it?"

"Like the early days. Before politics made a mess of everything."

"It was the psychedelics," he said. "Never should have stopped taking those psychedelics."

I suddenly felt very empty.

"I wonder, if people change, why doesn't the world change with it?"

"You're a poor, dumb son of a bitch."

"Why's that?" I said.

"You ask too many questions that don't have an answer."

"Think so?"

He nodded. We drank in silence. The bar maid came to check on us later. Stan nodded at her and she went to retrieve another pitcher.

"Why are you doing this, Stan? Really."

He looked over at me.

"Are you looking for ultimate causes here?"

"I'm always looking for ultimate causes."

"You are a poor, dumb son of a bitch."

"I've already admitted to that." He said nothing. "So?"

"I don't know. Maybe because it's a war I can win?"

"Do you feel that badly about 'Nam?"

"I wouldn't have, if it wasn't for all you goddamned hippies."

"Yeah, we screwed things up pretty good for you, didn't we?"

"It was a pretty goddamned simple world before you fuckers came along, that's right."

I drank from my beer.

"Yeah, well I had some pretty simple fucking dreams until you and your war came along."

"Yeah, we kind of fucked up that hippie shit, didn't we?"

"Yeah you did."

Stan was studying his beer. I was studying him.

"You think maybe you're just trying to make up for what happened over there in 'Nam?"

He looked over at me.

"You won't let up on a guy, will you?"

"I feel like it's my fault that Kip's in that prison. I'm trying to imagine your reasons for getting involved."

"Maybe so. It left a pretty bad taste in my mouth. That's for sure."

"Are there any good wars, Stan?"

"Let me ask you a question. You feel like dusting a few Mexicans after what you went through?"

"The thought has occurred to me."

"And would it make this world a better place?"

"No...Probably only make it worse."

"Then you know a little bit about how I feel."

I nodded and worked on my beer.

We went to have some grub once the day had cooled down, got back to the motel and packed it in early. It was Monday night. Visiting day was on Wednesday. By this time the following night, we'd be in knee deep. By the same time the night after that, we'd be up to our asses in trouble, with no turning back.

505

52

I heard someone pounding on the door and pulled the covers over my head, ready to kill whoever was out there. Thankfully the pounding stopped. With a quick look over my shoulder, I saw a faint light in the sky through the window curtains. The sun was still a dream on the eastern horizon. I could have slept for a thousand years.

A few moments later, the pounding resumed.

"Goddamn it! Who's there!?" I called out from the bed.

"It's the Pope, who do you think it is!?"

Pissed, I got up and opened the door for Stan. He was already showered and ready for battle.

"Close the door," I told him and climbed back into bed.

"Where the hell do you think you're going, soldier?"

I heard the bathroom door knock against the wall and the shower come on. Stan yanked the covers off me. He had all the lights on. Steam billowed out of the bathroom.

"Get your skinny white ass into the shower or I'll put you on recon."

Reluctantly, I crawled out of bed and headed for the bathroom.

Standing under the hot water, my doubts resumed. This going to war was a lousy idea. No one was making me do it. Like Stan that day in 'Nam, something was telling me not to take the chopper in.

Then I remembered my friend Kip and what I had told Caroline. I would have to live with my choice for the rest of my life. It was only a matter of bullets and how long it took you to die, when cowardice would live with you for the rest of your life.

I dried off and dressed next to the bed. Stan watched me.

"All right, let's get something to eat," he said when I was done.

"I'm not hungry."

"You never go to battle on an empty stomach."

I followed him out the door and across the street to the cafe. When the food arrived, I went through the motions with my eggs.

"You eat the son of a bitch. You don't play with it."

"Yes sir."

I looked at my watch and back at Stan. It was seven o'clock. He wasn't going to like what I had to say next. I waited until he had mopped up the last of the eggs with an English muffin before I threw it at him.

"We need to stop and get you a haircut."

"Like hell we do."

"I'm serious."

"So am I."

I worked on the tension in my forehead.

"The sheriff figures it's not going to look so good, him flying off with a couple of hippies."

"Well, good, he's only got one. And a redneck kid."

He nodded at me with his chin.

"Stan, come on, it's important."

"So's the hair."

"You don't think someone's going to be snooping around when this thing blows up?"

"So what?"

"So, the first place they're going to start looking is at the airport. However it comes down, you're going to stick out like a cat in the aviary."

"So to hell with them."

"Stan, remember. This is for Kip."

"You son of a bitch."

"I know. So, are you ready?"

"I swore."

"I know you did. Now let's go. We're running out of time."

"We're talking military style, aren't we?"

"Pretty much."

"And you knew this all along, didn't you?"

"For a few days."

"You rotten bastard."

"I know."

He walked with me down to a barbershop and took a seat without saying another word. When it was over, we headed for the airport. A delicate silence existed between us. I hated seeing it more than he did and chose my words judiciously.

"It's a nice, clean look, Stan."

"Shut up."

"I'm speaking from experience."

He gave me a quick once over.

"You're the one who said it. We're in the army now."

He eyed me again, not liking the taste of crow.

At the airport, we found the sheriff waiting for us. It looked like everyone had been to the same barber.

"Sheriff, this is Stan. Stan, Sheriff Prescott." The sheriff shook his hand with the manner of someone who was going to wash it afterward.

"Well, I'll say this much, you sure got him a haircut."

Stan walked off.

"We'd best leave that alone, sheriff."

I leaned on the hood of his car.

"Same story?" I said.

"Yeah, I got in touch with someone up on the reservation. They'll cover for us, if the time comes. But it'll take some money."

"If the time comes, I'll take care of them."

Stan wandered back over, reflexively rubbing his sideburns.

"Who do they think Stan is?"

"I told 'em he was a free-lance pilot. They don't give a shit how we met."

"And me?"

"You're the guide."

"Where are we taking you?"

"Around the back side of Mt. Lemmon. Now, if you're done askin' questions, let's get this thing over with."

"All right, after you."

"Now, wait a minute. They want a two thousand dollar deposit."

The sheriff watched with great interest as I pulled a roll of bills from my pocked and counted out the two grand. Stan went over to have a look at the chopper before following the sheriff and me into the office. With the owner filling out forms, Stan showed him his pilot's license. Stan signed the paperwork and the owner handed him a copy. We were turning to leave when the owner hit Stan with a question.

"One thing I was wondering. Why did you want the twin-turbine model? You won't really need it up there on San Carlos."

The owner looked at the sheriff and back at Stan. There was a long pause. Everyone was waiting for Stan to say something.

"Would you drive a Fiat when you could drive a Ferrari?" he said.

The owner laughed and patted Stan on the shoulder.

"Yeah, I suppose that's true enough. Well, have a good time and we'll see you in a few days."

"Depending on the hunting."

"Right. And don't forget to call if you get delayed."

Stan gave him a thumbs-up and we headed for the door. The owner watched from inside as we retrieved our gear. The sheriff had three rifles in buckskin covers. I had an assortment of camping gear in the Nova. With everything packed away, Charlie got up front with Stan. I climbed in back and slid the door closed.

A moment later, I heard the turbines kick over. The whine ascended to a high pitch. The whop-whop-whop of the rotor blades was chopping that sound to pieces.

Stan leaned over to say something to Charlie. I saw their lips moving but could not make out a word they were saying.

Stan called the tower, waved to the owner one last time and lifted off. The chopper banked to the north and climbed to 1500 feet in a rush. The fine homes up on Old Spanish Trail came into view, along with the downtown district and the south side. I saw the barren outskirts out by Wagon Wheel Drive. Success and failure were that close together when you looked down at them from the proper height.

Stan followed the highway past Old Tucson, then leaned into Mt. Lemmon. We were quickly around to the backside. The sheriff pointed to an open field about halfway up the mountain and Stan took us in for a landing. We were halfway between Catalina and Oracle. A trail led up from the plateau and a squad car was waiting there for the sheriff. He squeezed himself out and leaned over reflexively, holding onto his cowboy hat. I crawled around front and shouted over the noise.

"I'll call you when we get back."

"I guess I'd better wish you good luck."

"You know what they say sheriff."

"I don't give a shit what they say. Just get your ass back here. And remember what I told you."

"You've done your part, sheriff. If the shit hits the fan, I'll take the flak."

"You bet your ass you will."

I nodded and closed the door. When the sheriff was safely inside the squad car, Stan pulled back on the joy-stick, his feet and hands moving about in this strange mechanical dance. I gripped my seat and struggled with the sensation of my head and guts exchanging places. Stan clipped treetops, dove in and out of the canyons and continued to angle south. The mountain was on our right. A few housing developments dotted the dusty plain in the other direction.

When it was time to leave the cover of the mountain, Stan climbed out of a steep canyon and dove into the San Pedro River valley, where we could mostly stay under the radar from Davis-Monthan Air Force Base. If anyone saw us, it was a rancher or a stray hunter. Stan had done everything he could to steer clear of civilization.

Crossing Interstate 10, he turned west into the Coronado National Forest, climbed up the backside of Miller Peak and dropped like a hawk into Jake's hideout. We were safely on the ground, but I felt a part of me was still plummeting from five thousand feet. Stan cut the engines and climbed out. I followed him on wobbly feet. Tony and Bart were there waiting for us.

I caught a glimpse of Jake kicking dirt and shouting something out in front of his shack. Either he'd had too much whiskey or not enough. It was hard to tell which one from that distance.

"I told you we didn't need any more rope," Stan shouted at Bart.

He shrugged and threw me the additional line he had attached. With Tony's help, the cover performed gracefully and was a fine canopy in less than a minute. With a few more bodies we could do it in closer to thirty seconds. Everyone stood under the cover in near darkness.

"How about hitting the lights," Stan said.

Tony kicked over the generator and the lights came on. The spinning blades cast a shadow on the canvas above. There was four feet of clearance. One mistake and the canvas could easily sag into the rotor. It was hard to imagine the consequences of that much torque meeting that much resistance but you knew it wouldn't be pretty. Bart and I studied this.

"Looks okay," I said.

"Just make damn sure nobody lets go of their rope," he said.

He looked over at Stan and back at me.

"By the way, who's the new recruit?"

Tony chuckled. I cleared my throat.

"Careful or I'll leave you in Hermosillo, partner."

"Forgetting who saved your ass in 'Nam?"

Stan eyed Bart without another word.

The blades came to a halt and we gathered together beside the chopper.

"May as well get to it," I said.

"May as well," Tony agreed and handed out the sandpaper. "Not too much. Scuff her up easy, just so the paint will stick."

Tony arranged things with the compressor and paint. We masked off everything with old newspaper. When that was done, Tony hooked up his pot to the air hose and started to spray. The rest of us went outside to wait.

Fifteen minutes later, we rejoined Tony. The first coat was done. The chopper looked military green. I went over to look more closely. From a few feet, you could still make out the original colors.

"We don't want any more than that," Tony said. The less paint, the faster it'll come off."

He was already mixing the next color.

"This is going to stand out like a sore thumb in the desert. You know that."

"I know but we'll be hiding up in the mountains."

"You're the boss."

He went back to straining his paint.

"Can't say how this is going to turn out. Never painted military camouflage before."

"Anything close. We're just trying to fool the Mexicans."

"It'll be close," he said. He waited half an hour, sprayed some black here and there; then later some tan.

511

It was getting on towards sunset when Tony said it was safe to strip off the masking. Ten minutes later, we were down to the final pieces of newspaper. I climbed down and headed for the opening.

"Hey Clay," Bart called out. "What's for supper?"

"Pork and beans." There was grumbling. I walked over by the shack. The late afternoon was turning to dusk.

With an eye on surprising the troops, I had purchased some steaks to go with the beans, and also a couple of cartons of potato salad. I hadn't forgotten Stan's words. This might well be our last supper.

I got the fire going and grilled the steaks in an iron skillet. We would be down to eating out of cans after this and lucky to have it.

The sun disappeared behind the mountains and darkness fell quickly. I lit a couple of lanterns. Everyone spoke quietly over the meal and gave the subject of our mission a wide berth. Mostly, I listened to tales about cars and women, as these were the things that engaged men's hearts. The cars they could control and the women they couldn't. Occasionally, it was the other way around.

We turned in early and were up with dawn. I gave Bart a hand with the heavy box while Stan and Tony pulled the seats out of the back of the chopper.

Bart unlocked the big wooden box and revealed the assortment of military weaponry inside: a tear gas launcher, automatic weapons and, most prominent of all, an M-60 machine gun. Bart adapted the latter item to the bolt holes from the seat brackets, loaded several straps of bullets into the chopper and fed one of them into the gun for my edification. The tear gas launchers were taped under a bench along one wall of the cabin. Two automatic weapons were shoved into a small closet. Numerous rounds of ammunition followed. Bart then closed and locked the box. He looked at Jake sitting in front of the shack. Jake had run out of whiskey and steam about the same time. He had a beer and the shotgun in his lap.

"I'd hate to see him get into this weaponry," Bart said.

"He seems to have accepted what's going on," I said.

"Wait till he finds out the truth."

"Yeah, you're right. Let's hope he doesn't get into that box."

"Anyway, I guess that's it, brother."

Bart leaned against the M-60.

It was noon and everything was ready. We would be leaving in a short while. The idea was to blast in around three; not too near the end of the visit, but as late as possible, knowing we would have to ditch somewhere until dark. We had an hour and a half left to stare at each other.

"Let's go over everything again," I said to Stan.

"Hell, we've been over it a dozen times. What do you want to do, go over it backwards?"

"It couldn't hurt."

"You said there's four guards?"

"That's all I could see."

"That's all I need to know. As soon as we get a visual fix, you tell me where the front gate is and we'll do the rest."

I looked at Bart.

"You can take it from butch, here," he said.

Stan kicked Bart in the ass.

"Take it easy, Clay," Bart said. "When those banditos get a load of this .60 caliber, they'll be crawling all over each other to get out of the way."

Bart gave it an affectionate pat on the muzzle.

"Come on, let me give you a lesson on firing an M-16. That'll keep you busy."

He pulled one of the weapons out of the closet and tossed it to me from five feet. I looked it over, surprised by the weight. Bart brought a clip with him.

"You know anything about guns?"

"Never shot one in my life."

"It's a helluva time to start." He took the clip and shoved it home with a snap. "That's how you want to reload. No pussyfooting around."

He showed me how to remove it and had me practice.

"That's good. Just remember, when you hold down the trigger, it doesn't stop to ask questions."

"It would cut a man in two."

"That's right."

"Wow, I don't know if I could do it."

"When it's your life or someone else's, you will."

I stared at the gun and shook my head.

"Don't worry yourself about it. If anyone's stupid enough to shoot back, there won't be enough left of them to make two halves."

He patted the M-60 again.

Tony came over and asked some questions. I watched the wind stir in the trees down by the stream. The talk turned to hunting. Stan had been resting against one of the skids, half listening to the conversation and suddenly got up.

"Time for battle, gentlemen."

No one moved at first.

"Grab the ropes," Bart said. I got to my feet slowly and went around to the back of the cover. It was hard to imagine the appearance of this thing from the air. I looked up the steep canyon walls. On a fly by at six, seven thousand feet, the cover should blend right in with the desert terrain. If things went well, no one would have reason to come any closer.

Stan kicked over the turbines. I walked over to the shack with Tony and gave him half his pay, along with a note.

"Jake?"

"Trouble. That's all yer about is trouble."

"Jake, Tony needs your help while we're gone."

"I ain't helpin' nobody."

"I know this has been more than you expected. I'll pay you accordingly when we return."

"Ya couldn't give me enough fer all the trouble yer worth."

I looked back at Tony.

"I'm counting on you. Just be waiting for us when we make it back. If we don't, you know what to do."

"Good luck," he said.

I shook his hand and ran back to the chopper.

It was one-thirty but it looked like high noon in the desert. I climbed in front. Bart stretched out on the bench seat in back. Stan took us up easy at first, banking over his right shoulder, but once he had cleared the cottonwoods down by the stream, he wrenched us upwards in a fierce climb towards the southern peaks. Where my uncertainties left off and the wild feelings of inertia began, I quickly lost track, but Caroline flashed through my thoughts, along with a bit of the old tenderness. It was hard to imagine it, but I might never see her again.

On the far side of Millers Peak, Stan turned southeast and skirted over the ridges that fell away to our left. Eventually, we came to a deep canyon crossing the border and he nose-dived down into the bottom of it, following its sandy wash all the way into Mexico. On the south side of Cananea, he rose quickly back into the mountains, then jumped over into the Rio Sonora Valley at the first low point in the peaks. The valley was green and fertile beneath us.

Stan hugged the mountain as before, stayed low in the canyons and did everything he could to minimize our visibility. As the miles flew, I remembered how I had marched for days to travel the same distance. Now there was hardly time to have a handful of thoughts.

I glance over at Stan and saw the matter-of-fact look in his eyes. He had been in this place a hundred times before. It was not a time for hope. It was a time for resignation. You went and if your time was up, you didn't come back. Worrying and being afraid were pointless, but I had no other names for what I felt.

Just south of Huepac, I pointed and Stan jumped over the mountain into the San Miguel Valley, reversing the route I had taken on my journey north. I pointed down into the narrow canyon where I had nearly fallen to my death. Stan nodded and gave me a thumbs-up. That was where we would hide on the way back, assuming we made it that far.

Moments later, we were dashing down the San Miguel River and I began to think of all that could go wrong. What if they had cancelled the visit? What if they had thrown Kip in the hole for something? What if they knew and were waiting for us? And still it didn't matter. You went and if you did not come back, that would be the end of any concerns you might have.

Another ten minutes and we crossed the road from Carbo to Rayon. Two old trucks ambled along, one going in either direction. An old man and his children pointed as we crossed the open valley at one hundred feet. There were no signs of military vehicles, only these poor families who would think it strange to see a Yankee helicopter and go on about their business, as this had nothing to do with their lives.

Once past that crossroads, the hills along the San Miguel quickly rose up around us. Stan kept low, pushing one-fifty. I checked my watch, less than twenty minutes now. The night I had plodded heavily up this river came back to my thoughts. Caroline had been on my mind and I thought of her now.

Ten minutes later, we barreled out from between the steep canyon walls with the lake straight ahead of us. Hermosillo was in the distance. Sensing it was time, Bart came up and squatted between the seats.

"You hanging in there, Clay?" he said.

I nodded. He patted me on the knee. We were five minutes away now, everything moving fast, beginning ahead with a slow expansion of proportions, exploding in a blur of vision at our sides and unraveling into the past behind us.

Stan rose slightly to clear a row of trees at the edge of a lake, then dropped down so close to the blue water, it seemed as if I could feel the coolness through the seat of my pants. There was a nod between all three of us and we slipped on our ski masks.

Bart nudged me with his elbow and pointed to the people below us in their boats. All of them had paused to look up at our swift passing. Stan's attention was riveted on the horizon and town up ahead, his hands and feet constantly feathering the controls as he stared that way.

At the far end of the lake, he rose up again to clear the trees and continued in a slow ascent with the lay of the land. The prison was on the hill directly ahead of us, five miles away. Everywhere beneath us there were tin shacks, abandoned cars and poverty. Children jumped and waved as we flew by.

The prison sat atop its hill, a grim fortress firmly dug into the rock. A guard turret rose at each corner. The barred window openings were there, looking out over the desert. The women's block and northern foundation descended down the hill.

Stan stayed low enough to clip antennas off the passing rooftops. Bart went back and slammed open the cargo door. The controlled temperature rushed out. The dry desert heat rushed in. Stan turned off the air-conditioning and looked quickly over his shoulder at me.

"There, you see the road coming up from the west?" I shouted.

Stan nodded.

"And that's the main gate, where the van is parked."

"Where are the other two guard stations?" he shouted back.

"Directly opposite. You can barely see the tops of their turrets."

He nodded. We were a quarter-mile out now.

"You ready for battle there, Clay?"

"Yeah." I looked again at the prison. "What do you think?"

"Piece of cake," Stan said with a look back at Bart. They nodded at each other and looked back at me.

"Piece of cake."

53

Stan circled the base of the hill, positioned the chopper in line with the parking lot and began his ascent. Bart had the tear gas loaded. At the last second, Stan gave the collective lever full pitch and we popped up like a balloon, looking at the main gate from across the parking lot.

Bart got off two rounds of tear gas and hit the adjacent turrets with precision. The guards stumbled out of their towers.

"Clay!" Bart shouted.

I scurried back to him. He pointed at the front gate. We were looking down the long, arched hallway into the prison. The wooden doors behind the bars were open, as I had expected.

"Have Stan bring me in closer!"

Already aware of the problem, Stan was easing us across the parking lot. Two guards stood at the far end of the hallway, watching us, along with a crowd of prisoners and guests from inside the courtyard. Bart tossed a grenade in a lazy arc towards the gate and everyone scrambled for cover.

"Get up!" Bart yelled and Stan pulled out with a violent rush that quickly had us a few hundred feet in the air.

An explosion rocked the afternoon and a mass of deformed bars appeared out of the smoke below us. Then gunfire erupted.

Bart got the two nearer guards pinned down with the M-60 while Stan brought the chopper in over the courtyard. It was mostly empty now. Only a handful of prisoners had stayed outside to witness this spectacle, and they were huddled near the safety of the recessed hallways. One of them was Joe. I had yet to see Kip, Steve or Kristine. Bart tossed me a loaded M-16.

"Cover me!"

I unloaded an ammo clip in the direction of the far turrets as he loaded more tear gas and hit both of them. The two guards came out, groping their way along the wall.

"Bring her around!"

Stan did a 180 and Bart hit the first two towers again. The entire perimeter was a cloud of smoke and gas.

"Okay, the other gate!"

Bart waited until Stan had brought the chopper directly over it, then dropped the grenade just inside the tunnel.

"Get out!" Bart yelled over my head.

Stan pulled out and over to the front side of the prison. A few seconds later, another blast rocked the day. Stan looked at me.

"You're on, Clay!"

"Okay, lower level! I saw one of them!"

He pulled over the courtyard and eased down until the rotor was nearly kissing the rooftops. With the gate open and half the prison piling out towards the parking lot, it was total chaos below us.

I threw the ladder down but kept it out of reach until Joe was close enough to grab it. About the time he started to climb up, everyone in the chopper got a face full of tear gas. Coughing, I reached blindly for Joe and helped him in.

"Get up!" I yelled to Stan.

He quickly had the chopper out of the haze but the entire cabin was now thick with smoke.

"Where's Kip?!" I asked Joe.

"I don't know."

He was on his knees, coughing. Both of us were coughing.

"What do you mean you don't know?!"

He waved an arm at me.

I pulled the ski mask up over my mouth to filter the gas and leaned out the door, searching for Kip. Tear gas had flooded into all the cells, forcing those inside of them back out into the crowded courtyard. Faces appeared in and out of the smoke but none of them Kip.

Then an alarm went off and echoed across the town.

"Come on, Clay!" Stan yelled back. "You've got one minute!"

He made another turn and I saw Robby.

519

"Lower!" I yelled to Stan and motioned with my hand to show him the direction.

As he eased back down towards the roof, Robby was busy fighting with everyone else to get hold of the ladder. I was inclined to leave the little prick but manipulated the height and location until Robby alone could get his hands on it.

"Hurry, goddamn it!" I yelled down at him.

As he scrambled into the cabin, I noticed Steve and Kristine on the balcony directly below us and motioned for Stan to ease in even closer, then gestured at my neck when he was positioned just right.

Steve helped Kristine get hold of the rope and start her climb. I had my eyes peeled for Kip and was grabbing blindly for Kristine's hand when I heard a gasp, like the wind had been kicked out of her. Kristine's eyes went blank and her hand let go of mine. I lurched out and got hold of her arm before she fell. Joe helped me to drag her up onto the deck. She came face first and completely limp. By the time we had her all the way inside, both Joe and I were wet with blood.

"Goddamn it Bart, someone's unloading on us!"

Bart got back to squeezing off M-60 rounds. Steve had grabbed the ladder as Stan pulled away.

"Hang on!" I yelled. "Someone's on the ladder!"

Stan pulled up just in time to avoid clipping Steve into the roof. While Stan repositioned, we got Steve inside.

"Oh god no," he said, falling to his knees.

I was back to looking for Kip but glanced quickly as Steve turned Kristine over. The bullet had entered just below her ribs in back and exited through her heart in front. She had died in my arms.

"Oh god, no!" Steve kept saying as he gently shook Kristine. "Oh god, no, no, no, no, no."

Meanwhile, rounds were going off everywhere and Bart was returning fire indiscriminately. Stan yelled from in front.

"If you don't find that son of a bitch in fifteen seconds, I'm pulling out."

"Look, I've got to spot him, first. Come around facing east."

He frowned, knowing it left us with no cover, but did as asked. The courtyard below was still a scene of mayhem with half the people fleeing for the exit and the other half hoping to get hold of the ladder, Americans among them, Americans I had come to know during my restless days in the prison, but I callously held it out of their reach. My only thought was to rescue Kip.

Then I saw him and shouted over my shoulder.

"Get down as close as you can to the east end!"

Stan eased back and settled in. Bart came over and crouched next to Steve.

"Let's get her in back," he said gently.

"She's dead," Steve said.

"I know, I know," Bart said. "But we've got to get her out of the way."

"Just leave her in peace, all right?" Steve said.

"Look," Bart said coldly. "Get her out of the way or I'll have to do it for you."

I looked back. Bart was right. We had to clear the area, but it was still jarring, hearing him talk in that way.

Robby helped Steve place her gently in the far corner of the cabin. Steve remained over her body, quietly weeping.

I returned my attention to the courtyard. Kip was so close, I could see the blue in his eyes but he was beneath a balcony and restrained by dozens of other men down there trying to reach the ladder. Bart let off a few rounds but that did nothing to part the crowd. I watched Kip struggling to get free, half out of my mind with the futility of it.

"Come on, Kip! Get the fuck out in the open!"

Then we started taking fire again and a bullet clinked off the skids. Bart had reloaded the M-60 and returned fire but the bullets kept coming. I heard something rip through the fuselage up front.

"I'm getting out of here!" Stan shouted back.

"No! He's right there!"

"Goddamn it, Clay! We're taking fire from both sides!"

Bart nodded at him and Stan pulled out. I rushed forward with Kip growing smaller below us.

"Stan! We can't just leave him there!"

Stan ignored me and continued his climb. I went for the M-16 but Bart pinned me against the cabin wall.

"Goddamn it! Get your hands off me!"

I tried to wrestle free but Bart just held me tighter.

"Take it easy, buddy." He pulled his face mask off with his free hand. "It's over."

Bart stared until he felt certain I had accepted this fact and let go. I pulled off my face mask and went to the door. Stan was climbing and racing north. The prison had been reduced to the size of a matchbox. The sound of sirens filled the afternoon. I saw a line of army trucks moving down the main highway towards the prison. They looked like toy trucks from a distance.

I glanced back at Steve. He had placed his shirt over Kristine's wound. Joe sat against the wall with his head between his legs. Robby sat next to him, staring blankly into space. I looked back at the prison.

"Fuck. We could have had him."

"No, Clay. It was over," Bart said.

"No. We just ran like a bunch of cowards."

Bart grabbed me by the front of my shirt.

"Listen, you stubborn son of a bitch. You do the best you can and that's it. Any longer and we were all going down."

"So what."

"That's crazy talk. You don't think like that in war."

"Yeah? Well I would rather have died courageously than to feel like this."

"And I like living and you can call that whatever you want."

I looked down at Kristine. Bart did too and loosened his grip on me.

"Accept it, Clay. You had to try...so you tried and that's it."

I pulled away and looked out at the lake passing by. Bart reached back and slammed the door shut. Our eyes met before he went forward to sit next to Stan. I saw them talking but didn't care what they had to say. I kept seeing Kip in my mind, struggling to reach the ladder, like in a bad dream.

I cursed under my breath and went over to Steve.

"I'm really, really sorry, man."

"I don't believe she's dead, man. I just don't believe it."

"I know."

He brushed the hair from Kristine's face. I touched her arm. The skin was already growing cold. The little flecks of blood had started to coagulate in the warm air

"What do we do now?" Robby asked.

I shook my head, not knowing what to tell him.

We all rode in silence up the San Miguel Valley, everyone but Steve. He spoke to Kristine through his tears. I stared out the window and tried not to hear.

Five minutes past the road to Carbo, I went forward. A few miles farther ahead, I pointed and Stan banked hard right up a mountain pass. In time, the pass narrowed to a canyon and wound back and forth between a chasm of rock walls rising a thousand feet straight above our heads. A pilot flying by would hardly have a split second to make out the chopper, and that was assuming he had flown overhead in the first place.

Seeing the canyon closed off up ahead, Stan eased the chopper down into the sandy soil, cut the engines and jumped out. Bart jumped out with him. I followed. The blades were slowly whirling to a stop above our heads. Joe and Robby got out last, still uncertain of their freedom.

Stan and Bart were already around front inspecting the damage. I went around to join them. Bart had his finger in a bullet hole.

"We're goddamned lucky," Stan said over the noise.

"Went right past the avionics," Bart said.

They walked around the chopper, looking for more damage. There was one other bullet hole. It had gone in one side of the cargo area and out the other.

"We're goddamned lucky that didn't hit anybody," Bart said.

"Yeah. May as well top her off," Stan said.

Bart went to grab the jerry cans. Stan came over and put his hands on my shoulders.

"I didn't mean to be so hard on you, Clay."

"Yeah, Stan. Tell me about all the shit I need to accept."

"That's what life is, Clay. You do your best and accept the rest." I followed his gaze over my shoulder. Stan dropped his hands.

"Yeah, that's a goddamned shame. She was a beautiful lady. But they made their choices too. You didn't do it for them."

"So now what?" I said.

"We wait. They'll be along soon enough."

"Maybe we won't make it anyway."

He shrugged.

"We've got a better chance than we did a half an hour ago."

Bart came around the chopper with the jerry cans.

"I'll tell you one thing," Stan said. "We're not taking that body back with us."

"What would it matter?"

"Murder one, that's what."

"What the hell difference would it make?"

"Clay, they can try and pin any goddamned thing on us they want, but if we can just get back to the states and get the chopper painted, it won't stick. Even if we don't get it painted, they'd have to prove our involvement and that body in there is about all the evidence they'd need."

I looked inside the cabin. Steve was still sitting beside Kristine, staring off into space now with one hand idly stroking her hair.

"I suppose you're right," I said.

I knew he was. I just didn't like what had to happen because of it.

Stan waited.

"So, do you want to break it to him or should I?"

"No, I'll do it," I said.

"Okay. Get it done. We don't have much time to bury her."

He went to give Bart a hand with the fuel. I trudged back around to the cabin in the sandy soil, weighed down equally by the duty in front of me and the listless heat. Steve's pale face was flush. It was hard to tell where the heat left off and his tears began. His lips were moving as he stared down at Kristine but no sound came out. I stood over him and waited for the right moment.

"Steve," I said quietly.

He looked up at me with a blank stare.

"Steve, we've got to bury her here."

"No," he said, shaking his head

"Steve, it's not an option. It's sure homicide if we take her back."

"No," he said again. His eyes were focused off in the distance.

"I'll give you some time to get right with it but it has to be done."

His focus returned to Kristine lying in his lap, his lips moving again without words.

I walked over to Robby and Joe. Robby was in character: hands in his pockets and feet shifting. Joe just looked miserable. I explained the situation to Robby.

"Do what you can, but if he refuses, we'll have to do it for him."

Robby nodded and headed over to the cabin. I looked at Joe.

"How do you feel?"

"I expected to be a bit happier than this. I imagine you feel even worse."

"I don't know if there are words for how I feel, Joe."

"It would have been better if they had nailed me," he said.

"I've been thinking the same thing about myself."

Steve came out of the chopper, carrying Kristine. He moved heavily through the sand, his cheeks wet with tears. I grabbed the shovel and followed him. Everyone did. We slogged up the narrow trail, towards where I had climbed to freedom but a few weeks ago.

Steve stopped at some unspoken cathedral of rock and vegetation, looked up at the narrow opening of blue sky above us and set Kristine down. I started to dig but Steve took the shovel from me. Joe offered a hand at one point but Steve refused. We stood around for half an hour, watching him.

When Steve was six feet down, he nodded and we gently handed Kristine to him. Steve lowered her into the hole and arranged her arms over her chest. She looked peaceful enough, if that counted for anything.

We hoisted Steve out and gave him some time. The first plane went overhead while we waited. The afternoon heat had begun to fade. I could feel the sweat growing cool under my shirt.

Finally, Steve looked up at us and nodded.

I picked up the shovel and prepared to throw the first shovel of dirt.

"No," Steve said suddenly. "Not like that. We've got to cover her."

"There's a tarp in the chopper," I told Robby.

He ran off to get it. Steve climbed back into the hole and waited. When Robby returned, Steve spread the tarp over the body. We helped Steve back out.

Robby said something about God and eternal peace. Steve wept. The rest of us stood silently and waited.

When there was nothing left to say, I threw one shovelful of dirt in the hole. Everyone did the same and started back towards the chopper. Steve stayed alone to finish the job. When he returned, he was without the shovel. I figured he had left it as a grave marker.

By that time, jets were flying high overhead every few minutes. We could hear the occasional P-38 lumbering up the valley. Our plan was to wait until dark before leaving. Then we would see.

We had food but no one ate it. Words were spoken about what lay ahead and what we could expect but mostly it was quiet.

Somewhere in all the feelings, I remembered the day I had gone to see Stan. I remembered the feeling of apprehension in my gut as I pulled off for the airport and wanted to go back to that moment. I wanted to make that decision all over again. If I had followed my intuition then, if I had gotten back on the freeway, none of this would have happened. I leaned against the helicopter and closed my eyes, haunted by Kristine's death and Steve's sorrow.

The planes came less and less frequently as afternoon faded to dusk. Then darkness fell and they stopped altogether. Stan told us it was time to go. Bart got in front. I started to close the cargo door.

"No, please, leave it open," Steve said. "I'll feel closer to her."

I looked at Bart and he shrugged.

"Okay, Steve, until we pull away."

I backed off and left him alone. The turbines sparked to life. As soon as Stan had full power, he started to climb. Stan had agreed with me. The matter of wide open country aside, it was best to get away from the main highway and over into the Rio Sonora valley. We would skirt the mountain, stay clear of any villages and hope for the best.

Stan climbed to a thousand feet and stopped near the summit, not wanting to bank until Steve was safely inside. Steve had a grip on the door frame and was staring down at Kristine's final resting spot.

Sensing Stan's growing impatience, I reached out to close the door and looked with alarm all around the interior of the helicopter, not believing my senses. In place of a body, the cabin was suddenly empty.

"No fucking way!" Robby said. "No fucking way!"

Bart grabbed hold of him before he could get to the door. I braced myself, reached through the space where Steve had been and slammed the door shut. Stan's gray eyes met mine. The air between us now seemed vaporous and unreal. I nodded and he banked easily over the mountain, heading east.

54

Not a word was spoken on our run to the border. We saw the lights of towns along the river and those of homesteads scattered here and there against the hillsides but all was darkness high up along the mountain ridge. It was a moonless night and nothing disturbed our flight.

I tried to put the image of Steve falling to his death out of my mind but could not. It played over and over like a bad movie. Did I love Caroline that much, to give up my life for her? Was Steve brave to have done it, or simply a fool? I had no answers. Steve had left the rest of us behind to answer those questions. At least you could hope the two of them were together now, however naive that might seem.

I looked over at Joe and Robby in the darkness. Our eyes met briefly before looking away.

Stan was right. We had saved two men, but at the cost of two other very good people, and with having failed to rescue Kip. I had considered death. I had not considered how defeat might feel.

Then Caroline returned to my thoughts. I tried to imagine how she would take the news, if I even bothered to tell her. I doubted I would. Her perceptions of me would only be confirmed. I was a man going from one catastrophe to the next, a man who refused at every turn to seek another man's counsel.

Too, when considering what the attorney had told me, that little more than a long, legal battle awaited me back in the States, the choices which had brought me to this place seemed pointless. As to going back to face those purported crimes, I saw little reason to do so now, and failing that, I could not offer a woman like Caroline any kind of civilized existence.

Life had seemed like a simple matter of honor and courage but a few hours earlier. Now I did not know what to make of it. I had overcome cowardice, only to find disaster and confusion. Perhaps only fools expected to find peace in this world. Relish the battle, Achilles had said, and move on with no thought for the blood you have left behind. That sounded like a grand approach to life, if not for that thing you called a conscience.

I became aware of the drone of the chopper blades and the whine of the turbines as we raced towards the border. There were the stars and blackness and my restless thoughts.

In twenty minutes, we passed above Sinoquipe. The valley narrowed into a canyon and the first searchlight found us. I saw trucks and the spark of ground fire. Stan pulled up higher along the ridge. They would be waiting for us at Arizpe. We had to disappear into the mountains, either east or west. I went up front and crouched between the seats.

"Which way do you like, Clay?" Stan asked me.

"Towards that peak."

I pointed to the northwest where the backbone of the mountains rose up to Caliche.

"Stay on this side," I said.

"Where are you taking me?"

I didn't answer.

Before we reached Caliche, a valley opened up to the east of us. We could see the lights of Arizpe far below. I pointed due north this time.

"Do you see the ridge?"

"Yeah."

"There's a narrow canyon below it."

Stan banked right and shot up the ridge at full throttle. I held on and looked back. Joe and Robby had slid to the back of the cabin.

"You'd better strap in," Stan called out over his shoulder. "It's likely to get rough."

We cleared the ridge and could see a faint glow of lights beyond the next peak, probably from Nogales and the other towns along the border. There were also several cold lights from a plane coming right at us. I braced myself as Stan banked hard left, then did a

528

vertical dive into the next canyon. The bottom dropped out of me. Once he broke out of the dive, I let go of my grip.

"I wasn't so fond of all those pieces anyway."

Stan flashed a fierce look at me and went back to work with the controls. In five minutes, we came to the end of the canyon.

"What now?" he said.

"I was rather hoping you'd go up."

He did and I learned that acceleration worked the same, going up or down. My heart and balls seemed to be in the same location. Meanwhile, Stan crested the peak and leveled out over Jijiwa's plateau. We were surrounded on all sides by steep mountains.

"Good shot," Stan said. "Sitting ducks."

I glanced at him once while trying to get my bearings straight. I had been unconscious when the old man found me, never seeing the plateau from this perspective, and certainly not from this height. And I had only viewed the passes along the mountain ridge from the vantage point of the adobe hut. The wall of mountains looked impenetrable to me now.

"You want to tell me what we're looking for?" Stan said.

"There's a pass. But you can't see it until you're right on top of it."

"You hear that, Bart. We can fine tune things while we're picking the tail rotor out of our teeth."

"I'm trying to get my bearings," I said.

"Anytime, Clay."

The lights of a jet zipped by high overhead. The mountain loomed black and impenetrable in front of us, a half mile ahead and closing. I anticipated the Mexicans bearing down on us at any moment but nothing was clear in my head. And I only had one plan; disappear into the narrow canyon where Nai had taken me. I knew it would lead us to the northeast and towards the border, but Nai and I had skirted the mountain ridges on foot that day and Stan was now approaching the mountain straight on, in complete darkness and at one hundred and fifty miles an hour. Worse still, I had no idea if the helicopter could navigate along the narrow, winding walls of that canyon, the particulars of which I wasn't prepared to discuss with Stan at the moment. He already had enough on his mind.

"Goddamn it, Clay," he said. "Tell me something."

But I didn't know anything.

"Clay?!" Stan shouted.

"All right, turn east."

"East?!"

"Yes, east!" I said.

"That is not what I wanted to hear."

He banked hard and leveled out, heading straight into the teeth of trouble. The Mexicans would be coming over the mountain at any second.

With the mountain to our left, the steep spurs of it melted away into the valley on our right. Stan skimmed over each spur then down into a canyon, then up over the next spur and down into the next canyon. Each of them was there and swiftly gone before I had an opportunity to determine if it was the right one, or just another dead end.

"There it is!" I shouted, but Stan had already swooped up over the next ridge.

"That was it!" I shouted again.

In response, Stan pulled straight up and banked hard over his left shoulder, his maneuver met with the sickening scream of two turbine engines trying to overcome 8-Gs.

It was not good for human beings or machines, what Stan had done, but in the very second that we disappeared, the Mexican aircraft had cleared the mountain directly behind us. If Stan had taken the long, loping way around, we would have been left out in the open for half a mile. There was no telling if the Mexicans had seen us disappear, but if they had, at least they couldn't follow. Either way, we now had a small advantage.

Stan was forced to ease off the throttle and weave agonizingly up the narrow, switchback canyon, with all four of his extremities moving in rhythm and his mouth cursing at every turn. Everyone was cursing by the time we got to the top.

"I hate to ask what's next!" Stan shouted over to me.

"Your favorite thing," I told him. "A dive."

Stan shot up like an arrow and looked at me with a fierce smile before plummeting into a four-thousand foot vertical drop. I wedged myself between the seats and screamed. Everyone screamed. Stan appeared to be enjoying the hell out of it. It was over in less than thirty seconds, terminating with the sensation of my balls blowing back up through my heart.

"Come on, sweetheart, get us home," Bart said.

"They're going to need an air strike to stop me," Stan said.

We were bearing north by northwest now, along the base of the mountain, and searching for the gorge that had brought us across the border. Gauging by the lights of Nogales, the gorge was only a few miles to our west but we remained completely exposed until then.

The seconds ticked away. Then our luck ran out.

The DC-3 had circled back and was coming off the mountain to our west. Stan dropped down into the gorge just as 2.75 mm rounds started cracking into the rocks around us. I went to the back window and saw the plane making a wide turn to the east. Stan streaked north, blind except for straight ahead or directly above us.

"He's trying to get on my tail," Stan said.

"Can he outrun you?" I asked.

"You bet your ass."

"Watch my tail," he added. "If he comes in behind me, holler."

"What are you going to do?" I said.

"Play keep away," Stan said. "And hope like hell he doesn't have any friends."

A minute later I heard the roar and saw the lights loom over us like a flying battleship.

"Get out! Get out!"

Stan jumped the gorge and veered hard right then hard left and back into the gorge before the cannon shots caught up with us. The plane had lumbered out half a mile to the east again, trying to follow. As we dipped down into the gorge, I saw the pilot turning back. We had thirty seconds, maybe less.

"How far do we have?" Stan asked me.

"Ten miles."

"He won't go for that trick again."

"Let him pass us," I said.

"This ain't the interstate," Stan said.

Both he and Bart looked at me.

"Let him pass us," I said. "He'll never expect it."

Stan stared at me suspiciously for a moment before letting off the throttle. He was doing eighty but it felt like we were standing still. There was nothing. Then suddenly the plane swooped out over the gorge a quarter mile ahead and began to pull away.

"You're a sly son of a bitch, you know that? Look at this guy, Bart. He's a goddamned general."

Bart patted me on the knee.

After a minute the pilot realized something was wrong and pulled the plane out. Stan gave the chopper full stick and before the plane had time to lumber around again, we were blowing across the border. I pointed at the lookout tower and Stan skirted well past it before starting up the mountain pass. Another five minutes and we were diving into Jake's canyon.

"The truck's gone!" Stan shouted over the noise.

"No it's not. It's under the cover," I said.

Stan banked and I saw the frame of the cover out the window. Tony was running over from the shack. I scrambled back to where Joe and Robby were strapped in.

"As soon as we're on the ground, get out and grab a rope. We have to cover the chopper. And whatever you do, don't let go of the ropes."

"Where are we?" Robby said.

"You're in the States. What else do you want to know?"

"Wow, man, I'm just trying to figure out what's happening."

"I know you are, Robby."

He stared at me, his nervousness now caste in the amber resin of a dumbstruck stare. I stared back, wishing they had shot him instead.

"We'll be out of here by morning," I said, "but we've got to make this chopper look respectable before we do."

"Damn, that was incredible," Joe said.

"Don't look at me." I waved at Stan and Bart.

"That was far out," Robby said.

I looked away, not understanding why I had come to view him with such disgust.

The chopper settled in and Bart jumped out of the shotgun door. I slammed open the cargo door and followed him. Joe was right behind me, Robby right after him. Stan cut the engine and was on our heels.

"All right, you son of a bitches!" Stan yelled. "Pull!"

With a man on every rope, the chopper was hidden in less than thirty seconds. We went out in front and cautiously watched the sky. Several times we heard the roar of a jet engine high up and saw the lights among the stars, but nothing else.

"Never saw the shack and the outhouse," Stan said with a sly smile in my direction. "Thought the good lord had washed them away."

I looked around the end of the helicopter cover and saw the two structures were draped with tarps, just as Tony had been instructed to do.

"It was a last minute thought," I told Stan.

"You might have told me."

I shrugged. With the additional protection, someone would have to hover over the canyon to notice any signs of civilization, even in broad daylight. I looked back to the others.

"Did you gentlemen introduce yourselves?"

"Introduce ourselves," Stan said. "Hell, I know this guy." He wrapped one arm around Joe. "Didn't recognize him at first with all the hair."

"That's okay," Joe said, "you still look the same."

"You bastard. I'll take you back if you're not careful."

"You guys have already met?"

"Yeah, no shit," Joe said. "I hitched a ride with these dudes up to Khe Sahn one day."

"A lousy place to hitch a ride."

"Hell, I wondered then if he was trying to kill me."

There was silence.

"Hey, sorry, man."

Joe reached out his hands remorsefully.

"They're gone," I said. "Who are you going to offend now?"

"Let's say we get to work," Bart suggested. "It'll help all of us to keep our minds off the grief."

Joe looked at Robby.

"Hell, I feel the same way everyone does," Robby said.

Stan slapped him on the back.

"We all feel like hell, partner."

There was silence.

"Well, like Bart said, let's get to work, gentlemen. I want to put this slick back in the corral first thing in the morning."

"Hey Tony, where's Jake?" I said.

"He's sitting up in the shack with a bottle of Wild Turkey. Says he doesn't want anything to do with us."

"Where the hell did he get the bourbon?"

"I don't know. Must have been saving it."

"Probably lost it and found it again," Bart said.

"Who are you guys talking about?" Joe said.

"The old codger who's got a claim on this place," Stan said with a wink.

"No kidding, somebody lives out here?" Joe said.

"You're looking at a bit of paradise, my friend."

"Anything's paradise compared to where just came from," Robby said.

"Yeah," Joe said. "You'd be trying to bang Rosa right about now."

"Screw you."

"We're wasting time," I reminded everyone and started the generator. Tony handed out a couple of power sanders and some face masks. Those who didn't have power tools worked at the edge details with sandpaper.

I showed Tony the bullet hole in the cabin. It had gone through a plastic panel before exiting the fuselage.

"What do you think?"

"It's not too bad."

He climbed in and pulled one of the back seats forward.

"Here."

I crawled in back with him.

"These are identical," he said. "Just switch the panels. They'll never look back here."

"Good idea."

"I'll get you a screwdriver. Just leave this one off until I mix some bondo and fix the body."

Bart pulled the gun out and put the seats back in place. I changed the panels. In two hours, Tony was re-spraying the original colors. We all went outside to get away from the fumes.

"How about a beer?" I said.

"Yeah, figure I earned that much," Stan said.

"Wow, I thought I'd never have one again," Robby said. I walked up to the shack while the others kept talking about the adventure. Jake was sitting on the porch when I got there, the shotgun in his lap.

"We'll be out of your way in the morning."

"I'll be damned lucky if the Marines ain't overrunnin' the place by then."

"I didn't mean you any harm."

"Ya lied to me. That's what ya did. Ya lied to me."

I grabbed a couple of six-packs out of the ice chest and walked back down to the chopper, knowing it was true. I had lied to him. I had been willing to do anything to get Kip out that prison and had only failure to show for it, that and Jake's bitter words. I joined the others and passed out the beer.

"Thanks, Clay," Joe said. "Now how about a joint."

"Joe's not greedy," Bart said.

Joe shrugged. Tony came out and took his respirator off.

"I've got some bush," he said.

Joe put his arm around Tony's shoulder and gave him a hug. Everyone was smiling but me.

"I'd say Clay's losing his sense of humor, Bart. What do you think?"

I looked around and shook my head.

"I'm just tired, Stan. Tired of breaking the law. Tired of looking over my shoulder. Tired of trouble."

"Well, hell," Stan said. "It's a lousy time to be going clean."

Tony had rolled a joint and passed it around.

"You're not tired of breaking laws," Stan said after taking a hit. "You're just tired of what happens when you break them."

I passed the joint on without indulging.

"Cheer up, Clay," Stan said.

"About what?"

"Hell, you got Joe and Robby here."

"I know."

I looked both of them in the eye.

"But somehow it doesn't seem worth the loss."

"So now you know a little bit about war," Bart said.

"You guys have an answer for everything," I said.

Joe was coughing over the joint. When he had himself under control, he spoke.

"Damn, Clay. I feel bad enough as it is."

"I'm sorry, Joe. It's just hell remembering that look in her eyes. I'd swear she was trying to tell me something."

"You see why they don't let women in combat? The whole goddamned thing would grind to a halt over the grief."

I looked back at Stan.

"And wouldn't that be a shame."

"You're a dreamer, Clay," he said.

"So are you."

"Yeah. But I know where my dreams end and the world begins."

"You're right, Stan. I should have left well enough alone."

"That's what's wrong with your goddamned generation, Clay. Things get a little hard and you're all ready to throw in the towel."

Stan and I were standing face to face. The others looked on. There was a fine breeze coming down from the mountain. I could see a few wisps of clouds racing high overhead. All else was still as we looked into each other's eyes.

"I guess I'm giving it to you pretty hard," I said.

"You're not making it any easier," Stan said.

I looked over at Bart and back at Stan.

"You guys did a remarkable job. It's not your fault we didn't get Kip. Or the rest."

"We all could have been lying there in a pile," Stan said.

"No, you probably made the right decision. But still."

"The truth is, Clay, you never seem to be satisfied. With anything."

I nodded and headed up to the mineshaft alone. The surveillance flights continued to crisscross the sky. I saw the lights appear from over the mountain and disappear again. Someone cut the generator and the others sat against the canvas drinking beer. I heard occasional laughter but did not feel a part of it.

Much later, I went for a walk down by the creek. On my way back, I stopped by to see if Joe and Robby wanted a sleeping bag. It seemed plain nothing that was going to happen until dawn. There was talk about getting some sleep when Stan suddenly stood up.

"I'm getting out of here."

"Why the sudden rush?" Bart said.

"If these flights keep up until daylight, we'll never make it back without a reception party."

No one else moved.

"Call it intuition, boys, but I'm getting out of here."

That was it. Stan had made up his mind. Once the paint had dried, we stripped the masking. In the meantime, I got the truck ready and went over a game plan with Joe and Robby. It was agreed they'd wait while I went to call the sheriff. Tony and Bart would come with me.

If it all worked out, I'd return tomorrow sometime and get Joe and Robby on a bus. With a haircut and enough money, they could lay low for a little while. As for myself, I wasn't sure what to do next.

"As soon as Stan leaves," I told them, "strip the whole thing out and hide it in the mine shaft."

"Good luck," Joe said.

"For all of us," I said.

I handed Stan the keys to the Nova.

"See you at the motel."

He nodded and slapped me on the back.

I got in with Bart and Tony and headed for Tucson. We kept the lights off and worked the ranch roads south of Mt. Lemmon. An argument could have been made for pulling onto the highway at Sonoita but we opted to stay on the back roads. One road block heading north and we'd be doomed.

About five in the morning, we slipped into Tucson unnoticed and dropped Tony off. Back at the motel, Bart went to get some sleep. I called the sheriff at home. He wasn't very happy to hear from me.

"You're going to get my ass busted," he said.

"I take it you heard about it."

"Heard about it? It was on the evening news. Hell, it came over the squawk-box. And I'm being told that Kip's ass is still down there in that prison."

"Yeah, sheriff. His ass is still down there in that prison. Just get yours up there on the mountain. I'll have to explain the rest of it later."

I took a quick shower and lay on the bed for an hour without sleep. Once the streets were bustling with morning traffic, Bart and I ventured out for breakfast and hurried back to the motel. It was getting on past noon when Stan showed up.

"How is it out there?" I asked him.

"Hot."

"How hot?"

"The feds are crawling all over that airport. Your friend Charlie did a fine job."

"His ass depended on it."

"Mine too."

"Did they suspect you at all?" Bart said.

"They wanted to know what happened to the cowpoke, here. We told them he was still up bird hunting on the reservation. A couple of dicks were out there looking over the chopper while they questioned us inside. Seemed relieved to know the sheriff wasn't mixed up in this mess. You know, like they couldn't imagine it but weren't entirely convinced until they saw the evidence."

"Think I'd better skip the bus?"

"Yeah," Stan said. "I'd get them a haircut and drive 'em home. You'll be all right. Just keep moving."

"Yeah, I know all about that."

"What about that Caroline?" Stan asked.

"Probably best to leave her alone. She's likely to have a movie star on her hands by now."

I went to shake their hands but they hugged me instead.

"What can I do for you guys?"

"Nothing," Stan said. "I couldn't take money for that. Maybe if it had all worked out..."

I counted out a thousand dollars and stuck it in his hand. He looked at it once and back at me, weighing the money in his palm.

"Expenses," I said.

"All right. Fair enough."

Our eyes remained locked as he put the money away.

"I guess I'll see you guys again someday."

"Yeah, things'll cool down," Bart said. "Maybe when we get a new president."

"Sure, always when we get a new president."

"Meantime," Stan said. "You look up that lady of yours. Before you go off making any big time decisions."

He put his hand on my shoulder.

"To the best of all possible worlds."

"You're feeling awfully hopeful today, Stan."

Stan climbed into the truck and closed the door.

"Oh, give it time, Clay. This movie ain't over with yet. Forty years or so and we'll be bringing back the sixties."

I waved as they drove off.

Back in the motel room, I dropped to my knees, not sure if anyone was listening, and thinking it was just as well if they weren't, but I felt some powerful need to try. For all my efforts, I hadn't made the world a better place. I had only made it worse and there was an awful lot of grief associated with that recognition. It was a long time before I could get back up on my feet.

55

I lay alone on the bed, the curtains closed and the air-conditioner off, not wanting anyone to know I was in the room. At one point in the heat of the afternoon, I fell asleep for a brief spell but awakened in a sweat and spent the remainder of the day tossing and turning restlessly with my thoughts.

Towards sunset, with the drone of rush hour traffic increasing outside, I parted the curtains and considered whether or not to get lost in the bustle but decided it would be best to wait until dark. I went back to the bed and lay there for another hour, thinking.

Once all light had faded from the sky, I slipped out the door and headed south. I had no real desire to go in that direction but had given my word and was determined to finish at least one thing I had started.

I picked my way along the usual ranch roads and pulled into Jake's canyon an hour later without having seen any sign of the law. It was a clear night with countless stars. The place looked as if it had never been disturbed.

"Anything?" I asked Joe when he came up to greet me.

"A lot of planes overhead but we had this place spotless before dawn. Spent most of the day down by the stream or up in the mine shaft."

"How do you feel?"

"Doing all right. Hey, sorry about last night. I guess I'm used to war being hell. None of it was very funny."

"Don't worry about it."

Robby came up and I nodded at him. I saw hope in their eyes and knew again that Stan was right. We had accomplished something, though I still struggled with the cost.

"What are we going to do?" Robby asked me.

"I'm taking you home."

"Don't you think they'll be waiting for us?" he said.

"What do you think?"

He shrugged.

"I'll get you close and give you some money. You'll have to work it from there."

"They'll probably throw us back in jail."

"At least you're innocent until proven guilty now."

"Yeah, quit worrying," Joe said. "I know plenty of places to hide in Ohio."

"Okay, we'd better hit the road. We've got a long way to go."

I went over and handed Jake a roll of bills. He thumbed through it and a bit of warmth returned to his eyes.

"Thanks, old timer. You earned it."

"Got more'n I bargained fer but thanks jes' the same. Yer a man of yer word."

"Thanks for saying so, Jake. Maybe next time we'll go a little easier on the bourbon."

"Yep, 'spect that's some sound advice right there, partner."

"You take care. And your secret's safe with me." I patted Jake on the shoulder and walked back to the Nova.

Joe got up front with me. As nice as I was trying to be, I didn't want to be looking at Robby for a thousand miles. I ditched the ranch roads just south of Tucson but stayed off the main highway. West of Benson, I turned onto another back-country road and followed it east until Las Cruces. It was a hot desert night and the land was as dry as a bone but it changed as we worked our way north, as did the scent in the air. We kept the windows down until late and watched the stars pass overhead. Dawn was breaking when we hit Route 66 below Cuervo.

Robby had complained about hunger all night but we made do with a couple of beers and some of that packaged crap you find hanging around the front of cash registers. We stopped to get them haircuts in Amarillo and had breakfast. Joe and Robby were playing with the stubble around their ears as we walked back out to the car.

I knew the feeling. We looked like a trio of slicks from the rodeo circuit.

"You'll get used to it," I told them and handed Joe the keys. "You drive. I need to get some sleep."

"Hot damn, it's been almost two years."

"Just remember to stick to the speed limit."

I lay on the back seat with my eyes closed but not sleeping. The Midwest heat had my skin and clothes glued together. The drone of tires came through the floorboard with a strange feeling of nostalgia. It was the sound of driving home on Sunday nights with the folks, the sound of comfort and hearth and home; when all I had now was the road and weariness, and when I was tired, a little more road up ahead. Those other things had been stolen from me a long time ago.

I slept and awakened with a start east of Oklahoma City. It took a few moments to remember who I was and what I was doing. I sat up and saw the windshield splattered with bugs. It was a little before noon. We were surrounded by flat country in every direction.

Robby turned around once and looked away. I saw Joe's coke bottle eyes in the rearview mirror.

"How about we stop in St. Louis for a little fun?" he said with a grin.

"Come on, Joe, you've waited this long. You'll keep another night."

"What's the difference?" he said. "We could all use a good time."

"Yeah, Joe. We could all use a good time, but we're pushing through. We'll be in Chicago before dawn."

"Then what are you going to do?" Robby said.

"Get some sleep and move on," I said.

"Where to?" Joe said.

I shrugged. He stared at me in the rearview mirror for a moment and went back to watching the heartland of America.

My impulse was to drive up and corner Caroline at her movie set in Durango, but each time I imagined my arrival, I got a sick feeling in my gut. A nice fishing trip up in Manitoba sounded like a much better idea. Showing up out of the blue had the feel of a younger brother spying on his sister's first date. It was the wild and dangerous part of me, the part I knew I should avoid, yet the minute I tried to detour around the idea, the impulse returned.

The miles clicked by — Tulsa, Joplin, Springfield — until the trees and hills had grown dark around us and day was a pastel wash in the western sky. Then we saw a nice little cluster of lights up ahead, a warm and welcome sight on an otherwise empty road. Joe pulled into Ma's Diner. Ma thought we were all nice boys with our haircuts. I thought she made one hell of a fresh apple pie.

We pulled back on the road with a six-pack and a bottle of bourbon in our laps, and all three of us had a warm feeling inside by the time we hit the state line. Joe still wanted to hit a bordello. I told him to keep moving.

Somewhere out on the plains of Illinois, I took the wheel. Joe and Robby slept. We rolled into Joliet around two in the morning. I pulled in at the first vacancy sign and paid for three rooms.

"Get some sleep," I told them and took the bottle to my room, haunted by something inside as I lay there, like the wide, black plains under a night sky. Something was trying to speak to me but I poured more bourbon over those fleeting voices and made do with a few hours of restless sleep.

In the morning we had breakfast and I gave them each a thousand dollars. I had no idea why I kept giving everyone a thousand dollars. It just seemed like a nice round figure to hand out. They were talking about what to do when we pulled up to the bus depot. Joe went off to check the schedule. His parents lived in Youngstown and he was heading that way. I stood there waiting with Robby. Neither one of us knew what to say. He had his hands in his pockets and was shifting his feet, the way he always did. And I figured that was how I would always remember him.

"I'm really sorry about everything," he said out of the blue.

I looked at him

"So am I, Robby. I'm sorry about a lot of things but I'm not blaming you."

"I just wish we'd never gone down there."

"I know...I've said this a few times already but I'll say it again. You try to unravel how you got from there to here and pretty soon you're back in the womb."

"I just miss my friends."

Robby had a tear in his eye so I gave him a hug.

"I miss them too, Robby...I keep thinking there's a lesson in all of this somewhere...But hell if I know what it is."

We both smiled briefly, having no better way to process our grief.

Joe came back.

"Okay, are you guys all set?"

"Yeah, Robby's coming with me for a few weeks. Until things cool down."

Robby nodded.

"I've got your numbers. I'll try to check in on you someday."

"What do we say about Steve and Kristine?" Robby said.

"You'll have to decide that, Robby. I'm sure their parents will want to know. Just leave me out of it."

"How?" he said.

"I don't know. Tell them you hired two mercenaries."

"I'll try, but I don't think it's going to go over," he said.

"Haven't you learned anything, Robby?"

"Yeah, yeah, all right, I'll keep my mouth shut."

"Thank you."

"Thanks a lot," Joe said. "To old times, buddy."

I gave Joe a hug, then Robby again. I looked back at Joe.

"Try and stay out of trouble, you crazy son of a bitch."

"You should talk," he said.

I turned to leave.

"Thanks again," he said.

"Yeah, thanks, Clay," Robby said.

"Yeah, someday maybe we'll have a reunion," Joe said.

"Sure," I said.

Pulling out of the station, I looked once in the rearview mirror, expecting I would never see those two men again.

Heading west, I clipped across Illinois on Interstate 80. Iowa and Nebraska and were straight ahead, along with a lot of cornfields.

To hell with fishing, I decided. There was something I had to know.

I caught a burger on the fly and started counting miles. When I got bored with the mile markers, I tried telephone poles.

In the afternoon, clouds billowed up into the heavens. It grew dark, lightning flashed and a squall rolled across the land. Then, just as suddenly, the clouds parted, the sun appeared and the hot sweaty process started all over again. It was something only a farmer could love.

I made Grand Island at sunset, the big show on the plains. I had expected more after all those miles.

I found a cafe downtown and wandered in for a bite to eat. Everyone looked up like I was trouble coming through the door and for once they were probably right.

After the meal, I walked back to the Nova, considering a motel but feeling the urge to make a few more miles before I rested. I was looking for a lot of things in life, but Grand Island wasn't one of them.

It was pushing midnight when I pulled into North Platte. I felt reasonably good: as good as I was going to feel under the circumstances. I knew I could make Durango by nightfall the next day, not expecting to like what I found there, but needing to know anyway.

It was dawn when I checked out the next morning. The scent of the river and summer crops were on the early breeze. I stopped for some bacon and eggs and hit the road again.

All along the highway, there were stacks of hay and big, bruising farm boys standing alone, the plains as flat as a cornfield, the same scenery passing by me for miles and miles until just shy of Sterling. Then I started to feel the slow, steady rise of the land and saw the glimmer of something massive lurking below the sky on the far horizon.

I wasn't sure when, but I had looked away one moment and looked back to find a line of mountains spreading from one end of the horizon to the other, barely visible beneath the clear blue sky but all glistening white with snow. The road drove straight forward for hours, with the white peaks looming ever higher, until the foothills too had come into view and the Rockies had completely dominated the skyline. I passed by Denver a short while later, sickened to see all that wide, open country blemished by what felt like a junkyard but I turned south and quickly left that basin of smog and heartless commerce behind.

All down through Colorado, the mountains rose up tall and forbidding to my right and the plains sloped off free and boundless to my left and it seemed that those two things were a reflection of my life. Going up to Durango was the hard way. So why was I always choosing that route? Why not take the easy way for once? Grab all the money in that safety deposit box in Mazatlán and go somewhere far, far away. Abandon this endless turmoil that had come characterize my existence. Clearly, I had gained little from the current course of action, other than to find more trouble.

And yet it seemed that taking the hard way was etched into my karma, and even though I could see this, I was unrepentant and certain that things would turn out differently this time. In any case, I continued south towards Durango, driven on by a frenzy of uncontrolled impulses.

Well into the afternoon, I turned west at Walsenburg and started up into the higher passes. Aspens came to line the highway and evergreens rose up high against the blue sky. The going was torturous, sometimes ascending, sometimes descending, but endlessly winding back and forth. Like my life, I thought, up and down and all around on the way to Durango.

I wanted to feel innocence, but I didn't. I wanted to feel happiness at the prospect of seeing Caroline, but that too seemed beyond reach now. The thought passed through my mind several times. Just head back down to San Blas and enjoy the easy life with Faith. Nothing but heartache awaited me up ahead, but I dismissed these warnings and kept right on going.

In the chill and fading light of dusk, I stopped at the first saloon, hoping a drink would wash away some of these feelings, and if nothing else, warm my bones, but before I got the shot of Wild Turkey up to my lips, I caught the profile of a young brunette wearing a cowboy hat in the far corner of the bar and realized it was Caroline. She was sitting with another man and had just placed her hand on his forearm, in the same loving way she had once done with me. I watched her lean forward and whisper something into his ear and felt like a horse had kicked me in the gut.

I went ahead with the shot and somehow in that motion, Caroline turned her face and saw me. Her friend looked my way too. I went over to greet them.

"Clay?" she said.

She stood up to give me a hug and her cowboy hat clipped me on the chin. Her embrace was passionless.

"What are you doing here?" she said, standing back.

I looked from her to the man behind her and back again.

"Oh, I'm sorry, Clay, this is Bret Hart. He's one of the stars in the movie. Bret, you know, I've told you about Clay."

He shook my hand with the grinning menace that lurks between two men when they have met over the same woman. I was invited to sit down, which I did. I declined the offer of a drink.

"Hell, make yourself at home, partner."

I stared at Caroline.

"Clay, I don't understand. What are you doing here?"

"I need to talk with you." I looked at Bret and back to her. "Alone, preferably."

"Oh, Clay, we just got here. It's been a long day. Please, join us for a drink."

"It's important," I said with another look at Bret.

They shared a look and he got up.

"I'll be waiting for you at the bar, darling. And try to keep yourself out of trouble there, Clay."

He walked over to the row of barstools with a swagger and engaged the bartender in conversation. Both of them were wearing cowboy hats. Everyone in that bar was wearing a cowboy hat except for me.

I turned back and stared at Caroline, not wanting to believe I had interrupted a fledgling love affair, but knowing I had. One thing was clear. A lot had been said in my absence. I was about to speak up when Caroline beat me to it.

"I don't understand. How did you find me?"

"Purely by chance."

"You mean you just drove into Durango?"

"No. I spoke with your mother and she gave me the directions, so I drove up here and just happened to stumble into this saloon."

"Are you all right?"

"Not really. I suppose that depends on you."

"What did you think? That I was involved with Bret?"

I touched her forearm, the way she had touched him.

"Wouldn't you?"

"Oh Bret, I mean Clay...You know I have that habit. I'm sorry, I..."

She placed her hand on mine by way of explanation. I reached over and held it tightly.

"Do you still want me?"

"It doesn't matter if I do or I don't, Clay. I've come to accept that our lives will never fit."

"Perhaps I don't have what it takes anymore."

She shook her head.

"You're very humble whenever you want something."

"Whatever my failings, Caroline, I still love you. Or did you think that was an act too?"

She didn't answer.

"Look, I drove up here because I live with that truth every day and need to know. Do you still want to try?"

"Clay, how can I believe in you? One day you're off on some mad adventure. Then you show up without notice, expecting me to abandon everything I've worked so hard to achieve. Who knows what you'll do next?"

Somebody threw a quarter in the jukebox. I leaned over, trying to talk over the music.

"I asked you to stand by me until this one thing was over with. That's all."

"And I need someone I can depend on."

"Like Bret?"

"That's really none of your business, Clay."

"Oh, so it's none of my business now."

She had spoken with the dispassionate air of a woman who is done with one man and has started with another. It was like a fire that has burned through the ice and there is nothing left but a black hole and a wisp of smoke. I wanted to shake her and make the fire return, but I knew it wouldn't. Still, I tried.

"I'm going away now, Caroline. I think it's simple enough. Either you're coming with me or you're not."

"On that basis, I'm not." The waitress stopped by, called me honey and asked if we were okay. I waved her off as politely as I could.

"Caroline, I'm not ready to accept this. That I'll never see you again."

"I'm sure you'll get used to it."

"It sounds like you already have."

"I've grown tired of the heartache, Clay. I thought I would never say this, but I don't love you anymore."

She fidgeted with her Stetson, submerged in all her cowboy bullshit and far, far away from me.

"I don't understand how anything so warm can grow so cold."

"It happens when things die," she said.

She stared at me for a moment and looked away. I got up to leave.

"I've tried my best. I hope you can live with your part of it."

I waited, but nothing came.

"Good luck, Caroline."

I had gotten a few steps towards the door when she called out my name. I stopped and looked back, my heart beating wildly

"Yes, Caroline?"

"What happened with Kip?"

"It was all death and failure. Just like you figured."

"You mean Kip's dead?"

"No, but other people died and I failed to get him out."

"Oh, I'm so sorry," she said.

That was it. I turned away and walked slowly out into a summer evening in the mountains. Having seen this glimmer of warmth from the woman I loved, I wanted to believe it meant something deeper. I kept hoping that Caroline would run out of the bar and beg me to stay, but she didn't. I climbed into the front seat of the Nova, started the motor and drove away slowly with the warmth of the saloon lights spilling out into the darkness behind me.

Before I reached the outskirts of town, I searched for a decent FM station but kept finding country music. When nothing else could be coaxed from the radio, I gave it a good kick with my boot. It was going to take some work before it played any form of music again.

56

I cut across to Cortez and worked my way down through four-corners, with no earthly idea why I was heading back towards Tucson. I had no reason to be going anywhere at that point. I just figured a plan would come to me somewhere in the night.

Seeing my life before me, I thought it looked a lot like one of those noir films from the '40s, where the motives were money and women, and men got slapped upside the head a lot with guns; a place where no one ever got what they wanted, nothing ever made sense and everyone felt lousy at the end.

Early on, I had stopped for a bottle of Jack Daniels and rolled down the highway with that and my memories of Caroline to keep me company. They were bitter memories at first but a few shots of bourbon quickly turned that around. I wanted to deny that Caroline had been a good woman but the many images of her laughter and kindness worked in my heart.

Hell, I didn't like the hand I had been dealt. Why should I expect her to sign up for the show? There was nothing to do but wish the woman well and press forward with my own desperate set of circumstances.

Occasionally in the night, headlights appeared far off on the horizon, tiny dots that grew ever larger until they were bearing down on me, and there would be a sick urge to inch over that few feet, expecting the pain would be over quickly, silenced with final a mouthful of shattered glass. Then the lights would hurtle by and I would be alone again with the spires and mesas of nature's cathedral etched against the black, starry sky.

I thought I had known loneliness before but I had not. It was measured in how much you cared about people and how much of their companionship you had lost at any given time. And I had come to care a great deal about some people, and not a single one of them remained.

I knew this much for certain. Wherever my problems had begun and wherever they might come to an end, the responsibility for them lay squarely with me. The war had nothing to do with it anymore.

The bourbon and adrenalin began to wear off around Flagstaff but I pushed on until I saw a vacancy sign in Casa Grande. Somehow, it didn't seem wise to be stumbling into Tucson tired and the only car on the road. It was just before dawn when I checked in.

At a little past eleven, I was awakened by a maid knocking on the door. I told her I'd be out in half an hour and jumped in the shower. An hour later, I was in a phone booth on the outskirts of Tucson, talking to the sheriff.

"Boy, you got to be dumb to be anywhere near this town, let alone in this country."

"What about Kip, sheriff? Are we just going to let him rot?"

"Well, you can bet your ass he will after what you've done."

"Charlie, you know I've got money."

"Who the hell do you think you are? His parents got money and they can't get him out."

"They know?"

"Shit, the president knows by now. And he probably wants your ass, too."

"Me?"

"Your name has come up. Now I ain't said a goddamned thing but somebody's got you on the board. You'll be lucky if they don't come up and tap you on the shoulder while we're talkin'."

"Are you in trouble?"

"Not yet, but I wouldn't count it out."

"I'm keeping my end of the bargain, Charlie."

"Well, there may come a time when I can't help you no more, irrespective of what happens to my ass."

"To hell with it, Charlie. I just don't care anymore."

"Son, just get your ass out of town."

"You worried about me, Charlie?"

"Hell if I know, but I have to respect you for tryin'."

"I tried, goddamn it. I tried."

"I know you did. Now get your ass out of town before somethin' worse happens to ya."

"Thanks, sheriff."

"Don't be thankin' me. I may be the one who has to bust ya."

"Yeah, well, thanks anyway."

I went back to the car and sat there thinking. What now? Nothing came to mind, other than to sneak across the border and head back down to San Blas. The way things had played out, I probably never should have left.

Realizing it would be best to change my identity before heading anywhere, I decided to take another room. Maybe Danny could bring me some hair dye or a wig. Anything was safer than sitting out there on the streets.

I found a cheap place on the outskirts of town and parked the Nova around in back. Ma sat behind the counter with Pa sitting next to her, keeping an eye on things. They looked to do a brisk trucker trade from all the big rigs parked out on the street. The price reflected the Spartan appointments and lack of seclusion.

I noticed Ma glancing at her husband while I filled out the card. Something wasn't right, but I went ahead with paying for the room.

Fifty feet down the sidewalk, I found my door and was sticking the key in the lock when I noticed something out of the corner of my eye. I glanced back in the direction of the office but no one was there. I went inside and stared at myself in a mirror.

What's it going to be, old boy? Did you want to go on? Or just lie down and take it? I knew the law would be there soon; and giving up felt like death, when the spirit goes out of something.

But why go on? Why not just give up and serve my time? I stood there staring into the depths of my own eyes when it came to me.

Kip. I could not give up until he was a free man again. No greater love hath a man, than to lay down his life for a friend. Perhaps it was the only reason I had left for living, but goddamn it, it was reason enough, and there had to be some way of getting him out of that hole.

I started for the front door but stopped. It was best if Ma and Pa believed I was still in here. I went in to have a look at the bathroom window and it was the usual thing, small and high up, but the only way to escape without being seen. I removed the screen and shimmied through the opening with a great deal of effort. Having landed on my head, I jumped to my feet and hurried over to the car.

Bypassing the highway, I got completely around the airport before working my way east and south on the usual network of ranch roads. Early on, I had taken a couple of jolts from the bottle of bourbon to calm my nerves.

Two hours later, I was pulling up to Jake's shack. He sat on the porch and did not look the least bit happy to see me. There was hardly a glance my way as I got out.

"Hi, Jake."

"I don't recollect askin' fer no more trouble."

"You said I was welcome anytime."

"Well ya ain't, so there."

"I brought some whiskey."

He eyed me suspiciously from under his hat.

"Ya got somethin' up yer sleeve, tenderfoot."

"Trying to be nice, that's all."

"Well, I got my own whiskey."

"So, what? I can't stay?"

"Stay?! Who said anything about stayin'!?"

He stomped his boot on the porch steps once in saying this.

"Fuck it, Jake. I'm in trouble and need a place to hide."

He stared at me with his eyes twitching.

"Come on, Jake. I'm serious. I've got no place else to go."

"What kinda trouble ya in?"

"Shit, what kind aren't I in?"

He kept staring with his twitching eyes.

"Come on. Let's go sit down by the stream and I'll tell you about it."

Jake reluctantly got up and followed me.

Dusk had grown velvety around us by the time I concluded my tale. Jake and I were sitting quietly with our shoes off and our feet in the water. The stream murmured softly as it skipped over the shallows. The water was cool and clear from its source high up in the mountains. I swiped at the swarming insects and had another swig of the bourbon.

"Boy oh boy," Jake said. "Ain't that a laugh. Well, ya sure got yerself in a heap a trouble fer nothin', didn't ya?"

"It seems that way."

"Yessir, I remember I used ta think I had a string a cans tied ta my tail. But that's what you get fer fraternizin' with the human race."

"Yeah, I think the same thing sometimes, Jake, but how do you live this life without other people?"

"Ya pay a price fer everythin'. And that's the price I pay fer my peace of mind."

"Loneliness?" I said.

"Call it whatever you like, partner, but ya've seen the alternative."

I nodded and stared off into the growing darkness. I had never considered there might be a price to pay for a man's peace of mind. I always thought it was just something you stumbled onto one day.

Before night fell, I climbed up into the mineshaft and dragged out my old tent. The days passed without insight as to how I might rescue Kip. Every sort of silly and bizarre notion passed through my head, but nothing resembling a legitimate plan. There were moments when I ached over Caroline and imagined our blissful reunion. There were moments when I felt like Jake. Screw the human race, but in the end, my thoughts always came back to Kip. There had to be some way to free him from that prison but no ideas came to me and I was alone and without hope in the dust and emptiness of the desert.

On the fifth day, I heard Jake calling out from the far end of the canyon.

"Someone's a comin'! Someone's a comin'!"

He had been down by the columbine trees checking his rabbit traps and ran up out of breath. Panicked, I was already pulling on my boots.

"How do you know?" I asked him.

"I heard 'em comin' through the pass!"

He rushed into his shack and returned with a canteen and a bag of jerky.

"Here, this'll last you a day and a night! Now high-tail it."

With the car's approach echoing into the canyon, I crossed the stream in full flight and started up a narrow foot trail that wound along the folds of the canyon. A thousand feet up the mountain, I saw a Border Patrol vehicle pull to a stop in front of Jake's shack and ducked behind some brush to watch. Three men got out and confronted Jake, two of them in street clothes. One of the men pointed at the Nova. I knew from the way Jake was flapping his arms that he was trying to explain it away.

One of the men looked up in my direction and I ducked further out of sight. When I looked back, he was on the radio. They weren't buying Jake's story. I waited until everyone was distracted and continued up the trail at a desperate pace.

Nearing the summit, the absurdity of my situation struck me. It was a chess match in which I had lost some time ago, my circle of options increasingly smaller with each move, yet I refused to concede. I was Cochise on the mountain but wouldn't give up.

On the other side of the summit, I stopped to catch my breath. An expanse of desert and dry mountains marched off to the south of me, wavering in the midday heat. I glanced up at the blazing sun and everything was dark and blurred when I looked back.

I had to get someplace safe and set my sights on Nogales. Being on the other side of the border was perhaps my best shot. From Nogales, and with a disguise of some kind, I could probably make it down to San Blas. I did not stand a chance in the States, not without a car, and I had no illusions of buying one, at least not within five hundred miles of Tucson. They'd be looking for me at every dealer.

I was opening the canteen to have a drink when a chopper shot out from over the peak behind me. I dove for cover in the shade of the nearest mesquite. The chopper hovered overhead for a minute before heading west. I waited until it had disappeared before starting down the mountain in a full gallop. I wanted to be that much closer to the border, if and when it came back.

In my mad scramble downhill, I cleared the shoulder of the mountain and found a posse of men and dogs off to the west, combing the border and heading my way. There went my plans of turning towards Nogales.

Hearing the chopper come back, I dove for cover again. The pilot went a little farther to the east this time before turning around. I used the opportunity to make it a bit farther down the mountain. My mind went on struggling with my dilemma. My only hope was to get my hands on a car but there weren't many options. The lights of Lochiel were visible to the east, but it was not nearly far enough away from the dragnet I had set in motion.

In the fading light of dusk, I reached the border and crouched down out of sight. The search party was within half a mile now. It felt like the chase was over, and just as well. Everything was telling me to accept my fate. It was the only way I would ever find the peace in this world.

I was ready stand up and surrender when a cool breeze blew down from the mountain and an idea popped into my head. And a feeling of peace came with it. I pulled out a piece of beef jerky and looked again at the men working their way along the border.

To hell with you. I'm not ready to give up yet, and there's a place where I can hide, a place that exists in another time and dimension, a place where I'm respected and perhaps even loved, and where no one would ever think to look for me.

Once all light had faded from the horizon, I slipped through the barbed-wire fence and began a slow, steady lope towards the south. I rested once but continued on through the night.

Dawn had brightened the eastern horizon when I came around the last ridge and saw the valley below me. A wisp of smoke trickled up from the roof of the adobe hut. I stood and watched in quiet gratitude.

"I'm so glad to see you," I told Jijiwa when he came to his door.

The old man put his hands on my shoulders and looked into my eyes.

"Ah. You are a cowboy now."

"No. I don't like cowboys. Especially people who pretend to be one."

"Then why do you dress like this?"

"It was easier not to be noticed."

"Nothing makes sense in your world."

I laughed, the first honest laugh I had experienced in a long, long time. Then all the emotion that had been damned up inside of me since Kristine's death was released and I wept.

"Come," Jijiwa told me. "Sit and talk."

The women came to the door upon hearing voices but quickly closed it again out of respect for my grief. I heard them talking inside.

When my grief was spent, I explained all that had happened. Jijiwa listened intently without saying a word. The sun cleared the mountain peaks as I spoke. The first light of day warmed me in the cold morning air.

"What do you think?" I asked Jijiwa.

"You have lived a strange life."

"I don't care. I just want peace."

"Always the impossible with you."

"I don't know. Is that true?"

"Eh, who can say, but a strange life is a special life. Perhaps you will be wise someday...If you live that long."

I looked at him hopefully and he shook his head.

"No, I do not think you will."

His laughter resounded across the valley.

The women came out with their pole and baskets. The saguaro fruit was in full bloom.

"You are back," Toki said. I nodded and looked into her dark eyes.

"I am back."

Nai came out and stood behind Toki, refusing to look at me.

"Nai thinks I'm bad medicine," I said.

"No, she thinks you are too good medicine."

Nai broke from her mother and ran into the fields. Toki smiled.

"She missed you," Toki said. "But she will learn."

I stared at Toki, not knowing what to say.

"Are you going to stay with us?"

I nodded.

"I have nowhere else to go."

"Then you are like us," she said.

She touched my shoulder and followed Nai into the morning sun. Jijiwa watched his wife and daughter pass through the fields and disappear into the lower valley.

"You are a lucky man," I said.

"Eh. You call this luck? Someday it will be over for me and for Toki. Then Nai must go down and learn the new ways."

"There's nothing new about them."

"It doesn't matter, as long as young men think they are."

"You know of no one in your tribe who wants to live up here?"

"No...I think maybe the gods sent you."

He looked at me and away again.

"I wish I could be that simple. I mean, to stay here. I'm cursed with the white man's disease."

"Ha, what is that?"

"Always wanting to be someplace other than where you are. The Hawaiians told me that."

"They are a wise people."

"It's easier to be wise on a beautiful island."

"It is never easy to be wise, anywhere in this world."

"Yeah, I suppose. Anyway, I still have the disease. I want to go somewhere, but when I get to where I'm going, I want to be somewhere else."

"Some people never try. Which is worse?"

"I feel good when I'm here."

"Then stay."

He had said this seriously, but with indifference.

"I don't know, Jijiwa."

"No one knows. Come, let us hunt."

I followed him down into the valley and for that day and several more we traveled together like father and son. Jijiwa taught me to hunt and what plants were good and how to use them. There were only the sun and the sky and the wind and I began to understand what made this man what he was, and realized he was like the ancient sages who had written down the I Ching long ago. The world turned and a wise man learned to stay in tune with those changes.

Jijiwa and I ate and worked together beneath the sun, and when day was done, we sat beneath the stars in quiet reflection. And when we slept, Nai was very near. Growing uncomfortable with my thoughts, I spoke with Jijiwa.

"I don't know what to do with these feelings."

He stared for a moment before laughing loudly.

"Why do you laugh?"

"When there is one man and one woman, what shall they do?"

"Well, what do you think?"

"That is for you and Nai to decide."

"But what if I should leave? What will happen if there is a child?"

"Ha, do you think the world stops when you go away?"

"I don't know," I said, "I only know it gets screwed up when I arrive."

We laughed together for a long time.

"It is different here," I said at last.

"It is different, yes."

I looked at him.

"Do you think the child will have the white man's disease?"

"A wild seed cannot come to much harm in this valley." He waved his arm across the fields and mountains. "It will be a wild seed, don't you think?"

"I don't know if this is a good thing, Jijiwa."

He stared at me with his dark, watery eyes.

"Without a seed we will pass away from time."

When Nai returned that evening, I met her eyes in the fading light and she did not look away. The lingering warmth of the sun glowed on her skin. The folds of her muslin skirt moved with her.

After our meal, when darkness had fallen, Nai went out the door alone and did not come back. I followed a short time later and found she had made a bed beneath the sky. She pulled aside the blanket and showed herself to me. Her small breasts quivered in the cool breeze. I took off my clothes, and when I lay next to her she covered me with her warmth and was as kind as summer.

The next day Nai went off early with Toki. When they returned, it was with poles and fiber from the woods for making a bed.

I slept again with Nai behind the hut that night, and with each passing day, her kindness grew, but my sadness did not fade. I could not help but feel that with time, everything precious would be stolen away from me and that it would go on thus, always learning to care for things that I could not keep. I was unable to accept or understand the life I had been given.

The summer days raced towards fall, sometimes hunting with Jijiwa, sometimes working in the fields but often times running with Nai down by the stream where it wove through the woods. I did not think of days or count them. I had forgotten time. Until one day it returned. I remembered Kip and my promise to him, but still nothing was revealed to me. The more I concentrated on the problem, the more frustrated I grew. It was as if I stood in a maze and the answer was just on the other side of a hedge but I could not see it. The truth may as well have been on the other side of the universe.

Watching me one morning, Nai said something in her native tongue and went inside the hut. When she returned, it was with a bota bag. Understanding her intent, I stared long into her eyes before starting across the valley alone.

In time, I found the narrow canyon and walked where the rock walls were vertical around me and the way grew cool and shady. An hour later, I was sitting atop the rock ledge again, gazing across the vast, empty spaces of the desert with the snow-capped Sierritas on the far horizon. The wind whispered quietly in my ears. The warm, desert air rose up and grew cool around me.

I knew that Nai was right. The answer lay beyond impulses of the spirit. Even my attempts at logic had led only to more disaster. I needed to look deeper. It was time to have faith in something I could not see, for either the universe was the manifestation of some loving consciousness or we were all groping around pointlessly in the darkness.

As I searched for this deeper level, the forms of the world moved in the wind around me. Day passed away into night and there were only the stars in the sky. My own life came before me then, and I saw it as a man suddenly becomes aware of his hands as he is working. The haste and concerns of the world fell away and I wept to feel a great, loving power touch the knot in my heart, and knew with unspeakable certainty that my life could not have been any other way, that it had taken all these journeys and all this pain and hardship for me to be sitting where I was. It had taken everything I had experienced for me to become willing. I had searched so desperately for the truth, only to discover it was waiting inside of me.

When the world returned, I laughed at myself, for it seemed silly to have been crying with such frequency of late. And I laughed even further to think how real those words sounded within my own mind.

Then, with the tender hand of dawn, the answer for rescuing Kip came to me, and came with a wave of awareness so utterly simple, I laughed until I cried from the pain. It had sprung from the very depths of the universe. I laughed as someone who has searched all around the house for his hat, only to find it sitting on his head.

Before departing, I wept again, this time with a sense of surrender. I had been a fool, but it did not always have to be that way. In the cool morning air, I said a prayer for Steve and Kristine and started on my way home.

57

Jijiwa stood alone in the woods by the stream when I returned, as still as the old oak and sycamore trees whispering around him. I stopped before him and stared into his dark, watery eyes. After a long moment, he grunted and turned towards home with me at his side. There was no need to explain what had happened. Jijiwa knew the place where I had been very well.

When we arrived back to the hut, Nai and Toki were inside preparing the evening meal. Jijiwa and I sat in front of the hut and watched the sun go down behind the mountains. The passing of day had soon left the trees and mountains as black as ink.

"I think I must go and try to rescue my friend again," I told Jijiwa.

"Ha, more trouble."

"It is always possible with me."

He looked at me, his eyes full of mischief.

"And what is this new wisdom?"

"Who knows? Perhaps it is only doing the same thing but doing it differently this time."

He looked away.

"Your life may yet be a long one."

"Ha," I said like him and he laughed.

When Nai came outside, I stood up to face her. How long had it been? I placed my hands on her stomach and tried to piece together the passing months in my mind. Her dark eyes looked down at my hands and back up into mine. I took her by the hand and we went back down to the woods in that hour of dusk, and along the stream where the autumn wind moved gently in the trees and falling leaves marked the rhythm of life. Nai was a woman with child and certain of herself and I knew she would be a good mother and that Jijiwa would be a better father than I could ever hope to be. And yet I felt guilt at the thought of abandoning my new family and hoped in my heart that the universe would forgive me for leaving.

Before departing that night, I gave Toki a large sum of money. She shook her head but I forced it into her hand.

"Use it for the child."

"Children do not cost money in this place."

"Toki, the world is changing. If Nai ever has to go down the mountain, she will need it."

"If not, we will use it to start a fire."

"Then I very much hope it will start a fire."

We said goodbye to all we had shared, and though they were gracious, I again felt a great burden about leaving. The fool in me wanted there to be two Clays; one to go, and one to stay behind.

Jijiwa walked me to the backside of the mountain as before and we stood together watching the cluster of lights on the border.

"What is this sadness with my world, Jijiwa? I feel the weight of it in my heart already."

"The wind moves through the valley but the valley remains."

He looked at me. My head turned likewise.

"You think we are like the wind?"

"We must be, or why do we pass away."

"I felt like the wind today. I want to feel that way always."

"Then don't regret the good you leave behind."

I looked again at the string of lights against the darkness.

"Tonight, looking at Nai, I wanted to be everywhere at once."

"We are, I think."

I shook my head, unwilling to accept. He shrugged indifferently.

"We all come from one place, and there we return, so why worry?"

I reached down to hug him.

"You have been like a father to me, Jijiwa."

"I did not ask for this job."

"No, it is true. You are not much envied in this world."

We laughed together then.

I took his words and began my journey back to America, and far down the mountain, I heard Jijiwa chanting with his gourd. I marched to his steady rhythm until I heard it no more but in my heart.

I felt strong from all those days in the valley and loped along easily beneath the moonlight. Much later in the night, I passed by the sparse lights of San Lazaro and well before dawn, came to the base of the mountains, reminded of the many times Kip and I had scrambled up those peaks, but I was not headed there on this morning and turned west instead towards the backside of Nogales.

A little after daybreak, I caught a taxi in town and paid him for a ride to Tucson. I had some breakfast and slept all day in a motel.

Near dusk, I took another cab across town, got some change, found a phone booth and called California. I had the door open while the phone rang. It was a fine, cool evening with an autumn breeze blowing down from the hills.

On the tenth ring, Sarah answered. I closed the door.

"How many lives does a cat have?" she said upon hearing my voice.

"I don't know, but thank you for your help."

"I suppose you heard."

"Yes, though there still exists a litany of law enforcement agencies intent on returning me to my bondage."

"Where are you?"

"Would you like me to pinpoint the location? On the chance that someone is listening in?"

"The city will do."

"Tucson."

"Lovely," she said. "The last bastion of radical naiveté, if I'm not mistaken. A riot broke out at the local university not long ago."

"Are you hopeful yet?"

"Actually, I've been experimenting with domestic bliss."

"I knew it would come to that in the end."

"I was never revolting against domestic bliss."

"Indeed…Well, back to the reason for my call."

"Are you still trying to save the world?"

"Let's just say I have a mission that requires your help."

"And you wanted from me?"

"I need you to come to Tucson. All expenses paid, of course."

"That is the only way I would come to Tucson. Assuming I'd come at all."

"It's important."

"Okay. Explain more."

"Tomorrow night. I'll call you at six. Then I'll know more."

I assumed Sarah to understand me. Given her history, I would never call to explain the details on this phone line. She would know to wait for my call tomorrow evening at an old friend's place.

Either way, there would be no need for Sarah's presence in Tucson if the next call did not go over well. I closed the folding door against the rush of traffic and dialed the number, surprised to hear Caroline's voice.

"Hi, it's Clay."

"Clay! Where are you? What are you doing? Are you all right?"

"Slow down, dear. One question at a time."

"Oh god, I thought I would never hear from you again."

"Well, I'm here."

"I'm so glad."

"Yeah?"

"Yeah."

"Well, it's nice to know you care."

"Of course I do."

Not knowing quite how to respond to that comment, I left it alone. Then I sensed her crying.

"I'm sorry, Clay. I'm so sorry I hurt you and acted the way I did."

"I'm sorry, too, but let's not discuss it over the phone, okay?"

"Okay…But where are you?"

"In Tucson."

"What are you doing back there?"

"That will take some explaining."

"You're not in trouble, are you?"

"No, not at the moment, but you know me."

"Oh Clay, don't say that."

"Well, the fact is, I need your help. Any chance you could come to Tucson?"

"Won't you tell me anything?"

"It's really best if I explain things when you get here…So?"

"Okay. The fall semester doesn't start for a month so I've got at least that long."

"Good. And any chance you could come tonight?"

"I'd have to check with the airlines. It'll probably cost a lot at the last minute like this."

"Don't worry about it. I'll drive to the airport right now and make the reservation."

"You're sure?"

"Of course. I'll call you back as soon as I have a flight arranged."

"Okay."

There was silence.

"I love you, Clay."

"I love you too."

"Please tell me we can try again."

"I guess we are, huh?"

"Yeah, I guess we are."

"Okay. Let me get to the airport."

I took a taxi there and bought a first-class ticket on Western Airlines. Caroline arrived a bit after midnight.

"Oh Clay," she said, standing on her tiptoes to kiss my lips. "I'm sorry."

"Ssshhhhh. It's okay."

"I tried to forget about you but I couldn't."

"I know."

A tear rolled down her right cheek and she didn't bother to brush it away. I kissed that one and the others as they came and we were there a long time holding each other before going off to grab her luggage.

At an all-night cafe, we had sandwiches and talked and the many things we had shared together passed through my thoughts as we did, some of it sweet, some of it hurtful, and some of the hurtful things were very hurtful, but I had learned that emotions were ephemeral and only fools lived their lives bouncing from one feeling to the other. The wise let these memories and feelings come and go, like passing clouds, and stood firmly upon the virtues that withstood the test of time.

A few times, Caroline tried to press me about what I had been doing since our last encounter and I sidestepped the subject as best I could. No good would come of explaining my days with Nai, or from thrashing around in Caroline's love affair with Brett. I could wish that our journey together was pristine and without wounds, but that was not the way of life, and definitely not the one we had been given to live.

At some point, Caroline placed her feet up in my lap.

"Can I ask you a question," she said.

"Sure."

"Do you really respect me now?"

"Sure."

"Why?"

I weighed my response before answering.

"Because you're not nearly so foolish."

She kicked at me under the table.

"Of course, neither am I."

Her feet came back and she nibbled at her sandwich.

"Do you really think I was foolish?"

"It's what makes us human, don't you think?"

"That sounds awfully calculated."

I put my sandwich down and grabbed her feet.

"It was."

I laughed as her feet struggled in my hands.

Both of us stopped suddenly and stared into each other's eyes. I threw some money on the table and we hurried back to the motel in a taxi.

Undressing Caroline became an act of redemption, my hands, my teeth, my lips seeking the flesh beneath. When she was naked and standing next to the bed, I knelt down and nuzzled my face in her womb.

Her hands gently pulled my face upwards to look at her.

"What's wrong, Clay?"

"Nothing."

"You don't look happy."

I shook my head, again not knowing how to answer her.

"Just tell me how I can please you," I said

Her dark eyes studied me, her tongue toying with the birthmark on her upper lip. Then, without another word, she crawled onto the bed and looked at me over her shoulder.

Much later, I lay spooning her under the sheets. Cars passed by on the street and made patterns on the ceiling and walls. I watched them move in the darkness of the room. The scent of Caroline's hair was in my face.

"It's not nearly as five-star," she said.

I was surprised to hear her voice. I thought she had been asleep.

"That hotel in Burbank wasn't exactly five-star either," I said.

"It was a lot closer."

"I suppose."

"We're not going downhill, are we?" she said with wonderful dramatics.

A truck rumbled by and shook the walls.

"We're certainly getting closer to the street."

She laughed and pulled closer.

"Clay?"

"Yes."

"Let's get married."

"Sure. We'll get married as soon as possible."

"Do you really want to?"

"Yes, very much so."

She turned her head back and kissed me.

"I still want you to face your legal problems."

She stared into my eyes and turned away.

"At least look into it."

"Still trying to get me behind bars I see."

"Clay, I just said look into it." I laughed and she slapped me. "What's so funny?"

"I've already looked into it."

"And?"

"They've indicted dozens of people."

"For the bombing?"

"Yes. And many of them had perfect alibis."

She turned over to face me.

"A lawyer told you this?"

"Yes."

"So what does it mean?"

"It means it's a legal circus. I'm more likely to be imprisoned for flight than for the original crime."

"Then you're not going to turn yourself in?"

"It's doesn't seem to make much sense at the moment."

She played with the few hairs on my chest.

"There's more," I said.

"Is this about the draft?"

"Yes. The lawyer I spoke with knew someone who worked in the military."

"That's nice."

"Yeah, so when I was in Hawaii, I wrote a letter and mailed it to the sergeant-in-command at the local draft board."

"Why would you do that?"

"Because it said not to do so on my induction notice."

"That's so like you."

"Uh huh."

"So? What did your letter say?"

"I told them that I was on acid the day I reported."

"Were you really?"

"No. It sort of felt that way, though."

I made big eyes.

"Actually, I told them that I took acid on a daily basis. That I was in a cult and if they wanted to find me, I was living on a coffee plantation in Hawaii."

"I still don't understand. Why would you think to send them a letter?"

"Because Stan told me this one night when I was living in Hawaii. The sergeant-in-command at the local draft board is the only officer on that level who can re-classify you without consulting anyone else."

"And so? What happened?"

"They classified me 4-H."

"Is that like 4-F?"

"Somewhat. In this case, they might still call you up, but only if the Russians were landing in Manhattan. Of course, I didn't know for sure if I was a draft dodger or a deserter. I guess because I never swore an oath at the induction center, I was never officially inducted into the military."

"So it worked," she said.

"The draft part, yeah."

She stared at me, idly nibbling on a fingernail.

"What about Kip?"

"That's why I asked you to come here. So I could explain my plan."

"I've got a feeling this is the bad part."

"Could be."

"Okay…Go on."

I did. She shook her head while listening.

"Clay, please. You're just looking for more trouble."

"I assumed you'd say that and I respect your feelings, but it was something in here."

I tapped lightly on her chest with my fingers.

"Something deep inside. Something from the deepest reservoirs of my spiritual being and I can't help but feel it was divinely inspired."

"Well, even if that's true, I don't like the idea of working with one of your former flames."

"It can't work without her. It can't work without both of you."

"How do you know this Sarah would even want to be involved?"

"I talked with her on the phone a few hours ago."

Caroline turned over and faced the other way.

"Please," I said.

She looked back at me.

"Because I love you, I won't say no. But I'm not prepared to say yes, either."

"Fair enough, but if we're going to explore this, we'll have to meet with Sarah."

"Don't expect me to be enthused about that."

I held Caroline close to reassure her. A long silence followed.

"Clay?"

"Yes."

"Have you been with another woman?"

"No."

"You have. I can feel it."

"No," I said again.

I felt her starting to confess her own sins and put a hand over her mouth. I knew the truth, but for me it was better to pretend. The mind was a wonderful thing in what it could ignore. The other way was certain to be like a knife forever digging around in my heart. Where would the imagination draw a line? It was impossible to do so. I would want to know every sordid detail. And still, it wouldn't be enough. Better to cauterize the wound and forget things as best as we could.

Caroline had begun to cry again.

"Everything's going to be all right," I said.

"Oh, Clay, I'm so sorry. He turned out to be such a big liar."

"Caroline, please. We live and we learn. That's it. We can't change the past. Now I'm asking you again. Just drop it.

"Why does it have to be this way?" she said through her tears.

"I don't know. It just is."

She went on crying and I let her go on for a spell before pulling her around to face me and doing what I could to turn the old heartaches into new passions.

I pulled Caroline close afterwards and caressed her quietly.

"I wish we could start all over," she said.

"We are, I think."

She did not answer and I hoped we could leave it at that.

In the morning, we showered and walked to a nearby sidewalk café. The food was good and the cool, autumn day felt pleasant on our skin. Afterwards we walked to the university campus and watched people go by from the shade of a tree. Later we had Mexican food and wandered the streets window-shopping.

At six, I called Sarah. She arrived the next day, shortly before sunset. Caroline greeted her like a wary cat.

"Do you see what I mean?" I said after the introductions.

Caroline nodded.

"It makes sense, but it doesn't change the danger involved."

"Life is dangerous," I said.

Like all my assurances, that one didn't go over very well.

We had dinner together and continued to flesh out the details. I was encouraged when Sarah and Caroline began discussing things among themselves. I added my input here and there — the layout of the prison, the procedures and daily routines — but they did most of the fine-tuning on their own.

"Okay, what do you say?"

I searched both their faces.

"I'm willing to try," Sarah said. "But I think we should be honest with ourselves. At some point, it may be a matter of doing more harm than good."

"That's fair enough," I said and looked at Caroline.

"I guess I feel the same way." She looked at Sarah and back at me. "I'm willing to try. But I want to know something from you right here and now, Clay."

"What?"

"That you'll give up at the slightest hint of disaster."

I shrugged.

"I will be very confused about the universe to think I was wrong, but yes, I will relent at the first sign of trouble."

"As long as you promise me that," she said. "I'll try."

Over coffee, we refined the plan further. Then it was time for Sarah to head back to the airport. I called a taxi and gave her enough money to take care of any needs she might have in California.

The next morning, I gave Caroline a wad of cash and sent her off to buy a car, thinking it would be best for me to steer clear of car dealerships. As the day wore on with no sign of Caroline, I began to worry. About four o'clock she pulled up, accompanied by the growl of an old bi-plane.

"A Volkswagen?" I said.

It was a '58 rag-top with chipped yellow paint and a worn sunroof.

"I don't know. I thought it kind of resembled our romance. A little beat-up, but it runs and has a sunny outlook."

She stuck one hand through the top.

"Funny."

"I'm learning," she said.

I walked around it once and noticed that the hood did not latch properly. I tried closing it several times.

"What's the matter?" she said.

She got out and came around front.

"The latch is broken."

"Should I take it back?"

"No. Like you said, it resembles our romance. Old and a bit worn out but probably worth repairing."

I circled the car with Caroline chasing after me.

It took us most of that day to locate the makeup supplies Caroline required. Along the way, we stopped at a hardware store, where I purchased some rope to secure the hood of the Volkswagen. With that done, we returned to the motel in the late afternoon. I poured two snifters of sherry and Caroline went to work on me: first cutting my hair short, then dyeing it black and then applying a disguise to my face. It was half an hour before I was free to look at the results in a mirror.

"What a strange feeling," I said.

I looked at her.

"I feel as though I should act differently now…Ha," I added with a bow. She shook her head.

"I'll think of myself as Toshiro Mifune."

"Japanese-American will do."

"I've always gone for the dramatic," I said and feigned several sword thrusts. "Okay. Now what?"

"Scrub your face and let's head south…" We kissed with those all too familiar words trailing off into the dying afternoon.

58

We passed through Nogales at dusk with storm clouds low along the southern horizon. I rolled down my window to the crisp, autumn air, struck by that end of day déjà vu feeling, when twilight descends and people rush here and there and it seems as if you have always been in that very same hour.

I reached for Caroline's hand, glad to have her there with me and for once not wanting to be anywhere in the universe other than where I was, and more so, knowing that I could not be anywhere else but in that moment, with our history and dreams all bound together in what we had come to know as our fleeting lives.

But behind these contented feelings, my uncertainties lingered. Was I doing the right thing with this plan to rescue Kip? Or was this just one more of my headlong schemes? At times, I felt absolutely certain of my vision from up on the mountain. At others, doubts riddled my heart and I would think myself half mad. And all the while, the lights of a Mexican border town passed by, vividly etched against an evening sky.

Somewhere below Benjamin Hill, the storm met us on its way up from the gulf and the rain began to pelt the roof of the car in earnest. Ten miles north of Hermosillo, we passed through the checkpoint. The guards were all huddled together out of the rain and waved us through rather than get wet.

Five miles south of the checkpoint, I pulled off into the brush along a barren stretch of highway and held a flashlight as Caroline redid my disguise. With a final dab of mousse and comb through my hair, she nodded and I pulled back onto the highway.

Half an hour later, we were booking a room at the Hotel Anselmo, which we had heard was the only respectable place in town.

Opening the door to our room, I was struck by yet another déjà vu feeling. It was as if I had been opening that door for all eternity, planning Kip's escape, just as in another hour, Eric and Rebecca had been here planning mine. Always different actors but always the same drama and same moment in time.

Caroline placed her bag down and went off to use the bathroom. I parted the curtains and saw the prison through the wet evening sky. The conical hill was dark save for a glow of lights at the top.

"Look," I said when Caroline came back to stand beside me.

"Oh, it looks like such a horrible place."

"Yeah. You wonder if men used to lock each other up in caves."

She shook her head.

"It doesn't make much sense when you think of it like that."

I sat in a chair next to the window, facing into the room.

"Look, it's in the mirror."

Seeing this, Caroline draped a towel over the mirror.

After she had unpacked a bit, we walked downstairs to the cantina. The Mexican male patrons seemed greatly interested in our presence.

"Either Mexican men are not accustomed to seeing Japanese men or they've got a thing for you."

Caroline continued her visual reconnaissance without bothering to reply. When she sipped at her margarita, our eyes met in the mirror behind the bar.

"I suspect it's you."

She looked back at my profile.

"Are you getting jealous, dear?"

I looked over at her.

"Probably. Japanese men are very territorial."

"You should probably be quiet about that."

"Ah so. That would be in keeping with my ancient heritage."

She admonished me again with her eyes.

The bartender came to check on our drinks. I smiled and bowed imperceptibly to him. A thought occurred to me.

"Is there a special way of smiling in Japanese?"

For this I received another frown and a surreptitious slap under the bar. I smiled at myself in the mirror. It seemed okay. I paid for two more drinks. Caroline's chin was against my shoulder. I saw in the mirror that she studied my profile.

"I cannot remember there being any Japanese potentates."

"There are samurai."

"Yes. But still, it is a loss."

"A samurai and a geisha girl," Caroline said. "That doesn't sound so bad to me."

"You are right. In fact, why don't we go back up and see what a samurai and geisha girl can do to have fun on a rainy night."

We were soon back up in our room and stayed there for the rest of night.

The storm broke before morning so we went down to the lobby and inquired about a suitable place to camp on the beach. Our pretense was research for a book about the gulf, for which we received a great deal of advice, more than we really wanted, but decided by virtue of its description to head up north to the gulf area around Desemboque.

We had already purchased camping gear in Tucson and needed only to stop and purchase the necessary provisions in town and were on our way north on a crisp, sunny day. Again, five miles outside of town, and before the checkpoint, I pulled out of sight along the highway and Caroline removed my makeup. When she was done, I hid her kit inside one of the door panels and we continued north.

There was not much traffic on the highway that day, which afforded the guards at the check-point an opportunity to give each car a nice going over. They wore green trench coats and had M-1 rifles slung over their shoulder and the mood was exceedingly somber.

One of the guards pointed at the rope tying the hood and asked me to undo it. I did as asked and watched as he made a cursory look through the contents of our suitcase. With a final check of the spare tire compartment, he allowed me to close the hood again.

The lead guard went through the motions of searching the interior, but clearly it was just an excuse to have a better look at Caroline. Meanwhile, several other guards stood nearby trying to look impressive with their trench coats and M-1's.

Having found no contraband, the lead guard waved us through.

"We should bring them cigarettes each time," I said as we pulled away.

"Why? Do you think it will help to distract them?"

"Oh, I think you've distracted them quite enough already."

"Oh, my poor, jealous samurai potentate guy."

"Yes. It brings me great suffering to watch them ogle over my one and only geisha girl."

Caroline kissed my neck and let me know by way of her hands that I was still her one and only samurai guy.

A short while later, we came to Benjamin Hill, passed Santa Ana half an hour later and turned west on Highway 2. It was a bad road that led through Caborca and down to the gulf. We approached a tiny village as we neared the coast. Caroline got the map out.

"It's San Francisco," she said.

"Hey, we can stop at Fisherman's Wharf."

"Funny."

In less than a minute, we had driven into and out of the San Francisco. There were the remains of an old mission church and little else.

"All the big cities in the world have gone to hell," I said.

"I'll bet Desemboque is even bigger and better."

"I'll take that bet."

She looked sidelong at me.

We came to a bridge and motored across the mouth of the Rio Conception. A stiff wind was blowing in from the sea. On the far side of the bridge, we entered El Desemboque, which was perhaps even smaller than San Francisco.

I looked sidelong at Caroline.

"How did you want to pay?"

She laughed.

Beyond the village, we found a washboard road and followed it out to the sea. The wide shoreline was bordered by sand dunes and the dunes were white against the blue sea.

We parked, grabbed a blanket and found a comfortable place high up among the dunes. Grains of fine sand whispered about our legs and ankles. The edges of the dunes slowly slipped away as we watched.

"It's lovely," Caroline said.

"All the big cities of the world can go to hell." She crawled on top of me and stared with her dark eyes. "What? Were you thinking to get that payment out of the way?"

"Maybe we should put up the tent first."

I chuckled.

"I admire your practicality."

"Really?" she said.

"Yes...No."

She laughed and tried to tickle me.

"I admire your newfound honesty."

"Really?" I said.

"Yes...No..."

She fought off my attempts to tickle her and ran back towards the shore.

I deflated each tire a bit and we drove far down the coast in that late hour. The sand dunes were on our left and the blustery sea to our right, the endless whitecaps pushing in towards shore with the afternoon wind. Looking either way along the coast, there wasn't another soul in sight.

Having settled on a place to camp, we erected the tent, got things arranged inside and climbed back up among the dunes. The sun was just then setting across the gulf and the wind grew cold with it. Caroline nestled up closer to me.

"You look worried," she said with a glance in my direction.

"I guess I am at times."

"Have you thought of not doing it?"

"Yes, but like I told you. It was something in here." I tapped at my own heart. "Someplace deep inside."

I looked back across the gulf, knowing I could never explain how it had felt. The more you tried to convey a spiritual experience, the more it eluded you.

As we sat quietly, the sky along the horizon faded from warm pastels to gray-blue. The sea had been navy-blue and white-capped but was now gray and cold looking . Gulls crossed the darkening sky, going to wherever they went in that hour.

"I worry too," Caroline said and squeezed my hand.

"I know," I said and kissed her forehead. "But it really comes back to this question of what is behind the universe? I mean, if what happened to me was nothing more than a meaningless illusion, then

I'd feel pretty well screwed and none of the other stuff would really matter."

"Being in jail matters," she said.

"Yes, I suppose, but the way this plan was revealed to me. Well, if I'm wrong, I would just feel like the universe was pointless."

"I worry a lot, Clay but I have to trust you."

"Thanks. I wish I had more to offer."

She stared at me for a moment and put her head against my shoulder.

We returned to Hermosillo the following afternoon, stopping a few miles south of the checkpoint to restore my Japanese appearance. Then Sarah arrived that night. I kissed her cheek cautiously at the door.

"Well, Toshiro," she said.

I smiled and bowed.

"He's my role model."

"Hi Caroline," Sarah said on her way inside.

They hugged and Sarah made the additional gesture of kissing her on the cheek.

An awkward moment followed.

"Come, sit down and relax," I said.

Sarah sat cross-legged on the bed and patted for Caroline to join her. Caroline did so, but at a safe distance and with her feet on the floor.

"How was your trip down?" she asked Sarah.

"Fine, fine. How are you two making out?"

"Well, we had this totally groovy trip up to Desemboque. Wasn't it, Clay?"

I acknowledged as much with a nod of my head.

"I'm going to buy some paints and try my hand at watercolors. I'm hoping we can go there between every visit."

"Very cool," Sarah said. "And why, pray tell, is there a towel over the mirror?"

I pulled the towel away briefly so Sarah could see the prison reflected. Fascinated, she went to look out the window and I went over to join her. The prison was five miles away but bathed in lights and seemingly close enough to touch.

"Babylon," Sarah said absently.

"Yes," I said. "A hopeful young generation marched off to captivity. For...uh...why in the hell we were marched off to captivity again?"

"For being uppity," she said.

"Ah, yes. Thanks to President Nebuchadnezzar."

Sarah smiled at me and then at Caroline. She had remained sitting on the bed. I wasn't sure if she had gotten the historical reference or if I should bother to explain it.

"I've really begun to worry about this whole thing," Caroline said out of the blue.

Sarah and I glanced at each other and another awkward moment followed.

"Well, we'll have a much better idea tomorrow," I said.

"And if things go south, you'll be in there with him."

"So will I," Sarah said.

"Somehow, I don't find that comforting."

I looked at Sarah.

"Let's drink and be merry," she said. "For tomorrow we may die."

Somehow, Caroline didn't find that comforting, either. Sarah decided it was a good time to head out the door.

"I'll see you two down in the cantina."

I turned to face Caroline.

"Go on," she said. "I'll meet you there."

I followed Caroline into the bathroom.

"Why are you doing this?"

"Well?"

"Well, we're old friends."

"Yeah, old friends."

"Oh, Caroline. I can't change the past. I can only make today a good thing."

"With her around?"

"No, with you around."

Caroline stared.

"Please, just until Kip is out."

I tried to hug her but she resisted.

"All right," I said

Caroline was staring at me from the bathroom as I went out. Hell, I thought. This is the last thing I need. A cat fight on my hands, even a one sided one. If Caroline goes off on a jealous tangent, the whole mission will be doomed.

"You've got to work on comity," I told Sarah down in the bar.

Sarah paid for her drink and saluted me with the glass. She took a sip and placed the drink down.

"Don't worry yourself, Clay. I know how to play the bridesmaid. Caroline and I will get along just fine in the end. You'll see."

"To echo her most recent sentiment, yeah sure."

Sarah laughed and we were soon lost in conversation.

Caroline came down later and we spent a few hours drinking and talking together. Sarah did a remarkable job, both of getting Caroline drunk and making her feel the center of attention. The two of them were gabbing away like old chums by the time we headed off to bed.

The following morning, Caroline stopped me as I prepared to go out the door. She inspected my disguise then kissed me.

"Be careful," she said. "I don't entirely trust this Sarah."

"Oh stop," I said. "This Sarah. The two of you were old chums last night before we went off to bed."

I shook her face gently and kissed her lips.

"I'll see you this afternoon and we'll drive straight to Desemboque."

"Alone?"

"Of course."

"What's she going to do?"

"I don't know. Relax, Caroline. She just wants to be your friend."

I guessed this was her personal Durango of sorts, so I showered her with abundant affection, but she still seemed terribly uncertain about everything as I closed the door.

Sarah was waiting for me in the lobby and we drove straight across town in her rented car. Sarah had mailed Kip a note from the states, along with some money, telling him to expect an old friend and to have a private cell ready.

At the prison, we were confronted by something I had not expected, a platoon of soldiers. Two of them manned a large artillery piece off to one side. There was a bunker of sand bags around the gun. The remaining soldiers were milling around the parking lot.

"I think you may have offended someone," Sarah said.

"You know," I said. "It occurs to me that this is one revolution you could actually win."

"I wouldn't know what to do, I'm so accustomed to losing."

"The Mexicans can offer counseling in this area. They've been losing at things for five hundred years."

"What brave souls. I've grown disillusioned after only five."

We climbed out of the sedan and joined a long line of people waiting to enter the prison. There were many young mothers with children and old ladies alone. The old ladies wore black dresses, as usual, and clutched rosary beads in their hands. There were prostitutes, too, all of these women mixed together in line.

The line inched slowly forward towards the main gate, with those at the front eventually disappearing from bright sunlight into the dark, cavernous hallway.

"You can hardly tell we blew the place up," I whispered.

Sarah looked with fascination from the building back to the pageantry of Mexican culture around us.

"Where are the men?" she asked.

"I've concluded that Mexican fathers are too disgraced by their offspring. It's not very machismo getting caught, you know."

She turned to me.

"Speaking of fathers, did you know that Caroline's pregnant?"

"Good god, no. What makes you think that?"

"A woman's intuition."

"It takes more than intuition to get pregnant."

"You know, Clay. I sometimes wish we'd had a child."

"Perhaps you could prevail upon Caroline to share me."

"Do you think she would?"

"I think there's a better chance of pigs flying."

"Okay, we'll cheat."

"A woman's intuition, remember?"

"I'm only asking for a very small piece of your cornucopia?"

"You're treading on very dangerous ground here. And no, I can't."

I smiled at her.

"Do you think I smile okay in Japanese?"

"Yes. Is making love any different?"

"I'm sorry, Sarah. It's the way of the world. At least this particular version of it. Sharing bliss always gets back to the flesh.

582

And the flesh always gets back to territorial matters. And strange things happen when you get into territorial matters."

She took my hand and looked at me enticingly.

"Stop it," I said.

"No," she said.

"I'm serious. And by the way, you really have me worried about this pregnancy business."

"I'm fairly certain about that," she said. "Remember? A woman's intuition?"

She smiled but I didn't and began to fret. The specter of children and parenthood had always seemed like a matter of freedom lost to me.

Then it was our turn to pass through the front gate and into the wide, arched hallway. A guard sat watching everyone come in. A line of people stretched out before us. As my eyes adjusted to the dim light, I saw three guards waiting at the far gate. One of them was a female.

"I'm thinking it will be okay," I said. "But my heart seems to have other ideas."

"About the child," Sarah said.

"Well, yes, that, too, but I was focusing more on the potential for incarceration at the moment."

"Just think positively," she said. "We're boarding a train to Paris."

She came close and I put my arm around her.

One of the guards watched the gate and studied each person as they neared the front of the line. The other two guards were there to conduct searches. The female guard led Sarah into a booth. I waited my turn in the men's line. Rebecca's uncle was no longer at the gate. Perhaps he had retired with his newfound fortune. Perhaps he had been arrested.

Thinking of him, I remembered Rebecca with a sudden pang of guilt. I had used her and tossed her aside carelessly. I would have to send money. Something. If not for her, I would not have found freedom.

I was still papering over those guilty feelings when the new guard welcomed me into the booth to be searched. Sarah was waiting for me when I walked out and we passed through the gate together. The enormous weight of captivity weighed upon my soul again instantly. I had almost forgotten how hopeless it could feel.

Standing in the courtyard, we were surrounded by men who had been locked away from the world into which they were born; men who had failed somehow to do what society expected of them and were now cast into this place of purgatory for their sins. I knew all too well how it felt and wanted to forgive them all. I wanted to open the gates and give every man back his freedom, but I was only there to save one person and started across the courtyard in search of Kip. Sarah and I were almost to the other end of the prison before I spotted him. Once I had pointed out Kip to Sarah, she went over and introduced herself. I stood off to one side.

Kip looked from Sarah to me and back with a perplexed smile on his face. Plainly he had no idea who we were. I went over to shake his hand and spoke softly into his ear.

"It's your partner."

He stood back with the same smile, but his eyes were as big as saucers now.

"Did you get the cell?" I asked him.

"Yeah, yeah," he said and led us towards one near Cell 13. All along the way, Kip reviewed Sarah and especially me with a look of wonder.

We passed by Rosa along the way. Don was there, done up with lipstick and a babushka. I saw Green and Haynes up above. They had survived. Every American in sight watched us intently, but clearly none of them recognized me. They were just wondering who this Jap was and no doubt envying him for his slinky, blonde girlfriend.

The owner of the private cell greeted Kip, opened the gate to have a look inside and left. Sarah went in first. I followed. Kip closed the door and came over to give me a hug. He held me at arm's length.

"I figured you had forgotten about me, partner."

"No, no. I couldn't do that, my friend. I was forever back in Guaymas, knowing we should have waited for a train."

Kip nodded without saying a word.

"I was really bummed to hear about Steve and Kristine."

"There's no way to explain how I feel about that."

Kip nodded again, but sadly this time.

584

"Anyway, we came to get you out of here. Or at least to try."

"Wow, brother. You're taking a hell of a risk just being here."

"Yeah, but somehow I know you'd do the same for me."

Sarah had gone to lie on the bed.

"All right, you two. Enough with the melodrama. We don't have long in this cell."

"Yes, we'd better get down to business, Kip."

"By the way," he said. "Great disguise."

"It melts when things get hot."

"I've been trying to verify that fact," Sarah said. "But this Caroline's got him firmly by the ding-dong."

"Speaking of ding-dongs," I said with a squirm. "This rescue business could get to be a real pain in the ass."

"Personally," Sarah said, "I've never been banged and had so little fun."

She made a face at me. I made one back and looked at Kip.

"So, what's it like in here these days?"

"Ever taken a cold shower on a cold day?" he asked me.

"Yeah, I remember tripping on that thought when it was hotter than hell."

"Yeah, well. It's anything but a trip now."

"And your family? What about them?"

"Disowned me," he said. "At least for now."

"It's probably just as well. We don't need them coming around to mess things up. Things are bound to get a bit dicey."

"Well, Clay, you were right about one thing."

"You mean, ten years in this hole?"

"Yeah."

"Hey, transcending's a noble thought and all that, but…"

"Yeah…So, I'm all ears. I'm guessing this is another one of your crazy schemes."

"You bet. It will definitely take some explaining." I sat down next to Sarah. "By the way, did Harry get out?"

"Yeah, some people from the consulate came by last month and he was out the next day."

"Amazing what they can do when they put their minds to it."

"You have to remember, Clay. We're dealing with a major superpower down here."

"Yes, I saw the inter-continental taco launcher out front."

We laughed. Sarah took off her blouse and lay face down on the bed.

"How about a massage while you two are bullshitting."

Kip went over to work on her back.

"The plan?" he said.

"Ah, yes, the plan. Well, if this vision I had was truly inspired, and I sure hope it was, you're going to walk out of here a free man in one month. That or I'll be back in here with you...And Sarah too."

Kip went on giving Sarah a massage but looked up wistfully from time to time as I explained the details.

"You're nuts," he said when I was through.

"So we agreed long ago. But it could work, don't you think?"

"Yyyyyou know, you know, it jjjjjust might at that, there pilgrim."

"Good Jimmy Stewart," Sarah said. "Do it again."

He did and I played John Wayne and the rest of the hour passed by swiftly as we talked and laughed and refined the details. At one point I had to confess to Kip that much of his money was already gone.

He shrugged.

"However, if we can ever get back down to Mazatlán, I'll be happy to share what I have left with you."

Kip shrugged again with his wistful smile.

When our time in the private cell was through, he walked us out to the gate.

"See you on Wednesday, partner." He hugged Sarah and bowed almost imperceptibly to me.

The guard put his hand up and asked for our passes. He looked at them and back at our faces before nodding and instructing the other guard to open the next gate. After walking down the long, arched corridor, we were free outside, but my heart kept beating wildly as we drove down the hill.

"It seemed too easy," I said. "What do you think?"

"Anything can happen," Sarah said. "And of course, there's the last day."

"That has an ominous ring to it."

"By the way, am I invited to Desemboque?"

"Do you get the feeling that Caroline is marking out territory?"

"She's a sweet girl," Sarah said in response. "I've actually grown quite fond of her."

"Oh really...And what are you going to do?"

"I suppose head up to Tucson and iron out a few of these details. While you two screw on the beach."

We had arrived at the hotel and Sarah pulled around back. I gave her a handful of money.

"If you need any more, just holler. And thanks. We'll see you on Wednesday."

I got out.

"Have fun with Caroline," Sarah said as she drove off.

I went upstairs and held Caroline for a long moment before we hurried on our way to Desemboque.

Sarah came again on Wednesday and again things went without a hitch at the prison. We had arrived late and stayed until the end. The line was long and moving slowly at that late hour. When we reached the gate, I looked over to see Sarah rifling through her purse.

"Clay, I can't find the pass."

"Sarah, they are not going to like this."

The guard watching us asked for our passes. I gave him mine. He waited politely for Sarah but when she made it clear through various gestures that she couldn't find hers, things took a serious turn. I attempted to say something and was told to sit down inside the gate. Sarah was taken aside and made to dump out her purse. They called Kip and searched him in the booth. They searched Sarah, then me. When nothing was found, they took Kip to search his belongings. Sarah was taken into the director's office and he was summoned to the prison on his day off. It was dark and everyone else had long departed by the time Sarah came out. Not at all satisfied, but without evidence, they finally allowed us both to leave.

"Is everything okay?" I asked.

"He said they could imprison me for losing it."

"They can imprison you for anything down here."

"I know, but I think he really meant it."

"Yeah, that would be really fucked up, Sarah."

"Yeah," she said.

"Well, the question is, are we still on?"

"Why not? I guess if we survived that catastrophe, we can survive anything."

When we arrived back to the hotel, I got out and leaned in the window.

"Then you'll be back on Sunday?"

She nodded.

"Have you decided when the last day will be?"

"Whenever the moment seems right," I said.

"When the moment seems right," she said.

With the same faux jilted lover look, she drove away and Caroline and I soon left for Desemboque. The guards at the check-point stopped us long enough to make small talk and to get a better look at Caroline. They took our carton of American cigarettes and waved us through.

We arrived late and found a cold wind blowing down the shore at dusk. I shined the headlights on our enterprise and Caroline and I battled the wind while getting our tent in place. Caroline held one end, I staked the other and we laughed at ourselves in the bitter cold.

When everything was in order, Caroline made the interior cozy and the two of us went for a long stroll down the shore, huddled together against the wind. The sea was black and bristling white with surf and the stars sparkled high in the infinite sky above us. We had stopped for something to eat on the way up from Hermosillo and wanted nothing except to walk quietly.

The tent seemed especially warm when we returned. I lit a kerosene lamp and we sipped Mexican brandy together while reading our books, which was not altogether bad on a cold night along a desolate shoreline, with the wind singing against the canvas.

"What are you reading?" Caroline asked me. I showed her.

"A Hero of Our Time?"

I went back to reading but she pulled the book around to see the cover.

"Who's Mikhail Lermontov?"

"A Russian."

She made a face.

"I know that. You're always reading one Russian or the other."

"I like them the best," I said. "When they're sober. Maybe even when they're not so sober."

"Do you think being a writer and being a drunk go hand in hand?" she asked.

I laughed.

"It's true for many of them."

I went back to reading.

"Would you like to be a writer?" she asked.

I looked over my book.

"I guess it wouldn't be a bad job."

"You've got the drinking part down pat."

She smiled mischievously, but it was a beautiful smile.

"Do you like him?" she asked before I could continue reading.

I put the book down again.

"Yes."

"Why?"

"It's a good, simple story. Not altogether cluttered with thought."

She came closer.

"I know a good story," she said.

"I'll bet you do."

"And it's not too terribly cluttered with thought."

She removed the book from my hands as I reached to turn down the kerosene lamp.

We awakened early the next morning but slept again until ten and it was quite late before I was out lighting the Coleman stove and getting things ready for breakfast. We had bacon and eggs and the food was delicious in the fresh morning air, and especially with the great distances of the gulf around us and with the many colors of blue and green against the fine, white sand. When it grew warm, we went for a swim and I was reminded of the island we had visited off Mazatlán, though the water was cooler at this time of year and the locale even more remote. We had miles and miles of sand dunes and a shoreline all to ourselves.

I tried my luck at surf-fishing that afternoon and caught several corvinas but threw them back, knowing they were gamey and better when smoked. Going by the book I had bought about the Sea of Cortez, I gathered I would have to go a bit farther up the coast towards Puerto Penasco, where the bottom was rocky, in order to find any abalone or lobster but I searched for them anyway in the clear, shallow water close to shore.

As I went about passing my days in idle enterprise, Caroline grew quite accomplished at her painting. I tried not to be envious, but I was. It seemed that whenever Caroline wanted something in life, she just set her mind to it and struck off in this new direction. In comparison, my most natural vocation appeared to be daydreaming.

When I came back from the sea the next afternoon, I found her working on a landscape in watercolor. It was very haunting and alive and I told her I liked it.

"Will you take care of me when you're famous?" I asked amidst my unspoken insecurities

She smiled with a look at my burgeoning mid-section.

"I'm not so sure I can afford you."

"You are not exhibiting a true appreciation for hidden the powers of your samurai potentate."

She looked up from beneath her straw hat.

"And what would those powers be, my dear old potentate?"

I went over and pressed the hardness in my swim trunks against her naked back and kissed her soft skin. It was like the brown color of hazelnuts against the white sand. My kisses went up her spine and onto her shoulders.

"Let's go play in the dunes," I whispered in her ear. "And I'll show you my illustrious powers."

She looked back at me.

"You dirty old potentate."

"Only to play. I promise. "

I ran up from the lagoon and down into the folds of the dunes and heard Caroline's laughter following along behind me.

59

Our sojourn went on for nearly a month, broken every Wednesday and Sunday by a visit to the prison. The issue of the lost pass had never entirely blown over, making Sarah the recipient of additional scrutiny every time we came and went. Otherwise, things were the same. If one day an American prisoner was set free, the next day another unsuspecting fool had fallen fall into the trap. Some of the sentences handed down were favorable, but some, like Kip's, left the convicted man with little hope of being freed for the next five years.

It was October, 1971 and in reading the papers Sarah delivered to me from the States, I grew more and more disillusioned with the state of the world; disillusioned with empires, disillusioned with wars, disillusioned with what power did to the hearts of men. There was always talk of bringing Vietnam to an end, but it dragged on and every effort to protest it was met with an iron fist. If you dissented, it served to ruin your own life more than the machine, and so a generation grew lost in the wilderness, their hopes and dreams steadily extinguished.

As an expatriate, I had my moments of guilt, feeling that I should have been there on the frontlines and more engaged in the struggle, and yet without those of us who had renounced Vietnam by burning our draft cards, there never would have been an anti-war movement. And though our generation appeared to be crashing and burning onto the pages of history, the dream of peace and brotherhood lived on in my heart.

On a more personal level, I harbored fleeting emotions of every imaginable kind, from longing to visit old friends and places to missing the sound of a well-worn phrase to thoughts of stopping for a good burger at a roadside stand. When I dreamed of home, those were the day to day trifles that brought a quiet ache to my heart.

But as Sarah had been right, and Caroline was now pregnant, I had not only the plan to rescue Kip on my mind, but a child's future to consider, and as my once invincible convictions about the mission wavered, my anxieties about parenthood grew with inverse proportion. I had wanted to run off to someplace simple with Caroline. The thought of diapers and screaming babies terrified me as much as wars and prisons.

Sarah came to visit us early one Saturday and was practicing the next necessary disguise on Caroline. I sat on the bed, distracted by such thoughts.

"Let me practice on you, Clay," Sarah said.

"I've already been practiced on."

"You're no fun," she said. Caroline frowned good-naturedly at me.

"Okay, I've been worked over professionally," I said.

Caroline laughed.

"Perhaps you had better sit quietly, dear. Things aren't coming out of your mouth right today."

"It's my identity crisis. I fear I'll have to be a Mexican after this."

I saw Caroline's face in the mirror.

"Please, dear. We agreed, no negative thoughts."

I got up and faced Sarah.

"Did you ship the box?"

"Yes." She glanced at me once and went back to working on Caroline's face. "Yesterday, but who knows if it got through."

"We'll know soon enough," I said.

"That we will," Sarah said. "If you can be patient that long."

"I'll wait for you two in the bar," I said and went downstairs.

I was there an hour before Sarah and Caroline appeared. The bartender had asked me about them repeatedly. Clearly he didn't think I was much fun. When the ladies arrived, we ordered margaritas and drank them until we were good and high.

I left early, feeling like an intruder in their newfound camaraderie and was further saddened when Caroline returned very late and passed out without bothering to undress. I watched as she slept and felt lonely and thought it foolish to feel such things when someone who loved you was right there, but the feelings remained and I did not sleep until much later in the night.

During our prison visit the following day, Sarah coached Kip in the proper etiquette of being a lady. I kept watch at the door.

"Everything okay?" I asked as the time to leave approached. Kip nodded.

"Okay then, we go next visit."

Kip handed Sarah her shoes and she put them back on. She was now lying on the bed in her bra and panties and high heel shoes. Kip sat next to her and she rubbed his back.

"You don't mind, do you?"

I studied them for a moment.

"No, but you'd better make it fast. I melt in the sun."

I pulled back the curtain, closed the cell door behind me and went to watch a man making tortillas down one of the covered hallways.

How odd, I thought, this thing between former lovers. I had once been terribly jealous over Sarah, and she with me. Now, we were like a brother and sister. How these emotional attachments came and went was beyond me to understand. If I caught Caroline sharing intimacies with another man, I would want to kill that person, or both of them. I would die a thousand deaths inside. Could I ever feel such detachment towards Caroline in the future? The way I now felt towards Sarah? It was impossible for me to conceive.

I was glad for Kip, in any case. Men would not starve to death from a lack of love, but the absence of it exacted an even greater cruelty. Nothing civilized men more than having it, and nothing made them harder in their hearts than doing without.

As if to prove my point, Sarah and Kip found me fifteen minutes later, both of them walking on air. Sarah came over to me and we resumed our pretense of romance on our way out the gate.

In advance of the next visit, Sarah again came a day early and worked with Caroline on the disguise. Sarah attached a wig to Caroline's head and Caroline's hair then looked more or less identical to Sarah's hair. Then Caroline took off the wig and we went to dinner and passed the remainder of the night talking in the room.

I kept to myself, more than usual. My thoughts were of that day up on the mountain, when my vision had seemed as sharp and bright as a face in a mirror. Either that moment had happened, or it had not. Either I trusted in it, or I didn't. Either way, I said nothing to either of them about my doubts and reservations.

About midnight, Sarah got up to leave our room

"I've been thinking that you should ride back with Sarah," I told Caroline. Caroline and Sarah looked at each other.

"No," Caroline said. "We're in this together. Besides, it would only arouse suspicion, especially when you go through the check-point."

"I don't care," I said. "I'm worried about you."

"Well now it's my turn to be stubborn."

"Back me up here, Sarah."

Sarah smirked and went out the door. I looked at Caroline.

"I'm just worried, okay?"

"You asked me to place my trust in you, Clay. And now you have to trust in yourself."

I lay awake long into the night, thinking about that.

And finally, the day had come. It was a cold, dry morning with a wind blowing down from the mountains. The curtains in our room had been pulled tight to the world outside. Caroline was dyeing Sarah's hair brown in the bathroom. I lay on the bed, staring at the ceiling. When the dyeing was complete, Caroline curled Sarah's hair and placed the wig over that. When all that was done, they hugged each other and promised to stay in touch. Caroline hugged me a long time before I followed Sarah out the door.

We took our separate cars this time and drove over to the prison. The visitor line was especially long. As Sarah and I stood there waiting, I thought the extra crowds were probably a good thing, then worried that maybe they weren't.

Sarah had brought Kip a cardboard box filled with books and cookies. I had thrown in a carton of cigarettes. It was all inspected to be sure the factory seals were not broken. Then we were inspected and allowed inside.

Kip had rented a cell, but only for the last two hours of the visit. We had four hours to kill.

Finding a place in the bleak sun, we sat and watched the carnival of life go by. I passed the day as one does waiting for the gallows.

A few minutes before two o'clock, we went over and stood with Kip by the cell he had rented. Don came over to chat with us. He had a cardboard box and placed it down next to Kip's box. After several minutes, Don left, having picked up Kip's box instead of his own. Don went down the hall into Cell 13.

A couple emerged from our cell. The owner made a cursory look inside and ushered us in. Kip closed the gate and set his box on the bed. I pulled the curtain closed. Sarah went to work immediately.

"I need to practice again," Kip said.

"Okay," Sarah said, "but first shave your legs and change your clothes."

I stood guard at the door. People went by outside and my heart raced with each passing shadow. Sometimes the shadows stopped in front of the cell and my panic went off the charts. Kip and Sarah worked away at their chores. I was aware of their movements but mostly kept my focus on the door.

"Don't you think the dress looks a little tight on him?" I whispered to Sarah.

"All the better to distract the guards," she said. Then to Kip, "Try on the high heels."

Kip put them on and paraded around the room.

"I see Cell 13 in your future."

"Shut up Clay. Come back here, Kip."

Sarah worked intently now, as though she were back making Molotov cocktails. It was nearly an hour before she was happy with every detail. Sarah took off the wig and put it on Kip, then stood next to him and looked at me.

"Well, how is it?" she said.

"It's very good," I said.

"You bastard, give me a straight answer."

"Well, I'm damned if I do and damned if I don't. He looks like your twin sister, but you're still prettier. How's that?"

"Very diplomatic." She turned to Kip. "Where's the shawl?" Kip pulled it out of the bottom of the box and wrapped it around his shoulders.

"That's it," she said.

"Are you leaving?" Kip said.

"Soon as I change." She turned to me. "Are you okay?"

"I'm fine."

"Is that why you're biting your nails?"

"It's an old habit."

She nodded knowingly.

"How about you, Kip?" she said.

"Personally, I have nothing to lose."

He threw his hand out daintily. Sarah slipped out of her dress and reversed it. I stared.

"Enjoying yourself?" she asked me.

"I was thinking it might be my last chance for a while."

She kept her eyes locked on me and I kept my eyes locked on her stunning figure: tender and slim as a girl of sixteen. She tied a belt around the dress and smoothed it over her hips. It had been identical to Kip's dress before she reversed it.

"Nice of Don to help us out," I said.

"I hope he gets out soon," Kip said. "Hell, all of them."

"Let's hope we get out soon," I said.

Sarah checked her hair in the mirror, slipped her purse over her shoulder and prepared to leave.

"Do you have the pass, Kip?" she said. He showed it to her. "Remember, when in doubt, stare. It disarms men."

"The filthy dogs," he said and pretended to smooth over his dress.

"Good luck to both of you," she said.

"We'll be fine," I said. "We'll all be strolling together down Rue St. Michele in a couple of weeks."

"I'm holding you to that."

She kissed Kip, then me and checked the courtyard before going out the door. I watched through the parted curtain. She handed the guard her pass and was waved through the gate without a problem. I closed the curtain and gave Kip a thumbs up. He was busy pulling apart the cover of a Bible. The lost pass had been hidden inside.

"Saved by the disciples," I said absently.

"Careful how you talk to me, stranger."

I came back from my thoughts and laughed nervously. A great nervousness permeated everything we did now.

Our conversation fluttered about in the dry day and our hearts with it. Then the bell rang and it was time to depart. I opened the cell door for Kip and watched him walk gracefully out into the courtyard. He smiled and took my hand. He was quite a woman. Even his fingernails had been painted red.

We stood in line, waiting. The balconies were empty above us but we saw the faces of men watching from their cells as the procession slowly drifted towards the main gate. The soiled white prison walls had turned golden with the last light of day. I was thinking of all the things I enjoyed in life and hoping I would not have to wait a long time to enjoy them again.

60

Two guards waited in the passageway beyond the main gate, one of them seated on a stool, taking passes, the other one standing nearby with an M-1 in his hands, in case anything went wrong with the passes. The guard taking the passes checked each face without emotion. Both guards went about their business without emotion. Behind them, the wide, arched corridor led out to the parking lot. A breeze came from that direction. The exit was that close. There were the bars and these guards and perhaps forty feet of empty space separating us from freedom.

The line continued to inch forward, with people converging in the courtyard behind us. Then Kip and I were only five feet away. Three old women stood in front of us and the guard waved one of them through the gate, then another. Only one woman remained before it was our turn.

Kip had unconsciously dug his fingernails into the flesh of my palm. I pleaded at him with a smile and he relaxed his grip. I put my arm around his waist to help steady him on the high heels. I checked his makeup again and was suddenly aware of my own disguise. My heart beat wildly. When fear came, it was impossible to moderate. It engulfed and swallowed you whole.

The last old lady went through and the guard nodded for us to come forward. As the lady in this deception, Kip went first but caught his left heel on the iron bar that secured the bottom of the gate and lurched forward. The guard with the M-1 caught Kip with one hand. His other hand remained on his rifle. Everything had come to a halt. The guard glanced once at me and then back at Kip.

I was waiting for him to bark out a command but instead heard a woman's voice.

"Gracias, Señor."

It had sounded so foreign, I failed to realize at first that it was Kip speaking.

Then I heard the guard saying "De nada, Señorita" and saw Kip pull his hand free. He touched the guard's arm, then smoothed his dress and winked for the other guard. That guard took his pass and also mine and waved us forward with a final look at our faces.

Laughter followed Kip and I down the long hallway. I assumed the guards were having a little joke about the gringa Señorita and what they'd like to do to her when they got off their shift that night.

Kip and I walked out into the sunlight. The soldiers were seated behind the cannon and milling about the gravel parking lot, as usual. I felt an impulse to hurry but kept my arm around Kip's waist and continued on at a calm pace.

At the car, I opened the passenger door for Kip and went around to the driver's side.

"By the way," I said, getting in. "I know where you can find a quick date."

"You know what these Latin types do to me."

"Yeah. You trip all over yourself."

We had another nervous laugh while I started the motor and pulled into line. Dozens of cars were already converging towards the road. Groups of peasants walked past us and down the hill.

"Christ," I said, inching forward. "After all the weeks of planning, here we are, stuck in traffic. They'll probably be waiting for us by the time we get to the bottom of the hill."

"Relax, darling."

"I'll relax you." I checked the rearview mirror. "How long do you think we have?"

"About fifteen, twenty minutes."

I let out a sigh.

"Relax," he said again.

"I just hope no one notices you missing before la cuenta."

"Everyone's usually too busy talking about their cheap adventures to notice someone missing."

"You hope."

I kept stealing glances in the mirror, expecting a rush of troops at any moment, but there was only the car behind me and a driver looking as perturbed as I was about the slow pace.

"Fifteen or twenty minutes," I said, thinking out loud.

"It might be more, by the time they get around to my cell."

"And nobody notices you missing before then."

"And nobody notices me missing."

"Maybe half an hour then."

"Yeah, maybe," he said.

I knew the answer but couldn't help nervously thinking out loud. We had maybe thirty minutes, which was more than enough time to get past the check-point. I thought we would be fine after that.

It did seem that we could have organized this better but we had reasoned through countless other alternatives and every one of them had led us on another perilous journey, either to the south, or across the gulf, or had required that we put our fate in the hands of a Mexican pilot. In any case, if a better way existed, it was too late to be worrying about it now.

When we came to the bottom of the hill, I was able to satisfy my urge for speed and raced breakneck across town towards the hotel.

"Clay?" Kip said.

"I don't like the sound of this."

"Wasn't Don supposed to come by and pick up that box with my clothes?"

"You reminded him, didn't you?"

"I reminded him."

"Well, for the love of Jesus, let's hope he did."

"Yeah, let's hope."

"Maybe the owner of the cell will just take it over to your bunk and leave it."

"No. They'll look inside."

"Maybe they'll just think it's some new clothes we brought you."

"But they'll still be looking for me."

"Yeah."

"Maybe we should head down to the gulf instead."

"Oh fuck it. Let's just go forward with things as planned."

I had said this as if supremely confident but there was no getting my mind off of the problem now.

Back at the hotel, I parked in the driveway and walked calmly into the hotel, saying hello and smiling for everyone on my way through the lobby.

As soon as I was out of sight, I raced up the stairs and made the proper knock on the door. Caroline opened it and threw herself in my arms with a cry of relief.

"Let's hurry, sweetheart."

"Why? What's wrong?"

"Oh, nothing, nothing. But I really wish you'd take the train on your own."

"No," she said.

"Look, there's no reason for you to risk going through the checkpoint."

"No," she insisted. "We're doing this together." She came out and closed the door. "The guards will be suspicious without me."

I did not want to admit that she was right, but she was.

"All right," I said. "But let's hurry."

We rushed downstairs and waved merrily to the staff on our way out the door. The room was paid for in advance, as usual. Kip got out of the car and gave Caroline a hug.

"Hi, Kip. How does it feel to be free?"

"Glorious."

They stood there looking at each other with tears in their eyes.

"Okay, you two, come on," I said.

Kip climbed into the back seat. Caroline sat next to me. As soon as we were safely away from the hotel entrance, Kip lay down out of sight. A few miles outside of town, I pulled off into the brush. Caroline got her kit out and started to remove my disguise.

"Untie the trunk," I told Kip.

Caroline finished and I threw her kit into the brush.

"In there?" Kip said when I came around in front.

"Would you prefer the engine compartment?"

He took off his high heels.

"Here, don't lose these." I threw them into the brush, as well. Kip got in and curled himself into the embryonic position.

"I have to go to the bathroom."

"Oh for the love of god, Kip, hurry."

He ran into the brush and returned shortly. I stood there with my hand on the hood while he crawled back in.

"Okay?" I said.

He batted his eyelashes at me. I closed the hood carefully.

"Everything okay?"

"It's dark in here," he said.

It came through very faintly. I tied off the rope with several extra knots and got in.

"Is he okay?" Caroline asked.

"He said it's dark."

"Poor guy," she said.

I squeezed her hand and drove back out to the highway.

As we neared the check-point, we were confronted by a long line of cars, and each one of them was being stopped and searched. I checked my watch. It had been almost thirty minutes since we left the prison parking lot.

"I think they know," I said.

Caroline grabbed my hand.

"Maybe we should turn around and head the other way."

"No. A guard's up there watching."

"Okay," she said. "We're going to Desemboque, just like always."

"Yeah, just like always."

Caroline reached over into the back seat and grabbed the carton of cigarettes.

"Perhaps you should undo a few buttons."

She stared at me before turning the mirror on herself and going to work. I stole glances while she tossed her hair to one side and held it there with a tortoise-shell comb. Then she took off her bra and opened her blouse two buttons. A hint of her nipples was visible through the muslin cloth. Lastly, she put on red lipstick, turned the mirror back and looked at me.

"Like that?"

"Carmen."

I went to kiss her lips but she held me back.

"You don't want to smear it," she said.

"Yes I do."

She touched me tenderly.

"I love you."

"I love you, too. I want you to look that way when we get married."

"Oh honey, not like a whore."

"I don't care what you call it. I love it."

"Will we go away after this?"

"After this, yes, very soon."

"If we make it."

"We'll make it," I said. "We'll make it."

"It sounds better when you say it twice," she said.

"I know. Maybe we should chant."

She smiled funnily and looked ahead. I heard her repeating the words quietly to herself.

I inched forward as one car after another was waved through the checkpoint. Every person so far had been asked to open their trunk. As we got near, one of the guards noticed us and came back to say hello.

"Que paso, amigo?"

"Ee's one American. He is escaping from dee prison today."

I put up my hands in mock surrender.

"No, ee's not jyu."

I pointed at Caroline. The guard leaned in and gazed at her with a big smile. She leaned forward and winked seductively.

"Hola, hola. No, ee's not the Señorita."

We laughed. The last car pulled forward and the guard waved us up to the checkpoint. The lead guard leaned into my window. Caroline rolled down her window and allowed the other guards to get a closer look. They crowded around her window like a band of thieves.

"Jyu are looking especially beeuteeful today, Señorita," the head guard said.

Caroline reached across me and touched his forearm. I watched his eyes struggling with the sensory information. No doubt he was getting an eycful. His smile remained but his nostrils had flared.

"Thank you," she said.

Then remembering the cigarettes, she leaned over again. He was waiting with his smile.

"Thank you, Señorita."

Remembering his manners, he thanked me as well.

"So who escaped?" I said.

"Oh, eets one American. Hees getting loose from dee jail so they want us to check all dee cars. Jyu know."

"Maybe it's me?"

"No no no, Señor, please. Ee's one guy they think maybe was dressing like a woooman. Weeth the yellow hair. And one more guy, un chino."

"A what?"

"You know, like jyaponese."

"Oh."

I pulled up the corners of my eyes and they all laughed.

"Dat's perty good, Señor."

He looked quickly behind the seat at all our camping gear and back at us.

"Ees mucho work, all thees." He waved his hand over the line of cars and shrugged. I smiled and waved forward.

"Maybe just enough room for one Japanese guy up there."

He laughed and looked again at Caroline, fumbling with his carton of cigarettes. I didn't have to look to know that she was giving him another eyeful. He stood up and peeked around at the big knot of rope on the trunk. He looked back at the long line of cars then back at us: especially at Caroline.

Suddenly, a proud look came over his face and he waved us forward with a sweep of his hand.

"Too much trouble, eh? Jyu have a nice treep. Bring de beeuteeful Señorita back to see us soon."

"I will. We'll be back in a couple of days."

Caroline leaned over and smiled for him one more time. I waved and accelerated slowly onto the highway, watching the guard in the rearview mirror the whole time. He stared after us proudly for a moment, as if savoring his moment of authority, then turned and motioned for the next car to move forward. The driver got out and opened his trunk.

"Oh Clay, it worked, it worked."

"Yes, I think so."

"You don't think there'll be another checkpoint?"

"No." I turned to look at her. "We made it."

"Maybe we should try a different route north."

"No, we'll go straight through. We'll be in Nogales in a couple of hours."

"Clay, you were so brave."

"So were you."

"I was terrified. Didn't you hear my teeth chattering?"

"Those men will die wanting you."

She raised her eyebrows.

"Of course, darling. I will too."

Caroline smiled and put her head against my shoulder.

We drove straight ahead towards the border. Several times we saw troops near the road and various military trucks in the villages we passed, but there were no more roadblocks. I turned off to the east before Nogales and found the dirt road leading towards San Lazaro.

The sun had fled behind the mountains and the desert floor was growing black. The last light of day glowed on the towering saguaros. The evening was quickly turning cold.

When we were safely beyond the outskirts of town, I pulled over and untied the trunk. Kip emerged and stretched his atrophied limbs.

"Wow. It's like being born again."

Once he had limbered up, he paraded around in the dress a bit and we laughed.

"You can leave it on if you like."

He gave me a look while taking it off. The wig and dress went into the brush. I grabbed a pair of jeans and boots from a box in the back seat.

"Did you hear what happened at the check-point?"

"A bit. It sounded like a tight squeeze."

I nodded at Caroline. She had turned to put her bra back on.

"You sold her?"

"Kip, you turkey." She finished and turned to face us.

"We let them inspect the merchandise a bit."

She slapped my shoulder.

"Anyway, it was enough to blind a man to his duty."

"Far out," Kip said. He turned his attention to the expanse of surrounding desert with his nose up in the air. "Far out," he said again.

Caroline came over and all three of us hugged together in the approaching darkness. Then we were wiping at tears with a laugh.

"I suppose we'd better get going," I said.

"I hate letting you out of my sight."

"We'll be all right. Are you sure you can find your way?"

"I can always get directions."

I pulled out my wad of cash and handed most of it to Caroline.

"Put it down your pants when you cross. And don't forget to call Danny."

"Are you forgetting who got you here?"

I kissed her.

"No, I'm not. I love you, sweetheart."

"I love you, too. And you Kip." She gave him a hug. "Welcome home…Well, soon."

He stood there with a wistful smile on his face. I encouraged Caroline over to the car and helped her in. Then, remembering the trunk, I went around to tie it off. Back at the driver side window, I kissed her again.

"I don't suppose we'll ever fix that now."

"Never," she said.

I put my cheek next to hers and whispered.

"I'll see you before morning."

"Just be careful."

"I will." I kissed her several more times. "I love you."

"And please don't do anything foolish."

"Well, you know me."

She laughed and slapped at me playfully, but with a look of concern in her eyes. I pulled her hair back and kissed her neck and ear and lips again and watched as she turned the car around on the road. She blew a final kiss my way and headed west in a cloud of dust. The sky was still pale with twilight in that direction.

I watched until the car was out of sight before turning back towards Kip. He was staring off at the Patagonias. I heard the faint sound of the wind whispering in the brush and thorns. All else was quiet, as though one might hear the universe turning.

A shooting star crossed the sky and disappeared.

"Did you see that, Kip?"

"Yeah." He turned to face me. "By the way, thanks, partner."

"Oh hell. I wouldn't have been able to sleep at night, knowing you were still in there."

He shook his head as if still unable to accept his newfound freedom.

"Unbelievable, man. Unbelievable."

"Yeah. Now let's see if we can keep ourselves out of trouble."

He smiled. I looked back up at the mountains, overtaken in that fleeting hour by a feeling of terror and rapture all at once. My god, the enormity of it, and how little I knew; about life, about my reasons for being here or where destiny would lead me next. All I had was some kind of unspoken blind faith now, in a universe that I did not truly understand, and the courage to go forward, no matter what might come. I remembered Jijiwa's words…we are but the wind blowing through this world…and felt that terrifying rapture jerk in me again. How small we were. How fragile my hopes and dreams, and yet within my heart was everything.

Returning to the moment, I looked at Kip.

"You all right?" he said.

"Yeah, yeah. Just tripping on the journey."

"And what a long strange trip it's been."

I smiled and patted Kip on the back.

"What do you say we get moving?"

"Sure. I've got a hankering for a steak and some pie a la mode."

I laughed.

"Somehow I'm hearing Merle Haggard."

Now Kip laughed.

We stood eye to eye for another moment before starting off through the brush. Ahead of us, the desert floor had turned into an army of black forms, as far as the eye could see.

About The Author

The product of an Irish/Italian family, Mr. Corcoran was transplanted from the clapboard New England of his youth to the cookie cutter, stucco subdivisions that increasingly littered the old ranches and disappearing orange groves south of Los Angeles in the 1960s. Ever rebellious, and true to the folk music/coffee house idealism that helped shape my early worldview, he chose to resist the Vietnam War, was a man without a country for several years and, as recounted in this same novel, can count incarceration in a Mexican prison as one of his many colorful experiences from that era.

Having pursued a love of reading and writing in various forms all his life, Mr. Corcoran finally took that passion seriously around the turn of the millennium and has dedicated the remainder of his days to authorship. In completing the circle of destiny, he has returned to the New England of his youth and presently resides along the Rhode Island shore